Journey to HIDAYA

KAINAT AZHAR

Merrinore Press

ISBN 979-8-9880164-0-3

Cover design by Melisa Labra

Interior design by Lorna Reid

First edition April 2023

Kainatazharchughtai.com

To my grandfather, Ajmal Uppal, who promised to read my story when I would publish it. He is with God now, and may God have mercy on him and enter him into the highest level of paradise.

This is for you, Nana. Thank you for being one of my biggest support systems. <3

If there's a book that you want to read, but it hasn't been written
yet, then you must write it.

Toni Morrison

Author's Note

Assalaamu 'Alaikum (peace be upon you).

Welcome to all. Whether you are Muslim or not, this story is still for you.

Thank you for picking up this book. Allah (God) has brought you here, and He has brought you here for a reason. I hope that something in these pages touches your hearts, and it serves as a source of enlightenment for you. *Ameen.*

I've been writing ever since I was able to hold a pencil. It started with half-finished stories on scraps of paper. Then, as I got older, it progressed to frantic notes and hastily written scenes on my phone or in the margins of some notebook. Finally, when the pandemic hit and I suddenly had a plethora of free time on my hands, I got around to shoving my half-formed thoughts into coherent sentences and stories on Google Docs. During those two years at home, I was able to begin and complete my debut novel *Journey to Hidaya,* and bring to life a story that had been forming in my mind for a very long time. *Alhamdulillah,* all praise and thanks be to God.

Throughout my life, writing has been a constant source of comfort and happiness. I've traveled the globe; discovered alternate, fantastical worlds; explored fear, hope, love—all by putting pen to paper (or fingers to keyboard).

Why am I telling you this? As Martin Luther King Jr. said, "I have a dream." I've been dreaming of writing and publishing a book ever since I was a little girl and able to hold a pencil. Today, if this novel is in your hands, that means I was able to fulfill my dream.

And if you take away nothing else from this book, take away

this: If I was able to fulfill my lifelong dream, so can you.

Journey to Hidaya is a story that I'm sure we can all relate to in some respect, at some point in our lives. It's a story about the journey towards guidance and enlightenment; about discovering true faith versus the manipulation of it; and about learning to hold on to faith when it becomes especially difficult to do so.

This novel explores concepts such as domestic violence; mental health; spiritual reawakening; practices of blind faith; harmful attitudes in the religious community (which often turn people away from faith); and learning to trust God above all else. Since *Journey to Hidaya* is a story that deals with specific cultural and religious communities, translations and references are provided at the end of the novel.

I accredit much of my inspiration for this story to Umera Ahmed's *Pir-E-Kamil*, or *The Perfect Mentor*. As her book changed my heart, I hope that mine can change yours as well.

Margaret Atwood's *The Handmaid's Tale* has also been a driving force behind some of the messages in my book. *The Handmaid's Tale* delivers a powerful message of how religion is often abused and used as a scapegoat in worldly, political, and personal affairs.

Lastly, Yasmin Mogahed's *Reclaim Your Heart* has deeply influenced the last third of my story, which deals primarily with healing and mending your heart through your connection with God.

Before I go, here is an important disclaimer: I am no scholar. I am simply a woman who loves her religion and loves writing, and wanted to combine my love for the two into something that will (hopefully) leave a lasting impact on you. It is my attempt, as a person of faith, to write a story that is representative of the Muslim community, as well as the general faith-based community. That being said, none of us are perfect, and my characters (and I) *will* be flawed. Being imperfect is the essence of human nature—the test is how we address and attempt to rectify these flaws.

So once again, thank you for being here. I hope you enjoy this story as much as I enjoyed writing it.

Please remember to keep me in your prayers.

Wa 'Alaikum Salaam (and peace be upon you).

Content Warning

This novel deals with themes such as child neglect, emotional abuse, domestic violence, and mental health issues. Please read at your own discretion.

One

~

"Ms. Zoya?"

Auburn curls fly. A pretty face turns and *jhumkas* dangle from her ears. A sequined *dupatta* adorns soft shoulders, and the bangles on her wrist jingle merrily as she flips through the papers in her hand in frustration.

"This better be really important, Sameer."

The guy pauses, and the helicopter blades in his ribcage can be heard even from a distance.

"Uhh—"

"Stop stuttering and tell me what you want." Zoya slaps the papers onto the table. "And where the hell is this stupid file?"

After a moment of calculated silence, Sameer says, "Which file?"

"The one with the new designs and blueprints for the *sherwanis* and *lehengas*!"

"Where did you put it?" he dares to ask.

"On my head!" she shouts, glaring at him. "If I had known that, Sameer, why the hell would I ask you where it is?"

He stays quiet, knowing full well not to interrupt his boss in her rage.

Zoya sighs, closes her eyes, and pinches the bridge of her nose between her thumb and forefinger. She takes a deep breath. "You have two seconds to tell me what you disturbed me for, Sameer."

Sameer rushes forward. "Ma'am, there's someone here for an interview."

At this, her eyes fly open. She narrows her gaze. "Send him to Bill, *as we discussed.* And get me some chamomile tea, please."

Sameer turns to leave, then dares to run on knives and turns towards his boss again. "Ms. Zoya, are you alright? Why don't you take a little break?"

She flips her hair behind her shoulders and places a hand on her hip.

Once, Sameer's heart used to beat faster around her. And not out of fear. But whose heart hasn't and doesn't at least once beat irregularly around stunning Zoya Zameer?

"I'm okay, Sameer," she says, fanning herself with her *dupatta.* "Breaks can't be afforded. Especially not now, when the industry is booming and the demand for Pakistani clothes for Fashion Week and bridal occasions and so forth is higher than ever. Can you believe this? Dreams are coming true." She makes a grand sweeping gesture with her arms.

Sameer smiles and leaves it at that, exiting her office.

Zoya Zameer returns to searching for the black file.

~

The man behind the large oval desk clears his throat.

"I'm Bill Krenak, the senior manager here," he says, rifling through the file in his hands and pausing to eye the interviewee in front of him. "Haroun is your name?"

"Yes, sir."

"Am I pronouncing it correctly?" Bill asks. At the flash of surprise on Haroun's face, Bill chuckles. "As I'm sure you've noticed, Zameer is a very diverse company. We celebrate people of all backgrounds and value our employees' comfort here."

Haroun nods. "Yes, sir, thank you. You're pronouncing it correctly."

"Awesome. Do you have a preferred name?"

"No, sir."

"Tell me about yourself, Haroun."

"What do you want to know, sir?"

Bill raises a brow, intrigued. "Surely you're well acquainted with what interviews are supposed to entail? Considering you've come for one of the largest businesses in North America, correct?"

Haroun smiles. "I didn't realize interviews were supposed to be so thoroughly scripted and rehearsed."

Bill leans back and presses his lips together, staring Haroun down with an unmistakable spark of interest. "Perhaps not. But I'd like to know about you."

As Bill questions him, Haroun gives minimal responses, as if using too many words is exhausting. When the senior manager asks about his previous jobs, Haroun taps the desk with four fingers, the sound resembling hoof beats. A fissure appears between his brows, as if he's contemplating how best to word his next sentence. He seems to reign a sigh when he murmurs, "Have you seen my résumé?"

Bill raises another brow but quirks his lips. "Of course. That's why you're here. But I'd prefer hearing directly from you than from a file."

Haroun nods shakily. "Right. Sorry, I understand. It's just . . ." He trails off, eyes growing dark.

Bill scrutinizes him, a sympathetic expression coating the senior manager's features. He's seen many nervous interviewees, but something tells Bill that the man in front of him isn't trembling from nerves. "You know what, let me ask you something else." Bill closes Haroun's file as an attempt to put him at ease. "I'm curious; I've looked extensively through your CV and attempted to understand, but I've come up empty." Bill tilts his head. "You certainly have the experience and work ethic, given your recommendations, to pursue a higher position. Why are you interviewing for the position of an intern?"

Almost imperceptibly, Haroun's breath catches. Bill notices and leans back, eyebrows knitted.

Haroun takes a deep breath. "I understand your curiosity. It must seem strange . . ." He pauses. "The truth is—"

Just then, Zoya barges into the office and sets a black file on Bill's desk. She pulls strands of hair away from her face and says breathlessly, "What is this, Bill?"

Bill steeples his fingers and stares at her. "Surely this can wait?"

"No, it can't."

"I'm conducting an interview right now."

Haroun makes a small noise, holding back a smile. His shoulders have relaxed since Zoya's abrupt entry—he seems to be grateful for the interruption.

Zoya turns to him. "Who is this?" she asks in a friendly voice. She smiles sweetly at Haroun and bats her eyelashes, to which he replies by looking away.

"This is Haroun. I haven't gotten past too much yet, so if you would please—"

"No, I would not *please*. This file was supposed to be sent to the media office days ago. Why hasn't that been done yet?" As she speaks, Zoya continues to sneak unabashed glances at Haroun. Her eyes sparkle with uncharacteristic warmth.

Bill's eyes narrow at the expression on the CEO'S face. "I had spoken to Rana about it," he says, gesturing to the file. "He said it was sent to the media office for reviews and it wasn't accepted."

Zoya's momentary lapse in attention disappears, and she turns the full force of her gaze on Bill. "Wasn't accepted? What do you mean?"

"Meaning the designs were rejected."

Zoya laughs mirthlessly. "Okay, Bill Nye. I don't have time for your silly little games."

"I'm not playing games with you."

Zoya slams her palm on the table. Haroun flinches, but Bill is unfazed. "Tell them to come to *the CEO of this company* and give a valid reason as to why the designs were rejected." She slaps the table once more before she turns—hair flying—to stomp out of the office.

Bill sighs. He cannot even be annoyed with her because her anger is justified—the designs were magnificent and would surely have popularized their campaigns and further expanded their reach—but the media office rejected them. Bill and his team are all baffled.

He looks up at his guest. Haroun hasn't moved an inch and is tense with what may be anxiety.

Bill cocks his head. Considering Haroun's CV and what Bill has gauged from observing the man himself, needless to say he's both impressed and intrigued. He taps his fingers on the desk, mulling over a couple things, before he comes to a resolution with a smile.

"Welcome to Zameer Co. Meet your CEO, Ms. Zoya Zameer."

Two

ZOYA LETS OUT A peal of hysterical laughter. "You sent the media office *the wrong prints?*"

A stammering program lead tries to explain; Zoya merely stares at her with folded arms. "Ma'am, I was under the impression that those were the designs for New York Fashion Week." The employee's team—along with Bill and the new intern Haroun—are standing silently to the side.

Zoya takes a deep breath. "Do you realize what a *colossal* mistake it is to send the *wrong* designs to a *rival fashion company*? And that too to our old business partner, *Pak Enterprises?*"

The employee looks up meekly. "B-But Ms. Zoya," she dares. "Why does it make a difference? The prints were rejected anyway, it's not like they're actually going to be designed and . . ." She falters when Zoya's eyes flash.

Zoya places her palms on her desk and leans forward. "It matters, *Preeti*, because now the rival company has the inside scoop on what we are gearing our latest designs towards. Now they have *our* ideas. Whether they like them or not is irrelevant to the fact that they are definitely going to get something out of our designs and claim all credit."

Preeti nudges her glasses up her nose, comprehension and fear simultaneously dawning on her face.

"You're fired."

The employee's head snaps up and her eyes widen. "W-What?"

"You're fired," Zoya says simply. "I want you out and I don't want to see you again. You'll get the check for the next two months as promised in the contract, and then you're on your own."

Preeti seems to be on the verge of tears. Bill opens his mouth, "Ms. Zoya, if I may—"

"No, you may not." Zoya gathers her curls into a bun at the nape of her neck. "You may escort Preeti out. Thank you for your time, Preeti," she says dismissively, already starting to fan herself with her sequined *dupatta* as if this is all merely a bore to her.

Without another word, Bill leads a sobbing Preeti out. He's careful not to comfort her physically, adhering to Zoya's strict rules on professionalism in her work space.

Preeti's team—still in shock—starts to head out. Haroun—who has been watching the scene with apt horror and surprise—starts to follow when Zoya calls him.

"You," she points at him. The bangles on her wrist clink against each other. "Come to my office. I want to talk about work with you."

Once Haroun has followed Zoya to her office, she gestures to the chair in front of her desk. He wordlessly sits down. Zoya eyes him with the same open curiosity she had when he arrived two days ago. Her expression is so piqued, it seems as if the events of the past five minutes have been entirely forgotten.

"*Salaam*," she says with a sheepish smile, opting for a religious greeting given his Muslim name. His responding smile is polite but strained.

"*Wa 'Alaikum Salaam*," he responds.

For formality's sake, Zoya inquires, "What do they call you?"

"Haroun."

Zoya mulls over the name. *Haroun.* "Haroun," she tests it out on her tongue, liking the way it sounds.

He flinches a little.

Zoya lets out a giggle and sits down in her desk chair. "What would you like, Haroun? Coffee? Tea?"

He shakes his head. "I'm okay." Pause. "Thank you."

Zoya tilts her head, scrutinizing him. His gaze is shifted elsewhere, but that doesn't stop Zoya from noticing how captivating his eyes are. She reaches back and tugs the band out of her hair, letting her curls cascade down her shoulders, a scene that would turn most people's faces into heart-eye emojis.

Haroun blinks.

"You can't come to my office and not drink anything," she says in a matter-of-fact tone.

Haroun looks down. He seems to be avoiding her eyes. "Actually, if I may, I was called here. I didn't come on my own."

Zoya raises an eyebrow. "Day one and already so daring?"

Haroun purses his lips. "No, I didn't mean to—"

"So I'm assuming since you're here, Bill was really impressed by you. He has a habit of being nitpicky and slow to warm up to new employees but you . . . you caught his eye." *And mine.* Zoya leans forward and places her chin in her hand. "Tell me about yourself."

"The senior manager was really nice. He didn't seem at all nitpicky to me. And I'm sorry, but am I still here to discuss my job?" Haroun seems agitated, black eyes wary.

Zoya's eyes widen. "Of course. A boss must thoroughly know her workers."

Haroun raises an eyebrow at the word *thoroughly*. "With all due respect, Ms. Zoya . . . I don't think it's right for me to be in your company if it's not about work."

Oh, damn. A little religious. Interesting. Zoya places her chin in her hand and smiles at him, fighting off unpleasant memories of the last couple of religious people she used to know. "I respect that," she says. "But this *is* solely about work. I just want to get to know you better. I do so with all my new employees."

Haroun stays quiet. Zoya observes him brazenly, allowing her eyes to covet his sharp jawline and rosy lips balanced by the dark eyes that add mystery and secrecy to him.

He looks away, discomfort lining his features.

"Why do you want to work here?" Zoya leans back, resting her elbows on the arms of her chair. She steeples her fingers and eyes him expectantly, looking entirely like the CEO that she is.

"I need the money."

Zoya raises her eyebrows. *At least he's honest.* "Then why apply for the intern position?"

He hesitates before saying, "I want to spend more time with my mom. She recently had surgery, so . . ." he quiets suddenly.

Zoya waits for him to continue, but it seems that Haroun is a man of few words. She clears her throat. "I'm pretty sure you would have been able to find a well-paying job anywhere, especially considering the way that you look."

Haroun presses his lips together. Zoya drinks in the small detail: a dimple in his left cheek. He seems to be blushing.

"I'm not trying to embarrass you, Haroun. It's just the truth. Psychologically and in the business world, people tend to gravitate towards someone who is more"—she pauses to find the right words—"visually appealing."

For a moment, she wonders whether her prattling tongue and unflinching honesty might land her a meeting with HR.

Haroun averts his eyes. "I'm sorry, would you rather I not work here?"

"No, no. That's not what I said. I asked you why you wanted to work *here* specifically. At Zameer."

"Because it was the highest-paying job on my list of potential jobs."

Interesting. Zoya grabs a pen and twirls it between her fingers. "Do you know how I became the boss of this company?"

He shakes his head but doesn't indicate for her to continue.

She does anyway. "Grit. Hard work. Determination." Zoya uncaps the pen and absentmindedly draws on the palm of her hand. "It wasn't handed down to me. It wasn't through family connections. It was because *I* wanted it and I made it happen." She sets the pen down and leans forward to look into Haroun's eyes. Although her posture exudes intimidation, he doesn't seem fazed. "I expect the same level of commitment and determination from you as well, Mr. Haroun . . .?"

"Suleiman," he prompts.

"Mr. Haroun Suleiman."

He nods once. "Understood."

"Good." Zoya gives him her most sugary smile. Her eyes rove over him once again, and she notices that underneath the jean jacket he's wearing a black t-shirt. Everything about his posture and attitude and appearance suggest he never actually expected to receive the job.

"Oh, and I expect all my employees to wear at least one of the things we ourselves manufacture, whether it's clothing or accessories with Zameer's logo. It gives the company credibility and status in others' eyes, and depicts our dedicated work ethic." Zoya sweeps her hair to one side and tucks a wayward strand behind her ear. Everything about her is objectively intriguing as well as distracting; the merry bangles on her wrists, the sparkly *jhumkas* dangling from her ears, the luscious hair cascading down her back, the winged eyeliner, and the vibrant Pakistani clothes.

Haroun doesn't seem to be the least bit distracted. "Okay."

"Oh, and *kabhi kabhi meri Urdu nikal jaati hai.*" Zoya smiles at Haroun's raised brows and dares to voice her next, kiddish request. Just to see how he will react. For some reason, his politely aloof demeanor makes her want to dig for more to discover what's beneath the quiet exterior. "So I'd love it if you could respond in Urdu; it's always so nice having employees I can interact in my mother tongue with. I visited Pakistan frequently throughout my childhood and teenage years, so I always enjoy speaking Urdu with others." She briefly pauses before continuing, "That is, considering you're fluent in the language." She stares at him expectantly.

He doesn't deny it. "Right. Okay."

"So . . ." Zoya gestures in a pronounced fashion.

There's a pause before, "'*Okay*' is used in Urdu as well."

Zoya giggles. "I like you. No wonder Bill did, too. You're definitely staying."

"May I leave now?"

"You leave when I ask you to leave, sweetheart. Which, if I recall, I haven't done so yet." Finger twisting around one of her curls, Zoya bats her lashes at Haroun. "I'm sure Bill has already filled you in on your responsibilities. You're going to train for a week, and then

I'm going to personally monitor your progress and see how you do. Don't disappoint me." She gives him a lopsided grin, which he is hesitant in returning. "I don't believe you will. I am already content.

"I have a special job for you in the mornings. You're going to bring me coffee, tea, whatever it is I feel like drinking that day. Every morning. Understood?"

Haroun doesn't seem too excited by the prospect. "Isn't there anyone else who can bring you tea?" Zoya raises her eyebrows. He rushes to continue, "No—I mean—in a company this large, isn't there someone designated to handle these types of tasks?"

"*Mene tumse bola, to tum hi karo ge. Samaj aai?*"

He nods grudgingly.

"*Urdu me jawab de sakte ho, meri jaan?* Come on, just one little phrase." Zoya throws him a megawatt smile. "You'd make your boss very happy."

Haroun seems as if his patience is being tested, but he maintains a polite demeanor. "*G, samaj aai.*"

A jolt of shocked pleasure runs through Zoya when she hears him speak in her mother tongue. "Bravo. You sound good."

Running his fingers through his hair, he sighs. "Thank you."

"You may leave now."

He stands as if there is nothing on earth he would rather do. His flustered and agitated nature causes Zoya immense humor. She smiles at him. "I expect you to fulfill your responsibilities, otherwise you may end up like Preeti a few minutes ago."

Grimacing, Haroun nods and makes his way to the door. Before leaving, he turns around and murmurs, "*Salaam.*"

"*Wa 'Alaikum Salaam,*" she replies, even though he's already gone.

There's something, she decides. *I like this guy.*

Three

~

"THREE, TWO, ONE, HOLD still. Perfect. Now turn your face to the side. Beautiful."

Cameras flash, lights dance. The model in front of the green screen places a hand on her hip and turns the other way, the Pakistani *shalwar kameez* decorating her in bright and vibrant colors.

Zoya Zameer walks around the crew, fanning herself with her favorite flower-patterned fan. She decided to join the shoot after a very long time today, telling herself her decision had nothing to do with the new intern. She struggles to make good on that statement, however, as she steals frequent glances at Haroun Suleiman.

Zoya tilts her head and narrows her eyes, attention momentarily straying from him when she senses something off in the shoot. "Halt," she says, and everyone freezes in their tracks. She points to the model. "We need some of Abeer sitting. Maybe with crossed legs and the *dupatta* draped across the chaise. It's going to look fabulous," she singsongs.

The crew obeys her command and—when she isn't looking—the photographing lead shoots her a glare.

Haroun stands to the side with a clipboard in hand, noting the breakdown of the photo shoot. Zoya sees an opening and walks over to him, fluffing her hair and shooting him her perfect Colgate-teeth smile. His responding smile is polite but reserved.

Zoya flips her curls over her shoulders. "What do you think?" Her voice is sugary sweet.

He continues to take frantic notes. She notices how he avoids looking at the female model as much as possible, focusing instead on the props around her or flickering his gaze to the male photographer instead. "I'm sorry, about what?"

Zoya grins. "The shoot, sweetheart."

His jaw tightens. Zoya gauges it must be a response to the word *sweetheart,* which only makes her grin wider. "Oh," he says. "It's very nice."

She raises her eyebrows. "Very descriptive."

"I apologize," he says, looking up from his notes with a tired smile. "I'm just trying not to miss anything."

Zoya lets out a peal of high-pitched laughter. "Week one and already Zameer has gotten you into the nitty gritty of things?"

He nods, continuously glancing at the photographer, who is now focused on a male dressed in an intricately embroidered wedding *sherwani.* The prop team shuffles around and grabs things to add and take away from the set.

Zoya's eyes trace Haroun's features, and again she is surprised by how attractive she finds him. "So what do you think of *this* model's clothes?"

"Hmm? Oh, they're nice."

"Just nice?" she challenges. *Come on,* she pleads silently. *I know you've got more in you.*

Haroun stops writing and turns to Zoya. He's a good head taller than her, but with her confident posture and bright eyes, Zoya is able to intimidate all.

There is an agitated look on his face, and he seems distracted as his gaze darts around. But to Zoya's surprise, his voice still comes out courteous when he speaks. "It's fantastic, Ms. Zoya."

"Really? That doesn't sound very wholehearted, Mr. Suleiman."

He twirls his pen. "No, seriously, it's awesome. Really. Great job." With the way he's speaking, one would think he's picking cereal flavors rather than designed embroideries.

The lights continue to flash around them. Flora, one of Zoya's favorite and most dedicated workers, walks forward and sets a lamp on the table beside the chaise.

"I'm glad you like it. You know—" Zoya stops instantly, gaze zeroing in on the lamp. The soft orange light spreads in a halo under the umbrella of the lamp. Zoya's breath catches, and Haroun watches her expectantly, eyes boring into the side of her head.

"Ms. Zoya?"

No.

She cannot seem to speak. Her hand flies to her chest, bangles jingling merrily. Her heart starts to beat like helicopter blades, quick and persistent.

"Um, Ms. Zoya?"

The lamp shade squeaks as her hand flies to the bedside table, almost knocking it over. The sharp beads at the bottom of the lamp shade slice her wrist.

"Stop," she whimpers.

"Get that off the set," Zoya breaks out of the memory and finally finds her voice. "Flora, off the set *right now*. I don't want to see it again. Throw it away. Burn it. I don't care. Don't ever bring that in front of me again." Her voice holds so much venom in comparison to a minute ago.

A frantic Flora stammers something incomprehensible before rushing forward, grabbing the lamp, and hurrying away with it.

Zoya's breath comes in sporadic waves. She turns on her pale pink heel and rushes into the elevator, insistently pushing the button for the doors to close.

"Ms. Zoya, where are you going?" Haroun calls out, his voice revealing utter confusion.

Zoya spins on her heel, furrows her brows together as if in deep thought, then points to her wrist suddenly. "It's *Dhuhr* time," she declares, continuing to frantically push the elevator buttons.

Then the doors slide closed and Zoya's distressed face disappears.

~

Haroun continues to grip his pen and stare at the elevator in confusion. After a moment of silence, the shoot resumes, and a very confused group of employees direct the models back to their positions. The photographing lead is hissing at Flora: "How could you forget? Don't you remember that time when she—"

But Haroun loses focus on the rest of the conversation because something is nagging at him. *Oh,* he thinks suddenly. *It is Dhuhr time.* A bout of frustration consumes him at having not paid attention to the time, and he looks around at his environment with great distaste. Then he walks over to Bill and hands him the clipboard. "Mr. Krenak, do you mind taking care of this for a little bit?"

Bill raises his eyebrows. "Are you going on vacation?"

Haroun thinks of his five daily prayers. "Something like that." He sees the skeptical look on Bill's face and almost laughs. "I'm going to pray."

Immediately, the senior manager's face goes from disbelieving to serious. "Oh, right, sorry."

"Don't apologize. Do you know where I can pray? Where does Ms. Zoya usually pray?"

Bill rubs his chin. "In her office, I think. But you're not allowed in there unless it's strictly work-related." Bill shrugs. "You can use my office whenever you want. And we also have an interfaith room on the fourth floor."

Haroun's eyes light up. "Really? Thank you, Mr. Krenak."

"Bill. Call me Bill." He shoots Haroun a lopsided grin.

Haroun walks into the elevator and pushes the button to go up. When the doors slide open ten seconds later, he stops in surprise.

Zoya's back is to him, her head down and one hand pressed against the wall, the other clutching her stomach.

"Ms. Zoya?" Haroun says. She flinches in surprise but doesn't turn around. "Are you alright?" He can hear her laborious breathing even from a few feet away. Her shoulders are shaking.

"I'm fine." Her voice sounds distant. "Don't worry about me. You can go back to the shoot. I'll be there in a minute."

Haroun's body is positioned in the opposite direction, ready to leave, surprising even himself. Something tells him these are dangerous waters. But his heart keeps him rooted to the ground. "*I give you counsel that you be good to women,*" the Prophet Muhammad had said. His mother has strictly drilled that into his head.

"Are you sure you're alright?"

Zoya's curls fly as she whips around. "I said I'm *fine.*" Her eyebrows furrow, gaze resting at a point somewhere behind Haroun. She fumbles for the fan hooked to the side of her *kameez* and unclasps it, spreading it open and fanning herself. Her shoulders shake as she breathes heavily.

Suddenly she turns to Haroun and gives him a wide, artificial grin. "I'm okay, sweetheart."

Haroun grimaces slightly. *Sweetheart.*

"Did you need something?" she asks in a tone of forced calm.

"I just needed to pray. I was going to the interfaith room--"

"You can use my office," she interrupts, flashing him a bright smile.

But you're not allowed in there unless it's strictly work-related.

Haroun lowers his gaze. "It's okay. Thank you for the offer, but I'll use the interfaith room." And before she can say anything else, he steps back and walks away from the unsettling aura in that hallway.

When he's a safe distance away, he shakes his head, trying to stave off the disturbing feeling that has formed in his heart.

Four

"Allah, the eternal Refuge." (Qur'an 112:2)

~

ZOYA ZAMEER ISN'T ONE to display her weaknesses—being the CEO of such a successful company has taught her *that* valuable lesson—so when Haroun witnesses the end of her panic attack, a fire ignites within her.

For the next few days, she settles all her angry focus on him. Although he's only an intern, she gives him tasks that are quite above the expectations of his job description. And on top of these absurd tasks, she summons him for tea every morning. Her behavior is a combination of merciless and flirtatious. It's precisely the latter reason that causes Haroun to purse his lips when she bats her lashes and asks for more sugar in her tea.

"I added five packets, Ms. Zoya."

"Mmm." Zoya taps her chin, pretending to be immersed in thought. "Add six next time."

Haroun nods after a beat. "Yes, ma'am." A moment of silence later, he turns to leave.

"Oh, by the way," Zoya beckons with her index finger, the laughter already bubbling inside her in anticipation of his reaction. "I want you to see this."

He walks forward tentatively, hands shoved in his pockets. The way he carries himself amuses Zoya, as if he constantly believes he needs to be prepared to defend himself against potential attack.

On Zoya's desk lies a blue file. It consists of designs for the clothes of the next bridal shoot. She flips through the designs and stops at one particularly striking *sherwani*.

"You're wearing this."

Haroun's black eyes seem to darken further. "What?"

Zoya revels in the pleasure she feels at riling him up. At the tensing of his shoulders and the tightness of his jaw. She's never experienced this kind of thrill before, and it feels heedy and intoxicating.

"Yeah, you're going to be the model for this part of the show," Zoya says.

"But I don't even—I'm just—why do *I* have to model for it?" She can see the effort it takes him in reigning his anger in, and replacing it with polite indignation instead.

Zoya raises an eyebrow. He's too respectful to be outright rude towards her, but the storm beginning to swirl in his otherwise passive eyes is unmistakable. "Because I asked you to." *And I enjoy it far too much when I get under your skin.*

"But I'm an intern." Haroun holds his hands out, confused. "Besides . . ." he hesitates. "Is the company allowed to force me to do something that wasn't in the job description?"

She hears the additional, unspoken sentence. "*Are* you *allowed to force me?*"

Zoya leans back in her chair. Her gaze flicks to his hands, then to his face. His choice of words intrigues her. *Is the company allowed to* force *me?* Which tells Zoya he seriously sees this as a threat, a realization which only further fascinates her.

"Your concern is justifiable," she drawls, examining her nails. "But I'm assuming you're staying in this job for the long run?"

"I—" he seems too flustered, too lost for words, to form a response.

"Besides, did you read the company policies document in its entirety?" she dares to bluff.

Haroun furrows his eyebrows.

Check. He's taking the bait.

"Well, no . . ." he murmurs quietly, but rushes to continue at the triumphant expression on Zoya's face. "But Ms. Zoya, who *ever* reads the company policies document in its entirety? It's like the terms and conditions on an iPhone."

Zoya gives him a smug smile. "It's your responsibility to read it. Besides, if you ask anyone who's worked here for at least a year, they have all participated in a bridal shoot." She doesn't include the very crucial fact that their "participation" didn't necessarily consist of modeling.

"Not because we don't have models," Zoya continues. "Oh, honey," she giggles, flipping behind her shoulder. "We have *plenty* of models. But the business was deteriorating. And we needed something"—she pauses, biting her red lips in thought—"*phenomenal* to get the business booming again. So we used our own employees as models. And people loved it. And *you*, my friend," Zoya's eyes drop from his face and travel all over him before making eye contact again.

He fidgets under her gaze.

She smiles, flashing her impeccable teeth at him. *HR, HR, HR,* a small voice in her head tries to warn her. But she barrels forward, "With *you* on that stage, not only would the crowd go wild, but the business would topple through the roof, my dear."

Haroun flinches. "I don't want to be a model."

Zoya raises her eyebrows. "Why not?"

"Because," his voice roughens. "That's exactly why I don't want to be a model."

Zoya lets out a bubbly laugh. "Because you *look good*?"

"No. Because I don't want to be the object of unnecessary and uncomfortable attention."

Oh. Zoya sits back once again, rubbing her chin. She mulls over his words. *He doesn't want attention. Even looking like* that, *he doesn't want attention. Interesting.*

"Everybody has initial stage fright," Zoya says slowly. "We all get over it, eventually."

Haroun sits in the chair opposite Zoya and places his palms on the table. Zoya notices that his hands are trembling. "This isn't about stage fright, Ms. Zoya. I don't want people looking at me like that."

His shaky voice is a stark contrast to his appearance—to the hard set of his jaw and the fierce determination in his eyes.

Which tells Zoya that the prospect of potentially having to do this terrifies him, but he's still firm on his stance.

"Like *what*?" she challenges, knowing full well that this conversation is digging into his self-control.

"With . . . *desire*," he releases a breath and leans back, relieved.

Zoya stifles a laugh. "We've all modeled at least once. People forget about you after a while."

Haroun's eyes darken. He rubs a hand through his inky black hair and trains his eyes on the floor. "With all due respect, Ms. Zoya, I think it's . . . insulting for someone like you to model in front of others."

Zoya's blood boils. "Someone like *me*? *Insulting*?"

"Someone so . . . noteworthy. Someone so eye-catching." Suddenly, he grimaces and presses his lips together, regret etching into his features. Nonetheless, he continues moments later with a deep breath. "For someone like you—someone so respected and renowned—to be on a stage for others to ogle at." He says this quietly—with a steady expression—as if his comment can go in one ear and out the other.

But Zoya's heart—for the first time in a long time—stutters, then starts again.

Haroun clears his throat quickly and shakes his head. "Oh God. I'm sorry. It was absolutely not my place to say any of that. Really, forgive me, I—" He rubs his eyes with a loud, loaded sigh. "Bad habit I'm trying to break."

Still in shock over his previous words, Zoya eyes him quietly. *You have bad habits, too, Mr. Suleiman?*

Haroun stands, shaking his head again as if to clear it. "I think this conversation is over, Ms. Zoya?" He says it like a question. As if he's asking for permission. But Zoya can tell by his tense posture that it's just a formality.

He can't wait to flee.

"Yes," she murmurs quietly. "It is."

Haroun turns and exits her office.

Wait. Zoya freezes. *Did I just say yes?*

She grabs a strand of her hair and twirls it.

He's strange, Zoya thinks. He shows up with a casual demeanor not expecting to get the job. Then, when he gets the job, he throws his heart and soul into it in the span of a week. He's reserved and politely indifferent with his CEO, and politely indifferent—hell, *any* kind of indifference—is *not* what Zoya Zameer is used to.

On top of that, he's managed to make *her* speechless.

She cocks her head to the side, eyes trained on the wall hanging in her office. *There's something so . . . intriguing about him.*

Zoya flips her hair behind her shoulder. "To work, Ms. Zameer. To work."

Five

~

ZOYA SLAPS A FILE on the table. The employee flinches.

"What is this, Farhan?"

"Ma'am, it's—it's the concept designs you asked for."

Zoya leans back and stares him down. "Why are you stuttering?"

"N-No reason."

Zoya begins to giggle, and the tension on Farhan's face diminishes momentarily. "I was going to tell you that they're done really well." She pauses. "You had help."

Farhan fidgets, eyebrows furrowed. "I just wanted to get some of the concepts looked over and finalized with—uh—with the new intern. Haroun."

Zoya raises her brows. "I see." *Of course it was him.* "Leave."

"P-Pardon, Ms. Zoya?" Farhan's face contorts in worry.

Zoya stares at him pointedly. "We're done with this discussion. Good job. Great. I really have nothing else to say to you, and you're holding up my meeting with an agent, so leave."

"Uh—okay. Thank you."

When Farhan leaves, Zoya returns to the designs in front of her. "Interesting, Mr. Haroun Suleiman. You've already become friends with your coworkers."

For a distracted moment, she halts in flipping through the file and reaches into her desk drawer. An absentminded smile makes its way onto her face as she pulls out Haroun's résumé and brushes slow fingers across his picture.

"You're something, aren't you?" she whispers.

~

Meanwhile, Farhan rushes out of the hallway of Zoya's office, a frustrated look on his face. The balls of his feet barely touch the floor as he angrily heads to his cubicle.

He collides into someone and stumbles backward.

"Whoa, man. What's the hurry?" Haroun chuckles, then backtracks at the expression on Farhan's face. "Are you alright?"

"It's nothing. I was just gonna file a report with HR," Farhan replies angrily, then sighs at Haroun's raised brows. "Sorry, man. I just don't understand why that woman hates me so much."

Haroun knits his brows. "Are you talking about Ms. Zoya?"

Farhan's eyes widen. "Is it that obvious?"

Haroun purses his lips, shaking his head. "No, I was just—"

"Oh, man, it *is* that obvious. I *knew* I wasn't the only one who noticed." Farhan's eyes dart around before he leans in. "She's like a *chipkali*, man. A lizard." Haroun flinches, but Farhan is oblivious to his reaction. "She'll suck up to you when it's necessary, and then suddenly she's bolting high and far away from you. How can someone so pretty be so vicious? I don't understand what her problem with me is! She literally looks at me like she wants to squeeze my brain to a pulp. And mind you, there isn't much of it for her to squeeze, anyway. This job has weakened my entire prefrontal cortex, the *logical* area of my brain. Now I act on my emotions, my *amygdala*, constantly thinking, '*Oh, no, what will Ms. Zoya say?*' And God knows what top secret mission she's conducting in her office nowadays. She's having secret meetings with business contractors of other companies and international agents or something. If someone so much as walks by, she snaps at them."

Haroun seems thoroughly confused. "Business contractors and international agents?"

"I don't care, man!" Farhan says agitatedly, running a hand

through his hair. "She's *ruthless*. And you know what—"

Haroun places a hand on Farhan's shoulder. "Farhan, relax. I don't think you should talk about her like that, no matter how you feel about her—"

"No, no, let him continue," an amused voice says. Both guys quickly turn around.

Their CEO is leaning against the wall at the end of the hallway, arms folded and posture relaxed, eyes bright and eager. She absentmindedly tugs at her hair, pulling loose strands out.

Farhan looks as if he's going to pee his pants.

Despite the tense situation, Haroun holds back a laugh. *His amygdala is probably going haywire right now.*

"*Chipkali*, huh? That's pretty creative, I gotta tell you." Zoya wraps loose hair around her fingers and throws it in the trash can near her. Haroun's eyes stray to the large circle of fallen hair, eyebrows knitting. "Snake, I've heard. Witch, I've also heard. But *chipkali*? Now *that* deserves an award," Zoya laughs and begins to applaud.

Farhan's face turns ashen.

"N-No, Ms. Zoya. I wasn't talking about you—"

Zoya turns to Haroun and rolls her eyes as if to say, *Can you believe this guy?* "Farhan, save it. Can you please come to my office?"

Farhan looks as if he would rather pour hot tea all over himself. "I-Is that necessary?"

"Yes. You can say all those things to me in my office." She spins on her heel, then turns back around. "Oh, and you too," she points to Haroun before heading to her office.

An indent appears between Haroun's eyebrows. "Wait, why me?"

Zoya's footsteps slow. "I want to talk to you guys about something," she says without turning around.

Haroun and Farhan follow her to her office, the latter of whom clenches and unclenches his fists. "I'm dead. I'm finished, bro. After Ms. Zoya fires me, my mom is gonna make me work at her brother's IT company, and I swear I'm gonna plummet into depression after staring at all those computer screens for days. I'm gonna lose what's left of my freaking mind, I'm telling you. You *know* how much I *hate* comp sci, right?"

"You know IT and comp sci are two separate things, right?" Haroun says.

"Whatever!" Farhan huffs. "That just proves my point."

Haroun chuckles, his dimple flashing. To alleviate his friend's tension, he jokes, "Get ready to code in Python."

Farhan elbows him. "You're the worst, man!"

Zoya turns around when they're in her office and winks. "I hear Java isn't *that* bad."

Farhan gulps, and the CEO rolls her eyes. "Relax. I'm not firing you." For the fleetest moment, her eyes flick to Haroun, but she looks away so quickly he thinks he may have imagined it. "But I need you as the lead for this new project."

Farhan's expression shifts from fear to utter surprise. "What project?"

"We've been offered a place in the annual Desi World Fashion Show, and I want you to lead the project." Zoya pauses, cocking her head at Farhan. "I've talked to the board about this. We want you to assemble a team, figure out finances, meet with the designers, and finalize models. We would like to see a presentation with the logistics in two weeks."

Farhan's eyes are wide with disbelief.

Haroun, observing from a more objective point of view, gets a bad feeling. *From the little I know of him, Farhan cracks under pressure.* Begrudgingly he thinks, *And she* does *seem to be extra hard on him.*

"Ms. Zoya, may I give a suggestion?" he blurts out.

The CEO turns her full, intense focus on him. Haroun remains steady, resolute. "Is it possible for me to co-lead? Farhan will have some support, and I'll become familiar with the extensive Zameer experience."

Zoya taps a nail against her lips, contemplating his words. Farhan's breath hitches, and Haroun is shocked to see the intense warmth in his friend's eyes. "Hmm." She pauses for a few seconds. "I summoned you in here because I wanted you, as a relatively new employee, to participate in the project to some degree as well, but co-leading is a reasonable option. I'll run it by the board, but that's completely fine with me."

Haroun nods, glancing at his relieved friend. "Thank you, Ms. Zoya."

"*Koi baat nahi.* You guys may leave now."

As soon as they exit, Farhan grabs Haroun's arm. "First of all, what the hell? She's suddenly in a good mood. Second, she just gave me such a *huge* opportunity. And third, you *literally* saved my life back there. I would *not* have been able to do this on my own. Fourth, what the hell is your effect on her, man? She turns into an angel when she sees you." He halts. "What's going on? *Koi chakkar chal raha hai?*"

Haroun's face grows serious. "No, man."

Farhan shrugs. "Yeah, you don't seem like the type to me anyway."

Haroun furrows his eyebrows. "The type?"

"You know, the type who would start anything premarital. Especially not with someone like *her.*"

Haroun tenses and reaches up to run his hand through his hair. "*Yaar*, Farhan, I really like you. Please don't say things like that."

Farhan's eyes widen. "What did I say?"

Haroun's tone is soft, eyes apologetic. "Assumptions about her character. We never know the state of anyone's heart."

Farhan opens and closes his mouth, unsure of what to say. "Sorry, *yaar*. You took it to heart."

Haroun sighs. "No, it's not about me. Or you. I just—" he shakes his head suddenly. "Never mind."

Farhan reaches up and pats Haroun's back. "I get it, man. You're right. You're the kind of friend my mom would be proud I have. For once."

Haroun's eyes darken. "I'm not—"

"Oh, Mr. Suleiman?" Zoya reapproaches them from the end of the hallway. "Can I talk to you for a second?"

Farhan bites back a smile and nudges Haroun, who gets a nervous feeling in the pit of his stomach. Especially when he remembers her previous request: *You're going to be the model for this part of the show.*

He follows his boss to her office.

~

Once in her office, Zoya turns around, her curls bouncing around her face. "Close the door." Haroun gives her a strange look. "Please," she adds.

He does as she says and stands awkwardly in front of the door. Zoya fights off the laughter rumbling in her chest at his posture and clears her throat. "I've spoken to the board, and they approve of your collaboration on the project. But I wanted you to know that choosing you as co-lead was a conscious decision. I didn't do it because you requested it."

Haroun shoves his hands in his pockets. His eyebrows scrunch together as he smiles bemusedly. "Okay?"

His smile reveals the dimple in his left cheek. Zoya halts in twisting a curl of hair around her finger and eyes him brazenly.

Haroun looks away.

"I just wanted to let you know," Zoya says simply. She takes a few steps forward, and Haroun visibly tenses. She cocks her head to the side, a grin making its way onto her face. "Although I first appointed Farhan as the lead for this project, I think *you're* the much better choice for it."

"Then why appoint him?" he asks casually, twisting his watch around his wrist and avoiding her eyes. Then, as if he realizes how that might be interpreted, he rushes to add, "I mean, if you weren't satisfied with him leading the project. Not that *I* want to lead it."

Zoya moves closer and smiles. "*Meri marzi.* I don't need to tell you that."

"Okay . . . so is there something else you called me for, Ms. Zoya?" His voice is polite but strained as he rubs the back of his neck.

Zoya takes a few more steps until she's directly in front of him. *HR, HR, HR,* the voice in her head warns. But she's simply too curious.

She ducks her head to try to look into his eyes. He's actively avoiding her gaze, and it baffles her. After all, he *had* called her noteworthy and eye-catching—even if he seemed to have immediately regretted it. So were those all simply passing observations? Words he'd heard others say about her?

"Why won't you look at me?" she says softly.

Haroun looks up, gaze roaming around the office. He shifts so that he's at a considerable distance from her. When he sighs, Zoya can practically feel the tension emanating from him. "Was there something else you needed from me, Ms. Zoya?"

Zoya grins, intrigued by his behavior. He's still avoiding her eyes. "The point is, I want you and Farhan to work together, but I want you to have the upper hand. Clearly, you're already so practical and skilled in these organizational matters, as depicted by your résumé."

Haroun finally looks at her, a flicker of surprise in his eyes. As if he wasn't expecting her to have read his résumé, let alone think him capable. "You read my résumé?"

"*Jaan,* I'm the CEO." She winks, and he looks away once more. "I know everything that goes on in these headquarters. About each and every employee.

"So—and this is off the record—you're leading the project. And"—she snorts lightly—"I'm sure your assistance will be appreciated by Farhan. Someone like you, who is so skilled and"— Zoya pauses, daring to move closer.

Haroun has seemed to reach his breaking point. He steps away hurriedly, a muscle jumping in his jaw. "Uhh, anything else, Ms. Zoya, before I . . . ?" He gestures towards the door, slowly backing away to create even more distance between them.

Zoya flashes her brilliant smile at him. "No, darling. You may go." He exits quickly, and she's left standing in the middle of her office with a strange smile on her face, eyes contemplative and curious.

"I'll figure you out, Mr. Suleiman, I will. And if not"—she shrugs and throws her hands up in the air, bangles clinking against each other—"I'm not Zoya Zameer."

Six

"So verily with hardship, there is ease. Verily, with hardship, there is ease." (Qur'an 94:5-6)

~

AS ZOYA FINISHES PRAYING *Maghrib*, the orange hues in the sky begin to fade into indigo. She sits behind her desk and resumes working.

Zoya doesn't realize how late it's gotten until she's yawning and glancing absentmindedly at her clock. Widening her eyes at the darkness outside, she quickly begins to reorganize her desk and pack her things. She stuffs her keys into her handbag and almost trips in her haste to leave.

As expected, the headquarters are silent and empty save for the security guards. They nod at her as she leaves. "Good night, Ms. Zoya."

"Good night," she replies breathlessly, barely even looking at them.

Zoya hurries into the elevator, elbowing the button for the first floor. She fumbles in her handbag for her phone.

The elevator dings and the doors slide open. Zoya turns a corner—head now buried in her handbag to search for her phone—and gasps in surprise when she slams into someone. Her bag slips to the floor, her heel giving way as she collapses forward.

She grasps strong shoulders, and two hands reach out to

upright her. The contact sends waves of discomfort throughout her.

Zoya looks up and sees Haroun's dark, intense eyes.

As soon as he uprights her, Haroun immediately steps away and shrugs himself off. He reaches down to grab her bag and hand it to her. Zoya notices how careful he is not to touch her again, even by accident. "I'm sorry," he mutters. "Are you alright?"

"Yes . . . yes, thank you," she stutters. *Where did he come from?* She tucks her hair behind her ears and shoulders her handbag. "How come you're still here?"

He points behind him, avoiding her eyes. "Farhan and I were working on the project. I was going to get our UberEats order."

"Oh." *Pick your head up, Zoya, it doesn't suit you to be speechless.* Zoya straightens and flips her hair behind one shoulder. "Wow. You guys are pretty dedicated."

"We just wanted to get a head start," he replies quietly.

"Right." *Leave before you further make a fool of yourself, Zoya.* "Well, I'm—" she gestures to the exit and he nods with a "*Salaam*," backing away as if he can't wait to get away from her.

Zoya is escorted to her car —she'd wanted to drive herself this morning—and she bids the security guards goodnight.

As Zoya drives home, Haroun's eyes continue to distract her. So dark, so intense.

"*Kya hua hai, Zoya?*" she chides herself out loud. "He's just a man like half the world is. Nothing special." Someone in the car behind her beeps their horn. "*Kya hai?*" she yells. "Dumb people on the roads these days." She shakes her head, and as the person behind her switches lanes, she too switches to be in front of him. Zoya glances in the rear view mirror, scoffing at the middle finger the man is pointing towards her. "Yeah, yeah, go ahead. As if you have any other defense. *Paaghal hai sab aaj kal, yaar.* Everyone's *crazy*." The man switches lanes once more. This time, Zoya allows him. As he drives by, she watches his face—contorted in rage—switch to surprise as he sees her impeccable features.

Zoya flips her hair behind her shoulder. "Yeah, that's right," she murmurs haughtily. "You have no idea who you're talking to." She drives quietly for a few more minutes, again unsettled by how dark it is outside. She always tells herself to leave work right after *Maghrib* so that it's not too dark but manages to lose track of time.

Finally, after what seems like forever, Zoya approaches her manor and the gatekeeper buzzes her in. "Good evening." He hesitates. "You're late today, Ms. Zoya."

She sighs long and loud. "Work kept me."

After Zoya parks, the doorman Aman lets her in, gazing at her with that sad look that always confuses her. She's too tired to once again argue with him about it.

Zoya is about to make her way upstairs when her maid Mumtaz approaches her. "Zoya *bibi*, you're late today. Is everything okay?"

Zoya slams her keys on the foyer table and Mumtaz flinches. "Does everyone need to keep reminding me that I'm late? I *know* I'm late."

"*Bibi*, I was just worried because you get—"

Zoya's eyes flash. "I get *what*, Mumtaz?"

The maid looks down and quiets.

"I thought so." Zoya massages her neck and sighs. "Anyway, I'm hungry. Get the food ready while I shower."

Mumtaz nods eagerly and rushes to the kitchen.

Zoya heads upstairs to her room, trying to suppress the shivers that are beginning to consume her. She steps into the warm shower as quickly as possible, allowing the water to relax her shaking muscles. "I-It's okay," she whispers through clenched teeth, pressing her fist into the wall. The dark, ominous night sky continues to appear behind her closed eyelids. "You're okay, Zoya."

Once showered and changed, Zoya heads downstairs, tucking wet hair behind her ears. Mumtaz has set the table with some of Zoya's favorite foods: biryani, samosas, *dahi bhare*, and more. Zoya smiles and digs in. When Mumtaz still hasn't left, Zoya looks up at her. "This is really good," she mumbles reluctantly, and Mumtaz seems to glow with happiness.

The maid eyes Zoya closely and purses her lips, suppressing a laugh. Zoya sets down her fork. "What?"

"Uh, *bibi*, you still have some mascara running down your cheeks."

Zoya grabs her phone and flips open the camera. Sure enough, dull black lines run down her face just as they appear in movies, when the heroine cries over her pathetic, broken heart.

Zoya sighs and locks her phone. "Whatever. Did you guys eat?"

"Yes," Mumtaz replies, a look of surprise on her face at the uncharacteristic question.

When Zoya's done eating, she wipes her mouth with a tissue and begins to pick up the dishes. Mumtaz reaches out to stop her. "*Bibi,* it's okay. I can do it."

Zoya tenses at the contact. "I have hands, too, Mumtaz."

Mumtaz obliges silently at the flash in Zoya's eyes, and together they carry the dishes to the kitchen. Then, needing further distraction to suppress her shudders, Zoya washes the dishes while refusing Mumtaz's and the other maids' pleas to do them. The entire time she's at the sink, her jaw is clenched, eyes strictly focused on the water and the soap suds in an attempt to combat the terror crawling up her throat.

Later, when she's snuggled under her soft comforter, head lying on her black ice memory foam pillow, Zoya can't seem to close her eyes. Her shivers won't subside, even though the chandelier lights are on and the curtains are shut, concealing the darkness outside. The door of her room is open as well, light filtering through the hallways outside.

"Relax, Zoya," she mumbles through shivers. "You're okay."

Then, surprising even her, the image of a pair of intense black eyes flashes in her mind. Her hands remember the strong arms she gripped.

Her eyelids droop, the memory of black eyes never leaving her. She falls asleep imagining those strong arms around her.

Haroun's arms.

Seven

"Indeed, I am near." (Qur'an 2:186)

~

THERE'S A KNOCK ON the office door.

"Enter," Zoya says without looking up from the file in her hand.

Someone enters and walks up to her desk. "*Salaam,* Ms. Zoya."

Upon hearing his voice, she looks up. A slow grin spreads across Zoya's face. She sits up straighter, flipping her hair behind one shoulder. Shoving away thoughts of Haroun's appearance in her dreams last night, she replies, "*Wa 'Alaikum Salaam.* What's up?"

"Sorry to interrupt, but . . ." Haroun holds up a newspaper. He seems distraught. "I just wanted to show you something."

Zoya eyes the newspaper. She recognizes the title *Gup Shup News* and immediately guesses what this is about, but layers her voice with false curiosity anyway. "What's this?"

"I just"—he flips to the second page—"I wasn't sure if you had seen this already." He turns the newspaper over and sets it in front of her. At the top of the page, headlined in large bold letters, is: *Zoya Zameer, CEO of Zameer Co., Rumored to Have Reunited With Alleged Husband.* Underneath is a picture of the backs of Zoya and a man. The picture shows Zoya's longer auburn curls versus her shorter curls now. The news makes her blood boil, but she feigns indifference and looks up at Haroun.

"What is this?" she repeats.

"Ms. Zoya, actually . . ." Haroun fidgets, expression growing perturbed. "I was going to ask *you* that."

"What do you want to know?"

"I think it's . . . insulting for them to be spreading news like this."

"Ugh," she says, nodding vigorously. "Oh, you're so right." She points to the first line of the article. "'Twenty-*six* year old Zoya Zameer'? I'm twenty-five!"

This doesn't seem to lighten his mood. His brows knit as he says, "Seriously, Ms. Zoya. This is highly disrespectful of them."

Zoya laughs, running her hands through her curls. "Highly disrespectful? Haroun, it's a *newspaper* in the twenty-first century. It's not going to be anything *but* disrespectful. And who even reads newspapers anymore? Most people prefer digital media."

"It's not about whether newspapers are read or not. It's about these people"—he points to the reporters' names on the paper—"trying to ruin your reputation and by default the company's reputation." He pauses. "Forgive me for saying this, but stuff like this is deliberately done *especially* since you're a woman. And you know people nowadays jump at any chance to say things about women." A brief, dark look passes across his face before he shakes his head and gestures to the paper. "We should do something about this."

Zoya clucks her tongue and stands up. "*Bichaare*. You're so *masoom*." Haroun rubs the back of his neck at her declaration of his innocence. "Don't lose sleep over it. In a prosperous company like this, we're bound to have the media constantly spreading news. We cannot stop every report or article. So I'm telling you, leave it be."

"But . . ." He doesn't seem to be the least bit satisfied with her reply. "It doesn't bother you? To have people constantly say false things about you and the company?"

Zoya shrugs. "Why should it bother me? *I* know the truth. And . . ." She examines her nails for a moment before peering at him through her lashes. She doesn't know what makes her do it, but she murmurs, "Who says it's false?"

Haroun halts in running his fingers through his hair. Zoya hides her smile. "Oh." His entire demeanor changes. "Oh, I'm so sorry. I assumed it was—I shouldn't have"—he breaks off, uneasy.

Zoya walks around to the front of her desk and leans against it, closer to him. He immediately begins to step away. "It's alright," she says. "Thank you for looking out for me."

Haroun seems confused now, holding his hands up defensively. "I was just . . . I assumed it may be false, so I just wanted to make sure no harm would come to the company. That's why I brought the paper in."

Zoya smiles at his rambling. "Now my deep dark secret is out. Oh, *no.*"

"Are you—were you married?" he asks. She strains to pay careful attention to his tone but doesn't detect any underlying motives. Just plain curiosity.

"Yes," she says. Her lack of elaboration probably comes off as strange to him, considering Zoya Zameer loves to amplify and sugarcoat everything.

"Oh." Haroun smiles slightly, still too embarrassed to look up. "I'm sorry, I didn't know. That's really nice." He points behind him. "I'll go now. I just wanted to show this to you." He grabs the newspaper and turns around when Zoya's voice stops him in his tracks.

"And divorced," she blurts out. Again, she doesn't know what makes her say it. But she watches his back with a strict urgency, waiting for him to face her. "Married and divorced. Zameer is my maiden name." Saying her father's name out loud causes her heart to lurch painfully.

He turns. Slowly. "Oh," he says again. "Oh, I'm sorry." He immediately begins shaking his head. "Not because you're divorced, just--"

"I understand. No need to be sorry." She moves closer, and he moves farther. Like a dance. "*Jo ho gaya, so ho gaya.* And *qué será, será.*" She shrugs. "Whatever has happened, has happened. And whatever will be, will be. Life mottos."

"Right." He pauses for a brief moment before gesturing to the door. "With your permission, Ms. Zoya . . ."

Disappointed, Zoya returns to her chair. "Of course," she says. "I wouldn't want to keep you." Haroun murmurs a "*Salaam*" before shutting the door.

Zoya sighs, the image on the newspaper flashing through her mind. The one that's been plaguing her all morning. *Thank God it was just our backs. And where did they even find that picture from anyway? These people honestly have nothing better to do than grovel around in the dirt of other people's lives.*

"*Nikamme log*," she grumbles, shaking her head.

~

"Farhan, send me the presentation by tomorrow. Need to make sure you haven't made any mistakes before it's presented to the board." Zoya points an accusatory finger in his face. "Alright?"

"Uh—yes, Ms. Zoya," Farhan says nervously.

"And why are you always stuttering around me?" she snaps.

"Um—I—no, Ms. Zoya. I was just worried about the news from this morning."

"Is the news about *you and your alleged wife*?" Zoya asks him.

"Well, no, but—"

"Then there's no need for you to worry about it. It was about me. So *apne kaam se kaam rakho*."

"We were all just worrying about Zameer's image, Ms. Zoya," he replies defensively. "Just thinking of the repercussions of false news in terms of PR."

False news. Zoya mulls over Farhan's words. Although the news *is* false—no doubt a hatched plot of her rival Zaki Ahmed to attempt to unsettle her—Zoya hasn't yet addressed it with her employees. Farhan believes it's false, and he's closest to Haroun at this company. Meaning Haroun has defended Zoya after their conversation in her office. Meaning he knew it was something Zoya would want to clarify.

A slow smile spreads across her face.

Farhan looks confused as he says, "Ms. Zoya?" He tries to catch her gaze.

She breaks out of her stupor and flips her hair behind her shoulders. Adjusting her *dupatta* and *jhumkas*, she straightens. "You think this stuff doesn't occur to me, Farhan? *Jaan*, I'm the *CEO*. I think about what's best for this company *before* you do." She begins ticking off on her fingers. "PR is strengthening because of our advanced marketing campaigns, and the next course of action is launching our new clothing line. Then, this *bakwaas* news will become the last thing on everyone's minds. Besides, the media office is constantly working on getting useless news removed from all platforms." Zoya runs her fingers through her hair, pulling out loose strands. "Why do you think we've been going crazy having Flora and her team of designers work on all those prints?"

Farhan's eyebrows are raised. "Wow. As always, you never fail to impress us." He pauses, then dares to ask, "Did you know this false news was going to be publicized? Is that why you extensively prepared for it?"

Zoya giggles. "Keep your friends close and your enemies closer."

Farhan laughs nervously at her cryptic answer. Then his voice takes on a nasally monotone. "Right. But still, Ms. Zoya, we appreciate you for taking the necessary steps to combat the press. You're always two steps ahead." He seems to be holding his breath for her next words.

She stops giggling—suddenly remembering who she's talking to—and neutralizes her expression. "*Acha, acha.* Don't get too free with me. Go do your work."

He deflates and returns to his workstation.

Zoya sighs happily. "You're fabulous, Zoya Zameer, you are." She kisses her hand and heads back to her office, heels clicking against the floor, and *dupatta* flying through the air behind her.

~

That evening, Zoya is exiting the headquarters and heading to her driver when reporters begin to crowd around her. She continues walking, trying to shove their mics away from her face.

"Ma'am, is it true that you've reunited with an alleged husband of yours?"

"Ma'am, the media wasn't even aware that you were married. Are you currently in a marital relationship?"

Zoya stops, takes her sunglasses off, and flashes a smile at the cameras. She can already imagine the headlines: "*Zoya Zameer's Smile: Affirmation or Declination?*" She giggles out loud, surprising them. Taking advantage of their confusion, Zoya dashes between them and rushes to her driver's car, ignoring the cries of "Ms. Zoya!" behind her.

In the car, her driver raises his eyebrows. "Why didn't you deny their accusations?"

She shrugs. "Oh, Raheem. Sometimes it's honestly better just to shut the hell up. Opening up is going to give them what they want. They provoke us, so answering invites them to ask more questions and make more assumptions. It's a never-ending cycle." Zoya pulls out a tube of lipstick from her purse. She tugs down the visor from the roof of the car and begins prattling off almost absentmindedly as she applies her lipstick.

"Just my personal opinion, but I don't think *every* issue requires constant, *loud* resistance. Silence is often equally as powerful." Zoya smacks her lips together and fluffs up her hair. She furrows her brows, deep in thought. "Actually, I guess it really depends on the situation. Like, if a woman has suffered some form of harassment, it would probably serve her better *not* to stay silent about it." She stops suddenly, expression darkening.

Raheem switches gears and pulls out of Zameer's headquarters. "Unfortunately," he says. "Too many women are forced to be silent on issues like that, whether by internal or external forces."

Zoya's eyes widen at his words.

The next couple of minutes pass in tense silence until Zoya suddenly continues the conversation from where it left off: "You know what, though?" She stares at her reflection in the window. Brown eyes lined with winged eyeliner stare back at her. "Women who stay silent about stuff like that are cowards."

Raheem's eyebrows incline. "That's . . . a pretty daring statement."

"Is it?" Zoya retorts, heart beginning to race. She shakes her head in disgust. "We live in a world riddled with feminism. People nowadays will believe anything women say."

"Not necessarily," Raheem says. "I think that, *because* we live in a post-feminism era, people will often attribute everything a woman says or does to feminism. Which in turn will decrease the severity of any situation she's involved in."

Zoya rears back in shock, her driver's words piercing her somewhere deep. Words of people from her past filter through her mind.

Our son would never do that to a woman.

She's accusing him because of that whole #metoo movement.

All these women are making up stories now because they know feminists will have their back.

Raheem's voice interrupts Zoya's unpleasant memories. "You don't consider yourself a feminist?" he asks. "Every time I've seen you speak in interviews or campaigns, you've seemed averse to the whole idea of feminism."

"Feminism is a joke, to be honest," Zoya replies. Raheem does a double take at the venom in her voice. "Western feminism, at that." She mimics holding up a sign and contorts her face into an angry expression. "'*We want equality*'—actually, we say we want equality when really we want to be above men. '*Men are spawns of Satan and deserve to be buried six feet under! Women should cut off their hands before stepping into the kitchen!*'" She drops her hands and rolls her eyes. "What a joke."

Her driver furrows his brows. "I think we need to make a distinction here—I think you're against radical feminism."

Zoya mulls over it. "Well, yeah, I guess. But I think all kinds of feminism have subtly morphed into radical feminism." Zoya sits straighter and leans forward, briefly wondering how strange it is to have this conversation with her *driver,* of all people. "See, if we were to say that feminism is about women's rights, then of course I'm all for it. Which woman wouldn't be? But the problem is, that's not solely what it's about anymore. Now it's used as a tool for women to put down men and incessantly criticize them, often without reason. For instance, wives cooking a meal for their husbands are often reprimanded and thought to be doing so out of compulsion. Daughters asking their brothers or fathers for money are viewed as codependent and having no status of their own."

Zoya blows out a sigh. "Feminism has created a specific, limited agenda. One that only works for some women. For example, feminists will rave about a woman's right to work, but will never give that same energy to women who choose to be housewives or homemakers. Instead, they'll label them as oppressed or succumbing to the patriarchy. And, okay, maybe for some women, that *is* the case. But for *so many others*, that's a preference or a choice." Zoya glances at Raheem, who is listening with rapt attention. "I think the term feminism is often abused and used too loosely. People employ it very broadly to paint their own scenarios, or use it as an excuse to take advantage of certain situations. Like, yes, there are grounded versions of feminism, but there are also very toxic versions of feminism which, I think, veer off course."

Zoya takes a deep breath. "So, in conclusion: of course I support women's rights when *that's* what they're about. But no, I don't support radical feminism. Because it's rarely about women's rights anymore; it's more focused on extraneous things."

Raheem is silent for a moment before he says, "I understand that completely. And I'd have to say I agree. I used to be the kind of guy who bristled at the topic of feminism due to, sadly, what it's become about. But eventually I learned what it's *supposed* to be about. The whole thing is so much more convoluted than it seems, and I can't say that many men understand it or are even willing to understand it."

Zoya knits her brows. "Actually, yeah. Enlighten me, Raheem. Most men flee as soon as they hear about women's rights or feminism. I'm curious what made *you* so invested in the topic."

Raheem laughs. "I have three sisters. They knocked some sense into me. Otherwise, I promise you, I would have still been the guy fleeing from an important discussion."

Zoya chuckles, then immediately grows serious. "Isn't that so sad, though? Imagine how many people shy away from important concepts because of the way they're portrayed to them. Or how many people end up never learning the true essence of something because they're put off by its representation."

Raheem nods in agreement, and Zoya suddenly grows quiet at her own words, for reasons she cannot begin to explain.

For the rest of the drive, she leans her head against the window and watches the orange hues in the evening sky disappear.

Eight

The Prophet Muhammad (peace be upon him) said, "Leave that which makes you doubt for that which does not make you doubt."
(Sahih at-Tirmidhi)

~

ZOYA MAKES SURE NO one is around Farhan when she approaches him. "I want hydrangeas for the Desi World fashion show. Fresh ones in every single color."

"Yes, Ms. Zoya." He copies it down onto his clipboard.

"And get that ridiculous gel out of your hair." She gestures to his spikes, and he self-consciously pats his head. "I don't want my employees looking like reckless bike riders."

"Uh—yes, Ms. Zoya."

"*Phir* with the stuttering?" she huffs, stomping towards her office.

Two hours later, Zoya calls her receptionist. "Sarah," she says when the woman walks in. "I have a task for you. Give these images of carnations to Farhan and tell him these are the flowers I was talking about. The ones that will decorate the stage."

Sarah nods and takes the folder from Zoya, exiting the office.

Zoya leans back in her chair and taps her chin with a pen. A corner of her mouth lifts. "Sorry, Farhan. Unfortunately for you, you've become a pawn on the chessboard of Zoya Zameer's life. A piece in the game."

Suddenly, shouts erupt from outside her office door. Zoya furrows her brows before departing her office to witness the commotion.

Flora stands before Haroun with a clenched jaw. His eyes, as usual, are trained to the floor. But this time they are focused on the spilled coffee around Flora's feet.

"Can't you *watch* where you're going, Haroun? Just because you're now Ms. Zoya's *favorite* doesn't mean you can go around doing whatever the hell you feel like!" Flora rubs tissues over her pant leg, which has a dark brown stain on it.

Haroun looks genuinely confused when she says *favorite.* "I'm really sorry, Flora. I—"

"Just get out of my face."

"Whoa, whoa, whoa," Zoya laughs; the sound comes out too high. Her heart begins to beat faster and her cheeks flush--she's *angry.* Heels clicking loudly against the floor, Zoya approaches the two of them. "Flora, what's the problem?"

"He doesn't have *eyes* is the problem."

"Excuse me, Flora, but I don't appreciate my employees bickering with one another." With a sardonic laugh, she adds, "That's *my* job."

Flora narrows her eyes, the expression frighteningly bold, especially when the opponent is Zoya. "Well, we follow by example, don't we?"

Zoya scoffs, rolling her eyes. "You're lucky you don't piss me off, Flora."

Flora doesn't respond; she just continues rubbing her leg with the tissue. Haroun leans down and places tissues over the spilled coffee, pushing them around to soak the liquid into them.

Something about seeing him bent on the floor, lips pressed together and dimple creased in concentration, swirling tissues around in dirty coffee, sets Zoya's heart beating at an erratic pace. "Sarah," she yells. "Call the janitor."

Sarah obliges and disappears down the corridor.

"Leave it, Haroun," Zoya says, tucking her curls behind her ear.

Look at me, she wills silently.

He continues to clean it. "It's alright, Ms. Zoya. I made the mess, so I'll clean it."

"Damn right you will," Flora says angrily.

Zoya turns to her and raises her brows. "Flora," she says, batting her lashes. "Excuse yourself from my sight. *Now.*"

Flora widens her eyes—clearly surprised by Zoya's attitude towards her—before she spins on a heel and stomps away. Zoya turns back to Haroun, expecting him to be pleased by this, but he's quiet. Eyes filled with shame. With one last disappointed look, he turns and walks away.

Zoya stands there, utterly confused.

Flora plainly and openly insulted *Haroun,* the man coworkers bonded with very quickly due to his calm and welcoming nature. And although Flora is one of the few people who doesn't piss her off, Zoya dismissed her for insulting Haroun. He should be happy that he's experiencing the nicer side of Zoya Zameer.

Yet he's managed to awaken in her the emotion she felt only around her father. The lingering, the constant expectation for something more.

Zoya shrugs, mystified.

Sarah returns with the janitor in tow. Zoya pulls Sarah to the side and murmurs, "Go do what I've asked."

Sarah nods. Zoya walks back to her office slowly, Haroun's wounded eyes occupying her thoughts.

~

When Sarah finds Farhan pacing around with a clipboard in hand, she hands him the file. "These are the carnations Ms. Zoya wants on the stage."

"Carnations? But she told me she wants . . . hydrangeas."

Sarah shrugs. "She gave these to me."

Farhan knits his brows. "Carnations . . ." He flips through the images on the clipboard, then shrugs. "Well, alright then."

Haroun joins Farhan, and the two begin working on stage design and role designation. Farhan keeps eyeing Haroun, finding his quiet demeanor bizarre.

"*Yaar*, what's up with you?" Farhan finally says, setting his pen down. "Did Ms. Zoya say something?"

Haroun shakes his head. "No."

"Then what happened? I heard that there was some ruckus on the fourth floor. That's where you were, right?"

Haroun smiles, but it seems forced. "Nothing, Farhan. I'm okay, really. Just a bit tired."

"Hm." Farhan doesn't look convinced. "Well, alright, then. We'll take a coffee break."

At the word "coffee", Haroun's eyes fill with shame. Farhan bites his lip and narrows his eyes. "Whatever happened on the fourth floor—it involved you, didn't it? But what could *you* have done to piss anyone off? Did you accidentally walk in on one of Ms. Zoya's secret meetings or something? What happened?"

"I don't—it's not her fault. I was walking quickly and accidentally spilled coffee on Flora. Hot coffee."

Farhan sucks in a breath. "Ouch. I heard that there was some yelling—that was Flora?" He pauses, lips pressed together before he blurts out, "But she's always really nice."

A dejected expression takes over Haroun's face. "I don't think she likes me very much. She said something about being Ms. Zoya's favorite."

"Can't deny that." Farhan shrugs at Haroun's bewildered expression. "What? I told you this before. She favors you over everyone else."

"That's not true," Haroun insists.

"Yes, it is. But since you're not very fond of this topic, let's focus on the lineup of these models."

Haroun nods, still looking sullen. They spend the rest of the afternoon working on the logistics of the fashion show with the rest of the team. Farhan sighs happily a couple hours later, leaning back to stretch and then snapping back into a more professional position as Zoya walks over to them.

Immediately, Haroun busies himself with the images of the carnations.

"How's it going, boys?" She adjusts her *dupatta* over her shoulders.

"Great," Farhan replies animatedly.

Although she had asked both of them, Zoya's eyes are trained only on Haroun. "Mr. Suleiman?"

"Yes?"

"How's it going?"

"Good."

She nods slowly. "I don't expect it to be going any other way, with someone so qualified leading the project."

Farhan's eyes widen as he takes Zoya's compliment as directed towards him. But Haroun flinches at the statement.

"Excuse me for a moment, please," Haroun mumbles politely, standing and disappearing around the corner.

Zoya's eyes follow him, face screwed up in concentration. Farhan watches her carefully, monitoring the way she continues to stare at the space Haroun disappeared into, even many seconds later.

Suddenly, Zoya turns back to Farhan and readjusts her *dupatta*. "What?" she snaps.

Farhan stares at her indignantly. "Nothing, Ms. Zoya."

"Get back to work," she orders, turning on her heel to walk away.

Farhan sighs. "*Yes, Ms. Zoya.*" When she's out of sight, he murmurs, "Right after I finish my HR complaint."

Nine

THE NEXT FEW DAYS are spent in a wild chaos; the designers rush to complete the dresses for the staff, the media office is strictly preoccupied with news reports that have blown up about the prestigious Zoya Zameer, and on the day of the Desi World Fashion Show, Farhan is in a tizzy, walking around giving orders to everyone he sees.

"No, Mark, what the hell are you doing? I said those go in the *other* truck. The *other* one. Oh my God." He gestures wildly to Mark, who huffs and turns around.

Farhan turns to the group huddled around the mannequin of one particularly striking *sherwani*. They look up quickly as he approaches. "What's going on?" he says anxiously. One of the workers looks nervously at the others. "Guys, what is it?"

The worker says, "Nothing, Farhan. We were just—"

Farhan pushes past the group, smacking his forehead when he sees the damage. "You *ripped* the sleeve?"

"We didn't do it!" another worker says indignantly, shooting Farhan a nasty look.

At that moment, the loud click of heels at the end of the hall announces the CEO's arrival. After one look at the chaos, Zoya cups her mouth and yells, "*Quiet!*"

Immediately the loud chatter dies down, and all eyes turn to their boss. She shakes her head and approaches the group huddled around the mannequin. Taking one look at the ripped sleeve, a loud sigh escapes her. "Farhan, get me Flora. *Now*."

Farhan obliges, rushing away quickly. Zoya folds her arms and turns her piercing eyes to each individual in the group. They all look as if they may drop dead when Zoya says, in a deadly voice, "Which one of you good-for-nothings did this?"

Nobody replies, and Zoya rolls her eyes. "You're lucky we have Flora"---they collectively breathe out sighs of relief—"to fix your selfish mistakes." She turns on her heel and begins to walk away when someone behind her whispers, "Does she have to be such a *b*—"

Zoya turns back so fast that her hair flies around her face, curls bouncing against her shoulders. "Beautiful, amazing queen?" She raises her eyebrows at the employee standing to her right, who she knows for a fact was the one who spoke. She *tsks*. "At least wait for me to walk like five feet away before you curse me out, Jordan." Jordan's eyes widen, and he immediately shifts out of her line of sight.

Zoya turns back around and click clacks away, observing everyone else frantically doing their work. Her eyes roam around the hall, halting on one particular face.

His eyebrows are knitted together, his dimple creased in concentration as he flips through the papers on his clipboard. When he finds what he's looking for, he uncaps a pen with his mouth and scribbles something on it.

Zoya can't help the smile that blooms on her face. Even as she notices the weariness and tension enveloping him like a second skin.

"Ms. Zoya?"

She turns suddenly, cheeks reddening. Flora stands in front of her expectantly.

"Oh, right." Zoya clears her throat. "Go fix up that mess, please. And do it quickly." She gestures to the mannequin, and Flora obliges.

Zoya slaps her cheeks when she's sure no one is looking. "Stop it, Zoya Zameer. Why the red cheeks? What the hell is wrong with you?" She takes a deep breath, flips her hair over one shoulder, and straightens her back. "That's right. Back in character."

Farhan approaches her, wringing his hands. "Ms. Zoya, I'm really worried about the *sherwani*."

"It's being taken care of, Farhan. Calm yourself."

"But there are also the flowers—"

"Oh, my God, Farhan." Zoya makes a big show of placing her fingers at her temples. "Never consider a job even slightly higher than your capabilities, let alone the *CEO's* position. I thought you deserved the extended professional experience after having been with us for a while, but you're too uptight." Farhan's expression turns hurtful; Zoya huffs a dramatic sigh in classic Zoya Zameer fashion. "Go take a break, please. *Mera maghaz na chaato.* Stop irritating me. Literally, like, back the hell away from me, or I *will* pull a Jackie Chan on you because your second degree stress is *pissing me off.*"

He walks away from her with a wounded expression, and Zoya rolls her eyes.

After checking on everyone—particularly one person whom Farhan has now joined—Zoya makes her way over to Bill. "Bill, everything good?"

Bill nods. "Everything's set. And your dress has been ironed and is being sent to your house."

Zoya gives him a blank expression. "Did I ask for it to be sent to my house?"

Bill furrows his eyebrows. "Uh, is that not what you wanted?"

"If I wanted it sent to my house, I would have asked, Bill Nye."

Bill raises his brows. "And you just called *Farhan* uptight."

Zoya laughs, the tension in her shoulders loosening. "Stop defending that guy."

Bill smiles. "Just pointing out the obvious."

"Which is?"

"Come on, did you really not want me to send your dress to your house? You're just nervous, Ms. Zoya. And you don't have any other way of controlling it, so you're walking around pushing your anxiety onto everyone else."

"Oh, my God, you're *so* right. I should call you by a different name now—Bill Nye the *Psychology* Guy. Since you're so damn observant, aren't you?" Zoya narrows her eyes at him.

Bill stares at her, then bursts out laughing. "Bill Nye the *Psychology* Guy? Very original."

Zoya lifts her hand and moves it in a duck-like motion, signaling that he can keep talking and she won't care. "*Jaan*, I'm literally the *CEO*. I've been doing this for too long to get nervous about *anything* anymore. So thank you for your observation, *Freud*, but your critical analysis of me is unnecessary. This is a fashion company, not an English class."

Bill holds his hands up defensively. "Hey, I was just saying that—"

"By the way, did you ever believe any of that rubbish our English teachers would say? About what the authors of the novels we read in class were articulating? Teachers made so many damn speculations that made no sense." Zoya makes dramatic hand gestures and adopts a high-pitched tone. "'*The protagonist is eating these boiled potatoes. Now, these boiled potatoes signify the sufferings and the tribulations life has thrown his way, and the way he's eating them signifies—*'"

Bill begins to laugh boisterously, bending over to clutch his stomach.

Zoya is just about to tell him that it wasn't that funny and he can stop pretending to laugh with her when she freezes suddenly. She cocks her head to the side, eyes caught on something outside the headquarters' entrance.

Haroun uncaps a water bottle and hands it to Farhan, who begins pouring water over Haroun's hands. All the first-floor bathrooms have been closed for renovation, and it hits Zoya that Haroun is making *wudu* with a water bottle. He seems to have chosen stepping outside for a moment rather than using a bathroom on another floor.

Zoya watches him perform *wudu* with her feet glued to the ground, absolutely fascinated. He splashes water onto his face three times, then pulls his sleeves back and washes each arm carefully up until his elbow three times. Zoya observes him pass his hands over his head, and a strange sensation consumes her. As if water is rushing through her ears. He performs his *wudu* with so much reverence, so much concentration. In a whirlwind of passion and focus. As if—

"Ms. Zoya?"

Zoya breaks out of her stupor and turns to Bill, whose eyebrows are inclined. She blinks a few times, forgetting where she is and what they were talking about. Her gaze darts back outside, and by now Haroun has finished and is capping the water bottle. He runs his fingers through his hair, laughing at something Farhan is saying.

Zoya turns back to Bill, overwhelmed by disorientation and another feeling she can't name.

"Uh, I—" *Stop stuttering, Zoya. Confusion doesn't suit you.* "I just remembered that I have to tell Flora something." She turns and walks away, leaving Bill with a baffled expression on his face

Zoya rushes to Flora. The image of Haroun making *wudu* keeps flashing in her muddled mind, and she shakes her head to dispel her thoughts.

What about the scene she witnessed so unsettled her?

She knows the exact reason, but is unable to form the words. Her mouth—always ready to puncture and wound and maim with her words—seems at a loss for these very things now. It feels almost insulting to have witnessed Haroun perform *wudu* with such veneration and say anything harmful afterwards. As if by doing so, she may destroy the strange sensation of peace that has enveloped her.

Zoya collides into Flora, regains her balance, and backs away quickly. She clears her throat. "Have you fixed it?"

Flora gives her a bewildered look. "It's been like five minutes, Ms. Zoya. I'm good, but I'm not *that* good."

Zoya laughs shakily, attempting to rid herself of the unsettling feeling that won't leave her. *Back in character, Zoya Zameer. Back in character.* "I'm going to my office. When I come back down, have it done."

Before anyone can see the confusion splayed on Zoya's face or hear the way her breathing is rapidly increasing, she heads to her office.

Once there, she leans back in her chair and stares across the room at the wall in front of her. With furrowed brows.

With thoughtful eyes.

~

"Alright, guys." Zoya paces in front of her staff, the echo of her heels reverberating throughout the meeting room. "As you all know, tonight is an extremely important night. We are going to be scrutinized from every possible angle, especially after all those wild news reports." She mutters, "Since—you know—people just love wasting breath in their already miserable lives talking about me." She stares pointedly at everyone and clears her throat, raising her voice again. "We *cannot* afford any screw-ups." This she says while directing her gaze at Farhan, who stares back indignantly. "It's a crucial time that may determine the success or potentially lead to the downfall of this company."

Someone huffs and whispers, "She literally says this before *every* event."

Zoya turns to the speaker and smiles. "Correct, Jordan. Thank you for your observation." She twists a curl around her finger. "By the way, you should really break your habit of speaking ill of me literally *in front of me.* I have ears."

Jordan lowers his eyes, cheeks reddening as he shrinks back into the crowd.

"As I was saying, everyone needs to take heed of the importance of this event. Clean up nicely, in the clothes handpicked and designed especially for you." She fluffs her hair. "Because no Zameer employee is going to show up in front of cameras wearing anything but Zameer apparel."

Someone whistles, and the group begins to clap and let out whoops of excitement. Zoya nods and bows theatrically. "Let's show them what we've got. You have"—she glances at the clock on the wall—"five hours. See you at the Desi World fashion show. And be on time, otherwise I'll cut from your paycheck," she announces, head held high. Her staff has become used to this empty threat she uses as motivation, and everyone excitedly chitters before dispersing.

Bill is standing with Haroun and Farhan, eyebrows scrunched. His gaze is trained on Zoya with such intensity that Haroun squirms.

"You good?" Farhan asks Bill.

Bill nods, a corner of his lips turning up. "She really knows how to make people listen."

Upon hearing the admiration in Bill's voice, Farhan turns to him with a quizzical expression. "*You* sound awfully impressed," he says suspiciously.

Bill shrugs. "She has a way of articulating herself that—"

"Whoa, whoa, whoa." A grin spreads on Farhan's face. "Don't tell me *you* also fell into the Zoya Zameer trap?"

Bill shakes his head wordlessly but doesn't meet Farhan's eyes.

"Oh, man." Farhan begins to laugh. Even Haroun smiles gently, a faint trace of his dimple appearing. "*You fell for Zoya Zameer.*"

Bill finally looks up. "She may not be the nicest person, but you can't deny the reason that this company is successful is because she's so good at what she does."

Farhan nods vigorously. "I've been spearheading this project for only three weeks—which still seemed like an eternity. I don't know how she does it."

Bill continues, "The reason this company is successful is because—quite frankly—Ms. Zoya doesn't give a damn what rival companies think of her. She doesn't give a damn what *anyone* thinks of her, for that matter." His voice reveals raw admiration. "She doesn't allow personal matters to come between her and her work, and I think that's an incredibly important asset to have as the boss of such a large company. A fashion company, at that. In our industry, people are constantly throwing challenges disguised in compliments at you. Ms. Zoya artfully dodges these, and manages to portray Zameer as superior every single time."

Farhan chuckles. "Alright, alright, Romeo."

"No, seriously." He hesitates. "Let this remain strictly in confidence, but I still work here, don't I? Despite her notorious attitude—because the assets outweigh the liabilities."

"Why do you think I've never finished any of my HR complaints?" Farhan laughs. "Too bad you're just one of her *many* admirers."

Farhan, Bill, and Haroun turn to look at Zoya—who has appeared in the lobby and is now speaking intently with Flora. Flora is holding a magnificent sequined dress in her hands, one that Zoya keeps gesturing wildly to.

"She won't even look twice at almost any guy," Farhan murmurs with a smile in his voice. Haroun becomes very preoccupied with his watch as Farhan's eyes sear into the side of his head.

Zoya gives Flora an order, to which she obliges, before heading towards the three of them. Her heels click clack to a stop in front of Farhan. "Ready for tonight, Goldilocks?"

"Goldilocks?" he replies in confusion.

She rolls her eyes. "Because you *need* everything to be 'just right.'"

Bill bursts out laughing, and even Haroun lets out a few chuckles. Zoya turns her piercing gaze to the latter, and the iciness melts from her eyes almost immediately.

"Yes, I'm ready," Farhan replies in a wounded voice.

"Good. *Meri naak na katwa de na.*" Zoya turns and walks away, her curls bouncing against her back.

"Translation?" Bill says imploringly.

Farhan gives him a dry look.

Ten

~

ZOYA SQUEEZES HER EYES shut. The memory falls on her without warning.

She sits in front of the mirror and applies red lipstick. He stands behind her, watching. "More," he says.

Zoya stares at him in the mirror. "But it's already dark enough."

His coal black eyes pierce hers.

Zoya obliges, lathering more lipstick onto her already caked lips. She knows why he makes her do this. Her gut twists as she thinks of his illogical reasoning. Some strange part of him likes seeing her wear makeup as he roughly touches her. Because her painted face makes him feel less bad about the pain he causes everywhere. As if the front she puts up with her lipstick and her mascara can conceal the agony underneath.

It makes him feel masculine.

Zoya caps the lipstick, placing it on the dressing table. She feels his hands settle on her shoulders, and she flinches.

The first time, she excused the predatory feel of his fingers, the way they pierced into her shoulder blades like knives. She excused the dangerous glint in his eyes, thinking she may have been mistaking it for predatory when in reality, it was passion.

Now, months later, she recognizes the way his nails dig deep into her shoulders. Now, she has purple marks and fresh scars underneath her clothes to testify that the glint in his eyes means nothing but danger.

Zoya opens her mouth to say something when he cuts her off. "It's my God-given right," he murmurs. This shuts her up, and she presses her lips together to keep from sobbing.

The morning after, she will discover various new colors on her body.

Zoya's eyes fly open, her breathing harsh and laborious.

She's standing in her room, fully glammed up by her hairdressers and makeup artists. Now there's just one thing left to do.

She opens her desk drawer and pulls out a tube of lipstick, uncapping it.

It's bright red.

It's been years since she opened it, but the lipstick looks the same as the last time she wore it. Flat from constant use all those years ago.

Zoya takes a deep breath and lifts it to her mouth, where it hovers for a few seconds before she lathers it on. She's taken back to that dressing table in her memory. Under those dim, seemingly romantic lights.

Seemingly.

Once she's done, she stares at the woman in the mirror.

The woman looks fabulous, bold, fierce. Exactly the way Zoya Zameer should and always does.

She doesn't feel anything like she looks.

Tonight, when she does what she's about to do, she hopes that *he* sees it. And she hopes to God that wherever he is, he recognizes the red lipstick. She wants fire to burn within him when he realizes she's worn it by *will*. She wants him to lose sleep, knowing his memory isn't destroying her.

Even if it may not hold true.

Her ex-husband Farhan Hussain has plagued her mind since she ended things; now she's going to plague *his* mind by teaching him a lesson.

By using her success as a weapon—one that will hopefully destroy him. Only then will she be able to find some semblance of peace in her life.

Only when she makes a radical display of power will she be satisfied, even if there is the risk of collateral damage.

~

Sequined golden heels meet the red carpet as stunning Zoya Zameer steps out of her limousine, adorned in a fabulous sequined gown. Lights flash, and the cameramen go crazy, each attempting to capture her from the best angle.

Indulging them, Zoya looks down at the floor and makes a great show of tucking her hair behind her ear with one hand. She holds on to her clutch with the other. Bursts of bright light surround her across the red carpet, and she keeps her eyes pasted to the door of the hotel as she sashays by the onlookers.

Ready, Zoya? she thinks, smiling at one of the cameras nearest her. *This is going to be one hell of a night.*

Zoya stops in the entrance, nodding at some of her employees. Immediately reporters flood forward, extending their mics in front of her. Zoya lets out a boisterous laugh and clutches Flora's arm.

The first few questions a reporter asks seem arbitrary and harmless. But this is expected; their abrasiveness will escalate throughout the night. Zoya has been doing this long enough to predict everything that is to come.

"Ms. Zoya Zameer!" a reporter with a mic booms, approaching her. "Welcome to the annual Desi World Fashion Show. You are dressed fantastically, as always. Is that a Zameer dress?"

Zoya grins. "You know it."

"Zameer is always wowing us, but as of late, your company's designs and campaigns have surpassed everyone's expectations. Has any special occurrence catalyzed this?" His question sounds innocuous, but Zoya resists the urge to roll her eyes. *There are always challenges disguised in their compliments.*

"Just my employees doing what they do best," Zoya says, beaming as she turns to Flora. The reporter's face falls a bit, as if he had been expecting more.

"One more thing, Ms. Zoya, before we let you go to enjoy the night," he says. "Everyone is wondering whether you—"

"Oh, look, Zameer's fashion show lead is here!" Flora exclaims as she points to the limo that has arrived, out of which Farhan emerges. She grabs Zoya's arm and steers her inside the hotel.

Zoya flips her curls behind one shoulder. "Thanks, Flora."

The reporters hustle towards Farhan, immediately beginning to pester him with questions. Zoya watches with silent laughter in her eyes.

Her attention, however, immediately strays to someone else as the door to the entrance is pushed open once more, and in walks none other than Haroun Suleiman, tux and all.

Zoya freezes.

His already impeccable features are groomed to perfection, and the black suit and tie manufactured by Zameer Co. adorn him. He runs a hand through his hair, eyes darting around warily as he approaches Zoya and the others. Zoya immediately resumes motion and fluffs her hair.

"You clean up nice," she notes admiringly.

Haroun glances at her before he quickly looks away, nodding a polite *thank you*. Disappointed, Zoya tries again. "Not your scene?"

He blows out a tense sigh. "Not really."

"*Ooh*, well, what is *the* Haroun Suleiman's scene?"

He grimaces. "Not . . . here."

Zoya chuckles. "Get used to it, *meri jaan*. You're a Zameer employee. You'll be frequently attending events like this."

Haroun doesn't look the least bit excited by this prospect. Zoya is about to ask him why he's so glum, but becomes momentarily distracted when he bites his bottom lip, dimple creasing.

She looks away, a strange flutter in her heart.

For the next hour or so before the show starts, people mill around being interviewed and getting photographed. Many renowned members of the fashion industry—including her old business-partner-turned-rival Zaki Ahmed—approach Zoya, marveling over her attire and excessively admiring Zameer. She receives many offers of companionship—and even more offers to contract deals with businessmen—which she laughs off by flipping her hair around a lot and not making any promises.

Her interests lie elsewhere tonight.

The subject of her scrutiny seems to be at the height of discomfort, pacing near Farhan and keeping his gaze lowered as much as possible. When women of other fashion companies approach him--and there are quite a few who do--Zoya is surprised by the flash of anger that passes through her.

She soon realizes that she's vexed for no reason, because every time Haroun is approached, his nervous habit of pursing his lips and furrowing his brows emerges. He speaks to the women politely but succinctly so that after a few moments, they give up and walk away, disappointed by his lack of attention.

"—are you looking at, Ms. Zoya?"

"Hmm?" she murmurs absentmindedly, turning to a fellow CEO speaking to her.

"Oh, I was just wondering what you were looking at."

"Just the interior design of the hall." Zoya gestures around vaguely. "It's marvelous."

The man nods. "You like it?"

She flashes a smile at him and watches in satisfaction as his face goes from curious to taken aback. "Love it. Now if you'll excuse me . . ." She lifts her gown to take a step. Lights flash all around them. Zoya is entirely aware of the cameras following her conversation with this man.

"Wait. Will you consider my offer?"

Zoya bats her eyelashes at him. "What offer?" *The one that made me throw up a little in my mouth?*

He grins, and Zoya restrains a grimace at his shameless nature, at his lack of decorum. "The one that would solidify our companies' relationship and allow them both to excel further in the industry."

Zoya's eyes dart to the cameras before she looks back at him. "Is that your *only* reason for wanting to marry me, Mr. Hassan?" she says loudly. The cameramen move closer.

He has the decency to look embarrassed. Tossing him one last smile, Zoya turns around and heads to her distressed employee.

"Why so antsy?" she remarks airily. A waiter walks by with a tray of soda glasses and Zoya grabs one. Haroun politely declines.

"I'm just tired," he says.

She takes a sip. "Tired? Before the show has even started? Don't you want to see all the work you put into this?"

Haroun shakes his head. "No, not really."

Zoya is amazed at his reply. "No? How come?"

Haroun tilts his head back to look at the ceiling. A camera suddenly flashes in their direction. He flinches, clenching his jaw. "It's just . . . I'm not fond of this environment."

Zoya laughs. "Says the employee working in one of the most influential fashion companies in the United States."

"Sometimes man has to bend under life's wills," he murmurs quietly. "*Majbooriyan.*"

Zoya knits her brows. "Life gives you a chance to take control."

He smiles slightly. "True, but we are mere humans. Sometimes we're not in control."

Zoya is surprised by this claim. "Do you really believe nothing is in your power?"

"Not . . . no, that's not what I meant. It's just that . . . power, Ms. Zoya? Humans are merely *adequate* for sovereignty—absolute power doesn't lie in our hands." Haroun shoves a shaky hand through his hair. "True, we have . . . choice and free will, but everything happens for a divine, predestined reason. We choose, God controls." His voice is incredibly soft, incredibly careful. He seems to be warring with his own thoughts, shoulders tense and a pucker between his eyebrows. When he sees that Zoya is watching him with rapt attention—still willing to listen—he continues.

"But"—he hesitates—"you know, we *do* have the power to rewrite our destiny through our prayers and our choices." Suddenly Haroun shakes his head, the storm in his eyes clearing.

"When someone asked the Prophet Muhammad whether he should tie his camel and trust in Allah, or untie his camel and trust in Allah, the Prophet Muhammad said, '*Trust in Allah, but tie your camel.*' I have tied my camel." Haroun's eyes skim across the hall as he sighs softly. "Now I'm placing my trust in Allah. Because . . . even if our experiences aren't always conscious choices, they're what's best for us." He smiles gently. "And sometimes we're far too human to understand that."

There is pin drop silence between them for a couple of seconds.

Zoya always knew Haroun was religious, but he had never directly expressed his views until now. Although he just seems to have experienced some kind of internal conflict, it had been . . . *different* witnessing his innocent thought process. She cocks her head at him, expecting the slew of religious comments to make her blood boil. But something about his true, gentle nature always catches her off guard. Something about his rigorous belief—even when he doesn't say a word—renders her speechless.

Her jumbled thoughts are interrupted when the host of the show announces that it will start in fifteen minutes. He requests everyone to begin heading to the great hall and to their seats.

Zoya turns back to Haroun, unable to explain why she suddenly feels so . . . strange. Asking him to join her in watching a fashion show when he expressed his distaste about this very environment feels *wrong*.

"Coming?" she inquires anyway.

He rubs his temple and murmurs, "I'll just be a minute."

Zoya has a feeling he won't be coming anytime soon. With one last contemplative look thrown his way, she turns to join the show with the rest of her employees.

Farhan is, of course, nowhere to be found, probably bustling around and making sure everything is perfect.

For a moment, Zoya marvels over his and Haroun's friendship—about how he doesn't seem to be at all worried that Haroun is not helping him out.

As Zoya enters the great hall and focuses on the runway decorations, she takes a deep breath and reminds herself of her purpose tonight. She puts her restless thoughts of Haroun Suleiman aside and begins to walk forward, preparing for her façade. She ignores the looks darted towards her, as well as the cameras that don't stop following her.

This is your moment, Zoya. This is what you've been waiting for.

Reaching the end of the hall near the stage, she finds who she's looking for. Taking another deep breath, her expression shifts into a more appropriate one for this moment.

Zoya charges forward, curls flying behind her as she approaches Farhan.

Eleven

"WHAT THE HELL IS this?" Zoya snaps, pointing to the stage.

Farhan flinches. "What, Ms. Zoya?"

"Are those carnations I see?" she murmurs dangerously. "Where are the hydrangeas?"

"Ms. Zoya, you asked for carnations—"

"No, I did not!" she says fiercely. "I asked for hydrangeas and you *know* I asked for hydrangeas because we discussed this when I spoke to you."

"B-But, Ms. Zoya—"

"And here she is—the prestigious—ZOYA ZAMEER!" A reporter walks over to them and grins at Zoya. She's still having a fierce eye battle with Farhan, whose forehead has creased with worry.

Suddenly, Zoya turns to the reporter and flashes a huge smile at the camera next to him. "*Salaam,*" she chirps.

Belatedly, the reporter's eyes dart between her and Farhan. "Did we interrupt something?"

These damn reporters, Zoya thinks. *Always finding a way to appear friendly and harmlessly curious. As if we don't know their real purpose--to grovel around and find dirt in our seemingly perfect lives. Anyway—pick your head up, Zoya. Give them what they want. Give them a new headline in a newspaper. Something for these good-for-nothings to do in all the free time they have.*

"*Salaam*," Zoya repeats with an even wider grin. "How are you?"

"I'm great, thank you. How are you?"

"Fine, thank you."

"So how's it going? Are you enjoying the night?"

"Oh, I *was* enjoying the night. Until I began talking to one of my incompetent employees." Zoya giggles, and the reporter answers with a confused chuckle of his own, eyebrows furrowing as his gaze shifts from her to Farhan.

"*Shoot*," Farhan curses in a low voice, much to Zoya's delight. "I'm done for."

"Oh yeah," Zoya continues talking to the reporter. "His name is Farhan. He can't tell the difference between carnations and hydrangeas. Even with Google. Haha, isn't he funny?" She looks at Farhan with false affection, and his face turns a deep pink. "Oh, by the way, you're fired, *Farhan*." She enunciates both syllables, ice in her voice.

Farhan's shoulders tense, his eyes widening. The reporter laughs, but nervously this time, eyes full of questions. Zoya can gauge the source of his perplexity. He has probably heard of Zoya Zameer's ruthless attitude, but wonders what lengths she'll go to.

Well, she'll clear up his confusion.

"This is my favorite type of employee, by the way," Zoya says haughtily. "One who claims he's right to lead the project and proves himself to be unworthy. Bravo, Farhan Malik, bravo." In a low voice, she mutters, "You'll get your contract." Then she smiles at the unsettled reporter, flips her hair behind her shoulder, and saunters away.

Farhan stands there with his fists clenching and unclenching by his side. He throws the confused reporter a weak smile and excuses himself.

~

After having paced around in the lobby for a few minutes, Haroun enters the hall to find Farhan and ensure that everything's set, familiar with his friend's perfectionist nature by now.

His eyes scan the hall and land on Farhan, who is standing next to Zoya in front of a reporter and cameraman. Haroun moves closer to them, stopping short when he hears his boss' giggle, which Farhan goes rigid at. Haroun follows the conversation with widened eyes, shocked by the scene unfolding before him.

When Zoya walks away from an immobile Farhan, Haroun's jaw clenches as he's overtaken by a bout of frustration. He sits down for a second, rubbing his temples and taking deep breaths to calm himself.

Farhan sprints to him and grabs his arm. "*Yaar*, Haroun, please do something! Did you see what just happened? Please tell me that was a sick joke of hers in front of the cameras. Please, *yaar*. I can't do without this job. You may not want to admit it, dude, but she's smitten by you. She'll listen to you. Please, please, please help me out."

Haroun doubts that anyone is *smitten* by him, but he rubs his friend's hand reassuringly. "Don't worry, I'm gonna try to do something." Then, with a tense expression, he follows his CEO into the room she's disappeared in.

~

There is a knock on the door.

"Oh," Zoya turns her head slightly, rubbing her ear as she removes an earring. "It's you."

Haroun towers in the doorway, jaw clenching and unclenching. His emotion-filled eyes seem to increase his size tenfold. "Ms. Zoya . . . what was that for?"

"Uh, pardon?" Zoya takes off her other earring. "You're gonna have to be more specific. I'm not going to magically know what you're talking about, hun." Despite her flippant tone, she marvels at the way he approaches her. With controlled anger, without yelling. Despite the scene she knows he just witnessed.

"You . . . fired Farhan. On live TV."

Zoya laughs. "And?"

Haroun blows out an exasperated sigh. "And?" He rubs his forehead. "Ms. Zoya, do you realize what you just did?"

"He's incompetent." Zoya shrugs. "He couldn't carry out the simple job of separating carnations from hydrangeas. It's a colossal mistake."

"Ms. Zoya—" Haroun rubs the back of his neck. "It's not a big deal, to be honest. I'm sure a small logistical error won't bother anyone. The people are here for the fashion show, not what types of flowers are decorating the stage."

"He humiliated me in front of Desi World and those sleazy businessmen."

"But . . . was it necessary to humiliate him in return?"

Zoya shrugs as if to say, *of course.* "An eye for an eye."

She tenses as a memory falls on her.

This was one of her ex-husband's favorite verses from the Qur'an. He used to say it all the time, purposefully forgetting the continuation of the verse, which said that forgiveness and patience would yield a greater reward. Something Zoya only found out many years after.

When it was already too late.

"Haven't you heard that an eye for an eye makes the whole world blind, Ms. Zoya?" Haroun tenses and rubs his fingers over his temples. "Are Farhan's concerns true? Do you really not like him? Did you purposely ask him to lead the project so that he could be publicly humiliated? Were you banking on him screwing up?"" Haroun tenses, as if he reviles the words coming out of his mouth. "Forgive me, Ms. Zoya, if I'm making any wrong assumptions."

Even now, Zoya is amazed by his patience with her. By his dignified and respectful approach to what is obviously a stressful situation for him.

"Sweetie, I don't mix my personal and my work life." She loosens her curls and massages her hair with her fingers. "Farhan was incompetent, so he deserved what he got. I don't know where you're coming up with these baseless theories from."

Haroun shakes his head. "I'm sorry, but this isn't fair."

"Yeah? Well, a lot of things aren't fair! *Domestic violence* isn't fair! What can *you* do about it?" Zoya—always cool, calm, and collected—has her hands splayed out in front of her, begging for an explanation.

Haroun's face scrunches up in confusion. "Domestic violence? I wholeheartedly agree, but where did that come from? We were talking about Farhan."

Zoya swallows hard and turns away. "Anyway, Farhan is fired."

"Ms. Zoya, please don't do this. Give him another chance, please," he insists. "Besides, I was co-project manager, and technically *just* project manager in your eyes, so realistically you should be punishing both of us. The responsibility lies on both of us."

Zoya shakes her head. "I know there's no way you made this mistake."

"How can you know that?" Haroun holds his hands out, his voice breaking as it rises an octave. "I'm *human*. Why do you place me on such a high pedestal, Ms. Zoya?"

"Because there's goodness in you!" she cries out fiercely, whirling to face him again. "There is goodness in you! Like right now, you're willing to take responsibility for something you didn't even *do* because you want justice. This goodness of yours *eats* into my flesh." She gestures by slapping the inside of her wrist. "It *eats* into my flesh, Mr. Suleiman. It renders me powerless, and I do *not* like feeling powerless." For the first time since she's met him, she expresses the raw emotion she feels in his presence. "So *stop* being so good, for your own good. No one in the world is ever going to be able to match your goodness."

Haroun's hands drop limply to his sides, his jaw slacking at her words. "You overestimate me."

Zoya laughs mirthlessly. "*Okay*, Haroun." She shakes her head again and unclips her hair from the left side to readjust it.

Haroun shakes his head. "Really, Ms. Zoya." After a moment of tense silence, he murmurs, "And do you even realize the loss the company could incur because of this? You fired an employee on *live TV*. It could potentially ruin not only your image but the image of

Zameer as a whole. This could . . . backfire, and whatever you were thinking—whatever plans you made—could come crashing down on your unsuspecting shoulders." He says this quietly, with reservation. As if he's afraid to hurt her with the dangerous prospect of his words.

Zoya places a hand on one hip. "Unsuspecting? Me? Sweetheart, you're deluding yourself. Zoya Zameer never does anything without calculation."

"What do you mean by 'calculation?'" Haroun asks worriedly.

She huffs out a resigned sigh. "Farhan's not being fired, sweetheart. That was just. . . . a calculation." *A power move. A way for me to show my ex, Farhan Hussain, who's in control now. Even if that means my employee Farhan Malik has to suffer.*

Too bad they share the same name.

"But you just said . . ." Haroun's expression morphs into sheer confusion. "Did you *plan* this, Ms. Zoya?"

"Not a plan. Just . . ." She takes a deep breath. "I pray to God that the person who was supposed to see that saw it, otherwise it will have all been for nothing." She turns her face suddenly, afraid that she has exposed too much. What is it about him that causes her tongue to unroll of its own accord? "Now, if you would please leave, I need to take care of something before the show begins."

"Wait, wait." Haroun's voice is dangerously low. "Did you do this *intentionally*?"

Zoya lifts her head to the ceiling and closes her eyes. Her hands begin to tremble. Clenching them into fists, she thinks desperately, *not here, not now.* "Please leave," she repeats. "I need to take care of something."

Haroun presses his lips together and worry lines crease his forehead. "We can talk about this later." The firm statement is a promise, and he quickly exits the room.

After an anxiety-ridden moment, Zoya sighs. She pulls out her phone and dials a number.

"Hello?"

"Sameer?"

"Yes, Ms. Zoya?"

"Are the reports ready?"

"Yes, Ms. Zoya."

"Good. Contact the journalists and have the reports released now."

"Got it."

Zoya ends the call and tucks her phone away into her clutch. She takes a deep breath.

Pretending to fire Farhan on live TV was risky but absolutely necessary. But, since Zoya isn't stupid, she knows the press will need news of greater weight in order to forget the Farhan fiasco entirely.

Hence, the wisely timed announcement of this news.

Zoya smiles. "Let's see what the press remembers of Farhan Malik after they find out that Zameer is expanding its manufacturing to the international level."

Twelve

~

THE SHOW IS A BLAST.

Cheers and applause continue for quite some time before thank you speeches are made, people are hugged, and confetti scatters from the roof of the great hall.

People mingle in the lobby afterwards. Businessmen, employees, and reporters approach employees of Zameer Co. They are continuously marveled at and interviewed over their great work with the fashion show.

Farhan is approached frequently, and when one particularly blunt reporter queries, "Didn't Ms. Zoya fire you today?" Haroun steps in and adds that he doesn't know where the reporter is receiving this false information from.

The only person missing is the CEO herself. Zoya is nowhere to be found after a couple of interviews and propositions from other businessmen.

When she finally appears, people swarm over her like bees. She can be seen from a distance smiling and smoothly declining reporters' remarks and assumptions, claiming that she must have eaten something strange and needed to get some fresh air. Her flushed cheeks and the sweat beading on her neck support this assertion, and after a while people stop crowding around her.

Towards the end of the event, Zoya heads to her employees and smiles. "What a night!"

Farhan stares at her in furious astonishment. She is—quite plainly—pretending like everything is normal.

"Let's head home, yeah?" she says. Bill and the others nod their assent and head to the exit, where their limos have arrived. Zoya is left with Sameer, Farhan, and Haroun.

Farhan stares at her. "Ms. Zoya?"

"Hmm?" she says absently.

"Is everything okay?"

"Farhan, please stop pretending like you don't have any other motive than to ask me whether you're fired or not," she snaps, shoving her curls behind her ears.

"No, I wasn't—"

"You're not fired. Happy?"

He doesn't look the least bit happy. He seems perturbed to a great extent, and after telling Haroun that he's going to leave with Bill, he turns and walks out.

Haroun stands there, wringing his hands awkwardly. "You'll be leaving, Ms. Zoya?"

She nods just as Sameer says, "I gotta jet. Need to drop my dad off at the airport. Goodnight, guys." He salutes to Zoya and Haroun. He's about to walk away when his Apple Watch pings with a message. Sameer's brows furrow as he turns back to his boss. "Oh, no. Ms. Zoya, your limo's been in an accident."

Zoya hears Haroun's breath catch as he says, "What? Is the driver okay?"

Sameer shakes his head. "No idea." His forehead creases with tension as he murmurs to himself. "How am I supposed to get a limo rental right now . . ."

Zoya almost laughs at the shock on Haroun's face. This probably seems strange to him––for someone to be more concerned about her transportation than the well-being of a potentially injured driver. Zoya is obviously used to the ins and outs of the business world, where attitudes like this are normal, but Haroun is clearly still unaccustomed to it.

Sameer's narrowed gaze darts around the hall.

Zoya recognizes the look on his face and snorts. "I'm not leaving with any of the sleazy men who've offered. Imagine the embarrassment. The CEO of the company got left behind while her employees all ditched her, and she had to be rescued by one of these men." She shakes her head. "I can just visualize the headlines. These people have nothing better to do."

Haroun glances between the two of them. "Can't you order an Uber?"

Zoya bursts into laughter, and Sameer cracks a smile. "Are you kidding me?" she says. "We just successfully orchestrated one of the greatest fashion shows, and you want me to leave in an *Uber*?"

Haroun knits his brows and purses his lips. He seems to want to say something, but thinks better of it.

"I have a better idea, *meri jaan*." Zoya sidles close to Haroun, and he abruptly steps back. "Why don't I leave with you?"

Realistically, Zoya will have no trouble calling her driver Raheem and asking him to pick her up. But she's much more interested in Haroun's reaction to her request.

Zoya waits with bated breath, attempting to look nonchalant in front of her employee. But there is an earnestness in her eyes that she is unable to hide, one that Sameer seems to detect with an exhausted shake of his head.

Zoya can only be glad that Haroun has a habit of keeping his gaze lowered.

Zoya knows it's foolish. For her to give in to her petty desires, her absurd fantasies of this seemingly simple man, when he is very clearly not interested in her. But she *is* Zoya Zameer, and old habits die hard.

He mesmerizes her. Because she does not mesmerize him.

And for many other reasons.

Haroun looks around uncertainly. His eyes fall on the businessmen who continuously glance at Zoya. The reporters who were raving about what a sight to behold she is dart furtive glances her way. Haroun visibly flinches, and Zoya knows just by the tension in his jaw that he is disturbed by the brazen way these men watch her, as if undressing her with their eyes.

"I can take you home," he says. He doesn't meet her eyes, tension etched into his features.

Although Zoya triumphs at her small victory, she's still surprised.

Despite her intense desire for him to do so, she did not expect Haroun Suleiman to make this offer to her. Quiet, careful Haroun Suleiman, who flinches at the flash of a camera. To make this offer must be troubling to him since cameramen are still milling about; he'd be sure to get caught in their trap as leading his boss out of the hall.

"Really?" Zoya's voice is too high. She clears her throat.

He nods. "My car is just parked a bit far. I can run and drive it back here?" His question is phrased oddly. She detects a hint of uncertainty in his tone.

Sameer is darting glances between the two of them, eyebrows raised.

Zoya is momentarily surprised that Haroun arrived in his own car. But her shock wears off a brief moment of contemplation. Judging by the time that she's known him, Haroun would blanch at the attention he would receive if he arrived like everyone else did.

"No, it's okay," Zoya says quickly. "I'll walk with you. It's better for the cameras anyway. And I don't feel like talking to any more 'eligible men.' God, they have no shame in their requests."

Haroun looks simultaneously relieved and troubled. Sameer gestures between them and says, "O-kay, so this is done? I don't need to try to rent a limo? We're good?'

Zoya nods enthusiastically, and Sameer narrows his eyes at her. "Well, okay then," he says. "I really need to head out. See you, guys."

Then it's just Zoya and Haroun, the latter of whom seems to want to disappear into the floor. He takes a deep breath, shakes his head, and says, "Ready, Ms. Zoya?" She nods, and together they head out of the great hall. There are even more paparazzi outside, and Zoya—understanding Haroun all too well by now—quickly redirects them to the back exit in order to avoid the flashes of cameras.

He gives her a grateful look.

Haroun is quiet as they walk. He doesn't ask her again about why she pretended to fire Farhan on live TV, and she doesn't indulge in the topic either. She simply walks quietly at his side.

The night sky is pitch black. When they had arrived, the time for *Maghrib* had just ended, and the blue hues in the sky were fading into indigo. But now, the sheer darkness causes Zoya to shiver involuntarily. Everywhere she turns is formidable and mysterious, blackness creeping onto them like a cloaked hand.

Distract yourself, Zoya.

She turns to Haroun, observing him brazenly. Her eyebrows knit when she sees him carrying a drawstring bag in his left hand. She hadn't seen that before. She ponders over what he could possibly have brought to the fashion show.

His mom calls him as they walk. He speaks gently into the phone, telling her he'll be home in an hour or so, *Insha Allah.* Zoya struggles to hide her adoration at the soft voice he uses, the tenderness in his eyes. She feels a sudden, searing pain in her chest at the memory of parents.

They walk for about five more minutes during which— multiple times—Zoya wants to ask where the hell he's parked his car that requires them to walk this much. Instead, she remains quiet, sensing he's already at the height of discomfort. His uneasiness amuses her; she finds herself holding back a laugh at the way he walks at a distance from her.

While they're walking, a group of men pass by, closer to Zoya than Haroun. They flash her a smile; she smiles back dismissively— and as if automatically, Haroun shifts ever so subtly so that his tall frame blocks her from their view.

A shock passes through her--one that has nothing to do with the chilly night air. She stares in awe at Haroun, but he seems not to notice. A strange feeling courses through her, arresting her senses and taking hold of her heart, squeezing it.

Zoya shakes her head to clear her thoughts. Haroun tilts his head in her direction. "Are you okay?"

"Yes," she replies. Her voice is strangely muffled. "No, actually," she admits moments later.

Zoya stops and looks down at her feet. Although she's used to wearing heels on a daily basis, this day has stretched out longer than usual. *Besides,* she thinks bitterly. *It seems like whoever manufactured these heels added some sequins on the* inside, *too.*

"What's wrong?"

"These heels *mujhe maar dalein gi.* Like, they're *really* gonna kill me."

Haroun shakes his head, his eyes unexpectedly dancing with silent laughter.

"I'm gonna walk without them." Zoya reaches down to pull them off and lets out a relieved sigh. Haroun watches her as if she's crazy.

"You're going to injure your feet. These sidewalks aren't exactly made of marble."

She waves a hand at him dismissively. "I'll be fine." He presses his lips together, and Zoya rolls her eyes. "Really, Haroun, I'll be fine."

"Wait." He pulls his bag open. "I brought extra shoes. They're men's shoes, so I'm not sure how they'll fit, but it's better than walking barefoot."

Zoya stares at him, then bursts out laughing. "Haroun Suleiman, only *you* would bring extra shoes to a *fashion show.*" She pretends to wipe a tear away.

He furrows his brows and glances at his feet. "I knew I would be uncomfortable in these; I don't wear dress shoes too often."

She stops laughing. "So why don't *you* wear the extra shoes you brought?"

He shakes his head. "You need them more than I do." He lifts the shoes out of the bag. "I'm really sorry. They're not new. I hope you don't mind."

Her eyes trace his actions. She is unable to express her awe at his gentleness, his innocence. "No, that's fine."

He sets them down on the floor and holds his hands out for her heels. She stares at him. "I'm not putting my nasty, sweaty heels in your bag. No way." He tells her he doesn't mind but she shakes her head firmly. What an insult to her beautiful femininity for him to smell her clammy heels.

His hand is still held out, posture insistent. He seems to war with himself as he opens and closes his mouth, then finally says, "At least let me hold them." Zoya sighs and hands her shoes to him, noticing how careful he is not to touch her fingers. She tries his shoes on, and even though they're big on her, she manages to walk in them.

They walk silently for another minute or so before Haroun stops. Zoya looks up at him quizzically.

"I'm sorry," he says sheepishly. "We'll have to cross through here." He gestures to a narrow alley that leads to the other side of the road, where there seems to be a large parking lot.

Zoya lets out a peal of laughter. "Haroun, I get not wanting to ride in a limo, but did you think the FBI would tail you if you parked closer to the hotel?"

He shakes his head in embarrassment. "I just didn't want to draw too much attention. And . . . parking nearby was packed."

Once again, she marvels over his words. *This guy is something else*, she thinks. "Alright. Let's go." She gestures for him to walk ahead but he shakes his head firmly, indicating that she go first. Zoya—strangely touched by his protectiveness—obliges and walks ahead of him. He's quiet the entire way, and she wants so badly to turn around and look at his face. To see the expressions filtering across it. The firm protectiveness. The detached gentleness.

The protectiveness and gentleness he would offer to anybody, because that's just who he is, Zoya reminds herself.

Once they reach the parking lot, Haroun pulls out his keys and clicks the unlock button. A few feet away, a small car beeps. Zoya and Haroun follow the sound, and when they reach it, Zoya sees that it's an old Toyota Avalon.

This doesn't surprise her. She hasn't taken any wild stabs at

Haroun's economic status—only some speculations after his blunt "I need the money" confession when she first met him—but she senses that Haroun is the kind of person who would own this same car even if he was a millionaire.

So chivalry is not *dead*, Zoya thinks cheerfully as Haroun jogs forward and opens the door for her. She raises her eyebrows at his decision to open the back door instead of the passenger door, but doesn't say a word as she gets in. He would probably crash the car somewhere out of nervousness if she sat next to him, anyway.

Or, an unwelcome voice in Zoya's head prods. *He's setting his boundaries.*

Haroun gets in the driver's seat and puts on his seatbelt, placing Zoya's heels carefully on the passenger seat.

"What's your address, Ms. Zoya?" he asks. When she tells him, he backs out of the parking space and makes his way onto the road.

Zoya is surprised with herself. Although she would have flinched at telling anyone but a driver her address, she didn't think twice before reciting it to Haroun.

As Zoya observes him, she's amused to discover that Haroun even *drives* gently, one hand at 1 o' clock while the other drums the inside of the steering wheel at 7 o' clock. He seems to pass over every pothole with ease, and drives with a relaxing rhythm.

"Don't you need Google Maps?" Zoya says.

"No," he replies. "I'm going the right way."

She shakes her head. "I mean you know the way?"

"Yes. I've been around that area a couple of times."

"How come?"

He shifts in his seat. "I was looking for jobs there before."

"Ah."

The entire drive is spent in silence. But uncharacteristically for her, Zoya is at ease, leaning back and observing the interior of his car. Not a speck of dirt. Not a single gum wrapper or soda can. Scented Arabic calligraphy of the name *Allah* hangs from the rear view mirror, and the *du'a* for traveling is pasted to the dashboard.

This is even better than sitting in the back of a limo. This way, Zoya gets a small view into the quiet life of Haroun Suleiman.

After some time, Haroun furrows his brows at his surroundings before he mumbles, "I must have missed the exit." He drives for a few more minutes, trying to find the next exit and proceed to the local route. But after he does so, he only looks further perplexed. "I've been here so many times, why . . ." With furrowed brows, he tries to navigate the roads to find the right way.

"Did you forget the route?" Zoya asks, leaning forward slightly.

"I don't know, I—" he trails off unsurely. After a few more minutes of his confusion further plaguing him, he begins to visibly panic. He stops the car on the side of the road and presses his head against the steering wheel.

"Haroun, it's okay. I can just pull up the directions on my phone."

He shakes his head. "I'm straying off the path." His voice is low, pained. He presses his fingers against his temples.

Zoya is awed by witnessing this small moment of vulnerability into the quiet Haroun Suleiman's life. She would be remiss to say she isn't drinking it in like every detail she does of him.

"Haroun," she says. "Seriously, it's alright. Do you want me to drive?"

A moment later, he picks his head back up and shakes it, turning the key in the ignition. Watching him in the rear view mirror, she is confused by the expression of grief in his eyes, of loss.

"Do you mind looking up the directions on your phone, Ms. Zoya?" he says shakily. "Mine is dying."

Zoya nods and pulls them up, handing him her phone. With the guidance of Google Maps, Haroun is able to get back on the highway and find the right exit before he approaches Zoya's manor slowly, handing the phone back to her.

Zoya finds herself carefully observing his reaction when he first looks at her house. She is both surprised and disappointed to find that he doesn't display the same reaction that everyone else does; his eyes merely pass over it once before he looks back down.

His dimple has appeared, signaling that he's tense about something.

"Thank you so much, Haroun." Zoya shrugs off his shoes and places them back in his bag.

"No need to thank me, Ms. Zoya," he states professionally. "It was my responsibility as your employee."

Her face falls a little, but she isn't surprised by his words. Of course he would have done this for anyone. He would never find sleep if he left a woman in the midst of a bunch of leering men. It would strain his conscience.

She slips on her heels and steps out of the car to walk over to his side, throwing her hair behind her shoulder. Her gatekeeper looks between her and Haroun in amazement.

Zoya knows it's out of the question to invite him inside, especially at this time. So instead she says, "Can I get you anything? Water? Juice? Something to eat?"

He shakes his head. "No, thank you, Ms. Zoya. I better get going. My mom is waiting on me."

"Alright." She taps the hood of his car and steps back. "Thanks again, Haroun. I really appreciate it."

He nods and starts the car again.

Zoya can't explain why, but for some reason she finds herself not wanting to leave. She wants to stand there and watch the emotions that pass over his face. The worry, the discomfort, the fatigue.

She wants to understand this man. And this in itself shocks her. After her ex-husband, no man has ever stirred Zoya's heart.

Of course, the one who managed to do so has absolutely zero interest in her.

Haroun doesn't seem to be leaving until Zoya steps inside, so with one last wave of her hand and a hair flip in his direction, she proceeds through the gate to her manor. When Aman opens the door for her, she turns around, expecting Haroun to have left.

But Haroun Suleiman is still there, waiting patiently and earnestly as Zoya Zameer makes it safely inside.

~

When Haroun has parked outside his house, he turns the car off and leans against the steering wheel.

He bangs his head against it. Once. Twice. Thrice. Until he accidentally honks the horn, startling himself.

Haroun rubs his eyes and drags his hands down his face. His shoulders begin to shake.

God, if he didn't need to provide for his family, he would never have applied for a job at Zameer. He had been warring with himself when he arrived at his interview weeks ago. Part of him wanted desperately to be hired, so that he could pull his family out of their financial crisis. The other part of him secretly hoped that they would dismiss him, so that he wouldn't have to go through what he is now going through.

Zameer's environment is constantly testing him. The photo shoots, the paparazzi, the partying, the freemixing of genders (when it's unrelated to work), the job itself. Every day that Haroun goes to work, he feels as if he's hanging onto his sanity by a thread.

He almost lost it completely today. With the camera flashes, the fashion show, the journalists and reporters crowding around everyone—it was all too much. He had to rush to the bathroom multiple times just to catch his breath.

On top of that, being around his boss is akin to tip-toeing on eggshells. As if every day at the company isn't already torture, today he found himself alone with her, for reasons unrelated to work. His heart had been beating too fast the entire time. He was constantly thinking, *Is this necessary? Do I really need to be in this situation? How can I continuously clarify that I'm only doing this because she was in a helpless situation, and it didn't sit well with me to leave her there? Where men were watching her like predators watch their prey, right before pouncing.*

But Haroun had held her *shoes*, for God's sake. He'd given her *his shoes* to wear.

For a moment, when Sameer was trying to figure out her ride, Haroun had wanted to scream in frustration. Was it *so* difficult to find a ride home for one of the most prominent women in America?

Haroun blows out a sigh and runs a tense hand through his hair.

The longer he stays at Zameer, the more his faith and scruples will deteriorate, and the more exhausted and helpless he will become. Even when he thinks he'll be able to uphold his morality, eventually he'll succumb to his environment.

Is his faith so weak, though? That it can so easily be shaken? Isn't a test of faith remaining true to one's morality when it becomes most difficult?

Haroun gazes outside the window, eyes trained on his apartment.

Despite his personal struggles, it destroys him even more when he comes home every night, and his tired mother forces a weak smile for him. When his exhausted sisters crack jokes just for his benefit.

And he's given renewed strength to return to work the next day.

Thirteen

"It was thanks to Allah's mercy that you (Oh Muhammad) were gentle with them. Had you been rough, hard-hearted, they would surely have scattered away from you." (Qur'an 3:159)

~

ON HER DAY OFF, after a peaceful sleep filled with dreams of a certain dark-eyed, dimpled man, Zoya gets ready and leaves her house. She settles in her car and places sunglasses on her head. Her phone is thrown onto the passenger seat, the lock screen lighting up with notifications that she *knows* are from her board of directors about the press having released the news. They're going to be wild with glee at people's reactions, and her employees will understand why Zoya had constantly been meeting with international agents.

Additionally, ger PR team will be carefully observing Zaki Ahmed's reaction; because the CEO of Pak Enterprises—Zameer's number one rival company—will be losing his chill when he sees Zameer's shot to success.

Zoya grins. "Time to treat yourself, Zoya." She drives onto the highway with her windows rolled all the way down, pressing on the gas aimlessly, navigating through the lanes, and yelling at various drivers before taking her exit.

When she stops at the red light near her favorite restaurant, she drums her fingers on the steering wheel. Memories of last night replay in her head over and over again.

A single voice stands out.

Was it necessary to humiliate him in return?

Haven't you heard that an eye for an eye makes the whole world blind, Ms. Zoya?

I'm sorry, but this isn't fair.

And then afterwards, the pained, *I'm straying off the path.*

The light turns green, and Zoya presses on the gas. Suddenly, a strange sound grinds out of her dashboard. Furrowing her brows, she ignores it at first, but becomes increasingly worried as the insistent, rhythmic thrumming grows more pronounced with each passing minute.

"*Kya hai, yaar?*" She pats the dashboard in annoyance after a few minutes. "Please don't create any problems for me."

As if in reply, the engine releases a loud, guttural noise, and several signs light up above the speedometer, alerting her of potential danger. Her eyes flick to the rear view mirror, which showcases the small cloud of smoke rising in the back. A honk follows from the car behind her—probably somebody advising her to take caution. She panics and pulls over to the side of the road.

"What the hell, *yaar?*" Zoya whines, banging her head against the steering wheel. "Why?"

She pulls the key out of the ignition and sits there expectantly. "What the hell am I supposed to do?" Having never experienced a vehicular breakdown, Zoya is overcome by confusion. She opens her door and walks around to the front. Popping her hood as she's seen in the movies, Zoya pushes strands of hair away from her face and glares at the machinery.

"What the hell are all these?" she cries out, scrunching her face as she fingers the tubes running along the length of the engine. "What are these? Worms? And what the hell is this?" She points to what looks like a white bottle nestled into all the machinery. "What is this? Water?"

After several minutes of uselessly poking around at the machinery, Zoya is forced to resign and phone a towing service. She yells at them when she hears their towing cost. After negotiating it, she turns the phone off angrily.

"This was supposed to be my one-day vacation. I was supposed to celebrate the look I'm going to see on Zaki Ahmed's face," Zoya whines, back in her car. "Now I've got to sit here for hours, waiting for some idiots to come take my baby away." She pats her dashboard. "Why, oh, why? Couldn't you breathe for a bit longer? You've never given me issues, so why now?" She gives the steering wheel an accusing glare.

Zoya grabs her phone and dials her driver's number. He picks up on the fourth ring. "Hello?"

"Raheem, where the hell are you?"

Pause. "At the dealership . . .?" His tone suggests that this is obvious information.

"The dealership?" Zoya huffs. "What the hell are you doing at—" *Oh.* She smacks her forehead, suddenly recalling the reason for Raheem's visit to the dealership.

What a great time for me to have demanded a newer car.

Ending the call and throwing her phone aside with a groan, she observes her surroundings.

There is a cluster of buildings nearby, one of which is a mosque. Zoya immediately looks away from it.

When the time for *Dhuhr* comes, Zoya is tense, knowing there is nowhere to pray around her car. She briefly reviews her options: On the one hand, by the time she gets home, her prayer will be extensively delayed. On the other hand, praying inside her car will be cramped and uncomfortable, and there doesn't seem to be anywhere else to pray near this busy road.

Unless she's willing to risk being hit by a car.

She can already envision the headlines. *CEO Zoya Zameer: Run Over By Car.*

Grumbling, she grabs her purse and makes her way to the mosque. "It'll just be for ten minutes," she reassures herself. "I'll be in and out."

The mosque is clearly inspired by Ottoman architecture, with its exterior consisting of a royal blue dome in between intricately designed minarets, and its interior consisting of beautiful swirling colors and patterns. This, however, doesn't lift Zoya's mood in the slightest. She slaps her shoes onto the rack and begins to walk upstairs, where a small placard indicates the womens' *musallah*.

Please don't let anyone be here.

Unfortunately, her fears come true when she enters the prayer area and finds several women scattered about. She immediately averts her eyes and secludes herself to a corner, wanting to avoid as much interaction as possible. But she doesn't miss the way two women reading the Qur'an look up at her when she enters, their eyes raking over her outfit: a simple white dress and jeans, along with a sequined *dupatta*. A Zameer *dupatta*, of course, because the CEO never leaves her house without at least *some* form of Zameer apparel.

A neon board at the front of the *musallah* indicates that they will be starting *Dhuhr* in a few minutes. Zoya pulls out a less transparent *dupatta* from her purse and wraps it around her head.

Suddenly, a heaviness settles in her chest. She tries to control the short spasms that plague her breathing, but to no avail. Zoya presses her head into her hands.

All of it—the mosque, the intricate architecture, the shoe rack, the twirling ceiling fans, the women scrutinizing her with beady eyes—is too much. She is brutally elbowed back into that capsule of time where she was under similar ceilings, in a similar environment. Around similar beady eyes.

The *adhaan* begins, to Zoya's immense relief. The sooner the prayer starts, the sooner she will be able to leave.

The women begin to form two rows. Zoya reluctantly stands to join their congregation, ignoring the silent, watchful woman next to her.

All throughout the prayer, an extreme sense of discomfort plagues Zoya. Having gone almost six years avoiding congregational prayers, she wants nothing more than to break hers and back away from these women, who make her feel like a puppet attached to strings. Her breathing grows continuously laborious, and when the prayer finally finishes, Zoya hurriedly steps into the row all the way at the back to complete her *sunnah* and *nafl* prayers.

Once done, she grabs her purse and is ready to dash out when a woman clad in a long *abaya* and a voluminous scarf approaches her. "*Assalaamu 'Alaikum,* sister," she says gruffly. It's the same woman who had been praying next to Zoya. She holds a *tasbeeh* in her hand.

Zoya panics. "*W-Wa 'Alaikum Salaam.*"

The woman raises her eyebrows. "I have not seen you before. Are you from around here?"

Zoya shakes her head. "No. My car broke down, so I had to stop here." *Otherwise believe me, I'd rather fly to the moon and pray there.* "I better be going. My towing service might be here."

The woman extends a hand to stop her and Zoya blanches, slowly removing herself from the woman's grasp. "Sister, I just wanted to tell you that your prayer is not accepted in this condition." Between snippets of conversation, she moves beads along the *tasbeeh* and whispers prayers under her breath.

Zoya furrows her brows. "In what condition?"

The woman gestures to Zoya's attire, *tasbeeh* dangling from her hand. "In these clothes."

Zoya looks down at herself, then back up at the woman. Her blood begins to boil. *I should never have come here. I should have prayed on the busy street—to hell with the risk of being run over.* "What's wrong with my clothes?"

"Sister, have some *hayaa,* please. Don't be so immodest," the woman scoffs. "Do you really believe Allah will accept your prayer when you traipse around in fitted jeans like this?" She gestures to Zoya's legs.

Zoya clenches her jaw and fires a question of her own at the woman. "Do *you* really believe you know who Allah accepts and who he doesn't?"

"*Astaghfirullah.* Hold your tongue, sister," she responds sharply.

Zoya shakes her head. Her tongue itches to spit out more to quell the fire erupting within her heart. The fire that has been dormant for so long and has suddenly been revived after coming to a *masjid,* of all places.

But it isn't worth it.

"I really need to get going," Zoya snaps.

"You see that girl over there?" the woman continues, pointing to a woman around Zoya's age. "She's just like you. But she's wearing modest clothing, you see? Her skirt reaches her feet, and her scarf hides all of her hair." Her tone is harsh, eyes disapprovingly lingering over Zoya. Their conversation has caught the attention of several other women around them.

Zoya laughs mirthlessly, having reached the height of her patience. "This is the problem with you so-called 'religious' people. You walk around decorating your mosques and inviting others to Islam, yet you don't have the decency to speak properly to people. You keep prayers on your tongue and run around with *tasbeehs* in your hands, but you have the audacity to openly shame others. You *love* making comments about other people's dressing or their outward spirituality. You point fingers and make judgments, trying to play the part of God." Zoya shoulders her purse in disgust. "A piece of advice: Please fix your own attitude before you decide to walk around making assumptions about anyone else. Or worse, attempting to preach a religion you don't seem to know much about yourself."

The woman opens her mouth to say something else, but Zoya shakes her head and rushes out of the *musallah*. Footsteps follow her, but she pays them no heed, flying down the steps in an attempt to leave the *masjid* as quickly as possible. However, she's not quick enough; the footsteps approach her from behind, and someone taps her shoulder.

Zoya whirls around. "*What?*" It comes out as a spit.

It's the other woman, the one around Zoya's age. She stares at Zoya in amazement. "Sorry, I just wanted to ask you something."

"Yes?" Zoya says curtly, one hand on the door handle of the exit.

"You're Zoya Zameer, right?"

Zoya is surprised by the question. She nods.

"I *knew* you looked familiar!" the woman exclaims. "I was really surprised when I saw you come in. I didn't expect to see you *here*."

Zoya clenches her teeth. "Why? Am I some spawn of Satan who can't enter a mosque to pray one of my daily prayers?"

"No, I didn't mean—"

"I know exactly what you meant. Please keep your lousy opinions to yourself. You'll probably never see me here again anyway, especially not since I've *once again* discovered that coming here causes me to encounter people like *you*." Zoya pushes open the door to the exit. "So thank you for ripping the temporary blindfold off my eyes. I thought I could spend *ten minutes* of peace in here to pray, but I guess I was wrong." She huffs out an angry sigh and exits the mosque, leaving the woman behind, whose expression has morphed into one of shock and hurt.

Zoya stomps towards her car. "Don't know who they think they are," she mutters loudly, capturing the attention of several passersby. "'*Have some hayaa*'—you and your *mom* need to have some *hayaa*. Acting like I'm some spawn of Satan who doesn't know anything about her religion." Zoya huffs out an exasperated breath. "'*You see that girl over there? She's just like you*'—oh, for God's sake, give me a damn break. I should never have come here. Next time I really *will* pray on the road. I don't give a damn."

This past half hour has rudely pushed her back into *that* time, when she was around different people, but met with the same attitudes. Zoya always tries her best to ignore any place that reminds her of *him,* yet somehow finds him hiding in nooks and crannies everywhere, waiting for the perfect opportunity to jump out and unsettle her.

She is in a very foul mood after that. When the towing service arrives, she yells at the poor guy for taking such a long time. He listens without fighting back, and that makes Zoya even angrier as she storms off into her Uber driver's car. A last resort—otherwise she would never be caught dead in an Uber.

Fuming silently along the way, Zoya eyes her jeans. As soon as she gets home, she's going to rip them off her legs and throw them into the fireplace. She does not want any reminder of that mosque.

The driver stops for gas, and Zoya exits the car to get some air. She regrets it immediately, however, when a cameraman and reporter with a mic approach her from the car behind. *Were they following me?*

"Zoya Zameer!" he greets her cheerfully. She throws him a smile through clenched teeth. "How are you?"

"Perfect, thank you. And you?" *I want to shove your camera up your nose.*

He smiles. "Great! Would you be willing to answer a few questions?"

Her first instinct is to say no, but after realizing this is inevitable, she nods tightly.

"Just last night, Zameer announced that they will be expanding internationally. What brought on this decision?"

Hopefully, somewhere out there, my father will see it and be proud of me. Zoya shakes off the intrusive thought and gives the reporter a weak smile. "I have always envisioned overseas expansion for my company, as our merchandise and campaigns have been met with significant approval and demand in many domains. By expanding internationally, Zameer will be able to broaden its scope in order to cater to a wider demographic, and thus become even more involved in the business sphere."

"Fantastic. Now, Ms. Zameer, there have been speculations that your company scheduled this news to be released at a time when the press was attacking your personal life. People have speculated that in order to cover up this news, you—"

The reporter's words fade into the distance. It's all too much. Her car, the mosque, the reporter's questions brutally hammering her already thinning patience.

Zoya shakes her head and cuts the reporter off, "I do what I do because I feel that it's necessary. Not because anyone has prompted me to do so. Thank you very much and have a great day." Placing her sunglasses back on her eyes, Zoya opens the car door and slides inside, leaving the reporter standing there with a baffled expression on his face.

The driver glances nervously at her in the rearview mirror. Zoya's eyes pierce his. "Drive," she orders.

The car speeds away with her heart hammering wildly in her chest.

Fourteen

"And be patient over what befalls you." (Qur'an 31:17)

~

WHEN ZOYA RETURNS TO work the next day, she yells at anyone who comes into her office. Hushed mutters spread like wildfire; everyone is wondering what has gotten Zoya Zameer so riled up. After all, the fashion show was a huge success, and the news of Zameer's international expansion has been met with an incredible burst of support. Consumer demand is continuously rising, and the company is skyrocketing to even greater success.

The staff's confused whispers reverberate from room to room and person to person the entire day.

What the hell is wrong with her?

She's worse than usual.

Did somebody forget to put the sixth sugar packet in her tea?

The subject of everyone's conversations is sitting in her office, knee bouncing up and down as she reviews recent consumer demand statistics with her CFO. When a knock sounds on her door, she barks "Enter!" without looking up.

Someone approaches her desk and sets a mug down on it. "Your tea, Ms. Zoya."

His voice shocks her into the memory of the night of the fashion show. Zoya looks up from her tablet and sees Haroun standing before her, waiting for any other commands.

For some reason, the sight of him causes Zoya's fists to clench in anger. Haroun—quiet and religious—is a brutal reminder of the women at the mosque.

He probably thinks of me just like they do, she thinks bitterly. *He just doesn't say anything.*

Zoya had begun to think that Haroun was the only Muslim in the world who didn't have the ability to piss her off, but she realizes now that she was wrong. It's a hoax. *He's* a hoax. She should not have fallen into his trap and believed for even a second that he was different.

They're all the same.

There's no way every Muslim Zoya has encountered is like those women at the mosque, while Haroun is gentle and forgiving. *He must have some ulterior motive,* Zoya thinks resentfully. *Otherwise no one is this kind and patient with me.*

In a second, her entire perspective of him shifts.

"You can leave," she says curtly. Haroun looks a bit surprised, but he nods and exits wordlessly. This further pisses Zoya off.

Why didn't he argue with me?

"Zoya?" The CFO breaks her out of her stupor, and she returns to the tablet. But her seething mind is elsewhere.

"Robert, you're not understanding what I'm saying," Zoya tells him exasperatedly after a couple minutes. She points to the graph. "That's an exponential curve. And it didn't rise just last night. This dates back to the seventeenth—over a week ago. Meaning consumer demand has shot up since then. But why? We need to analyze the events of that week to determine what caused this."

Robert shrugs, rubbing his red-rimmed eyes tiredly. "As long as it's going up, it doesn't concern me."

His comment peeves Zoya. "Oh, *okay,* Mr. *CFO,* whose literal *job* it is to be concerned about this. So if I'm not mistaken, as long as a curve on a graph keeps increasing, you don't give a damn if it's due to murderers or sexual traffickers or *whatever.* You just want it to keep going up. Correct?"

"Murderers and sexual traffickers?" he blinks, eyes bleary. "This is a fashion company, Zoya. You're getting off track."

"You *know* what I mean!" she says angrily, hands splayed out.

"No, I really don't—"

"Just get out." Zoya points to the door. Robert raises his eyebrows. "I said *get out*. If you don't leave right now, I'm gonna spill this tea all over your crusty, mop-like hair. It would do you some good, anyway."

Surprise flashes across Robert's features. He grabs the files from her desk and obliges, throwing her one last quizzical look before he leaves.

"Everyone is *crazy* here, I swear to God. Everyone's *nuts*."

Her mood does not improve for the rest of the day. When she arrives home, she yells at Aman—who listens wordlessly—for not "opening the door right" and for always looking at her with "puppy dog eyes." Infuriated by his lack of argument, she makes her way upstairs, prays, and flings herself onto her bed.

"The world is crazy," she mumbles. "Everyone's crazy." Eyelids drooping, she drifts off into a restless sleep.

Sometime in the middle of the night, Zoya shakes awake. Her room is plunged into darkness. She panics and sits up in bed, placing a hand over her heart. It's pitch black—so dark that there is no difference whether her eyes are open or closed. She fumbles around for her phone but comes up empty.

The door is shut. *Why is the door shut?*

Zoya begins to breathe heavily. Her surroundings are a jumble; nothing makes sense to her. The windows reflect a dim slab of moonlight on the ground, and the bend and crawl of it over the floor is eerie. It plunges her into an unwanted memory, and she shakes her head roughly.

"Stop it, Zoya," she whispers. The sound of her own voice in the silent room scares her, and she takes a deep breath before standing up to find the light switch.

By now her breaths are coming in short gasps, spasms of fear.

Relax, Zoya. Deep breaths. She stands, but is immediately gripped by a spasm of terror and falls back down.

It's too dark. Too dark to see, too dark to hear, too dark to breathe.

Zoya musters the courage to stand again and is halfway across the room when an intense fear grips her yet again. Knees bending, she collapses to the ground with a heaving breath.

What's happening to me?

Just then, she feels as if someone is in the room with her. Zoya spins around, but the darkness masks her eyes like a blindfold. Wild panic grips her and she croaks out, "Who's there?"

Silence.

If I can't find these damn lights right now, I'm going to scream. She attempts to stand again but falls back down, her breaths huffing out with great effort.

Without warning, hoarse screams erupt from her throat. Her high-pitched, terrified voice reverberates throughout the silent manor.

The absence of light is suffocating, as if a cloaked hand is gripping her lungs and squeezing them. Before Zoya can block out the memory, it closes in on her.

"Come here, Zoya."

"Please—"

"I told you not to argue with me. Come on, Zoya."

She obliges, keeping her eyes lowered. Focusing on the sliver of moonlight peeking through the curtains. He grabs her wrist and pushes her down.

She starts to sob.

Footsteps pound toward Zoya's door before it swings open. Someone gropes around for the light switch, and the room is suddenly sheltered with harsh beams of light. Zoya's screams die down, and she blinks blearily at the doorway. "Mumtaz?"

"*Bibi,* what's wrong?"

"Why was the door closed?"

"I don't know, *bibi,* you must have closed it."

"Do I ever close the door? Do I ever turn off the lights?" she screeches. "Do I?"

"No, *bibi,*" Mumtaz says in a low voice. She approaches Zoya slowly, as someone would a wounded animal. "Are you alright?" She reaches out a hand to help her up, but Zoya stands of her own accord. Seething, she glares at Mumtaz.

"The next time this door is closed or the lights are off, I'll kick you *all* out of here. I don't care how helpless you are. Do you understand me?"

Mumtaz nods wordlessly, and Zoya gets back into bed. Sweat beads her forehead; her breathing is still ragged.

Suddenly, a face flashes in her mind's eye. Pursed lips and a dimple in his left cheek. The shadow of long eyelashes cast across cheekbones as he trains his eyes to the floor. Zoya closes her eyes, and one of his rare smiles blooms in her mind.

Zoya's breathing becomes less laborious, her fear momentarily subsides.

As this image projects from her mind's eye, her muscles loosen. Her heart—which had been beating erratically only moments before—slows to a much more normal pace.

"Thank you, Haroun," Zoya whispers as she drifts back to sleep.

~

Zaki Ahmed paces around in his office, tension lining his features.

When the knock he's been waiting for arrives, he quickly swivels around. His assistant enters, a file in her hand.

"Sir, the photos are ready."

"Let me see them."

He hastily opens the file and sets the printed pictures on his desk. Upon observing them, a slow, wicked smile appears on his face. "You thought to challenge *me*, Zoya Zameer? You made the biggest mistake of your life in breaking off our partnership. I'll show you what it means to piss Zaki Ahmed off." He begins to laugh maniacally, and his assistant stands by with a troubled expression on her face.

~

When Zoya returns to work the next day, having applied a little extra concealer to cover the dark circles, she's in no better mood than she was the previous day. In fact, she's even worse, and she lashes out at all her employees. Despite hearing about carefully collected reports on Zaki Ahmed's outrage at Zameer's growing success, her spirits aren't the least bit lifted. She continues to tug agitatedly at her hair and wearily rub her eyes.

When Haroun arrives with her tea, Zoya is immediately reminded of last night. Of how her mind had conjured him up as catharsis. She expects to feel some relief at seeing him, but her heart has different ideas. It beats quickly. Angrily.

Apparently, Zoya's heart is not happy that she chose him as a source of comfort.

Haroun sets the mug of tea along with a familiar-looking golden clutch on the table. Zoya eyes it, realizing with a start that it's from the night of the fashion show. *I left it in his car?* Unbidden memories of that night filter through her head one by one.

Haroun stands before her expectantly. Zoya notices faint bags decorating the area under his eyes, and for a brief moment she wonders, *what keeps* him *awake?*

She clears her throat. "Why are you still standing here?"

He purses his lips. Zoya isn't happy with herself for recognizing his nervous tell. "I was wondering if you needed anything else."

"If I needed anything, I would have said so."

He nods. "With your permission, then." He gestures to the door.

"Actually, no. Wait. I do need something." She sets her pen down and makes her way around the table to him. Very subtly, he backs away, but instead of amusing her like it usually does, this infuriates Zoya.

"Why did you bring this back to me?" She taps the clutch.

He looks surprised. "Because you left it in my car, Ms. Zoya."

"Why did you think I needed it back?"

"I assumed . . . I assumed you would want it back."

"Don't assume as such next time," she snaps. "I have plenty of clutches."

He nods wordlessly.

Say something, dammit. Prove my assumptions about you correct. "Also . . ." she racks her brain to give him something to do, standing there for so long that he says, "Yes, Ms. Zoya?"

Ugh. "You can leave," she snaps, flipping her hair behind her shoulder and plopping back down in her chair. By the time she settles down, Haroun has already left.

So silent, Zoya thinks. Her anger has dissipated, replaced by confusion. Her mind plays tug-of-war, battling with itself.

If he's just like those women at the *masjid* and the people of her past, why didn't he say anything? Why didn't he argue with her stupid claims?

Her image of him is constantly tested. Especially later, when she's about to finalize a list of charity organizations with her board of directors, and comes across Haroun.

He's mopping the floor.

Doing a double take, Zoya quickly performs the calculations in her head. *Three o'clock. Tuesday. Janitor Jay sweeps and mops the floors.*

Zoya approaches Haroun and folds her arms. "What are you doing?"

He gestures to the floor. "Mopping the floor, Ms. Zoya," he replies politely.

"I see *that.* I mean why are *you* mopping the floor?"

"Jay needs a break from time to time. Everyone does," Haroun says with a smile in his voice.

Later, she almost walks into the lobby when she stops, having heard the passionate discussion of her two employees. She peeks around the corner.

"No, man. It just sucks." Farhan shakes his head in disgust, and Bill and Sarah listen intently. "We're told from a certain age that we *have* to do this and we *should* do that and if we don't, we're going straight to hell."

"But that's what I'm saying, Farhan. I *understand* why people would express distaste in religion. I understand why *you* do. Because so many times, the 'religion' we're shown—especially as children— isn't representative of the religion at all. It's a hoax, a fabricated religion fueled by interferences of culture and society." Haroun shakes his head. "The religion isn't the problem; the way it's demonstrated is."

Zoya leans back, pressing herself against the wall. After hearing this brief monologue, her breath seems to be getting caught in her throat. Haroun's eloquence always baffles her, but hearing his views on religious matters further intrigues her.

Haroun continues speaking, his voice laced with revulsion. "On top of being raised to resent Islam, Muslims are bombarded with news screwed up by Western media. With the decades-old narrative of 'evil and oppressive Muslims.'" He pauses, and Zoya holds her breath. "Maybe we Muslims don't always do a great job of demonstrating religion, but mainstream media doesn't cut us any slack either. It doesn't bother to recognize true Islam versus the manipulation of it."

The bitterness in his voice roots Zoya to her spot.

"Like . . ." It's Bill who speaks next, pausing as if thinking of how best to word his thoughts. "News of terrorist organizations. Those who use the name of religion as a scapegoat."

"Oh, definitely," Haroun's voice is strained, as if he's holding himself back from erupting. "These people yell *'Allahu Akbar'* or *'Allah is great'* before slaughtering innocent lives. They violate and oppress, then carry the banner of Islam over their heads, leading everyone to believe this religion is violent and unjust."

Zoya turns slightly to observe the expression on Haroun's face but whips back around when his gaze sweeps around the room. "I never understood how anyone could call this religion violent when its very greeting begins with sending peace upon the other person. And a verse in our holy book clearly states that killing an innocent life is equal to killing *all of humanity*." Zoya risks peeking around the corner again and briefly witnesses his distraught expression. "But sometimes it seems like people's negative assumptions of Islam are—to some extent—justified."

Farhan raises his brows.

"Yeah, the media screws us over, but we're human. We often believe what we're told and what we see on TV, unfortunately without conducting our own research. How is anyone *not* supposed to be hostile towards Islam after all they've seen of it is violent images and glaring headlines portraying manslaughter and other atrocities?" Haroun rubs his hand down the length of his face.

"These sickos drag Islam's name through dirt and make other Muslims look bad as well. So that everyone who walks by and sees a woman in *hijab* or hears a Muslim name at the airport becomes wary and afraid."

"Well, yeah, we *don't* do a great job of showcasing religion," Farhan says bitterly. "Have you seen Ms. Zoya? She prays, but that's about it. Everything else is *halal*—permissible—for her. She's rude, she's selfish—"

Zoya has half a mind to abandon her hiding spot and rush towards the neanderthal to teach him a lesson of just how *rude* she can be, but Haroun beats her to it. Much less violently.

"Farhan," he interrupts, his tone placating. "That's not the same thing. I understand your frustration, but . . . we don't know what goes on in people's hearts. We don't really have the right to twist someone's story, to ruin their image because of what *we* see, you know what I mean? Sincerity can't always be determined by us humans." Haroun pauses, observing Farhan's reaction. He must see that Farhan is still willing to listen, because he continues.

"Do you know what God says in the Qur'an? '*Your Lord knows best what is in your hearts.*' So if we as humans try to"—he holds his fingers up in air quotes—"'*measure someone's level of spirituality,*' I think I'd understand why they would become bitter with us and towards religion. If we act like this towards other Muslims, what will the larger Muslim community become? We'll all become bitter towards one another, and the true message and purpose of this religion will be lost." He runs his fingers through his hair, agitated.

"But . . ." Sarah hesitates. "So I was raised with the Methodist Church. I'm not the most religious person, but I remember one thing from my childhood. My family *always* preached no judgment, which is obviously important, but I felt like that didn't ever help anyone grow to be a better person."

Haroun nods. "Yeah, I get what you mean. I can't speak on other religions, but from an Islamic perspective, we're definitely told to hold off on judging others or trying to identify what's in their hearts. But we're also told to fix wrongdoing when we see it, and to advise others in a manner that suits the action. Because yeah, like what you're saying, if we were to just constantly allow wrongdoing to occur because we don't want to be judgmental, that doesn't really help anybody. We only grow and develop and become better practitioners of our respective faiths when we're given advice and guidance." Haroun blows out a sigh. "That being said, the advice also needs to be given in the right manner. For example, if someone has just converted to Islam, and I'm reprimanding him or her for not praying their five daily prayers, that's just extremely insensitive of me and an unrealistic expectation to have. But if one of my friends is purposely missing a prayer because he's attending a party instead, then it becomes my responsibility to counsel and advise him. Advise, not judge."

Haroun pauses, forehead creased in thought. "I think I was referring more to so-called practitioners of faith who are merciless and constantly admonishing people who already struggle with faith. That's also a way that growth—in terms of faith—is hindered." Haroun's expression becomes sad. "Kicking someone when they're down."

Bill and Sarah begin asking genuine, curious questions, and the four employees continue to converse. Zoya turns away, unable to explain why she suddenly feels out of breath.

For days afterward, Haroun continues to prove her assumptions wrong, often without having to say a word. Flora yells at him several times for things he isn't at all involved with, but are nevertheless fitting with his job description, such as a broken printer or a lagging computer. Each time, he stands silently before her, attempting no defense.

Slowly, Zoya's opinion of him reverts to what it was before the *masjid* incident. She's surprised to feel an intense guilt at having thought of him as anything but the pure, quiet human being that he is. She used the people of her past and those women at the *masjid* as a template for all other Muslims in the world, and completely disregarded the careful opinion she had crafted of Haroun Suleiman after her own thorough examination. She had blatantly disregarded the caution she had warned herself to take for the past six years—to not allow *him* to taint her image of others.

Somehow *his* memory still ends up traversing throughout her life, manipulating her emotions and serving as a base through which she views others. Even after all of Zoya's caution, *he* still ends up shadowing her every move, haunting her with the past she has tried so hard to forget.

Days later, Zoya calls Haroun into her office. When he sits down, she watches him brazenly with her chin in her hands.

"Yes, Ms. Zoya?" he says, eyes trained to the floor as usual. His passionate conversation about religion from days ago flits through her mind.

She is about to reveal why she summoned him when his gaze falls upon the article opened on her tablet. It features a picture of Zoya speaking to a distressed employee at the Desi World Fashion Show, and the article speculates about a relationship between them.

That employee being Haroun.

Haroun's eyes widen, mouth agape. "Ms. Zoya . . . what is *that*?"

"This? Oh, it's nothing. Just another despicable attempt by my rival to break me down. Haha." She reaches forward to lock the screen when his shaky voice stops her.

"May I see it?"

Reluctantly, she unlocks the tablet and pushes it towards him, watching as his expression goes from shocked to distraught.

A strange pang resonates in her chest.

"This . . . this is . . ." He seems too distressed to form words.

"*This* is nothing to worry about." Zoya laughs and twists her hair around her finger, trying to lighten the mood. To no avail, however, because Haroun's breaths become quick and shallow.

Zoya stops laughing. "Haroun, *meri jaan*, it's okay. It's the business world; people do this all the time. I'm used to false news about me."

He must be seriously distressed because even her use of *meri jaan* doesn't seem to affect him. "But—but this says—a relationship—"

"So what? We're not actually in a relationship, right? So it doesn't matter." To her surprise, her words come out bitter. She remembers that upon first seeing this news, a glow of happiness had unexpectedly radiated throughout her. Because the article, as tawdry as it was intended to be, had given her the glimpse of a possibility . . . even though she knew that the journalists had nothing better to do than accept large sums of money from angry businessmen.

"But I—" Haroun's hands begin to shake, and Zoya stands to grab the tablet before it falls.

"Haroun," she says gently. "Breathe."

He places his head in his hands. "This is why—this is why I didn't want to—"

"It's okay, Haroun. Relax. We're working on canceling further printings. The media office is already tracking down the source. Since we know it's probably Zaki Ahmed—given his thirst for revenge—it won't be long before we find the culprits." This seems to calm Haroun down a bit, and Zoya hands him a water bottle. "Drink."

She observes him carefully, baffled by his reaction. Is it that bad to be seen in a romantic manner with his CEO?

But deep down, she knows it's not being seen with *her* specifically that bothers him, but false news as a whole. He's too gentle, too pure for the harsh business world.

"I'm giving you a raise," Zoya blurts out, wanting to alleviate his agony. "And a promotion. You're going to be the senior manager's— that is, Bill's—assistant, considering your education and your work ethic since you've joined us. Honestly, you were qualified for a higher-ranking job as soon as you stepped into Zameer." Zoya shrugs nonchalantly as she reveals the news that had been her intent in summoning him to her office.

Haroun looks startled. "A raise? How come . . . all of a sudden?"

Only you *would object, Haroun Suleiman.*

Zoya shrugs and tucks a curl behind her ear. *Because you'll be around me more often now.* "I'm the CEO, *meri jaan.* I can give these privileges to whomever I feel like, whenever I feel like . . . depending on their work ethic."

"But I don't understand . . ." he trails off uncertainly, so baffled that again, even her use of *meri jaan* doesn't break him of his stupor.

Of course you don't. I don't understand. "You've worked really hard, and I think you deserve it." She pauses, twirling a curl around her finger. "You will receive your contract soon."

With furrowed brows, Haroun stutters, "Thank you. I really appreciate it." Zoya nods, smiling at his shaken response. But she notices that his eyes still harbor a dull darkness, as if he isn't entirely happy with the news. When he leaves, she settles her chin in her hands and stares at the spot he had been occupying.

"How would *you* understand, *meri jaan*?" Zoya smiles to herself. "No one's ever been promoted as early as you have at Zameer. I, Zoya Zameer, still have trouble understanding why and how I made this decision. And I *never* have trouble understanding *any* of my decisions."

Fifteen

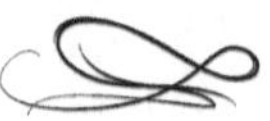

The Prophet Muhammad (peace be upon him) said: "Shall I not tell you whom the (Hell) Fire is forbidden to touch? It is forbidden to touch one who is always accessible, having polite and tender nature."
(At-Tirmidhi, classed as Hasan)

~

THE NEXT DAY, ALONG with Zoya's cup of tea, Haroun carries a gift in purple wrapping paper. Zoya looks at him quizzically.

He shifts uncomfortably. "*Salaam*, Ms. Zoya. Um—" He sets the box on her desk. "This is from my mom."

She furrows her brows. "For what?"

"For my promotion."

Zoya laughs. "You deserved it!" She eyes the gift. "But tell your mom I say thank you! That is so sweet of her."

Haroun nods and is about to leave when Zoya blurts out, "I heard you went ziplining yesterday."

Smooth, Zoya.

He turns. "Yes."

"Did you guys have fun?" She doesn't bother hiding her brashness, having done an in-depth investigation of who had been on the trip the night before: Haroun, Farhan, Bill, and a couple of their other male friends outside the company. Zoya had been searching for a file in her office and asked Sameer to locate it for her, who passed it over while scrolling through Farhan's Instagram.

Zoya's eyes had caught a glimpse of a picture—featuring Haroun and the other guys—and she had done a double take.

"Is that Haroun?" she had asked. Sameer smiled and nodded.

Her curiosity piqued at seeing her gentle, kind employee against the backdrop of such a wild adventure. She eyed the longing on Sameer's face. "How come you didn't join them?"

Sameer had given her a bewildered look and simply pointed to her office as if it was obvious. "I'm working."

"Yes, ma'am, we did. Thank you." Haroun's voice breaks Zoya out of her thoughts. *What did I ask him again?* Zoya nods absentmindedly and Haroun leaves.

As soon as the door shuts, Zoya stares at the gift before grabbing it. "'From my *mom,'*" she repeats snidely. "Would you *die* if you pretended and said it was from *you*? You really know how to make a woman happy, Mr. Suleiman." She rips off the wrapping paper, revealing a large silver-studded box. Inside rest the most gorgeous pair of *jhumkas* Zoya has ever seen, bedded on pools of white satin. Zoya lifts the satin and lets out a gasp. It's a floor length white dress, elegant and shimmery. She rubs the material between her fingers, astonished at how this woman could have been so familiar with her taste in clothes.

Nestled next to the gifts is a small note card written in tidy print. Zoya reads it out loud.

"'This is nothing compared to what you have done for us. May Allah bless you and reward you. We would love to have you over for dinner on Friday if that works for you.'"

A strange lightness spreads throughout Zoya. Having never seen her own mother after she passed away during childbirth, receiving such a heartfelt message from someone else's mother feels like the answer to a secret prayer.

Zoya mulls over the request. *Dinner on Friday.*

"Why not?" She shrugs and places the note card back in the box, stowing the gift away.

She shifts her attention back to the tabloid featuring her picture. The headline reads: *Zoya Zameer—CEO of Zameer Co.— Announces International Expansion of Her Multi-million Dollar*

*Business.*Below the bold words is a picture of Zoya from the Desi World fashion show, followed by an article that details her decision, throwing in a few speculations about the sudden announcement.

Speculations rarely bother Zoya, since they are an inevitable part of the life she has cultivated for herself. She usually doesn't even bother reading news about her personal life—the media office and her PR team do that for her—but one of the rumors in the article grabs her attention. Thrown in between a few lines about her company's victorious appearance at the fashion show are comments about "suspicious motives," one of them detailing a description of her alleged husband.

Zoya locks the iPad screen and settles back in her chair, thoroughly disturbed. Her mind is too preoccupied to think about the meetings she has planned for today.

~

The two employees are braced in front of each other, one with flared nostrils and crossed arms, while the other looks like he wants to sink into the floor.

"That's it. I'm sick and tired of this!"

Haroun remains silent in the face of Flora's irate outburst, his head bowed.

"Because you know what? Before *you* appeared, *I* was Ms. Zoya's favorite." On a quieter note, she adds, "She did *me* favors."

Haroun opens and closes his mouth, brows furrowed. "Flora, it's not what you think. There are no favorites—"

"No favorites my *foot*," Flora snaps, her eyes pooling with furious tears.

"Flora, it really wasn't my intention to hurt you. I'm really sorry if—"

"Oh, *please* stop with your whole '*holier than thou*' attitude. It's phony and it *pisses me off*!"

"Please, I never—"

"Yeah, yeah. It's clear with the way you carry yourself that you believe you're better than everyone here. Is that what your religion teaches you? To bash others and make them feel terrible?"

Haroun shakes his head, his forehead creased with worry. "No,

Flora. Of course not. I don't think I'm better than anyone here."

"Clearly you do. *Clearly* Ms. Zoya only likes you because you're *Moslem* and so is *she*." Several employees who are watching the scene gasp at her words—Flora has crossed a line.

One of the onlookers leans in to whisper, "*She's mad as hell about his promotion*" to another.

Haroun presses his lips together and keeps his eyes trained to the floor.

Flora shoves her finger in his face. "See? You think you're too good to even give me an answer. Pick your head up and talk to me like a *man*!"

Haroun still doesn't say anything. At that moment, the sound of clicking heels draws closer, and Zoya—having heard the chaos—turns the corner to face her two employees. By now, everyone in the hall is watching them with bated breath.

"What's going on?" Zoya asks, her voice quiet and deadly. Her gaze snaps between Flora, whose jaw is now twitching with fury, and Haroun, whose hands are clasped before him. Zoya has witnessed variations of this scene repeatedly over the past few weeks—of Flora lashing out at Haroun for one thing or another.

"This man believes he's better than everyone here," Flora huffs, gesturing to Haroun.

Zoya raises her eyebrows. "Why do you say that? I don't get that vibe from him." She pauses, then dares to add, "Contrarily I think he constantly humbles himself and believes he's of lower status than everyone here."

Flora glares at Haroun. "See? *Of course* you would say that, Ms. Zoya. It's because he's fooled you like he's fooled *everyone* with his innocent and meek façade. But *I'm* not falling for it."

Zoya turns to Haroun, waiting to see whether he'll defend himself. But he keeps his mouth shut, gaze searing into the floor.

His words from days ago filter through her head: *But we're also told to fix wrongdoing when we see it.*

Zoya continues to watch him, thinking, *Won't you fix* this *wrongdoing, Mr. Suleiman? Or do your rules not apply to yourself?*

Haroun remains silent.

Zoya smiles and turns back to Flora. "Alright, Flora," she says, clapping her hands. The onlooking employees exchange anxious looks at the oddly calm tone of her voice. "Let's settle this once and for all—since this is clearly a permanent issue for you. Forget about the majority—if even *half* the people in this room agree with what you say, I'm firing Haroun. And I swear by the God Who gave me life that I'll do it."

Haroun's head snaps up in alarm.

"Everyone gather round," Zoya raises her voice, and it resonates throughout the hall. "Join the circus show," she mutters to herself before continuing, "Gather round now. Quickly! I need everyone here!"

Everyone drops what they're doing either eagerly or hesitantly and makes their way to the three people in the middle of the hall.

Zoya turns to Haroun and smiles sweetly. "Close your eyes, Haroun."

Haroun hesitates. "Just do it, sweetheart," Zoya insists. His brow furrow—either at the word *sweetheart* or at the tense situation—but he does as she says. Zoya turns full circle to everyone in the room. Flora looks stricken, her face taking on a sickly yellow pallor.

"Alright. Raise your hand if you think that Mr. Haroun Suleiman over here"—she gestures to him—"gives off the vibe that he believes he's better than everyone around him. And be honest. Your integrity is on the line. Raise your hand if you think he displays a—as Flora says—'*holier than thou*' attitude." Zoya eyes each employee and waits.

No one raises their hand. Not a single person. Not even Flora's friends, who shoot her apologetic looks.

As expected. "Great." Zoya chirps, turning back to her two employees. "We have a unanimous vote. Not a single person in this room agrees with your statement. So Flora, you're fired." Zoya gives her a sickeningly sweet smile.

Flora's head immediately snaps up; her eyes widening. "W-What?"

Zoya nods. "You're fired. Do you wanna hear it in Spanish? *Sal de aquí.* Get out of here."

Flora's face turns ashen. "No wait, Ms. Zoya. I'm sorry, I—"

Zoya tucks her curls behind her ear, turns around, and begins to walk away. Haroun looks even more worried than before, and Flora throws him one last resentful look before she rushes after Zoya. "Please, Ms. Zoya. It was a mistake. I'm sorry, I—"

"Nobody is allowed to insult my employees, Flora," Zoya snaps, continuing to walk as Flora trails after her. "And I don't tolerate injustice at Zameer. Do you know what the word *zameer* means, Flora? It means conscience. What kind of conscience would I— *whose last name is Zameer*—display if I allowed you to stay here despite what you've done? No, I won't tolerate it. This *world* may target the harmless and the innocent, but *I* won't allow that in my company."

"No, please, please, please, Ms. Zoya. Don't do this. Come on, it's me! It's Flora! I'm the *lead designer*. What happened to being one of your first employees—one of your *favorite* employees? Please don't do this to me. It was a mistake. I take it back, I—" Desperately, Flora grabs at Zoya's arm since Zoya continues to walk away, *dupatta* trailing carelessly behind her. Zoya's sleeve rides up, revealing faded scars lining her arm.

Immediately Zoya shakes her arm out of Flora's grip and looks around hurriedly. To her dismay, Haroun's eyes, as well as many other employees' eyes, have followed Flora's actions.

"Don't *touch* me," Zoya spits out through gritted teeth, eyeing Flora hatefully. The kind of hatred that, to an objective eye, would seem much too intense for this moment alone. "You can't take things back; you can *never* take things back when they're over. Once you've done something, the scar of it remains forever, whether you regret it or not." Zoya rubs her arm. With one last glance at the watching employees, she rushes towards the elevator to head to her office.

Flora continues to follow her. "*Please*, Ms. Zoya." Angry tears pool in her eyes but Flora swipes at them, attempting to hold herself together. She points to herself. "Please. It's *me*, it's *Flora*! I'm your lead designer!"

Zoya turns and gives her a small smile. "Yes, I know that."

"So please don't do this to me, Ms. Zoya. Not to me."

A corner of Zoya's lips turns up. "You could be Bill Gates." Her smile vanishes. "And I would still fire you." She turns and walks away, heels clicking against the floor. Flora's tears begin to fall, and Haroun stands there with an even more troubled expression on his face.

Sixteen

"So whoever does an atom's weight of good will see it. And whoever does an atom's weight of evil will see it." (Qur'an 99:7-8)

~

"Zoya, come sit with me for a minute."

Ecstasy grips Zoya as she abandons her task and follows her father's voice. "Yes, Papa?"

He shifts closer to her and strokes her hair. Zoya has to control the wave of happiness that washes over her, but she can't help the confusion that also arises at his unexpectedly affectionate gesture.

"You're my amazing daughter, aren't you?"

Zoya nods her head earnestly. "Yes, Papa."

"I found a guy for you."

Zoya's face falls for a second, then brightens up quickly. "Really?"

"Yes. He's an investment banker, and he's really wealthy. He's religious, too. His name is Farhan."

Zoya listens with rapt attention. All she can focus on is the plea in her father's voice.

"Do you want to meet him?"

Zoya observes her father, sees the tender way he's looking at her. She feels his hand stroking her hair, and all she can think of is how she had forgotten what this felt like.

She smiles. "No. I agree."

Her father's eyes brighten, and Zoya's heart lurches. "Really?" he says.

She nods firmly, no hint of regret on her face.

"Oh, Zoya." He leans forward and embraces his daughter. For a few moments, Zoya's eyes widen with shock. Then she throws her arms around his shoulders, reveling in the sweet pleasure of the embrace.

Zoya jolts upright, panicked. Bright light from her chandelier pierces her eyes as she gropes around in her blankets, unsure of what she's looking for.

Realizing that she's awake, a sudden, fierce pain grips her. She draws her knees up to her chest, trying to numb the aching of her heart.

"Papa," she mumbles. His face—so vivid, so clear—has come to plague her dreams again. She closes her eyes, trying to preserve the memory that had manifested into a dream. Tears begin rolling down her face. "Ugh." Shocked at herself, she swipes angrily at her eyes. "Stop."

Although nineteen-year-old Zoya had no idea what horrors that day in her dream would lead to, twenty-five-year-old Zoya would do anything to fall back onto her pillow, close her eyes, and see her father's face again. Feel his hands stroking her hair again. See the adoration in his eyes again.

So Zoya Zameer falls back onto her pillow, closes her eyes, and mumbles, "Good night, Papa."

~

Later that day in the office, there's a knock on Zoya's door. "Enter!" she barks. Footsteps proceed towards her desk and she glances up, distracted.

Haroun sets her tea at her desk and stands before her. "*Salaam*, Ms. Zoya. My mother was asking if you'd be able to make it tomorrow."

Oh, shoot. With the events of the past few days and the numerous interviews for new designers (which Zoya had insisted on conducting herself), the invitation has completely slipped her mind. She twists a curl around her finger. "Oh, yes, yes. Tell her yes."

Haroun nods and turns to leave, then stops midway to the door. Worry lines crease his forehead.

"Ms. Zoya, it's just been bothering me for the past couple of days and I . . ." He blows out a deep sigh, shoving a hand through his hair. "You didn't have to fire Flora because of what she was saying to me. I'm simply your worker, as everyone else here is."

Zoya knits her eyebrows. "What makes you think it was because of you? I fired her because I don't tolerate injustice. And I don't tolerate her lashing out at my employees."

"I understand, but she was the *lead designer.* And you were more fond of her than—"

"That should give her no sense of entitlement; she has no right to go around stabbing defenseless people with her words. Yes, it'll be a sad loss to the company. But I cannot keep such character at Zameer."

"Please just give her another chance," Haroun whispers quietly. "She didn't mean anything she said, and I wasn't offended by it."

Zoya laughs. "A bomb exploding on the other side of the world doesn't cause physical destruction here, where we stand. But that doesn't mean the bomb didn't explode." She shakes her head. "Look at you; you still continue to defend Flora after she demoralized you. Bravo, Mr. Suleiman, bravo."

"She didn't mean any of it. I know she's a great person. I may have done or said something that upset her or—"

Zoya rolls her eyes and folds her arms, walking towards him. He stands silently before her, gaze fixed to the ground. "You are the epitome of goodness," Zoya says, voice low and solemn. "Morality and righteousness is—is *packaged* into your human body." She points to her window. "You see this twisted, corrupt world outside? This world has *no room* for people like you. *Stop* being so good. I'm warning you; one day this goodness is going to come crashing down on your unsuspecting shoulders. It's going to be thrown in your face, and you'll regret all the good that you ever did for anyone." She pauses, cocking her head to the side. "You know this piety that beats inside your heart? This faith in everyone's 'clean' motives, and this belief that everyone is inherently good? It's going to destroy you, Haroun Suleiman. And you'll be left standing in the debris of your destruction, remembering what I'm saying. You mark my words."

"Ms. Zoya, you place me on such a high pedestal, please don't, I—" He rubs his face with his hands. "Please," he says helplessly. "Give her one more chance."

Zoya snorts. "*Life* doesn't give second chances. Why should I?"

Haroun bites his bottom lip and furrows his brows worriedly, as if debating whether he should speak or not. After a moment he says, in an almost imperceptible whisper, "The guilt is too much."

Zoya steps closer to him. "*Pobrecito*. This guilt that beats inside your heart is just more proof of your clean character." She turns around and walks back to her chair. "Understand that you're lucky to feel this emotion. Not a lot of people do." She chuckles mirthlessly. "And understand that, inevitably, this emotion will eat you inside out. Better to restrain it before it's too late."

Haroun remains standing for a couple seconds, a helpless expression on his face. Then he turns around and exits the room.

Zoya is not given much time to ponder over this conversation because she receives a call from the receptionist, notifying her of the designers' arrival.

"Send them both to my office."

Zoya has always been fond of group interviews so that she can get rid of more people at one time. Finding an assertive and professional employee nowadays is difficult, and tackling them with the group method better highlights a probable candidate.

Zoya freshens her lipstick and fluffs her hair. Satisfied with her reflection in the mirror, she waits for the designers'.

Before they arrive, Farhan brings documents for Zoya to sign. She scans the documents, then grabs a pen and hastily signs them. Farhan wordlessly takes the file back, turning to leave when Zoya's voice rings out.

"Farhan," she says, pausing as her dream floods back to her. Shaking her head, she continues, "I'm pretty sure you have a tongue in that mouth. Considering it runs pretty wildly when you're trash talking me."

He turns slowly, eyes wary. "What do you want me to say?"

Zoya shrugs nonchalantly. "At least acknowledge your boss' existence."

Farhan hesitates. "Hi, Ms. Zoya."

Zoya rolls her eyes and shakes her head. "Never mind."

Farhan exits quietly, and Zoya is left to stare at his retreating back, mulling over how guarded he has become around her since the Desi World Fashion Show. Even more so than before.

A knock sounds on the door, interrupting her thoughts. "Enter," Zoya shouts, flipping over the hourglass on her desk.

A man and a woman a little older than Zoya step inside. Upon seeing the man, Zoya grins and tosses her curls behind her shoulders coyly.

"Have a seat, please," Zoya says. The man smiles and extends a hand for her to shake, to which Zoya immediately shrinks back. "Oh, no. I don't—"

"Oh, I'm so sorry." He sits down with his hands in his lap, and the woman follows suit.

"Do you guys know each other?" Zoya points between the two of them. They shake their heads. "Great. Now you do." Zoya opens the file in front of her. "Sana, meet Alejandro. Alejandro, meet Sana. Tea or coffee?"

They look taken aback at her forwardness, then Sana quickly says, "Coffee is good for me."

"Same here," pipes up Alejandro.

Zoya calls Sarah with a request for Haroun to bring two cups of coffee.

"None for you?" Alejandro asks politely.

"I don't drink coffee," she replies curtly before setting her chin in her hands and staring them both down. Alejandro squirms under her gaze.

"So," Zoya says. "What will you bring to my company?"

They look at each other before Alejandro says, "Well, the designers are sort of the backbone of the fashion industry."

Zoya raises her brows. "Why? In essence, all you guys do is draw. People all over the world draw; not everyone gets paid for it." Alejandro and Sana turn to each other in bewilderment. Zoya laughs, twisting a curl around her finger. "Are you offended? It's the truth. Let me ask you a question. Would you ever work as a barber?"

Both of them look thoroughly confused by this onslaught of seemingly random questions.

Sana slowly says, "If it was the last job option I had."

Zoya turns to Alejandro. He presses his lips together, and Zoya is suddenly reminded of someone else with the same habit. "I don't think so, no," he says. "Unless I had no other options, like Sana said."

Zoya smiles. "Right. Do you know why? Because it's *degrading*. The term barber has negative connotations." She pauses. "What if I told you that you're now Kim Kardashian's personal hairdresser?"

Sana exclaims, "I'd love to be her personal hairdresser!" while Alejandro looks shrewd and says, "I see where you're going with this."

Zoya nods. "We live in a twisted world that claims equality yet really favors the wealthy. A barber is a barber and an occupation that people scorn, but if you're *Kim Kardashian's hairdresser*, then oh My God, you've become like *the* coolest person to ever walk on earth. It's about privilege. It's about wealth and status and who you *serve*, not about what occupation you have."

Alejandro nods. "Understood."

"Now tell me." Zoya turns her piercing gaze to him. "What will you bring to my company?"

"Well, without designers, you don't have designs. And without designs—"

Zoya holds a hand up. "I know very well the job description for a designer, thank you." Alejandro's cheeks redden, and he opens his mouth as if to elaborate, but Zoya cuts him off.

"I asked what *you* will bring to the company. Not the designer in you." She turns to Sana. "Yes?"

Sana raises her brows. "Ms. Zoya, we speak as designers when we come here. I can say that I myself will bring a plethora of new ideas into the market—"

Zoya shakes her head in frustration. Alejandro interrupts, "May I ask why you're giving more weight to this than our skills and capabilities, Ms. Zoya? You've probably seen our résumés, assuming that we're here . . ." He trails off at the expression on Zoya's face.

Zoya leans forward and sets her clasped hands on the table. In the quiet room, her bangles clink noisily against each other, and the interviewees flinch. "Because, *Alejandro,* I value character more than talent in my company. And fortunately for me, I've been able to handpick people from all over the nation who harbor both of these traits." *Well, that's ninety-nine percent true. Sorry, Flora,* Zoya thinks bitterly. "Integrity is the baseline for every form of work. It either makes or breaks you. *That's* why this holds more weight."

Alejandro nods, looking shaken by her response. "I understand."

Zoya sits back in her chair. "You two may leave."

They exchange confused glances. Alejandro says, "But—"

Zoya smiles sweetly. "Yeah. I can ask my receptionist to show you out of the building. And if you need a ride, I can arrange that for you." She bats her eyelashes at him. *I'm not arranging anything for anyone.*

Sana grabs her purse. "No, thank you, Ms. Zoya. We'll find our way out." Her voice is cold.

Zoya nods vigorously and examines her nails as they leave. Once the door shuts, she grabs the hourglass on her table and slams it upside down. "Idiots," she snarls. "Flora, couldn't you just keep your mouth shut about Haroun? Because of you, I have to go through all this."

Someone knocks on her door. "*What?*" she yells. Haroun walks in, a tray of two coffees in his hand. He looks around quizzically.

"Take it away," Zoya snaps. "Drink it. I don't care. I sent them away." Suddenly, Zoya remembers that he no longer has to handle tasks such as serving coffee, but still continues to do so when asked by Zoya.

Haroun remains in the doorway for a second. "Is everything alright, Ms. Zoya?"

She sighs, making a big show of shoving her curls away from her face. "*Yes,* Haroun. Everything's fine."

Without another word, he leaves.

"Oh, Haroun," Zoya laments to the ceiling. "Would it kill you to stay for a *second* more and ask me again if everything's okay?"

Seventeen

~

ON FRIDAY, ZOYA GOES to Haroun's home.

It's a pretty, clean little apartment nestled into a homey-looking neighborhood. She's wearing the dress and earrings Haroun's mother gifted her, as well as one of her best (Zameer Co., of course) *dupattas*. Upon ringing the doorbell, Zoya's heart hammers in her chest; an inexplicable, unanticipated fear rises in her. A mantra plays over and over in her head: *Keep your damn attitude in check today.*

Having this thought in the first place surprises her. Why does it matter so much to her what these people think of her?

Pressing her palm flat against her ribcage, she feels the quick, persistent heartbeats underneath.

"Stop it, Zoya *Zameer*," she murmurs, emphasizing her last name to remind herself of one of its meanings: dignity.

The door flies open, and a pretty teenage girl adorned in a soft red *dupatta* stands in front of Zoya, locks of raven hair framing her face. A lovely aroma wafts from inside the house.

Abruptly, Zoya remembers that she knows nothing of Haroun's family—how many siblings he has, what his parents are like.

"*Salaam*," she blurts out, hoping that her awkwardness isn't apparent to the girl.

The girl grins broadly. "Ms. Zoya! *Salaam*. We've been *so* excited to meet you." She reaches forward to embrace her and Zoya—too surprised by the gesture—is unable to shrink back from the touch. She stands awkwardly for a second, trying to quell the anxiety rising within her.

The girl doesn't seem fazed as she pulls back and beams. A sweet, playfully angry voice from inside the apartment says, "Invite her in, won't you, Aisha? Or will you just stand there all day? *Allah, Allah.* Have I not taught you manners?" The girl smiles sheepishly, stepping back for Zoya to enter.

Zoya smiles, reaching up to tuck her curls behind her ear out of habit. Her hands drop awkwardly to her side when she remembers that her hair is piled into a neat bun at the back of her head.

As the young girl—Aisha—closes the door behind her, Zoya hears her whisper to herself, "She's even prettier in real life!"

Inside, Zoya is greeted by an older woman, who must be Haroun's mom, and a young woman around Zoya's age. Probably younger. She sports a broad smile and has the most captivating brown eyes.

His mother's face is soft and fragile, gray streaks lining the black hair that peeks under her *dupatta.* Her forehead is dully lined, and her dark eyes lack shine, as if someone extracted the happiness from them. Her features are quite simple, yet one could tell by looking at her that she had an exquisite face in her youth. Looking at her immediately makes Zoya recognize where Haroun's softness comes from. This woman exudes warmth and valor.

Zoya is inexplicably drawn to her. "*Salaam,*" she murmurs.

His mother smiles. "*Wa 'Alaikum Salaam,* Ms. Zoya."

"Just Zoya," she corrects, smiling. "*Aap mujhe Zoya bulaa sakti hai.* This is for you." She holds out the gift bag she bought at the last minute, recalling how her father would always take treats to a new home.

His mother smiles and reaches forward to hug Zoya, who holds her breath. *It'll just take a second.*

Yet she's surprised to discover that she doesn't feel any sense of suffocation or anxiety when this woman embraces her.

"We don't know how to thank you, Zoya," the woman says

when she pulls back. "Haroun's promotion is a huge blessing for us, *Alhamdulillah.*" She gestures to the gift bag. "And honestly, you didn't have to bring this. You have already done so much for us."

Zoya is appalled by these words. She giggles nervously, flattered. "No, no. It's no big deal. I just gave Haroun what he deserved." She looks around. "Speaking of him, where is he?"

Something clatters in the kitchen. Haroun steps out a moment later, placing a salad bowl on the table before approaching Zoya. He ducks his head. "*Salaam,* Ms. Zoya."

It seems as if the atmosphere in the room shifts. The heat pressing down on Zoya feels so thick that she pauses for a second, simply staring at Haroun. Something about his homey appearance causes her legs to feel like jelly, and she is abruptly afraid they will give way and lose function.

"*Salaam,*" she replies a moment too late, hoping no one notices.

"Did you find our place okay?" he says.

She nods, still slightly breathless.

"Please, come sit!" His mother ushers Zoya into the living room. It's a small space, but somehow the bursts of color such as the vases of vibrant flowers and the bright, tranquil paintings on the walls make the apartment seem lighter, happier.

They make the apartment a home.

"Naima, your chicken is ready." Haroun tells his sister. The older one lets out a frantic gasp and rushes into the kitchen. Aisha follows Zoya and her mother into the living room.

Where is his father? Zoya wonders.

"What would you like to drink?" Aisha asks. "Water? Juice?"

"Water is fine, thank you," Zoya replies. Aisha disappears into the kitchen, leaving Zoya alone with Haroun's mother.

It's been a long time since she's been in the presence of elders outside of work, so Zoya Zameer struggles to find words. But the woman's calming presence dispels all of her fears and anxious thoughts.

"How are you, Zoya?"

"*Alhamdulillah.* And you?"

"*Alhamdulillah.* We have much to thank Allah for. May He

bless you for what you've done for us, too."

Zoya is flustered by the woman's sincerity. "Really, auntie, it was nothing. Haroun deserved it. He's a hard worker." She absentmindedly reaches up to twirl a curl, hand dropping awkwardly in her lap a second later.

The woman smiles. "Haroun tells us *you're* a really hard worker."

Zoya's eyes widen. *Haroun talks about me at home?* She chuckles. "Oh, that's so kind of him."

After Aisha arrives with cold water for Zoya, the three of them engage in easy conversation until Naima calls them to the dinner table.

Zoya doesn't ask about Haroun's father.

The table is set with the most tasteful and artful dishes. Biryani, loaded fries, samosas, roast chicken, Chinese noodles, and more. "Oh my God!" Zoya squeals, to which they all laugh. "No, really, this is amazing. Thank you guys so much!" She remembers the line her father always used to say, "You didn't have to do—"

"Oh, no, none of that." Aisha shakes her head and gestures for Zoya to sit down.

The five of them talk over food, which the mother, Naima, and Haroun collectively made. Haroun is mostly quiet but occasionally chuckles at something someone says, and Zoya's eyes shoot to him, drinking in the scene.

She learns that Naima is in her second year of college, making her around five to six years younger than Zoya, while Aisha is in her junior year of high school. Both girls work part time as well as attend school full time, which takes Zoya by surprise. Their faces and happy-go-lucky attitudes don't betray any hint of the burden placed on their shoulders at such young ages.

"Naima's looking into getting married soon," Haroun's mother comments casually. Zoya's ears perk at this. She looks over at a smiling Naima.

His mother continues, "And Haroun's been looking for a while, too." She smiles in a secretive manner. "*Alhamdulillah.*"

Zoya's head snaps up; her eyes widen. She has no words to

explain the unexpected panic that jolts through her.

Haroun's gaze darts her way at the sudden movement, and a pucker appears between his brows.

Haroun's been looking for a while? An alarmed voice in Zoya's head shouts. *And what does Alhamdulillah mean? God, what does it mean? He's found someone? He's tying the knot? WHAT DOES IT MEAN?*

And then another, calmer voice. *Breathe, Zoya. Breathe. One, two, three.*

She inhales through her nose and forces a weak smile. All she can manage to say is, "Really? Interesting." She's afraid to ask for clarification, afraid of the answer she might receive.

Zoya turns to Naima to distract her addled mind. "Has anyone caught your eye?"

"Naima isn't interested in *anyone*," Aisha laughs. "*Nada*. Zilch. Zero. But she wants to get married."

"Well, Naima, I think that's pretty great. That you have no one specific in mind, no expectations. Makes it a little easier to get used to a marriage once you enter it, because you're not harboring any unrealistic fantasies." Zoya's voice comes out unintentionally bitter. "If I could give you any sort of advice, I would say not to get married at all, but"—she laughs—"I understand that people have different desires and aims in life."

Haroun's mother smiles at Zoya. "You seem to be talking from experience?"

Haroun coughs on his drink, and Aisha pats his back. He glances briefly at Zoya before looking away.

So he hasn't told anyone. Zoya's heart hammers rapidly in her chest, and she has to stop the smile from spreading on her face.

"Are you alright?" she asks him. He nods.

Zoya turns back to his mother. Something about the softness in the older woman's eyes prods her to say, "Uh, yes. I was married."

"Was?" Naima asks quizzically. Her aura exudes gentleness like her mother's, just as the meaning of her name implies. *Comfort, tranquility.* A perfect antithesis of her carefree, bubbly sister. "I'm sorry, I didn't mean to be so blunt," she quickly adds.

"No, no, it's fine. Yes, I was married. And divorced. Not a lot of people know."

For a brief moment, there is a charged silence in the room. The four family members exchange quick glances before turning back to Zoya.

Naima doesn't say anything, and a dark look passes over Aisha's face before she murmurs, "I'm sorry."

Haroun's mother clucks her tongue. "Aisha, don't say that." She looks at Zoya. "Zoya, *beta*, whatever happened, happened for your own good."

Zoya stares into the eyes of this calm, strong woman who is so accepting of her. Of *Zoya Zameer*, whose life is rudely displayed and scrutinized under glaring—seldom true—headlines, inviting people to make the worst assumptions. This woman, who hasn't attempted to intrude upon her personal life, and has only complimented and thanked her.

Zoya smiles. "It was. Besides, I don't think there are many men left on this earth who possess *ghairat* or shamefacedness." She shrugs, and the two sisters share a look. Zoya points to Haroun. "One of the exceptions is your son, auntie. I have never seen a more respectful man." Haroun reddens slightly, and his mother beams.

They spend another hour simply talking. Zoya is enjoying being around his family so much that—to her surprise—she finds herself not wanting to leave.

On her way to the bathroom a little while later, she passes by the master bedroom. Her eyes flick to the lamp on the bedside table, its light spreading in a soft halo around the room.

Zoya freezes in her spot.

Her legs become immobile, heart rate speeding up. She shakes her head to dispel the memories trying to resurface but fails miserably as a particularly horrifying one rushes over her head and pulls her under.

"Please, I can't."

"What do you mean, you can't?" *His voice is a soft, soft purr.*

Zoya wipes the tears beginning to stream down her face. "I'm not ready."

He steps forward and presses his fingers sharply into her shoulders. "Are you refusing me?" he murmurs softly, voice low.

She shakes her head weakly, wincing. "No, I'm just telling you that I'm not—"

He reaches forward and loosens her nightgown. It falls open and cascades down her shoulders, lying in a silky heap on the floor. Such a pretty, pretty purple color.

Zoya wraps her arms around herself, feeling exposed and distraught. "Please, I—"

He leans down to Zoya's ear slowly, and she flinches. "This is my God-given right, Zoya, do you understand?" His voice is still soft, seemingly romantic. To outside ears it would seem like a seductive purr.

When she doesn't answer, he repeats the question. But his voice rises several octaves this time. Zoya covers her ears.

"Are you ignoring me?" he asks quietly. For a moment, it seems like a harmless, curious question.

Abruptly, he steps closer. Zoya—panicked—jerks back quickly. Her back hits the lamp on the bedside table, and the beads decorating the umbrella pierce through her skin, slicing it open.

She lets out a yelp. "Please, Far—"

"Come on, Zoya." His voice is dangerously soft, a threatening purr. He leans down, attempting a gentle expression. But his fists are clenched as he gestures to the king-sized bed. "Come on."

And then he becomes more characteristic, more pressing. Zoya winces as the force of his words hits her, her entire body trembling at the memory of last time's scars.

She obliges silently as he unbuttons his shirt.

"Ms. Zoya?"

With a gasp, Zoya's eyes fly open. She's collapsed against the wall, and Haroun is kneeling at a distance from her with a worried expression on his face. She breathes harshly, shoving some strands of escaped hair away from her face.

"Are you alright?" His voice is laced with concern. He turns around and calls out, "Naima, bring some water, please."

"I'm fine," Zoya huffs out, standing up. He follows suit, and she almost collapses forward onto him but grabs the door handle for support.

"You don't seem fine, Ms. Zoya," he says. Worry lines crease his forehead. "Are you sure you're—"

"I said I'm *fine*," Zoya snaps. Then, appalled at her own abrasiveness towards him, she turns around. "I'm going to head out now."

Naima arrives with a water bottle and hands it to Haroun. Her eyes dart between the two of them. "Is everything okay, *bhai*?"

He hesitates before quietly replying, "Yes, everything's fine."

Zoya turns around and flashes Naima a weak smile, throwing her hair behind her shoulders in classic Zoya Zameer fashion.

Her hands are still shaking.

"Yes, *meri jaan,* everything's okay. I get a bit claustrophobic sometimes. Your worrywart brother freaked out."

Naima looks concerned. "Oh, no! Then you should definitely drink some water. And come to the living room. I'll open the windows. So sorry about that."

The three of them make their way outside, and Zoya begins to insist that she must make it home as it's getting late. They invite her to stay longer but she declines, thanking them profusely and trying but failing to resist the gift box Naima places in her hands.

"Your parents must be worried," Haroun's mother says. Zoya flinches at the mention of parents and catches Haroun throwing her a quick glance.

His mother seems to have realized something and places a hand against her forehead. Instead of elaborating on the topic, however, she continues with, "Haroun? Girls? Drop Zoya off to her car, please."

"No, auntie, there's really no need to—"

She shakes her head firmly. "It's late." She leans forward and embraces Zoya once more, and it takes Zoya a moment to remember how to breathe again.

Once outside, the four of them make small talk until Zoya reaches her car. Aisha excitedly requests Zoya to visit again, and Zoya thanks her and makes the same offer.

However, the difference is that Zoya's offer is far from genuine. It's been too long since she's had people in her house. She can't imagine ever having guests again.

As Zoya pulls out of the parking space, she waves to the three figures becoming smaller and smaller in her rearview mirror. Letting out a breath she didn't realize she was holding, she takes one last peek at Haroun Suleiman.

He's leading his sisters back to their apartment, arms wrapped securely around their shoulders.

Eighteen

"Why do you see the speck that is in your brother's eye, but do not notice the log that is in your own eye?" (Luke 6:41)

~

ZAKI AHMED STEEPLES HIS fingers and stares at his desk. His secretary fidgets nervously in front of him.

"We are experiencing an enormous loss, sir, especially with the resignation of one of our designers. And—"

"I'm aware of that."

"And as for the printing of the news about Zoya Zameer, the reporters were coerced into canceling further printing. They were offered large sums of money."

Zaki slams his palm on the desk. His secretary flinches. "This is all *her* fault," he seethes. "This is all Zoya Zameer's fault. Ever since she broke off our partnership, we've been . . ." He trails off for a moment, lost in thought, before he adds, "She must have offered no less than thousands of dollars to the reporters."

"Correct, sir."

Zaki laughs suddenly. "It doesn't matter. The news about a possible relationship with her employee wasn't enough to rile our audience. After all, everyone is familiar with her reputation anyway." He sneers. "What we need is something more . . . uncharacteristic. Something more destructive."

His gaze drifts away as he falls back into deep thought, plotting the downfall of his rival. His secretary watches him warily, concern etched into her features.

~

Sameer knocks on the door to Zoya's office and peeks inside. "The designer is here for her interview."

"Sameer, will you ever give me good news?" Zoya sighs loudly, breaking out of her disturbed thoughts of last night. Something about Haroun's young sisters coupling the burden of working along with studying won't leave her mind. That, and the comment their mother made about Haroun looking into getting married.

"Send her in quickly," Zoya tells Sameer. "Hurry up, oh my God. You are *so* slow, it makes me want to puke!" she huffs dramatically.

Frustrated by the last several interviews for potential designers, Zoya can only hope that this one doesn't make her lose her mind. And since she doesn't trust anyone with this task but herself, she cannot be tempted to leave the interviews to Bill, as always.

Minutes later, a woman Zoya's age enters. She's clad in a long, simple dress, her hair pulled back in a neat ponytail. A plain shawl hangs around her shoulders and falls over her chest.

"*Salaam*," Zoya says, opting for the Muslim greeting given the interviewee's name on her résumé.

"*Wa 'Alaikum Salaam*." The woman's voice is soft, eyes lowered.

"Sit," Zoya orders. For introduction's sake, she says, "Name?"

"Sumaiya. Sumaiya Akhtar."

"Sumaiya . . ." Zoya trails off. "Coffee or tea?"

"I'm okay, thank you."

"Tea it is," Zoya says, calling Sarah to send Haroun with tea; old habits die hard, and she isn't satisfied with anyone else delivering her beverages. "So, Sumaiya." She flips her hourglass upside down, and Sumaiya's eyes follow her actions. "Why do you think you can be the lead designer?"

She clears her throat. "Ms. Zoya, I believe I have the potential."

Zoya raises her brows and flips open Sumaiya's résumé. Haroun knocks and enters with their tea, and Zoya is too immersed in her file to notice the way Sumaiya's cheeks tinge pink at his arrival.

While Zoya is scanning the résumé, Haroun sets the tray of tea on her desk and turns to leave. Again, Zoya misses the smile he directs at Sumaiya as he exits.

"Worked as the lead designer for three years in Pak Enterprises," Zoya reads from the résumé as she leans back. "You do know Zameer Co. and Pak Enterprises are like Harry Potter and Voldemort, correct?" She doesn't hesitate to lay her rivalries with other companies on the table. What can people put in the media and use against her that she isn't already prepared for?

Sumaiya laughs. "I'm sure the entire fashion industry is aware, yes." She takes a sip of her tea.

"Why would you leave such a secure job? I'm flattered, really, I am," Zoya drawls in a bored voice. "That you decided to come here. But why the sudden change? *Ooh*." She leans forward excitedly as a thought occurs to her. "Were you fired?"

The woman laughs. "No, Ms. Zoya. It just . . . didn't fit with my ideals. And I was tired of the team dynamic."

Zoya perks up, interested by this peek into Pak Enterprises. "Team dynamic? Interesting. What about it tired you?"

Sumaiya meets Zoya's eyes, and suddenly her expression becomes wary. "Just . . . wasn't the best," she murmurs vaguely.

Okay, Zoya thinks. *So she's not naïve. She's still guarding her previous job's honor. Check.*

"Just so you know, I wouldn't be able to pay you like they did," Zoya remarks, fingering the top of the hourglass.

Sumaiya shakes her head. "I'm not concerned about that. I think I have some wonderful ideas and designs on modest bridal wear that I'd love to bring to the market."

Modest bridal wear. So she wants to do something bigger than earn Benjamins. Check.

Zoya inclines her brows. "I value modest wear. Walk anywhere in my company and examine any mannequin and you won't find what we offer in many other places in the world. Because unfortunately, a lot of us believe that we need to compromise our beliefs and rid ourselves of old traditions and cultures to be seen by others." Zoya gestures to her office, to the luxurious furniture and the thousand-dollar decorations. "Yet look at Zameer."

Sumaiya nods in agreement, smiling.

There's something about her that sticks out to Zoya. Something she didn't feel in the presence of the many other people she interviewed. The woman exudes a uniquely calm aura, something that eases the restlessness in Zoya's heart from the past few days.

"You're hired." Zoya shuts her file. Sumaiya's eyes widen. "You have the experience. And the passion. And my intuition tells me you're a good fit." *Most importantly, you seem to have integrity.*

"Thank you so much, Ms. Zoya," Sumaiya says. She stands and holds her hand out. Zoya stares at it pointedly before deciding to shake it, realizing she likes her.

When Sumaiya leaves, Zoya makes a quick call to Sameer. While she trusts her instincts, she's also not stupid.

He picks up on the first ring. "Yes, Ms. Zoya?"

"I've hired a new lead designer; she's a former Pak Enterprises employee." Zoya hears abrupt shuffling on the other end. "I need you to keep an eye on her twenty-four seven. Keep constant tabs on her and report back to me."

"Got it. Her name?" Sameer doesn't even question her. Zoya knows he has become accustomed to strange requests like this from her.

"Sumaiya Akhtar."

"Alright." He ends the call. Zoya stares at the phone, irritated that he cut the call before she did.

She heads to a meeting room per the request of her board of directors and PR manager. The issue of profit margins comes up, around which they express concerns about possible consumer decline due to Zoya's recent "shenanigans." Zoya sharply reminds them that the CFO has been tracking the exponential increase of their revenues, especially after her announcement of Zameer Co's international expansion.

"But we still have to remember this," Ibitoye, one of Zoya's directors, cuts in. "Rival companies, especially Pak Enterprises, will exploit Zameer's image by using any chance, any opening that they see. They'll dig up some dirt, use backhanded methods, and make seemingly harmless things appear questionable, which could have an immensely detrimental impact on us. Especially considering recent developments. You know what they say; the bigger they are, the harder they fall."

Zoya twirls a curl around her finger and rolls her eyes. "Say what you wanna say in clear words, Ibitoye."

Ibitoye looks her dead in the eye. "We can't take any risks. No more funny business, Zoya."

Another director, Raj, says, "She's right, Zoya. You're spearheading one of the most successful and fastest growing businesses in the fashion industry; people won't miss any chance to bring you down."

Zoya nods nonchalantly, examining her mascara in a hand mirror.

When she dismisses them twenty minutes later and returns to her office, she unlocks her iPad. Her eyebrows furrow upon reading the tabloid article.

Zoya Zameer: Orphaned?

She leans back in her chair, letting out a huff. "The lengths these people will go to," she mutters, tapping her nails on the desk. "Because they have no lives of their own, they *love* stooping around and digging up dirt on other people's lives." Zoya slams her hourglass upside down, watching bits of sand fly out of the slightly cracked glass.

The ring of the phone jostles her out of her stupor. Picking up, she drawls out a bored "Yes?"

"Ms. Zoya," Sarah hurriedly says. "Literally *every* Pakistani news channel overseas has called to ask for an interview with you. And a couple local American news channels as well. What do you want me to say?"

A corner of Zoya's lips lifts. "What do they want to know?"

"I'm sorry?"

"Obviously, they're digging for something. Did they drop any hints, give any suggestions as to what they're looking to, ah, *unveil* me for now?"

"Not directly, no," Sarah murmurs, seeming unsettled. "Mostly they sound like they want to know what sparked international expansion, whether you were ever married or not, and why you fired an employee on live TV. Oh, and they suspect you're orphaned." She says the last bit quietly, as if afraid to anger her.

Is this not direct enough for you, innocent little Sarah?

Zoya laughs. "People are interesting, aren't they? Seeing others lead successful lives causes them to pull out binoculars and begin examination."

Sarah remains silent on the other end.

"Which news channels?" Zoya asks absentmindedly. Sarah begins to prattle off names of news channels as Zoya mulls over them. She knows the press wants a statement—or several statements—and as her PR team has been advising her, not appearing before them will make her look bad (which could undoubtedly have a ripple effect). And Zameer cannot risk that, especially with the number of improvements these past few weeks.

Zoya sighs loudly and pinches the bridge of her nose. *All of this is getting exponentially messier.* "The evening gala for our new project is in a little over a week. They can all see me then."

When Zoya shuts off the phone, she remains immobile for a long time. Her eyes are closed—brows knitted together, fingers pinching her nose—when there's a knock on the door.

"Enter," she barks without looking up, thinking it may be Farhan with another document for her to sign. Whoever it is walks up to her desk quietly and waits.

Zoya opens her eyes to see Haroun Suleiman standing in front of her. Quickly, she adjusts her tired expression into a flirtatious one and throws him a smile.

All the while trying to ignore what his mother meant by her statement last night.

"*Salaam,*" he says quietly. "I just wanted to thank you for coming last night. It meant a lot to my mom."

She leans forward, *jhumkas* dangling. "*Just* your mom?"

"And my sisters."

This guy is hopeless. Disappointed, Zoya leans back again and drums the table with her fingers. "No problem. I enjoyed it." Pause. "Thank you for your hospitality."

Haroun nods. And then there is that thick, pressing silence.

Please don't mention what happened at your house.

"Ms. Zoya, I also wanted to ask you something."

"Ask away." *Please don't mention it. Please don't mention it. Please don't mention it.*

"Are you okay?"

Zoya raises her eyes to his, but he's fingering the edge of her table absentmindedly. His eyelashes cast shadows like spiderwebs over his eye bags, which have grown considerably darker recently, as if he hasn't slept in days. A lock of raven-colored hair falls over the top of his forehead. So artful, so natural.

Zoya is suddenly struck by how *beautiful* Haroun Suleiman is. Of course, she's always known this, ever since the day she laid eyes on him. But to see him in this fatigued, concerned state, with dark bags under his tired eyes, and his hair artfully strewn around on his head—so natural, so *vulnerable*—awakens a feeling within her. A feeling that has long been dead.

"I'm okay," she replies quietly, ignoring the thrumming of her heart. The question he asked—the one she hasn't heard in a while— seems to reverberate through her core. "Why do you ask?"

He shifts, resting his hands in his pockets. "You just seem . . ." He mulls over the right terminology. "On edge."

Zoya grabs a pen and begins clicking the end of it. Her bangles clink against one another, awfully loud in the silent room. "I'm okay," she repeats.

If you ask me one more time, there's a ninety-nine percent chance I might burst into tears.

Haroun nods, but the skepticism doesn't leave his face. Without another word, he leaves the room.

Zoya stares at the door he disappeared through, for the first time feeling unsettled. She shakes her head, occupying herself in arranging a meeting with her board of directors. They need to discuss the statement she'll give to the media.

Ibitoye is the first to arrive in the meeting room, and she walks in on Zoya tugging at the end of her hair to pull out loose strands. She wraps the strands around her finger to form a ring of hair. The two women lock eyes, and Zoya throws Ibitoye a cocky grin, offering her the circle of hair.

Ibitoye scrunches her nose. "No thank you."

Zoya raises her brows and shrugs. "No? Okay. I was giving you my DNA and an open chance to clone me, and *who* wouldn't want that? But you refused." Zoya sighs theatrically and throws the hair in a trash can. "What will the world do with just *one* Zoya Zameer?"

Ibitoye gives her an exasperated look.

~

Haroun is absentmindedly typing data into his laptop when—with a shock—he sees someone he's been thinking about standing a few feet away. He stands up quickly and rushes forward, desperately eager to apologize. To untie the knots that have been in his stomach since the day she was fired.

"Hey, Flora. How are you?"

She doesn't reply. Her back is turned to him, shoulders stiff.

"Can I please talk to you?" he says.

Flora still doesn't turn around. "I just had to get some of my belongings. I don't have much time. I parked my car against the curb."

"Please, Flora? I won't take too much of your time." Haroun's forehead is lined with stress.

She shifts slightly so that the side of her head is visible. "Make it quick."

Haroun sighs, walking around to face her. "Look, Flora, I—"

"Don't," she interrupts, clenching her fists. "Just *don't*."

"I need to," he whispers. "I've been feeling . . . weighed down by guilt since that day. I need to apologize. Flora, I am *so*—"

"It's not you." Flora squeezes her eyes shut and reopens them. Tears begin to pool at the corners. "It's not you," she repeats slowly, reluctantly. As if she doesn't want to admit what she's saying. "So don't apologize."

"I feel like it's my responsibility to—"

"No, everyone's right about what they say about her." Flora nods. "I was too blinded by her affection for me to see it before, but everyone's right. She's inconsiderate and cruel to the max. She doesn't give a damn about anyone's feelings. I know this is the *'corrupt corporate sector,'* but I have seen plenty of humane bosses in this *'corrupt corporate sector.'"*

Haroun quiets. "With all due respect, I think she's just been through a lot."

Flora's fists clench. "Yeah. You may be right. But that gives her *no* license to ball her pain up and throw it around in other people's faces," she snaps. Haroun's eyebrows shoot up in surprise. "Yeah, *you* also seem like the kind of guy who's been through a lot. I used to hear you always worrying with Farhan. About your mom and her medical expenses. About your sisters and their education. About how you feel like you can't provide for your family or whatever. You've been through a lot, too. But you don't allow the pain that's packed in you to hurt others. You don't." Flora pauses. "You really are a great person, Haroun. I guess even at the age of twenty-seven, jealousy and neglect from my parents got to me." She sighs.

Haroun presses his lips together, suddenly overwhelmed by the words he doesn't deserve. "Have you found a job yet?"

Flora looks up at the ceiling, around the pipes surrounding it, down to the racks and mannequins covered in designer clothing. "No," she says. "I'm unemployed, single, and I have an elderly mom to take care of. I don't know what I'm going to do. Even the money from the contract is going to be gone eventually and then—" She looks around again and tears up. "It's been a good few years here." She laughs a little. "I'll miss pinning dresses on mannequins, and staying up late to cut cloths, and . . ." Flora trails off, her smile disappearing.

Haroun attempts to lighten the mood. "I have a . . . suggestion for you," he says. Flora looks up at him curiously and he shrugs. "Get married." Her eyebrows furrow. "You won't solely be burdened with a job, and you'll have more financial stability." He grins. "And you'll even have a life partner, isn't that crazy?"

Flora stares at him, then bursts out laughing. "'And you'll *even* have a life partner?' As if that's not the exact reason people get married. That's like saying I went to the White House and *even* got to meet the President." She laughs again, then gets serious. "You really are a good person. And . . . I'm sorry for all the things I've said to you."

Haroun shakes his head. "Forgotten."

She smiles, grabbing her bag.

Haroun hesitates. "I hope . . . I hope your journey ahead brings you happiness and success."

Flora gives him a weak smile, a well of tears in her eyes accompanying it. Then she rushes out of the headquarters.

Haroun stands there with a soft smile, feeling as if the burden of the sky has been lifted from his shoulders.

Nineteen

"Many people think that punishment is limited to one's health, his wealth, or his children; however, having a sick and corrupted heart is truly the worst kind of punishment." —Sheikh Salih al 'Uthaymin

~

THE EVENING GALA APPROACHES quickly. Zoya, as a test for her new lead designer, instructs Sumaiya to design a dress specifically for the event.

"You got everything down, Sumaiya?" Zoya drawls, twisting her hair around her finger. She has been watching Sumaiya like a hawk ever since she hired her, and Sameer has been reporting back frequently with the same news: *Hardworking, nice girl. Comes to work, goes home. Nothing fishy as of yet.*

Sumaiya nods, jotting down a few more notes.

"This needs to be done by Friday." Zoya examines her nails. She gauges that Sumaiya has most likely familiarized herself with the attitude of her new boss, that Zoya will stop at no lengths to humiliate her if she designs something that humiliates Zoya.

Sumaiya nods.

Zoya scrutinizes her. *What is with this girl?* "That's two days from now."

Sumaiya smiles. "I know."

Zoya huffs out a sigh and spins on her black heel, dismissing her.

Someone knocks on the office door and peeks in. "Ms. Zoya?"

"Yes, Sameer."

"The meeting room is ready."

Zoya nods. "Gather everyone. I'll be there in a minute." Collecting some files, she takes a deep breath and makes her way to the meeting room, where her employees are arriving. Her eyes dart to Haroun, who settles next to Bill with a notepad in hand.

"Good afternoon," Zoya says, placing the files on the large oval desk. Sameer begins to pull out the board but she waves a hand, signaling she won't be needing it. Zoya gestures at Sumaiya dismissively and announces, "I'm sure you have all familiarized yourselves with our new lead designer." She darts a quick glance around the room. Haroun, who is concentrating on the papers in front of him, looks up briefly and smiles.

Zoya's brows furrow.

"Alright. So our CFO Robert has been closely monitoring international expansion, which has significantly raised our revenues. We're being bombarded by positive feedback. Funding has also increased; net margins are skyrocketing. Of course, this means we're working on further expanding with workers and locations. And the press is continuously demanding our attention.

"As you all know, the gala is in three days' time. That is when I'll be giving the media my statement, as well as introducing the new project we've been offered."

The staff throws each other quizzical looks.

Zoya takes a deep breath. "We've been offered to take on a project regarding domestic violence. Contractors of a Pakistani organization geared towards domestic violence issues have reached out to the board. They've requested for Zameer to partner with them and help spread their message as well as *creatively* portray these issues, since they're not receiving enough media attention."

Confused glances are exchanged around the room. Haroun bites his lower lip, eyebrows knitted.

"Well, this is new," Bill comments, breaking the silence. "What do we get out of this?"

Zoya examines her nails, hoping nobody can hear her rapid

heartbeat. "The press has been bombarding us with questions and speculations. This is our chance to address all their assumptions and allow them to see what this company really stands for. Trust me, the media will go so wild with this that they'll forget about anything else."

"*Creatively* portray?" Haroun interrupts quietly. Everyone's attention turns to him, since he speaks minimally during these meetings. His cheeks tinge pink, but he barrels forward. "How can we *creatively* portray domestic violence? That seems . . . insulting."

Heads nod in agreement. Zoya's heart rate skyrockets, but she attempts to keep her cool. "I agree with you. But this organization's campaigns aren't receiving as much press coverage as they need, and they recognize that the South Asian community tends to brush off these issues. What they need from us is a different way of spreading their message, something other than senseless marketing and flyers shoved under people's noses. And I *know* we can make that happen. With our increased funding, this should be a piece of cake."

Seeing the collective head nods, Zoya takes another deep breath. "I need you all to listen to me very carefully." She begins to propose her ideas on the various designs the team can construct to catalyze this project. As she speaks, eyes begin to light up, heads nod vigorously, and notes are taken. Once she finishes, she asks, "Any questions?"

"Ms. Zoya, who will be leading the project?"

"I will," she says simply, ignoring the raised eyebrows in response.

As the meeting ends and employees begin to file out of the room, Zoya cocks her head to the side and fluffs her hair. "Haroun?" she says sweetly. Sumaiya's gaze darts to her. "Stay for a minute." He nods after a beat of hesitation.

The last person to leave is Sumaiya, her face harboring a strangely troubled look.

When Zoya and Haroun are alone in the meeting room, Zoya begins playing around with her *dupatta*. "What do you think of the new project?"

Haroun nods. "I'm glad you took the offer."

This catches her attention. She looks up quickly, *jhumkas* dangling. "How come?"

He seems surprised by the question. "Because it's something that needs to be talked about. And if it's not receiving enough public attention, what better way to achieve that than have a renowned company like Zameer represent it?"

Something in Zoya stills. Wind rushes through her ears, causing her head to pound. Her vision blurs, and she almost topples off the desk but grabs the chair to steady herself.

"Ms. Zoya?" Haroun remains at a distance. But there is concern in his voice. Polite, detached concern. "Are you alright?"

She reaches up to press a hand against her forehead and nods. "Yes." Zoya raises her eyes to his, sensing the achingly wide distance between them. The distance that feels as if it's crackling with electricity. As if she can reach across the space and feel the firecrackers exploding from her touch.

His face is impassive, reflecting none of the feelings beating in Zoya's heart.

She suddenly remembers his mother's statement about how Haroun has been searching for a spouse, but shakes her head immediately to brush it off.

For some reason, Zoya feels compelled to tell Haroun the truth about the new project. A wide, gaping chasm has made room inside her and hungers to hear what else he has to say about the topic.

She peeks at him through her lashes. "I took on this project on my own."

"Yeah?" is all he says.

"Yes. Matters like this are neglected too much, and unfortunately smaller people cannot do much bigger things. And unfortunately, most bigger industries feel it is not their responsibility to worry about 'small' things like societal problems and such. So in the end, who is left to carry the burden?" Zoya covets the expression on his face—the admiration in his eyes, as well as the hint of a smile playing on his lips. She stands and moves forward, and he automatically steps back. "I think sometimes bigger industries forget about the power that they are given, the things that they can do."

Haroun nods vigorously, and a strand of his inky black hair falls over his forehead. "You're doing really noble work, Ms. Zoya. You don't realize how much initiatives like this are needed."

"Oh, trust me," she says. "I do."

"I pray Allah blesses you and makes it easy for you."

Her breath catches in her throat at his words.

When Haroun leaves, Zoya falls back in a chair and massages her forehead. "Please let this work," she whispers.

~

A few hours later, Haroun approaches Zoya cautiously, requesting a moment to speak with her. Zoya sets aside everything on her desk and leans forward, hands folded under her chin. "Yes?"

Haroun fidgets nervously. "I . . . wanted to ask you for a favor."

"Of course."

"I—" he takes a deep breath and sighs loudly, a frustrated look sporting his face. "I'm sorry, it's just a bit difficult to ask for. I know it's kind of out of the question to ask for a favor like this when you work at a company this large. To be honest, I don't even know if this is *allowed*. I understand if—"

"Haroun," Zoya says, eyes widening at his strange behavior. While he tends to be shy and aloof, he's never like this. Never this anxious, this nervous.

He lifts his eyes to hers for the slightest second before focusing his attention back to his feet. "I was wondering if you would be able to let me leave work earlier?" Pause. "Every day?"

Zoya's eyebrows incline. "Well, that was unexpected."

He runs a hand through his hair. "I know it's a crazy and highly unprofessional request."

She leans back in her chair. "Not crazy if I know why."

Rubbing his neck, he reddens slightly. This further piques Zoya's curiosity. What's making *him* embarrassed?

"Uh . . . it's work. Something I do outside of working here. And it's a bit flexible, so timings have changed and I"—he tenses—"can't be available during the new times anymore. Unless . . ." He sighs. "Ms. Zoya, I've been working with you for a few months now. Do you trust me?"

His question is posed very professionally, with no underlying motives apparent. "Of course I do," Zoya replies, then backtracks, realizing she may have said that too fast. She flips her hair behind her shoulder and titters nervously. "I trust everyone, haha."

"Then can you please trust that I'm not feeding you some made up story just to leave early?"

Zoya holds back a smile at his restless attitude. At his bouncing knee and trembling hands. "Of course I can. But you know, as your boss, I need to be given a valid reason in order for me to even consider your request. Plus, the board will also want a proper explanation."

Haroun nods. "Yes, I know, I expected as much. Um . . ." His shoulders sag in defeat. "It's humanitarian work."

Her interest is further piqued. "And why were you so hesitant to tell me this?"

He doesn't answer, just bites his lip nervously.

"Humanitarian work." Zoya mulls over it. "And you want this request to be granted right after I gave you a promotion?"

Haroun runs a hand through his hair. "I know it seems strange, but I was actually committed to that long before I started working here. I compromised hours for them because I needed to focus on my job. But—"

"But your work there is voluntary, correct?"

"Correct."

"So . . ." She waves her hands around, attempting to communicate something obvious.

A crease appears between his brows. "So?"

"So is it necessary?"

He perks up. "Yes, Ms. Zoya."

Is he lying? Although highly faulty, this is the only explanation Zoya can think of for his strange behavior. Because she hasn't once heard him mention this humanitarian work in all the months he's worked for her.

"Okay," she says thoughtfully. "So it's necessary. But if you knew you had this volunteer work to do, why didn't you tell me this when I promoted you?"

He blows out a sigh. "We needed the money." By "we," Zoya guesses he's speaking of his family. "Besides, who turns down a promotion, right?" There is a hint of bitterness in his voice. A symbol of deeply buried resentment.

Now she's perplexed. Especially because she gets the feeling that he didn't want the promotion. "Do you not need the money anymore?"

"We do," he murmurs quietly. "We all wanted Aisha to be able to quit so that she can focus on school, but she insisted on working. Naima's also still working, but I know the burden is a lot on her, with college and all. My mom's started baking and selling sweets at home to try to—" He presses his lips together. A red tint appears in his cheeks, and Zoya knows it's not shame.

It's guilt.

He sounds so helpless, so vulnerable that Zoya steeples her fingers to cover her trembling lips. She asks the question that has been bothering her since she visited his house. "What about your father?"

There. She detects the slight clench in his jaw. But other than that he remains composed. "My parents are divorced."

Her mouth widens into an *O* before she quickly shuts it. Her heart begins to race rapidly as some puzzle pieces finally click together. "I'm sorry about that."

He shakes his head. "Don't be. It's like my mom said to you—whatever happens, happens for our own good."

She knows she's pushing the invisible barrier surrounding him, but breathlessly she asks, "And does he not send you guys any support?"

He shakes his head.

Zoya feels a strange sensation cloud her heart. To hear about Haroun's father reminds her of her own. And the pain Haroun has faced and continues to face because of him—as well as the haunting past Zoya has survived—seem so parallel, so alike, that she remains speechless.

This organ in her body—this strange organ that throbs and aches and manages to continue beating after the terrible excuse of a life she's lived—feels strangely attached to the human being sitting in front of her. As if the gate to the castle of her heart has opened, and the bridge has extended to let Haroun Suleiman in.

Zoya breaks out of her reverie. "So then shouldn't you be working extra hours?" She backtracks at the expression on his face. "I mean, considering you need the money, the last thing you should be doing is decreasing work hours to do something voluntary."

Haroun drops his head in his hands, and Zoya's eyes widen at the defeat in the motion. "I should. That would be considered the *'plausible'* option. But my mom always tells me that even if life is difficult, we shouldn't stop doing good for people. She says that we're still so much better off than others who have less than us. And she's completely, entirely right. We have so much to be thankful for. But—" He rubs his temples. "It kills me to see my sisters having to sacrifice time from their education and their social lives to make sure we can pay off the expenses of my mom's surgery and pay the bills every month. They shouldn't have to worry about all that. And now my mom . . ." He trails off, hair falling over his forehead as he holds his head in his hands. "But not doing it . . . not doing it makes everything worse. I need *some* semblance of sanity. I need *some* tranquility in my life, *something* to set the seesaw straight. I need to know I'm fulfilling at least a *part* of the purpose I was made for." His fists are clenched, regret etching into his features. He bites down on his lip to keep himself from speaking any more.

I need some *semblance of sanity.*

He must have been harboring these feelings for quite a while if he let them slip in front of *Zoya,* someone he is normally quiet and reserved around.

"Haroun," Zoya says gently, ignoring the thumping of her heart from his pained words. "It's okay. Relax." He heaves in a deep breath. "You can leave early if you please. I won't cut from your paycheck."

He looks up suddenly, then shakes his head. "No. You can't do that."

She watches him with a perplexed expression. Clearly he and his family are in a financial crisis, yet he still won't give up his *voluntary* humanitarian work in order to spend more time at his job.

And when Zoya—cruel, arrogant Zoya—offers to allow him to leave *and* to pay for his time off, he won't accept that either.

He baffles her more than anyone she's ever met.

"*Jaan,* I'm the CEO," she replies gently. "I most certainly *can.*"

His lips begin to tremble. "You can't. You've already done too much for us. Besides, it isn't right. Don't give me any favors that you wouldn't give to another employee." Pause. "Please."

She wants nothing more than to deny his plea, but she shrugs nonchalantly and says, "Okay, if you insist."

He thanks her profusely, tells her he will only leave an hour earlier every day, and exits.

Zoya Zameer returns to her work, flipping through files and papers distractedly. Observing designs with glassy eyes. Receiving and making phone calls mechanically. All throughout this time, seven words occupy her head space entirely.

You've already done too much for us.

Inside her heart, a war wages. Haroun is clearly troubled with financial difficulties, rife with emotional ailments. And he has always been a calm, resolute man. Rigorous in his faith, blindly trusting God. Always doing good for others, even when they fail to compensate. Doing unnecessary work which is overburdening him and would make his life easier if he gave it up.

Yet he allowed himself to be vulnerable in front of her for a minute. even if he regretted it immediately, and all Zoya had been able to do was watch, shoulders sagging. Because once again, he had managed to make *her* speechless.

And somehow, he still told her that she has done too much for him.

Zoya rubs the worry lines on her forehead.

Not enough, Haroun. Not enough.

Twenty

"And if you should count the favors of Allah, you could not enumerate them. Surely, mankind is (generally) most unjust and ungrateful."
(Qur'an 14:34)

~

THE DAY BEFORE THE gala, Zoya makes a cryptic announcement to her staff about having to run an errand. When she's in her car, she enters the directions Sameer looked up for her in Google maps.

"Ms. Zoya, I ran their names through some databases. The younger one works as a part time cashier at a Walmart nearby."

"And the other one?"

"There's a Panera Bread close to the Walmart; she works there part time."

"Great. Pull up the addresses and send them to me."

"Alright."

Zoya follows the Google Maps directions, speeding across the highway. Once she reaches her first destination, she pulls a scarf out of her handbag and wraps it securely around her head. "Time for Zoya Zameer to go," she murmurs to her reflection, grabbing a makeup wipe and rubbing it over her face. Adjusting the Ray Ban's over her eyes, she takes a deep breath and exits the car.

While she's heading into Walmart, she passes by a few people who either nod or smile at her. Zoya Zameer is used to being respected for being such a prominent figure in the fashion industry, but having this blind respect and regard from others who don't even recognize her is startling. Especially because she has a nagging feeling that it's due to the piece of cloth resting on her head.

Once inside, she asks customer service where the manager of the store is, and—after gazing at her leather handbag and Gucci belt—they direct her to his office. As Zoya is waiting for the manager, her eyes sweep the area, and she makes sure to stay out of Aisha Suleiman's view.

A couple minutes later, an aged man enters the office. "Hi, I'm the manager," he says as Zoya stands. "My name is Ben. You asked for me, miss?" She notices his eyes travel over her headscarf, and immediately he pulls back the hand he held out, nodding politely instead.

"Yes, I did. How are you doing?"

"Well, and yourself?"

"Great. Actually, I wanted to talk to you about one of your employees." She gestures outside the office to who she's talking about, and the manager swivels around.

"Sure," he replies, somewhat confused.

"I need you to promote her to a higher position."

Ben blinks at her. "Excuse me?"

Zoya pulls out her business card from her handbag and hands it to him. "I'm Zoya Zameer." Ben doesn't seem to recognize her name and looks at her again, even more confused. "CEO of Zameer Co. It's a Pakistani fashion company." Her tone implies that this is obvious information.

A glimpse of recognition and surprise flash across his face. "Yes, yes, I think I've seen you on Fox News once."

Zoya rolls her eyes behind her sunglasses. *Of course you have.* "I need you to promote her or find her a more well-paying job. Something part time but not as . . . *exhausting.* You're the manager of this Walmart. You have connections; it'll be a piece of cake for you. Trust me, I run the business world. I know the things you have control over."

Ben furrows his eyebrows. "But . . . why should I do that?"

Zoya pulls out the other *accommodation* she brought with her.

Ben's eyes widen as he darts a quick look around, gulping.

"This is why," Zoya says.

Part of Zoya wants for him *not* to reach out for the wad of bills in her hand. Part of her wants for him to cross his arms and raise his brows and say his integrity can't be bought.

Of course, this part of Zoya is also well accustomed to the way the world works, especially the corrupt business world. So she isn't too surprised when Ben's eyes further widen and he asks, "Who *are* you?" in amazement.

"I've told you. Zoya Zameer."

"But why are you doing this?"

"Think of it as a miracle," Zoya says airily, adjusting her sunglasses. *Ben, once I figure out why I'm doing this, I'll be sure to let you know.*

She gestures for him to hold his hand out and presses the wad of bills into it, careful not to touch him. "Do as I've asked."

Ben's eyes glaze over as he observes the bills. *He's probably losing his mind, wondering how his average Thursday morning turned into a lottery in the afternoon.* "Okay, but . . . I still don't understand."

"You don't need to." Zoya adjusts her handbag over her arm. "Oh, and please do me a favor and don't mention our little meeting to anyone. God forbid we would want Fox News to say anything about me. Or worse, about your little Walmart." She narrows her eyes.

Ben shakes his head. "No, miss. You can trust me." He glances at the bills again, eyes still widened in disbelief. "I'll find her a job as soon as I can. Don't worry."

"Good. My number's on the card. I'll be expecting a call from you when you've done what I've asked." She smiles. "And remember, *don't tell a soul.*"

Ben nods vigorously as Zoya heads out. She heads to Panera Bread and requests to speak to the manager. When he arrives, she launches into her purpose for being there.

This one is a little harder to convince; he asks several questions and tells her he won't accept a "bribe" and place his integrity on the line. Zoya patiently listens to him, secretly pleased with his attitude and firm stance. He gives her hope that honest people still exist in the business world.

But she has a job to finish, so she sits and smiles at him through gritted teeth, twirling her hair and asking about his family. He tells her about his two daughters and wife. When Zoya places the wad of money on the table, his eyes almost bug out.

"I-I can't accept this, ma'am."

"Of course you can. I'm gifting it to you."

"I can't accept your gift."

She raises a brow. "Do you know who I am? I'm *Zoya Zameer*; I run one of the greatest industries in America. And I get *really* offended when people don't accept my gifts." The man's shoulders sag in defeat. Having done her work, Zoya tells him she expects a call before she heads out with a flourish.

Zoya mulls over the meetings in her car. "Man is so easy to deceive. So easy to please," she murmurs, pulling out an apple from her handbag. "In life, power, money, and status can get you anywhere. But where do character and decency take you?" She laughs scornfully. "Where do people value honesty and integrity anyway? No matter how much a lower-class person may make claims on their integrity, when they're offered what they haven't had their entire lives—wealth—then to hell with integrity and honesty. All mankind can do is laugh at morality; virtue has become comical. All humans are the same."

Briefly she thinks of Haroun, and how yesterday he had refused the money that would surely have eased many of his problems.

Zoya takes a bite of her apple and steers with her left hand. "Greed and power have blinded mankind; even a man with the most decent character is bound to hang his head before power and wealth, utterly defenseless to their unruly obligations. He's bound to allow his inner desires to take control." Zoya sighs, lamenting to her steering wheel. "After all, what is man but a puppet, and society the puppeteer?"

Suddenly, she straightens in her seat. "What is this, Zoya, Broadway? You're not Hamlet. Shut up."

When Zoya is back at her office in the headquarters, Sumaiya tells her she wants to show her something. In her hands is a clothing bag, and she's practically hopping in excitement. Zoya raises her eyebrows.

"Your dress is ready, Ms. Zoya."

Zoya folds her arms. "Well, let's see it, then."

Sumaiya pulls down the zipper, and out fall heaps of silk and net, intricately woven and delicately laced. Zoya's arms loosen, and her eyes momentarily widen before she clears her throat and maintains a neutral expression. Sumaiya pulls the entire dress out and holds it in front of her. It's baby blue, with silver patterns threaded as a delicate net over the layer underneath. It's simpler than most of Zoya's dresses, and not nearly as flashy, but it screams elegance and beauty with a single look at it.

Sumaiya fidgets nervously as she looks up at her boss. After a few moments of silence, she ventures to ask, "What do you think?"

Zoya rubs the fabric between her fingers. All of it has been put together in such a precise, orderly, and delicate fashion that Zoya can't help the smile that blooms onto her face. Sumaiya smiles tentatively in return, relieved.

"I'm impressed." Zoya tucks a curl behind her ear. "When did you finish it?"

"This morning," Sumaiya replies. "I started when you told me that you needed it by today."

That means she probably worked the last two nights on it. Zoya's eyes rove over her employee's face, detecting the faint bags underneath her eyes and the haphazard concealer smeared there. A corner of Zoya's lips lifts. "Good."

Sumaiya's face falls for a brief moment before she resumes her bright smile. "I'm glad you liked it. I know we talked about color schemes, but I was just wondering what you thought of this shade of blue? I figured it was more soothing, and considering the project you're about to launch, having a tranquil appearance is going to help facilitate your message, don't you think?"

Her words shock Zoya. Flora and her team, as was their duty, were invariably careful about Zoya's appearance. But their motive was always tied solely to PR relations and business trends.

To have Sumaiya so carefully view Zoya's appearance from the perspective of the impact it will have on her message is astounding.

She's something else.

Zoya nods. "Color's great. Now, listen to me very carefully." Zoya describes in detail the finishing touches required for the employees' attire.

When Sumaiya leaves, Zoya saunters back over to her dress.

"You've really outdone yourself, girl. Zaki'll be sorry you ever left." She twirls the dress around in her hands. "Now *this* is art. Flora was amazing, but . . . there's something about this dress that tells me you *really* give a damn about what people think of the company. And by default, of me."

Zoya hangs it beside her desk. Throughout the day, as she works, she continuously sneaks glances at the dress that captivates her more and more with every look.

~

A few hours later, Zoya receives a call from Ben, who notifies her of Aisha's new job per his referral. Zoya smiles smugly and thanks him in a lilting voice.

She busies herself in work again, eagerly anticipating the other call. It arrives two hours later as she is meeting with her directors and consulting her CFO. Zoya excuses herself and steps out of the room with her phone pressed to her ear.

The manager of the Panera Bread reluctantly tells her that he has completed her request. "That was fast," Zoya can't help but taunt him. He simply huffs out a breath and shuts the call.

Instead of angering her like it normally would, this only makes Zoya feel giddy. She lets out a sigh of relief and heads back into the meeting room to continue discussing plans with her board.

Twenty-One

~

ZOYA RUSHES THROUGH THE *forest, whipping her head wildly around. The footsteps continue to pound against the floor behind her, reverberating throughout the jungle and causing her to tremble in the darkness of the night.*

She whips back around and focuses on putting one foot in front of the other as she flies through the dark forest. Terror seizes her insides and grips her heart. The sound of feet slapping on the asphalt behind her propels her legs forward at a faster speed.

But nothing, nothing can stop Zoya from recognizing the imminent doom heading her way. No matter how fast she runs on her blistered feet, no matter how loud she screams, those footsteps will eventually catch up to her. Those footsteps that take twenty steps towards her for every ten that she runs ahead; footsteps that manage to make her so breathless that her body teeters at the edge of defeat.

Abruptly, dread takes such a hold of her that she lets out a huff of air and falls forward, bruised hands hitting the ground. Scrapes and fresh cuts pierce her skin, and she lets out a cry of pain. "NO!" she screams. The darkness is suffocating, pressing down on her like a gnarled hand and cutting off her supply of oxygen.

Zoya whips around and holds her scraped hands above her as a shield, squeezing her eyes shut. Suddenly, a heavy weight falls on her, pressing her already bruised back into the cobbled asphalt. She screams, but a heavy force blocks off the sound and continues to weigh itself down on her. Excruciating pain takes over and begins to numb her. Zoya writhes and thrashes, trying to grope around in the suffocating blackness of the night to pull the weight off of her and scream her throat raw.

But there is nothing there.

Zoya flies awake, breathing heavily. With wide, disoriented eyes, she gazes around her bedroom.

Despite the cold sweat running in rivulets down her body, she wraps her blanket tightly around herself and begins to rock back and forth. Clamping her mouth shut to suppress the screams, she balls her hands up into fists and sets her head on her knees.

Weeping silently.

~

Zoya smiles in front of the cameras, her PR manager, Lucas, standing faithfully by her side. After thoroughly relaying her script to the frenzied press that firing Farhan was a colossal misunderstanding and that she wishes to keep subjects like her parents private, Zoya flashes a brilliant smile at the cameramen. They begin to back away from her just as the host welcomes everyone to the gala and requests for them to settle down.

After many tedious announcements and scripted speeches, the moment everyone has been waiting for arrives.

"And to speak about this project herself, I would like to invite Ms. Zoya Zameer!" the host announces.

Loud applause ensues. Zoya makes her way to the stage in her powder blue dress, flipping her straightened hair behind her shoulder. As she approaches the podium, the applause dies down, and everyone listens with rapt attention.

"Good evening, ladies and gentlemen." Pointing to the chair at the center of the stage, she turns to the host beside her. "Can I sit there with the mic?" A look of confusion passes over his face before he stutters out a surprised "Of course." Zoya grabs the mic and settles down in the chair, smiling around at her audience.

Resisting the urge to roll her eyes, she begins with the scripted line her PR team and directors had discussed with her: "This project is very close to my heart." As she continues speaking, eyes watch her with wonder, carefully taking in her every movement, her every casual hair flip, attempting to undress the meaning behind these seemingly arbitrary acts.

"Ms. Zoya, why have you agreed to take on this project?" a reporter asks after Zoya's speech, notepad and pen ready in his hand.

Zoya smiles. "I believe that in the South Asian community, domestic violence is just a problem to sweep under the table. Something else to add to the growing pile of issues collecting dust in some forgotten corner. Why? Because we're raised to believe that condemning domestic violence is 'feminism.'" A harsh laugh escapes her as she remembers her conversation on feminism with her driver. "Furthermore, we as children are shown a distorted image of marriage, so that even when something seems odd or off, it is our *normal*. It's all we've been told and all we've seen in TV shows.

"Thus, domestic violence is heavily underplayed and given the misleading title of feminism to make it seem more . . . arbitrary and casual. No offense to feminism," she adds hastily. "That's just how I think it's generally perceived.

"And those experiencing issues such as domestic violence are scared into silence. I'm just interested in washing away this wave of misconceptions and doing what I can to give more power to those powerless." Zoya shrugs lightly, and her directors nod approvingly.

Anyone watching her would take her words as a politician's words—strong, well articulated, and spoken with the intention of gaining rhapsodies of praise. But anyone observing carefully—like a certain dark-haired man with his dimple creased in tension at the far end of the room—would gauge that her poetic words hold some experience.

Another reporter raises his hand. "You mentioned South Asians. Do you really believe that issues of domestic abuse and rape are marginal issues?"

The PR manager's voice rings through Zoya's head. *Keep your cool and stick to the script.* She takes a deep breath and attempts to follow these instructions.

"Do you know what generally happens to people in South Asian countries, sir?" she asks. He does a double take at being addressed so directly. "They get kidnapped, they get raped, and when they're thrown back on the road after they've been used and their oppressors have tired of them, they're *blamed*. Do you know what happens when they come back home?" The reporter squirms under Zoya's intense gaze. "People avoid speaking to them and avoid making eye contact with them. Because they don't see them as people oppressed and robbed of their peace. They see them as people who went *gallivanting* and lost their honor and respect." A mirthless laugh escapes her, and something shifts in the audience. A strange thickness that wasn't there before.

Zoya tries. She tries so hard to clamp her lips shut and heed the warning glances of Lucas and her board of directors, but seconds later a physical force seems to pry her mouth open and she continues.

"People don't see them as *victims* who have been robbed of self regard and self-respect. Instead, these victims are scrutinized and blamed for their every action. Because at the end of the day, in the people's eyes, the abuser is only *partially* at fault." Zoya sighs long and loud into the microphone, but underneath the pretense of a powerful and professional leader, her heart beats rapidly within her chest.

"More precisely, it's the *woman's* fault for having the organ in her body that makes her *desirable* to others less capable of controlling their heinous, unlawful desires. It's not the man's fault for being characterless and discarding his *ghairat*—honor or shamefacedness. Not the man who dared lay a hand on a woman's honor and dignity, destroying her self-respect and sense of safety in the world."

Across the hall, Lucas stares her down and shakes his head subtly. It's an almost imperceptible movement, but there all the same. *The script,* he mouths.

Zoya swallows, her brief silence sending an uneasy ripple throughout the audience.

She cannot be silent now. Not now, of all times.

"As I was saying, dear guests." Her voice is uncharacteristically shaky, and Lucas pinches the bridge of his nose between his thumb and forefinger. "The crimes of abuse and rape are split three ways: physically, emotionally, and psychologically. What we as society do is break down what's left of the oppressed by running back and blaming *them* for it, as if they haven't already been through enough! First they are abused by a person, then they are abused by *society*." Zoya lets out a bewildered laugh. "Where is the justice in that?"

For a moment, there is pin drop silence. Zoya's heart beats so persistently against her chest that she fears it may thud into the speakers through the mic in her trembling hands.

Maybe I said too much.

"But, Ms. Zoya," the same reporter from before interrupts her thoughts, raising his hand hesitantly. "Do you really believe that this is just a South Asian issue?"

"It's an issue everywhere," Zoya responds in a clipped tone. "But I think that the issue has the opportunity to be resolved much better in more developed countries. In many South Asian countries, however, the abuse of power is unreal. So it is only fit to solve the problem somewhere that the problem doesn't have the opportunity to be solved." She scrutinizes the reporter with narrowed eyes.

Her string of words thrown together seem to confuse him, but he nods and quietly continues taking notes.

Another woman raises her hand. "Zoya, ma'am, we've noticed that a lot of your previous projects and initiatives have focused on women and feminism. The previous ones have been a bit more subtle, but this new one is a bit more pronounced. We were just wondering what catalyzed this turn of events and shifted the focus of your company's campaigns."

A corner of Zoya's lips lifts. "Actually, I would like to ask *you* a question." Lucas and the board of directors turn to one another and shake their heads, sighing. "Can you tell me when and where—in any of my company's initiatives—we have mentioned that we're doing what we're doing for women? Or for feminism?" The reporter, like the previous one, looks startled to have been addressed so directly. "No, I don't mean to single you out, really. I'm just curious. See, this is the problem with the media. People don't have an understanding of me or my company and then make strange assumptions and accusations."

The reporter opens and closes her mouth, perhaps to say that she wasn't making any accusations. In the far corner of the room, Ibitoye sighs and buries her face in her hands. Raj pats her shoulder as if to say, "there, there."

"Can you tell me, miss, why when a woman stands up for another woman, people call it feminism?" Zoya says. "If you pay so much attention to my projects and initiatives, you should know that I've never once mentioned I'm doing my work for women. I think you should take a look outside your window, get your head out of your notepad and pen for a second to see that the world is ugly and twisted. Because who are the oppressed? My dear, you call it feminism because you know for a fact that men are rarely the oppressed. Of course, don't get me wrong, it *does* happen with men. But statistically speaking, the *overwhelming* majority of victims are women.

"Just take a look, for example, at domestic violence." Zoya sets her mic aside and crosses one leg over the other. Her blood feels like it's boiling, and she clenches her fists together to contain the rage coursing through her. "I've taken on this project, and suddenly I'm told that my 'feminist campaign' has become more pronounced, although I didn't mention just *the wives* being oppressed. But if you say that I'm standing up for women, then sure, to entertain your belief, let's say I'm standing up for only women. Even then, my speaking out and standing up for another woman shouldn't be called feminism. It's just *insaaniat. Humanity.* And if the world is suffering, why can't my company try to do what it can to help?

"To clear up your misconceptions, let me paint you a picture of the outside world, since you don't seem to know much about it," Zoya says in a tone of forced calm. Bill exchanges a disbelieving glance with Lucas, and Zoya can tell that they're burning with frustration. This was definitely not part of the script.

Zoya sits up straighter in her chair and leans forward, holding the full attention of her audience. Something in her warns her against losing her temper so quickly, but it's too late. The reporter's pen is suspended in midair, a look of shock on her face at the shift in conversation. "Most of the time, when a rape case is filed in South Asian countries, do you know what happens? *Aurat ki izzat pe aik daagh lag jaata hai.* Meaning a woman's dignity is stained. People go around saying things such as '*Moo kaala kar diya*'—that she rubbed her face in dirt. Nobody talks to her, nobody marries her, people cut off all ties with her. She becomes *badnaam,* blamed. If you can tell me of even a single case in a South Asian country, in which a woman who has been raped is married off with dignity and respect and happiness, then let me know, please."

Ibitoye, who had been shaking her head disapprovingly before, now listens with curious attention.

"Not to mention how divorcées are treated after leaving abusive marriages, because the South Asian world chokes at this idea. In their eyes, this problem doesn't exist. And if a woman recognizes that abuse and—say, decides to get a divorce—first she is emotionally divorced from her husband, then legally divorced from her husband, and then mentally divorced *by society!* Because outside eyes that claim to know better about her relationship don't *approve* of her choice.

"However, that isn't the point here," Zoya continues, shrugging nonchalantly. She begins to play around with her hair to conceal her shaking hands.

She wants to stop talking, she wants her tongue to knot and twist and settle silently in her mouth. Because she knows the potential consequences of allowing this dormant volcano to erupt.

But all her tongue seems to want is to keep moving and keep talking.

"Most of the time, abused or raped women in these countries are not married off happily. Instead, they are ridiculed by us, by society. You know what we should be saying instead?" Zoya's voice rises an octave. "When we hear of a woman's rape, we should hunt down the oppressor and ask him what *disgusting* blood in his body made him want to commit such a crime. Because in rape, who has control?"

At this last statement, people shift uncomfortably in their seats. The host steps forward as if to ask her to stop but Zoya holds a hand up. "Please let me finish what I came here to say." He backs away reluctantly. Zoya returns to the audience, detecting her rival Zaki Ahmed's stony face in the crowd. "I know all of this may seem taboo and uncomfortable to talk about, but that makes it all the more important, right?

"As I was saying, who is in control? And note that I'm referring to general and more widespread cases, statistically speaking." She pauses. "*Generally*, whose body has the power to label this crime a rape?" Zoya spreads her hands out. "Man! And still we don't call him *behaya*, lacking modesty, or *besharam*, shameless." She shrugs in defeat and stands, making her way off the stage.

Pin drop silence follows Zoya's talk, and she tosses her hair behind her shoulders as she approaches her team. Delayed applause and hushed whispers erupt behind her. Some people gaze at Zoya approvingly, others give her strange looks. Zaki Ahmed's jaw is clenched so hard it seems at risk of breaking.

Zoya's team's eyes follow her, silently questioning her unplanned performance. She can already feel the wrath of Lucas and her directors but shrugs it off, busying herself in adjusting her appearance. She's running trembling fingers through her hair, and doesn't realize where she's walking until she bumps into someone and stumbles backwards.

Haroun's smoldering eyes bore into hers as he quickly backs away from her touch. As soon as they make eye contact, he drops his gaze, flustered.

The brief glimpse into his eyes tells Zoya that unlike everyone else, his gaze didn't harbor anger. Instead, there was gentleness in it, a different question from the one everyone else was asking.

Are you okay?

"Sorry," Zoya whispers a second too late, stepping away to create even more distance between them. Her heart thumps wildly.

The rest of the night passes excruciatingly slowly, with Zaki and Zoya shooting each other clipped smiles the entire time. As soon as Zoya and her team step into the limo to head back home, voices erupt all at once. Angry voices.

"Zoya, what the hell was that?"

"We talked about how dangerous it is for you to get on anyone's bad side right now!"

"There was no need to say all of that."

She ignores them at first, gazing outside the window, until Ibitoye tells her, "You crossed the line."

Zoya lashes out at her, unable to hold back further. "Oh my God, just *shut up* already! How can you be a *woman* and say that?"

"It's not about my being a woman or not being a woman. It's about not taking arbitrary comments and questions to heart. It's about looking well-rounded and composed in front of the cameras, and to hell with what you do backstage!"

Zoya bares her teeth at Ibitoye. "Stop this fanatically professional BS. I've been CEO for almost seven years now. I have never '*stepped a toe out of line,*' and the one time I speak up when it's important, you want me to stay quiet?"

"You're getting too emotional," Ibitoye says frankly, and Lucas nods in agreement. "Being the CEO, you've also known for the past seven years that personal and professional life should not mix. You've been doing a great job at keeping that up. But now? Lately all the tabloids and magazine articles have been about your outbursts. All of them have started speculating about you and your personal life because *you gave them an opportunity to.* When you sat back and showed them the lack of effect their words had, you were more successful. Now you're giving them a chance to unveil you."

Zoya's chest rises and falls with her rapid breathing. Rage clouds her eyes in a red haze. But instead of snapping out several choice words at Ibitoye, she sags back against the upholstered leather and closes her eyes, harsh memories filtering through her mind.

Her ex-husband's constant, threatening reminders about God's dislike of divorce, a strategy to force her to stay in the abusive relationship. Her attempts at placating him every time his jaw tensed even the slightest. His eyes flitting carelessly over the scars decorating her body.

Zoya clenches her fists, veins popping against her skin. She desperately tries to reign in her panic, but is unable to stop her chest from tightening in response to the memories.

Her directors exchange dubious glances. At the far end of the limousine, Haroun watches her quietly. Observes the clenched fists, the trembling shoulders, the telltale *thump thump* of her toes rapidly tapping against the floor.

He averts his gaze, swallowing hard as he makes a silent *du'a*.

Twenty-Two

"Indeed, it is We Who created humankind and (fully) know what their souls whisper to them, and We are closer to them than their jugular vein." (Qur'an 50:16)

~

THE PHOTO SHOOTS FOR the project follow immediately after the gala. The team huddles around the cameras and the green screen, excitedly clicking shots and taking notes. The CEO herself paces around the set; as the lead of the project, Zoya had wanted to monitor the progress at every milestone. She observes the model with her chin in her hand, then cocks her head to the side.

"No, not like *that.*" Zoya walks exasperatedly towards the model and adjusts her hands. "Like *this. Feel* the role. Make it believable."

The model nods, somewhat agitated since this is the third time Zoya has given this order. She schools her expression carefully as she has been instructed. Her hands lie in the same position Zoya had adjusted them, but moments later Zoya clucks her tongue and shakes her head. For the next few minutes, she criticizes the model, complaining that her facial expression isn't real enough, it isn't "good enough." Eventually the model becomes frustrated and snaps, "Ms. Zoya, maybe *you* should model for this project, since you know the perfect poses and the perfect expressions to make!"

The model must not have realized these words were a recipe for disaster. Zoya's eyes flash, her fists tightening. "How about you stop telling me what to do and just do your job right instead of behaving in such a lousy manner?" she retorts sharply.

The model's mouth forms a wide *O*. She resumes motion, but her shoulders are stiff, posture rigid.

Zoya whirls around. She looks up and sees Haroun leaning against the far wall with a notepad in hand. His stance is casual, but when their eyes lock, there is an inexplicable depth in them before he looks away.

Zoya's cheeks flush.

"I want these photos ready to review by tomorrow," she shouts at the quiet studio. Pin drop silence follows her announcement. Zoya rushes past everyone, avoiding Haroun as she makes her way into the elevator.

However, Zoya is unable to ignore the pang that resonates in her chest when she sees Haroun in her peripheral vision. He rushes forward to grab a box from a female employee's hands, careful not to touch her. The employee smiles gratefully at him, and Zoya cannot thank God enough for the elevator doors sliding closed.

In her office, she phones Sarah and hesitates before asking her to send Sumaiya. Minutes later, there's a knock on the door.

"Enter."

Sumaiya walks into the room and stands in front of the desk expectantly. Sameer's words run through Zoya's flustered mind. *I'm keeping track of her every move, Ms. Zoya. She goes straight home from work and comes straight to work from home.*

"*Salaam*, Ms. Zoya. You called for me?"

Zoya flips through a duplicate file of designs and stops at one. She points to the drawing. "This is what the model is wearing, correct?"

Sumaiya nods.

"Why is it blue?"

Her eyebrows incline. "I'm sorry?"

"Why. Is it. Blue?" Zoya repeats.

"Um, Ms. Zoya, we talked about this. Extensively . . . remember?" Sumaiya settles down in the chair across from her CEO. "I had initially made it blue to match your dress at the gala, but then we discussed that half of the cover photo would be in black and white anyway."

"So why isn't it black?"

"Because . . . you said that blue didn't look as harsh in the black and white tone. And you wanted some semblance of a normal girl in the picture, someone not so 'obviously' affected by the issue that the project is revolving around." Sumaiya hesitates. "Remember? We discussed how issues of abuse are not always apparent to an outside eye, so we wanted the campaign to have a realistic portrayal of it."

Zoya taps her fingers on the desk agitatedly. *I know, sweetheart, I know. Say something else. Distract me.*

"Is . . . everything alright, Ms. Zoya?" Sumaiya asks tentatively.

Anything but that question. Abruptly, Haroun's eyes flash in Zoya's mind. Dark, intense, probing. "Yes," she replies curtly. "Can you bring me the rest of the designs? I left them downstairs."

Sumaiya nods. "I think Haroun has them. I'll get them from him."

Zoya straightens suddenly, not wanting another accidental interaction with Haroun, with his eyes that make her feel as if he can see everything inside her. "Bring them yourself."

The employee looks startled at this request, but she nods and exits.

The model's words filter through Zoya's head. *Maybe you should model for this project, since you know the perfect poses and the perfect expressions to make.*

Zoya's fingers are trembling. Someone knocks on the door, and she balls her hand into a fist.

Haroun enters with Sumaiya following behind, and Zoya immediately averts her eyes. It's a new move; she isn't used to not staring him down and twirling her hair and giggling while speaking to him. She rifles through the files on her desk, hoping he can't hear her thrumming breaths. Hoping he can't sense the *thump thump* of her heart, since he seems to be able to break down all of her carefully constructed shields.

She can't forget his eyes.

In the past few years of Zoya's life, she has never done anything without careful calculation and consideration. But unexpectedly, Haroun Suleiman has turned out to be the one piece on Zoya's chessboard game of life that she hadn't anticipated. He flummoxes her. Even with all her careful plays, subtle thoughts and actions, and skillful consideration, somehow Haroun has ended up being king on her chessboard game.

While she hasn't even moved a single pawn.

"He wanted to ask you something," Sumaiya says by way of explanation, breaking Zoya out of her stupor. "That's why he brought the file." She watches her boss carefully.

Zoya nods, attempting nonchalance, and turns to the file Haroun is now pointing towards her. He flips through the papers while Zoya sneaks a peek at him. *Have his eyelashes always been this thick and long?* she wonders. They cast shadows over his dull eye bags. Zoya quietly observes him, and he must feel her gaze because his eyes flick to her for just a second before he focuses back on the file.

Zoya's cheeks heat. She uncaps her water bottle to preoccupy herself.

"I just wanted to make sure these are going to be omitted." Haroun points to the page.

"Yes. They are."

"Okay." He shows her something else and discusses some details regarding finances before closing the file and standing before her expectantly.

Sumaiya steps forward. "Ms. Zoya, I know it might be a little late for this. But I was telling Haroun that I was wondering if the previous *kameez* I designed sends a stronger message? I know that in our last meeting, the majority vote was for the second one. But Haroun and I were looking at the first one again and I think the patterns are more insistent."

Haroun and I? Zoya's eyes dart between the two of them. Disregarding everything else Sumaiya said, Zoya settles on these three words. She points between them. "Do you two know each other? Like, outside of work?"

Sumaiya glances at Haroun quickly. "Well, yes."

"Interesting. Like, apart from being coworkers?"

Sumaiya nods tentatively.

Zoya's heart rate skyrockets. "How?" Looking for something to do to decrease the trembling of her hands, she uncaps her water bottle again and takes a large sip. She crosses one leg over the other, appearing indifferent and harmlessly curious.

Appearing.

Suddenly, Haroun's mother's unwelcome words filter through Zoya's head. They've been intruding on her thoughts at spontaneous times ever since she heard them, deeply unsettling her.

Haroun's been looking for a while, too.

Alhamdulillah.

Zoya can't explain the surge of panic that overtakes her.

Sumaiya interrupts the chaos slowly unfolding in Zoya's mind when she says, "Well . . . we're engaged, Ms. Zoya."

At these words, the chaos in Zoya's mind erupts. Full blown mayhem, absolute destruction.

Zoya's eyes widen; she chokes on the sip of water in her mouth and begins coughing profusely. She bangs her fist on the table and places a hand over her chest. Sumaiya and Haroun exchange a worried glance before Sumaiya rushes forward, patting Zoya's back. When she finally stops coughing, Zoya shrugs out of Sumaiya's grasp and takes another sip of water with trembling fingers.

We're engaged, Ms. Zoya.

It seems as if ice cold rain is being poured into Zoya's wounds. Lightning is coiling around her veins, electrifying her insides. Debris rains on her, weighty and suffocating. Her breath begins to shorten, but Zoya maintains the façade of a genuinely surprised CEO. "That's"—she manages to choke out between coughs—"lovely."

Haroun's mother's words finally make sense.

Sumaiya watches her worriedly. "Are you alright, Ms. Zoya?"

"I'm fine," she replies, her voice oddly calm. Her eyes search Haroun's slowly, and she doesn't know why betrayal seems to suffocate her. He never made her any promises, never indicated anything beyond professional loyalty. There should be no reason for her to feel as if she is standing in the middle of a battlefield, being pierced by her own sword.

Haroun's eyes are steady, resolute. Zoya fights the urge to scoff. And why shouldn't they be? He knows he never promised her anything; for him his relationship with his CEO is strictly business-related. She recalls him taking the box of tools from that woman's hands just a little while ago and wants to laugh mirthlessly. He is good to everyone; there is nothing special about her for him.

Isn't my relationship with him also strictly business-related? Zoya thinks. *I never said anything about . . . I never felt anything for—*

"Are you sure you're okay?" Haroun asks politely.

She nods tightly. "So, when's the wedding?"

"We haven't decided on a date yet," Sumaiya says, eyebrows knitted at Zoya's shifting moods. "My parents are in Pakistan. They'll be coming later, so we're waiting for them."

"Wonderful!" Zoya exclaims too loudly. She clears her throat and fans herself with her *dupatta*. Avoiding their eyes, she says, "How did you guys meet?"

"We frequently go to the same *masjid*," Haroun says. "And our families have mutual friends."

"We met at a gathering at someone's house," Sumaiya adds. "And we found out that we'd both been looking . . . Ms. Zoya, are you okay?"

Zoya realizes she had frozen mid-fanning herself. She looks up at the two of them and nods. "Yes. Continue." Her voice comes out steady, to which she silently congratulates herself.

Sumaiya hesitates, scrutinizing Zoya. There's a strange kind of tension on her face, but it disappears so quickly Zoya wonders whether she imagined it.

"We met a couple times with our families after that. Talked and got to know each other. And . . ." Sumaiya shrugs and smiles. "It just kind of happened."

"When was this party?" Zoya says. "Where you two first met." If the two of them find Zoya's intrusive questions strange, they don't mention it.

Haroun knits his brows as he thinks. "About two months ago."

"And when did you guys get engaged?"

"About two weeks ago."

Zoya's heart rate skyrockets. Her voice comes out unintentionally snarky as she says, "Bit of a quick decision, don't you think?"

Haroun smiles, and for the first time Zoya wants him to stop. She doesn't want to see him smile. She doesn't want that happiness to bloom on his face. Not when the topic at hand is about his upcoming marriage. "Ms. Zoya," he says softly. "When you've talked and gotten to know each other, when your families have been involved and are on board with the entire process, when you *know* you've found the right person—what's the point of waiting?"

Zoya stares at him, at the content smile on his face. Her heart thumps wildly against her chest. His words only add to the chaos erupting in her mind.

"Congratulations," Zoya deadpans. *I want to throw my water in your faces and I don't know why.*

"Thank you," Haroun and Sumaiya say simultaneously.

"You guys need to leave. Now. I need to talk to Raj about something." Zoya rummages through her drawers, feeling awfully displaced, and Haroun and Sumaiya exchange another confused look before exiting together.

The scene causes Zoya's throat to clog, despite the fact that they walk at a careful distance from one another.

Zoya rubs her forehead. Grabbing the front of her *kameez*, she pulls it back and forth from her chest, suddenly feeling an inexplicable heat. Sweat beads her neck and forehead, and she hastily wipes it away.

We're engaged, Ms. Zoya.

~

The domestic violence project is launched, and a few days later Zameer Co. is met with a buzz of mixed feedback. Some of it negative, but most of it positive. There's a thrill in the media over this new project that Zoya claimed was "very close" to her heart. Magazine covers are populated with the famous shot: one side of a woman adorned with jewelry, smiling under bright lights and vibrant colors; and the other side of her in black and white shadow with a shackled wrist, weeping.

Zoya's CFO and board of directors review the statistics one week after the launch of the campaign. While some concerns are expressed, overall satisfied smiles are exchanged over the campaign's climbing success. Cakes are made, celebrations take place in the company, and throughout it all, Zoya Zameer says little more than a few words.

A silence has seemed to settle above her like an ubiquitous cloud. In front of watchful eyes and cameras, she smiles and attempts to make witty remarks, but behind closed doors she sets her head in her hands and can't stop shaking. Trying and failing to rid her mind of those *two words* that keep haunting her ever since they were spoken.

Two weeks after the launch of the campaign, Zoya receives a call from her receptionist. One that momentarily distracts her from her misery. "Yes, Sarah?"

"Ms. Zoya," Sarah exclaims. "Security has been trying to hold him off and even threatened to call the police since he came, but he won't budge without speaking to you."

"Who?" Zoya inquires. A wry smile lights her face when Sarah says his name—a smile that has disappeared since the surprising news from two weeks ago. "Send him up."

"What?" Sarah's voice lilts in surprise.

"Yes. Send him to me."

"Um, okay."

Zoya places her chin in her hands smugly, waiting. A knock sounds on her door, and after her reply of "enter," someone storms in, followed by two of Zoya's security guards.

"What the hell is this?" He slams the fashion magazine down, with Zameer's campaign against domestic violence featuring the front cover. Security steps forward and stands on either side of him, the expressions on their faces a warning.

A smile spreads on Zoya's face as she flicks her wrists casually at the guards. "Mr. Zaki? What a pleasant surprise. It's been a couple of weeks. Have a seat, please."

Her business-partner-turned-rival clenches his jaw. For a

moment, his gaze flits to a file on her desk—a file with Haroun's name on it—before Zoya subtly shifts it to the side and he looks away.

"What is this?" Zaki repeats, pointing to the magazine's front cover.

"Looks like a magazine to me, Mr. Zaki."

"Don't try to be smart with me, Zoya. You know exactly what I'm talking about."

"Maybe a *kameez,*" she pretends to guess again, pointing to the attire the model is wearing. "A really nice one, too." She gasps in surprise. "Oh, wow, would you look at that? It was designed by Zameer!" She points to the description on the page.

"Zoya," he says sharply.

Zoya raises her eyebrows. "Excuse me? I'm sorry, but with all due respect, in these four walls—in fact, *anywhere* in the world— you need to learn how to talk to someone with respect."

"Respect is *earned,* Zoya."

"I agree. It's also mutual, and if I haven't done anything to you, I see no reason for you to speak to me this way. So please, with all due respect." She gestures for him to continue.

He still looks a little angry, and Zoya wants to laugh. How comical it is that men like him get mad when shown their place, when asked to return the respect they so easily earn.

"What is this?" Zaki points to the model's face on the magazine cover. "This is bad for marketing."

Since when are we still partners for you to care? "Pardon me, how is it bad for marketing?"

"Because—" he seems to be struggling to provide a response. "Because it's—" Zoya raises her brows, arms folded, patiently waiting for an answer. "Because you have to think about your audience, *Ms.* Zoya."

"Who's my audience?" she says quizzically, almost laughing at his forced use of "*Ms.*"

"This is strictly a Pakistani clothing company. Who do you think your audience is?"

"Culture can be appreciated by those not a part of it as well."

"Yes, but your work focuses solely on the South Asian population—South Asian men and women—and a demographic requiring bridal wear and formal cultural attire. You have to think about the *men* that will be seeing this—"

"And?"

"Ms. Zoya, if you want overseas success and expansion, you have to think about not just the South Asian-American demographic but the South Asian demographic *living in South Asia* who are seeing this. They don't want to see feminism—"

"*Don't* you dare call it feminism," Zoya snaps, appalled at his nerve and at having to explain this yet again. She shoves her curls away from her face, remembering her conversation with her driver and thinking of how right he was. When he said that people lessen the severity of issues like women's rights by attributing them to radical feminism.

"It's *not* about feminism, it's about *respect*. It's about *humanity*. It has nothing to do with feminism. I could have put a man on this but unfortunately, statistics tell us the real story. That women suffer from this the most. And I want the *people* you're referring to to get it out of their sick, twisted heads that this is not about feminism, it's about *insaaniat. Ghairat.* It's about gaining and earning respect and staying within your limits no matter who you are. And most importantly, it's about *not* stigmatizing and scandalizing those who speak of these *illnesses.*"

"What illnesses?"

"Oh, please, Mr. Zaki." Zoya waves a hand at him dismissively. "You think it's not obvious that the men you are defending are simply showcasing their power over others, their fabricated sense of strength? Because in case you didn't know, Mr. Zaki, this spousal abuse is often seen as the husband making a *'brave'* show of masculinity. Trust me, though, masculinity is *nothing* that these muscled, heavy-handed men show." She sighs long and loud but barrels forward. "Part of masculinity is honoring a woman's dignity and self-respect, elevating her respect in other's eyes, and guarding her name behind her back when people say things about her. *That's* masculinity—not mustaches, beards, or muscled abs."

Zoya lets out a huff of exasperation. Zaki simply shakes his head at her. "You won't understand," he says, shoulders sagging.

"*I* won't understand?" Zoya can't hold back her mirthless laugh. "Mr. Zaki, since when are we still partners for you to feel as if you can simply barge into my office and tell me what I will and won't understand?"

"I know why you're doing this." Zaki barks out a short laugh. "You need to show people you support things like this so that you gain more recognition. And let me tell you, it's working."

Zoya leans forward, chin set casually in her hands. Although he's standing and she's sitting, the waves of fury emanating from her cause Zaki to shrink back slightly. "Do you know what one of the meanings of *zameer* is, Mr. Zaki? *Conscience.* It refers to those who, before doing something *questionable*, feel the telltale *dharkan* of their hearts, the quiet signal from their conscience that what they're setting out to do isn't right. The whisper to stop. The warning to halt. *That's* what *zameer* is. And *mai apne naam par qaaim rehti hun, to mujh par jhoota aur ghatiya ilzaam lagaane se pehle is naam ka soch kar lehaaz kar liya kare*, please. *Kyun ke* I'm the daughter of Zameer, and I *am* Zameer."

Zaki simply stares at her, jaw clenched.

"Don't think I don't know why you came here, Mr. Zaki. You don't *approve* of this, and you're scared our old partnership will get in the way of the press, and they'll turn around and point fingers at *you*, questioning your company's values. You only give a damn about yourself, you despicable human being." Zaki looks infuriated by this but doesn't reply, and Zoya points to the door. "Kindly exit. Thank you."

With one last shake of his head, he storms out the same way he came in, fists clenched so tightly that his veins are popping out. Security leads him into the elevator.

Zoya sinks her head into her hands, nails digging into her auburn curls.

I'm spiraling downward.

She had attempted to talk to Zaki Ahmed in a placatory fashion, knowing losing her nerve would do none of them good. But when he spoke, Zoya abruptly remembered her ex-husband and his favorite line.

This is my God-given right.

Zoya shivers. Once, and only once, she mustered up the nerve to question this continuous statement of his, countering with a curious "*What are my rights?*" and asking for a more detailed explanation of his.

She shivers violently once more, remembering how that ended.

Twenty-Three

"My mercy embraces all things." (Qur'an 7:156)

~

ZOYA BURIES HERSELF IN her work, often yelling at someone, threatening to fire an employee or two, and then secluding herself to her office. If her tea so much as comes in with less than five packets of sugar, she swirls up a storm and is snappish for the rest of the day. And the poor intern serving her tea leaves her office a stuttering, stumbling mess.

To everyone else, she is the same harsh Zoya Zameer, perhaps just a bit moodier than usual. Nothing new.

Only she herself knows the difference.

Sumaiya has started wearing the *hijab* and positively *radiating* in it, something that angers Zoya in a way that she can't explain. Often she summons Sumiya to her office and harshly evaluates her designs, criticizing what she doesn't see, pulling out mistakes that aren't there.

The warm, kind girl simply nods and takes her boss' insults, but that isn't to say that she isn't utterly confused by her behavior. Sumaiya has become used to scarcely being appreciated by Zoya Zameer and even handling her jibes here and there, but this? This wild hostility, this cold nature? It leaves Sumaiya feeling more baffled than ever every time she exits the CEO's office.

She does not want to confirm her suspicions about this new,

cold attitude, so she stamps out any whispers in her heart. Shakes her head to dispel her thoughts. Leaves the room quietly.

It seems that the employees of Zameer Co. have more to worry about, however. For the entire month after the domestic violence project launch, tabloids upon tabloids are released. The press has done a full blow-by-blow of Zoya's outburst at the gala of her project launch. Other media outlets highlight simple, arbitrary expressions on Zoya's face and make them appear questionable, speculating what they "really mean." Others go back to the Desi World Fashion Show and even farther back, as if digging up her grave.

Zoya is unfazed. She disregards most of the tabloids that are released, and tries to avoid as much news about herself as possible. Her PR manager and marketing team check in with the media office and notify her if they believe a certain news is "stepping out of line."

Zoya occupies herself in observing Haroun Suleiman. It's not as if she hadn't been doing so before, but she now keeps an extra careful eye on him. If she ever sees him speaking to Sumaiya within company hours, she quickly calls one of them over to "discuss something."

Not that the two betrothed speak much, and even if they do, it's always about work. They know their limits, and for some reason, this infuriates Zoya.

Because deep down in her aching heart, she knows they are perfect for each other.

Haroun leaves an hour earlier every day, as he had requested. Days pass, and Zoya's curiosity is piqued. What does he do that requires him to leave early *every single day*? He had mentioned humanitarian work, but for some reason Zoya finds that hard to believe. She knows he would never lie simply to leave work early, but the way he had approached her about it stirs her suspicions.

Do you trust me? he had asked. She has to shake her head to dispel his words from her distraught mind.

Back in character, Zoya Zameer, back in character. She's been chiding herself with these words every day, ever since she heard of Sumaiya and Haroun's engagement. *What's your greatest asset? Being unfazed. So be unfazed.*

One day she approaches Farhan, who has been reserved with her ever since the day of the Desi World Fashion Show. She's noticed how his attitude has slowly changed since Haroun's arrival. Whereas he used to become agitated at the smallest things, now he can be seen exerting great effort to bite back any groans of frustration. A couple days ago, when Zoya criticized him for a minor mistake, he rushed off muttering, "Fifty shades of Zoya Zameer!" and she had to hold back a laugh. Especially when he covered his mouth quickly, as if in regret.

It doesn't make her despise him any less, though.

Farhan is closest to Haroun within the company, and perhaps outside of it as well. With this in mind, Zoya saunters by him, dropping a file on the desk next to his. "Eduardo," she says to the employee sitting there. "Review the points I've highlighted. Good work." She's about to walk away but feigns surprise when her eyes meet Farhan's. "Oh, Farhan, you're still here?"

Farhan smiles weakly. "Uh, yes, Ms. Zoya."

She nods absentmindedly. "Hmm. No, I was just wondering." She twirls her hair. "Like, no plans? You're not hanging out with Haroun or anything? Like, every day from now?"

Farhan watches her carefully. "Uh, no. He has some important work to do at this time."

He knows! Zoya nods, trying to seem unbothered, although her mind roils with questions. *What important work? Where? Why? With who? And why every day?*

Instead she says to Farhan, "Oh, I see . . . Like, just some random thing? Some work related to the company?"

Farhan blinks. "No." But he doesn't elaborate, and Zoya has never wanted to squeeze him into a pulp more than she does right now. Perhaps he senses her agitation, because he turns quickly away from her.

A day later, when she's had enough, she waits for Haroun to leave work, then orders Sameer to cancel the rest of her meetings for the day. Grabbing her handbag, she rushes into the elevator and out to the lobby. She catches sight of Bill, and barks out his name authoritatively.

He turns around with both eyebrows raised.

"Come with me," she whispers.

His brows knit. "Where, Ms. Zoya?"

In irritation, she snaps, "Drop the *Ms.*, please. As of this moment, we're no longer at work."

Bill's eyebrows rise again. "Okay, but where—"

"Just come with me!" she hisses. He obliges with a confused shrug and follows her out of the building. Zoya tosses him her keys. "You're driving."

He catches them, even more confused now. "Why?"

"Because if I drive, Bill Nye, you'll lose your damn mind. So let's go." She gets into the passenger seat, tapping the window impatiently for Bill to hurry up. He enters the car and twists the keys in the ignition.

"Follow that car," Zoya orders, pointing to Haroun's car ahead. Bill stares at her pointedly as she places her handbag at her feet and puts her seat belt on. She looks at him and throws her hands up. "What? Did I speak in French? I said follow that car, Bill."

He obliges reluctantly and presses on the gas. Zoya shrinks down in her seat, hiding herself from outside view. Her flustered nature causes an amused smirk to play on Bill's lips. "Ms. Zoya, if this is something that I end up in jail because of—"

She gestures at him dismissively. "Yeah, yeah, you'll get your money as promised in the contract."

"That's not what I—"

"Can't you go any faster, Bill? Like, damn, have you never played Grand Theft Auto?" She gestures to the highway in agitation. "I didn't drive because I don't want anyone to see me but can you literally not go *any* faster?"

"If you want us to crash, sure," Bill replies dryly. "It's *your* car. Also, call your driver next time you want to do something . . . questionable."

Zoya narrows her eyes at him and sighs in frustration. "Just shut up and keep driving, Bill Nye."

A few moments later, Bill queries, "So if this car goes all the way to—let's say—Florida, we're going all the way to Florida?"

"Yes," Zoya responds curtly. Tangentially she wonders, *Does he not recognize his friend's car?*

"Ms. Zo—Zoya, if I get arrested because of this—"

"Yeah, yeah, you'll get bailed out. And you'll still have the job, don't worry."

Bill laughs. "It's not about the job, Zoya. I just want to know what I'm risking—"

"We're following Haroun, okay?" she snaps. "Happy? And aren't you getting a little too comfortable with saying my name?"

"You told me to. And Haroun?" Comprehension slowly dawns on his face. "Oh, *that's* whose car it is."

They reach the local area about twenty minutes later. An angsty Zoya (with the worst possible thoughts floating around in her head) looks out the window, and she is taken aback to find Haroun stopping in front of a dilapidated area with broken blinds at the windows. The building is sagging with wear; the paint is peeling, and the sign above the alcove barely visible. She knits her brows before stepping out of the car to follow Haroun. "Stay here," she orders Bill. He opens his mouth to protest but she continues, "I mean it. Someone needs to be by the car. And keep the key in the ignition!"

In case I need to make my escape.

Zoya rushes up the cracked stairs of the building and enters, seeing Haroun's back disappear through the door to the right. She is about to follow when her eye falls on the reception desk and the "ID required" sign at the front. With no time to grab her handbag, and knowing that a first-timer like her probably won't be allowed so easily into a place like this, she bites her lip nervously. She does not want to go back to the car in case she misses the opportunity to see what Haroun may be doing.

As a last resort, Zoya rushes up to the guy at the reception desk, pretending to look flustered. He looks to be in his early twenties. When he glances up and does a double take, Zoya knows this will be a bit easier.

"Hello, ma'am. How can I help you?" he says breathlessly.

Zoya grabs a strand of hair and twirls it around her finger, morphing her face into a concerned expression. "Hi," she says earnestly. "I'm so sorry to bother you"—her eyes flick to his name tag—"Eric, but"--looking around desperately for something, her eye falls on the schedule behind him with the day and night shifts. It's almost five o'clock now, so Zoya prays he has just started his shift. "Actually, I left something here when I came earlier in the morning." She pouts and makes a show of wiping a false tear under her eye. "It was very valuable to me, you know. My—my mother gave it to me."

Eric observes her mournful face. "I'm so sorry about that, ma'am, but I can't let you in without ID."

Zoya pouts and scrunches her eyebrows close together. She hears Eric's breath catch. "The thing is, it *is* my ID," she bluffs. "My mother was my greatest help in passing my driving test. It's just . . . the last memory I have of her, you know?" She dabs at her eye theatrically and dares to say, "If you want, you can check your cameras to see when I came in earlier."

Eric's eyes rove over her face before he shakes his head. "No, that's alright, ma'am. Go ahead."

A jolt of surprise passes through her. Zoya has half a mind to stand right there and begin yelling at him about the lack of integrity he carries in his work ethic, but instead she flashes a smile at him. After all, he's been a great help to her. "Thank you, sweetheart. God bless you." Blowing the flustered guy an air kiss, she rushes away and follows Haroun's footsteps. She stops when she approaches a room at the end of the shabby hallway, scuttling to the side to hide herself from view.

Inside, Haroun enters and smiles at a group of . . . children? Once they see him, they stand up excitedly and rush over to hug him. Haroun leans down and embraces the children, planting kisses on each of their heads. They're all clamoring to talk to him, and Zoya strains to hear what they're saying. Her forehead creases in wonder. "Who are these kids?" she whispers.

A sudden thought occurs to her. *What if he's already married and these are all his kids?* Her eyes dart around the room. *No, seven kids is too many, right? He's only, like, two or three years older than me.*

Or what if he already married Sumaiya and these are her kids? No, Sumaiya doesn't look like she birthed these many children. And he never mentioned being married before. Besides, the children don't all look the same.

You crazy idiot, why would he come to an establishment like this to meet his own kids? He said it was humanitarian work . . .

Hyperventilating, Zoya watches Haroun and the children for the next fifteen minutes. The children continuously throw themselves at Haroun and he kisses their cheeks, and when another worker walks in to give him bags of food, he sits there and helps feed them. While the children finish eating, he talks to the worker with a strained look on his face, pointing to the rickety building and the tattered clothing of the children. Whatever the worker is saying seems to have a great effect on him because he rubs his temples and sighs. She tries to catch snippets of their conversation but is only able to lip read the words "sponsors" and "orphans." It seems that the worker is about to leave the room, so Zoya quickly steps away from the door and rushes back out.

She barely notices the receptionist as she trudges by, her mind a mess of muddled thoughts. The children are orphans. And Haroun came to clothe and feed and spend time with them. And he does this every day.

What had Zoya been thinking? What nightmares had she been entertaining?

He has been sacrificing money and time every day to come to this ramshackle, desolate building. Just to spend time with these orphan children.

A searing pain blossoms in her chest, a gaping ache that this man is engaged to someone else. She is at a loss for words.

"Were you able to find what you were looking for?" the receptionist asks. Zoya looks up quickly, having forgotten his presence. A lost, faraway look envelopes her face. "Yes. Yes, I was." She walks out slowly and stumbles into the car, ignoring Bill's questioning glance.

"So?" Bill says. "Did he kill anyone?"

"Far from it," Zoya replies breathlessly, leaning her head against the car window and refusing to elaborate. Bill stares at his boss with knitted brows, surprised at her dramatically changed demeanor before going into the building versus coming out.

"Are you alright, Ms. Zoya?"

She flinches. The same words from someone else's mouth ring in her ears.

Are you alright?

Are you okay?

Do you trust me?

Zoya nods weakly. "Just drive us back," she murmurs.

An increasingly nagging emotion tugs at Zoya, rooting restlessness in her heart. She has been antsy for days, pondering over what Haroun may be doing in the hours he takes off work. She's lost sleep many nights, coming up with bizarre scenarios to satisfy her burning curiosity.

Now she feels empty, undone. And she's scared to admit it, but she feels *ashamed* at the thoughts that have crossed her mind the past couple of days.

Her father had always told her that guilt was the worst feeling in the world. Guilt, regret, shame. They would all snowball into one and destroy a person. She never understood him before, much less given a lot of thought to his warnings. Not even when he left. Because she had become scornfully accustomed to the compulsion of this emotion.

Now she is beginning to understand.

Twenty-Four

~

THAT NIGHT, DARK EYES plague Zoya's dreams. Quiet, intense, and probing. She tosses and turns in bed restlessly.

Do you trust me?

~

For Zoya to say that she didn't expect the various reactions to her new initiatives would be a lie. In the business world, it's never *just* positive or *just* negative. Fluctuations are her best friend.

The Zameer Co. clothesline has released various new designs in bridal wear, most of which are met with admiration and approval. Yet, as Bill quotes Newton, every action has an equal and opposite reaction. Meaning every time they majorly succeed, they will also majorly screw up.

Zoya tells him to shut up.

The board of directors and other staff are gathered around the table in the meeting room. They're mulling over the latest statistics and worrying over the slight decrease in consumer demand. Zoya leans back in her chair and watches all of them, amused. She has been concerned about the decrease as well but maintains her indifferent façade.

Something about pretending that she doesn't give a damn about things is very appealing to her.

Haroun settles in the corner of the room, taking notes and busying himself with inputting new catalogs into the system. Zoya steals a glance at him. He rubs his eyes wearily, faded shadows decorating the area under them.

"I don't think this decrease has anything to do with our actual products," Ibitoye says, staring pointedly at Zoya.

Zoya begins examining her nails nonchalantly.

Bill's eyes dart around the tense room. "Perhaps it's the change in designs?" he proposes.

"No, I don't think that's it, either," Matt, another director, says. "Sumaiya's wonderful, really. Her designs have a touch that spectacularly show the essence of the company. Flora was amazing, but I don't think her designs always highlighted that."

At the far end of the room, a corner of Haroun's lips turns up when Matt compliments Sumaiya.

Zoya wants to hurl her *jhumkas* in Matt's face but nods grudgingly. "Agreed."

Raj clears his throat. "Actually, I beg to differ. Regarding the decrease in consumer demand." He pauses. "Do you guys remember what Mr. Zaki was wearing at the evening gala?"

"A whole lot of arrogance and attitude," Zoya says in a clipped tone.

Raj ignores her cynicism. "He and the rest of his employees were wearing clothing designed by their own company."

"So? We do the same."

He shakes his head. "What I mean is, their clothing catered more to the audience there."

This catches Zoya's attention. She stops examining her nails for a moment and leans forward. "What do you mean '*catered more to the audience there*?'"

He takes a deep breath. "I think the reason we are experiencing some downfall is because we need to cater to a wider group of people. Mr. Zaki and his employees adjust according to the styles and standards of a broader demographic. Being the CEO, he parades his most renowned employees around in their best clothing, and it receives showers of praise because he knows what *people* want. Especially in the fashion industry."

"And we don't?"

"No, I—" he stops, seeming to calculate his next words. "I think that being the CEO and making . . . *adjustments* to his and his staff's style . . . wins them more success."

"So what are you suggesting?" Zoya says somewhat sharply.

"Ms. Zoya . . . maybe since *you* don't make these adjustments to your own style despite being so renowned . . . it . . . turns people away."

There is pin drop silence. The sound of Haroun's furious typing halts, and for a moment there is only thick tension in the room. Eyebrows are raised, heads are bent, and a few scared, subtle nods of assent follow Raj's observation. Perhaps others know better, however, because they widen their eyes or solemnly shake their heads. Ibitoye and Bill included.

"Excuse me?" Zoya says after a moment, eyes glinting dangerously. "What are you saying?"

Raj bites his lip anxiously but stands his ground. "I'm not saying that what you're doing is wrong. I'm just saying that maybe you should consider changing up your style a little bit in order to reflect a broader demographic. It may be seen as . . . ah, *liberating* to others, which would be vastly celebrated, especially since you're the CEO." Zoya almost laughs at how he purposely avoids the word "feminism" and opts for "liberating" instead. "Other companies are skyrocketing because their employees aren't averse to showing what people want in fashion, and sometimes that may be a bit more skin or—"

Zoya cuts him off. "All I hear is *bakwaas*, I swear." Her staff has been with her long enough to know what this particular word means. "I'm absolutely awed that you, as a *man*, are saying this to me. If you had even the tiniest inkling of what respect is, you would be looking out for me and making sure people don't lay their nasty, unlawful eyes on me in the wrong ways. Yet *you* are turning around and telling me to show '*a bit more skin*?' And that too in the name of business? What kind of a man are you? Okay, maybe don't respect me—I'm *Zoya Zameer*. But don't you have respect for *any* woman?

You immoral—" she stops, balling her fists.

Raj looks a bit wounded, perhaps at having his masculinity challenged, but to defend himself he says, "Of course I do—"

"If you respected me or were familiar with my morals at all, Raj, you would never tell me to '*show a bit more skin*' in the name of liberation and empowerment. You would recognize my values, would want to protect me, would tell me that the world has nasty eyes and views women as specimens, as objects. And my '*showing a bit more skin,*' as you advise, would not liberate me. It would place me in jeopardy of those disgusting eyes and that disgusting mindset. Especially considering your conviction that women exist solely to undress or cover up for the pleasure of men."

Zoya is so mad with rage and disgust that she wants to spit. "I'm liberated. I'm empowered. I don't need any more of this one-sided, one-track feminist rubbish, so please stop. If you want to do all this, go ahead. If you don't agree with Zameer's ideology, start up your own company. Better yet, go work with Zaki Ahmed. But I'm not going to compromise my beliefs and the integrity in my company just for a few dumb statistics to change. I value my respect and honor more than that." With that, she pushes against the desk and whirls out of the room.

Haroun's fingers hover over the keyboard, but the blank expression on his face signifies his attention has strayed far from the catalogs he's supposed to be inputting.

The remaining directors all stare at each other until Ibitoye sighs. "You *had* to bring that up, did you?"

Raj holds his hands up indignantly. "If I knew it was going to make her react like that, I never would have said it! Like always, I was just thinking of ways to combat recent issues."

"Raj, you've been here long enough to know," Bill scolds him. "I understand what you were trying to say. But how could you not recall that things like this are her biggest pet peeves? She doesn't believe in sacrificing her own morals for temporary success."

"And maybe others wouldn't be offended by a comment like that," Ibitoye adds. "But you know how she gets when it's about various views on feminism, and what she believes respect entails for women."

The directors in the room continue to argue back and forth.

Outside, Zoya fumes as her heels click sharply against the floor. Once she's inside her office, she grabs fistfuls of her hair and closes her eyes.

Control. Breathe in. Breathe out.

As of late, she's noticed that it has become increasingly difficult for her to suppress what bothers her most. She can't afford this lack of control, not when she's on such a high, public pedestal.

"Back to normal, Zoya," she chides herself as she adjusts her curls. "Become who you were. Spine straight as a ruler. *'I don't care'* façade stronger than a tied knot." She glances at herself in the mirror hanging on the wall. She looks the way Zoya Zameer always does—impeccable, breathtaking. Not a hair out of place.

A bit more skin.

Suddenly, she is thrown back into *that* time. Another memory hits her like a brick to the face, like being dunked in ice cold water.

"I don't understand why she took such a rash decision for a divorce. And this . . . this doesn't make sense to me."

"Ayaaz, this girl has become trouble for us. Have you heard the things she's mumbling about? Abuse, beatings, what is all this nonsense?"

The man is hesitant when he says, "Salma . . . her face and arms are covered in bruises. And those are the ones we can see."

"Do you think she's honestly telling the truth about our son? He would never harm an ant, let alone a woman."

"Then how do you explain those scars all over her body?" His voice is conflicted.

A scoff. "I know how women work, Ayaaz. After all, I am one. They have a way of making themselves seem innocent."

Silence, then, "Do you think she will take legal action?"

A sigh. "I don't think so. She knows better than to do anything like that."

Outside the door stands the young woman they are speaking about. She turns to leave and sees him *standing at the far end of the hallway. His eyes bore into hers before trailing down to her exposed arms. Because lately he has stopped marking her in unseen places and has resorted to marking her everywhere he desires, heedless of possible repercussions.*

Perhaps because he knows there will be no repercussions for him.

She hastily covers herself up with her dupatta and turns quickly away from him, walking in the opposite direction.

Her lifeless eyes are trained to the ceiling.

A knock sounds on the door. Zoya's eyes widen as she is thrown out of the brutal memory, and her heels swivel around at lightning speed. She grabs the first thing on her table and hurls it across the room, where it smashes against the wall and scatters into smithereens on the floor.

The door to her office opens, and Haroun stands there with a file in his hand. He enters with a panicked expression on his face. "I thought something happened—" He glances at the broken glass at the same time that Zoya realizes what she broke.

The hourglass. The one her father gave her.

A strangled cry escapes her. She rushes forward just as Haroun does, attempting to grab the pieces of glass and do anything, *anything* to put them back together.

But the hourglass is broken beyond repair.

Her throat constricts; it feels as if the air is being sucked out of the room. Zoya falls to her knees, stunned.

When she reaches forward to try to collect the pieces, Haroun bends down and quietly says, "Don't touch them. You might hurt yourself." Zoya wraps her arms around her knees and simply sits there, glassy eyes staring at the broken hourglass.

She wants to say something, *anything*. Wants to hold a conversation so that he cannot witness how disarrayed her emotions are. Wants to explain why this hourglass is so significant.

Words fail her as she stares at the shattered hourglass.

Haroun looks around the room, perhaps searching for a brush to sweep the contents into the trash can. When it's nowhere to be found, he grabs a piece of paper and a file instead. Zoya watches him through eyes thick with tears. Using the paper as a funnel, he brushes the glass onto the file and is about to reach out to carefully take hold of the larger pieces when Zoya shakes her head. "No." Her voice comes out raw and strained. "You'll hurt yourself."

He shakes his head. "I won't. It's okay."

"No," Zoya says. "Don't do it."

After a pause, Haroun stands. "I'll go get a broom." Before leaving, he hands her the water bottle that was sitting on her table. "Drink some water, Ms. Zoya."

She simply stares at the broken hourglass, which she herself blew to smithereens in her uncontrolled and uncalculated rage. The sand is strewn across the floor.

A fresh wave of sobs overtakes her.

A moment later, the janitor steps inside and rushes forward to clean up the mess, but Zoya shifts to block it. He gives her a confused look, while Haroun stands helplessly behind the janitor. "He wouldn't let me," he says.

"No." Zoya says firmly. "I don't want him to do it." She grabs the broom out of the janitor's hands and begins sweeping the glass together, but Haroun stops her by clearing his throat.

"Ms. Zoya, let me do it."

And Zoya, too overridden by grief to argue, simply watches with lost eyes as Haroun takes the broom from her and collects the mess into an empty trash can nearby.

Zoya walks over and pulls the plastic bag out of the trash can, attempting to tie it securely and place it on top of her desk. But her hands are shaking too badly. She fumbles with the knot, a tear trailing down her cheek.

Wordlessly, Haroun reaches out for the bag.

Do you trust me?

Zoya hands it to him. He ties the knot effortlessly and places the bag on her desk. "Are you alright?" he asks quietly. "Did you get any cuts from the glass?"

She shakes her head no.

After a tense, charged silence, he murmurs "Okay." He turns to leave but then pauses and retrieves the file that had been in his hand when he walked in. Hesitantly he says, "I fixed the problem with the catalogs and printed out a copy."

Briefly, Zoya laughs inwardly at the thought that her board of directors knows her so well, they sent Haroun for this task. Knowing that in her current state, she would probably fire any other person who walked through her door.

Zoya nods at Haroun. "Thank you." Her voice sounds strangled. She cannot be near him right now. His demeanor, his thoughtfulness, it's all too much.

He is engaged to someone else.

"Are you alright?" he asks.

"Yes." Zoya's answer is quick. Too quick to believe.

Quietly Haroun replies, "Okay."

With that, he leaves.

And Zoya is left staring at the plastic bag that carries one of the last remnants of her absentee father.

Twenty-Five

"But they plan, and Allah plans, and Allah is the best of planners."
(Qur'an 8:30)

~

"I'M GOING TO QUIT, MAN."

"Why?"

"Why? *Why?* Are you seriously asking me that question right now, Haroun?" Farhan's pent up frustration is clear in his voice, like an explosion waiting to happen.

"Yes," Haroun deadpans.

"Do you need me to explain to you once again how she's literally been treating me like chewed up *gum* on the bottom of her heel? Actually, scratch that, it's not accurate enough—"

"Farhan—"

"Maybe more like a rat. You know that show where those rats kept exploding because of some virus? *Teen Wolf,* it was called, I think? Yeah, she thinks I'm those rats—"

"Farhan—"

"She may think I'm a lizard, actually. I think she's still really pissed about that *chipkali* thing, even though she was laughing about it." Farhan shudders. "When she laughs, it's so terrifying. It's like insects are crawling over my skin and—"

"*Farhan*—" Haroun exclaims in exasperation, stopping in the middle of the hallway. Farhan's hands drop, his fingers halt in imitating insects crawling over his arms.

"What, bro?" Although he has tried his best to keep his mouth shut on the slow, agonizing journey to self-improvement, his spool is coming undone now.

Haroun raises a hand to his forehead and rubs it down the length of his face, stopping at his chin. "*Relax.*"

"That's easy for *you* to say. She doesn't *step* all over you."

"She doesn't—"

"Don't feed me the same cock and bull story about her not acting *any* different towards you."

Haroun smacks his forehead. "Farhan, I'm getting *married.* Can you please drop that now?"

Farhan folds his arms. "*Haroun,* I'll drop it when I see that it isn't true."

Haroun glares at him.

"Besides, we're getting off topic. We were talking about how she treats me like the spawn of Satan."

"Farhan, I think she's going through a tough time right now."

"Tough times don't call for inexcusable behavior."

"You have to think about the burden placed on her shoulders. She's younger than both of us, yet she's managed to shoulder a multi-million dollar company *and* she's managed to do it successfully. It's not easy living a life constantly under the spotlight, scrutinized from every angle. She has to double check her every move, second guess her every step, be painfully aware of every word that comes out of her mouth."

"Yeah, well, she didn't do a very good job of that when she *fired* me on live TV," Farhan grumbles, but Haroun's words have their intended effect, and he quiets down.

Haroun sighs. "I know it doesn't make sense to us and seems unfair, but maybe it was a mistake on her part. She *did* say it was a misunderstanding. When we're stressed, we do and say stuff we don't realize, right?" Haroun places a reassuring hand on Farhan's shoulder. "And I'm sorry about what you had to go through, bro."

Farhan stares at him for a few moments, blinking. "Man, why are you so hell bent on making everyone look human?"

Haroun lets out a surprised laugh. "Is everyone not human?"

"No, just—" Farhan shakes his head frustratedly. "I don't understand how you make everyone seem redeemable."

"I think everyone *is* redeemable," Haroun responds quietly.

"*Everyone?*"

"Yes. If they've been given the proper chances, known the right people. I mean, I don't think anyone is born inherently evil. Sometimes I feel like it's the actions we take in response to what's happened to us that make us look evil." Haroun shrugs, running a hand through his hair. "In reality, I think most of what makes us look bad can be justified with a proper explanation. That doesn't mean some of our actions can be excused, just that we're . . . human and probably had a reason for doing them." He pauses, face screwed up in contemplation.

"Allah *always* gives people chances. Over and over again. He says that even the gravest of sins are forgiven if humans just turn to him and repent. That's all He asks for. But us humans . . ." Haroun rubs the back of his neck. "You and I, we're cheap when it comes to giving people chances." He shakes his head sadly.

His words seem to have struck a blow on Farhan, because he's quiet after that.

Farhan has always despised talks of religion in regular, casual conversations, perhaps because of the way religion is handled in his home—like shoving rods down one's throat by force. But whenever Haroun speaks of God or religion, there is no anger creeping up Farhan's neck, no impatience. Somehow the logic that builds the foundation of this religion has never been apparent to Farhan until Haroun entered his life. Whereas before, rulings and regulations in Islam seemed burdensome and suffocating to him; after meeting Haroun, he is slowly beginning to learn that there is sound judgment and reasoning behind these rulings and regulations. The logic and judgment he had never been given the chance of learning on his own, and had only been conditioned to be hostile towards.

On top of that, Haroun loops himself into the problem at hand. Whatever it is, even if it has nothing to do with him. He never explains something and makes Farhan feel bad for it, a feat Farhan has not at all been exposed to. All his life, his family and the so-called religious practitioners that he's met have all had one common problem: pointing out the faults in others. They have used bits and pieces of religion to back up their claims, and rebuked any forms of disagreement or curiosity. Farhan's genuine questions and curiosity have always been seen as forbidden and blasphemous, but Haroun makes it seem otherwise. He has never pointed out Farhan's faults and rubbed them in his face, never explicitly laid out Farhan's sins before him to be on full display. Instead, he has garnered an altogether different approach—friendship. He's *befriended* Farhan, something none of these religious scholars or family members did. Thus, he allowed Farhan to see the true meaning behind giving advice to others and helping each other improve.

"You good?" Haroun asks, eyes narrowed at Farhan's uncharacteristic silence.

"Yeah, bro, I just—" He throws an arm around Haroun's shoulder. "I just love you, bro!"

Haroun smiles quizzically. "Okay?"

"When are you coming over again? It's been a while, and my mom keeps crying that *'he's forgotten us, he's forgotten us.'* And have you looked in the mirror lately? Your eye bags would put Dracula to shame."

The two of them walk away like that, arms thrown over one another's shoulders, their laughs reverberating throughout the halls.

"Zameer's favorite duo," an employee watching them says with a smile.

At the corner of a hallway, Zoya stands still and silent, her breath caught in her throat. She has just heard Haroun and Farhan's entire conversation, and she is speechless. Why does Haroun's insistence on guarding her name never fail to baffle her? She has known him for quite some time now, known that he would protect anyone's reputation no matter who it is. So why the surprise?

Abruptly she shakes her head. "No, Zoya. He said it himself. He's getting . . . *married.*" Saying it out loud causes her heart to squeeze painfully. "Stop this . . . fascination. Whatever this is." She breathes deeply. "No more of this . . . obsession with Haroun Suleiman, okay?"

He makes that a little hard to do.

Angry at herself, Zoya huffs up to her office.

She phones Sarah, and after hesitating at the recollection of their last encounter, asks her to send Haroun.

"No more pretending," she says to herself. "Time for confrontation."

Haroun arrives, and Zoya gestures for him to sit down across from her. Hands shaking, she clears her throat and trains her gaze on him.

Be cool, calm, and collected. Just like Zoya Zameer is always supposed to be.

The last time they had been in each other's presence, Zoya had been far from cool, calm, and collected. She wonders what he thinks of her now, especially since he had no context of her emotional outburst.

"Are you alright, Ms. Zoya?"

Almost choking on her own saliva at his question, she nods nonchalantly.

Haroun's eyes roam around the room as he waits patiently. Gaze settling on the expensive decoration piece across from where he's sitting, he scrutinizes it carefully.

The air thickens with the possibility of unsaid words.

Zoya Zameer has never had trouble opening her mouth ever since she entered the professional world. She's certainly never had any difficulty saying what's on her mind in front of entire crowds. So why does her tongue seem to have locked in upon itself in front of this one man?

Start off with something easy, a voice in her head says. She wants to ask him about the orphanage, about why he hid it from her. Was he keeping it a secret, or did he not think she was important enough to tell?

Something tells her it was probably the latter reason.

Perhaps she should ask him about his engagement? About whether the date of the wedding has been fixed? As soon as this thought crosses her mind, Zoya's heart rate rises considerably.

How can she ask him about it when her own heart stubbornly refuses to accept the harsh truth? After her initial shock at finding out, she has sat down for hours at a time and thought about it. How had she not known? Zoya observes everything about Haroun Suleiman, from his polite and upright demeanor down to the casual clothes he wears on to the kind of coffee he likes to drink. So how had she missed this one key detail?

Perhaps, the voice in her head nags at her. *Perhaps it's because they both don't make a big deal out of it. They know their limits; they know that they have made a commitment, and that's it.*

This realization suddenly makes everything all the more unbearable.

And why had she frightfully dismissed his mother's comment about him searching for a spouse? Why hadn't she conducted further investigation?

What could you have done, Zoya? Stopped the engagement from happening? You heard Haroun; he's content with his decision, and is convinced that he found the right person.

Taking a deep breath, Zoya leans forward, bangles clinking noisily in the quiet room. "How are you doing?"

"Good, *Alhamdulillah,*" Haroun replies. "And you?"

She deflects his question. "How is your mom? Your sisters?"

A smile blooms on his face. "They're doing great, too. My sisters have both been promoted."

The ecstatic expression on his face causes Zoya to flush with pleased warmth. She grabs her water bottle and feigns surprise. "Really? That's amazing!"

He nods happily. "It's a blessing, honestly. They both have higher-ranking positions but are not as exhausted, and they can focus more on school." He pauses, eyebrows furrowing. "It's honestly kind of surprising. I'm not sure how it happened all of a sudden, and that too to *both* of them . . ." he trails off. "*Alhamdulillah.*"

Zoya coughs on her water, throwing him a sheepish smile. An awkward silence settles over them again.

Time to get real.

"Why do you feel the need to defend me every chance you get?" Zoya blurts out.

Surprise flickers across Haroun's face at the sudden change in conversation. "I'm sorry?"

Zoya shrugs lightly. "Countless times, I've heard you stepping in with others who say negative things about me. Why does it bother you so much?"

He's still surprised, but doesn't miss a beat. "Because I don't think it's right for you to be disrespected."

"Just me?" A flicker of hope rises within her.

"Everyone deserves to be given a chance to defend themselves, but when they're absent, they deserve to be defended by others."

"Everyone?" The flicker dies out.

He pauses. "*Be merciful to those on the earth, so the One above the heavens will be merciful to you.*"

Her eyebrows rise. "Where is that from?" Although she's pretty sure she already knows the answer.

"It's a *hadith*—a Prophetic saying."

Once again, she realizes with a shock that his mention of religion doesn't cause steam to swirl from her ears. Instead, the words he quotes soothe her heart.

Zoya leans back in her chair. "But why does *me* being disrespected matter to *you*? People talk all the time. And I'm not even there to hear it ninety percent of the time. So what difference does it make for you to say something in my defense or not? Why would you bother speaking up at all? It's not like I would ever know that you didn't and penalize you for it."

"It's not about whether you hear me or not, it's about my responsibility to guard someone's reputation."

She feels a pang in her chest at these words, knowing that they only prove he would stand up for anyone. Nothing is special about her for him.

Of course you're not special to him, a voice in her head whispers. *He's getting married to someone else.*

Haroun must be alerted by her uncharacteristic silence because he takes a deep breath, as if he's about to say something very serious. "Ms. Zoya, why do people protect *anything*? Why bother to take care of or defend anything?"

Zoya cocks her head to the side. "Because it's valuable."

"So is your honor."

Zoya's breath hitches. Suddenly the room seems too small, too compact, for Zoya to be able to breathe. She's becoming unbalanced, teetering off the edge of the only cliff she's ever known. Especially when she thinks of this man promising himself to someone else.

A sensation equal to falling rapidly overtakes her.

With a haphazard flip of her hair, Zoya attempts to regain her sanity. "Too bad not everyone thinks like you," she says. "Let people do the bullying. You don't have to speak up in my defense. Just stay out of *their* way and you won't have to suffer harassment because of *me*."

I hope he can't hear how fast my heart is beating.

Haroun's eyebrows incline. "Are you asking me to be a bystander to the bully?"

"I'm asking you to stay out of business that doesn't concern you."

"People's reputations *do* concern me."

Raising her head to the ceiling, she blows out a sigh. "You're infuriating, Haroun Suleiman."

After a pause he says, "Ms. Zoya, a woman's reputation is really delicate. Unfortunately, people are quick to believe what they hear about her, no matter how absurd it may be. No matter how senseless it is. So defending women against oppression is really important. Defending *anyone* against oppression is really important."

She swivels around in her chair, too rattled to form a response.

Once again, *Zoya Zameer* is speechless. She's been rendered powerless by Haroun's words, his tackles to her heart's fortressed walls.

Ironically, she is bitterly reminded of her ex-husband by Haroun's words. In some of her last days with him, he had told her he didn't like her liberal feminism. And she had said, *"What is it? You don't like women standing up for themselves when they're being mistreated? Well, maybe if men like you stood up for us, you wouldn't have to see this 'liberal feminism.'"*

He never understood the word oppression. And how could he? He wouldn't *want* to even if he could; what he did to her fell no short of oppressive. And God forbid he would taint the perfect image he had of himself as the perfect Muslim if he acknowledged that he was the oppressor, that he was the one at fault.

Perhaps reading her silence as contemplation, Haroun clears his throat and asks, "Did you know that Allah revealed verses of the Qur'an specifically in defense of the Prophet Muhammad's wife Aisha?"

A startled look appears on Zoya's face. *This is new.* She shakes her head and leans forward with her chin in her hand.

He nods. "They were traveling with a caravan and Aisha, may Allah be pleased with her, went to use the bathroom. When she returned, the caravan had left, thinking she was already sitting in the palanquin. After falling asleep in the desert, she was awoken by the sound of a man." He begins to gesture with his hands. "In the old times, one man would travel a little further behind the caravan to make sure everything got safely to its destination. So when he saw the Prophet's wife, he took her back home safely and in a dignified manner. But they experienced a delay in returning, and false allegations were laid on her. Her pure reputation was stained, and for weeks, people mistrusted her and made misleading accusations. We're talking about *Aisha*, one of the most chaste and pure women."

The corner of Haroun's mouth turns up in a half-smile. "During a time when her integrity and purity were being questioned, when even her husband still loved her but became distant from her—after all, the Prophet *was* human—Allah sent down verses in *Surah Nur* to defend her. To claim that He, *God*, was a witness to her innocence."

Zoya gasps in surprise, having never heard this story in her entire life. "That's . . ." She struggles to find words. Why is it that things like this were hidden from her? Her father had never been particularly religious, but why had her ex-husband never told her this story or similar stories when he constantly preached about Islam to her?

Perhaps he was too busy telling her that she was basically the spawn of Satan, before he would sit down to read the Qur'an and make *tasbeeh* on his fingers. He would remember Allah's name consistently with the same mouth he used to puncture and scar her soul.

Zoya, the oppressor only speaks of what benefits him. He will never speak of things in your favor.

Haroun clears his throat. "So, Ms. Zoya, if *Allah* defended a woman's reputation, who am *I* to stay silent?"

Zoya remains mute, too shocked by the story and by Haroun's fierce determination to be able to say anything. He seems to sense that she needs to be alone, so he stands, says, "With your permission . . ." and leaves after her shaky nod.

After sitting in shock for a few minutes, Zoya realizes something.

Haroun is nothing like the other religious people she anticipates with dread. Every time he comes around, she does not feel an inevitable fear, nor does she feel like a sinner. Most other religious people she has met in her life have made her feel as if she's doing *something* wrong. They've always made her feel lesser, inferior somehow.

Haroun presents himself as not only inferior but humble as well; he does not make any assumptions about her spirituality to her. Hell, he does not even make claims about his *own* spirituality to anyone. His rigorous faith and demeanor are strong in that he carries a sphere of gentleness exuding from religion out of him, and this sphere touches the hearts of everyone he meets.

Zoya has been psychoanalyzing him with every passing day and continues to do so in her office, in a state of wild confusion. She's always known that there was something different about Haroun Suleiman from the moment she met him, when he refused to look in her eyes and rake his gaze over her pretty face and impeccable features, something no man can resist doing. She knew *something* made him keep his gaze lowered, *something* made him humble himself even around her—*Zoya Zameer.*

He doesn't walk around forcing religion down people's throats, as many practitioners of faith often do. He simply conducts himself in a way that makes people ponder what makes him so gentle and humble. In this way, he silently carries the banner of Islam and presents it to everyone he meets; every time he lowers his gaze in front of a woman and talks to her with respect, every time he serves as the judge in a friendly dispute and selects the fair choice, every time he talks admiringly about his mother with other employees, and every time he greets someone in his gentle manner.

He does not have to say a single word, yet represents a message so heavy, a feat so powerful, that it's rendered impossible for someone *not* to develop a strong liking for him and what he represents.

In the stillness of her office, Zoya shakes her head to herself. Being left alone with her thoughts is always dangerous for someone like Zoya, because solitude means thinking. And when Zoya thinks, she plots. And when she plots, it never ends well for anyone.

All her life, she has been baffled by every man she has met, thinking *"Is this what they are all like?"* When one man finally comes across who not only makes everything easier to understand, but is gentle and caring and respectful and beautiful and so many other things as well, she's just going to . . . let him go?

"No." Her voice is loud and clear. Right then and there, she makes a decision. "*Agar mera naam Zoya Zameer hai,* there is no way I'm letting him get married to someone else."

Twenty-Six

DESIRE.

To think that this simple word has so many innuendos. So many insinuations.

Yet it is simply the act of wanting. A greater power of wanting. Wanting something so badly that it makes every breath an ache, every blink of the eye arduous, every footstep misplaced.

It makes every heartbeat quicker.

Zoya has never felt such an intense desire in her life, such an ache to want something so badly. Zoya has always *wanted* more, but has never *desired* more. She *wants* every single day, more and more than she had the last day, and she makes sure she can do whatever is in her power to gain what she wants. She is *Zoya Zameer*, CEO of Zameer Co., one of the most renowned women in America—of course she can obtain whatever she wants. She wants it, she makes it happen, and *poof*, it's there.

So wanting something and not being able to have it? That is outside the scope of Zoya's sphere. Hell, that is outside the scope of Zoya's entire *galaxy*.

To her, the word *desire* has always held negative connotations. It has always meant lust. She has known no other definitions of the word, no other side of the coin. Life has shown her nothing but the ugly side of desire, the corrupt side.

The penetrating, the trespassing of property, the violation of privacy, the thieving of dignity, the coercion. This is the only thing desire has shown her.

So when she finds herself quietly observing Haroun and Sumaiya; the way they only speak if it's absolutely necessary, faithfully adhering to religious limits despite heading for marriage; the way Haroun keeps his eyes lowered around Sumaiya as well; the way he carries himself and speaks to others; the word *desire* is given a new meaning. She doesn't *want* Haroun Suleiman; she *desires* him.

And not in the connotative sense of the word, the sense that the world has given it. But in the sense that a strange thumping and squeezing sensation overrides her heart when she thinks of him promising himself in marriage to someone else. Something sick stirs within her, something aches. An emotion she hasn't felt in a long, long time.

She desires for this strange organ in her body—which continues to somehow beat—to be in line with his. She desires to place her head over his heart and hear the rhythmic beating, hear the proof that goodness like him exists and breathes in this cruel and corrupt world. She desires for him to continue to say things that make her breath hitch and cause her brain's gears to stutter, that make her reconsider every thought she has ever had. She desires to hear his voice, see his smile and the creased dimple, be allowed to stroke his cheek every time he blushes in an uncomfortable situation.

She desires to press gentle fingers to his dark eye bags and ask him why he is so tired all the time. Her heart aches to pour out all of her life's worries to him, to lay down her trials and tribulations into his caring, protective hands. To hear him give her reassurances that she will eventually begin to believe.

And none of this can be accomplished while he is promised to someone else.

She has to be the one. She has to be the one whose hands he holds every night, whose hair he brushes back from her face every night, whose tremors he stops every time she flies awake from a nightmare, rapidly breathing with eyes full of terror. She has to be the one he provides comfort to during times of stress, the kind of comfort she has only felt in her father's presence, and now Haroun's presence.

Ironically, both times she is the one pining after the man. First her father, now Haroun Suleiman.

Regardless, it cannot be anybody but her. She needs to be the one who attains this valuable jewel in a world of rock hard stones.

It has to be her.

Twenty-Seven

"Then which of the favors of your Lord will you (humans and jinn) both deny?" (Qur'an 55:13)

~

"WE'RE GOING TO PAKISTAN."

Instead of glancing at Ibitoye, who made the announcement, the staff turns to their CEO, who sits at the desk with steepled fingers.

Her mind flits back to the disturbing dream that had caused her to fly awake last night. She had darted her wild eyes around and covered herself tightly with her blanket, warding off unseen threats.

She can still recall the sensations in her dream. The pressure, the force, the imaginary threat, the helplessness.

And worst of all, the unbearable anxiety she had felt when she tried to open her mouth to scream, to cry for help, but had succumbed to a terrifying helplessness that only allowed her to mumble indecipherable sounds of utter fear.

"Zoya?" Mark prompts.

She blinks and shakes her head, attempting to rid herself of the disturbing effects of her dream. The executives are all staring at her quizzically.

Bewildered by their surprise, Zoya exclaims, "What!"

"Isn't it a bit early?" Bill says.

It takes her a moment to remember the conversation at hand.

"Early? Bill Nye, we talked about this," she huffs out exasperatedly. "Why do you always make me repeat myself? It's been weeks since we announced international expansion. Zameer's second base now resides in Pakistan. I'd say our visit is rather overdue."

"Ah, right . . ." Bill trails off, a pucker between his brows.

Zoya turns her steely gaze to him and tugs at her hair, pulling loose strands out. She knows he won't dare to ask her the question burning in his throat, so she snaps, "Yes, we could have conducted our visit earlier. But we couldn't allow the media to think I'm escaping all the . . . *allegations* laid on me, now, could we? Had to clear a few things up first, as Lucas and PR advised. But we've been keeping in touch with the contractors and advertising managers based in Pakistan's site, *as we discussed* in the past few meetings. The launch party will take place in about two weeks, and our presence will be the cherry on top."

"When you say 'we,' you mean . . ." Bill trails off.

Grabbing the ends of her sequined *dupatta*, Zoya begins to fan herself, causing locks of hair to sway around her face. Despite the tension coiling inside her, she holds back a smirk at the expression on Bill's face. "A select few of us will be going. A list will be sent out later. Moving on, Sumaiya wants to propose an idea."

Venom laces her throat while she says the other woman's name.

Sumaiya clears her throat. "Hello, everyone. So, as we discussed in the previous meeting, we've scheduled for a bridal shoot before attending the launch party in Pakistan. I wanted to briefly touch on the logistics of that, as it's going to be a little different from Zameer's usual bridal shoots."

As Sumaiya speaks, Zoya watches her carefully. No matter how hard Zoya tries, she cannot hate the woman. Sameer has not been able to detect anything off-putting about her either. On top of that, she's compassionate, patient, professional, and worst of all, easily likable.

No wonder Haroun wants to marry her.

The thought flares her up inside. She huffs out an impatient breath, signaling for Sumaiya to hurry up.

At least she can still pretend to hate her.

"So the shoot will take place at Ms. Zoya's manor," Sumaiya finishes.

At this, heads snap in the CEO's direction. Zoya rolls her eyes and faces skyward.

Bill is the first to speak. "At Ms. Zoya's . . . how come?"

"This needs a homey environment. Something cozy and not over-the-top. And Ms. Zoya herself proposed that her home would be the best place to do it."

"Since you think it unnecessary to explain *why*, dear Sumaiya, let me go ahead and tell our very curious audience." Zoya sighs long and loud. "I have a classical garden behind my manor, decorated by the finest experts on the East Coast. It's gorgeous, obviously. And it's the perfect site for the shoot so as to avoid it seeming too practiced and planned. This needs to be natural."

"I don't understand. I don't think it needs to be at your manor to be natural—"

Zoya's withering glare forces Bill to lapse into silence.

Lucas perks up. "Do you think it *wise*, Zoya, for the press to discover your place of residence?"

A peal of laughter escapes her. "Sweetheart, you think the press is clueless? These people find out everything they want to know. The only reason they haven't broken into my house yet is the fear of being caught. Besides, we don't have to explicitly mention that the site of the shoot is my place of residence. If they know, they know. If they don't, they don't." Zoya shrugs lightly. Despite knowing that this is nowhere near a satisfactory explanation, she doesn't bother to continue with a better one. "Besides, I just won't sleep at night afterwards. What's new?"

Seeing her foul mood, nobody further questions her.

~

"I thought I told you to get rid of those lamps? Get them out of my sight *right this moment*."

"String those lights up over there. *Yes*, over there. Man, why are you so slow? What am I paying you for? Ugh, give that to me." An exasperated breath later, Zoya reaches up to stretch out the lights and adjust the lanterns above her.

Her staff continues to filter in, admiring their surroundings. The shoot is taking place outside, but curious, wondrous eyes can't help but pass over the modern architecture of Zoya's manor, glass windows and all. It screams extravagance, and clearly alerts to the wealth Zoya is submerged in.

In the back, apart from the classical garden is a large, luxurious pool. The edges are decorated with petals of every color. Surrounding the entire vicinity are small, twinkling lanterns catching the sun's rays.

Although frustrated at her workers, Zoya's hospitality is unstinting; gazes sweep around to the small square tables strewn around the garden, the smell of Chinese catering wafting through the air. The garden is huge, with geometric patterns weaving in and out of rows of gorgeous flowers. Flowers in every shape and every color.

"Wow. I must say, this is incredible." Bill's voice is filled with awe. Zoya glances at him for a second, grins, then returns to adjusting the lanterns.

He coughs profusely, walking away with a red tint in his cheeks.

Most of the staff has arrived, and the prop team gets to work making slight alterations to the surroundings. Half an hour later, Zoya becomes antsy and begins bouncing on her feet, searching the crowd of employees. Her gaze sweeps across the entire garden strung with garlands and lights and lanterns.

"He's not here yet."

She turns to the speaker. Sameer's face splits into a knowing grin.

"Who?"

"Haroun, of course."

Zoya narrows her eyes. "Who said I'm looking for him?"

Sameer rolls his eyes. "Your eyes say it all."

Her heart begins to beat faster. "And how, pray tell, would *you* know what my eyes say?"

"I'm no love expert, but . . ." He begins to back away slowly, hands in his pockets. "I'd be stupid if I didn't recognize the look in your eyes every time you see him." He turns and walks away before

Zoya can even open her mouth to counter him.

Hands trembling, Zoya clears her throat nervously. Is her . . . *admiration* of Haroun that obvious?

Shaking the thought as well as her growing concerns about his absence out of her head, she makes her way to the two models for the bridal photoshoot.

Sumaiya had proposed that the models be a real life married couple; she felt that this would be more *authentic*. Although Zoya hadn't pressed the matter, she knows that was probably not the main reason for this suggestion.

Zoya knows Sumaiya's *authenticity* consists of maintaining integrity and modesty, even during the shoot, and sticking to her religious values. She knows Sumaiya wants to make sure that she won't be responsible for two people gazing at each other lovingly yet unlawfully.

Sumaiya hadn't been lying when she said she wanted to bring modest ideas to the fashion industry. Unlike the many phony people Zoya had interviewed, Sumaiya had chosen a few wise words and convinced Zoya of her passion for change in the fashion industry.

Adding on to the list of reasons she needn't be despised, of course.

Zoya approaches the models for the shoot and haughtily says, "I'm assuming I need to remind you not to overdo the love act."

The male model, Salar, glances at her quizzically. "Why would we overdo it?"

"Oh, you know. Newlyweds tend to do so." There is a hint of resentment in Zoya's voice.

The female, Inaya, raises her brows and gives her a quizzical look. Probably because the very point of the shoot is to ooze newlywed love and excitement. "Don't you worry, Ms. Zoya," she says. Zoya turns around with a shake of her head as the photographing team begins preparing for the shoot.

Suddenly, Zoya's eye falls on the person who has just arrived and is standing uncertainly at the far end of the garden. Her heart beats persistently against her ribcage, remembering Sameer's words.

Haroun's eyes dart warily around. Fumbling with the collar of his shirt, he glances at his wristwatch with a pained expression on his face, sighing before making his way to his coworkers.

Zoya's eyes follow him until he reaches Farhan, who throws an affectionate arm around him and shakes him roughly. The ghost of a smile appears on his face. Farhan says something to him, something Zoya can't hear, and she automatically draws closer when Haroun lets out a resounding laugh.

Approaching them, she makes out a, "Well, look who finally made it" breathlessly. Everyone turns to look at her, and she suddenly becomes hyperaware of Sameer's eyes boring into the side of her head.

For a moment, Zoya forgets who she is and where she is. She forgets about all of her projects, her initiatives, her vengeful claims about destroying Zaki Ahmed. She forgets that she is one of the most wealthy and powerful businesspeople in America.

She forgets that she's Zoya Zameer.

And for this split moment, Zoya would be lying if she said that she isn't reveling in the pleasure of the feeling. Basking in the warmth of not being who she is.

Until her illusions are shattered by Haroun's reply of, "*Salaam,* Ms. Zoya."

"*Wa 'Alaikum Salaam.*" Pause. *Calm down, Zoya. Act normal.* "You're late?"

"Uh, yeah." He rubs the back of his neck. "Traffic."

"Mm." Zoya turns to glance at the quiet roads across from her manor. Haroun seems to be uncomfortable with his lie, but Zoya doesn't push the matter. "Alright, everyone, let's get started."

Throughout the early evening and into the twilight, the team works on the photoshoot. The lights strung around the garden coupled with the sun's rays cast various hues upon the couple with the passing of time. Zoya settles into a chair near them, a mug of tea in her hands.

While the shoot takes place, Zoya gestures around wildly and cups her hands around her mouth to yell something from time to time, pausing only to pray *'Asr* in congregation with some Muslim employees.

While praying, she is completely out of focus, continuously reminding herself to breathe and relax as she fidgets next to the women.

They wrap up after praying *Maghrib*—Zoya concocts an excuse and hurriedly finishes prayer in her room alone—and everyone begins eating and socializing. Chit chat and laughter echo across the garden, along with the occasional clink of cutlery.

A quiet smile hovers on Zoya's lips. She had quelled the initial anxiety she felt at inviting people to her home, convincing herself that these are her employees. She's known most of them for too long to become uncomfortable with the idea of them in her house.

And now, days later, when her garden is crawling with people after years of the grounds being empty, she can't help but feel strangely lighthearted.

Zoya climbs the staircase, halting in surprise when she sees Haroun and Farhan at the far end of the hallway. Haroun is whispering something frantically to Farhan, who shrugs and whispers something back. Farhan pushes open doors, peeking through doors before moving on.

Zoya's fists clench as she charges forward. Farhan's eyes widen when he sees her, and Haroun simply places a hand on his forehead.

"Can I help you?" Her voice is icy.

"Uh, sorry, Ms. Zoya. We were looking for the bathroom," Farhan croaks out, and Haroun gives his friend a bewildered look at the word "*we.*"

Zoya stabs her thumb in the direction behind her and says through gritted teeth, "It's that way. You should have just *asked* me instead of—" Her voice stops, eyes widening when she sees which door Farhan is standing in front of.

Zoya hadn't realized she had walked in this direction. Knees trembling, heartbeat hammering, she moves closer slowly. It seems as if the air has stilled, a menacing draft seeping out of the walls.

"You can go," she orders Farhan. Haroun's head raises at the tone of her voice. She sounds strangled, as though she's trying to suffocate the emotions within her chest. Zoya's barely repressed anger is clear, evident in the clenching and unclenching of her fists.

Farhan walks away with a pucker between his brows.

Closing her eyes and taking a deep breath, Zoya's voice is muffled as she says, "Haroun. Can you do me a favor, please?" She knows she is probably imagining it, but a chilly, threatening draft seems to creep out of *that* room, caressing her with dangerous memories. Memories she cannot afford to crumble under *here,* in front of *him.*

"Yes, Ms. Zoya," Haroun replies. The sound of his gentle, quiet voice begins to calm her down. She focuses on it as if it is a melody.

Zoya opens her eyes. "Close this door, please."

And just like that--without questioning anything, without a comment—Haroun's fingers wrap around the knob as he shuts the door.

Zoya releases a breath. "Thank you."

"Are you alright?" His voice is quizzical.

Zoya nods.

"I'm really sorry about that," Haroun says sheepishly. "I know we should have asked you where the bathroom was. That's what I was trying to tell Far—"

"It's fine. You can head down. I'll be with you guys in a minute."

As Haroun trudges down the stairs, Zoya reaches up to clutch her chest. Her heart aches at seeing him go.

And that's when she knows that seeing him in her house is what she has needed all along. His mere presence is like a repellent, something to ward off the evil memories threatening to drown her under. His footsteps in this house are what chase away the footsteps of her horrible memories. His calming presence is exactly why she had wanted this shoot at her house in the first place, thus why she had invited so many employees who didn't have anything to do with the photo shoot.

She hopes that his memory will appear in corners of her house whenever she's feeling exceptionally distraught by her haunting past, whenever the memories become truly unbearable.

She'll remember him here. And that will be enough.

~

When the staff is mingling and enjoying themselves under the glow of lights, Zoya traipses over to one of the prop team members. She looks a bit younger than the rest—maybe a nineteen- or twenty-year-old intern—and Zoya's gaze roams over her once before she eyes the boxes of tools by her feet. "What's your name?"

"Jadyn, ma'am." Her voice is high-pitched, like the pretentious, privileged voices of youth who've never heard the word "no."

"Jadyn, can you ask some of those workers to grab these boxes and place them near the tables?"

Jadyn's head turns to the male workers Zoya pointed to, then back to Zoya's tired face. Her eyebrows rise as she places her hands on her hips. "Are you implying that I can't carry these myself because I'm a woman?"

Zoya's eyebrows fly high; needless to say, she's astounded. This is the last thing she had expected to come out of the girl's mouth. "Excuse me?"

"That's what you want the men here for, right? Because you think I can't carry these by myself?"

A hysterical, impatient laugh bubbles out of Zoya. She raises her hand to her forehead, closes her eyes, and inhales deeply, attempting to maintain her sanity. *Why the hell did Bill hire you?*

This must be one of *those* interns. Those fresh-out-of-high-school, one-year-into-college, "I can do anything" interns.

Patience wearing thin, Zoya looks back at the girl. Then, just to vex her, just to see how she will react, Zoya says in a tight voice, "*Yes.*"

Jadyn cocks her head to the side, not backing down. She must be relatively new if she dares to be this brash with Zoya Zameer. "I mean, I know I'm no man, but that doesn't mean I can't—"

Zoya snaps. "Sweetheart, if you want to break your back in the name of this supposed feminism, then go ahead. I won't stop you." Abruptly she remembers her conversation with Raheem, when he told her he believed that she was against radical feminism.

Day by day, he continues to be proven right. Zoya stumbles upon so many instances of radical feminism that anger her, and in those moments she can't help but remember her driver's words.

By now the men, having heard the commotion, approach Zoya

and dart glances between the two. One of them says, "Zoya, ma'am, should we take these boxes over there?"

"Oh, no, no," Zoya says. Her voice has taken on a high pitch. "No, Jadyn over here will take them."

Their eyes shift to the girl in front of Zoya, who now that her challenge has been accepted, doesn't seem all too confident anymore. She eyes the boxes filled with expensive lanterns, stringed lights, and many other heavy tools, before biting down on her bottom lip nervously.

"Are you sure, Ms. Zoya?" the man says.

"Oh, yeah," Zoya nods vigorously. "Positive. Actually, why don't we call everyone here to watch her?" Before anyone can stop her and before the plea in Jadyn's eyes begins to manifest, Zoya signals for her employees to head towards her.

She gestures to Jadyn. "Our sweet employee here would like to show you guys a magic trick." The staff exchanges glances, wariness settling on their faces.

Jadyn has reached the height of embarrassment, her eyes becoming guarded and her hands beginning to tremble. After a moment of uncertain lip biting and tense silence, she grabs the first box. She stands, wobbling for a second. The man reaches out to steady her, but she shoulders the weight and trudges to the tables with all eyes on her. Some confused, some pitiful. When others reach out to help her, Zoya's withering glare causes them to halt in their tracks.

Jadyn continues to come back and forth, head bowed, with everyone's attention and Zoya's eyes trained sharply on her.

Zoya has to give her credit; the girl doesn't say a word, stubbornly carrying the boxes back and forth.

As Jadyn is finishing, Haroun approaches the crowd from a distance, shutting his phone call off. His eyebrows furrow before they incline when he witnesses the scene before him. He whispers a question to a coworker, who murmurs an explanation. Comprehension dawns on his face.

Zoya applauds, but no one follows suit. "Awesome, Jadyn. See? I knew you could do it."

Lips wavering and tears pooling in her eyes, Jadyn looks at her once before she turns around and rushes towards the end of the garden, disappearing from sight.

Zoya gives her twenty minutes before approaching her once more at her table. Jadyn's eyes are puffy and red-rimmed, cheeks tinged pink. Zoya simply raises a brow at her. "Are you happy now, Jadyn?"

Jadyn averts her gaze, looking as if she may burst into tears again when everyone sends her pitiful glances. Bill even responds with a "Come on, Ms. Zoya," but Zoya continues to batter the girl down ruthlessly.

"Let me tell you something, *Jadyn*." She spits the name out like a curse, sneering. "God has made man and woman different in many ways. Anatomically, physically, mentally, emotionally, in *many* ways. He's made us balance one another out. We're each born with our own set of strengths, capabilities, and weaknesses sometimes similar and sometimes contrary to those of the opposite gender. Just because there's something a man can do that a woman can't or vice versa, or something a man or woman can do better than the opposite gender, doesn't mean there's anything less valuable about her or him. She has her own assets, and she doesn't need to try to claim *his* assets as well in order to attain respect and self-worth. She, herself, is enough."

Jadyn averts her gaze and says nothing. Zoya leans towards Bill and says sharply, "Why the hell did you hire her?"

"She was—"

"I don't care. Fire her," Zoya states before walking away.

Some time later, Haroun approaches Zoya to bid farewell. "Thank you for your hospitality, Ms. Zoya." His voice is uncharacteristically cold. Withdrawn.

Zoya ducks her head to try to look into his eyes. "Are you angry at me?"

He gives an unconvincing shake of his head.

"Yes, you are. I can see it written all over your face."

"I'm not angry at you."

"Lying doesn't suit you."

Haroun finally lets out a defeated, frustrated sigh. "Was it necessary to do that with Jadyn?" he asks softly.

Zoya shrugs. "She wanted a chance to prove herself. So I gave it to her."

"She's young . . . you know how they can be."

"She also thinks she's invincible. I had to put it through her thick skull that life isn't as black and white as she thinks it is."

"Ms. Zoya," he says slowly, as if building caution for his next words. "You know the way you feel when somebody talks about religion?"

A shock passes through Zoya. She stares at him for a few moments, unable to fathom how he could possibly have gazed so deeply into her scarred soul. She wants to ask, "How *do* I feel?" or "What are you talking about?" But she cannot deny him. Of all people, not him. He breaks down her metal barriers and leaves her defenseless. He does not give her a chance to draw her sword, and he dismantles her before she even raises her shield.

He continues in the same soft voice. "From what I've seen, the religion *you're* familiar with makes you disgusted. And it's not your fault. I guess you weren't shown any other way." He pauses, allowing her to catch her breath. Because Zoya Zameer is breathing harshly, and her eyes are wide as his words unravel her.

"Jadyn is young. She has different perceptions and different ideologies. Her image of certain things was shown to her another way." He begins to retreat, hands in his pockets. "We have the chance to show her a different way."

Zoya wants to say something, to argue with him. She wants to say that no one in her life has ever been compassionate towards her, so why should she be compassionate towards anyone?

But as usual, Zoya's tongue ties itself into knots in front of Haroun Suleiman.

Murmuring a "*Salaam*," he turns and trudges up the path to his car. Zoya speechlessly stares after him. His figure grows smaller and smaller by the second before it is engulfed by his surroundings.

The ache returns to her chest.

"Ms. Zoya?"

She turns. "Yes, Sameer?"

His eyes twinkle mischievously. "I've arranged for cleanup. Don't worry about this, just get some rest."

Nodding, she mutters a grateful "Thank you."

When the last of the people have left, Zoya retreats upstairs. She pauses in the middle of one of the hallways, at a crossroads between her past life on her right and her present life on her left. Her head turns slightly, gazing at the corridor she hasn't stepped in for years until today. The corridor with *that* room.

The cold draft returns, slithering up her spine.

We have the chance to show her a different way.

How can Haroun possibly have gauged Zoya's past, her feelings about religion, her disgust? She never made it publicly apparent. At least, she tried not to.

He's just too observant, Zoya thinks. Quiet, gentle Haroun. Who somehow discovered Zoya's secret when no one else did.

And he was bold enough to tell her that she should not be limiting her approaches. That she should take a different approach, the way she wishes one had been used with her. That she should give people the chances she wasn't given.

Zoya shakes her head, turning her back on her past life and strolling into her room on the left.

If only she knew that all of her answers lie in taking the right path and battling her monsters head on.

Twenty-Eight

~

THE EMPLOYEES BOARD THEIR respective private jets in their assigned groups. Once inside, immediately Farhan makes a beeline for the bathroom. Zoya settles onto the lavish, button-tufted leather sofa, already feeling nauseous as she mechanically murmurs prayers under her breath.

She is vaguely aware of Haroun walking around and joking with the staff, making sure everyone—especially those who fear traveling by plane—is comfortable. He begins to approach Zoya as well.

Haroun sits across from her on another sofa, and despite knowing he only chose this spot to sit next to Farhan (who wanted to be near the window), Zoya is happy that he's there.

Leaning her head back, she closes her eyes and breathes deeply.

Zoya has always tried to wriggle her way out of traveling by plane. She either makes excuses about not liking the attitudes of the air hostesses (nonexistent) or hating the plane toilets (perfectly fine) or claims she prefers trains, buses, and cabs regardless of the amount of time they take.

In truth, however, the memories of travel always haunt her. Because they remind her of her father, and the various trips they took overseas for his job. Especially their frequent trips to Pakistan, which were one of the few times her father would animatedly speak to her, even if it was just to explain the significance of historical sites or point out important landmarks.

"Are you claustrophobic?" a quiet voice interrupts her thoughts. Zoya's eyes fly open, and Haroun gestures to her clenched fists and rapidly bouncing knee.

She sighs and looks around before replying quietly, "A bit, yes." Her cheeks color.

He shrugs. "It's nothing to be embarrassed about."

Her knuckles tighten as air hostesses flit by, preparing for taxi. Farhan still hasn't returned yet, and despite her dislike of him, thinking of him all alone in a portion of the jet elevates Zoya's nausea.

"Ms. Zoya. Just breathe. Relax," Haroun says calmly, repeating the same mantra he said to all the other staff. "Don't think about it."

She throws him a bewildered look.

He's quiet for a moment, turning his head towards the window. His eyes rove over the scene outside wondrously, even though it's nothing but runways and taxiways and open sky. Moments later, as if out of habit, he opens his mouth and begins reciting something from the Qur'an. His voice is low, soft, and so melodious. Zoya closes her eyes and listens to him.

As he recites, her fists unclench slowly, her knee halts in its bouncing, and the indent between her eyebrows smooths out.

Five minutes later, when Farhan has returned and is busy searching for a movie to watch as the plane prepares to take off, Haroun stops and glances around at everyone. His eyes fall on his boss as well, whose chest heaves up and down as she breathes deeply.

"She's asleep," he murmurs absentmindedly.

"What?" Farhan asks, clueless.

"Nothing." Haroun continues reciting the Qur'an softly.

~

When they step out of the jets, weary and spent, Zoya's heart palpitates against her rib cage. The humid, thick air of Pakistan coupled with the lights in the distance awaken a tearing feeling of nostalgia within her. An overwhelming, burdensome feeling.

She hasn't been to Pakistan since the last time she accompanied her father on one of his trips. And all of it—the plane, the memories of traveling with him, the distant but all-too-familiar lights of malls and roads—is too much. She descends the stairs and presses her face into her hands.

"You okay, Ms. Zoya?" Sumaiya presses a hand to her shoulder lightly.

Zoya shrugs her off and snaps an "I'm fine" through gritted teeth.

They travel to their assigned hotels in Karachi by limousines, calling their families to notify them of their arrival. Zoya is the only one who stares out the window silently, watching the familiar surroundings with a heavy heart.

While her roots are tied to Punjab, Zoya and her father used to visit every corner of Pakistan. Karachi was the most frequently visited, due to her father's job and it being a commercial hub.

After her divorce, Zoya used to come across little trinkets and souvenirs she got from bazaars in Pakistan. They would make her heart ache terribly, especially because the one who had bought them for her had fled after her divorce. He had been too ashamed to face her, had claimed he was wholly responsible for what happened to her.

Weeks after he fled, while Zoya was still observing her *'iddah*, she stumbled upon a dress he bought for her during one of their trips to Pakistan. When he gifted it to her, she remembered feeling like it was the most gorgeous piece of clothing she ever laid eyes on. Especially because her father had gone to the bazaar and bought it *himself*, something he seldom did without Zoya accompanying him.

Seeing the dress again, she had burst into tears, clutching the fabric to her chest.

After that, she felt that the only way she could remain connected to him was through Pakistan. She felt that the only thing which would make her father come back was if Zoya made him proud, and if she did it in a public manner.

She had always been passionate about fashion, and had been studying it in college before she was forced to drop out. After her *'iddah*, Zoya used all means necessary—conventional and unconventional, truthful and manipulative, patient and power-hungry—to establish a successful business and gain recognition. She exerted herself to the point that there were often nights blending into days, in which Zoya had done nothing but work, work, work. She ate only when her stomach growled in protest, and took breaks only to use the bathroom and pray.

At one point, she became so haggard that she stopped looking in the mirror, for fear of what she might see.

But despite the hurdles, she knew it was worth it. And she would do it all over again. Just to snip that red ribbon in front of Zameer's headquarters and smile proudly at the cameras.

Zameer. The company she named after her father. In the hopes that he would one day return to his daughter.

Zoya is hauled out of her memories from the past when the employees arrive at the hotels. Someone opens the door of her limo, and Zoya blinks up at the chauffeur. It takes her a moment to recalibrate her senses.

She steps outside and almost stumbles to the floor. The chauffeur reaches forward as if to upright her, but backs away when Zoya bares her teeth at him.

After groaning at Zoya's sharp announcement of a nine A.M. meeting, the staff disperses into their respective rooms.

Zoya doesn't sleep for a long time, standing on the balcony with her nightgown billowing behind her, staring out at the sea.

She had heard Haroun and Farhan talking about their favorite views for an ideal vacation a few days ago. Farhan had been grumbling about having unpleasant memories in the water as a child, and Haroun had been saying that if he could spend the rest of his life by the sea, he would.

So naturally, the hotels near the water had been booked. To Zoya, it seemed like a win-win. Annoying Farhan, and comforting Haroun.

Now, as she stares out at the waves lapping onto the shore under the light of the glowing moon, she knows it's definitely a win. The night breeze and the sound of the waves momentarily calms her distressed heart.

Zoya heads back inside, attempting to sleep for three hours before waking up during *Fajr* time again.

~

It is said that the early hours of the morning are the most peaceful and serene time of the entire day. Zoya stirs awake to calm waves slapping against the shore, the sound of birds slowly waking up, and the sky's hues softly changing as sunrise arrives. She heads outside after praying *Fajr* and leans against the balcony railing, staring out at the sea as the wind gently twirls her hair back and forth.

A figure by the water catches her eye. She squints and, with a start, recognizes Haroun. He stares out at the sea silently, still as a statue.

Hurriedly changing into proper clothes, Zoya makes her way out of the hotel and ushers her guard away, heading towards Haroun. She doesn't bother applying makeup to her bare face. It's just him, after all.

He sees right through her anyway.

She approaches him quietly and stands at a distance, not wanting to disturb the peaceful silence. He fidgets, his grip tightening on the shoes he's carrying.

"*Salaam*," he murmurs without looking at her.

"*Wa 'Alaikum Salaam.*"

They simply stare at the water as the morning sun's hues mirror across the rippling waves. "So peaceful," he observes quietly.

Zoya nods.

The silence between them isn't deafening and expectant, as it sometimes tends to be, pregnant with the possibility of spoken words. It's tranquil, peaceful.

"You told me once that doing humanitarian work provides you with a sense of relief and sanity," Zoya begins unsurely, voicing the question that has been plaguing her subconscious for some time now. With the image of Haroun's dark eye bags in her mind, she continues, "So . . . how come you're so restless all the time?"

He looks surprised by this observation and lowers his tired eyes to the ground beneath his feet. "It's temporary comfort. This world begs for us to worry—problems, worries, issues that never stop in this *dunya*—that's what makes us human." He smiles softly. "It's a brutal but effective reminder that we'll seldom be at complete ease in this life. But our struggles and our efforts won't be overlooked. That's what gives life balance, right? Allah says that with every difficulty, there's ease." He quiets for a moment. "Besides, if the journey of this world was easy, patience would never be one of the doors to paradise." Pause. "And for me, doing this work fulfills a sense of purpose that no other thing in my life can."

She remains quiet, not knowing how to reply to that. Moments later, a thought occurs to her. "What is one thing you want most in this life?"

"*Hidaya.*"

Zoya inclines her brows. *Guidance.*

"*Hidaya?*" she repeats. Haroun nods. Zoya gives him a once over—from his lowered gaze to his clasped hands and dignified demeanor—and a corner of her lips turns up. "I think you've been granted that already."

Shock flits across his face as he shakes his head firmly. "I'm human. I can never say for certain that I've been granted *hidaya*. It's not a one-time lesson or a single experience. It's a combination of lessons, an entire experience. Something lifelong, something you're always trying to obtain." He rubs his forehead. "Something you have to keep praying for every day."

"How do you know you don't own it already?"

A soft smile blooms on his face, causing Zoya's breath to halt. "There are so many things that we can own in this world, wealth being one of the largest and probably most wanted of these things. But there's one wealth that no one can ever truly own, and that's *hidaya*. Because it doesn't come from anyone but Allah, and He grants it to whom He pleases, whenever He pleases."

Haroun shakes his head, running a hand through his hair. "No human can grant it, and no human can ever be completely sure they have it, which is why it's something that constantly needs to be prayed for." There is a twinkle in his eyes. "It's . . . the light at the end of the tunnel, the breath of fresh air to the drowning man, the only comfort to the agonized soul."

Zoya cocks her head to the side, observing him brazenly. His eyes flit from the rising sun to the crashing waves in the distance, as if taking in the vastness of it all.

"What is one thing *you* want most in this life?" Haroun asks quietly.

Zoya is shocked by him throwing her question back at her, rendering her speechless yet again. How can he know that she doesn't already own everything she wants? She successfully leads one of the fastest growing businesses in America, has an insanely high net worth, owns one of the largest manors on the East Coast. Money is her right hand; wealth pools at her doorstep. Her success continues to skyrocket, and her face flits across virtually every major news channel and magazine.

And all of this is only increasing.

Yet Haroun Suleiman seems to have known what no other person in this world has known about her—that she always craves more. That she is never satisfied. That running after all the wealth and success in the world is actually a cover for what she is truly chasing.

"Contentment," she whispers.

Haroun continues to stare at the sky as he says, "'*And your Lord is going to give you, and you will be satisfied.*'"

Zoya gazes at him, knowing the tender look in his eyes can only mean that this is a verse of the Qur'an.

"Through sun, rain, snow, or whatever situation it may be, everything happens for a reason. Anything you may be experiencing is in Allah's *hikmah,* or ultimate wisdom." He looks down and drags a finger across his wristwatch absentmindedly. "Personally, I find peace in knowing this, because everything Allah has planned for me is a thousand times better than what I think I want. How can I not find peace in trusting Him?" He pauses, chuckles softly. "His love and mercy for his creation are immeasurable and infinite."

Zoya stares out at the water, listening to Haroun with strict intensity.

"Whatever trials you're suffering through, whatever weight you feel like you're crushing under, everything will pass with Allah's plan. There's a verse in the Qur'an that says, '*Your Lord did not abandon you, nor did He forget.*'" Haroun turns to her, keeping his gaze lowered. "So even if the world seems to be crashing down onto your unsuspecting shoulders, or contrarily your life is going exactly the way you want it to, know that both scenarios are out of His ultimate wisdom. And sometimes we're far too human to understand that."

Zoya remembers these last words, the ones he had spoken at the Desi World Fashion Show, seemingly ages ago. The ones that had rendered her powerless for the first time in a while. The ones that had made her drop her sword weakly and attempt to shield herself halfheartedly. Hearing them again elicits almost the same reaction. Her guards have fallen, her façade is wearing thin, and Zoya Zameer is *tired*.

Tired of carrying the burden of her haunting past, tired of being Zoya Zameer, tired of having no one to depend on, no one to trust.

Haroun shakes her out of her stupor by bending down to put on his shoes. He turns to leave but pauses for a moment. "I pray that Allah grants you the contentment you're trying to find." And with that, he trudges back up the beach.

Leaving Zoya more speechless than ever.

~

After their morning meeting, during which Zoya averts her gaze and avoids Haroun's presence instead of the other way around, the staff mingles in the hotel's lobby, eating breakfast together.

Zoya sighs loudly. Sameer raises an eyebrow at her. "What's with you today, Ms. Zoya? You've been avoiding him like the plague."

Her gaze snaps towards Sameer. "Avoiding who?"

"You and I both know who we're talking about."

"I'm not ignoring him," she scoffs. Sameer inclines his brows at her stiff posture, at her back turned to Haroun. "Oh, shut up." She gestures to the expression on his face. "Stop that—this—whatever you're doing!"

"Okay," he says in a voice that means it's not okay at all and he's only dropping the topic due to her discomfort. "Would you like a bagel?" He offers one to her.

She shakes her head.

He throws a hand up as if coming to a realization. "Ah, of course. Haroun doesn't eat bagels either." He begins to place it back in the tray when Zoya snatches it from his hand and takes a large bite out of it.

"I do not choose my food preferences based on somebody else's." She rolls her eyes while Sameer simply smirks at her. "Wipe that smile off your face, Sameer, or you'll get a letter in your email pretty soon. And it won't be a promotion."

He immediately stops smiling but clamps his lips together, eyes twinkling mischievously.

Zoya sighs, continuing to chew the bagel.

How can she admit that her conversation with Haroun has been plaguing her heart and fracturing her carefully built composure? How can she say that she, *Zoya Zameer*, is *embarrassed* that Haroun has witnessed her vulnerability? That he knows all of this—the business, the success, the wealth—is a façade?

And worst of all, how can she explain that Haroun committing himself to someone else in marriage is just about the deepest sorrow she has felt in her life since her father left?

"Besides," Zoya mutters as she turns to Sameer. "He's getting married. Stop trying to break up his marriage." She rushes to continue when Sameer triumphantly smiles at her. "I mean, it's unfair towards his to-be wife to constantly tease me about him." Although she doesn't care about this reason in the slightest, she doesn't reveal that to Sameer.

Sameer shrugs. "They're not married yet, they're just *engaged*. Haven't you seen them? They don't even spend time with each other outside of work because they stick to their religious limits. They met, talked, involved their families, and made a commitment. But they're not *married* yet." He pauses, scrunches his brows. "Although I *did* hear that since they're in Pakistan right now and so are her parents, they may tie the knot here." He waggles his eyebrows at her.

Zoya stops mid-chew. "What?"

He nods vigorously, applying cream cheese to his bagel. Zoya darts a glance behind her at Haroun and Farhan, who are immersed in conversation on one side of the room while Sumaiya and Ibitoye are on the other.

She turns back to Sameer, eyes widening.

They figured, why not?" Sameer says. "The only reason they were waiting is because her parents were in Pakistan. And now *we're* in Pakistan."

Zoya's heart begins to beat frantically. "But—but Haroun's mom? And his sisters?"

Sameer shrugs lightly, pouring coffee into a cup. "Maybe they couldn't make it. And instead of delaying it any longer—"

"Please tell me this is some stupid joke of yours," Zoya whispers anxiously, leaning forward.

Sameer takes one look at the expression on her face and bursts out laughing, placing his drink on the table and clutching his stomach as he shakes with mirth. Zoya turns to see her staff staring at them, and her cheeks color when Haroun's gaze flits to the two of them. Turning back to Sameer, she hisses, "You *idiot!*"

He pretends to wipe a tear from his eye as his laughing fit dies down. "You should have seen the look on your face. All of my theories have been one hundred percent confirmed."

"I will bury you in the ground, Sameer Mirza, I will," Zoya threatens. Sameer chuckles, unaffected by her anger. "Disappear from my sight before I do something, and you regret ever opening your unfortunate mouth," she seethes.

Sameer holds his hands up. "Okay, okay. No need to be so feisty." He grabs his breakfast and starts walking away before he turns to her with a much more grave expression on his face. "But I'm serious, Ms. Zoya. You're losing your chance. You don't wanna regret this for the rest of your life."

He turns away, and Zoya stands with her fists balled, glaring at his retreating back. Although she is angry at him for teasing her, she is even angrier at him for his suggestion. He is blatantly telling her to break someone's marriage up, and even though the thought has crossed her mind multiple times since she found out about the engagement, it's still jarring to hear someone else say it aloud.

She has not yet had the courage to do something about this thought.

However, she is Zoya Zameer.

Whatever she wants, she makes it happen.

~

Two days later, Zoya bites her lip and gazes off at the sea, expression full of angst. From her balcony, she can hear the waves riding softly over one another, and the sound provides some comfort.

She takes a deep breath and clicks her pen.

Dear Papa,

I'm in Pakistan. I can smell chai everywhere, hear the distant honks of the city, see the crowded bustling of the streets far away.

All I can think of is you.

You are in every crevice, every nook, and every cranny of this place. I can smell that perfume you always wore. It had such a strong smell, even from afar, because I know you didn't like when I got too close to hug you. I feel like I can see you talking agitatedly to some rickshaw driver, negotiating with the man at the bazaar, clenching your jaw at the men leering at me.

I know you weren't very fond of me, but you had it in you to want to protect me from their unlawful gazes. It was one of the few times I felt like you might be able to love me.

I ate a bagel today, and it reminded me of the way you would scrunch your nose whenever we were served bagels. You would push them to the side and eat everything else on the plate, and I would watch you with my childlike eyes, wondering how anyone could hate bagels.

But I loved you. So I wanted to do something that might have brought you a little closer to me. That would finally, finally make you proud of me. That would erase the anguish and the repressed anger in your eyes every time you looked at me. So I too shoved my bagel to the side and ate everything else.

You simply looked at my plate and wiped your face with a napkin.

I faintly remember your thin beard. The way you rubbed the napkin over it after you ate. I'm scared I will forget the way you look. Because every time I close my eyes to imagine you, a small part of you fades away every day. It has been too long since I've seen you, and you intentionally tried to leave nothing behind for me to remember you by.

You are somewhere on this broad expanse of earth. And the thought makes my heart somersault with dangerous hope. Maybe you are somewhere close, maybe you are somewhere far. You're hiding from me, too ashamed to show me your face.

The last time I was in Pakistan was with you, when we were visiting the Northern areas for your business trip. And I have never wanted to set foot in this damn country again after you left. Because I'm afraid my conflicted heart has become much too frail to handle this. To handle being here without you.

Yet coming here has been bittersweet in every way. I am able to remember you a little more.

Even if it breaks me inside.

Papa, I forgive you. It was not your fault. My failed marriage was not your fault. Jo ho gaya, so ho gaya. But I need you. Please come back to me.

Haven't you guessed yet that I hold no grudges against you? That even when I have become one of the most successful people in the business world, who have I named my business after?

I hope that somewhere out there, you see Zameer and you're proud of me.

And I will let that thought comfort me in your absence.

Your daughter,

Zoya

Zoya's eyes roam over the words once, a tear trailing down her cheek. With trembling fingers, she ignites a match and holds it close to the paper.

"I love you," she whispers.

The paper alights and the flame begins to spread slowly across it, charring the surface. Erasing the words and traces of Zoya's vulnerability from the page.

Forever.

Twenty-Nine

"And I did not create the jinn and mankind except to worship Me."
(Qur'an 51:56)

~

"WHAT IS THE PURPOSE of our existence?" Farhan mulls.

Zoya slaps her palm over her face. "Please, Goldilocks, not right now."

He stiffens when she responds, as he tends to do every time Zoya speaks to him now—stiffen and become reserved.

Zoya's eyes flick to Haroun as he observes his friend's clenched fists and set jaw. And Haroun, ever the Good Samaritan, jumps into the conversation. "In what aspect, do you mean?"

"In *every* aspect," Farhan says exasperatedly.

Haroun turns to him. "There is a simple answer to your question, but this might be a long conversation."

"Go ahead."

Haroun opens his mouth, but Zoya's breath begins to race. He cannot speak here, not now. Otherwise he will once again manage to instill in Zoya that helpless feeling that she is becoming increasingly familiar with around him. And feeling powerless while attending an important milestone in her career is *not* what she had envisioned.

"I'll tell you what the purpose of *your* existence is, Goldilocks," Zoya interrupts before Haroun can say a word.

Farhan turns to her slightly, but stares at the window behind her head rather than at her.

"To not piss anyone off. Can you manage that, sweetie?" She leans forward, batting her eyelashes at him deliberately.

Farhan's jaw tightens. Haroun's eyes dart between the two of them. He opens his mouth, but Zoya cuts him off once more, "I'll take that as a yes."

The limousine stops in front of the hotel and the staff heads inside, greeting people and flashing smiles. Zoya is invited to speak on behalf of Zameer during the launch party, and she holds the attention of every single pair of eyes in the room—except for one—as she speaks.

Haroun trails over to the beverage tables and fixes his gaze on the lavish assortment of coffee and tea machines. The company label for the beverages reads, "*Quench with a purpose.*"

He cocks his head to the side and scrutinizes the label, sighing.

He has been waiting to hear the fundamental question of existence from Farhan's mouth for a while now, seeing how his friend struggles with finding meaning in his life. And he has tried his very best to prepare an appropriate and guided answer for him, yet his tongue seems to have rolled in upon itself, making it difficult for him to voice what he wants to say.

At the stage, the Q&A session has begun, and various questions are asked from all around the hall. Questions like, "*Who has been your greatest support?*" to which Zoya replies with a "*Myself, of course. And my employees.*" She continues to rave about her accomplishments, her successes, her journey to this lofty and conspicuous position. Her words heavily imply that without status, wealth, and power, man is nothing.

Haroun listens to her halfheartedly, unable to gauge whether he believes her political words or not. How can she say all of these things on stage after she's hinted to him that it's all a façade, that she has not yet found what she's seeking?

Or has he misread her?

He shakes his head. His perplexed thoughts bounce between his boss and Farhan, both of whom seem to be fighting the same battle, but on different grounds. Farhan's issue is not about belief, but about the way belief has been handled with him. Yet the CEO's issue is deeper, more far-rooted. It isn't simply an issue with the way faith has been shown to her, but an issue with faith itself.

Haroun paces around the beverage table, deep in thought.

Farhan has not been given the chance to love religion. He believes that all the Muslims he's met are cookie cutter representations of Islam. He believes some lines of reasoning to be faulty, has been burdened by rulings and regulations. Before he was taught to love Allah, he was taught to fear Him.

Applause follows Zoya's speech, breaking Haroun out of his stupor, and he turns to see his boss descending the stairs of the stage. Her eyes search the crowd quickly, roving over faces before she catches his gaze and a warm smile touches her lips. She begins to approach him.

Haroun turns away, rubbing his temples with the thumb and forefinger of his right hand.

And then there is Zoya Zameer. His boss. Who seems to want to rain debris on everyone she sees except for him. Who firmly believes in his supposed goodness, is blinded by her insistence to trust him. He cannot understand why she is so adamant about believing the virtue she apparently sees in him. It places him on an unrealistically high pedestal, causing him to double check his every action.

When he joined the company, Haroun quickly became aware of his boss' eyes following him everywhere, became acutely conscious of the way she spoke to others about him and the way she began looking up to him. Even while brushing off Farhan's claims about her change in attitude towards him, deep down he could not ignore what was so plainly obvious. It became unbearable, really, when Haroun knew how badly he was struggling with trying to maintain his faith in the midst of the challenging environment he was in.

Now, not only is he battling with keeping a firm hold on his faith given the circumstances, but he's also struggling to uphold strong character.

From the get go, Haroun managed to gauge that Zoya Zameer never had the chance to experience goodness in her life. And for some reason, she sees it in *him*. And if Haroun can become someone's source of strength, if he can become someone's reason to want to believe in Allah's mercy again, is that not something for which he will be rewarded? Is it not something for which he desperately seeks his Lord's pleasure, something that gives him a sense of purpose in life?

To be someone's anchor to Islam?

Haroun's mind wars with itself. With what he has observed, he has become a point of constancy in his boss' life, like the North Star to the early navigators. And his consistent attempts to please his Lord through helping her may cause her attachment towards him to grow, and he cannot risk hurting any human being in this way.

Has he led her on in any way, or has he simply attempted to guide her? Has anything he said to her been needless and caused an unnecessarily personal attachment?

Is it not his responsibility to attempt to lighten someone's burden?

Should he withdraw and risk a wounded heart? Will she stop trying to understand and love religion? Just how much of an effect do his efforts have on her?

And if he should not withdraw, then is he causing her to hang onto him expectedly? Is anything about his demeanor or his character unintentionally leading her on to believe in something that isn't there?

Haroun sighs deeply, head pounding as the reality of his exponential situation hits him fiercely.

"Migraine?"

He turns at the sound of her voice. Zoya smiles at him and he looks back at the coffee labels, shaking his head.

"Not your scene, right?" she says.

He shakes his head again.

"Do you want to get some fresh air?"

"It's alright, Ms. Zoya. I'm okay. Thank you for your concern," he says politely before taking a few steps back and disappearing into the crowd. His mind is a mess of swirling thoughts, threatening to drown him under the tide of fear and concern.

Zoya is left behind him, looking crestfallen.

~

Farhan sets his chin in his hand.

"I think . . ." He struggles with words. "I think I understand."

"Are you sure?" Haroun says, voice far from exasperated even after conversing with Farhan for over an hour.

His friend nods slowly. "It'll take some time to fully settle in, but . . . I think I get it."

Haroun leans back and uncaps his water bottle, taking three sips after whispering a *Bismillah*. Farhan observes him carefully.

"I think what really hit me . . ." Farhan steeples his fingers, staring thoughtfully at the night sky. "Is that your *trust* in God is what essentially determines your relationship with Him. The stronger it is, the easier you are able to navigate through life, since you have that to rely on. Like a point of constancy," he rehashes carefully. Haroun simply remains quiet, allowing his friend to sort out his existential crisis.

Farhan turns to him after a while. "You know, I've never been allowed to question religion."

Haroun sighs. "Ironically, I think that's one reason so many people lose faith. Either they don't receive proper answers to their genuine questions, or they've been told that questioning is blasphemous."

Farhan nods thoughtfully.

"You know, having genuine doubts is okay. Having genuine questions is okay. That doesn't make you any less of a believer; it just means that you want to be able to comprehend things better in order to strengthen your faith. Your trust in your Lord doesn't mean that you always understand everything He decrees, but it's more that you're willing to let go of things you may not fully understand *because* you trust in His wisdom and trust that He's planned everything in perfect order for you. And you trust that sometimes, our humanity limits us from understanding God's wisdom and His decisions."

"Trust," Farhan drags the word out slowly. Then he shakes his head with a snort. "It surprises me that it's as simple as trust. Everybody always says *'Read the Qur'an and you'll feel better! Pray and you'll feel better! Make this du'a and do this and that and you'll feel better!'* Well, does feeling better just come from mechanically doing things that I'm not even putting my heart into?"

Haroun tilts his head to the side, contemplative. He shakes his head and says carefully, "No, I think knowing why you're doing what you're doing for your Lord increases your trust in Him. Our religion doesn't tell us not to be discontent and sad—that's human nature—but you can't *force* contentment onto someone by handing them religious books and calling it a day. The relationship of love and trust in God is more important than anything. Then yes, making *du'a*, reading Qur'an, and praying *will* undoubtedly bring you peace. And these acts of worship are also catalysts to developing a better connection with God.

"A lot of times when we're young, we're taught to mechanically worship. We aren't taught the feelings associated with worship. The love, the compassion, the beauty, and most importantly, the *peace*. As kids, the way we're sometimes taught to worship is with anger, punishments, and scoldings, which builds a resentment for the message being taught." Farhan nods vigorously at Haroun's words. "The message isn't the issue; the way we're taught is the issue."

Farhan's eyes are filled with silent wonder and anguish. He brings a hand up to cover his face. "*Yaar,* this is all so much. I've been in the dark for too long."

"It's okay," Haroun says gently. "Darkness eventually yields to light; night eventually becomes day. It's a process, not a single moment."

Both friends sit quietly in front of each other, gazing up at the sky sprinkled with stars. Though their own thoughts threaten to overwhelm them, they both recognize that even the night sky's darkness is scattered with glowing stars.

A sign that hope is never lost.

As Farhan sits by the friend that has changed his life, he begins to understand that as long as he trusts God, darkness will always lead to light.

~

Zoya paces around in her room, absently yanking at strands of her hair. She weaves them around her fingers like yarn, then throws the circles of hair in the trash can. Clutching her head, she mumbles, "Why did stupid Goldilocks have to open his mouth about the purpose of our existence and all that? *Nikamma aadmi.* Seriously, *is ne kabhi zindagi me koi acha decision liya bhi hai ya nahi?*"

She doesn't want to admit it, but her subconscious continues to prod her with the obvious answer to her distress—she is dying with the curiosity of what Haroun could have possibly said to Farhan. What answer could he have had to this question? What does he know that Zoya doesn't?

More importantly, why does it matter to her what the answer was?

"No, no, no," Zoya mutters, shaking her head. "I don't care. I don't care what his answer was." She settles down in a chair and opens her laptop, typing gibberish into the search box.

Irritably, she slams the laptop lid back down and shoots up, knocking her chair to the floor. Her lips tremble, her hands shake. *Why does it matter what the answer to that question was?* a voice taunts Zoya again in the back of her mind. *Aren't you fulfilling the purpose of your existence?*

She freezes in her tracks. *Am I?* another voice, loud and clear, whispers in her head. *Am I fulfilling the purpose of my existence?*

She mulls over the thought, freezing in the middle of the room. Slowly, she takes a deep breath and allows herself to be honest. Allows her thoughts, those that have been desperately repressed by a mental dam, come flooding out to haunt her.

Zoya settles down on the bed, eyes lingering on her launch party dress still lying on the couch. Her gaze shifts to the suitcases she packed, which are bursting with folded heaps of fabric and expensive jewelry. Then to the files tucked in another suitcase, pages upon pages of catalogs and statistics and designs and plans.

Climbing the corporate ladder has never seemed like a daunting job to Zoya Zameer. But . . . lately, she feels that she's been doing everything that she has for no meaningful reason, especially after her talk with a certain employee by the beach. She works hard day and night, weekday and weekend, to make a name, to earn respect. For what? For being the CEO of a company and leading employees who design and market . . . clothes?

The voice inside her head begins to whisper tauntingly once again. *Imagine growing up with people telling you that you have the ability to change the world, whether it be in micro amounts to fully blown out game-changers, and you wake up and go to school to learn how to expand a business that designs . . . clothes?*

"But clothes are a necessity," Zoya whispers weakly.

Her mind continues to tease her. *The types of clothes my company produces are far from a necessity. Nobody in the world is going to die without designer bridal and fashion wear. People can get by with far simpler clothes.*

Is this what the purpose of my life is? she thinks to herself suddenly. Zoya has never been a religious person, and if she ever had the potential to be, the scum from her past took that opportunity and desire away completely. But for a moment, she thinks of all the things Haroun has said that have left her baffled. Which is basically almost everything he utters. She ponders whether her existence is supposed to have a higher meaning, a greater purpose.

Surely she couldn't have been born, grown up, and raised simply to build a career concerning *clothes*, to become one of the most notorious businesswomen in North America? Or to make as much money as she makes? Or to be known by others?

And *feared* by others.

Surely, her life had been written with a greater purpose? Will she continue on this way? Going to work every day, yelling at employees, firing some from time to time, working tirelessly with designs and files, arguing with her directors, dodging her rival's plans to uproot her, reviewing statistics and experiencing temporary happiness at her success, discussing news about herself in the media and ways to cover it up and overcome the next steep climb, the next rude headline on a tabloid—is this her life?

Is this the reason she had been created, the reason she had been fashioned from a single blood clot, given life, given the ability to stay in a protected vessel before she met the world? The reason her mother carried Zoya in her womb for nine months and birthed her, the reason her mother had experienced the excruciating agony and pain of labor, the reason she had died because of it? Is this the reason? So that she can live a life constantly plagued by the bad eyes of others, suffer the risks of being a notorious figure in the corporate world, and deal with the repercussions of her every action? And then?

Then what?

She'll continue to run her business, she'll grow old, and for the rest of her life she'll live alone in her million dollar manor with its endless rooms and silver-studded couches and gold-plated decorations. Living the epitome of the life everyone wants, yet never attaining the happiness she so desperately seeks.

Zoya blinks with a start.

Never attaining the happiness she seeks.

What will happen then? What will happen after she grows old and retires one day, if she lives that long? She'll spend the rest of her days wasting away in her manor. All alone. Being given the torturous element of time so that she can be brutally forced back into her hollow memories every day. Depending on others to lift her up, take her to the bathroom, take showers, eat food, just to crawl back into bed again. Having no one to give love and affection to, having all the time in the world to think about the parents she had hardly ever known, the husband she had made the mistake of marrying. And then dying off, being buried six feet under and leaving behind . . .

Leaving behind what?

Leaving behind a manor that costs more than anyone can afford, and a business that makes no meaningful difference in the first place?

No, Zoya thinks with a shake of her head. This can't be it. This can't be all.

Right?

She grabs her purse and shoves her shoes on, preparing to head to Haroun's hotel. Outside her room, her two guards are asleep. The sight momentarily distracts Zoya. It takes all of her willpower not to chuckle at the scene, especially when she thinks of how furious Sameer will be when he discovers this.

Zoya quietly shuts her door and swiftly sneaks past the guards, refocusing on the matter at hand.

She needs to talk to Haroun. She needs to know what the purpose of her life is. She needs to know. Because how can *he* know but she doesn't know?

Are people chosen to know?

With a wildness so overwhelming that it practically blinds her, Zoya leaves her hotel and rushes across the street, crossing two blocks and making a turn before dashing towards the hotel looming into view, where half of her staff is staying. Karachi is still very much alive, with people—mostly men—milling about, laughter echoing, smoke from cigarettes curling up into the air, clusters of them huddled around something with sinister chuckles escaping them. The kind of chuckles that make people's skin crawl, especially women.

Zoya hardly notices any of these things. Not even the dark night sky that usually causes her to tremble, since bright lights and vibrant colors still make the city around her seem very much alive.

Zoya flies into the other hotel, and the receptionist eyes her flustered appearance with a raised brow. "Can you tell me which room Haroun Suleiman is checked into?" Zoya says breathlessly. In her haste, she left the list of employees and their rooms back in her hotel. And the only other person who has the digital document is Sameer, whose triumphant smile she doesn't want to see when he finds out who she's visiting.

"Ma'am, that's confidential."

Zoya points to herself with barely repressed fury. "*Hello*. I'm Zoya Zameer, and I don't have time for your BS. That's my employee. I'm his boss. I need to speak with him."

The receptionist's brows only rise further at Zoya's words. Zoya wants to slap the stupid smirk off her face. How vile for her to think anything even remotely wrong or dirty in relation to Haroun Suleiman!

Zoya pulls out her business card and shoves it under the receptionist's nose. "Zoya. Zameer."

"I know who you are," the receptionist says, a corner of her lips turning up. Zoya experiences a moment of blinding rage at the woman's insinuations about her supposed reputation.

But this rage is trumped by another feeling. The overpowering desire to know. The craving to fulfill the emptiness within her, to have all her questions answered.

The receptionist makes a few clicks on her computer. "He's in room B141, ma'am."

Zoya slaps the counter, making a mental note to rid this receptionist of her job by morning. She rushes into the elevator, hastily pressing the buttons to make her way up.

Once, when her ex-husband would drag her to gatherings, she heard a lecture that actually caught her attention. The speaker was saying that when a person embarks on the path of knowledge, Allah makes it easy for them. He automatically takes down barriers, clears paths, opens doors, and catalyzes their journey. That isn't to say that there aren't thorns of hardship in between, but even roses have thorns.

Zoya Zameer has never believed more than now that her path to knowledge is being cleared by Allah. In the streets of Karachi, no matter how established or industrial the area, she—a strikingly beautiful woman—had rushed out of a hotel and ran two blocks away to another. It was an extremely dangerous situation in and of itself, yet Allah had protected her. Allah had guided her along, and His omnipresence that she is suddenly aware of begins to scare as well as exhilarate her.

The elevator doors ding and slide open, and Zoya rushes to B141 and stops in front of it, taking a deep breath. She rings the doorbell, then knocks on the door repeatedly before finally stopping. She paces impatiently in front of the door, wringing her hands and muttering, "The purpose of my existence" under her breath. When a few seconds pass and still the door hasn't opened, she raises her hand to knock again. And again. She's raising her hand one last time when the door finally opens, and there stands none other than Haroun Suleiman. He's halfway through pulling on a robe haphazardly and he squints, eyes thick with sleep.

"Ms. Zoya?" he says tiredly, rubbing his eyes, voice colored with surprise.

Was he expecting someone else?

Don't be stupid, Zoya. This is Haroun *you're talking about.*

Her breath catches in her throat. "Haroun. Were you sleeping?"

After a brief silence, he nods, expression indicating that this is obvious information.

"I need to talk to you." Zoya's voice is urgent.

Haroun is still rubbing his eyes when something occurs to him. He glances around them, looking behind Zoya into the hotel hallway. "Did you come here alone?"

"Yes."

He glances at his watch before his head snaps up and he stares at her with a look of horror. "Ms. Zoya, it's one A.M."

"I know. I'm sorry. But I really needed to talk to you—"

"Do you know how dangerous it is for you to come here alone at this time?" All traces of sleep are gone from his voice, and his eyes are wide with alarm. Zoya realizes he never interrupts her. Or anyone, for that matter. He must be really upset or concerned about her showing up at this time for him to interrupt her. He must be really worried about her safety.

A warm feeling spreads throughout her chest.

"It's fine, no one harassed me or anything," she says quickly, shrugging off his concerns.

"You could have called me, Ms. Zoya. We could have met in your lobby," he argues exasperatedly. "It's not safe."

"Haroun, I'm telling you it's fine." Zoya sighs. "Can we talk, please?"

"Where's your security?"

"I sneaked past them. Now *please*. I need to talk to you."

Haroun gives her a baffled look before rubbing his eyes again. "Okay." Stepping inside for a second to splash water over his face, he grabs his hotel key card from the foyer table, shoves his phone into his pocket, and tightens his robe around himself before stepping out.

"Oh," Zoya belatedly realizes that he would rather come outside than invite her in. Of course he would; he's Haroun Suleiman. The insinuations, the implications of that, even with him being the pure person that he is, would taint Zoya's image as well. Just like the receptionist had thought. And that's something neither he nor her would want.

After the past couple of years in the business world, Zoya is unused to this respect and decorum. Any other man would shamelessly step aside for her to enter the hotel room, but Haroun has once again reminded her that dignified people still exist.

She can't help the smile that blooms on her face.

"Shall we go to the lobby?" Haroun asks, breaking Zoya out of her thoughts. She nods and rushes ahead of him to the couches. She sits down and waits for him to catch up, and he takes the seat across from her, at a safe distance. At a distance where Zoya can finally breathe without her throat choking up just looking at him.

"Is everything alright?" His voice is laced with concern. Zoya can't help but eye him brazenly. Somehow, his disheveled appearance is even more attractive than his clean, put together one.

It reminds her that he is human, just like her.

She dismisses any thoughts of his attractiveness by reminding herself that he's *engaged* and nods. "Yes, yes, everything's fine. I just—" She takes a deep breath. "You told me that you do humanitarian work because it makes you feel like you're fulfilling the purpose of your existence, right?" He looks perplexed at this sudden, unexpected question, but nods all the same. "Well, what is it?"

"What is what?"

"The purpose of your existence."

Haroun's mouth opens and closes in surprise. He probably hadn't been expecting a heart to heart conversation with his CEO at one in the morning, but he seems to catch up quickly. "The purpose of *my* existence, Ms. Zoya, or simply the purpose of existence?" He speaks as though he has been waiting for this, as if he always knew that sooner or later, she would approach him with this question.

Zoya wrings her hands. She stares outside the window next to them, overlooking the central lobby. A quiet breeze lifts a strand of her hair, and she realizes with a start that it's not a window at all; it's a balcony overlooking the lobby. Upon closer examination, she sees right through what she had supposed was glass before.

She wishes Haroun could see right through her so she would not have to go through the arduous task of explaining her dilemma to him. "What is the purpose of existence?"

"To worship God," Haroun says simply.

Zoya twists her bangle around her wrist, taken aback by his brief and simple answer. "I mean, how do you know that that's your purpose? How do you know that you're fulfilling a part of your purpose by doing this humanitarian work?"

"Because I feel peace when I'm there. *Sukoon.*"

She starts at his use of the word. "How do you know that it's peace?" Her voice is an almost imperceptible whisper.

"Because no matter how tiring or excruciatingly stressful the work can be sometimes, it's one of the most fulfilling things I've ever experienced. No matter how much it exhausts me, I still wake up every day feeling so blessed that it's a part of my life. That if Allah wills, I, as the insignificant human that I am, am able to take a small part in trying to make this world a better place."

Zoya stares at him, dumbfounded. He sits calmly in the chair opposite her, unaware of the effect of his words on her. "So fulfillment means peace, which means purpose?"

Haroun shrugs lightly. "There's no dictionary definition. But if there's something that gives you comfort from the hurdles of this world, that is your peace, granted to you by Allah. The kind that brings you closer to Him. And you'll know it when you feel it." He pauses, then carefully says, "You have to find your peace, Ms. Zoya. Open up to your Lord."

She looks up at him in surprise, déjà vu from the day at the beach striking her. "How do you know that I haven't found my peace?"

He eyes her wringing hands, the restless tapping of her feet. She becomes acutely aware of her actions under his scrutiny and quickly stops. Only Haroun has this effect on her—unraveling her without her even noticing.

"Ms. Zoya, have you ever felt like doing this work, spending all day at this job, coming back home, going to sleep, and then doing it all over again has given you peace? Have you ever felt that it was what you were made to do?"

He can see right through me. Zoya flushes. She feels as if his eyes are piercing through her soul, unleashing years of doubt and questions she has tried so hard to cage. Suddenly, her wish for him to see through her, for herself to become transparent, unsettles her.

"You don't need to answer me," he says quietly. "That's for you to think about."

Zoya looks up at him. "I . . ." *Stop stuttering, Zoya Zameer!* "I don't know what to tell you."

Haroun fists his hand and places it under his chin, staring at the glossy marble floors.

Zoya places her hands over her face, but catches a glimpse of him through her fingers. "Do you think . . . do you think that I'm a bad person? A coward?"

Surprise flickers across his face. "Why would I think that about you, Ms. Zoya?"

"Because you know . . ." *You know who I really am.* "You know what I really feel, and you see me still leading this business and doing this work and . . ."

His eyebrows furrow. "Everyone is fighting their battles. I can't assume who you are, Ms. Zoya, and your life isn't my business. But I can assure you that you're far from a bad person. You took the risk of leaving your hotel at this time of night to seek something beneficial to you, and I would hardly call that an act of cowardice."

"Yes, I am," she mutters, ignoring his words. "I'm a coward. I'm too far in and I can't let go. I-I should be . . ." She pauses suddenly, raising her head to see Haroun watching her expectantly. He quickly shifts his gaze away from hers.

What is she doing? She's *Zoya Zameer,* so why is she displaying her vulnerabilities so openly? Why is she allowing him to loosen her tongue, to unlock the cages she has spent too much time oiling shut? Had she not vowed never to become the same woman she once was: vulnerable and helpless? So what about him is causing her to slowly let down her guarded walls?

When Zoya is in Haroun's presence, a part of her past self returns to her. And she cannot afford to be that woman again. She cannot afford to be weak and helpless again.

"I should get going." Zoya grabs her handbag and stands.

Haroun looks startled, but he doesn't question her as he follows suit. "Is everything okay?"

"Yes."

He hesitates, seeming to war with himself, before he says, "I'll drop you off to your room."

She shakes her head, but he's already making his way to the elevator. After ten seconds of uncomfortable silence, the doors slide open, and the two head to the exit.

The receptionist eyes them with a barely suppressed laugh, and Zoya has half a mind to claw the woman's eyes out, but decides to ignore it. She'll have Sameer speak to the hotel manager tomorrow, anyway.

When Zoya and Haroun arrive at her hotel room, Zoya's security guards—who are now awake—startle at the sight of her and exchange wide-eyed glances with each other. Their panicked states momentarily distract Zoya from her quandary, and the ghost of a smile appears on her face.

"M-Ms. Zoya?" One of the guards—Caden—knits his brows.

"Caden? Did you fall asleep or something? It was *your* shift," the other guard—Warner—says. His eyes are full of raging disbelief.

Caden clears his throat, rubbing the back of his neck. "Sorry, Ms. Zoya. I think I'm still jet lagged."

Warner narrows his eyes. "Commander Jay is going to hear about this. And Sameer is going to have your head."

"Guys, guys," Zoya cautions. "Calm down. I just went for a little walk. No need to get all worked up." For a moment, she reflects on the revelations she had in her hotel room, and thinks of how crazy this entire situation is. Of how she's valuable enough to be guarded, but has nothing meaningful to offer to the world.

"How did you get past *both* of us?" Caden says, adjusting his earpiece and glancing sheepishly at Warner.

Zoya shrugs. "All these years of being Zoya Zameer have taught me a thing or two."

Both Caden and Warner look deeply perturbed as they realize that this may not have been Zoya's first time getting past them.

While the two of them are bickering with each other, Zoya turns to Haroun, all traces of lightheartedness dissolving. She mumbles out her thanks, avoiding his eyes. After a moment of hesitation, she adds, "I'm sorry for disturbing you at this time and I trust that you won't . . . disclose anything about tonight to anyone else."

Haroun shakes his head firmly. "Of course not. My lips are sealed." He opens his mouth as if to say something else, then changes his mind. "Good night, Ms. Zoya."

Zoya stands absolutely still as he walks away. Her knuckles are white as she grips the doorknob, conflict roiling in her heart.

Thirty

~

ZOYA DOES NOT FIND sleep that night.

Open up to your Lord.

The words have been engraved into her mind, painfully knocking, scratching, itching at the walls of her skull. Demanding her attention. She tosses and turns in bed, but those five words keep her awake.

Rolling over and staring at the ceiling of her hotel room, the thought runs through Zoya's mind again. *Open up to your Lord.*

She scoffs, covering her face with her hand.

"Open up to my Lord?" She laughs mirthlessly. "The Lord who doesn't want to see me? The Lord who left me to fend for myself after what happened to me?"

What had her ex-husband told her? That praying is done for Allah and Allah alone, right? "I still pray, don't I?" Zoya says aloud to her quiet room. "And *supposedly*, that should give me what I'm looking for. So where is my peace?" She shakes her head. "I built myself this life. I rose up from my ashes. Nobody helped me. So who is left to open up to?"

Haroun's voice filters through her head. *If there's something that gives you comfort from the hurdles of this world, that is your peace, granted to you by Allah.*

You have to find your peace, Ms. Zoya.

She scoffs again. "Peace? This is not a term I am familiar with, Haroun Suleiman. Unfortunately, the Lord that granted you peace has somehow forgotten about me." She tugs at her hair in frustration.

"Besides, where is this coming from, Pakistani Kate Spade?" Zoya turns her sarcasm onto herself. "What's going on in here?" She taps her temple. "Why are you thinking about all this useless stuff? You're happy. You're at peace, right? You have everything anyone could even begin to hope for. Of course you're at peace."

Saying this out loud does not lessen the heaviness in her chest in the slightest.

One of the questions from the Q&A session flits through her mind. One reporter had bluntly asked, "Are you happy?"

Zoya had coughed, shocked by the question, before she replied, "Of course I'm happy!" Her voice had dripped with condescension. What kind of a silly question had that been?

But had there possibly been another reason for her hesitation?

Zoya continues to think out loud, "Maybe I'm too horrible. I've done too much and God does not want to grant me peace. Maybe I'm not worth remembering." She rubs her hand over her face and sighs. "Maybe I will just have to find this peace myself."

Haroun's voice flits through her head again: *Granted to you by Allah.*

Seven years ago, when she had requested her ex-husband to get her in touch with a therapist, he had viciously mocked her, asking what she needed a therapist for when she had Allah.

Is Haroun saying the same thing?

"No," she objects to herself, immediately knowing that Haroun is nothing like her ex-husband. "He's not saying the same thing." Haroun had said that contentment comes from trusting God's plan, but he didn't say that it comes from trusting God alone. What had he told her at the Desi World Fashion Show? *"Trust in Allah, but tie your camel."* Wouldn't that mean to seek out the means one has *while* placing their trust in God, rather than pinning it all on Him?

Zoya bites back a howl of frustration as she lays sleepless

throughout the night, despite her mattress foam bed.

~

During their return to America, Zoya seems to be going through withdrawal. Sameer arranges for a jumbo jet so that Zoya has a living and bedroom all to herself, as she requested. At one point, she has difficulty breathing; she holes herself up in her room and clenches her fists until the suffocation goes away. She avoids the others like the plague the entire flight, and rushes off as soon as the announcement is given to depart.

Reporters and the flash of cameras follow the crew around as soon as they step out of the jets, descending the stairs towards their private cars. Security ushers the frenzied crowd away, most of them calm, some of them irritable and agitated at the intrusive press.

Zoya keeps her head down for the duration of the walk to the private cars waiting for them. Their luggage is transported to another van, and upon reaching their respective cars, the staff mumbles departures and stumbles into their seats. Everybody is weary from the journey.

When Zoya reaches her manor, her guards greet her and ask about the visit, to which she gives short, clipped replies.

She rushes into the shower and scrubs herself raw, squeezing her eyes shut and attempting to expel every moment of her stay.

What is the purpose of existence?

Zoya angrily shuts the water and dries herself off. Once she's snuggled into the comfort of her bed, she blinks blearily up at the ceiling.

"Stop," she whispers to herself. "Don't think about it. Don't say it. Don't remember it."

She succeeds for a couple minutes until she begins to absentmindedly massage her aching, heel-accustomed feet. And then *it* comes rushing back, prompted by the reminder of what has her so worn out in the first place.

Her chin begins to tremble.

Zoya does not want to remember Pakistan. She does not want to remember her father's face, the familiar roads that she traveled with him, the smoke of transportation curling up into the air. It is too painful, too dangerous. It prods at her harshly stitched wounds, threatening to split them open.

And now she has a new memory of Pakistan. The memory of a cold, breezy night. Running across the road to approach another hotel. Feeling the intense urge to quench her thirst for answers. Knocking upon her employee's door and becoming breathless with the answers he procures for her.

Before . . . before Zoya had a clear cut aim in life, a clear goal: rise up in the industry. Destroy her rival Zaki Ahmed. Become one of the most successful people in the nation. And maybe make her father proud somewhere along the way (although she had subconsciously given up hoping for that after all the years of his absence).

Now?

Now her thoughts are scattered in disarray, her mind swirling with confusion. She is beginning to doubt herself, something she has never done before. She is now second guessing her every step, her every decision. Looking back over her shoulder as if waiting for someone to point out what should have been obvious to her all along. And this is *not* who Zoya Zameer is supposed to be.

Zoya squeezes her eyes shut. It seems as if the pain is a circular tumor, rolling upon itself and festering inside her, beating like a heartbeat in all the wrong places.

Governing from the heart rarely enables people to emerge victorious. It is the mind that plans algorithmically, the mind that gears logic and reasoning to produce an emotionless, clinical plan. Zoya has always allowed her logic to guide her, attempting to keep a firm reign on her emotions.

So then why, all of a sudden, is she beginning to lose all control?

~

After finally falling into an exhausted sleep, Zoya wakes hours later for *Fajr*, then settles down with her laptop. A text from one of her directors pops up on the screen. It had been sent at 1:42 A.M. and reads: *Heard Mr. Zaki fired an employee. Something about him being in a really bad mood ;)*

A smile blooms on Zoya's face, immediately brightening up her glum mood. *So Zaki Ahmed's ego can't handle Zameer's success. Check.*

Her intention for flying to Pakistan had been to attend the launch party and deal with some minor matters, but Zaki Ahmed's anger is the much needed cherry on top. Satisfied, Zoya checks up on a few other things and finalizes several overseas contracts sent by Sameer before closing her laptop and making her way downstairs.

"Good morning, *bibi*," Mumtaz greets her as Zoya blearily reaches the bottom stair.

"Morning," she mutters. "My chamomile tea?"

"On the table, *bibi*. What would you like to eat today?"

Zoya taps her chin, thinking of her options. "Do something with eggs."

Mumtaz nods. "How was your trip?"

"Good."

She stands there unsurely. "Would you like a massage today? You must be tired—"

"I'm not tired."

The maid pauses, a skeptical look on her face, before she nods quietly and disappears into the kitchen. Zoya makes her way into the first floor dining room. She absentmindedly grabs her tea, letting out a yelp when the hot liquid sloshes over her hand. The porcelain cup clatters to the floor, smashing into bits and scattering around Zoya's feet.

Mumtaz rushes out of the kitchen, eyes widening at the sight before her. "Zoya *bibi*, are you alright?"

Zoya begins to quiver uncontrollably, an unwelcome flashback gripping her mind.

Farhan finishes giving his lecture on respect, and men stand to greet him, praising his eloquence. Once he has exited the men's musallah area, he sees a woman speaking to Zoya in the masjid lobby and quickly walks towards his wife, draping a casual arm over her shoulder. "This is my wife," Farhan says to the woman, gesturing at Zoya.

The woman smiles, somewhat bewildered by his sudden

appearance. "Oh, how wonderful. Well . . . it was a pleasure meeting you . . ." She waits expectantly.

"Zoya," Zoya prompts. She glances swiftly at Farhan to gauge his reaction.

"Pleasure to meet you, Zoya."

Zoya nods meekly and smiles, unsure of what to say now that Farhan is here. Her eyes dart to her husband once again, whose jaw seems to be ticking through the happy-go-lucky façade he is putting up.

Zoya's heartbeat rises.

"Well, I'll see you around, Zoya. Salaam." The woman smiles once again before excusing herself, still perplexed by Farhan's sudden appearance.

Farhan is quiet the entire ride home from the masjid. Zoya glances at the tension in his jaw, the tightened hands over the steering wheel. Fearful anticipation builds up in her heart.

Once they are home and have been served tea, he finally says, "What did that woman approach you for?"

"She was telling me about some programs at the masjid—"

"Do you know who that woman is?"

Zoya flinches at the low tone of his voice. "N-No? She said her name is Amber but that's all I—"

"That woman used to be a prostitute!" Farhan spits venomously.

Zoya swallows, afraid to voice her next words. "I know. She told me . . . but that was months ago. She's a different person now. She turned to God and repented, and has been at peace since. And she's been trying to be a better person."

Farhan laughs mirthlessly. "She told you? And you still stood there speaking to her?"

Zoya's body is tense with dread, but the words on her tongue spill out before she can stop herself. "If . . . if G-God can forgive her, can't . . . can't we?"

She should have known the destruction this sentence would cause, and known better than to utter it.

Farhan's hands tremble with rage, his teacup dropping from his grip to smash into the floor. He ignores the shattered porcelain and slowly advances on Zoya. She cowers away from him, any sense of anger at his bigotry vanishing into thin air, replaced by fear instead. "'So?' I don't want you to be friends with people like that!"

"I-I'm sorry! She seemed like a nice woman," Zoya weeps, all efforts of trying to change his perspective gone. Attempting to placate him, she lightly touches his arm, but he shrugs her off. "I'm sorry, Farhan."

"Yeah, you should be!" he snarls at her. He closes his eyes in frustration, breathing deeply. Zoya watches him with wide, scared eyes, horrified by his unwarranted rage. Moments later, he huffs out a breath and reopens his eyes. "I do this because I care about you, Zoya." He lifts a hand to gently caress her cheek. Zoya balls her fists at her sides to avoid flinching. "I wouldn't want the angel on your left shoulder to be busy, right?"

With that, he stomps his way upstairs.

Zoya stands there staring at the shards of porcelain scattered on the floor, tears pooling in her eyes.

She hadn't known he would react like this. She hadn't known at all.

The woman had been so nice.

Of course, as Zoya later discovered, Farhan just needed a scapegoat to lessen the severity of his own flawed character, hence the excessive anger towards someone who was trying to be a better person.

Zoya bends down, attempting to dislodge the broken teacup pieces from where they have wedged themselves into the chair's exterior. Her palms scrape the ground, and shrapnel-like pieces pierce her skin.

She lets out whimpers of pain.

Mumtaz dashes into the room. "Zoya bibi!"

"Zoya *bibi!*"

Mumtaz shakes Zoya's shoulders roughly. Her eyes refocus, and she blinks sharply at the room around her. The same room. The same dining table. The same floor.

"Are you okay?" Mumtaz's voice is frantic, panicked.

Zoya stumbles backwards into the dining chair, breathing

heavily. Mumtaz yells for a cook to bring some water as her hands hover around Zoya uncertainly.

"Zoya *bibi*, are you okay?"

Zoya nods slowly, eyes flicking towards the smashed porcelain. Her heart beats quickly, staccato.

A cleaner hurriedly rushes into the room with a broom and trash collector in her hands, sweeping away the mess. Zoya seizes the glass of water with shaky hands, gulping the drink.

She remembers how her father had visited her and her husband that same day. He had entered and seen Zoya's red-rimmed eyes, and despite his usual lack of affection, his face had contorted in concern.

"What's wrong, Zoya?"

"Nothing, Papa." Zoya smiles at him, facial muscles aching. "I was just cutting onions in the kitchen."

"Oh."

There is a heavy silence. Then, "Come inside, Papa! Don't just stand at the door. Have a seat in the living room, and I'll prepare some chai for you."

Zameer nods and makes his way into the house, eyes gazing in wonder at the expensive decorations and the extravagant furniture. Zoya knows that look, notes that no matter how many times he enters her house, the lavishness of it all still seems to take his breath away, even though the father and daughter were pretty well off themselves. Just not this *well off.*

Farhan descends the stairs and perks up at the sight of his father-in-law. "Uncle! Assalaamu 'Alaikum wa Rahmatullahi wa Barakaatu!" They shake hands.

The two men exchange pleasantries and start talking about politics and the stock market. Zoya arrives with their tea, and Farhan pats the space next to him for her to occupy.

"Zoya, how are you doing?" her father asks.

"Good, Papa."

"Alhamdulillah," Farhan murmurs as a reminder.

"Alhamdulillah, Papa. And you?"

"Alhamdulillah. This is good chai." He gestures to his teacup.

And despite the day's events, that one, seemingly small comment causes a bright smile to bloom on Zoya's otherwise haggard face. "I'm glad you like it." She doesn't mention the constant degradation that caused her to improve her chai.

Then her husband begins talking about the da'wah workshops taking place at the masjid, and her father nods along, smiling.

The maid glances at Zoya worriedly as Zoya's eyes flutter open. "*Bibi?*" She reaches forward to shake her again.

"Don't *touch* me," Zoya spits. Her eyes refocus, and she glances around at the crowd she has gathered. Her maids, cooks, and guards all stand in front of her expectantly, concern etched on their faces. Mumtaz's eyes follow Zoya's heaving chest, worry lines creasing her forehead.

"What?" Zoya snaps. "Is this a circus show? Get back to your work. I don't pay you for doing nothing."

Reluctantly, all but one of her workers trudge out of the dining room. Mumtaz stands before her with a pill and a glass of water in her hands. "*Bibi*, take this. It will make you feel better."

Zoya's eyes sharpen into steel. "There is nothing wrong with me. I don't need your stupid medicine." She stands and shrugs past Mumtaz, wrapping her arms around herself to conceal her quivering form.

But her maid sees through it all.

Thirty-One

"The retribution for an evil deed is its equivalent. But whoever pardons and seeks reconciliation, then their reward is with Allah. He certainly does not like the wrongdoers." (Qur'an 42:40)

~

A GIFT BEARING AN invitation perched on a bouquet of roses arrives at Zameer Co. In an elegant script, the invitation requests Zoya's presence at the launch party of Pak Enterprises' new project.

Upon reading it, Zoya snorts and tosses her hair over her shoulders. Sameer raises his brows.

"Idiots," she mutters.

"Will you accept the invitation?" Sameer says.

Zoya turns it over in her hands, eyeing it absentmindedly. "Of course. Mr. Zaki wants a show . . ." She trails off. "So I'll give him a show."

Sameer clears his throat. "What do you mean?"

She snorts again and throws the invitation on her desk, where it falls next to the gift and the bouquet of roses. The gentle white petals threaten to snatch her into a disturbing memory, but she quickly looks away.

"It's business, baby," she says, holding up her fingers to count on them. "Obviously, he wants to rub his company's success in our faces after seeing our launch party in Pakistan all over the news. He's *still* angry that we broke off the partnership, and he's been braced to fight since I told him off the other day. Why give him the satisfaction of not showing up? Oh, we'll be there." Settling down in her seat, she waves lazily at the gift and the bouquet. "Get these out of my sight."

Sameer nods and does as he is told. Zoya is left staring at the space where the gift had been. *White roses.*

She's once again shoved down the rabbit hole of her memories.

He holds the bouquet out to her. Zoya takes it, murmurs a thanks, and stands there unsurely.

Stepping closer, he raises a hand towards her cheek. The deeply colored, unnaturally red cheek. She flinches, and his jaw clenches. "Don't I get some compensation for that gift?" His voice drips with false sweetness, and he watches her expectantly with a glint in his eyes.

"What compensation?"

He steps closer. The roses fall out of Zoya's hands.

A knock on the door jolts her back into her senses. She shakes her head quickly, adjusts her posture, and takes a deep breath. "What?"

Sumaiya enters, hesitating by the doorway. "Ms. Zoya, I wanted to run through some designs with you."

Leaning in her chair with her relaxed posture makes it seem as if she has all the time in the world, but to spite her Zoya says, "Does it look like I have the time for designs right now?"

"Um . . . I met Sameer outside and found out you'll be attending the launch party for Pak Enterprises, so—"

Suddenly, it seems as if a lightbulb flickers over Zoya's head. "You!" she exclaims. "Oh my God, yes! Come here."

Confusion is plastered across the designer's face. "Yes, Ms. Zoya?"

"Yes. This is perfect. Zoya Zameer, you are one incredible human being." Zoya kisses her own hand, while Sumaiya simply watches with raised brows. "You're my plus one to the launch party."

"Your plus one? But—"

"So I need a striking dress. It has to be really simple, but let it make a statement." She gestures wildly with her hands. "And your dress needs to be simple, too. That way, it won't be obvious why I'll be parading you around."

"Parading me around? But I—"

"It's in one week. Zaki will be expecting some of my staff there, but that's not important. I'll select who's going with me later. The point is, *you're* with *me*."

Sumaiya furrows her brows. "Ms. Zoya, I can't guarantee that I'll be available."

"Excuse me? You're my lead designer. I don't pay you for nothing. You need to be available at all times whenever I need you."

"I understand, but—"

"You'll be there." It's a curt statement, and Sumaiya presses her lips together. "Have the design for my dress ready by tomorrow. We'll go over some pointers with the board then. *Adios*."

With that, Zoya gestures at her dismissively, and after waiting for a perplexed few seconds, Sumaiya turns and leaves.

~

A week later, Zoya turns to the three employees who rode with her in the back of the limo. They're all spaced apart and watching her anxiously. "Zaki Ahmed is a despicable man, and he will stop at nothing to humiliate his rivals in public. But he has a way of doing it that, I'll give him credit, makes his victim look like the oppressor." Ignoring Haroun's frown at her statement, Zoya turns to Sumaiya. The employee looks exquisite, clad in a long, simple blue gown paired with a camel-colored *hijab*. "Stay by me *at all times*. Do you understand?"

She nods.

"Good." Zoya's gaze falls on Haroun, who seems to be uncomfortable already. He has seemed worried ever since Zoya mentioned the launch party. "Be distant, but be polite so that they still admire you. If anyone compliments you or the company, smile and don't say too much. Those are just insults and challenges disguised in pretty words. Besides, you won't have to do much to make people like you." She smiles at Haroun.

Sumaiya fidgets next to her.

"And lastly . . ." Zoya turns to Farhan and immediately

grimaces. He opens his mouth indignantly. "Just . . . stay out of my sight. You're only here for *his* comfort." She nods in Haroun's direction.

They're almost inside the event venue when Haroun stops suddenly. "Wait," he says, as if he finally realizes something. Turning to Zoya and Sumaiya, comprehension dawns on his face. "Sumaiya worked with Pak Enterprises before." His voice is slow and careful.

"Yes, love." Zoya gestures for her staff to head inside.

"And Zameer and Pak Enterprises have been long-time rivals."

She cocks her head to the side. "Correct."

Worry lines his features. "Is that why you brought Sumaiya here, Ms. Zoya?"

For the love of God, please stop being so damn observant. "Sweetheart, you're being vague," Zoya says, examining her nails. "What do you mean?"

"Ms. Zoya, I . . . ." He trails off and presses his lips together, probably refraining from saying something disrespectful.

"It's business, baby," Zoya replies flippantly. "Either you're an asset, or you're a liability."

"Or *human*," he says, distressed.

"What's going on?" Farhan interrupts them. Sumaiya doesn't say anything, either not wanting to make a scene or wisely choosing to remain quiet.

Haroun continues as if he hasn't heard his friend, which signals his extreme distress. "And . . . it's not fair to parade her around and make a spectacle of her in the name of business."

Even though Zoya knows Haroun would probably defend any person in Sumaiya's position right now, it still causes her blood to boil to see him defending *her*, his betrothed. Knowing that Zoya would never be the only person whose honor he would protect. "Sweetheart, I *run* the corporate world," Zoya says in a clipped tone. "I know how to do my job."

"Will someone tell me what's going on?" says Farhan.

"Please shut up," Zoya snaps at him. Despite the dread beginning to settle in the pit of her stomach, she turns away from Haroun.

At the entrance of the hall, a man and a woman speak to each other in hushed tones. When the man sees Zoya, he clears his throat and straightens up, and the woman turns in the opposite direction and disappears.

Weird.

Once inside, Zoya loops her arm through Sumaiya's and glances at the marvelous hall. Cocktail party tables are artfully placed every fifteen feet and people mingle about, chatting animatedly. Men in suits and women in flowing dresses laugh and slide compliments into their conversations, artfully extracting information about the opponent's company. Because nobody here is friends. Or acquaintances. Everyone is the competition. Everyone is fair game.

Inside the hall, two men greet them. Zoya giggles, acting flustered and fluffing up her curls. One of them smiles in response, but the other simply stares at her.

"Ms. Zoya Zameer? Mr. Zaki has reserved a special seat for you," the first man says, pointing to the front of the hall.

"Thank you." She walks in that direction, blowing him an air kiss and watching in satisfaction as his cheeks turn from pale to crimson.

"Can I ask you something?" Sumaiya hesitantly says. "If you don't mind."

"Roll right on."

"Do you enjoy that?"

"Enjoy what?"

"Like . . . getting a reaction out of people?"

Zoya swivels her head to her. "Of course I do."

Sumaiya looks surprised by this blunt answer. "How come?"

A lifetime of neglect trains you to make sure no one ever neglects you again. "All's fair in love and war."

"So . . . you love all men?"

Zoya almost chokes on her own spit as she bursts into laughter. "No, sweetheart. All men *are* war."

Perhaps even more baffled by Zoya's ambiguity, Sumaiya shakes her head. "I'm sorry, I shouldn't have asked. It's not my business."

"Correct." Zoya throws her a sugary smile.

By now many of the guests have noticed Zoya's arrival, and are either casting her furtive glances or coming up to greet her enthusiastically. Moments later, when Sumaiya and Zoya are alone, the designer turns to her boss. "Ms. Zoya, I know why you brought me here."

"Oh, really?"

"Yes."

"And why, pray tell, have I brought you here, sweetheart? Other than for you to accompany me as my plus one."

"Because I'm an asset." Zoya raises her eyebrows at the dejected tone of Sumaiya's voice. "I've worked at Pak Enterprises, and I'm the perfect person to throw around in their faces. I'm the perfect piece to play in the game." Her eyes shine with tears, and for the first time in a long time, a strange sensation nags Zoya. Something disturbing.

Damn you, Haroun, my jaan. You and your spot-on observations.

Zoya doesn't even bother denying Sumaiya's words."Well, why have you come with me if you knew what you were going to be used for?" she says.

Tears well in the lead designer's eyes. She tries very hard not to blink, but is unsuccessful. A teardrop trails down her cheek, and she hastily wipes it away.

The tugging sensation intensifies in Zoya.

Zoya makes the mistake of looking away, and her eyes fall on Haroun across the room. He's watching the two women carefully, his brow creased with distress.

For some reason, this infuriates Zoya.

She turns back to Sumaiya and sighs, observing her nails. "There are *people*," she hisses.

Sumaiya nods, trying to rub away her tears before anyone catches sight of her. Or worse, before the cameras do.

"Control yourself," Zoya commands.

Sumaiya simply takes a deep, shaky breath and stares into Zoya's eyes, expression strangely steady despite her breakdown.

"I asked you why you came if you knew your use."

Sumaiya still doesn't reply, simply looks away, lips trembling. The sight irks Zoya.

Just then, Zaki approaches them, and Zoya watches as Sumaiya takes a deep breath and plasters on an expression of professional courtesy.

"Ms. Zoya Zameer!" he says animatedly, as if he's forgotten their last meeting and the spitfire that erupted between them. "Well, well, well. You made it." His eyes trail down her dress. "Looking marvelous as always."

I want to punch you in the throat and claw your eyes out. "Thank you, Mr. Zaki. You don't look too bad yourself." She tugs Sumaiya closer to her. "This dress is a product of my lead designer, Sumaiya. You're probably familiar with her already." Her voice is laced with contempt and scorn, all strange feelings having disappeared.

Zaki smiles through his teeth. "Of course." He nods at Sumaiya. "Good to see you again." He turns back to Zoya and loudly exclaims, "It's just so wonderful to see you here! I feel like we haven't had a proper conversation in a long time!"

Proper conversation. Zoya is distinctly aware of the photographers having turned their cameras towards the two business rivals. She grins. "It's wonderful to see you as well."

"Please, allow me to introduce you to some of my staff." Mr. Zaki leads them to their reserved table. Zoya's staff waves to her from another table, and she waves back. She quickly glances behind her to check on Haroun but does a double take when he is nowhere in sight. Farhan is busy conversing with a businessman, hands moving around animatedly.

Idiot. He had one *job.*

Zoya searches the room for Haroun, but he is nowhere to be found.

Zoya breaks out of her investigative glances when a man stands and approaches her. "It's such a pleasure to finally meet you, Ms. Zoya. I'm Hamza," he says.

Something about his face disturbs her. He's clean, well groomed, and combed to perfection. Yet something is off-putting, because as soon as Zoya looks at him, her heart begins to beat rapidly.

It's his face, she realizes. *This man looks just like* him. *He looks like—*

Sumaiya nudges Zoya, and Zoya jolts back to her senses. "Pleasure's all mine," she grits out.

At the table, everyone introduces themselves and begins chatting animatedly. Since Sumaiya is familiar with some of these people already, she makes easy conversation. One of the women asks Zoya about her campaign against domestic violence, and everyone at the table turns to the two of them. Zoya resists the urge to claw out Hamza's eyes when he looks at her.

Relax, she chides herself. *It's not him.*

Zoya begins talking about her domestic violence project, carefully revising her mental script. Mr. Zaki watches her contemptuously, and she wants to hurl her glass of soda in his face.

As she speaks, she surreptitiously glances around for Haroun, becoming more antsy with every passing minute. Where could he have gone? She sees everyone else. All of the guests. All of her staff. But where is Haroun?

The woman who was whispering at the entrance earlier is heading outside. Immediately, Zoya gets a bad feeling. Her concern for her employee only increases.

Maybe he needed a break from the environment and went outside to get some fresh air. This does not lift Zoya's spirits in the least. It worries her to think of Haroun—with his good will and good nature, too innocent for the cutthroat business world—standing in the midst of all these predators like easy prey.

"I think it's fascinating that you took on this project," Hamza marvels, breaking Zoya out of her anxious thoughts. "It will really boost your company's name."

Zoya's fists clench in her lap. "Of course. However, that was not my sole intent."

"Oh, we know all about your *intent*," Zaki says with a dismissive wave of his hand. It's a casual statement, and he grins at her afterwards as if they are old-time best friends, but Zoya knows it's a dig.

"*Do* you, now?"

"Of course."

"Enlighten me, Mr. Zaki." There is a threat hiding under her playful tone.

He walks towards her with a glass of soda in his hands and opens his mouth to speak. But when he takes his next step, his dress shoes slip on the table's cover.

It all happens so fast. One moment he's smirking at Zoya with all the confidence of a predator who's caught his prey, and the next he's flying backward, collapsing onto the marble floor. The soda spills onto his crisp suit, dark black tainting his clean white button-down. The glass rests sideways on the floor.

For a moment, everyone in the hall turns in shock. Then, Zoya breaks the silence with peals of hysterical, uncontrollable laughter. Once she starts, she can't stop, even as she realizes that every pair of eyes and cameras in the hall has turned to focus on her. Even when Sumaiya nudges her and murmurs something incomprehensible, Zoya clutches her stomach and doubles over in laughter.

Hamza is no longer smiling at her, his eyes reproachful and critical. For some reason this irks Zoya, and she finally quiets down. She hiccups, pressing her fist to her mouth to stifle any laughter threatening to pour out.

Zaki Ahmed is no longer smiling smugly at her. Instead, he scowls, shaking off his employees' hand when he tries to lift him up. He's shed the façade of playing nice, casting aside the mask of false friendliness.

"Sorry," Zoya says, her lips still curved in a smile. "Are you alright?"

Before anyone else has a chance to react, a shrill voice echoes around the hall as footsteps thud towards the crowd.

"Help!" someone screams. Zoya scrutinizes the woman running into the hall, and realizes that it's the same woman she had seen when they first entered the hall. The one who Zoya immediately had a bad feeling about.

She looks far from composed—her hair is a mess, lipstick badly smeared, mascara running down her face. Her shirt hangs loosely off one shoulder, as if it was used to drag her around.

She begins to sob. "This man is trying to harass me!" Crying out, she points to the entrance.

Where none other than Haroun Suleiman stands.

His eyes widen, and for a moment they lock with Zoya's. There's a clear message in them. *I didn't do anything.*

Gasps and murmurs break out all across the hall. The attendees' eyes flicker from the woman to Haroun, who stands there mutely, his tie haphazardly hanging from his neck. Several men rush towards him furiously, attempting to grab him, but security releases him from their clutches.

At the far end of the hall, Farhan stares at the scene unfolding before him, mouth opened in a wide *O*. He pushes forward.

Zoya elbows her way past the throng of guests and hastens towards the commotion, Sumaiya following closely behind. Upon approaching the woman, Zoya says, "Whoa, whoa, whoa, *excuse* me? What did you just say?" Her heart is thumping frantically.

"This man tried to harass me!" the woman shouts. "I was heading outside for some fresh air, and he came out and attacked me from behind! He grabbed my shirt and pulled me to him and— and—" Unable to complete her sentence, she shakes with raucous sobs and falls to her knees. Some women approach her and help her stand, consoling her.

Zoya is unable to control the laugh that bubbles from her lips. For the second time, confused gazes turn to her. "You're *insane*. That man would never harm an *ant,* never mind a *woman*. You're mistaken," she says firmly.

For a brief moment, Zoya's statement reminds her of something. Of when her ex-mother-in-law uttered the same words about her son.

Turning to Haroun, she silently wills him to look up at her. When he does, his eyes harbor the same urgent message: *I didn't do it.*

Zoya scoffs internally. *As if you need to prove that to me, Haroun Suleiman.*

The sobbing woman collapses against the women holding her up. "No, I'm not! He tried to harass me, and I barely got away." She continues to sob hysterically, and Zoya resists the urge to roll her eyes.

Yet her heart begins to beat more frantically. Why would this woman accuse Haroun of such a vile thing?

Zoya turns back to him. Anyone with *eyes* would be able to tell that he didn't take any part in this vile act.

For the first time, Zoya sees Haroun rendered completely vulnerable, eyes wide open and terror lining his every feature. "You guys can't possibly believe her," Zoya says. "I've known this man for almost a year now. He is the most kind, respectful, and dignified person that I have *ever* met. His fiancée is standing right here, you can ask her if you don't believe me." She gestures to Sumaiya.

Sumaiya's eyes are wide as they dart from Zaki to Haroun. Zoya watches her as she trembles, wondering if she shouldn't have said that last statement.

The crying woman's shoulders sag. "How could you say that? How could you tell me that I don't know the face of my harasser? He . . . he tried to—" she breaks off, weeping dramatically.

"Wow, Ms. Zoya," Zaki says with a shake of his head. "Are these the kinds of people you keep in your company?" He strolls towards her. "I'm disappointed."

"Now just wait one second—" Zoya is about to negate his stupid accusation when her eyes widen. Comprehension dawns on her face. "Wait." She laughs suddenly, panic rising in her throat. "Oh, my God. I know what you're doing."

Zaki simply raises a brow.

She laughs again, but this time with a note of hysteria. "Oh, my God." *He's framing him. He's framing Haroun.*

Zoya had underestimated Zaki's anger in her office that day. And she *never* underestimates her enemies.

Shock begins to race throughout her body.

It's a trap. A brutal, vicious trap to lay the integrity of her business on the line. A trap to question Zameer's morals and drag her company under the spotlight, and by default defame Zoya Zameer.

"Please, Ms. Zoya. Clearly, you can't handle these types of employees in your company, so you bring them along to—"

Zoya surges forward, wild in her sudden rage, but Sumaiya grabs her arm and drags her back. Lucas has made his way through the crowd and approaches Zoya quickly, shaking his head furiously at her.

"Let me go!" Zoya screams, but Sumaiya's grip is suddenly ironlike. Zoya whirls around to her audience, curls flying, and trembles in rage under their accusatory glares. "Don't you guys see what this man is doing? He's setting Haroun up. He's setting *me* up. Don't you see?" She struggles against Sumaiya's hold, to no avail.

The guests share doubtful glances with one another. Lucas steps closer and murmurs something to Zoya, but she pays her PR manager no heed.

"Now what would I gain from that, Ms. Zoya *Zameer?*" Zaki says. The crowd does not seem to detect the malicious edge to Zaki's voice when he says her last name, but Zoya recognizes it, and fury flares up within her. She knows he's taking a jibe at her, reminding her of who she is, reminding her of her monologue about being proud of her *zameer.* About being proud of her character and conscience.

"Ms. Zoya, I think it's time for you to leave," Zaki says quietly. Zoya stares into his eyes, at his feigned innocence, at his mask of professionalism, and rushes towards him once more. The logical area of her brain, the part that controls her every decision, has suddenly gone silent.

"You filthy piece of—you vile, immoral human being. How *dare* you do this? How *dare* you lay such an accusation on my company? I'm going to throttle you, you stupid man—" Dimly, Zoya registers that causing a scene will backfire badly in her face and she should step back and remain composed, but she is wild with rage that someone could accuse *Haroun Suleiman* of such a foul, immoral act.

Lucas rushes forward and pulls Zoya back roughly, and the shock at being touched by a man causes Zoya to halt for a moment. Lucas lets go immediately with an apologetic glance but shakes his head firmly. *No.*

Zaki dejectedly shakes his head. "I'm afraid that this is a police case, Ms. Zoya. Your employee harassed mine—"

He's choosing his words wisely, doing everything that he can to throw the accusation back in her face and taint her company's image. Because he's *furious* at her success.

"Wait!" Zoya screams, eyes wide. "This isn't true! Your stupid employee went out *after* Haroun did. I saw it with my own eyes!"

For a moment, there is pin drop silence and a flash of doubt in Zaki's eyes—a bare, almost imperceptible flash but a flash all the same—before it vanishes.

"Check your cameras. Do it *now* if you're so honest."

The audience, resisting being ushered out by security, turns from Zoya to Zaki with questioning glances.

Just then, sirens sound; moments later, two policemen enter the chaotic hall. They look around at the scene swiftly, and Lucas presses a hand to his forehead. The "victim" surges forward.

"Sir, sir! This man tried to harass me!" She points to Haroun, who looks dejected and weary. His eyes are trained to the floor, and he's not putting up a fight against the security guards holding him. His shoulders have sagged.

Angrily Zoya thinks, *Don't you dare accept defeat, Haroun Suleiman.*

"That's a lie," Zoya counters smoothly as she steps forward. At this point, she is far from caring about her company's image, far from thinking ahead to the consequences her actions will have despite Lucas' constant efforts to calm her down. Because she is *livid*, and this anger can be seen in the flash of her eyes, in the rage emanating from her body language.

"I'm Zoya Zameer of Zameer Co. Mr. Zaki here requested my presence at his launch party tonight, but it was clearly a setup since his intent was to lay false claims on my employee."

"That was certainly not my intent, Ms. *Zameer*, but the accusation isn't false," Zaki replies calmly.

"Oh, it most certainly is."

"Really? Then how do you explain this?" He gestures to the victim woman's haphazard appearance.

Zoya's lips press firmly together. The two policemen's gazes dart from Zoya to Zaki as they ask questions.

Zoya's board of directors is ushered back. Security maintains crowd control and tapes the perimeter with barricade tape.Within seconds, only eleven people stand within the large hall. Zoya, Zaki, Lucas, Sumaiya, Haroun, Farhan, the woman, the two policemen, and two security guards.

They question the woman first, who sobs and retells her story with trembling hands.

When they turn to Haroun, he looks up tiredly and explains what happened in an oddly detached voice. His story is, of course, different from the woman's. Zoya watches his face as he speaks. Watches the face she has come to yearn for. Listens to his voice, which is laced with honesty and innocence. The innocence that is always wrapped around him like a second skin.

There is no way this man could have done what the woman claims he did.

The cameras are checked, and Zoya carefully observes the footage displayed, ignoring the woman's constant sniffles.

Her mouth opens in shock. Because of the position of the cameras, the woman appears first in the line of sight and Haroun appears after. Rage rises within Zoya, but she attempts to maintain her composure so that she can watch the rest of the footage carefully.

The woman walks toward the edge of the camera's view. Her lipstick is badly smeared, making it seem as if someone tried to wipe it off her face harshly. After a minute, she suddenly surges forward, clutching Haroun's tie. He yells out a panicked, "What are you doing?" There is a scuffle as she cries out, and Haroun attempts to disentangle himself from her hold, but she holds on tighter and screams, "Let me go!" His watch catches on to the fabric of her shirt and he tries to pull back, dragging her shirt along in the process.

Zoya demands a replay. And another. Before Zaki turns to her and murmurs, "You can replay it as many times as you want, Ms. Zameer. You're going to see the same thing."

"She *clearly* pulled him towards her!" Zoya protests loudly. "And her lipstick was all over the place before she even came into view!"

"The footage doesn't lie."

"Your cameras are very specifically positioned. You *planned* this."

One policeman steps forward, notepad in hand. "Ma'am, we will need to conduct further investigation, but with the testimony of the victim and the footage displayed, for now we have to—"

"No!" Zoya yells fiercely. At this point, even steady Sumaiya is trembling with dread. "No, don't say another *word*." The policeman raises a single eyebrow.

Lucas steps forward. "Sir, with all due respect, given the technicality of the cameras and the lack of substantiality of the footage, not to mention the additional details that aren't adding up, it isn't feasible to—"

"You gonna tell me how to do my job?" the policeman says, raising his brows.

Zoya shoves past Lucas. "Are *you* gonna do your job properly?" she seethes. Lucas shakes his head at her and gives her a warning glance.

"Ma'am, please step away," the policeman says. For a brief moment, he shares a look with Zaki Ahmed. And that look tells Zoya all that she needs to know. Her body shakes with anger; she feels as if her heart may explode at the injustice she is witnessing.

"Haroun Suleiman, you are under arrest."

Thirty-Two

"Indeed, Allah is with the patient." (Qur'an 8:46)

~

He stabs a fork in his salad. Zoya flinches.

"What happened to your cheek?"

Zoya sputters, glancing up at him in disbelief. "What . . . what do you mean?"

"Your cheek." He reaches out to flip the page of the newspaper, and she shrinks away from his hand.

Zoya doesn't know whether he's joking or not. But then again, they are rarely on joking terms with one another. "I . . . it was from . . . that day."

"What day?" He flips the newspaper closed and settles back in his chair, turning his piercing gaze to her.

Her breath catches in her throat and her eyes widen. Her palms begin to sweat, perspiration beading on her forehead.

Casually, he grabs a tissue and dabs at his mouth, murmuring a habitual "Alhamdulillah" after finishing his food. Glancing at her again, he says, "What day, Zoya?"

The way he says her name, low and dangerous, causes shivers to crawl throughout her body. The intensity of his gaze is so overwhelming that Zoya looks down, away, heart beating like helicopter blades inside her chest.

"I . . . um . . . it was just an accident. I . . . fell on the stairs."

He stands, and Zoya's heart stutters alarmingly. "Good." And, having done his work, he drops his napkin on the table and leaves the dining room.

Sitting there with tears streaming down her face, this was the first time Zoya Zameer realized that those given power hardly ever use it for good. That those in power scare the weaker into silence. This was the first time she truly realized that life was a game played with pawns on a chessboard. A game in which this man was manipulating and puppeteering her.

This was the first time she realized that before the battle had even begun, she had lost.

Zoya surges through the chaotic crowd, all hurling questions at her. She roughly shoves mics away from her face, and grits her teeth at every flash of a camera. Haroun is being led—handcuffed—to the back of a police car, and more reporters swarm the area as security guards attempt to restrain them.

When Zoya approaches the police car, a security guard warns, "Ma'am, step away."

"*Haroun!*" she screams. *Look at me, please.* "Haroun!" Cameras train on her and lights flash.

The policeman holding him stops and allows him to turn around. Haroun raises his tired eyes to her helpless, agonized ones for only a second, but it's enough for her to call out, "I know you didn't!"

Haroun pauses for a second before being led into the back of the police car. Lucas steps forward and attempts to maintain the situation, giving the reporters brief, clipped responses. Zoya's breaths come in short gasps. She sags against Sumaiya, who helps support her weight.

"Ms. Zoya, relax. If he's innocent, Allah will protect him. He'll be okay."

If? *If?* Does this woman—his *fiancée*—actually have an inkling of a doubt in him? Zoya releases herself from Sumaiya's grip and rushes forward. Security swarms around her, attempting to stop her before she snaps, "I'm going to the police station. Get out of my sight before I call my lawyer." The crowd parts for her like the Red Sea, and she slides into her limo. Sumaiya breathlessly makes her way into the limo as well, and Farhan stumbles in at the last second.

"Follow that police car," Zoya orders the driver.

Zoya's phone rings, and Sameer's face flashes on the screen. She answers with a clipped "What?"

Sumaiya's eyes dart to her, fists clenched in her lap.

"Ms. Zoya." His voice is rushed, hasty. "I think I found something about—"

"Not now, Sameer. Not now." She ends the call and throws her phone back on the seat.

Sumaiya's fists relax.

Zoya's jaw is clenched the entire ride. She is bombarded by resurfacing memories. It angers her, how her brain is putting things together *after* the fact. Especially since she has always trained herself to anticipate anything.

She begins to remember everything. The way Zaki Ahmed had been carefully following news of her company and snidely complimenting her on it. The way he had barged into her office and seen Haroun's file on the table. The way he had released the news with the photo of Haroun and Zoya at the Desi World Fashion Show to test her reaction. He had put the pieces together.

And today, he's skillfully driven her to the brink of madness. He invited her at a big risk—a risk that she may or may not bring Haroun along. But he knew she would, as he seems to know a lot of things about her now. He's been planning this for a while.

The woman whispering with the man at the entrance today was planned. The woman taking advantage of Haroun's kind nature, knowing he would never try to harm her and would be willing to help her, was planned. The woman smearing her own lipstick and playing the victim card, banking on people's sympathies of crying women, was planned. The position of the cameras was planned. The way that Zaki locked eyes with the police officer—who is now making a joke of the integrity he has promised to hold in his position—planned. Hell, even Zaki slipping and falling may have been planned. It would have been a small sacrifice for him to make in order to place himself and thus his business in everyone's good books.

All planned.

Zoya should have known. She should have known that a man like Zaki Ahmed would never let her insult of him slide easily. He would get back at her, and he would make sure it would be unforgettable.

Zaki had continuously tried to break down Zameer Co. but when he saw that the company's dynamic was stronger than he thought, he decided to break the CEO down personally.

She destroyed him with her success; he is destroying her by sabotaging her business's reputation.

And he is succeeding.

He has ruthlessly tied her down and humiliated her in front of cameras, breaking her at an intimately personal level.

Zoya had underestimated his cunning nature. He had clearly gauged from the media and his own close observations that Haroun was important to her. What better way to rip the carpet out from under her feet than to pin the blame on an employee she values most? What better way to reveal her nasty, not-so-composed side to the cameras than to take hold of what she wants to protect the most? What better way to throw her own words back in her face, to throw her company's fame back in her face, than to taint it with an unforgettable smear?

A quiet voice whispers in her head, *Did you not also exploit Sumaiya? Take pride in throwing her and your accomplishments in Zaki Ahmed's face? To prove that you are Zoya Zameer, that you can obtain anything you ever want. That you are powerful, that you can ruin an entire business if you feel like it. That all you have to do is snap your fingers, and people will fall at your feet.*

And in return, Zaki Ahmed exploited you, taking what you value most and throwing it in your face.

Zoya shakes her head, trying to quell her anxiety.

I want to crack my skull open on this limo's window, she thinks. *Better yet, I'll make someone else do it for me so that I realize how stupid I've been.* She turns to Sumaiya, but seeing the woman in such a tense state herself, thinks better of it. Her eyes flick briefly to Farhan, who is uncharacteristically silent, worry lines creasing his forehead.

You will reap what you sow, Zaki Ahmed, Zoya thinks venomously. *You mark my words.*

And to think that he had felt *so* threatened by Zoya and Zameer Co. that the only way he felt secure was by publicly humiliating her and her company.

The thought brings a bitter smile to Zoya's face.

When they arrive at the police station, Zoya flies out of the car. Frustrated screams lodge in her throat when reporters who have managed to follow her attempt to step inside, but Lucas exits his car and wards them off.

The officers in the police station eye her with furrowed brows. Zoya, in her pink dress and floral *dupatta* and styled hair, looks exactly like someone who does *not* belong in a police station.

Blind panic grips her when she catches sight of Haroun, and the hallways fly by as she dashes after him. Officers surge forward to stop her, but she's too quick. She approaches Haroun and the policeman—the same one who exchanged that traitorous glance with Zaki Ahmed.

"Ma'am, you need to step away right now." There is a clear threat in his voice.

More officers pile in behind her. "Ma'am, step away. You are not allowed in this vicinity."

Zoya laughs harshly. "Oh, yeah? You seem to follow your rules pretty strictly, don't you?" She directs her attention to the policeman in front of her. His expression remains composed, but she detects the hint of panic in his eyes.

Zoya steps closer. "If you can do what you've just done, it should be no problem for me to do what I'm doing."

The two stare each other down quietly before he gestures to the other officers to step back. They follow his order, but cast one another confused glasses. Zoya trails after her shaken, sagging employee. They turn a corner and approach a row of cells. The officer inserts a key into a cell and pushes Haroun inside, closing the door.

"You have two minutes," he mutters to Zoya.

"I can ruin your entire life," Zoya whispers to the policeman's turned back. He freezes. "Oh, yeah. You must have *no idea* who I am if you've just committed this act. I don't know how much money or what else Mr. Zaki promised you, but—"

He whirls around. "Shut up, you b—"

"Say it, I dare you," Zoya taunts. "One snap of my fingers, and you'll lose everything."

"Who would believe you?" His tone is arrogant, but she can detect the underlying fear.

"Don't you know by now?" Zoya's voice lilts, threateningly sweet. "The world loves to sympathize with women, regardless of their dishonesty."

He stares at her for a few moments, battling with what to say. Finally, his clenched fists relax and he steps away, footsteps quietly thudding around the corner of the hall before he disappears.

Zoya's fleeting moment of pride disappears, and she looks back at her distressed employee. Grabbing a bar of the cell, she croaks out, "I know you're innocent, Haroun."

He remains quiet.

"Despicable people are skilled in getting their ways. I just—I underestimated Zaki's cunning nature, his cruelty, his thirst for revenge. I should have known, I—"

"It's not your fault," Haroun mutters.

"No, I should have known. I know the way he is. I've known him for so long. I should have known he would do something like this to—" her voice breaks, and it becomes one of those rare moments that Zoya Zameer's fortress walls tremble, threatening to fall. "He's a horrible man. And to spite him, I attended his launch party and dragged you guys along. None of this would have happened if—"

"Ms. Zoya. Relax. It's okay."

Her breath hitches, and before she can fathom it, tears pool from her eyes and stream down her cheeks. She wipes them away furiously. It's strange to see him so calm and comforting her while *he's* the one inside the cell, blamed for assault, and she's the one standing outside the cell, helpless. "*Tumhari izzat aur ghairat pe koi daagh lagane ki koshish kare, ye mere se bardaasht nahi hota. Jis tarha tumhe istemaal kia gaya hai, ye mere se bardaasht nahi hota.* I can't handle it."

He listens to her quietly.

"How . . . how are you so calm, Haroun?"

"Because Allah knows I'm innocent. And that's all that matters."

His words throw her into shock. Such blind belief, such rigorous faith she has not seen in anyone else her entire life.

Quietly, Haroun continues, "My mom says this all the time: *Zaalim taaqat-war nahi hota, hum us se dar ke us ko taaqat-war bana dete hain.*"

The oppressor is not powerful; we fear him and thus make him powerful.

His lack of fear, his powerful faith, shakes her to her core. Attempting to regain her composure, Zoya says, "Do you know why you were accused, Haroun?" She pauses, scanning his face. "Because in life, you'll meet four types of people. The first group consists of those who lack faith. The second, of those who use their religiosity as a weapon and throw it in others' faces to make them feel guilty. The third, of those who hypocritically force things upon you yet have a lack of knowledge themselves. And the fourth, of those who are good in reality and are unfortunately pushed around by the world and the many unjust people in it. You, Haroun Suleiman, fall into the very small fourth category."

Shaking his head, he murmurs, "You think too highly of me, Ms. Zoya."

"Because there's goodness in you. Goodness that is too much for this corrupt world."

He scoffs, rubbing a hand along the length of his face.

"That's why people like you are taken advantage of. And that's why you're thrown into situations like this."

"I trust that there's *khair* in this, too."

Her eyes widen. "How can there possibly be anything good in a situation like this?"

He presses his lips together, his dimple flashing. "Allah's delay is never Allah's denial. He expects us to be patient and wait for His ultimate plan, which is better than what we could ever do for ourselves." Haroun reaches up and presses his palms against his eyelids wearily. Even now, trapped in a jail cell for a crime he didn't commit, his faith in God doesn't waver.

Again, he has managed to render Zoya speechless. He's taken a crack at her guarded inner fortress, allowing a sliver of light to peek through, and causing the distressed shadows to hurl away from the light in panic and disappear.

"Can you do me a favor, Ms. Zoya?"

She nods vigorously.

"Please tell my mom not to worry. I'm worried about her health."

Another tear escapes her eye and she wipes it away, nodding. "Okay."

"And I know my sisters will be okay, but just tell them I'm sorry."

"For what?"

He shakes his head. "Just tell them. I don't want them to worry that their brother isn't home. And . . ." His voice becomes uncertain. "The humanitarian work? The sponsors were supposed to meet tonight. But since I won't be able to, do you mind letting them know why? I'll give you the manager's phone number. It would just be more credible coming from you."

"Sponsors?" She throws him a baffled look. Even now, he's worried about his other responsibilities.

He sighs defeatedly. "Yes, the sponsors for the orphan refugees. I volunteer at an orphanage."

"Okay, but . . . is it wise to let them know the reason for your absence? I mean, what will they think? What if they deem you . . . incapable or something?" Zoya abruptly fears that she may have said too much. He never specified his work to her; what if he becomes suspicious about how much she knows?

He falters at her questions, then shakes his head. "They know me. They'll understand . . . hopefully. Besides, you don't have to give them details." He chuckles mirthlessly. "Actually, they'll probably see the news anyway, so . . ."

"Okay . . ." She cocks her head to the side, wanting to ask the question that has been bothering her. "Why didn't you tell me about this work before?"

"I did."

"You didn't give me the specifics."

He places a hand at his forehead, rubbing it along the length to wear out the worry lines. "I couldn't."

"Why not?" Her voice is firm.

"Because . . ." He sighs, long and loud. "Ms. Zoya, the sponsors have a certain financial eligibility to meet, and at the time that I requested you to allow me an early leave every day, I didn't meet it. I didn't tell you about it because you would have given me more favors; and you've already given me too many favors that I'm unable to return. I'm already indebted to you."

Zoya steps back in surprise, her hand falling from the bar of the cell. The way he spoke made it sound as if he wasn't speaking to Zoya, but to someone else. Someone kind and respected and revered, someone merciful and caring.

Not Zoya Zameer.

Not a lot of people have treated Zoya as if they believe there is good in her, yet Haroun hid this humanitarian work from her because he believed in her goodness. Haroun's unwavering belief has always bothered her, especially because she doesn't understand how someone who has so much to lose can be so trusting, and can submit to God so fully. But being on the receiving end of this unwavering belief causes her tenderness for him to grow even more. Because he believes that even *she* has an inkling of good in her.

Somehow, he manages to get through to her. Through his actions, sincere and gentle; with wise words that have more of an impact than any self-proclaimed *religious* people she has come across.

Zoya, averse to any forms of religious zeal and always ready to mock religion, now pauses when the subject matter is Haroun Suleiman. He does not make her blood boil or force her to go to sleep feeling as if she is a sinner.

Instead, he makes her feel gentle. He makes her feel that even in her, there is something worth salvaging.

Something worth saving.

Thirty-Three

"And your Lord does injustice to no one." (Qur'an 18:49)

~

"USE YOUR INDICATOR, YOU stupid guy!" Zoya swerves, barely missing the other car as she honks her horn and speeds by, overtaking them.

A voice blares from the car speakers. "Ms. Zoya, I spoke to Lucas and the directors, and a court hearing—"

"I don't care, Sameer." Zoya keeps checking her rearview mirror, hoping her reckless driving doesn't land her another meeting with the police. "We're gonna bail him out."

"I just need you to think about this logically, Ms. Zoya. If these allegations have been lodged against a Zameer employee, and subsequently against Zameer, the press is going to go wild. It already *is*, from what we're monitoring. And bailing him out is *not* going to be good for our image."

"I don't care. The damage has been done, so *any* action we take is not going to be good for our image."

"Just think about it reasonably. If we don't want to look guilty, we'll wait it out. Especially with a charge as serious as assault."

"I *am* thinking reasonably," Zoya snaps, impatiently waiting for the red light to turn green. "Waiting it out or not waiting it out doesn't matter. Don't you see, Sameer? This is exactly what they want. Why give them the benefit of the doubt? They've already laid this false claim against us. Now no matter what we do, fingers will be pointed at us. Besides, the policeman was *bribed,* Sameer. Zaki paid him *big money* to do this. We have to get this policeman to confess his crime."

"You're right, but in everyone else's eyes, this was a lawful arrest. And unfortunately for you, you're not above the law, Zoya Zameer."

Zoya tenses, hand tightening on the steering wheel. This is probably why Lucas and her board of directors had Sameer speak to her. He knows how to get under Zoya's skin without getting fired by her. But her mind is too focused on other people to be angry at Sameer.

"*Above the law?*" She laughs scornfully. "Those who are supposed to *enforce* the law are the ones *violating* it. So law is just an arbitrary concept. Nothing means anything anymore."

"I understand, Ms. Zoya. But even so, waiting for a properly scheduled court hearing is less risky than—"

Zoya nearly goes ballistic, almost slamming into the car in front of her. "Are you insane, Sameer? Like, are you actually right in the head? I told you we're not waiting, so *we're not waiting.* Do you understand?"

There's a moment of silence before Sameer—voice a little shaken now—says, "Well, in that case, I've already contacted the station, and they've scheduled a court hearing for bail in two hours. I've arranged for a bail bond to be purchased. Keep in mind that he may have to attend public court hearings later, which is possibly even more detrimental."

After a pause, Zoya furrows her brows. "If you already arranged for it, why waste my time by arguing with me?"

"Just trying to talk some sense into you."

Zoya wants to laugh in relief and cry in frustration at the same time. She's about to cut the call when she remembers and blurts out, "Oh, and Sameer? Find dirt on this police officer. A lot of it."

"Got it. Speaking of dirt, I need to talk to you about something else. I think I may have found something—"

"Not now, Sameer." She cuts the call before he says anything else. Drumming her fingers on the steering wheel, her mind keeps replaying Haroun's words.

I trust that there's khair in this, too.

His statement bewildered her then and it bewilders her now. She's always seen his belief as faulty, his blind trust in Allah as strange. She doesn't understand how a human can be so dependent, so trusting of God when he has so much to lose. Zoya herself has been so self-assured for the past few years, containing everything within her and trusting no one else. How, after witnessing the world's horrors and corruptions, can he be so rigorous in his faith, so firm in his belief?

Shaking her head as the light turns green, she speeds towards Zameer's headquarters. Once there, Sameer introduces her to one of the best lawyers on the East Coast, who will fight Haroun's case. All the while, one vengeful, bloodthirsty thought runs through Zoya's mind.

I am going to destroy you, Zaki Ahmed.

~

"Auntie, are you alright?"

Haroun's mother has been staring into the distance ever since Zoya explained to the frantic mother and daughters that it would be best for them not to visit Haroun right now.

"She was so shocked when she saw the news," Aisha whispers dejectedly.

Zoya sits down next to his mother. "Auntie?" The older woman finally looks at her. There is no hint of tears in her eyes, but grief is written all over her face.

"Auntie, I promise that I will bail your son out. The process is already underway," Zoya assures her.

His mom finally speaks. "Please let me help you," she says.

"Don't worry about anything," Zoya says. The older woman is about to protest, but Zoya shakes her head firmly. "He was implicated because of his involvement with Zameer, so releasing him is no one's responsibility but ours. Don't worry about any of it. I'll take care of it."

"I know you will, Zoya." She sighs shakily. "I'm more worried about something else. Haroun is very sensitive to reputations. I don't know if he will be able to handle this. And when his father sees this news . . ." She tightens her hands into fists.

This surprises Zoya. Is that the kind of person Haroun's father is? Someone who will immediately become angry at his son instead of waiting for an explanation?

To reassure the women, however, Zoya says, "Your son is very strong. He has firm belief. Trust him."

"Sweetheart, I trust him more than any man in this world. I know he is innocent. I'm just worried about his mental state. And about why somebody would accuse him of such a terrible thing."

Zoya gulps. How is she supposed to tell Haroun's mother that he has become the collateral damage in a catastrophe that had nothing to do with him in the first place? "I promise you that I will grant your son justice," she declares. Haroun's mother simply reaches forward and grasps Zoya's hand tightly, a silent *thank you* written in her eyes.

"May Allah bless you and aid you. Please let us know if you need anything."

Zoya's gaze flicks to young Aisha, who harbors no trace of her usual happy-go-lucky demeanor. Then to Naima, who is quiet as usual but has a sullen expression on her face. "I know this is a tense situation for all of us, but I need you all to relax, okay?" She stands. "I have to get going now. Don't cook anything. I'll send food your way." And before they can protest, Zoya exits the apartment.

Back in her car, she orders food for Haroun's family, then inputs the address to the orphanage in Google Maps. Once there, she enters, shows her ID and proof of her acquaintance with Haroun, and introduces herself to the manager and the other sponsors. She explains that she is present on Haroun's behalf. The manager discusses their partnership with an orphanage overseas and potential sponsors for the refugees. When Zoya hands the manager her card, his eyes widen considerably. She tells him that she is willing to contract a deal with the orphanage and be on the lookout for sponsors. Besides, after the emerging news on Zameer, this humanitarian work might lessen the blow on her business somewhat.

After the meeting, Zoya returns to the police station with Sameer, Lucas, Farhan, the lawyer, and the bail bond agent. At the station, she catches sight of the police officer Zaki bribed. She walks up to him, her eyes turning into slits.

"Funny that you're still wearing that uniform."

He looks down at himself. "Just doing my job."

"Really?" She folds her arms, and his eyes trail down her body shamelessly. She snaps her fingers. "Eyes up here. And you have some nerve telling me you're *doing your job.*"

He folds his arms as well. "You don't scare me."

Zoya snaps her fingers again. "Sameer?" He approaches her and hands her a file. Zoya opens it nonchalantly, humming. She turns the file around to the police officer and points to an image of a woman.

His eyes immediately widen, and he whips his head around. "She look familiar?" Zoya purrs. He watches her speechlessly, shaking with anger. "Do you have *any* idea how easy it was to make your victims talk?" Zoya presses a nail to her chin thoughtfully. "Apparently, you've terrorized more than just one innocent person. Surprise, surprise."

He tries to reach forward to pull her aside but Zoya steps back. "Don't you *dare* touch me. What, are you afraid your coworkers will see this?"

"What do you want?" he demands through clenched teeth.

"You know what I want."

"I've already given it to you."

Zoya throws him a quizzical look.

"He wasn't officially arrested, just detained. Nothing's on file. He's free to go."

Zoya experiences a moment of fleeting relief. So there won't be any public court hearings. This will eventually be buried by some other news. They can all regard it as a really bad memory and an urgent lesson.

Then simmering anger boils to the surface.

So everything was a show. The public accusation against Haroun, the "arrest," all of it was carefully planned so that the blame would forever tarnish Zameer's reputation, but Haroun would still be free to go.

With the burden of this accusation and a ruined reputation on his shoulders.

It is a huge threat. A "*try me again*" from Zaki Ahmed.

And Zoya's response is going to be, "*Yes, I will.*"

The entire ordeal infuriates Zoya to no extent. Especially the unlawful "arrest" of Haroun. Something her hands are tied about, because there are people more powerful than her in the world, she slowly realizes.

At this thought, her internal voice nags again: *Now you see how everyone else feels around you.*

"So you took heed of my previous words?" Zoya finally says to the policeman, shaking her thoughts out of her head.

He continues to watch her warily.

Zoya hands the file back to Sameer. They share a silent nod before Sameer walks away.

"So what are you going to do with that?" The policeman nods to the retreating file and shoves his hands in his pockets, attempting to remain nonchalant. But Zoya can sense the tension rolling off of him.

She shrugs lightly. "That's for me to know and . . ." She backs away, a smirk playing on her lips.

After Sameer and Lucas dismiss the bail bond agent and the lawyer with profuse apologies, Zoya and Farhan accompany Haroun home. When they're standing in front of the door to his apartment building, Haroun turns to her.

"Ms. Zoya, thank—"

"I spoke to the manager of the orphanage. So . . . don't worry about that." She doesn't tell Haroun that she *met* the manager and contracted a deal with him; she can tell that he'll become increasingly stressed out by this information.

"Thank you *so* much. Really." He sighs wearily. "You've done too much for us. We're indebted to you."

She waves a hand. "I don't expect you to return any favors, Haroun. That's not why I gave them."

He shakes his head. "I will return them, *Insha Allah*." He focuses his attention on both Zoya and Farhan. "You guys should join us inside. You look exhausted. Eat with us."

Zoya shakes her head. "It's late. I have to get going. And . . . your family is worried. You should be with them."

Farhan nods. "I should get going, too. But I'm always here if you need anything." He embraces Haroun tightly. Haroun is still for a moment before wrapping his arms around his friend. "You remember what you told me, buddy?" Farhan mumbles. "You said to *trust*. I know this is a crazy situation, but I also know *you* of all people have it in you to trust."

Haroun smiles slightly and says something back to Farhan. Something inaudible to Zoya.

Zoya feels as if she is encroaching on this scene and is about to leave when Haroun says, "Thank you, Ms. Zoya."

She freezes for a moment, breath caught in her throat at the emotion in his face. Then she resumes motion, descending the stairs to climb into her driver's car. Her knee bounces up and down in the backseat as she waits for Farhan.

He enters a few minutes later. Despite her dislike of him, Zoya refrains from passing any snarky comments.

And quietly they are driven back to their homes.

Thirty-Four

~

LUCAS IS CONFLICTED ABOUT whether the employees taking a day or two off will be beneficial or detrimental to the company's image. Zoya makes the decision for her PR manager, telling him that the damage has already been done, and announces a two day break to her staff. Which may prod at the press' suspicions, but will allow Zameer to clear some things up.

Either way, the seesaw teeters wildly.

Zoya drives around aimlessly, attempting to gather her thoughts. She is so furious that she has half a mind to barge into Zaki Ahmed's office and give him a piece of her mind. Her already shaky balance has become further rattled by his actions.

Zoya is so focused on her mission to destroy her rival, so blinded by her anger, that she doesn't realize where she's driving until she's directly in front of the headquarters of Pak Enterprises.

Letting out a groan, she presses on the gas pedal and is about to turn her car around when her phone rings. Glancing at the caller ID, she huffs out a sigh. "Not now, Sameer. Not now." She declines his call. Seconds later, however, her phone rings with his call again. She declines once more, but when it rings for the third time, she gives up and is about to receive the call when someone catches her eye. Abruptly, she slams on the brake.

Because walking out of the headquarters of Pak Enterprises is none other than Sumaiya Akhtar.

Zoya's eyes widen, confusion coating her features.

What is she *doing* here?

Sumaiya's eyes are red-rimmed, and she's blowing her nose with a tissue. Her hood is lifted above her head to conceal part of her face, and she glances around before edging towards the parking lot.

Zoya's foot on the brake loosens in shock, and she almost slams into the car parked in front of her. She parks her car and grabs a scarf from her backseat, knotting it around her. Grabbing her sunglasses and settling them on her face, she steps outside and begins to follow Sumaiya from a distance.

A man rushes out of the headquarters and approaches Sumaiya. He too glances around cautiously, gesturing at Sumaiya to head into a well hidden alcove to their left. The two disappear from Zoya's sight.

Zoya is extremely confused. Her heart rate begins to escalate as she inches towards the alcove, careful to stay close enough to hear but far enough to run away if need be. A sick feeling settles in her stomach, and she pulls out her phone and presses the record button.

". . . can't do this anymore. I've told you already," Sumaiya sniffles.

"You weren't doing a very good job of it in the first place," the man hisses. "Chumming up more than necessary to Zoya Zameer—"

"You told me to make her trust me!" Sumaiya says indignantly. Zoya presses a hand to her mouth to stifle her gasp.

"You know damn well she trusted you quickly enough! *You* got too attached. You didn't want to do this in the first place, and making designs and organizing photoshoots that increased their sales like crazy was *your* way of making your *guilt* go away. I *told* Mr. Zaki we could have hired *anybody*—"

"No, I just—"

"You just *what*, Sumaiya?"

Zoya leans closer, eyes wide. She hears a loud sob, then a series of sniffles. Zoya feels as if the rapid staccato of her heart may stop altogether.

"Oh, *please* stop this drama. I don't have time for this," the man spits. "You had *one* job, woman."

"But . . . But I did it! Ms. Zoya trusts me now," Sumaiya cries out, indignant. Zoya's breath catches in her throat.

"There's more to it than that. Make her trust you, and then when something bad happens, support her through it. Let her see she can still trust you during a bad time. And then your job is over. But you didn't have to *chum* up to her so much. You didn't have to be so damn supportive of the company. If that incident with her employee hadn't happened, Zameer would have continued on its happy and forever upwards journey. Because of what *you've* done for them."

"Are you even hearing what you're saying? You're literally contradicting yourself. How could I have distanced myself while simultaneously showing her my support during a bad time? Besides, what's the point?" Sumaiya mumbles bitterly. "She trusts me, you got what you wanted, so I should be allowed to quit all this now. You destroyed her company's name and . . . and ruined Haroun's reputation. Who, by the way, Zaki promised he wouldn't include—"

"So *that's* what this is about?" Comprehension dawns in the man's voice. "You weren't supposed to get attached to the *bait*," he hisses furiously.

Sumaiya continues to weep. Zoya remains immobile in her hiding spot.

"That's what it is, isn't it?" he whispers angrily. "You got attached to your *'fiancé?'*"

There is absolute silence for a few seconds, save for more sniffles from Sumaiya, before she whispers, "Have you *met* Haroun Suleiman? It's hard *not* to fall in love with him."

Zoya feels if she is having an out-of-body experience. This is too much. What with everything that has already happened, *this* is too much. Her phone clatters to the floor, and abruptly the hushed conversation stops.

The man steps outside the alcove and squints for a moment before he recognizes the person standing in front of him. He swears loudly and slaps a hand against his forehead. Sumaiya follows behind, stumbling against the brick wall when she sees Zoya.

Zoya grabs her phone from the ground and holds it in front of her like a shield, eyes darting between the two of them. Her heart is beating wildly. "You have two seconds to tell me what the *hell* is going on here," she says in a steely voice.

And there it is. That stupid, stupid voice in Zoya's head again. *But you already know what's going on, don't you?*

"Ms. Zoya, I can explain—" Sumaiya starts.

"Shut up and don't say a word." Zoya says, her eyes piercing Sumaiya's. "I'll talk to *you* in the car." She turns to the man. "What the hell does Zaki Ahmed do for you that you all fall at his feet? Huh? What is it that he gives you or holds over you to make you guys commit such atrocities?"

The man holds a hand up, eyes on the phone in Zoya's hand. He's clearly aware that she is recording his every word. "Ms. Zoya, I need you to relax. This is all just a big misunderstanding—"

"Shut up," Zoya says, voice barely a whisper. "Don't say another word." Then, to drive home her power over him, she snarls, "I will take this to court."

His eyes flash with panic. He abruptly steps forward, trying to grab the phone, but Zoya steps back quickly. "Don't you dare come near me. Oh, yeah, I'll take this to court. Let's see what your beloved Zaki does about *that*," she scoffs. "He's going to let you rot in jail, do you realize that? He doesn't give a damn about anyone unless they're useful to him somehow."

The man holds both his hands up in surrender. "Hey, listen, I was just following orders."

"Aren't we all?" Zoya says mockingly as she takes a step back, keeping her eyes on him.

He lunges forward, attempting another snatch at the phone. In doing so, he wraps his arms around Zoya's upper body.

She freezes in shock.

Her eyes widen as she is thrown back into too many horrible memories to count, and she feels as though an invisible hand is closing on her windpipe.

But she does not let go of the phone.

Sumaiya stands there helplessly, watching the tussle. "Stop," she whimpers. "Please."

Zoya is overcome by disgust. The man's hands seem to be all over her, everywhere. She screams at him, curses at him to let go. Her vision begins to turn black, flashbacks resurfacing through her mind, and her grip loosens on the phone.

Suddenly, the weight of the man's hands is lifted off of her. He is thrown back onto the ground, glancing up in shock.

And in front of Zoya stands Sameer, breathless. His eyes are wide, chest heaving up and down as he turns to Zoya. "*This* is why you should pick up my calls."

Thirty-Five

"And mix not truth with falsehood, nor conceal the truth while you know (the truth)." (Qur'an 2:42)

~

ZAKI AHMED SMILES IN satisfaction.

His PR manager gives him a withering glare. "I've highlighted the possible repercussions of that. I've told you what's at stake. I can't force you not to do anything; I can only warn you."

Zaki nods. "I understand. But I don't agree."

"What don't you agree with?"

"I don't agree that it will be detrimental for us."

"We would be risking confidentiality by trusting these reporters. If the spies were to be caught and our name came out, it would result in an enormous loss."

"*If*," Zaki says, emphasizing the word.

His PR manager nods stiffly. "Yes. A big *if.*"

Zaki spreads out his hands. "Well, then, they just won't get caught."

"You cannot guarantee—"

"I can, actually." Zaki gives him a smug smile.

The PR manager sighs. "Are you blackmailing them?"

Zaki stands and buttons his suit coat. "Not blackmailing. Just . . . taking certain measures. Everyone has something to lose." He strides to the door of his office.

"And the girl—Sumaiya? What will you do about her?"

Zaki shrugs nonchalantly. "The damage to Zameer has been done. Her loyalty makes no difference to me anymore. Rest assured that she will not speak of our business to anyone." He chuckles softly. "She too has something to lose.

"As for what we're about to do . . . this will be the last blow. I promise. Because it won't be necessary to do anything else after this." He stares thoughtfully into the distance.

"This will be enough to destroy Zoya Zameer."

~

Zoya feels as if someone has gripped her, dragged her across a cobbled road, and thrown her onto quaking, unsteady ground. Sumaiya's betrayal weighs down on her like boulders.

Zoya's snide inner voice is cackling, mocking her incessantly. She always knew something like this would happen. She always knew it was a mistake to allow herself to place even the smallest amount of trust in anyone other than herself.

Zoya sits in the driving seat, unable to look at the woman sitting next to her.

Sumaiya is silent, head bent towards her lap. Both women radiate tension.

"Why?" Zoya manages to speak, using all of her willpower in making this one word sound nonchalant. Not tortured, not like every inner wound has been ripped open. Inhaling deeply, she turns her head to the woman in the passenger seat.

Sumaiya doesn't say anything, just continues to stare into her lap. Zoya's eyes rake over her pained face, her clenched hands. Her gaze settles on the *hijab* wrapped around her head, and Zoya has to restrain herself from scoffing. She wants to spit, wants to throw up at the sight of the piece of cloth resting on this deceiving woman's head. Day by day, every single Muslim she meets gives her another reason to despise the whole lot of them.

Additionally, Zoya wonders whether Sumaiya and Zaki had secretly mocked her, wonders whether her pride at his launch party had been the topic of laughter in conversations with his employees.

"Why?" Zoya repeats, more firmly this time.

Sumaiya looks into her eyes, and a stab pierces Zoya's mutilated heart. "He was threatening me." Her voice quivers.

"With what?"

Sumaiya inhales sharply. "He has pictures with me. We . . ." She pauses, cheeks flaming. "We had a . . . sort of . . . commitment. But it turns out it was all a lie, as it was with so many other women. And he threatened to release our pictures to the press. I could not have him ruin my reputation. I could not."

Zoya's fists shake. Her rage at Sumaiya softens momentarily, while her fury at Zaki Ahmed simply increases. So Zaki Ahmed had committed himself to Sumaiya, too. How many more women has he attempted to deceive and charm with false sweetness?

Zoya's eyes rove over Sumaiya's attire and her lowered eyes. "You don't seem like the kind of woman who would make a commitment with Zaki Ahmed. But then again"—Zoya scoffs—"you didn't seem like the kind of woman who could do something like this either."

"I was different before. Weaker, more naive. And . . . you don't know what it's like," Sumaiya whispers, her watery eyes attempting to pierce Zoya's icy gaze. "To have this need to protect your reputation—"

A mirthless laugh bubbles out of Zoya. "I'm sorry? *I* don't know what it's like to have my reputation ruined? Sweetheart, I'm *Zoya Zameer*. I can't think of a time where my reputation *hasn't* been tarnished." The fire in her eyes burns brighter as she stares Sumaiya down. "You probably know all about that."

Sumaiya remains quiet.

A painful thought occurs to Zoya. "Tell me something. Is your engagement to Haroun even real?"

Eyes raised to the ceiling of the car, Sumaiya begins blinking rapidly. "He thinks it is."

A heavy weight settles on Zoya.

Pure, kind Haroun. To have been backstabbed this brutally will not be a soft blow on this gentle man. The news will destroy him.

Haroun, who smiles happily at just the mention of his fiancée.

"It wasn't real at first," Sumaiya rushes to explain. "Zaki Ahmed just wanted to get under your skin. But . . . Haroun has changed my perspective on so many things."

Zoya's brows furrow as she performs calculations. "Based on what you told me in my office a couple weeks ago, you have been engaged for over two months now. And you've been working at Zameer for less time than that . . ." Zoya trails off, jaw clenching. "So Zaki's been planning this for a while, huh? He had you fake an entire engagement *before* you infiltrated Zameer and before anyone could even fathom what was going on."

Zoya's blood burns, but she has to give Zaki credit for his cunning plan. He has been paying far more attention to her than she ever would have guessed.

Although Zoya believes she might know the answer, she asks anyway. "How did Zaki think to exploit Haroun at his launch party?"

"I swear I had nothing to do with that, otherwise I wouldn't have allowed—"

"Answer my question."

"He . . . he's been observing you for a long time—"

"You mean *you've* been observing me." Zoya's voice is icy.

Sumaiya swallows hard. "He's been observing you for longer than that. Before my arrival. Anyone can tell with the way you look at Haroun that . . ." Trailing off, she bites her lip anxiously.

To this, Zoya cannot seem to say anything. A nagging sensation in her had known this all along. Sameer, who scarcely speaks to her about non work-related issues, had pointed this out as well. Even with all her caution, are her feelings still blatantly obvious to everyone?

Thinking of Sameer, another thought comes to Zoya. "How come Sameer didn't know about this?"

"Zaki Ahmed is two steps ahead of you, Ms. Zoya. He has been aware that I'm being watched and has arranged for my protection. Sameer actually . . . saw me the other day and has been trying to tell you ever since. Today was . . . today I came to tell Zaki that I'm not doing this anymore." Her breath hitches. "I'm tired of this game. I want . . ." She begins to cry, And Zoya's jaw sets in a hard, merciless line. "I can't do it anymore."

When Zoya speaks, her voice is sharp as steel. "And where did this sudden change of heart come from?"

"Haroun Suleiman is a good person. Too good." Sumaiya's tears continue to trail down her cheeks, but Zoya's jaw remains clenched. "I've learned so much from him. He deserves the kind of goodness that is equal to his. He does not deserve *me*."

"You're right. And—to put it more accurately—*you* don't deserve *him*."

Sumaiya continues to weep silently.

"The company will not take any legal action against you," Zoya says slowly, the shock wearing off and allowing her mental gears to shift to practical details. "Because our reputation is tarnished enough as it is, thanks to *you*. The press will go wild if they discover that Zameer was infiltrated by a *spy*. No, Zaki has very carefully planned this out . . ."

Zoya slams her hand against the steering wheel in fury, and Sumaiya flinches. "You have ruined *everything*, do you realize that?" Zoya shouts at Sumaiya. "You have destroyed *everything*, you *sick*, despicable human being." Sumaiya's shoulders shake as she cries. "This man is used to threatening others—you fell into his trap and decided it was okay to ruin someone else's life in the process? *Chalo*, don't give a damn about *me*—I'm Zoya Zameer; *nobody* gives a damn about me—but at least you could have thought of *Haroun*. He didn't deserve this. He didn't deserve this at all."

"I know, I know," Sumaiya sobs. "That's why I've stepped back. I didn't know what else to do. Zaki was—"

"Don't you *dare* tell me you had no other choice. Before ruining someone's life, you *always* have a choice."

Even as the words leave her mouth, Zoya's inner voice whispers to her, "*Oh, is that so?*"

She shakes her head to dispel the thought, but to no avail. She is forced to consider her own actions through a different lens.

Is this what she has been doing to others? Manipulating them into helpless situations so that they are forced to do things that may not comply with their morality? She thinks of Ben from Walmart, of the manager from Panera Bread, of all the people she has somehow bent to her will.

She hasn't been doing the same thing, has she?

She shakes her head slowly. No, she hasn't.

Right?

Besides, she's Zoya Zameer. She doesn't need to be merciful with anyone who's done her wrong, and she will not be.

"I'm sorry, I'm so sorry—" Sumaiya starts again.

"I don't want to hear it," Zoya snaps. "Do you know what I want, dear Sumaiya?" The woman nods quickly. "I want you to vanish from my sight. I don't ever want to see your wretched face again in my life."

Sumaiya trembles, but nods all the same.

"And do you know what else I need from you? Remove yourself from Haroun's life." Zoya quiets for a moment before continuing, "And here's how you're going to do it: you're not going to tell him the truth. You're going to tell him that you don't want to marry somebody who has an admirer already. You're going to say that you don't want to compete with Zoya Zameer."

She gives several more instructions before Sumaiya's eyes widen. "You—you're willing to—"

"After you speak to him about this, disappear from our sights. I mean it. Or I'll do you over worse than Zaki Ahmed ever could. Now get out."

Sumaiya pauses, hand resting on the car door. "Ms. Zoya, I'm *so*—"

"Get out!" Zoya snarls, pointing to the door. "I said *get out!*" Her throat is raw. Sumaiya opens the door and steps out quickly. "And don't you *dare* try to come back and beg for forgiveness at my feet. Because I'm Zoya Zameer, *aur Zoya Zameer kabhi kisi ko maaf nahi karti.* I *never* forgive anyone. Leave, and if I ever see you again, I'll be no less than *Shaitan.* Leave!"

Sumaiya rushes away, trying to stem the flow of her rapid tears. But she breaks out into fresh sobs as she turns a corner and disappears from sight.

Zoya slams her steering wheel. Once. Twice. Surprising her, her own tears begin to flow. "Ugh." She swipes at her face in annoyance. "Ugh, what the hell, Zoya? What is this?" She rubs her tears away and takes a deep breath. "That's it, good. Inhale. Exhale." Gradually, her breathing begins to return to normal.

Until she thinks of Haroun Suleiman. The gentle man who trembled at simply seeing fake news about him and Zoya. The man who placed so much trust in this woman--his fiancée--who exploited him.

And Zoya's face crumples all over again.

Thirty-Six

~

SUMAIYA AKHTAR BITES HER lower lip nervously, knee bobbing up and down. When the man she has been waiting for arrives with his mother, her heartbeat rises. She glances at her parents quickly, and her father nods solemnly.

Haroun Suleiman greets her parents, hugging her father and nodding politely at her mother. The sight further increases the agony within Sumaiya.

When the pleasantries have been exchanged, the parents excuse themselves and settle at a distance from Haroun and Sumaiya. Close enough to monitor them but far enough to give them privacy.

"How are you?" Haroun asks. A soft smile touches his lips; his eyes are lowered to the menu in his hands, but she has known him long enough to recognize that he is busying himself so as not to make her uncomfortable.

It makes this all the more difficult for her to do.

She clears her throat. "Good." Pause. "*Alhamdulillah*. You?"

"Good, *Alhamdulillah*."

Sumaiya marvels at how he manages to say this after all that he's been through.

An uncomfortable silence settles over them. Sumaiya doesn't

know how to approach him about this issue. Any side that she tackles it from, there is a risk of heartbreak. Besides, he and his mother probably think that they're about to decide the date of the wedding.

The thought crumples all of her resolve.

"So the thing is, Haroun . . ." Sumaiya begins. Hearing the tone of her voice, Haroun swiftly glances at her before averting his gaze again. "The thing is, I'm going to get straight to the point." He nods for her to continue. After releasing a breath, she blurts out, "We can't get married."

Although Haroun is not one to brazenly look into a woman's eyes, Sumaiya knows he can't help it when he raises his gaze to hers in bewilderment. "What?"

Please don't make me say it again. "We . . . can't get married."

He is quiet for a few moments, as if waiting for her to elaborate. Finally, he says, "Are . . . you're serious?" His eyes are wide, voice uncertain.

Pull yourself together, Sumaiya. "Yes."

He remains too baffled to speak for a moment. Eventually he says, "Where is this coming from?"

Sumaiya's chin wobbles. Words fail her.

"Is everything okay? Did I do something?" An indent forms between Haroun's brows. "Did I say something that upset you or—"

"No, no. You did nothing, Haroun."

Hurt and confusion are written all over his face.

"It's just . . . look, I'm really sorry for having to say this, but I can't marry you while someone is prowling at your back all the time."

"What are you talking about?" He sets the menu to the side. "Who's prowling around me?"

She keeps her head down. *Follow your script, Sumaiya.* "Come on, Haroun," she says softly. "Don't tell me you don't understand who I'm talking about?"

"If you're talking about Ms. Zoya—"

"The fact that you know who I'm talking about means you understand this. And don't worry, I'm not angry. I know it's not your fault. I just . . . forgive me . . . but I *cannot* compete with Zoya Zameer."

"What?" Haroun looks baffled beyond measure. "Sumaiya, there has never been any competition. I respect both of you in different regards. I respect Ms. Zoya in her own way, and I respect you in your own way. My choosing you has nothing to do with her."

"I know that for you it doesn't. Trust me, I know. But I can't live my life with you in the constant fear that Ms. Zoya will be waiting for the right moment to pounce on us and separate us somehow. And I can't live in competition with her." She flinches at the scripted words coming out of her own mouth.

"Sumaiya." There is a helpless look on Haroun's face. "I'm telling you that this isn't about competition. I respect both of you. But this has nothing to do with her." When Sumaiya doesn't reply, concern etches onto his face. "Please . . . don't do this."

"You're a decent man," Sumaiya murmurs. "And almost getting married to you made me think I was a decent woman. Since Allah says in the Qur'an that the decent women are for the decent men. But Allah has different plans for us, Haroun." Saying Allah's name on the same tongue she used to commit her atrocities makes her want to recoil in disgust at herself. "I cannot marry you. I'm sorry, but this is my final decision. I've talked to my parents about it, and they just wanted me to talk to you about it." She gestures to her parents and Haroun's mom, whose face is now tensed in concern as they talk about the same news.

"So you've made your decision." Haroun's voice is awfully quiet.

"I just wanted you to know. I can't leave you without an explanation. I can't live my life in the constant fear that my husband may be taken away from me at any given moment. That he may be lured into someone else's trap. Someone waiting in the wings."

At this, his eyebrows rise. "Do you have such little faith in me? That you think I would be 'lured' into someone else's trap so easily if we were married?"

Sumaiya's fists clench. *This is an awful mess.* "No, I didn't mean it that way. I trust *you*, but . . ."

"But you're doubting Ms. Zoya's character." His voice is heavy with sadness.

Not knowing how to respond, she shifts gears. "Everyone can tell by the way she looks at you that she loves you."

Haroun scoffs. "Ms. Zoya does not *love* me." He pinches the bridge of his nose between his thumb and forefinger. When he looks back up, his eyes are watery.

"It's because of the incident with Pak Enterprises, isn't it?" he says miserably. "You're covering it up by using Ms. Zoya but it's about that, isn't it? You believe the accusation?"

This frustrates her so much that she wants to cry. How can she explain to Haroun that he is the last man on earth she would ever believe committed that act?

Zoya's words ring through her mind. *Let him believe whatever he wants to believe. Throw me under the bus as many times as you have to. Just don't tell him the truth.*

He takes her silence for affirmation. "The whole world can believe I committed that heinous act, but I never thought . . ." He clamps his lips together. Even now, he seems afraid to hurt her with his words.

Oh, Allah. What did I do to deserve the pleasure of meeting such a man?

"You . . . you always said that if someone values something, they're determined to go through all lengths to protect it," Haroun says unsurely. "But you're backing down so easily."

He's hurt, Sumaiya realizes with a pang in her chest. He is *so* hurt because otherwise, he wouldn't have said something like this. Haroun Suleiman doesn't manipulate other people's emotions, or make negative, pessimistic assumptions.

She really has struck a hard blow.

"I'm sorry," Sumaiya manages through trembling lips. "Really, I am. I didn't want it to happen this way."

His eyes are anguished, but he nods all the same. Bracing his hands against the table, he stands. His eyes lock with his mother's, and there is so much grief in their gazes that Sumaiya looks away.

Haroun's pained voice shatters her already quaking resolve. "I appreciate your . . . honesty." She can tell it costs him a lot to say this; it stands in stark contrast with the look in his eyes. "And . . . I hope you find someone who makes you happy, someone who brings you closer to your Lord, and . . . " He takes a deep, agonized breath. "I pray he's someone you value, and someone whom you think is worth standing up for."

Sumaiya's lips tremble as Haroun turns away, grief pooling in his eyes. The words that will refute all his assumptions are at the tip of her tongue, ready to be voiced.

But she bites her tongue. *Let him think what he wants to,* Zoya had said. *Anything but the truth.*

And if she can even hope for redemption, if she can even hope to rectify all the mistakes she has made in her life—especially the betrayal she has inflicted upon Zameer and its reputation—it will only do her good to keep her mouth shut right now.

Even if it makes her insides twist in misery. Even when an uncomfortable feeling settles in the pit of her stomach—like a large, hard rock—as she watches Haroun Suleiman bid her and her parents goodbye. As she sees the solemn expression on his face, his mother's arm around his waist as they exit the restaurant.

She watches him helplessly, her hands and tongue tied.

Thirty-Seven

"But perhaps you hate a thing and it is good for you; and perhaps you love a thing and it is bad for you. And Allah knows, while you know not." (Qur'an 2:216)

~

ZOYA STARES AT HER employee, fearful anticipation for his inevitable decision causing her heartbeat to quicken.

He says, "Ms. Zoya, I—"

"Don't," Zoya manages to whisper. Her fists are clenched, jaw tightened, as if her very body is pleading her not to resort to this helplessness.

Haroun's eyebrows furrow at her demeanor. "I have to, Ms. Zoya."

"Please." The word sounds strange and ugly coming from *her* mouth.

His dimple flashes as he presses his lips together, but after a moment he barrels forward. "I have to leave."

A tense sigh escapes Zoya, something she has been holding in for quite a while. "Haroun."

"I can't work here anymore, Ms. Zoya."

Her fists tighten.

"I'm sure you understand. So much has happened. Not only would it be unfit for me to stay, but I no longer have the strength to."

"I know." Her voice threatens to break. "But . . ."

"But? There are no buts anymore, Ms. Zoya. I've reached the end of this precipice. It's time to head back." His voice is determined, unwavering.

Since Pak Enterprises' launch party, Zoya has been nagged by this possibility, by the threat of Haroun's leave. She's been brushing it off because she is too used to his presence to even acknowledge the possibility of his absence.

Now the looming threat has come to pass, and Zoya cannot avoid it.

"Your character has been laid a finger on. That's not easy for me to see, either, since you're my employee. But the media office is working on repressing the news. And the statement I gave about it being a false accusation should clear the air, at least a little."

Haroun shakes his head, his smile weary and defeated. "The damage has been done. It's like . . . paper. Once it's crumpled, it can never be completely restored to its original state." He runs his fingers through his hair. "Besides, this was already written for me." He shrugs lightly. "Destiny."

A crawling sensation emerges in Zoya's throat. *Screw destiny if it takes you away from me, Haroun Suleiman.*

"In a way, this has helped me," he continues. Zoya stares at him in bewilderment. "I've been trying to leave for a long time. This gave me the courage to finally do it."

"Why were you trying to leave before?"

Haroun gazes up at his surroundings. Zoya observes the way he looks at the gold-plated decorations, the extravagant furniture, the expensive flooring. "As you've known, Ms. Zoya, this is not my scene."

Do not cry, Zoya Zameer. You're not supposed to cry. "Is it really that bad?"

He shrugs lightly. "I feel like it serves no purpose for me. I feel like I'm mechanically working"—he makes a gesture with his hands, miming puppets—"puppeteered by strings. I can't do it anymore. I was weak, but this . . . incident gave me strength. There was *khair* in it." A victorious smile blooms on his face. "I was finally able to grow my wings."

Zoya's lips tremble. She cannot hear these words from him. They are slowly tearing her down.

"Why did you ever work here in the first place, then?" she manages to ask.

She notices his fists clenching. "We needed money for my mom's gallbladder surgery. Urgently. My dad hasn't supported us since my parents' divorce, but he offered to help cover the expenses for my mom's surgery." He sighs and rubs a hand over his face. "My mom refused his money, understandably, and I still needed to find a job that would earn me money quickly, so . . ."

He shrugs, then becomes thoughtful. "You know, it's scary that I didn't realize how much I relied on money to provide my family comfort and relief. It was all about the *money* that would help us, the *money* that would pay the rent, the *money* that would put food on our table." He rubs his temples. "I feel like I neglected the One who provided us with that money, the One who made it possible. And in order to get that money, I robbed myself of my faith and peace."

Zoya stares at him incredulously. "Working here robbed you of those things?"

Haroun sighs. "Working here has been conflicting with my faith."

At this Zoya's eyebrows rise. "*Your* faith? You do realize we're part of the same faith, correct? We follow the same religion."

"Correct," he echoes quietly.

"Then are you trying to say I'm not as faithful as you are?"

Haroun chuckles wearily. "Far from it. I'm human—I don't know what's in your heart. Allah knows better."

These words send a chill through Zoya. She becomes abruptly aware of the telltale thumping of her heart, as if every beat is an assent to Haroun's words.

She leans back and clears her throat. "You realize that your reasoning for requesting to let you go is making implications about my spirituality?"

"Ms. Zoya? I'm not here to question your spirituality *or* make claims about mine. We all"—he gestures with his hands—"lie on different spectrums of faith, and are constantly striving to do better. I'm here to request you to let me go." His voice is resolute, unwavering. Zoya knows he is merely asking her to allow his leave from work, but it seems like so much more than that. In a softer tone, he adds, "Give people chances, Ms. Zoya. Everyone is not out to get you."

A blush creeps up her neck. Scrambling for another topic of conversation, she blurts out, "What happened of your marriage? Won't you invite your boss to the ceremony?"

His face falls a little, but he shakes his head. "It's not happening. The engagement was . . . broken off."

To maintain her façade, Zoya says, "How come?"

He holds his hands out, palms facing up. "It just . . . wasn't meant to be. We weren't written for each other."

She leans back and mulls over his words, ignoring the surge of grief rising within her at the expression on his face and the burst of anger when she thinks of the source of it. In his eyes—according to what she had instructed Sumaiya to tell him—Zoya had cost him a potential wife. And still he does not harbor any animosities towards her.

"I'm very sorry about that," Zoya murmurs.

I'm not the least bit sorry.

Haroun shakes his head. "Don't be, Ms. Zoya. It wasn't written for either of us, and it wouldn't have happened no matter how much we tried if it hadn't been decreed from above." Taking a deep breath, he says, "And I'm . . . okay with that. Besides, we were written in pairs, weren't we? It's just taking a bit longer to find mine." He smiles softly.

She's yet again surprised by his words, by his blind acceptance. His strong belief. "So you believe there's still someone out there written for you?"

Haroun smiles. "Of course."

She fires another question at him. "Do you believe there's someone written for *me*?"

He seems surprised by her question but nods firmly. "It's not about what I believe, Ms. Zoya. It's the truth. It's what's been written already. Our entire lives are predestined; we make the right or wrong decisions that lead us down the exact path that we're supposed to tread. It's like"—he opens and closes his mouth, struggling to explain—"everything's set in stone, right? But we have the important job of choosing which pen we want it to be engraved with." He becomes quiet once more, eyes harboring a faraway look, which signals that he's contemplating his own words.

He is talking about the concept of power and free will again, about the balance between God's plans as well as human beings' responsibilities over their decisions. Zoya remembers this from the Desi World Fashion Show, and hearing it again causes her hands to tremble. She balls them into fists under the table and feigns indifference.

"Ms. Zoya, may I ask you something? It's been bothering me for quite some time." When Zoya nods, Haroun continues, "Why did Zameer and Pak Enterprises break off their partnership?"

Zoya smiles hollowly, knowing this question is inevitable. "Zaki Ahmed proposed to me."

Haroun's jaw slackens. "The same Zaki Ahmed who's the CEO right now? Like, the same exact person?"

Zoya laughs at the disbelief on his face. "Yes, the very one."

After a few moments, comprehension dawns on his face. "That's why he's so *angry*."

Zoya nods. "I broke off the partnership the very next day, sold my shares, cut off all ties."

"If I may ask, why?"

She laughs again. "Have you *met* Zaki Ahmed?"

"I mean, I didn't know him before your rivalry. I don't know what he was like without the . . . anger of your rejection."

She snorts softly. Of course Haroun Suleiman needs to give everyone a chance. "He was . . . too much of a typical, egotistical man. Some of his ideals were questionable. Besides, he was angry because he thought I used him as a ladder in the start of my career to make a name for myself, then dumped him when the business boomed." Zoya shrugs lightly. "He may or may not have been right, but I wouldn't have married him anyway."

"Would you have married him if he wasn't a businessman? Assuming that's what made him questionable."

She shakes her head. "Absolutely not." She watches Haroun with a longing gaze. "I don't intend to marry anybody else."

His brows furrow. "Anybody *else*?"

Shoot. Zoya's eyes widen, and she clears her throat quickly. "Anybody, I mean. For the rest of my life."

He quiets.

"Well," Zoya says, reluctance seeping through her voice. "You have two weeks to tie up any loose ends and then . . ." Her throat constricts. "And then you can . . ."

As always, Haroun understands without Zoya finishing her sentence. "Thank you, Ms. Zoya." His voice is diplomatic. No hidden meanings, and entirely professional. Like an open book.

It makes everything in Zoya ache.

Haroun stands, and Zoya's breath catches in her throat. She never envisioned this scene. In all her time with him, she never imagined saying goodbye to Haroun Suleiman. And if something isn't written in Zoya Zameer's to-do list, all hell breaks loose.

That's because this doesn't have to be goodbye, an urgent voice whispers in Zoya's head. *Do something while you still can.*

"Thank you for your hospitality." Haroun's voice breaks her out of her thoughts. "For giving me this job. For all the favors you've done for my family and I. For everything." His voice carries so much gratitude. He pauses with a hand on the doorknob. "I pray to Allah that you find your peace." Before Zoya can reply, he twists the knob and exits the room.

A quiet, painless exit for him.

Yet everything for Zoya.

And something in her threatens to break. Tears pool in her eyes, her hands tremble. She clenches them into fists. *You can't cry, Zoya Zameer.*

Although her mind, her body, and everything in her conscious being wants to obey this command, the tears finally spill over.

And Zoya Zameer cries.

~

When Sameer enters her office after what feels like hours, Zoya hastily wipes her tears away. To no avail, though—mascara is smeared around her eyes, lipstick is smudged on her mouth, and concealer is wiped across her cheekbones.

"You look horrible," Sameer comments.

"Oh, shut up, Sameer Mirza."

He settles down in the seat across from her. "Do something."

"You have something for me to sign?" Zoya asks absentmindedly, avoiding his gaze. She opens and closes drawers, pretending to find something misplaced.

Perhaps that something is her.

"You know what I mean."

"I have absolutely not a single clue what you're talking about."

"For someone who pretends she knows everything, you sure aren't doing a great job of it right now."

Zoya turns her withering glare to him, but Sameer doesn't budge. "You've become daring, Sameer. Spending too much time with me, I presume?"

"Like boss, like employee."

Zoya scoffs. "I'm an enigma, sweetheart, an enigma. You can't be anything like me."

"And what an open book enigma you are." Sameer's tone is flat, eyes serious. After a pause, he conveys the message Zoya knows he's been wanting to say since he came in, "Tell him how you feel."

"What are you—"

"You *know* what I'm—"

"*Don't* interrupt me when I'm speaking," Zoya snaps. The two stare each other down. Zoya is not the first to look away.

Sameer's sigh resonates throughout the room. He pinches the bridge of his nose between his thumb and forefinger. "Ms. Zoya."

"Don't '*Ms. Zoya*' me. Get out."

"Look, you have to do it."

"And who are *you* to tell me what I *have* to do?"

"Someone who's known you long enough." He opens his eyes and looks at her again. In a softer tone, he continues, "You have to tell him how you feel. Who knows? He might even evaluate his own feelings. And even if he doesn't, trust me. Haroun's not the kind of guy—"

"Are you giving me relationship advice?"

Sameer pauses before shrugging. "I guess I am."

"Daring, aren't you?"

"Too much time spent with you, am I correct?" He cocks a grin, and although she feels terrible, Zoya manages a smile.

"You're not very good at this," she remarks.

"You haven't even listened to what I have to say."

Zoya leans back in her chair, folds her trembling arms, and stares her employee down. "Spill, then."

"Tell him how you feel." Sameer's voice is soft. "He's an honest and kind person, and he would never disrespect you, even if his feelings aren't mutual."

"Which they aren't," Zoya interrupts.

"You don't know that."

She scoffs. "Have you *met* him? Haroun Suleiman doesn't—he doesn't . . ." She falls silent, unable to say the words at the tip of her tongue. *He doesn't want people like me. He wants people like Sumaiya. Not people who are battered and bruised. Not me.*

Uncontrollably, fresh tears pool in her eyes. She blinks harshly and looks away; to Sameer's credit he peels his eyes away from her face to give her the privacy she is so desperately seeking.

"He's shocked and confused right now because of his engagement breaking off, and he doesn't even know the real reason yet," Sameer murmurs. "He would probably appreciate some emotional support. Someone who understands."

Zoya laughs mirthlessly. "You say that like it's easy, Mr. Hollywood. This isn't a movie. This is real life."

"At least *talk* to him," he says exasperatedly. Hands out, palms up.

Zoya eyes his hands, and for some reason the helplessness in his posture causes the tears to spill down her cheeks. She sniffs and looks away, pressing her lips together. She shakes her head. "I can't."

"Why not?"

Because he won't want me. And maybe Zoya Zameer will finally fall over the ledge she is barely teetering over with the possibility of his rejection.

"Look," Sameer says. "I know you're probably thinking he wouldn't choose someone like you to be his life partner, someone who lives a life so different from his. But you really can't know that without communicating with him. Besides, he's the kind of person who gives everyone chances."

Sameer, everything you're saying is right. But he won't want me. Zoya shakes her head again. "I can't."

"Ms. Zoya." His voice is strained. "You have to *try* to tell him how you feel. Otherwise you'll spend your entire life not knowing what the alternative possibility could have been."

I'm going to do something. I just . . . can't tell him how I feel. "How *do* I feel?"

"Do you need me to tell you that?"

"He's . . . my employee." Immediately, Zoya grimaces at the lie.

At this, Sameer snorts so loudly that it startles Zoya. He shakes his head with silent laughter in his eyes. "You can't make anyone believe that. Especially not me."

"Oh, yeah? What makes you so sure?"

"I'm your *secretary* and your *personal assistant.* I've been by you twenty-four seven and I've seen you in all your moods. I've seen the way you change around Haroun, the way you talk about him, the way you talk *to* him, the way you act around him. I'm not stupid, Ms. Zoya."

"You sure about that?" Zoya says halfheartedly, attempting to lighten her own mood.

Sameer laughs. "Positive." He pushes against the desk and stands, expression becoming grave again. "I don't know if what I said had any sort of effect on you, but you have to try, Ms. Zoya. You have to."

"Why does it matter so much to *you*?" Zoya fires back at him.

Sameer gives her a lost, wounded look. And it's so different from his usual expressions that Zoya does a double take. "Because sometimes, I wish I had taken my chances, too." With that, he backs away slowly, exiting the room.

Which chances did he not take?

Thirty-Eight

"I only complain of my suffering and my grief to Allah." (Qur'an 12:86)

~

"MR. ZAKI, HERE'S THE information you requested."

With steepled fingers, Zaki Ahmed stares at the file his secretary places in front of him. "You got everything?" he says.

"Everything we could find, sir."

"And what would that be?"

"We tracked down and spoke to some of Ms. Zoya's distant relatives. It was difficult to get them to speak, but . . ." The secretary shrugs.

"I understand. Thank you. You may leave."

"Yes, sir."

Zaki opens the file, and a smile plays on his lips. "Zoya Zameer," he murmurs. "You would have done yourself a favor by just marrying me."

He sifts through the files, eyes landing on a picture of a small marriage ceremony. He can already envision the headlines.

The Marriage and Divorce of Zoya Zameer.

~

When Zoya steps into Zameer's headquarters the next day, with concealer haphazardly dabbed under her eyes and her auburn curls a mess, her employees are all watching her with fearful expressions on their faces. She sets her purse on an employee's work table and folds her arms.

"Do I look like I'm paying you all to stare at my face? Get to work before I start firing people. And trust me, I'm in a horrible mood today, so it *will* happen. Don't try me," she barks. "Already the reporters and security outside have eaten what's left of my brain this morning. I barely escaped them. What the hell is going on?"

Nobody budges. Bill and Lucas edge forward cautiously, as if approaching a wounded animal. Bill murmurs, "Ms. Zoya, have you seen the news?"

She scoffs. "What? More speculation about my marital status? About the identity of my parents? About my employees, who are allegedly sexual offenders?" She grabs her purse and begins walking away from them, heels clicking noisily in the dead silence. "Tell me something I *don't* know, Bill Nye."

When everyone continues to stare at her, Zoya stops and furrows her brows. "What is it, Bill?"

Please say nothing. I can't do it anymore.

"Let's go to your office," Bill's tone turns placating. He leads her there as her staff's eyes trail the two of them.

Zoya's heart begins to thump frantically.

"Bill Nye, if this is some sick joke—" She stops when she sees the formidable expression on his face as they enter her office. Bill turns the TV on, and is about to switch to another news channel but stops.

He doesn't need to. The news is everywhere.

With a loud gasp, Zoya's purse slips from her hand as she brings it up to cover her mouth. Her fingers tremble, and her heart begins to beat at an alarmingly quick rate. Bill attempts to reach forward to comfort her but pulls back, the pity on his face revealing that he knows she doesn't like being touched, and he finally understands why.

Because written on the TV screen in large headlines are the words: *Zoya Zameer's Abusive Marriage and Divorce.*

"No." She manages to find her voice. Shaking her head back and forth quickly, she repeats, "No, no, no. Oh, my *God.*" She slides down to the floor and continues to shake her head with wide eyes. Bill hurriedly looks around and locates a water bottle, handing it to her. But she is too shocked to move.

No. Oh, God, no. Everything else, but not this.

"Ms. Zoya, are you okay?" Bill asks her worriedly. His voice is oddly far away, as if she's hearing it through a warped glass.

And then Zoya faints.

~

She wakes to muffled conversation.

"—saw the news."

"Poor Ms. Zoya. No wonder she's—"

"Is it true, though?"

"Should we call a doctor?"

"Look, she's awake."

Her eyes flutter open to meet some of her employee's worried gazes, but she only registers what's going on when she sees a particular person standing at the far back. Her eyes widen, and she attempts to sit up straighter, temporarily forgetting about the source of her distress.

"Haroun?" she croaks out.

The staff exchanges glances.

Haroun flushes bright red at the attention but waves awkwardly nonetheless. "You doing okay there, Ms. Zoya?"

"I'm okay. What are you doing in my office?"

He gestures to the door behind him. "I was wrapping up some things down the hall and heard . . . a commotion. Are you sure you're alright? Can we get you anything?"

"Water."

Sarah, whose eyes had been traveling between the two of them, quickly reaches behind her and grabs a water bottle from the desk. She uncaps it and hands it to Zoya.

Zoya sips greedily, hyperaware of the sound of her gulps in the quiet room.

Unexpectedly, she blushes.

"Ms. Zoya—" Sarah starts.

"Not now, Sarah." Bill gives her a warning glance just as Lucas shakes his head firmly at her.

The news.

Zoya's breath constricts, the room becomes small. The bottle slips out of her hand, and water spills across the floor.

"Get out," she whispers. "Everyone."

They hesitate for a moment before obeying her command. Bill is the last to leave, frowning with concern as he exits.

Zoya knows the staff will talk about this behind her back. They will speculate about it, question one another, remember minor details to patch their stories together. But as always, they will never ask Zoya Zameer for the truth.

Before, that never bothered her. Better their speculations and their fear in asking her than her wasting time telling them the truth that doesn't matter.

But now? Now with *this* news out, they will make the worst of it. And they will treat her differently. They will *pity* her. And God knows Zoya doesn't want their pity. She has worked too hard to build herself a life that is vastly different from what it used to be. She cannot return to the same person she once was, cannot allow others to see her that way again.

That helpless, poor girl.

She feels a powerful rage deep in her chest towards the obvious source of this news: Zaki Ahmed. Her fury is so strong, so fueled by hate that it steals her breath. She will destroy him, and only then will she find the peace that she has been seeking The peace Haroun Suleiman told her he would pray for.

For the millionth time that week, hot tears rapidly spill down her cheeks. The tears splatter against the floor, where remnants of Zoya Zameer's vulnerability will forever be etched into the ground.

No.

Zoya throws herself at the floor, smearing her tears with her hands. She rubs at the wet splotches, scratches, tears at them until she is no longer wiping away tears but clawing at the floor. Until she pulls back with cracked nails. Whimpers escape her, the sound of a lost and wounded animal, and she presses her face to the ground.

No matter how hard she tries, her past won't leave her alone. It will follow her to the grave.

~

Half an hour later, Zoya exits her office and takes the elevator to the first floor. Her makeup is redone, her hair re-fluffed, her bangles jingling, and her heels clicking louder than ever. The staff throws her looks of surprise, looks of pity, looks of confusion. She ignores them all and approaches Bill, slapping a file against his chest.

"Have these signed."

"What are these?"

"Excuse me, did I put a question mark at the end of my sentence?" She gives him a withering glare, which he returns with a look of surprise. "I thought so."

Turning back around, she stops in the middle of the hall when she feels eyes on her. "Is there something on my face?" she demands furiously.

Pin drop silence.

"Then peel your eyes away from me or I'll start firing. I'm aware that I'm irresistible—thank you for reminding me—but frankly, I don't need the reminder. *Get back to work!*" she screeches at the silent hall. Papers begin to shuffle, the thrum of voices picks back up, and the staff returns to work.

Zoya takes the elevator back up to her office, her heart beating frantically. She doesn't think she can pull a performance like that again, which is problematic because she is going to have to spend the rest of her days like this. Even more closed off, more insufferable. But if that's what it takes to keep their pity at bay, then so be it.

She won't be losing much, anyway.

There is a knock on her office door before Sameer enters.

"Do *not* say anything—"

"Have you talked to him?"

Her dark eyes blaze with violence. "Do you have a death wish, Sameer Mirza?"

"Maybe. You didn't answer my question."

She balls her fists at her sides. "*Don't* give me orders."

He quiets.

She sighs. "Leave me alone." *Please.*

"You okay?" His voice is soft, tentative. Everything Zoya doesn't want right now.

"I said *leave me alone*."

He holds his hands up. "Okay. I'm sorry." And he quietly retreats.

Grabbing anything to distract herself, Zoya makes her way to the printer room with a file in hand. Opening the door, she gives a single glare to the employees inside, and they scuttle out quickly. This is what she likes. The power. The control. Instilling the fear.

Because it makes her so much more than her past. Than her pain.

Farhan Malik is the last to leave the room, and Zoya jerks forward just as he passes by to scare him. He flinches, backing away from her quickly.

Slamming the door behind her, she edges closer to the printer and pulls out papers from the file. Random papers from the contractors in Pakistan. No longer important.

It is then that she realizes—she hasn't had to print out anything for as long as she can remember. Sameer, or someone else, is always doing these menial tasks for her.

The possibility of being incompetent at something doesn't sit well with her, so she enters the printer password and gives it a long stare. She clicks on the area that says "scan" and wedges the paper into the tray as she remembers. Then she waits.

Nothing happens.

She furrows her brows and leans forward, clicking scan again. And again, nothing happens. The printer stays silent in the eerie quiet of the room. No whirring, no clicking. Nothing.

Zoya slams the "scan" button again and again. "Work, you *stupid*, useless thing," she snarls. Somewhere along the way, she loses it and begins banging the printer from the top and from the sides. Punching, kicking, and pushing at it. She grabs the papers in the file and tosses them all over the floor.

The printer remains silent.

Zoya lets out an animalistic yell before erupting in loud sobs. Her breath hitches, her body quakes, and sniffles escape her. She vaguely registers the door opening but doesn't look up. Belatedly, her eyes fall on the sign taped to the side of the printer.

Out of order.

At that, she weeps even more. Something deep in her shifts at seeing these words. Something terribly aches.

She looks up to see who entered and makes out a face through watery eyes.

Haroun's face.

Ugh. She swipes her cheeks with the back of her hand. *Why does he always see me like this?*

The expression on his face is one of pure surprise. His eyes travel around the room, at the scattered papers strewn across the floor, at the printer Zoya unplugged while she had been assaulting it.

"Ms. Zoya?" His voice is startled.

"What are you doing here?" she asks him yet again, avoiding his eyes.

"I came to give Matt this file . . ." He trails off, still confused. His dimple creases, signaling his tension.

"Matt's not here." Zoya's voice breaks out into a sob, and she clutches her stomach to attempt to reign the pain. Haroun steps into the room unsurely before he grabs a chair and places it behind her. She collapses into it.

And quietly, he exits the room.

He left.

Just like everyone else.

Zoya's face scrunches up and her throat turns raw, hot tears pooling down her cheeks as she cries harder than before. The pain is too deep, twisting inside her as if it has a life of its own, scarring her already jagged edges, flames licking her wounds.

Minutes later, however, the door reopens and Haroun returns with a cup of steaming tea in his hands. Chamomile.

He sets it in front of her. "This might help." His voice is small, unsure. As if he knows these are dangerous waters he is treading.

He takes a small step forward, but leaves the room door wide open.

Zoya manages a warbled "Thank you" as she clasps the cup, reveling in its warmth.

Warm, like everything about Haroun Suleiman.

Something about him standing there brings fresh tears to her eyes. He is her safe haven, her sanctuary.

So what does one do when their sanctuary leaves?

"I'm sorry about what happened," Haroun says quietly, breaking her out of her thoughts.

She scoffs. "Why are *you* saying sorry? This was just one of *many* of Zaki Ahmed's plans to uproot me. The only difference this time was—" Her breath hitches. *It worked.*

Haroun settles down across from her. At a distance. "What will you do now?"

The question that means nothing yet everything at the same time.

"I don't know," she whispers honestly. Somehow, he makes her tongue unroll with the truth. Every single time.

He's quiet. Not uncharacteristic of him, but with the tension thickening in the room, his silence makes everything all the more unbearable.

Zoya's shoulders shake as she begins to cry again, a fresh wave of tears streaming down her face.

"Ms. Zoya . . ." He sounds helpless. She remembers his words when she first hired him, that he didn't think it was right for him to be in her (or any other woman's) company if it wasn't about work. The discomfort is clear from the tension in his body; he seems conflicted as to whether he should stay or leave.

Finally, he says, "Trust Allah. He is going to grant you justice."

Zoya shakes her head. "He didn't grant me justice back then and He won't grant me justice now."

"God's delay does not mean God's denial." Gentleness exudes from his tone.

These words cause her brain's gears to stutter. *Then what does His delay mean?* she wants to ask, but fears she is incapable of hearing his response. It will knock down her guarded steel walls.

Instead, her spool begins to unwind. Her mouth opens of its

own accord, and everything she's held back for too long comes rushing out.

"I built myself a carefully crafted image by becoming the CEO of what later became one of the fastest growing companies in the world," Zoya whispers. "The fashion industry is well acquainted with my name, and I command a certain type of respect, even if everyone may not like me."

Haroun hands her a box of tissues as she cries messily, still averting her gaze from him. "Being a powerful female in the corporate world . . . you're always pointed fingers at. Much more than men are." Zoya blows her nose. "I wish people could see my femininity as something other than a source of pleasure. I wish they would stop looking at me as a *woman*—or someone to be toyed around with and taken advantage of—and start looking at me as a *human*."

Haroun tenses, his fists clenching. Zoya realizes her words have probably confirmed the speculations on the news.

"You think I was always this way?" A hysterical laugh bubbles out of her. "I groveled in dirt to become the CEO of this company so that I wouldn't have people leering at me." Her breath catches in her throat, another sob threatening to escape. "Being a random employee or intern wouldn't grant me the justice I needed. Being the CEO would give me the right to shoot these people down, to put them in their places. So that when someone even looked at me in the wrong way, I would have the right to do what I chose with them."

Zoya runs her hand under her nose, disgusted by herself. "Zoya Zameer *this*, Zoya Zameer *that*. Why can't people just mind their own bloody business? What do they receive from digging up people's graves?" She quiets suddenly, lips trembling. Her thoughts are scattered, each one demanding to be voiced. "Everybody has made so many guesses as to who Zoya Zameer is that even *I* don't know who she is anymore." She laughs scornfully. "I'm a shell encased in a shell encased in a shell. Hollow like a coconut. Latching onto any form of display." Her chin wobbles. "Bruised and beaten inside. Confident and gorgeous as ever outside."

Something in her shifts at having said these words out loud—

something vulnerable. The logical part of her brain warns her to stop talking, to stop displaying her weaknesses so openly. But her logic has turned to hysteria, and the tears streaming down her face along with the ache in her heart prod her to continue speaking.

Because someone is finally listening.

"I have no identity," Zoya murmurs quietly, clutching the cup tighter as she thinks of *him*. "Every time my ex-husband gave me another scar, he took away a part of me. Killed a part of me. I became sucked into his vortex of lies and claims and senseless regurgitations, which he wrongfully took from the Qur'an. He wielded religion as a sword, and like a puppet, I bent to his will. He sabotaged every piece of my scarred soul until there was none left. So who is Zoya Zameer?" She laughs. "Even *I* don't know."

At this, Haroun's jaw tightens, and an indent appears between his brows. But for the first time, Zoya pays him no heed.

Her spool is still unwinding.

"You know every time I pray, I remember his voice telling me that I'm praying for God," she whispers as a violent shiver comes over her. "I feel like a doll, a puppet. He puppeteers me with his words, his taunts, his sneers. Even when he is nowhere near me, he has complete control over me. I am who I am because he made me this way." She blows her nose.

And then there are the unsaid words: *And I employ his same manipulative tactics because I never want to be placed in that position of helplessness again.*

For the first time, Haroun seems to be speechless with shock. He leans forward to balance his elbows on his knees and steeples his fingers as he listens quietly.

Finally, he clears his throat. "I . . . Ms. Zoya, I am so, so sorry. For everything." His voice is a low thrum, tentative and scared. Like a mouse when it dances precariously around the cheese trap, confused as to how to approach it without causing any damage.

Zoya scoffs. Hearing this from anyone else would have angered her, but Haroun's concern is not pity; it's empathy. "What are *you* sorry for?" *You're the only one who has made it all a bit more bearable.*

He shakes his head. "Nobody should have to go through that."

"People do. Every day."

He's silent for a moment as the weight of her words hits him. "Ms. Zoya, do you realize how strong that makes you?"

Her brows draw together in confusion.

"You hid your ex-husband's sins. You left him up to Allah. And your Lord loves you for your trust in Him and His justice.

You left him up to Allah.

Had she, though? Had she left her oppressor's verdict to God, or had she simply felt that no jury would ever grant her justice? Had the fear of her own reputation driven her to keep silent, or had it been the threats from others?

Your Lord loves you.

Does her Lord love her for anything? If He loves her, why does He cause her so much suffering? Why does one thing after another continue to pile on top of Zoya until she is crushed by debris over and over again?

Haroun's words have once again shaken her to her core. He sees her *silence* about her abusive relationship as her *trust* in God. He sees her *fear* as her *certainty* in God's justice.

He sees everything that isn't there.

"Have you ever been able to talk to anyone about this?" he asks quietly. "Did you ever try reporting it or . . . taking it to court?"

Despite the tears rolling down her face, she snorts. "Court?" Zoya's laugh is strangled as she rubs her hands across her face. "God, Haroun, do you know what it's like out there? People in power are so secure—nobody would dare go against them." She is abruptly reminded of her own self by these words. To shake off the tangle of conflicting emotions, she addresses Haroun's first question. "And apart from talking to *you* right now, I told my father." Her laugh turns hysterical. "But he was so ashamed that he took off. Never looked back."

It is so difficult for Zoya to say the words out loud. But for some reason, opening the dark, shadowed door of her past to Haroun Suleiman does not seem dangerous at all.

"Took off?" Haroun says. "As in—"

Zoya nods vigorously. "Oh, yeah." There is scorn in her voice that she never realized she felt, but it seems that her subconscious tried to bury this feeling away along with all her other painful memories. "My father felt too *guilty* for 'choosing' my ex-husband for me, even though he had consulted me and I had consciously agreed to marry him. So when I . . ." Her breath hitches. "When I needed my father the most, he . . ." She trails off, unable to finish.

Haroun rubs a hand down the length of his face. "Oh, God." His voice now carries the baggage of the knowledge he's just received. The baggage of Zoya's past.

They sit in silence for a while, Haroun's posture as strained as ever as Zoya's tears continue to stream down her cheeks.

"You're unbelievably strong," Haroun says quietly, voice full of awe. "After everything you've been through, you managed to build yourself up from your past—"

"Build myself up from my past?" Zoya laughs mirthlessly. How can she tell him about the nightmares, the constant terror, the flashbacks, the agonizing memories that haunt her every day, the periods of time where she can't seem to breathe?

She can't tell him.

"You struggled through everything alone," Haroun says. "You didn't tell anyone, didn't talk to anyone, were coerced by forces outside your power to let your oppressor go." He sighs heavily. "And everything that you've managed to do after all that . . . you are incredibly strong."

"I'm not mentally afflicted," Zoya interrupts through clenched teeth. "Just so you know."

"Of course not, Ms. Zoya. I know that." His voice is careful.

"So there was no need to talk to anyone, because there was nothing wrong with me." Her fists are clenched so tightly around her teacup that the heat begins to burn her fingers.

"People don't talk to others only when something is wrong." Haroun's voice is sad, almost pitiful. Immediately, Zoya's walls shoot back up. "We talk to others to find *sukoon*."

Zoya chuckles mirthlessly. "Again, Haroun Suleiman, the *sukoon* that is so readily available to you refuses to find me."

"Open up to your Lord," he echoes his words from that night in Pakistan. Carefully, quietly. As if he's soothing a vicious animal. "Not only will you find *sukoon,* but He will heal all your wounds. He will heal all your afflictions."

"There are no afflictions to heal."

"Open up to Him regardless. Unlike humans, He is a constant sanctuary. For pain and pleasure both."

A shock passes through Zoya, her walls halt in their ascent. Had he read her mind when she thought that Haroun was her sanctuary? Is he combating this thought now?

How is he so easily able to read her?

Moisture gathers in Zoya's eyes once again. "Haroun." There is a plea in her voice. The plea that has nagged her ever since she laid eyes on him, ever since he spoke and something stirred in her previously dead heart. The words are at the tip of her tongue, ready to finally be voiced.

But she can't. She can't.

Haroun Suleiman was not made for people like Zoya Zameer.

She is emotionally distraught, and he is offering her comfort. How many times has it indirectly been him who has soothed her distressed heart? How many times have her darkened days been brightened by his gentle sunlight?

And how many times has he been someone else's source of comfort as well?

Haroun is the light that reaches so many people's eyes. His glow is not limited to Zoya Zameer alone. Countless people can attest that Haroun has served as a beacon of comfort and guidance in their lives at some point.

He won't want Zoya.

At least not by choice.

A dangerous thought plants itself in her mind, seeding itself into the crevices of her brain. A sudden, violent thought, but an appealing one as well. A thought that needs nurturing before it turns into an act. Zoya carefully tucks this thought into the back of her head, saving it for the right time.

She continues crying silently, everything tumbling over her

once again. All of her plans to uproot and destroy Zaki Ahmed—gone. He is too powerful, has too much on Zoya, has targeted her weak spots and made her crumble. So that she is unable to retaliate without burying herself deeper into the quicksand.

Let it go.

Fire burns within her at the mere thought. How can she let her oppressor go?

You did it before, didn't you? a sad voice whispers in her mind. *Do it again.*

Not this time.

"Haroun, I . . ." Zoya presses her lips together for a moment. "I just want consistency. I don't want something new every morning. I don't want another headline on the news every day, another surprise attack before I sleep. I don't want . . ." She shifts in agitation. "I don't want turbulent waves; I want a calm shore. I want constancy. A North Star." She looks up at him through teary eyes. "Something that remains unchanged, something that promises to stay despite the turbulent waves." Zoya quiets, coming as close to a confession as she can.

"You want constancy, Ms. Zoya?" There is something new in his voice. Wonder, excitement. "Look at the world around you. Do you see constancy in the shifting politics, in the shallow relationships we now call real, in the quick pace of the business world? Do you think any of this is constant?"

She shakes her head.

He points to the window. "Look outside, Ms. Zoya." She turns her head and takes in the vastness of the sky. The glittering rays of the sun, the faded crescent moon. "In his search for God, the Prophet Ibrahim thought that maybe he would find Him in the sun, the moon, or the stars. But then the sun set and the moon came up, and then the moon faded and the sun came up, and the stars vanished and the sky cleared. And the Prophet Ibrahim said that if something vanished so easily, there was no way it was divine. If he could not trust even the sun to stay when it neared evening, this could not be God. Nor could the vast sky we all look at—sprinkled with stars at night that inevitably fade by morning. God could not be in these inconsistencies—the Prophet realized that."

Haroun pauses, shifts so that he's facing Zoya. He places a palm over his chest.

Right over his heart.

"But this, Ms. Zoya? This small, seemingly insignificant organ in comparison to the entire universe? This organ beats. It beats constantly. It beats consistently. It's minuscule compared to the vast sky and the sparkling stars, but it's constant. Even when the sun goes down and the moon rises and the stars appear, even when the stars fade and the sun goes up and the moon disappears, this heart continues to beat. In all forms, in all creatures. It beats and it beats and it beats. Constant, persistent.

"And this small, seemingly insignificant organ in comparison to the entire universe, is where we feel a connection with God. This is the root of it all; this is where we love Him, and this is where our relationship with Him lives. Not in the untrustworthy sky, or the untrustworthy stars and planets. But here." Haroun taps his chest. "This is the secret to knowing Allah."

Zoya begins to tremble uncontrollably. She becomes aware of her every breath, her every heartbeat, assenting to his words.

The sudden exhilaration robs her of speech. It instills in her a feeling that she cannot fathom or explain.

And that is when she knows for a *fact*.

She cannot let Haroun Suleiman go.

As if adding fuel to her thought, he continues, "There's always potential to change and grow. A person has even the smallest inclination in their heart to change, and Allah guides them along their path to reach their goal." Haroun stands, halts for a second. "I hope your pain eases. Let me know if you need anything." He gestures to the cup in her hands, but she senses he's referring to more.

Zoya simply nods, unable to repress her tremors.

Thirty-Nine

The Prophet Muhammad (peace be upon him) said: "There are three signs of a hypocrite: When he speaks, he lies; when he makes a promise, he breaks it; and when he is trusted, he betrays his trust." (Sahih Bukhari and Muslim)

~

"I'M SURPRISED THAT YOU called me to meet you here."

"Yeah, well, don't mistake my *majboori* for actually wanting to see your face." Zoya takes a sip of her tea, refusing to make eye contact with Sumaiya.

Sumaiya settles down in the chair across from Zoya and glances at their surroundings. "Nice place." She gestures to the restaurant logo, *Tea For Me.*

"Yeah, least conspicuous. Because Zoya Zameer would never be caught dead in a boba tea shop." She finally looks at Sumaiya, ignoring the pang in her chest. Her eyebrows furrow when she sees the headscarf wrapped around the woman's head. Zoya makes a vague gesture towards it. "Why are you still wearing that?"

Sumaiya's eyebrows rise. "Excuse me?"

"You heard me."

"I don't understand."

Zoya shrugs. "After everything you've done, you think you still deserve to have that on your head?"

Sumaiya's eyes widen, taken aback. "Ms. Zoya, I understand

that you're still angry. You have every right to be. And I don't know how I'll ever be able to tell you how sorry I am, truly—"

"Skip the theatrics. Answer my question."

Sumaiya takes a deep breath. "One mistake doesn't mean I'm destined to be left in the dark forever. That's . . . *Shaitan's* motto." She looks at Zoya cautiously, worried that her words will trigger Zoya's anger. "But God is always merciful. And if I allow myself a second chance and turn to Him in repentance, He too will give me chances. His doors of mercy and forgiveness are open for me until I stop breathing.

"And . . ." Sumaiya waves a hand over her *hijab*. "I'm not wearing this because of who *I* am. I'm wearing this because of Allah and because of the person that I *want* to become. Wearing it doesn't make me sinless or perfect, but it ensures that I'm willing to try."

Zoya squints. "Where was this whole *holier than thou* attitude when you threw Zameer under the bus? When you betrayed your '*fiancé*?'"

Sumaiya sighs heavily, resting her gaze on her lap. "*He* is what helped set me in the right direction. Through his personality and his devotion to faith." She looks back up at Zoya. "I am so, so sorry. Truly. If I could take it all back, I would."

"Mhm." Zoya doesn't hide her skepticism as her eyes rake over Sumaiya. "Speaking of second chances, let's get to the point. I need you to do something for me."

Sumaiya's head snaps up, hopeful at the chance for redemption. "Anything."

Zoya laughs mirthlessly. "You sure about that?"

Sumaiya bites her bottom lip, expression becoming wary.

"Well, it's not like I'm giving you a choice." Zoya takes a sip of her milk tea and pretends to gag. "Ugh, horrible flavor."

"What is it, Ms. Zoya?" Sumaiya presses.

Zoya flinches. "First of all, keep my name out of your damn mouth." She taps a finger against her lips. "You can call me '*miss*,' or '*your highness*.' Second, I need the pictures Zaki threatened you with."

Sumaiya's brows knit. "What?"

"Let's skip the part where you pretend like you can't hear me."

"I can't give those to you," Sumaiya replies immediately. "You know I can't."

Zoya gives her a blank stare, then waves a hand in front of her own face. "And what about my expression, dear Sumaiya, gives you the inkling that I give a damn?"

Sumaiya shakes her head continuously. "The whole reason I was forced to become a spy was because—"

"Save the sob stories for later. You said you wanted redemption, right? That you wanted to be rid of your guilt? Well, think of it this way. If you could reverse time and *not* do the things you now regret, how would it have gone down? Zaki would have released those pictures to the press." Zoya shrugs. "I'm doing the same. It'll be as if all the things you did never happened. All's right in the world."

Sumaiya's forehead creases with worry. "It's not just that. If I gave you those pictures, not only will my reputation be at stake, but so will my *life*. Zaki will harm me."

A giggle bubbles out of Zoya. "He will do no such thing. Because your face and identity won't be disclosed to the press."

"He'll know anyway," Sumaiya whispers. "He's not a fool. He's going to make sure I pay the price."

After a moment's hesitation—during which Zoya's conflicted inner voices battle—she shrugs. "Well, we all reap what we sow, don't we?" Zoya stares down the woman in front of her, no hint of remorse on her face. And yet, that voice nags at her again.

Zoya is determined to ignore it.

Sumaiya's eyes shine with tears.

"This is a way for you to right your wrongs, sweetheart!" Zoya exclaims. Sumaiya stares down into her lap. She sits still for so long that Zoya rolls her eyes, sighs, and says, "What is so interesting in your damn lap? Enlighten me, please."

Finally, Sumaiya looks up. A single tear rolls down her cheek and Zoya huffs, looking away. She dislikes the twinge in her chest caused by that tear. It infuriates her. She is not supposed to feel this way, not after what Sumaiya did.

"Okay," Sumaiya finally whispers. "I'll do it."

"Great!" Zoya beams. She shoves her bubble tea away from her with a grimace. "Glad this didn't take too long. Otherwise I would have been forced to drink this horrid tea. You know, because somebody is holding me at gunpoint to do so." She gives Sumaiya a knowing look, pays the bill, and stands. "You have twenty-four hours."

And with that, Zoya exits the bubble tea shop with a flourish.

~

Six hours after her request, Zoya receives the pictures from a reluctant Sumaiya. She arranges with a very distant Sameer to have them released to the press as soon as possible. When she asks him what his problem is, he simply shrugs and says, "You're just doing the same thing she fell prey to. She told you she didn't have a choice, and you wouldn't hear a word of it. Now you have the chance to make a different choice, but . . ." He shrugs and looks away.

Ignoring the discomfort his words bring her, Zoya settles for an accusatory tone. "Well, *Mr. Righteous*, if you're *so* against this, why are you doing what I say?"

A knock on the office door interrupts their conversation. Bill enters and says, "Haroun just dropped by to return this." He sets a file on the desk by the entrance and leaves the room.

A pang resonates in Zoya's chest when she hears his name. Her heart hurts. It hurts so bad.

Zoya clears her throat and turns back to Sameer, who seems to be contemplating something after Bill's arrival and the mention of Haroun. "Yes?" she queries peevishly. "Answer my question."

After a few moments of deep thought, a new look dawns on Sameer's face. A scared, but determined look. "You know what?" he says, setting the pictures in his hand on her desk. "I *do* have another choice."

And then he leaves the room.

Zoya stares at the pictures on her desk, open-mouthed. "Well, Sameer Mirza." She clears her throat, trying to ignore the conflict settling in her heart. To no avail, however, because her inner voices begin to whisper incessantly, rising to a fever pitch.

"I'll just have to do this on my own, then," Zoya says, picking up the phone to call the journalist.

~

When the news about Zaki's alleged affair comes out, the press goes wild. They call it the *Zaki-Zoya Tug-of-War.* Zoya flicks through every news channel in her office, letting out a deep sigh of relief when she sees Zaki Ahmed's face plastered on the screen, along with a heavily blurred picture of Sumaiya and her anonymous statement.

Now Zaki will not dare to retaliate. If he does, it is an indirect affirmation of his actions. Zoya tells this to a distressed Lucas, who continues to look angry despite her attempts at reassurance. He discovered the news along with everyone else, and he's still furious with Zoya for not consulting him.

Zoya pays her PR manager no heed.

Because a feeling has settled within her at seeing her rival's life turn upside down. Something close to the satisfaction she has been seeking.

But not quite there.

There is still a hollow chasm in her heart, an emptiness. Something is urgently missing.

A few hours later, Sameer—who has barely spoken to Zoya since his refusal to do her dirty work—barges into her office, breathless.

"What?" Zoya drawls, observing his haphazard appearance.

"There's been an accident."

Zoya closes the file in her hand and stands. "What sort of accident?"

"A car accident. Sumaiya is in the hospital."

The air whooshes out of Zoya, the cocky smile vanishing from her face. She stares at Sameer, rendered speechless by his announcement. "What?" she finally says in a shaky voice as Sumaiya's words filter through her head.

Zaki will harm me. He's going to make sure I pay the price.

Sameer nods. "She's in the ICU, in critical condition."

Zoya's mouth opens, but she seems to have momentarily lost

the ability to form coherent speech. She stares at him dumbly, unsure of what to do.

She warned you, the voice that has been haunting her for the past few weeks awakens once more. *But you shrugged it off as a bluff.*

And now she's going to die.

Zoya shakes her head, clearing her throat. She grabs her handbag and pulls out a scarf to wrap around her head. "Let's go," she tells Sameer.

"This is your fault," he says quietly. His voice is trembling, but he barrels on. "Do you realize that?"

Zoya whirls around to face him, one hand on the doorknob. "No, it's not," she snarls. *Is it?* "I'm not the one who crashed her car."

"No, but you're the one who could have stopped this from happening," Sameer shoots back shakily.

At that moment, Zoya wants nothing more than to pounce on Sameer, to hurt him with her words the way she does not want to admit he is hurting her with his. Instead, she takes a deep breath and fights back the urge to yell at him. "Are you taking me to the hospital or not?"

He rushes past her without a word, and she follows him to his car.

When they arrive at the hospital and are escorted to the waiting room, Zoya settles down with a jolt in her knee and dread in her heart.

This is not my fault.

Is it?

No, it's not.

Could I have stopped this?

It could just be a coincidence.

At this thought, she makes an incomprehensible noise in her throat, and Sameer shoots her a disapproving look.

When the doctor leaves Sumaiya's room, Zoya rushes to her. "How is she?"

"She's suffered a lot of internal bleeding and has three broken ribs, but she's stable now."

Zoya releases a breath she hadn't realized she was holding. The doctor walks away, and she stumbles against the wall for support.

She's alive.

When Zoya gains her bearings, she looks back up at Sameer, unable to meet his eyes for reasons she cannot explain to herself. "No one can know about this, Sameer. Okay?" Her voice is barely a whisper. She cannot fathom it, but for some reason she feels ashamed at her request.

He stares her down for a moment, his gaze unwavering. "Whatever you say, *Ms. Zoya.*" His voice is full of venom as he turns and walks away

Zoya simply stands there, a heavy feeling settling in her chest.

Zaki actually harmed Sumaiya to make a point. He actually had no regard for human life.

Do you *have regard for human life?* The accusatory voice is back in her head.

She intakes a sharp breath. *Yes, I do.*

Then why did you allow this to happen?

She begins to tremble with dread.

What would Haroun say? Zoya thinks. *He would probably say that it wasn't in any of our control, that it was God's will. Right?*

She reassures herself by this thought. But her face pales when she realizes what he would probably say next.

But Allah gave us the power to make choices.

Zoya closes her eyes and sinks to the floor against the wall. She presses her palms to her eyelids. Her body begins to shake, and the tears that attest to all the emotions she won't speak begin to flow out of her. She cries and cries, right there on that hospital floor.

Haroun is leaving her life, and she has found no way of trying to keep him of his own will. Sameer, one of the few people Zoya has formed an unspoken attachment with, now abhors her. Zaki Ahmed will stop at no lengths to destroy her, and Zoya is *exhausted* by the constant back and forth between them.

Her father left her years ago and never once looked back, and his absence burns holes in her heart every day.

Zoya Zameer has nobody. Nobody to love her. Nobody to care for her.

And when all of this comes crashing down on her overburdened heart, she makes another selfish decision.

And this time, she *really* believes that she has no other choice.

Forty

"They (think to) deceive Allah and those who believe, but they deceive not except themselves and realize (it) not." (Qur'an 2:9)

~

"WHAT HAPPENED?"

"Doctors are saying she was distracted and in shock, so she didn't look where she was going and tripped. Fell down a flight of stairs and hit her head. Might have a concussion."

"Oh, God. Is she gonna be okay?"

"Let's hope so."

Bill, Ibitoye, and Lucas rush through the hospital, heading to the ICU. Once there, they rush to room A123. A nurse stops them at the entrance. "I'm sorry," she says. "She cannot have visitors right now."

Bill holds his hands out. "*Please.* We just need to know that she's okay."

The nurse has the detachedly sympathetic look on her face that most doctors do. "I'm sorry. We'll update you with any news. The doctors are checking up on her. She may have suffered a traumatic brain injury."

"Oh, God," Ibitoye whispers.

The nurse nods and walks away, leaving the two directors and the PR manager standing there with shock on their faces.

After what seems like hours of lip biting, nail chewing, and aimless pacing, the three of them rush to the doctor that steps out of Zoya Zameer's room.

"How is she doing?"

"She's stable now," the doctor says, not meeting their eyes. They let out relieved breaths. "But she's suffered a minor concussion. What she needs is to be away from any source of stress right now." The doctor wipes her hands on her coat. "She needs time to relax, and she's requested not to allow any visitors." She tucks a curl behind her ear, and there is a slight tremble in her fingers. "She has also requested to keep this quiet. She does not want anyone in the press to know."

Lucas nods. "Okay. Just as long as she's okay."

The doctor nods and walks away quickly, throwing them one last furtive glance before disappearing around the corner.

"How are we gonna keep this quiet?" Ibitoye frets.

"We'll worry about that later," Lucas says. "Besides, not many reporters are aware that she's here. The ones who are will be paid to keep their mouths shut."

Rushed footsteps approach the three of them, and they look up to see Sameer and Farhan.

"Is she okay?" Farhan asks breathlessly. Bill nods, explaining the situation.

"Are visitors allowed?" says Sameer.

Ibitoye shakes her head. "They're saying that she needs to rest. And that she doesn't want to see any of us."

Just then, a nurse from Zoya's room approaches them. "Are any of you named Haroun?"

The five of them glance at each other quizzically before comprehension dawns on Sameer's and Farhan's faces. "No, but we can get him," Sameer says.

The nurse nods and retreats.

"She wants to see Haroun?" Ibitoye says, confused.

Sameer shares a knowing glance with Farhan. "Obviously."

"He has a meeting with the sponsors of the orphanage," Farhan says. "But I can call and let him know."

Sameer nods. "You do that. I just need to talk to Ms. Zoya's doctor for a sec." He jogs backward and disappears around the corner.

Farhan dials his friend's number and gives him the news over the phone. When the call ends, Farhan says, "He's coming."

~

Haroun enters, his mother following closely behind. There are worry lines etched into her forehead, which relax upon seeing Zoya.

Zoya turns her head when they come in, and she pushes her palms into the bed to lift herself up. Haroun's mother rushes forward and pushes her back down gently. "Don't move too much."

Zoya smiles at her. A real smile.

"These are for you." Haroun's mother sets a bouquet of flowers down on the food table. "And . . . I thought you might want some homemade food." She sets a plate of rice and roast chicken down as well. "I pray Allah grants you a speedy recovery."

"Thank you," Zoya says, her voice raw with emotion.

Her eyes fall on Haroun, who looks away when their gazes lock. "How are you feeling?" he asks, voice low.

"Better now." Zoya's voice shakes as she responds. She gestures to the chairs. "You guys can sit down."

After a few moments of silence, Zoya slowly says, "I'm sure you're wondering why I asked to see you."

Haroun simply nods for her to continue.

The tearing feeling comes back at the sight of him, and something aches in Zoya's chest. Her breath hitches, and she begins to cry.

His mother gives her a look of surprise and worry. "Are you okay? Should I call the doctor?"

Zoya shakes her head as tears spill down her cheeks, partly due to his mother's genuine concern and partly due to what she is about to say. When she gains her bearings, she looks back at Haroun. "I wanted to request your son for something."

Haroun's brows knit. "Yes, Ms. Zoya?"

Zoya sniffs, taking a deep breath. "I could get worse." Before his mother can say anything, she continues, "My doctor said that although it's been treated, there's the constant threat of possible internal bleeding again. And if that happens, next is possible organ failure and . . . who knows? Maybe I'll die young."

Haroun's mother reaches forward and brushes a hand over Zoya's forehead. Zoya starts, overwhelmed by the softness of the touch. It makes what she is about to do so much harder.

But she has no other choice.

"What if I don't recover? I could die, Haroun." She shrugs. "And I'm okay with that. I have lived a miserable life and would be better off dead."

Haroun shakes his head. "Don't say that." His voice is weak.

"It's the truth. And it doesn't bother me." Her tears continue to silently stream down her face. She braces herself for the words she is about to utter. "But you know what bothers me, Haroun?" She breaks out into loud sobs, drawing her knees up to her chest. "That I'll die, and *he* will be the last man who married me. Who touched me. That he'll be the last man I was with."

Haroun's eyes widen, laced with pain at her words. His mother darts a glance between the two of them, confused. Zoya turns to her. "Did you know, auntie, that my ex-husband beat me?" Her eyes widen, and Zoya nods vigorously. "Yes, and not just that; he beat me, yelled at me every chance that he got, and told me he was doing it for God. And he always messed with my head, playing with my emotions. He would . . . he would . . ." She buries her face between her knees, shaking.

Haroun's mother watches her with horror and pity in her widened eyes. Haroun shakes his head in disgust, shoving his hands through his hair. Because hearing the story more than once doesn't seem to decrease his horror and anger, and perhaps it never will.

Zoya picks her head up, eyes shining with tears. She is a mess. Eye bags darker than ever, lips trembling, face wet with tears, hair disheveled. "Haroun" Her hands are clasped in a plea. "I'm begging you. Don't let him be the last man I was with. *Please*, Haroun."

After a long, charged silence, comprehension dawns on his face. Pure and clear. Haroun leans back, mouth opening and closing, unsure of what to say. His hands tighten into fists, every inch of muscle tense.

His mother looks at Zoya. "*Beta*." She tilts her chin up so that

Zoya's tearful eyes are looking into the woman's strong, resolute ones. "What are you trying to say? I don't understand."

Zoya points at Haroun. "Your son does."

His fists are clenched, back ramrod straight.

"Haroun?" his mother prompts.

He places his head in his hands, tension etched into every crevice of his body.

"Please," Zoya whispers through trembling lips. "Please ask your son to marry me. If I die, I do not want to die with any trace of *that man.*"

I want to experience comfort and happiness at least once in my life.

The room is silent for a few agonizingly long moments. Zoya's shoulders continue to shake, Haroun still has his head in his hands, and his mother's face is impassive, nothing detectable.

"I know I'm asking a lot of you, Haroun. I know I am. But *please*, I'm *begging* you. You're a good man. I don't . . . I don't deserve someone like you. But out of the goodness of your heart, please do this for me." She holds her hands out, clasped tightly together in an urgent plea. Her heart hurts. It hurts so bad for what she is doing to him.

But she knows she has no other choice.

Finally, after what seems like hours, Haroun picks his head up. But instead of looking at Zoya, he glances at his mother.

His mother reaches down and covers Zoya's clasped hands with her own, her touch a soft embrace. She looks back at her son, her face determined, his helpless. There is a silent agreement between them, and she gives him a bare, almost imperceptible nod.

Haroun continues to watch his mother with that helpless look in his eyes. The look that—for the first time—scares Zoya. Because it reminds her of who she is, of what she is doing to get what she wants.

But there is no turning back now.

Then Haroun turns to Zoya and nods quietly.

Forty-One

~

"YES, I DO."

"Yes, I do."

Tears prick at Zoya's eyes. She looks around at the hospital room. Haroun, his father, and Farhan are serving as the witnesses, the *imam* is serving as Zoya's *wali*, and a second *imam* is performing the *nikah* with the agreed *mahr*.

Strange feelings makes a home in Zoya's heart. She's hit with a burst of happiness, and simultaneously a wave of anxiety-filled déjà vu from her last *nikah*.

Her father is not here. During one of the most important moments of her life, he is not here. Sameer had several people try to track him down for the purpose of Zoya's *nikah*, but he was nowhere to be found. As if he doesn't even exist.

He has hidden himself really well.

God knows where he is.

Her thoughts are interrupted when someone gently caresses her hair. Gold bangles are pushed up her wrists, and Haroun's mother smiles softly at her. All around the small room, smiles and congratulations are exchanged. To her and her new husband.

Her new husband.

Warmth spreads throughout Zoya at the thought. Haroun is

now her *husband*. She is tied to him for eternity. He is hers. She is his.

She has achieved her life's greatest desire.

As the *imams* and Farhan leave after a collective *du'a*, Zoya sneaks a glance at Haroun.

She has never been shy to look at anyone before, never been bothered by the thought of staring mercilessly into someone's eyes.

But for some reason, the way Haroun makes her speechless, today he makes her . . . shy as well. After her stolen glance at him, she sees that he is staring right back at her. Heat spreads through her cheeks, and she turns away quickly, clamping her lips to keep from smiling.

Until she remembers how this all went down, how she made it happen, the haunted look in Haroun's eyes.

Easy, Zoya, she tells herself. *You can worry about that later.*

But *that,* it seems, does not want to escape her conflicted mind.

No matter how much force she pushes it away with, glancing around at her hospital room and the IV pierced into her skin throws her into it all over again. And again she becomes preoccupied with worrying.

No need to feel guilty, Zoya, a voice nags at her. *You did what you had to do.*

She nods slowly. *Yes. I did what I had to do.*

Did she, though?

~

The two directors, the PR manager, Farhan, and Sameer all congratulate Zoya and Haroun before leaving. Before exiting the room, Sameer darts a knowing smirk at Zoya, but his eyes are also full of questions.

Haroun's parents congratulate the couple once again—his father shares a tense hug with him and an awkward pat on his new daughter-in-law's head—and begin to head out. His mother lags behind for a moment, waiting for his father to leave the vicinity before she turns in the opposite direction. Leaving Zoya and Haroun alone.

The last time Zoya had been alone with Haroun, he was just her employee. An employee she had pined over for months.

Now he is her husband.

The label causes Zoya to feel giddy, jittery, and terrified all at once.

She turns to him, suddenly unsure of what to say. His expression is wary, which further worries her.

Did he really not want this?

"Are you okay?" she asks tentatively.

He looks up, directly into her eyes. Then, flushing because he isn't used to it yet, he turns away quickly. "I'm okay. You?"

"I'm okay," she replies. She leans back a little, wincing as the IV cuts deeper into her skin.

He notices. And stands. And moves his chair closer to her.

Zoya's heart rate speeds up. She has never felt this thrilled, this exhilarated, *this* out of control around him before. Or around *anyone*, for that matter. She's Zoya Zameer—she's supposed to remain composed at all times.

It's scary and simultaneously exhilarating, the effect he has on her.

The monitor showcases the embarrassing speeding up of her heart, and Haroun's eyes dart to the screen. Surprisingly, a smirk plays on his lips, but the look doesn't reach his eyes. "Are you sure you're okay?"

A nervous laugh escapes Zoya. "It's just—this was hurting." She points to her IV and shrugs nonchalantly.

"Do you want me to call the doctor?"

"No, no. It's okay."

Haroun becomes serious again, turning his face towards the window. He is too quiet, and something about his silence scares Zoya.

How much did he not want her?

"Thank you," she whispers. When he looks at her again, she continues. "For doing this."

Thank you for doing this? What a stupid thing to say to your new husband.

He rubs his face tiredly but gives no reply, just a slight nod.

"Is it that bad?" The words are out before she can stop them. Before she can calculate all the ways that his answer could hurt her.

He sighs. Then, as if he can read her thoughts, he says, "I don't want to upset you."

"Nothing you say will upset me." *Lies, Zoya.*

Haroun is quiet for a few long moments, and Zoya thinks he may not answer, but then he opens his mouth and says, "It's not you, Ms. Zoya—" He catches himself, chuckles softly at the slip-up, shaking his head. "Zoya," he corrects, and her heart skips a beat. "I . . . don't think I was ready for a commitment yet. So soon after . . ." He hesitates, taking a deep breath. "I don't want to live a life under constant scrutiny. I don't want my privacy invaded by the media. And you—" He meets her gaze, and the anguish in his eyes brings the uncomfortable, tugging sensation back to Zoya. "You're all over the news. Constantly. Everywhere."

He presses his lips together suddenly, a flash of guilt passing over his face.

"I understand that," Zoya says, her voice softer than it ever has been. "And I know that after Zaki messed with your reputation, you probably want nothing to do with me and . . . my world. But—" *But I'm selfish. And I need you.* She struggles to explain it to him because truthfully, she does not have an explanation that will satisfy him. "With time, you'll understand," she ends lamely, the words sounding all wrong to her.

Stop blaming yourself, Zoya. You had to do this.

Haroun's gaze is trained outside the window again, passively roving over the skyline and the arch of the buildings. The light from the windows across the hospital sparkle like stars in the darkness of the night. The two sit in tense silence for a few moments before he turns back to her. "Are you hungry?"

She is still not used to the intensity of his gaze, and it seems that he isn't used to looking either because he turns away quickly. "No." She doesn't mention that they just ate an hour ago. She senses he's already nervous enough as it is and is attempting to make conversation despite their tense situation.

Haroun Suleiman, ever the Good Samaritan.

Zoya's eyelids begin to droop, and at one point her head lolls to one side before she snaps back up. Haroun turns at the sound, and a small smile plays on his lips. "You should rest," he says, standing up and reaching forward. Zoya tenses for a moment, thinking he might touch her, but he reassures her with his soft eyes and simply adjusts the pillows behind her head.

She is disgusted at herself for being afraid of his touch. This is *Haroun*. She has no reason to fear him.

And yet.

Her past continues to haunt her every day.

Zoya snuggles into the pillows as Haroun presses the button on the side of the hospital bed to decline it into a sleeping position. He reaches for the blanket and tentatively drapes it over her.

All this he does without intentionally touching her.

Zoya stares at him brazenly when he's not looking, her heart turning softer than it ever has. Seeing him tuck her in so carefully, so caringly, pushes away the regret that has been nagging at her. The regret that she made him commit himself to her. Instead, she grasps at the new feeling that is beginning to surround her. The quiet, comforting feeling. Blanketing her, arresting her senses. The ghost of what she could have if she spends more moments like this with Haroun Suleiman.

Peace.

As her eyes are closing, Haroun settles back in the chair across from her. She regards him for a moment before murmuring, "You can go home, you know. I'll be okay."

He shakes his head and leans back. "You are my responsibility now."

The words send a shock through Zoya. They're spoken with such intense care that after a long time, Zoya finally feels as if she can drop her shields and stop guarding her walls.

Because someone else may be defending them for her.

"And don't worry." The thrum of Haroun's quiet voice breaks Zoya out of her heart's warm reverie. "I will not touch you until you are okay with it."

And these words, on top of everything, seal the deal. She cannot feel regret anymore, not after the way he is acting and the things he is saying. Not after she has finally gotten Haroun Suleiman.

There is no need for her to regret anything she has done, because if it means she can witness more moments like this, Zoya Zameer is willing to take that decision not a hundred, but a thousand more times.

Because her desire for Haroun Suleiman's love is endless.

Forty-Two

*The Prophet Muhammad (peace be upon him) said, "The worst people
in the sight of Allah on the Day of Resurrection will be the double faced
people who appear to some people with one face, and to other people
with another face." (Sahih Bukhari)*

THE DOCTOR SAYS THAT the hospital cannot keep Zoya when her
vital signs are clear and there is no immediate threat. But she tells
Haroun that if Zoya experiences any dizziness, weakness, or low
blood pressure, she should be brought to the hospital immediately.
She shares a glance with Zoya and strictly says to Haroun, "You *must*
bring her to me––no other doctor."

This, to Haroun, seems like a strange request, but he nods all
the same.

When Zoya is discharged, Haroun brings her to his home, as is
customary in Pakistani culture. His mother and sisters welcome the
two of them happily. Decorations cover every inch of the house, and
Aisha places a necklace of jasmine flowers around each of their
necks as they enter. Zoya gives them genuine smiles, while Haroun
tries to crack a smile for their benefit.

Even though he is at odds with how he really feels.

They feast together, and Haroun's mother fusses over Zoya
while Zoya continuously reassures her that she's okay. His mother
pleads with Zoya to call her *Ammi*, and Zoya's eyes sparkle with
warmth at the request.

Even with the way everything went down, the heavy feeling that has settled on Haroun's heart lifts slightly when he sees that Zoya Zameer finally has someone to fuss over her, to take care of her. He can tell that she is flattered and comforted by it. He can tell by the soft gleam in her eyes and the way that she laughs with confidence, voice void of any animosity or mockery. The kind of confidence that only comes from someone knowing that they might be okay.

He is baffled by her. He continues to watch her. He watches her as she eats, as she talks to his sisters, as she startles when she catches him staring. He can tell that she's unsettled by his gaze, but he also can't seem to look away.

He has never watched her like *this* before, and it strikes him suddenly how breathtaking she is. With her auburn curls framing her face and her smile seeming to light up the room.

This does not seem like the same woman who cried in front of him, begging him to grasp her outstretched hand. This does not seem like the woman who told him she was weak and was tired of her weakness and didn't know what to do with herself.

This woman seems . . . happy. Even if only momentarily. Because every time she thinks nobody is looking, she breathes a deep sigh and furrows her brows together. Haroun can tell that something is nagging at her, but she shakes her head and tries to brush whatever it is off.

Nonetheless, there is a softness in her face that wasn't there before. A gentleness . . . a glimpse of happiness.

It makes Haroun feel worse than ever, knowing from her words and actions that *he* is the cause of that look on her face. Knowing that *he* is the cause she had breathed a deep sigh of relief when they both said "*Yes, I do.*" Once again, he feels as if he's been forced onto an unrealistically high pedestal by Zoya Zameer. She expects him to keep supplying her with happiness, but he has no idea if he can do that for her.

Haroun is upset and distressed. He's been put into a very strange situation and doesn't know how he feels about it. At the moment, he can't even make *himself* happy, not to mention this woman.

His wife.

Haroun has always sensed that Zoya Zameer had a secret. A deep, dark secret. From the get go, he saw in the way that she spoke to others and the way that she flinched at the mention of religion that somebody had hurt her. That she had been let down too much in her life.

After his mother's divorce, Haroun has always felt inclined to help others out. Especially those who are heartbroken, because he saw what it did to his mother. And he had sensed that Zoya was more than heartbroken, that she had survived a very difficult life. That's why, even though many of her actions had seemed questionable, he had tried to defend her as much as possible. Because he felt and still feels that behind her every word, her every insult, her every angry jibe, is a deep-rooted pain that nobody can reach. And he has wanted her to realize that her wounds can be healed.

But he didn't think she would see *him* as the source of her comfort. He never intended for it to be that way.

But that's the way it turned out. Haroun, with his annoying desire to help people heal—as if he's some dang motivational coach or therapist—has landed himself in an uncomfortable, helpless situation.

Throughout dinner, Haroun remains tense. Clutching his fork harder than necessary. Smiling with more force than necessary when he's spoken to. He doesn't know how he's feeling, and it frustrates him to be unable to explain his emotions to himself.

He can tell that he's angry, but at *what*? Or at who? At himself? At Zoya?

But why should he be angry at her? Isn't this his fault? He allowed her to become too attached. He allowed her to trust him, to want to share her pain with him. All the while, he thought he was trying to do something good for her, trying to make her realize that she needed to open up to God to heal her wounds. That a lot of her issues were rooted in her distrust of God. He thought he was doing it in a professional, detached manner.

But had he overdone it?

On top of that, there is Sumaiya.

Sumaiya, Sumaiya, Sumaiya. Haroun's chest squeezes painfully when he thinks of her. Although they had only made a commitment and he thought he hadn't gotten attached to her, he had been wrong. The few times they had spoken, Sumaiya had always seemed like a generous, caring person.

More importantly, they had a really good understanding of one another. He thought this would allow them to trust each other in any circumstance, but she had stepped away after the mere assumption of Zoya's affection for Haroun.

Haroun cannot even keep himself happy—he is too upset by Sumaiya's decision—so how does his wife expect him to keep her happy?

Another thought nags at him—if he got attached to Sumaiya after such little time, how can he blame Zoya for getting attached to him after all the time they've known each other?

Haroun's head aches. He doesn't want to think at all.

His angry swirl of thoughts is interrupted by the clank of dishes as everyone stands to put them away. Haroun stands as well, sneaking a glance at Zoya only to find that she is staring directly at him, her eyes seeming to pierce into his.

He flushes a deep red.

When the table has been cleared and the dishes have been washed, Zoya and Haroun are led by the three other women to Haroun's room, which has also been decorated. It is soft, beautiful, and elegant, with candles lit everywhere and rose petals scattered about the room. Garlands of flowers are strung from the ceiling into a sloping canopy around the king-sized bed.

Haroun turns to Zoya. Her eyes are full of awe as they rove around the room, then settle on the lamp on his bedside table. Immediately, terror mars her features. Her eyebrows furrow, her lips begin to tremble.

Haroun watches her, perplexed. His mother and sisters also watch her, excitedly trying to gauge her reaction to the room. But she pays them no heed. Instead, she brings a hand up to her heart, eyes fixated on the lamp. Haroun can hear her laborious breathing from a foot away.

"Does she not like the room?" Aisha whispers dejectedly.

"Zoya?" his mother says tenderly. "Are you okay?"

A memory suddenly hits Haroun like a brick to the face.

"Get that off the set. Now!"

Zoya's voice, from over a year ago, rings in Haroun's head. Loud and clear. He doesn't entirely understand why, but he realizes that the lamp is the source of her distress. He rushes forward quickly, unplugs the lamp, and stows it away in his closet. His mother gives him a strange look, but he simply shakes his head. He doesn't know how he'll explain that to her.

When the lamp leaves her vision, Zoya's hand drops from her chest. She swallows, then turns to Haroun. There is fear in her eyes, but it's quickly being replaced by warmth. She is surprised, he realizes, that he remembers her aversion to lamps.

He tugs his eyes away from hers, discomfited by the emotion in them.

Zoya reassures his mother and sisters that she's okay, that she loves the room, that she just got claustrophobic for a second, but when she turns back to Haroun, her eyes tell a different story.

Haroun's mother ushers for Naima to bring a pitcher of water and Zoya's medicines to the room before instructing Zoya to get some rest.

When they're alone, Haroun gestures to his bed. "You can take the bed."

Her footsteps halt behind him. "Where will you sleep?"

He points to the reclining chair by the window.

Silence. Then, "This bed is big enough, I think. I'll be okay."

He can tell it costs her a lot to say this, so he shakes his head. "It's okay. You don't have to do that." He shrugs. "Besides, I'm not sleeping right now. But you should get some rest."

She nods. "Okay, but . . . you can come whenever you're about to sleep. And I just need to pray *'Isha* first."

"We can pray together."

Zoya's eyes dart to him quickly before she looks away. She is uncomfortable by the idea, he realizes suddenly, but before he can say anything, she nods.

They both make *wudu* and Haroun begins the prayer. When they finish, he sits and holds his hands out in an earnest *du'a*.

Minutes later, when they're both done praying, Haroun turns to Zoya. He is taken aback by the emotions in her gaze. The wonder, the fascination.

He clears his throat and says, "You should take your meds."

Zoya gives him an unfathomable look. "Right now?"

"Yes . . . your doctor said one every night."

She nods reluctantly, and he brings her a glass of water. When she takes it from him, their fingers touch. She pulls back suddenly, sloshing water over her hand in the process.

"Sorry," Haroun murmurs automatically, handing her a napkin.

When she's all tucked in with her arm resting under her head, Haroun perches at the edge of the bed, careful not to touch her. He pulls out a blue velvet box from his pocket and sets it on the bedside table. "Your ring," he says, holding up a hand and wiggling his fingers. "I'm wearing mine."

A smile blooms on Zoya'a face.

Once again, Haroun is taken aback by her beauty, especially when he sees it from this close. Voluminous lashes frame her dark eyes, and tangled curls sweep around her exquisite face. Haroun has always found it somewhat strange that people write odes to a person's beauty, but now he thinks he is beginning to understand.

"When you're ready, I'll put yours on your finger, too," he says.

Zoya gives him another soft smile, and it's so different from the way she usually regards people that he turns away, hands tugging the back of his neck. "Is there, uh, is there anything else I can get you?" She shakes her head, continuing to stare at him in that way. Haroun nods, stands, and heads to the reclining chair, glad to be away from her unsettling gaze.

"Should I turn the light off?" he murmurs.

"No," she says quickly. "No, keep it on, please."

Haroun nods. "Okay, good night." He doesn't say anything, but sleeping with the light on is not going to be easy. He can't sleep if it isn't pitch black, and lately he's already been having difficulty sleeping, hence his "Dracula eyes," as Farhan likes to say.

Haroun settles into the reclining chair, opening his Qur'an to the page he left off on. Minutes later, when he looks up to check if Zoya has fallen asleep, he's startled to discover that she's staring directly at him.

~

A couple more days pass with this strange silence between the two of them. This uncomfortable, stretching silence. Haroun frets about Zoya's health, but he doesn't utter more than a few words to her. He smiles at her occasionally when he catches her staring, asks her if she's okay, if she needs anything. He murmurs sorrys over accidental touches and speaks casually about insubstantial matters. He plays the part of husband really well, maintains his responsibilities really well, but that's it. Forced smiles. Empty conversations.

Zoya is on the verge of falling into despair as a result of it. She doesn't know how to reach him, doesn't know how to approach him when he is so close but seems so far away. She has never had trouble speaking to anybody, especially not him, but somehow their sacred bond has seemed to change everything.

One night, Zoya is lulled to sleep by Haroun's Qur'an recitation. She wakes sometime around three in the morning, startled by a muffled, strange sound. Zoya blinks blearily, rubs the sleep out of her eyes, and looks around the room in alarm.

The sound seems to be coming from outside the room, so she takes a long gulp of water to expel some of her sleep and trudges out of the room.

The apartment is dark and quiet, both things Zoya is not particularly fond of. But she hugs her arms around herself and continues to walk towards the source of the sound. She emerges into the living room, and there, sitting on the sofa with his head in his hands, is Haroun. His shoulders shake and his breath hitches as he cries.

The sight causes Zoya's chest to squeeze painfully. Haroun has been her peg, her column of support, the person she has relied on to be her foundation.

But her foundation is crumbling in front of her, and suddenly Zoya feels unsteady.

She steps forward slowly, and the floor creaks beneath her. Haroun's head shoots up. He registers Zoya standing in front of him and rubs his face hastily. But not before she sees the stream of tears pouring down his cheeks, the puffy redness of his eyes, a look so *wrong* for him.

"Haroun?" she says softly, stepping closer.

"I'm sorry, did I wake you?" He attempts a laugh, but it sounds all high and wrong. "I was just—" But just what he was doing Zoya doesn't get to hear, because he turns away as his shoulders begin to shake again.

Zoya has never been put into a situation like this, has never really cared enough about someone for her to feel uncomfortable when they are upset. But as she watches her husband, all of her certainty in herself suddenly flies out the window. She is unsure of what to do, unsure of how to comfort him, unsure of how to ask him what is afflicting him.

Especially because she is afraid to hear his answer.

So instead, she settles on the sofa next to him, listening to him cry. He tries to control it, tries to fist his hands and cover his mouth so the sounds don't disturb his mother and sisters, but he's only able to contain so much.

It makes Zoya's insides twist uncomfortably, to see him this way and think that she might be the root of it.

Zoya lifts a tentative hand, and it hovers in midair for a moment before she rests it on Haroun's back. He tenses for a moment, during which Zoya also feels strange to be touching somebody like this. But she shakes the thought out of her head, reminding herself of the many times she has linked elbows with Flora at events, the times she has shaken female employees' hands.

With this in mind, she rubs her hand slowly on Haroun's back. She moves it in a circular motion, jaw clenching at the shudders of his body as he cries. But she focuses on her single job of comforting him with her touch, since she has never been one who can comfort with her forked tongue.

His shudders lessen somewhat, his sniffs decrease. Zoya's hand continues to rub soothingly on his back before trailing up to his shoulders, then his hair. She strokes her fingers through it, and for one stupid, distracted moment, marvels at the texture of it.

Eventually he stops crying and turns to Zoya, her hand still in his hair. "I'm sorry." His voice cracks.

"You have nothing to be sorry for," she whispers, and the words feel right.

Maybe I can do this after all.

He gives her a weak smile, then reaches up slowly. His eyes ask permission, and Zoya's respond with a tentative *yes*. He grasps the hand in his hair with a gentle touch, bringing it down to hold in between his hands.

A shock of revulsion passes through Zoya at the feel of a strong, masculine hand on hers. But she shoves the feeling away angrily, focusing on Haroun's face to remind her of who is touching her.

She hates feeling this way. She doesn't *want* to feel this way. She doesn't want to shudder in disgust when he traces the shape of her nails, when he plays with her fingers absentmindedly. She wants to be able to cover his hands with her own, wants to be able to smile at him without feeling the disgust roiling through her.

She is an anomaly, then. One who shrivels at the act of touch and human contact—so forbidden to her—yet has taken every opportunity to sidle up to every male she encounters. To test out her theory about mankind's never-ending capacity for lust.

And yet, despite being the notorious Zoya Zameer, she cannot handle this one man's simple, gentle touch. Although she despises this vulnerable feeling, she pulls her hands out from Haroun's gently after a few moments, her eyes communicating a fervent apology.

"I'm sorry," he says automatically. "I didn't mean to—"

"It's okay." Zoya tries for a soft smile. "It'll just take some getting used to."

He nods.

"How about we go back to sleep?" Her voice is soft, gentle. So unlike the way it normally sounds. But Haroun seems to do this to her.

He nods and allows the pressure of her hand between his shoulder blades to guide him back to their room.

Forty-Three

The Prophet Muhammad (peace be upon him) said that Allah the Most High said, "I am just as My slave thinks I am, (i.e. I am able to do for him what he thinks I can do for him) and I am with him if He remembers Me. If he remembers Me in himself, I too, remember him in Myself; and if he remembers Me in a group of people, I remember him in a group that is better than they; and if he comes one span nearer to Me, I go one cubit nearer to him; and if he comes one cubit nearer to Me, I go a distance of two outstretched arms nearer to him; and if he comes to Me walking, I go to him running." (Sahih Bukhari)

~

ZOYA AND HAROUN'S NIGHTTIME bonding doesn't last long. In the morning, the same heavy silence settles between them. Zoya goes to work mechanically, despite the protests of her mother-in-law, who worries for her health and tells her to heed her doctor's warnings. Haroun goes to his temporary job every day, and although he doesn't mention it, Zoya knows he's worried about providing for his family, especially with a new member added to it.

At work, those who dare—such as Bill and Ibitoye—ask Zoya what she will decide to do about her hushed marriage. The press inevitably found out about it, despite Lucas' attempts at hushing the news. She tells them there may be an official reception later, but for now this is something she doesn't want to bring too much attention to. Already her days of absence from work have left the media baffled and confused, scrambling around for explanations despite Lucas' insistence that everything is fine and under control. She is approached by reporters to and from work, whom she tries her best to ignore. Sameer even temporarily hires a twenty-four seven bodyguard—much to Zoya's chagrin—to escort her places and ward off reporters, but they're insistent. They take any chance they can to shove their mics in Zoya's face, and even threats from security barely keep them at bay.

Although it's horrible having to face them, it also takes the press' mind off of Zaki Ahmed and the tension between him and Zoya. It distracts them from the accusations leveled against Haroun.

However, the damage has been done. Zoya overhears Haroun frequently fretting to his mother over job offers being withdrawn from him due to the accusation laid by Zaki. The concern and hurt in his voice circles constantly around Zoya like a plague.

Zoya feels as if she's been shoved off a steep, slippery slope, falling and falling and falling into a deep, suffocating darkness. Even after retaliating against Zaki Ahmed and having obtained her life's greatest desire, the emptiness doesn't leave her, only dulls slightly. The horrible, hollow emptiness that she thought would disappear after she finally grasped Haroun in her clutches.

But it doesn't.

It gives her the sensation of crawling inside her own skin—only to find that it doesn't fit—and then crawling outside her skin—only to find that the world outside provides no comfort either. It gives her the experience of itching herself until she is raw and red. Yet she's unable to feel anything at all. It doesn't help that Haroun is so distant from her, too. She would argue that he is even more distant than before their marriage.

Zoya Zameer is *tired*. She's so tired of what she cannot understand or grasp. She's so tired of her success, something she always wants more of but never seems to have enough of. It feels as if she is inhaling and inhaling without ever exhaling.

She's tired of being pushed around by political demands, tired of being held back by decorum and constraints. She's tired of pretending, tired of primping and beautifying herself only to find that the world still expects more from her. She's tired of this constant craving, itching restlessness that she can't even come close to putting a finger on, yet it seems to have her in its entire grasp.

On top of that, she feels suffocated in Haroun's apartment, even though it's customary in Pakistani culture for the bride to move in with the groom. It's not about the size of the apartment itself; she's just around more people at home than she's been around in her entire life. Even though these people treat her nothing short of a princess.

And although it holds terrible memories, she misses her manor. The garden, the pool, even the servants.

She knows Haroun senses this, too, but he doesn't speak to her about it. He doesn't speak to her much about anything except to ask her if she's okay and whether she took her meds.

His demeanor makes her feel worse than ever. It forces her to continue to think about what she's done to attain him, about what she's risked. And when she thinks of him ever finding out, her throat clogs up so painfully that she's unable to breathe.

About three quiet weeks into their marriage, Zoya approaches Haroun in their room, settling on the bed next to him as he reads a book. He notices her presence, looks up, and closes the book. "Everything okay?"

"Yes. I just wanted to talk to you about something."

Immediately a wariness takes over him, but he nods and sits up. "Sure."

Zoya places the file she brought in between them. "I wanted to talk about . . . my house."

Realization dawns on his face, as if he expected her to bring this up. "Okay."

"Look, I know you're not telling me, but you're looking for a new place. And this temporary job you've gotten will not be enough to sustain you and your family. And . . . me. We both know it." Zoya pauses. He looks uncomfortable but doesn't say anything. "I want us all to move into my manor."

He sucks in a sharp breath.

"I know it's a tough decision for the four of you to pick up everything and move in with me, but I want to repay you for what you've done for me." *And maybe it will make this nagging feeling go away for what I've done to you.*

Haroun shakes his head. "It's not about that at all. You don't have to repay us for anything. Relationships don't work that way—as if we're trading or making a transaction. They're built on trust and mutual understanding." A sharp pang pierces Zoya's chest when he says the word *trust.* "It's that *I'm* responsible for *you*, and that *I'm* to provide for *you*. And you're in no way obligated to provide for *me*, not to mention for my family."

Zoya nods. "I thought you would say that." She nudges the file towards him. "But there's nothing *wrong* with me wanting to do so as a choice. I earn enough to last us a *lifetime*." She laughs, and there is a hint of scorn in it. "You can continue searching for a more suitable job, and we can all live together in my manor." Zoya shrugs. "Everybody's happy."

Haroun watches her helplessly.

"And . . ." Zoya opens the file and turns the first page towards him. "If you're worried about living in *my* place, I'm ready to put the manor in your name alongside mine. You just need to sign these papers."

He gives her a look of pure shock, and suddenly Zoya remembers the last time she had someone sign these property papers.

The door to their room swings open, and her husband steps out. He swivels his head this way and that, looking around in confusion. "Zoya?"

A cold, metal point touches the small of his back. He freezes, probably getting a nasty feeling about what the object is.

"Move," Zoya says. Her voice is shaking. She hates herself for it.

"Zoya? What's going on?" He sounds so innocent, so unlike the monster that he is. But she will not be fooled by him.

"I said move." *She digs the knife deeper so that he lets out a little yelp, but he obliges nonetheless.*

"What is going on, Zoya?"

Zoya's hands shake. Her body shakes. Her very heart trembles. But she nudges him forward into a chair, quickly gesturing to the guard standing by. He nods and begins zip tying and binding her husband's hands behind his back and his feet to the chair. Her husband swivels his head around, a look of utter bewilderment on his face.

"Don't—don't say a word," Zoya stammers, slowly walking so that she's standing directly in front of him. The look on his face scares her, as it has scared her so many times, but she cannot cower before him now. Not when she's so close to getting what she wants. "If—if you try to do anything . . . there are guards surrounding the house. They won't hesitate to hurt you."

The utter shock on his face gives Zoya a sense of satisfaction.

This is the only defense she has. Using his money to bribe the people who usually follow his orders. Taking valuable things and finding somebody needy enough to accept them.

She wields her knife like a sword, putting on a show of strength that hides how she actually feels.

Zoya gestures to the papers on the table. "You will sign these, and then you will leave."

"What?" His voice is pure confusion now, mingled with oncoming rage. Rage she is so familiar with.

"Those are the property papers for this house, and those are the divorce papers. Sign them now and—and you won't be hurt."

Now he looks entirely perplexed, with his eyebrows furrowed and his mouth wide open. He looks almost innocent, but she knows him too well. "Zoya, tell me what's going on, for Allah's sake—"

"Don't!" she yells fiercely, hating the last three words that come out of his mouth, the phrase that always surfaces when he's angry. "Don't ever say that in front of me again."

"Can we just talk about this? What do you mean 'divorce?'"

"You know what I mean." She steps closer to him, knife held out before her. And although he is the one tied to the chair, utterly helpless, and she is the one with a weapon wielded before her, she's still scared out of her damn mind. "Sign the papers."

After a few moments of silence—during which Zoya is entirely sure he can hear her pounding heartbeat—he says, "Well, I can't do that if my hands are tied, can I?"

Zoya laughs. It's a terrified, nervous laugh. "You think I'm going to untie you that easily? All you've done to me is lie." As she grows closer to the freedom she has planned for months, Zoya's shivers decrease. "You have ruined my life. The least you could do for me is let me go. Leave my life, and never return."

"Can we talk about—"

"There's nothing to talk about," she barks, and he flinches. Good. She likes that she can elicit that reaction from him. "Right now I will call a guard from outside. He will untie you—don't even think of doing anything—you will sign these papers, and then you will leave and never show me your face again."

His eyebrows rise, and Zoya's heart falters for a moment. He's supposed to be afraid. Why isn't he afraid? "Allah doesn't like—"

"Don't tell me what Allah does and doesn't like!" Zoya screams. "I don't care! You will sign these papers, and you will get the hell out of my life."'

"Is this about the supposed 'abuse' you're speaking of to our parents? You know, it's my God-given right to—"

"STOP!" Zoya screams. "Just. STOP." Her chest heaves up and down as she breathes heavily. She steps closer and presses the tip of the knife into his chin. He flinches back, but she advances forward. His eyes flick to the guard, who stands motionless behind Zoya, making no move to rescue him.

All these months of being terrified in his presence have left Zoya reeling for even a sliver of comfort or safety. Every time, every time she thought of doing this, of overpowering him, her heart cowered in a way it never had before. Because in some twisted way, as he gradually cut off all her ties of security, he became her only source of solace and familiarity.

Mustering the courage to take action left her more exhausted than ever. Blackmailing those who usually respond to his beck and call felt like consuming poison and hoping she wouldn't keel over.

Now all she wants is to sag in relief. To exhale after months of only inhaling.

"Sign the papers," Zoya says, her voice deadly. "And nobody gets hurt."

He looks into her eyes for a moment before he swallows. "Okay."
His voice shakes, and satisfaction rushes through Zoya. "Okay, I'll do
it."

"Zoya?"

She blinks suddenly and registers her surroundings. Haroun. Their room. The present.

Haroun.

His eyes are worried, piercing deep into hers.

As she looks at her safe haven, she loosens a breath she didn't realize she was holding. "Sorry," she murmurs automatically. "Just . . . remembered something."

He reaches forward as if to comfort her but pulls back quickly. Zoya doesn't know whether that makes her glad or upset.

Instead, he nudges the file back towards her. "I can't. This is your property. *Yours.* I can't take that away from you."

"But I'm *willingly* giving it to you. And you're not taking it away from me—it will be under both our names."

He shakes his head. "I can't."

"Please," she says, exasperated. "*Please* come back and stay with me. Chase away his memory from there. From every nook and cranny of that place."

There is a moment of charged silence as Zoya realizes what she just admitted to.

Haroun stares at her, baffled. "Zoya . . . if the place hurts you so much, isn't it better to leave it? Start fresh. Start over."

Zoya shakes her head and smiles. "You fight your demons in hell, don't you? You never fight them anywhere else. You never fight them in paradise. The only way they go away is if you stand your ground and uproot them where they came from. If you run away, they haunt you."

His hands inch forward once again to reach her fingers. He wants to provide her comfort—she can tell by the pained look in his eyes. But he maintains the distance, allowing their hands to simply rest in close proximity to one another. Close, but not touching.

It comforts her all the same.

"You know," Haroun says softly. "Islamically speaking, you're allowed to charge me for living in your house. You have every right to—as my wife—if you choose to do so. Because it isn't your responsibility to take care of me."

Zoya smiles, a warm feeling spreading within her. Every time he speaks, he gives her more reasons to fall in love with him. He's *giving* her power, something she's not used to obtaining without snatching. He's telling her something that is advantageous to her and possibly detrimental to him, but he's making her aware of her rights as a Muslim woman.

And in her, a small part shifts. The tiniest, smallest step. But a step all the same.

Close to God. For giving her this man.

~

"You ready?" Zoya looks at Haroun. He peeks into the room where the press conference will take place, taking a deep breath and nodding slowly.

Farhan swings an arm around Haroun and tugs him close. "Don't worry, buddy. Once this stupid press conference is over, we'll go out to your favorite food place. And then we'll go zip lining."

Haroun looks outside the window, where it's heavily pouring. He raises his eyebrows.

"Okay, maybe not zip lining," Farhan says. "We'll go out to the city."

Zoya gives Farhan a blank look, but makes a mental note to weasel information out of him about Haroun . . . things she needs to know, like his favorite restaurant.

The board of directors stands to the side, throwing the couple a thumbs up. When Lucas and them had first suggested a press conference to Zoya a couple days ago, she had been livid. But after some contemplation and some time talking to Haroun, she had reluctantly agreed. She knew this was the most feasible option, no matter how wary she had become about press conferences.

As if he's reading her mind, Lucas says, "This should hopefully clear up some of the press' concerns, if not all."

Zoya nods, tucking her curls behind her ear. She slips off her handbag and thrusts it out to whoever is closest to her as she leans down to fix the strap of her heel. When she looks back up, Farhan is holding her handbag awkwardly.

She snatches it away from him. "Get your hands off my things."

"But you *gave*—"

"Guys," Haroun says, exasperated. His eyes dart between the two of them, but linger on Zoya for longer. There is an exhausted plea in them.

She huffs and shoulders her handbag, throwing Farhan a piercing look. When she isn't looking, Farhan makes a funny face at her back.

"Alright, guys," Ibitoye says, ushering the couple into the conference room. "You got this. And remember—" She touches Zoya's shoulder gently. "Remember to let Haroun speak first, okay? The press needs to know there was no coercion involved in this, so not only does what you two *say* matter, but so does the order of events."

Lucas nods in agreement. "And as always, keep this in mind: *You are not obligated to answer anything you feel is too personal. Anytime their questions are too probing, you do not need to say a word.*"

Zoya nods and everyone follows her inside.

There are cameras poised everywhere, and where there is no room for cameras, mics from various news channels take their place. Haroun shifts uneasily; the last time he had been in the presence of these many cameras was at Zaki Ahmed's launch party. Zoya gives him a small smile of reassurance as they walk to their seats. Bill, Ibitoye, and Lucas position themselves at the side of the room. Sameer and Farhan stand at the other end, performing a mock salute at Haroun.

News reporters welcome the couple, and introductions are passed for the sake of the cameras before Haroun takes a deep breath and gives them his statement.

His voice is steady, calm, despite the trembling of his fingers under the table. His statement consists of only a few sentences, but from time to time he turns to his wife. Something in her face must give him reassurance, because he turns back to the cameras with a newfound fervor in his voice.

When he is about to say that he was not in any way manipulated into their marriage, he hesitates for the smallest fraction of a second. A fraction Zoya is sure the media will scrutinize. Her body tenses.

But then he says it, and she hopes nobody can hear her sigh of relief.

Only then does she realize—relief does not make an appearance unless there was initially something to be worried about.

The reporters begin asking them both questions, most of which Zoya answers. At one point, one of them says, "Speculations have risen that to maintain your company's image, you"—he gestures to Zoya—"were coerced into marriage by your employee, who allegedly sexually harassed—"

"He did not," Zoya says sharply.

The reporter pauses for a moment, his expression shrewd. "Right, that's why I said *allegedly*—"

"There is no need for you to bring that up at all, sir, since it is false. And it was proven to be a ploy when Zaki Ahmed's own character was brought into light." Her voice has taken on a deadly calm.

He pauses again, then clears his throat. "Right. What I mean is, Ms. Zoya, people are speculating that after this . . . accusation was leveled against your employee, your rushed marriage was a way to maintain Zameer's image."

Beside Zoya, Haroun visibly tenses.

Zoya clears her throat, shoves her curls behind her shoulders, and throws the cameras a tight-lipped smile. For anyone who knows her well enough, that smile is not a good sign. "Sir, for some reason, I feel as if there's a threat to my privacy in this room." She reaches up to rub her eyes, pretending to ward off faux tears. From the right side of the room, Lucas gives her a small nod. "I would like to maintain *some* dignity by keeping certain things private, such as the nature of my marriage with Haroun."

The reporters begin shuffling around, seemingly flustered. *Checkmate,* Zoya thinks. The journalist who had been asking Zoya the most questions ventures, "I understand that, Ms. Zoya. But if you would like to be rid of presuppositions, wouldn't it be better for you to address them for the media?"

Zoya nods, maintaining her false bravado. "Of course. I understand that." She darts a glance at Haroun. At the pained, expectant look in his eyes. "But sir, no matter how many things I try to clear up, there will always be more. How much will I go around countering?" She shrugs. "One of the cons of my position, I guess."

He nods reluctantly, quieting.

"But . . ." Zoya says slowly, and mics inch closer to her. She waits for a long second, contemplating her next words before speaking them. "As you all have . . . become aware of my previous marriage . . ." She trails off. Under the table, her fists clench and unclench.

For Haroun, she thinks, and just as she does, a warm hand caresses the top of her clenched fist.

She doesn't dare make a noise, doesn't dare gasp. She is being scrutinized from every angle. But as the hand tugs gently at her, no hint of a threat, she spreads her palm open. Slowly, slowly, Haroun's fingers trace up her palm and entwine with hers. Firm and unyielding. Zoya's own fingers respond to his touch and slowly, as if she has all the time in the world, she curls her fingers around his.

Their hands fit like a lock and key.

"Ms. Zoya?" the reporter prompts, breaking her out of her reverie. From the corner of her eye, she sees Haroun staring straight ahead, posture entirely diplomatic and professional. But underneath the table, his thumb makes a slow trek across her hand. Back and forth. Back and forth. A promise of solace. A beacon of comfort in this dreary, suffocating room.

Zoya shakes her head to ward off the heat rising in her cheeks and clears her throat. "Right. As you've all been made aware of my previous marriage, I would like for you to ponder over this for a moment. Having escaped from a relationship like that . . . do you honestly believe I would . . . begin a relationship with someone like that again? I think that should tell you enough about what kind of man my husband is." She looks at Haroun, and for a moment he stares back at her. To gaze into his eyes like this—knowing that he's clutching her hand underneath the table where no one can see—spreads warmth throughout her body. As if they are sharing some secret of their own.

Briefly Zoya's thoughts are intruded by the disturbing fact of research she came upon a couple months after Farhan left. That despite the opposite expectation, women like her tend to fall into the same kinds of relationships, the same cycles of abuse.

She wills the thought out of her mind and gazes deep into her husband's eyes. "Choosing Haroun was an entirely conscious decision, made with a sound mind and heart." Zoya turns back to the cameras. "Thank you for your time."

Despite Zoya and Haroun having answered numerous questions, protests of "Wait!" and "One more question!" follow as soon as they begin to stand, which Zoya's PR manager and directors try warding off. Before they're able to, however, Haroun tugs Zoya's hand and motions for her to sit. He turns to the cameras.

"I just . . . I want to say one thing." The clamoring dies down. Cameras hone in on him, and reporters ready their notepads and pens. Microphones are shoved closer. Even Lucas, Bill, and Ibitoye exchange looks of surprise. Haroun shrinks back slightly, clearly unnerved by the attention. But he clears his throat and takes a deep breath.

"I just want to say . . . the reputation of a woman is very delicate. It's often tarnished by a single word or a single false assumption, something I don't think us men will ever understand." He blows out a sigh. "And . . . I think in the corporate sector, we often view people as objects. As assets, liabilities, prizes, brand images. Nothing more, nothing less. Just . . . objects to pigeonhole." Haroun pauses for a moment, turning to Zoya. She remembers his distress when she had called Sumaiya an asset at the Pak Enterprises launch party, and a smile plays on her lips. The look in her eyes is enough to prod Haroun to continue. "I wanted to request you all to put aside the binoculars and the notepads, even if it's just for a moment. Get rid of the scrutiny and the strict inspection. Take off the corrupt lens the corporate world has placed on you. And . . . remember that at the end of the day, just like the rest of us, Zoya Zameer is . . . human."

He's quiet for a moment, during which there is a responding pin drop silence. And then he stands, Zoya's hand still in his grasp, and leads her down the stairs.

The people burst out of their stupor, rushing forward with more cameras and more questions, as if his words mean nothing. But some of them have bewildered looks on their faces, looks of surprise.

Looks of contemplation.

As the couple heads out of the room, the PR manager and directors follow while simultaneously thanking the media for their time. Once they've all exited, Bill claps and Lucas nods appreciatively. Ibitoye throws her hands up in the air. "Yes!" she says. "Guys, that was amazing." Ibitoye's gaze turns to Haroun. "The hand holding was a *great* idea. I don't know why I didn't think of it myself."

"Oh." Haroun laughs nervously, and as if on cue, he drops Zoya's hand and reaches up to run his fingers through his hair.

Zoya tries not to let the disappointment show on her face. He hadn't done it for the cameras, had he?

The intimacy in his gentle touch had told Zoya otherwise.

"Woohoo!" an all-too-excited voice yells right behind Zoya. She flinches before turning around, already knowing who it is. Farhan reaches forward and does the guy handshake with Haroun before clapping him on the back. Zoya has a strange urge to throw her handbag in his face but decides against it, since it was too expensive.

"We're going out1" Farhan exclaims. "Food's on me."

"On you?" Haroun says happily.

"Did I say 'me'? " Farhan says. "I meant Sameer." Sameer rolls his eyes as the two of them lead Haroun away. At the last second, right before they're about to exit the room, Haroun turns around.

His eyes pause on Zoya before he gives her a soft, tentative smile.

Forty-Four

BACK IN ZOYA'S MANOR—which is now in both Zoya's and Haroun's names (after much convincing from her)—the couple is met with excited servants and extravagant decorations. Mumtaz has outdone herself; she's called the best designers and caterers on the East Coast for Zoya Zameer's first entry into her house with her new family by her side.

Immediately, the servants take a liking to Haroun, asking him for water, juice, anything he needs. He seems taken aback by the number of them, murmuring "No, thank you" to each one with a slight tremble in his hands. His eyes rove around the place, but instead of being wondrous as is the norm for most people, they are tentative. Afraid, almost.

Haroun's mother and sisters had been even harder to convince. *Ammi,* as Zoya's mother-in-law had requested her to say—kept saying it was very unconventional and borderline inappropriate for them to move in with their daughter-in-law. Zoya had huffed and said these things were only "unconventional" because society made them seem so, and that as far as she knew, religion did not at all prohibit this. And indeed, this was something *Ammi* could not argue with.

In the end, they had only reluctantly agreed because they were to move in with Haroun's grandparents a short time later anyway.

At the manor, it only takes a few hours for Haroun and his family to settle in with their immediate belongings. They politely refuse any help from the servants, insisting that they are able to do everything on their own.

At around eight in the evening, the doorbell rings. A guard comes in, informs Zoya of who it is, and after a confused moment, she nods for him to be allowed entry.

Haroun's father steps in, darting his eyes around quickly. He greets Zoya with a smile as she leads him into the parlor room.

"Mumtaz?" she calls. The servant appears immediately. "Some tea and samosas for Haroun's father. Oh, and inform Haroun of his arrival."

Mumtaz nods and disappears.

Haroun's father—Suleiman—is still gazing around with wondrous eyes full of light. The way he looks at everything makes Zoya uncomfortable—as if he intends to gobble it all up with his eyes.

For a heartbreaking moment, it reminds her of the way her father used to gaze wondrously at her manor.

Haroun appears, a tight expression on his face, but he greets his father politely all the same. He settles next to Zoya, and she's so unused to this that she inhales sharply, all too aware of his proximity.

"I came to bring you a housewarming gift." Suleiman picks up the gift bag and places it on the table between them.

"Aw, uncle, there was no need for this," Zoya recites one of her rehearsed lines. "Really, thank you."

"Yes, there really was no need for this." Haroun's voice is tight, like an elastic band stretched too far.

There is a tense moment of silence, during which Suleiman stares at Haroun unflinchingly. The latter, despite his tense posture and clenched fists, keeps his eyes lowered.

Haroun's sisters walk in, and the bubbly air seems to dissipate out of Aisha, while Naima becomes more reserved than ever. They greet their father formally before sitting at a distance from him.

The room seems to thicken with the possibility of unsaid words. Zoya tries her best to carry out a relaxed conversation with her father-in-law, and every time she laughs or gestures for him to eat or drink, she can feel Haroun's eyes searing into the side of her head.

And then Suleiman asks his children, "How is your mother doing?"

There is a sharp intake of breath from Aisha. Haroun's jaw tightens. Naima remains quiet.

Zoya barrels forward. "Uh, she's . . . she's doing well, *Alhamdulillah.* She went to bed early."

Suleiman's eyes pierce his children, for a moment paying no heed to his daughter-in-law.

"Is she okay?"

And then, like breaking the surface after drowning for so long, it is Naima who speaks up—not bubbly, talkative Aisha; not strong-willed Haroun—but Naima who says, "Papa, you're our father. We cannot disrespect you, but please don't put on these false niceties." She takes a trembling breath, and Haroun's head shoots to her, a warning in his eyes. "You haven't looked after us for a long time now, haven't bothered to see how we're doing for eight years. Please don't ask us how we're doing now. We can maintain a respectful distance, but . . . please, Papa. Don't pretend to care."

Suleiman is clearly surprised by Naima's uncharacteristic forthrightness. He casts her a shocked, hurtful glance. His mouth opens and closes, but no words come out. Without another word, he stands and exits the parlor despite Zoya's confused protests of "Wait!"

Zoya turns to Naima, taken aback by the tears streaming down her face.

"Naima," Aisha cautions softly, reaching for her sister's arm.

Naima pulls back. "Don't, Aisha. Don't 'Naima' me. We've stayed quiet for too long. He hasn't lived up to his title of father for so many years, and now he walks back into our lives when he sees the potential in his *wealthy* daughter-in-law and wants to pretend that everything is okay?"

Zoya's eyebrows rise at these words.

Naima points to the gift bag. "He hasn't given us anything for years, while he's showered his wife with endless gifts." Zoya restrains a gasp. Haroun's father is married? Her eyes dart to Haroun, a pucker appearing between her brows. She tries to recall a moment during which this information may have been disclosed to her. But she realizes that with the hasty way everything went down between the two of them—where they went from boss and employee to wife and husband in a matter of hours—they never had the opportunity to talk about their personal lives.

Naima continues speaking, breaking Zoya out of her trance. "He left us in such a state that we have struggled and struggled and are now living in our *brother's wife's* house." Her eyes are dark with shame, and Zoya is shocked by her sister-in-law. She is surprised by these words coming out of her mouth, surprised that the young girl spoke so much in just a few moments. And in a few short sentences, spoke so clearly the point she was trying to get across. With an eloquence Zoya is surprised by.

Haroun throws his sister a pained glance. "Naima, I know how you feel. I'm so sorry—"

"Sorry? Why are *you* sorry?" Naima laughs mirthlessly. "*Bhai,* you're supposed to . . . you're supposed to *explore* at your age. You're supposed to go out with your friends, camp, travel, have fun. You have responsibilities, yes, but you gave up *everything* so that Aisha and I could live comfortable lives. You're so young." Her voice cracks into a sob.

"You don't deserve to have your happiness sacrificed because of us. You don't deserve to be given such huge responsibilities at such a young age. You worked a job that pained you every second and gave you sleepless nights just so we could have a worry-free education. *Bhai,* you're *twenty-eight,* but you've been a father for much longer than that," Naima weeps. "You've done all that *he* was supposed to do. So he doesn't deserve to walk in here and ask us how we're doing. He doesn't." She buries her head in her hands while Haroun watches her with shocked, watery eyes.

Zoya senses this to be a private moment between siblings, so she stands silently. But Haroun turns to her, eyes full of grief, and suddenly she is rooted to the ground.

"Naima." Haroun's voice comes out a whisper. "In what world do you think you're a burden to me? You are my responsibility." He tries to catch her eyes, but she stares at the floor, crying silently. Haroun reaches forward and grasps both hers and Aisha's hands. "You guys have made everything worth it, do you know that?" In his voice there is an attempt at a smile. "I didn't do what I did to see you in this state. I did it so I could see *you*"—he gestures to Aisha—"laughing and making everyone around you laugh and so I could see *you*"—he nudges Naima—"finally realize how much potential you have." He wipes Naima's tears away with his thumb. "Don't you dare feel guilty for me doing what I'm supposed to be doing."

"You're not supposed to be fathering us—you're supposed to be a big brother whose shoulder we lean on to cry. Not someone who gives up everything for us."

"I'm supposed to take our father's place when he isn't present, so everything I do for you is my responsibility. And who says I'm unhappy?" Haroun says, smoothing his thumb across her cheek. "It only makes me unhappy when you say things like this and when you cry like this. I don't want to see these tears." He takes a deep breath. "And I know you're upset, but don't talk about him like that, okay? He's still our father, and we need to respect him. You should apologize to him."

Zoya expects his sister to lash out at him for this, to tell him she has a right to slander the one who is causing her pain. But Naima only nods shakily and leans into her brother's hug. This perplexes Zoya—to see someone so readily accept a request that they may not favor. Is this what it means to be open-minded? Or is it an acceptance of defeat?

Zoya simply stands there watching them, a strange warmth pooling in her chest.

The three siblings hold each other tightly. Naima weeps against her brother's chest silently while Aisha runs her fingers through his hair softly. But Haroun is not looking at her. Or at Naima.

Instead, his eyes are on Zoya.

~

Later that night, when Zoya is working in the living room, she dials Sameer's number and asks about recent developments.

"How's everything, by the way?" he asks towards the end of the call.

Zoya is startled by the question. She pulls her phone back to stare at it. "What do you mean, Sameer?"

There is a short laugh on the other end. "Only *you* would be surprised by a '*how are you?*' Are you looking for an ulterior motive? Maybe you think I'm just asking you out of courtesy. Maybe you think I'm asking because I'm trying to distract you in order to fulfill my *real* motive. Maybe—"

"Sameer," Zoya warns.

"Okay, okay. I was just joking. Forget I asked."

"Everything's fine," she answers anyway.

"*Ooh*, how much did it cost you to say that?"

She rolls her eyes, then becomes serious. "How's the media looking?"

"Bad. But it could be worse. I talked to Lucas and the rest of PR. We're trying to get everything under control. The press conference helped, but it raised a hell of a lotta new questions."

Zoya massages her temples. "We'll deal with them."

"As we always do."

"Goodnight, Sameer."

"Take care."

The call ends and Zoya sighs. As much as she pretends to be annoyed by Sameer's banter, she can't help but feel relieved. At least he doesn't hate her as she thought he did when that whole Sumaiya ordeal occurred.

He doesn't hate you because he doesn't know what you did.

Zoya shakes her head, angry at the voices in it. She rifles through papers on the table and gives up when she can't find the one she's looking for. Opening another file, she scans the pages of new designs on *sherwanis* and *lehengas,* frustrated by the lack of a proper lead designer.

Looking at the designs reminds her of Sumaiya—of what she

did and what Zoya did to her in return. A stab pierces her chest as she shuts the file with more force than necessary.

Zoya rubs a hand over her face, trying to massage the sleepiness away. She knows that as soon as her head hits the pillow, she will again be haunted by what she has done.

"You alright?"

She jumps at his voice. It's so quiet that it's barely audible. Haroun emerges from near the pillar by the doorway, two mugs in his hand.

"Sorry," he says as he sets a mug of hot chocolate on the table and sits next to her. "I didn't mean to scare you."

Zoya eyes the mug, then him. "How long were you standing there?"

He flushes a deep red but doesn't answer her question, taking a sip from his mug instead.

It is so eerie to be sitting with him here, in the middle of the night, when it is so silent. Usually they are around people when they talk, and the background noises help facilitate conversation. Or Haroun is reciting Qur'an as Zoya falls asleep. But here there is only silence, making them hyper aware of each other's every movement, every expression, every whisper.

"What are you working on?" He gestures to the mess of papers.

"Just looking over some designs. And files of potential designers."

At the indirect association with Sumaiya, his knuckles tighten around the mug, and Zoya immediately regrets saying anything.

"Have you interviewed any yet?"

She shakes her head. "I'm finding it a little hard to go to the office nowadays." They share a quick look full of unsaid words before Haroun looks away. Zoya rushes to fill the silence. "Has Naima calmed down a bit?"

"She's still moody, but better. Mama's with her. Told her to call Papa and apologize."

Zoya nods.

"I hate it when they say things like that." He sighs, shoving a hand through his hair. "As if I'm some outsider doing them some big favor."

Zoya shrugs. "They feel guilty, you know? You do so much for them."

"They shouldn't feel guilty." He rubs his forehead. "It's a duty."

"If they didn't know what you were sacrificing, maybe they wouldn't."

He eyes her. "What am I sacrificing?"

She thinks of how he told her he *had* to stop working with Zameer. Of the bags under his eyes and his constantly fatigued aura at work. Of the way he smiled when he told her he had finally grown his wings to leave.

"You were sacrificing your faith," she whispers. He continues to stare at her, an unfathomable expression on his face.

He clears his throat and switches the topic. "Thank you for what you did today, by the way." His voice, too, is a whisper. She wonders why in her big, silent house, in the middle of a dark night, they are whispering.

Now it's her turn to question him. "What did I do today?"

"You welcomed my dad. Showed him hospitality, talked to him, kept him company. I want our relationship to work out, but . . ." There is a bitterness in his voice that she is unused to.

Zoya circles the mouth of the mug with her fingers, recalling the new information she learned today. About his father's remarriage. "What—if you don't mind my asking—what happened with him?"

Haroun turns away so that she's unable to read his face. "He married a second time. In secret. We didn't know until three years later, when his wife already had a baby on the way. Unfortunately, she had a miscarriage, but . . ." He rubs his forehead. "My mom was devastated, and she demanded a divorce from him."

He quiets suddenly, forehead creasing in contemplation. "I know the timeless Western narrative is that polygamy is evil, but I think we have to remember that Western ideals aren't representative of the entire world's ideals. Truthfully, polygamy is a part of our religion, But, like so many other things in religion, it needs to be executed in the right manner." Haroun pauses, turning his head to the ceiling and closing his eyes. "If my father had told us he wanted to marry a second time, we could have sat down and talked about it." Haroun sighs, and Zoya wants nothing more than to reach up and stroke his hair. Cup his cheek. Trace the shape of his jaw. But she clasps her hands tightly around her mug to resist the urge.

"The issue was how he handled it," Haroun says quietly, opening his eyes and looking at her. Zoya is so startled by his intense gaze that her breath catches in her throat. "Deceiving us, having no consideration for my mother's feelings, essentially traumatizing her and dismissing what was important to her. The way he went about it . . . that was the biggest issue."

Zoya abruptly remembers his words from his conversation with his coworkers months ago: *The religion isn't the problem; the way it's demonstrated is.*

"Aisha was a bit young to fully understand what was happening," Haroun continues. "But Naima understood, and she's been so . . . quiet since then." He shrugs, not meeting her eyes.

Zoya's eyes glisten with tears. She can feel *Ammi's* pain at finding out something of such magnitude much, much later. How heartbreaking it must have been, to live and love somebody only to find out later that they had been occupied with someone else? No wonder Haroun's mother looks as if someone has extracted light from her eyes, why her smile never quite lights up her entire face.

"When my parents divorced, my mom didn't tell anyone but close family the real reason why. They would eventually find out on their own, anyway. Instead, she allowed people to make their own assumptions. She allowed people to come and tell her that she should be more compromising, that she should try to make the marriage work. She took it all quietly. She knew there was no point in defending her choices because our society would turn around and blame her for it. *'It's probably because you weren't good enough.' 'You should have compromised more.' My mom would rather take the false assumptions than the lack of support. She didn't want to risk a ruined reputation."* He scoffs. *"Yet our society manages to make everyone seem ruinable somehow, doesn't it? Even when she* was not at fault, society found a way to blame her for it."

Zoya listens to him silently, glad that he is finally speaking to her. She senses that he has been waiting to say this for a long, long time.

"Aisha, when she began to really understand what was going on, vowed to build a heart of steel and allow nothing to faze her. Naima took a hard hit, turned fragile and reserved. She has so much difficulty trusting anyone." He quiets for a moment. "But I know she wants to marry, so that she can prove to herself that all men aren't the same. That there are people out there who are not deceptive or inconsiderate."

Again, Zoya is rendered speechless. She doesn't know what to do, doesn't know what to say that will make him feel comfortable or at least put him at ease. She doesn't have the right words. Instead, she counters with another question. "And you? What happened to you?"

He laughs mirthlessly. "I went through a faith crisis. A major one. I questioned Allah, questioned why He let this my dad handle it the way he did. Questioned why my mom had to find out about his second wife the way she did. We had been robbed of the support from over our heads, my mom's heart had broken from the lies and the way it all happened. Why?" He inhales and rubs his eyes. "Until I learned that everything happens for our own good."

Zoya gives Haroun an appalled look. Somehow, she can never imagine Haroun to be the kind of person who questions God. She has only ever seen one side of him. The believing, trusting one. The faithful one. It shocks her to know that he once was just as she is now. Faithless, questioning God.

Human.

"How did you learn that everything happens for our own good? After what happened to you?"

He circles his hands around the mug. As Zoya watches his fingers, she feels the strange urge to capture his hand in hers and lace her fingers through his. To feel the same safety she felt the day of the press conference.

She has never wanted to touch anyone so freely after what happened with her ex-husband, but she finds herself wanting to lean her head in the crook of Haroun's arm, to have him run his fingers through her hair softly.

She blinks back to reality when Haroun says, "God tests us all differently." He laughs, low and pained. "My test was to trust Him during a time when that became especially hard for me to do. Isn't that the point, though? To manage to hold on when it's most difficult to do so? We never remember Him in comfort, only in pain and displeasure. But He's always there for us.

"I didn't learn my lessons overnight. But it was something small that really hit me." He blinks almost too quickly, and Zoya fears he may cry, and again she will not know how to comfort him. She will not be able to hold him to ease his sorrows even while wanting to so badly. "I used to open . . . this book that my mom read all the time. It was about the names of Allah. She would leave it around everywhere, especially after her divorce, and when I became most frustrated with God, I would open and close that book angrily." He shivers slightly, and Zoya reaches back for a blanket to drape over his shoulders.

When he glances up at her, his eyes are shining with tears, but he smiles at the gesture nonetheless. "Sometimes I would look down at the book, and every single time . . ." He pulls the blanket over himself, but that doesn't stop his shudders. "Every single time, it would land on the same page. With the same name. *Al-Muhaymin*. The Guardian, The Protector, The Overseer.

"I never actually read it. Until one day, when I was especially angry, I flipped the book open and it landed on the same page as usual. And I just . . ." Haroun shrugs. "I just began to cry. And my tears dropped on the page and . . ." He takes a deep, laborious breath. "I finally read it.

"There was a verse from the Qur'an on that page, from *Surah Baqarah*. It went, '*But perhaps you hate a thing and it is good for you; and perhaps you love a thing and it is bad for you. And Allah knows, while you know not.*'"

Haroun raises his gaze to hers, and in the pin drop silence of the night, his eyes carry so many words. "And it just . . . hit me, I guess. A realization. Like . . . the first breath of air after drowning for so long."

"Wow." Zoya's voice is full of awe. "That sounds like a real miracle. Not many people would be satisfied with just that." *For example, people like me.* She sits absolutely still, pondering over his story. A story that undoes her, like everything else about him.

For a long time, Zoya has felt like she needs to be somebody better around Haroun, especially because he sees goodness in her. And this push to change is not a forceful one, as she has been accustomed to within the religious community, but one that is authentic.

Haroun interrupts Zoya's thoughts. "It was Allah's mercy that He allowed me to see past my anger."

The silence that follows his statement makes Zoya's ears ring. She is too awed to speak, and as she absentmindedly stares around the drawing room and at Haroun, she wonders how she lived here alone for the past few years. Without family, without anyone she cared about.

"You should sleep." His soft voice breaks the silence. He shakes out a pill from the medicine bottle on the table and hands it to her with a glass of water.

Zoya takes it, pretends to swallow it, then smiles at him. "Thank you."

He nods. "I thought you should know—I took a separate room. I felt like you might need your space. And whenever you're ready . . ."

Zoya merely watches him with warmth in her eyes. Even without her saying anything, he understands her so well. What has she done to deserve such a man?

Something horrible.

Zoya squeezes her eyes shut to clear her mind. "Thank you," she repeats, reopening them. "Really, thank you for being so . . . understanding." *And caring. And thoughtful. And beautiful.*

He shakes his head, letting out a low chuckle that sets butterflies racing in Zoya's stomach. "No thank yous." With that, he stands. "You wanna head up with me right now?"

She nods, shuffling her papers together in a messy heap and standing. He grabs the mugs, and Zoya is about to protest and tell him that the servants will take care of it, but he's already walking towards the kitchen.

Once upstairs, Haroun stops and turns to her. He gives her an awkward little wave. "Good night."

"Good night." Zoya can't help the smile that spreads on her face at the fact that he has chosen the room right across from hers.

Haroun stands at the entrance of his new room, looking entirely nervous. It calms her a bit, to know that she isn't the only one afraid of all of this, and that she hasn't entirely lost her ability to make people squirm. Because that's where her power lies.

He gives her a slight nod, backing into his room awkwardly. His eyes fall on the chandelier brightening up her room. Although she has slept with the light on for the past couple of weeks, he points to the chandelier and asks, "You'll fall asleep?"

Zoya nods.

There is a brief, unfathomable expression on his face before he waves again and goes into his room.

Zoya retreats into her quiet, well-lit room, the ghost of a smile on her face.

When she's sure that Haroun has settled in bed, she spits her pill into the trash can.

Forty-Five

~

AS ZOYA STEPS OUT of her room, fully glammed up a little while after praying *Fajr*, she glances swiftly at Haroun's room.

He's not there.

Frowning, she makes her way downstairs into the dining hall. He's not there, either. She hears the clink of cutlery from the kitchen and heads towards the sound.

Haroun is at the stove, dressed in a black tracksuit and a green cap, flipping pancakes. At the sound of Zoya's bangles, he turns and offers her a small smile.

She returns it. "You can make pancakes?"

"Good morning to you, too," he retorts, and Zoya thinks she may have offended him until he throws her a cocky grin.

It doesn't, however, reach his eyes.

"Sorry. Good morning."

"I love pancakes." He sets them out on two plates, then proceeds to sprinkle sliced strawberries and blueberries over the pancakes, topping them with whipped cream and maple syrup. He slides a plate across the table towards Zoya, then hands her a fork and pours out hot milk for the both of them.

"Thank you." She's breathless, stunned by the unexpectedly domestic sight of him in the kitchen. She finds it surprisingly comforting. He settles across from her and digs in. "How did you find the stuff you needed?"

"Mumtaz *bibi* told me where to look."

She is startled by his use of *bibi* for Mumtaz. "Why didn't you just ask her to make them?"

He swirls his strawberry around in maple syrup before popping it into his mouth. "Why would I do that when I can make them myself?" A tentative smile plays on his lips, and Zoya's answering one is as bright as the sun.

"You don't seem like a pancakes-for-breakfast kind of guy to me," Zoya remarks.

His response is a surprised laugh. "Really? What kind of guy do I seem like, then?"

She knows he is asking in regards to breakfast, but looking at him in all his beautiful glory, she thinks, *The kind who makes my throat clog and my heart want to keep beating.* "The kind of guy who eats a sophisticated breakfast, like omelets and sliced avocados with toast. Brown bread toast, not white bread."

He chuckles. "I do like omelets, yeah. But I prefer white bread."

They lapse into silence. Zoya steals glances at him as he eats. She cannot get over her surprise at seeing him in this way—dressed in comfortable clothes, eating *pancakes*, and talking to her as if the events of the past few weeks are all a bad memory. Somehow, it makes him more human than ever.

But she also notices the wariness in his eyes, the way his smiles seem a little too forced, the tension in his every movement. As if he's bracing himself for something bad to happen. As if it's taking all of his willpower to appear normal.

Haroun picks up his glass of milk and is about to spoon the froth out from the top when Zoya says, "You don't like that part?" He shakes his head. "Can I have it?"

"Go for it." He nudges his glass towards her as she swipes her finger in one clean motion over the top, licking the froth off. She grins, and his eyes hold hers for a beat.

To distract herself from the rapid beating of her heart, Zoya gestures to his cap. "Going somewhere?"

"I used to take walks in the mornings and evenings." He gives her a swift, seemingly nonchalant glance when he says the word *evenings*. "Just trying to pick the habit up again."

"Mm," Zoya manages to say, unable to voice what she really wants.

But he voices it for her. In a tentative manner. "Do you—would you want to come with me?"

Trying not to seem overly excited by the prospect, she nods indifferently. "Yeah, sure."

When they clear up breakfast, Zoya—wanting to impress him despite having multiple dishwashers as well as many, many servants to do so—pushes back her sleeves and begins washing the dishes. Mumtaz enters the kitchen a few minutes later, widening her eyes when she sees Zoya. "*Bibi*, what are you doing?"

"What does it look like I'm doing, Mumtaz?" Zoya replies. Haroun grimaces at her tone.

"I know—I just—I haven't seen you doing this for a long time, so I was shocked. Forgive me—" Mumbling to herself, the maid walks away.

Zoya is too embarrassed by her failed attempt at impressing Haroun to look him in the face.

When the two step outside the manor gates, the birds are chirping and the sun is rising, soft hues playing over their faces. For a moment, the couple glances at one another, light sparkling in their eyes, before Haroun breaks the stare and turns away.

Zoya tries not to look too disappointed.

They walk in silence for the first couple of minutes, silence that becomes deafening and unbearable for Zoya. *Even these damn birds are chirping and talking,* she thinks scornfully. *Why not us?*

She is about to ask Haroun what he's thinking when a soft sound emerges from behind the trimmed bushes. Haroun darts his head towards the source of the sound.

The leaves ruffle, and out steps a small white kitten, big brown eyes gazing intently at the two of them. Haroun lets out an adoring gasp and bends down, reaching forward slowly so as not to scare it.

But Zoya, remembering that kitten all too well, backs away.

"Haroun," she hisses. "Stay away from that demon."

He turns around and knits his brows. The sunlight reflects on his skin, giving him an ethereal glow. "What?"

"That cute and fluffy and seemingly harmless thing is a monster," Zoya argues, remembering the last time she met it. "I was going to pet it, but it scratched me instead, the little devil!" She points to a mark near her hairline. "See?"

Haroun's gaze travels to her forehead, then back to her eyes. He gives her an amused look. "Really?"

"What, you don't believe me?" Zoya folds her arms. The kitten's eyes trail slowly between the two of them.

Haroun holds back a smile. "I don't know, I mean . . . she seems okay."

"Outwardly, everyone does." Zoya's voice is a little too sharp.

There is a knowing look in his eyes before he turns back to the kitten. "This little baby seems pretty harmless."

Hearing the coo in his voice, Zoya grows soft. Haroun reaches out slowly to pet the kitten, and Zoya releases a breath she didn't realize she was holding when the animal leans into his touch.

Before Zoya stomps her foot and folds her arms, causing the kitten to flinch under Haroun's hand. "That's not fair! The little devil is trying to win you over."

"Doesn't seem to be the only one trying to win me over right now." His voice is a low thrum as he throws her a playful smile, but it still manages to bring color to Zoya's cheeks. He fixes his attention back on the cat, running his fingers through her fur as her eyelids lazily droop. She burrows herself deeper into his touch. Haroun pauses for a moment before reaching down to lift the kitten, who thrashes for a moment before relaxing in his grasp.

"That's pure evil," Zoya whispers, but her voice seems to get lost in her throat when she sees Haroun soothingly stroke the kitten and rock her against his chest. He whispers soft words of adoration to her as she snuggles deeper into his chest, and a strange feeling settles consumes Zoya.

"You'd be a great dad," she blurts out, then pauses as she realizes the words that have come out of her mouth.

I want to bang my head against a wall.

If Haroun notices her embarrassment, he pays it no heed. "You'd be a great mom, too."

Zoya snorts. "What, by becoming jealous that my child is more attached to his father? There is nothing maternal about me."

He gives her a surprised look. "Why would you say that?"

"Because it's true."

"Debatable."

"Really? Tell me one thing about me that would make me a good mom."

Haroun shifts the kitten's weight into his other arm. She purrs in contentment. "You are fierce and determined to protect those you love at all costs. If that doesn't make a great mom, I don't know what does."

Zoya is stunned into silence by these words. How does he always do this to her? Like cutting the strings of a kite so that it roams aimlessly, uncertain of its destination.

As always, he doesn't seem to notice how he unbalances her. Or maybe he's just really good at pretending not to see it.

The kitten's eyes open at the sudden silence, and Haroun cocks his head to the side and looks at Zoya. "You okay there?"

"Yeah." She tries not to sound breathless. Slowly, she steps forward and lifts her hand to pet the animal, who shrinks back into Haroun's chest warily. Her eyes remain guarded, staring Zoya down.

Zoya lets out a sound of frustration and spins around, about to stomp away when she feels a hand clasp her wrist. She turns back to see the plea in Haroun's eyes, and her eyes travel to the hand wrapped around her. He lets go hastily, a fervent apology in his eyes.

"Don't give up so easily," he murmurs. "Give chances." He steps forward and strokes the kitten to calm the animal as Zoya reaches up once more to pet her. She doesn't know how to be soft, doesn't know how to touch the tiny animal without making harsh strokes with her hands. She has never had to be gentle; trying it now feels like attempting to fit herself into a new skin. A skin that isn't hers.

Oddly, it doesn't feel wrong.

The two of them simply stand there, stroking the small kitten together as she purrs beneath their touches and eventually succumbs to Zoya's attempt at gentleness as well.

And when Zoya looks up to offer Haroun a small, scared smile, his responding smile is soft and real.

~

After *Maghrib*, Zoya has several conference calls with Sameer as well as various journalists. She also receives some calls from very few concerned employees (Bill, Ibitoye, Lucas). By the time she ends her last call, she's exhausted, massaging her temples.

Haroun has returned from work, and after freshening up, he approaches her. He's dressed athletically again, this time switching his green cap for a blue one. He looks ethereal. Every time Zoya looks at him, she feels as if she is seeing him for the first time.

Haroun's eyes trek Zoya's movement's as she massages her forehead. He reaches forward as if he wants to aid her and then pulls back almost immediately, shifting his eyes. He swallows hard. "Are you okay?"

She flushes at the weird change in atmosphere. "Yes, yes, fine. Just tired of doing work." Her voice is surprisingly bitter as she shapes out the word *work*.

To break the thick silence that has settled between them, Zoya gestures to his outfit. "Going somewhere again?"

"Yup. You ready?" he asks her, adjusting his watch.

"For what?"

He points outside as if it's obvious. "A walk?"

"Oh." Zoya realizes far too late what he means. She aims for a nonchalant tone. "Oh, no that's okay. I was thinking I'd skip nighttime walks."

His eyebrows rise. Even he knows by now that Zoya would jump at any opportunity to spend time with him, even if he may not directly address it. "Scared, Zoya Zameer?" His tone is playful, but his eyes are serious.

Hearing her full name from his mouth awakens that desire within her again—the desire to answer to a challenge. She cocks her head to the side, staring him down brazenly. "Not in a million years."

"Come on, then."

Zoya rushes upstairs to change before returning, a challenging smile on her face.

Together they walk out, and the first few minutes are spent in that same uncomfortable silence that Zoya is becoming all too used to. Because there is something between them—an unspoken tension since the day of their marriage. Since the day Zoya's walls crumbled and she begged Haroun to marry her. Since the day her vulnerabilities were laid out in the open and Haroun felt helpless to refuse her begging.

"Why are you afraid of the dark?"

The question is sudden, disguised as casual. Haroun has always been a very straightforward person, so Zoya doesn't understand why she is surprised.

She giggles, hoping he doesn't hear the anxiety in it. She desperately wants to change the topic, but doesn't know what to say without seeming as if she's obviously deflecting. Instead, Zoya lifts a finger to wrap it around one of her curls, moving extra swiftly so the clink of her bangles is loud and distracting. She lifts her head and turns to Haroun with a very Zoya Zameer smile on her face.

His eyes are on the road.

She pouts, fluffing her hair dramatically until he turns to look at her. His gaze roves over her face and her movements before he gives her a confused look. "Something in your hair?"

Damn it, Haroun Suleiman.

"No. I mean, yes, I think." She continues to run her fingers through her locks, agitated that he doesn't seem the least bit distracted.

"Need some help?" he asks, seemingly clueless.

"What?" A nervous laugh bubbles out of her. "No, I'm okay. Thanks."

"So?"

"So what?"

"Why are you afraid of the dark?"

You won't let this go, will you? Zoya sighs. "I'm—it's not something big. It's just a common fear in children, you know? And mine passed on into adulthood." She shrugs, feigning indifference.

"Hm." His tone is disbelieving.

"What?"

"Nothing, just . . . I'm thinking of why you wouldn't want to tell me."

Zoya inhales a sharp breath. He's not going to believe anything but the truth. "It's nothing, okay?"

"Zoya." His voice is soft, and immediately her skin tingles. "Open up to the people who are close to you."

The implication that he is, indeed, someone close to her brings a smile to her face, which quickly vanishes as the memories his question brings resurface in her mind's eye.

"My ex-husband . . ." she begins, stepping slightly closer to Haroun. If he notices, he doesn't acknowledge it. "He . . . when he would . . ." She stops, squeezes her eyes shut. Upon reopening them, she is startled to see that Haroun is staring directly at her. His eyes are intense, serious. All hints of playfulness gone. "He hurt me mostly during . . . during nighttime. When it was dark and I"—her hand comes up to rub the length of her face—"when I felt most helpless. Most suffocated. When he knew no one would dare intervene."

Haroun breaks the silence. "Thank you for telling me," he murmurs gently. "Did your servants and guards know what he was doing?" There is barely any pity in his voice, nothing that would make Zoya wary and distant again. She has a feeling that he is trying very hard to control his emotions, and she cannot help but appreciate the effort.

Zoya shrugs. "I'm not sure. If they did, they never acknowledged it. But it would have been impossible not to hear . . ." She gulps, shakes her head. "He was a powerful, wealthy investment banker. He probably silenced them somehow. When we got a divorce, I dismissed all of his guards and servants except for one—"

"Mumtaz *bibi*," Haroun says suddenly. "Right?"

She nods.

"That's why she cares so much about you." His voice is full of awe.

Zoya gives him a surprised look. "What?"

"She's always asking about you, always worried about you. Wondering if you've taken your medicine and how you're feeling."

Zoya ponders over this for a moment. She never gives Mumtaz much attention except to give her an order, but she wonders if Haroun is right. Mumtaz is certainly always by Zoya at home, even if the constant pestering annoys Zoya. "I guess you're right."

"So . . . I know you didn't take it to court or anything like that, but what about his family members? Or yours? Did you tell anyone about what happened?"

Zoya scoffs. "First of all, nobody believed me when I said he was . . . harming me. And I never would have told them had they not demanded to know why I wanted a divorce. They asked me for *proof*." She laughs scornfully, absentmindedly tugging her sleeves over her arms riddled with scars. "In their eyes, everything I went through was telling the story that I had been a disobedient wife, and I had paid the price for it. Naturally, when I got a divorce, so many people came to tell me my decision was wrong. They told me the same things you said you were afraid your mom would hear afterwards." She pauses. "And . . . when I needed my father's support the most, he vanished.

"My ex-husband's sister approached me—literally with printouts of rulings and regulations—and shoved them under my nose. Telling me that I had been disobedient, that in Islam my husband had every right to . . . bed me and . . ." Zoya quiets, unable to say more.

Haroun lets out a frustrated sound, reaching up to rub his temples. "Oh, God, give me patience," he murmurs. "You know what one of the most dangerous things in this world is, Zoya? Telling only half the story." He shakes his head in disgust. "Like your ex, his sister and all those people completely ignored the fact that it was his duty to provide for you and take care of you in a *loving* manner. They disregarded his lack of respect for you and his inhuman treatment of you."

"Nobody remembers the other side of the story, the flip side of the coin," Zoya days, laughing bitterly. "Then what did anyone expect of me if not to despise religion?"

She startles suddenly, realizing that may be the first time she's ever said that out loud to anyone.

"I think alongside teaching people Islam, it's equally important to be showing it to them." Haroun says, an indent forming between his brows. "This is just my opinion, but I think people focus excessively on preaching rules and having theological battles that they forget the essence and beauty of being Muslim. The compassion, the devotion to faith, the community spirit, the *sunnah* of the Prophet Muhammad. We don't always have to shove rules and regulations under people's noses, especially not if they are already wary of religion. There's a time and place for everything. And I think sometimes it's just as powerful to hold the flag of Islam through our actions. Our demeanor."

Zoya listens to him quietly, surprised to find herself nodding in agreement. The two of them turn the corner of the sidewalk, taking another round about the neighborhood. "Sometimes . . . people pick and choose parts of the religion to use for their own benefit. It's like . . ." Zoya struggles to speak, afraid of voicing something that has been brewing in her mind ever since she became acquainted with Haroun and was forced to reevaluate her perceptions of religion. "It's like reading a single chapter in a book without context. My ex would frequently quote *ayahs* at me as justification for his actions. And then I would come back from it all hating him and hating the *ayahs* he quoted, thus hating Islam. And I hated it because he *made* me hate it." Zoya turns to Haroun, begging him to look into her eyes. He does.

"And then I met *you*, and you confused me. Because everything you said and did was gentle and . . . compassionate. And yet you are just as devoted to religion as he was." She furrows her brows. "You just have . . . a very different approach." She reaches up, wanting to touch his cheek. Instead, her trembling hand falls limply at her side.

"Farhan took everything out of context." Saying his name aloud causes a shiver to run up Zoya's back, even though she has been saying it for as long as she's employed the other Farhan. "So I rebelled after my divorce." Zoya shrugs. "I rebelled against every act he forced me to do. I wanted him to get angry at everything I was doing against his supposed judgment. Until I realized when I met you that all the things he forcefully threw in my face were God's words, twisted and warped to look evil and oppressive. Behind the warped mirror that he showed me was"—Zoya's eyes shine as she gazes into Haroun's—"purity and gentleness in God's words?" The last phrase comes out as a question.

Haroun blows out a tense sigh. "Zoya, I need to ask you this. I need to understand." She nods for him to continue. "How come you still prayed? After everything that happened to you, after everything you heard about Islam, you still had the strength to stand in front of the God everyone manipulated you into despising. Most people would abandon religion altogether—how did you manage to hold on?"'

Zoya shakes her head in disgust. "It wasn't even about God. It was about me and my own ego. Farhan told me that praying was done for God and God alone. It was the one thing I didn't do for *him,* essentially. So I wanted to prove to myself that there was *one* thing my ex-husband didn't coerce me into doing."

They are both quiet for a few long moments, pondering over their conversation. Then Zoya remembers how this discussion began. With Haroun asking about her fears.

He seems to remember the same thing because he asks apologetically, "Does walking in the dark right now scare you?"

Zoya swivels her head around at the dark streets and sidewalks, given a little relief by the street lamps. The air is still and silent; the crickets are chirping. "No, not really."

"How come?"

"Because you're here with me." The words are out before she can calculate them. She is scared to look at Haroun, but when she finally does, his eyes are wary. And yet also soft, warm.

"You trust me that much?" he murmurs.

"Of course I do." *Damn it, Zoya Zameer. Shut up, will you?*

"Thank you." The words are barely a whisper.

Puzzled, Zoya asks, "For what?"

"For finding me capable of trust. Trust doesn't come by easily, and if broken, it's even harder to repair."

Zoya freezes in her tracks, a feeling of dread settling on her. His words shock her to her core, like being dunked in ice cold water. She remembers her lie, the way she manipulated him, and her heart threatens to rip out of her chest with the ravaged way it beats.

"Zoya?"

She breaks out of her trance, watching him with tears brimming in her eyes. His confused gaze turns worried. "Are you okay? Is your head hurting? Do you feel faint?"

Zoya staggers back against the gate of a manor and Haroun reaches forward, hesitant about whether she would prefer steadying herself or him touching her.

Zoya pushes herself forward by planting her fingers on the wall of the gate. "I'm okay," she confirms breathlessly.

"Are you sure? Did you take your medicine—"

"I said I'm *okay*." She holds a hand up. He quiets, and instantly guilt dredges around her heart. A different guilt than the one she felt moments ago. He believes he's talking to a sick woman who could possibly land herself in the hospital again.

"I'm really sorry, Haroun," she says when she regains her bearings. *For all of it. For everything.* "I . . . just felt faint for a second," she lies.

"It's okay. Do you need anything?"

She shakes her head.

"Do you want to go back home?"

Home.

Zoya turns her face away from the street light so her tears aren't illuminated. "No, I want to stay here." *With you. Where I can continue to pretend that I haven't hurt you in the worst way possible.*

The thought brings on a fresh wave of tears. Zoya stumbles back against the gate again, trying to grasp anything to avoid falling down the deep, narrow hole she has dug for herself.

"Zoya, you really don't look okay to me. Maybe we should go home—"

He stops when she starts to take deep, heaving breaths. Stepping closer slowly—as if for every step forward, he wants to retreat one—he lifts a hand that hovers around her. Hesitant.

Zoya tugs at her hair, trying to quell the rising anxiety. But his words keep ringing through her head. *Trust doesn't come by easily, and if broken, it's even harder to repair.*

What will he do when he finds out what she has done? How will he react?

Zoya is broken out of her state when a gentle hand touches her back, rubbing soothing circles on it. She looks up in surprise—momentarily less panicked—to find Haroun's eyes filled with uncertainty. He seems to have realized that she isn't physically hurt but having a panic attack. He continues to comfort her, his hand making very slow motions across her back, as if he will pull away at any moment.

Zoya's emotions are battling, stuck in that constant tug-of-war of wanting to push Haroun away yet at the same time lean into him. She is disgusted at herself for feeling this way, for shrinking away from his touch after fantasizing about being able to hold him for so long. She wills herself to focus on the softness of his hands, of his fingers. To focus on the lack of pressure and the gentleness of his touch. To listen to the way he's murmuring "breathe, breathe." Zoya wills herself to look into Haroun's eyes in order to comfort her palpitating heart, to remind it of who exactly is standing in front of her. All this calms her down and she dares to move closer, allowing her head to drop against his chest. He hesitates, then circles his arms around her.

She hears his heartbeat. Quick, persistent, rhythmic. She focuses on it as if it is a melody, feeling the way his chest rises and falls underneath her head. Her muscles begin to relax. Haroun seems to notice that she is calming down and facilitate at the process by rubbing his fingers between her shoulder blades. His movements are slow, like he's afraid he will have to pull back at any moment.

To Zoya's surprise, she revels in the pleasure of the embrace, in being able to touch someone like this.

Until she remembers what she did to him, and immediately she steps back, the warmth rushing out of her and the anxiety rushing back in. She is unable to listen to his heartbeat any longer. His heartbeat which continues to prove what a pure, clean person he is, as well as remind her over and over of what she's done to him.

"Okay." He's tentative. "You're okay?"

Zoya manages to nod.

Haroun steps back quickly and adjusts himself, eyes on the floor. Zoya stands there dumbly. Something about his tense posture tells her he couldn't wait to get away.

"Let's walk back home, yeah?"

They continue to walk. Zoya needs to say something. She needs to talk about *anything* to distract herself from the horrible, unspoken feeling dredging around her heart.

He breaks the silence. "Do you often have panic attacks?"

Zoya turns her head away, heat coloring her cheeks. "Sometimes."

"Maybe you should . . . see a doctor," says Haroun. He rushes to continue. "I mean—I know you're not mentally afflicted or anything—but if you have such frequent panic attacks, you should tell a professional about it. Maybe they can help you—"

"I don't need help." A short, clipped reply.

Pause, then, "It's not about that. It's that these attacks clearly disturb you, and quite frequently at that. It isn't . . . healthy. Maybe someone could prescribe you medication that would ease—"

"I said I don't need anything." They've reached the manor now, and Zoya turns her piercing gaze to Haroun. "I'm fine."

His eyes rove over her face for a moment before he lets out a deep sigh. "Okay," he mutters, and as the gate opens, he disappears into the mansion.

When Zoya enters, Aisha greets her with a perplexed smile. "Zoya *aapi*, is everything okay? I just saw *bhai*—" She breaks off at Zoya's curt nod. "Oh, okay. I just thought—did you guys go out to eat?"

"No," Zoya says. Aisha watches her expectantly and Zoya sighs, forcing a smile. "We went on a walk, actually. Your brother said he's been trying to pick up the old habit."

"Wait, what old habit?"

"He said he used to take walks after sunrise and sunset."

Aisha's brows arch. "*Bhai* said that?" Zoya nods. After a

moment, the younger girl giggles. "*Bhai* didn't walk all that often. Sometimes in the mornings, but never at night." At Zoya's puzzled look, she shrugs.

Zoya stares at the staircase where Haroun dashed upstairs. Something nags at her memory. The way Haroun went quiet when she jumped at the darkness. The look on Haroun's face when he had gestured to her lit chandelier last night. The way his eyes had quickly darted to her when he mentioned walking in the evenings. The quiet challenge in his eyes when he had asked her whether she was scared. And the careful, nonchalant way he had asked about her fears.

Comprehension dawns on Zoya's face. It was all intentional.

He was trying to help her.

Forty-Six

"You are not a drop in the ocean. You are the entire ocean in a drop."
—*Rumi*

~

HAROUN WAKES IN THE middle of the night, eyes opening to mostly darkness save for a sliver of moonlight peeking through the windows. He rubs his eyes, sighs wearily, and rolls up into a sitting position.

The clock reads 1:43 A.M.

He shakes his head and pours himself a glass of water, knowing this will only make it harder to fall back asleep but drinking it anyway.

After setting the glass back down, he stands and trudges to the door, peeking into the long hallway.

Every single chandelier is lit and Zoya's door is wide open, lights brightening her room up as well.

Haroun hesitates before heading to her room. He peeks in, observing Zoya's appearance. She's in a t-shirt and leggings, blanket half covering her and half swept across the floor. One hand rests underneath the right side of her head, and the other dangles near the edge of the bed.

Her face is smooth of any animosity, any hostility, any fear or pain. It's soft, open.

Vulnerable.

Haroun steps inside and walks over to her slowly. He pauses when he's close enough, surprised as well as saddened by the scars riddling her arms. The arms she never exposes—probably for this very reason—except in the comfort of her own presence. For a moment, he simply stares down at her, wondering how someone who is so bitter most of the time can look so peaceful in sleep.

His mother's words ring through his head suddenly. *Be there for her. She needs you right now.*

He recalls his words, his frustration. His watery eyes. *I just need some time, Mama.*

And the more time you take, the more guarded she will become. She sees you as a source of comfort.

But I shouldn't be her sole *source of comfort.*

Haroun, do you think it was easy for her to beg you to get married like that? Can you imagine what amount of helplessness made her resort to that as a last option?

Haroun adjusts the covers, tucking them carefully around Zoya. She shifts a bit, curls falling forward onto her face, eyebrows furrowing slightly, hands warding off unseen demons. The scars on her forearms become more visible with her movement.

Haroun freezes, but breathes out a sigh when the wrinkles in her forehead smooth out and she snuggles into the blanket. As he watches her, he recalls the conversation they had earlier that night. She had said her ex's name for the first time—*Farhan*—and suddenly so many things had made sense to Haroun.

And then he remembers talking to Mumtaz *bibi* about Zoya. The elderly woman had said that Haroun entering Zoya's life was a huge blessing, and that she had observed Zoya's affection for him. She said that maybe Haroun could be the one to help Zoya confront her past and heal, to help her change.

Haroun had shaken his head. *If change comes, it will be by Allah's hand and by Zoya's own will. Besides, I feel like true help and advice come after two people are comfortable with each other. I don't want to force anything on her when she's especially vulnerable and hard on herself. She already thinks she lacks any goodness—one wrong word from someone she cares about, and she'll never see potential for growth and change. I think she needs to believe in herself and trust God before she's ready to tackle her past and her insecurities.*

Haroun stands over Zoya for a second before turning to exit the room.

At the door, however, a strange gravity tugs at him, forcing him to turn back around.

And then he leans against the doorframe, folds his arms over his chest, and continues to watch his wife sleep.

~

At the breakfast table, Aisha chatters excitedly about an art gala taking place at her school, where a couple of her paintings will be showcased. Zoya and Naima cheer her on as she does a little celebration dance in her seat. Her mother smiles at her.

Haroun, however, is quiet. Occasionally, his eyelids droop and his head jerks towards his cereal bowl, but he snaps back awake with a disoriented gaze around the room.

When Zoya had watched him pour his milk, she had choked mid-chew and almost spit out her food, to which Haroun had given her a raised brow.

"You put the milk *before* the cereal?" she had exclaimed.

His answering smile had been riddled with fatigue. "I feel like it lets me control how much cereal I take."

Zoya had stopped chewing despite the casual way in which he had phrased his statement. That was not what she had expected.

She had then realized something with an uncomfortable twist in her stomach.

She has no sense of organized control the way Haroun does, especially when it comes to forcibly taking the things she wants. The concept of delayed gratification is foreign to her. She needs everything in her grasp at the exact moment that she desires it.

And then there is this man—who measures his milk carefully so that he doesn't take too much cereal.

Zoya blinks, trying to shake the ever-present thought out of her mind. The thought that she has not done good to Haroun Suleiman.

"Calculating the electrons in your milk, *bhai*?" Aisha queries in a casual tone, but Zoya doesn't miss the concern on the young girl's face.

"What?"

"Nothing. Everything okay?"

"Yeah." He rubs his eyes.

Ammi's all furrowed brows. "You didn't get enough sleep?"

For a brief moment, his eyes shift to Zoya before he turns back to his mom. "I couldn't sleep last night."

Ammi runs a hand through his hair. "*Chalo,* you have some time before work. Get some rest, then."

He shakes his head. "Can't. I have a job interview at a bank today."

Once the breakfast is cleared, Haroun bids them goodbye. He gives a kiss to each one of his family members, then turns to Zoya as Aisha waggles her brows suggestively. He leans close, gives Zoya a swift peck on the forehead, and backs away quickly.

Zoya feels a mix of relief and disappointment.

Once he leaves, the women sit together for a bit before each scatters to her own work. After a phone call with an investor in Pakistan, Zoya trudges upstairs to get ready for the office.

On the way to her room, she passes by Naima's and hears sniffles inside. A moment of hesitation later, she knocks on the door. "Can I come in?"

There's a short laugh from inside. "*Bhabhi,* this is *your* house."

"*And* your brother's," Zoya reminds her as she enters, stopping short. Naima is sitting in the midst of scattered pictures, hastily wiping her cheeks. "What's wrong?"

"Oh, it's nothing." Naima forces a laugh. "I was packing some of my stuff before we go to our grandpa's place and found these. Just got a little nostalgic."

Zoya bends down, observing the pictures. With a start, she realizes that they are all of Haroun and his family. Through all ages. Pictures of two little girls and one older boy laughing and splashing around in a pool. Pictures of the three of them at the amusement park. Pictures through monumental moments in their lives—their graduations, their other accomplishments, and their parties at home. In some pictures, their parents stand on either side of them, laughing and watchingthem with adoration in their eyes. As the years pass, one parent begins to disappear from the pictures, but the children who have grown older still smile for the camera.

Sharpness pricks at Zoya's eyes. What must it feel like to have a wholesome family like this? To capture memories through laughs and tears to be looked at and reminisced over later? Zoya's childhood consisted of crayons and papers bought of the highest class, which she had excitedly used for drawings upon drawings of the perfect family to show to her dad. She expected him to appreciate the talent but was always grossly disappointed when he simply turned his face away with storms in his eyes.

Zoya raises her gaze to Naima. "Wow," she manages to say. "These are beautiful."

Naima smiles wistfully. "Yeah." She points to one. "This is when *bhai* went ziplining for the first time. Aisha was crying because she was too young to go, while I was scared to even watch *bhai* go. But he was so, *so* excited." She chuckles. "He was always fearless. Always wanting to try new things."

"Was?"

Naima sighs. "He's . . . different now. It seems like he's afraid to enjoy himself. Afraid to be happy."

Zoya settles into a more comfortable position. "How come?"

There is a sad smile on the younger girl's face. "After what happened with our dad and then"—she glances quickly at Zoya—"Sumaiya, I don't think he really allows himself the liberty to be too happy. I've seen how much he struggles with placing his trust in Allah in this matter. He wants to be happy without thinking of the consequences, but we're all human, aren't we?"

"Wow." Zoya's voice is full of awe. The way Haroun thinks about happiness is startlingly similar to her own mindset.

Naima's expression darkens. "It's a horrible thing, isn't it? To know that a single incident can change your entire life?"

Zoya shrugs. "Maybe sometimes the change is good."

"Yes," Naima murmurs. "But in gain, there is always loss."

This quiets Zoya. She becomes thoughtful for a moment. "You

know, Haroun really doesn't seem like the guy you're describing."

Naima laughs sadly. "That's because he's closed off most of the time. Battling his demons all on his own. He hardly shares his problems with anyone." She rubs a hand over her forehead in a motion laced with fatigue. "Have you seen him? He has these permanent eye bags and carries himself like something's weighing down on him, but he bottles it all in. Throws a forced smile when he catches anyone staring."

This, more than anything, concerns Zoya, because she knows that Naima is right. She has seen Haroun's exhausted demeanor, has been plagued at work by thoughts of what could be bothering him. But she has also always seen Haroun as stable, a pillar of strength. Untouchable. Unshakeable. And this description of him makes him utterly human.

"But he always seems so . . . composed," Zoya says.

Naima's responding laugh is bitter. "That's the talent, isn't it? He fools everyone. But I've woken up so many nights hearing him crying in his room, and I've been too afraid to comfort him. He's the kind of person who . . . feels as if he shouldn't talk to loved ones about his problems."

"But that's what they're *for*," Zoya argues.

"Exactly. But I think he feels like he's *burdening* people by telling them about his issues. He thinks people have their own battles to fight, and that he's just adding more baggage by sharing his own."

Zoya scoffs. "That's insane and foolishly selfless. He needs to take care of himself before he takes care of others. Otherwise, he'll be pouring from an empty cup all his life."

Naima sighs. She runs her fingers over the pictures absentmindedly as the two women stare into the distance, lost in thought.

"What does your brother dream of doing for a good time?" Zoya's voice turns mischievous to lighten the mood.

Naima's lips turn up. "Adventurous things. Dangerous things. Like ziplining or rooftopping or riding a helicopter above New York City or something equally exciting. He likes taking chances like that, experiencing new things. Him and Farhan are always embarking on some new adventure."

Zoya thinks of Haroun's lowered gaze and his dignified demeanor. "He really does keep it all in, doesn't he?" When Naima gives her a quizzical look, she clarifies, "I mean, no one would be able to tell by looking at him that he enjoys wild things like that."

The younger girl chuckles. "You're right. If he wasn't my brother, I would think he would call reading on a Friday night a fun time." She pauses, then backtracks quickly. "Not that reading on a Friday night isn't a fun time."

Zoya turns to her, observes her features. While Aisha looks every bit like Haroun, with her glossy raven curls and dimpled cheeks, Naima is pretty in a softer way. A big-brown-eyed, less-curly-haired way. Looking at her, Zoya thinks of the day Naima told her father not to put up the pretense of caring. Zoya had been surprised to hear the younger girl say that. Not only because it was unexpected, but also because while Aisha is boisterous, quick to trust, and finds comfort in the tensest of situations, quiet Naima is more careful, constantly fidgeting. Carrying herself as if she believes she weighs a little too heavily on the ground.

"What's *your* idea of a fun time?" Zoya asks her.

Naima grins. "Reading on a Friday night?" The two of them break out into giggles

"What about the future? What are your plans after college?"

"I want to get married and be a mother." She smiles dreamily before an immediate wariness settles over her face.

Zoya offers her a smile, and the girl relaxes somewhat. "Yeah? I can totally see that."

Naima's eyes spark. "I want to marry somebody who makes me fall in love with him every day. And I want to have children with him."

It's such a simple, small request. But the magnitude with which she says it coupled with the longing in her gaze tells Zoya how much this means to her.

Months ago, perhaps Zoya would have sneered at this girl. Rolled her eyes and told her she was too high up in the clouds. But something has changed in her after being surrounded by this gentle family, especially Haroun. So instead of passing a snarky comment, she says, "And you shall."

Naima shakes her head, scoffing. "Too bad not everybody thinks like you." She turns to her *bhabhi,* hesitant. "Do you know how difficult it is to be surrounded by Western ideology, having people constantly shove radical feminism down your throat? To have them sneer at you and call you oppressed or backward when you say you'd rather be a housewife than work towards a career, simply because your idea of a successful life is different from theirs?" She scoffs again, turning away to focus her gaze on the pictures scattered about the floor.

Zoya raises her brows at this. Having spent the majority of her working life in the business sector full of people from all walks of life, she can definitely attest to this reversed bigotry. She has certainly met some radicals in regards to feminism in her time—on both ends of the spectrum—and it has made her realize how truly complicated the issue is. With some people masking their beliefs for fear of ridicule, and others misinterpreting the entire issue, and others being overpowered due to their opinion's lack of popularity.

Time and time again, Zoya recalls her conversation with Raheem, where her driver had said, *I think you're against radical feminism.*

To which Zoya had responded with: *Feminism has created a specific, limited agenda. One that only works for some women. For example, feminists will rave about a woman's right to work, but will never give that same energy to women who choose to be housewives or homemakers.*

Hearing yet another person point out these things—especially Naima, this reserved, gentle girl—rattles Zoya once more.

"I think that's stupid." Zoya says with a shrug. "Every woman wields her power in different ways."

Naima laughs without mirth. "Unfortunately, the world is not as open-minded as you, *bhabhi.* In one of my classes, I made the mistake of saying that I'd rather be a housewife than a working woman. And a girl turned to me and said, '*Yeah, well isn't that, like, a part of your culture anyway?*" Naima lets out a sound of pure frustration. "I've learned that it's so difficult to earn respect as a woman in today's society if you're not a working woman. Because somehow, being less conspicuous makes you less intelligent or ambitious. I have nothing but respect for working women, but I don't appreciate this one-sided ideology."

Zoya lifts a tentative hand and squeezes the younger girl's shoulder. Words bubble to her lips, but all of them taste wrong. What can she say to make this torn girl feel better?

After a moment, she takes a deep breath. "I think you're incredibly admirable for saying those things in a classroom full of people who are opposed to your ambitions. And it doesn't matter what they think. Your strength lies here." She taps Naima's temple. "You are just as fierce as those women on battlefields or those women at the forefront of every protest or those women in the cutthroat corporate world. You are not limited to a single definition."

Zoya stands up and smiles, satisfied. Naima gives her a bright, real smile in return.

"Well," Zoya blows out a sigh. "I better get to work. You know, because my worth lies in my being a working woman." Naima laughs as Zoya edges out of the door, her heart unexpectedly light with happiness.

~

In her office, Zoya calls Sarah and asks her to send the good-for-nothing man in. When he knocks and enters, Zoya gestures for Farhan to sit down.

"You asked for me, Ms. Zoya?" Farhan says. He trembles a little less around her now, though the tense expression never truly leaves his face.

What Zoya wants more than anything after her past has been exposed is for people not to pity her, to treat her like she's normal. Haroun is like that. And, as much as she despises him, Farhan is like that, too. This attitude causes her to be a degree less frustrated around him.

Just a degree.

Zoya slides a file towards him. "I need you to go over this again."

He opens the file, scans it briefly, and nods. Zoya discusses some other matters with him, and while she's speaking, Sameer continues to periodically come into the office. First he sets some files at the desk near the door, then he enters with a crystal jug of water which he sets on her desk, and later he simply peeks in and glances at them. Frustrated, Zoya says, "What, Sameer Mirza?"

"Just checking to see you haven't killed him."

Zoya scrutinizes her secretary. "Do I look like I'm capable of murder?"

Sameer hesitates. "Do you want me to answer that?"

"Get out," she says instead, and Farhan covers his laugh up with a pathetic excuse of a cough. Zoya turns her narrowed eyes to him. "*Tumhe bari hasee aa rahi hai, huh?* Think this is so damn funny, don't you? *Chalo, tum bhi niklo. Jao.* Get out." Farhan picks up the file, uses it to cover his widening grin, and quickly exits her office.

Zoya rolls her eyes, catching her expression in the ornate hand mirror on her desk. "I wouldn't kill anyone," she scoffs.

Not literally, anyway. Only metaphorically, her inner voice nags.

Zoya gazes at her reflection in the small mirror, then turns her eyes skyward, deep in thought. Finally she murmurs, "Oh, shut up, Dr. Jekyll and Mr. Hyde."

Forty-Seven

"And rely upon Allah; and sufficient is Allah as Disposer of affairs."
(Qur'an 33:3)

~

ZOYA AND HAROUN DECIDE to have a reception in their manor. Something simple, with close friends, family, and coworkers. After everything that's happened, the last thing they need is more forced media coverage on their wedding.

They had a small *walima* a couple days after the *nikah*, but with the way the marriage occurred, the atmosphere had been strained and tense. It hadn't felt like a marriage banquet at all; hence the desire for another celebration.

A single group of reporters has been invited to their reception upon Zoya's hire. After the press conference, people had even more demanding questions, and Zoya and Haroun thought it best to clear them voluntarily on the day of their reception rather than have people make and publicize assumptions afterward.

The next two weeks are spent with Zoya's mother-in-law and sister-in-laws planning and preparing for the reception that will take place in one month. The three of them have moved in with *Ammi's* mother and father, but they visit almost every day. Every time Zoya settles down to join them in their planning, they usher her out of the room with urges to relax—Naima especially. She physically drags Zoya out of the room while Aisha threatens her that if she sees Zoya trying to plan her own wedding again, she will spill tea on all of her designer clothes. Which earns her a scolding from her mother but fit of giggles from Zoya.

So Zoya busies herself in her company's work, having taken on a new project with some wealthy investors. This is something she used to find great pleasure in doing but now seems like a burden to her. This burdensome feeling was seeded during her trip to Pakistan—when she had voiced to Haroun her hesitations regarding the industry—and has been growing like a poisonous flower ever since.

Zoya sighs as she flips through files in her office. She calls for a meeting with her board of directors, and tense sighs and furrowed brows travel all around the room as the finance manager goes over the recent decrease in revenues.

"Have we contacted the investors in Pakistan?" Zoya asks with an impatient tap of her pen.

Bill gives her a surprised look. "No."

"Why?" Her gaze is piercing.

"Ms. Zoya, *you* always do that. We assumed you had taken care of that already."

Zoya breathes out a deep sigh, her pen insistently tapping against the desk. *Damn,* she thinks. *He's right. And I can't even yell at him for not reminding me because the last time he did, I got pissed off at him.*

She's never going to say this out loud, though. Because that would admit that she has been distracted with other things.

Namely, Haroun.

After the meeting, Zoya unlocks her phone, fingers hesitating over the call button before she presses it. He picks up on the fifth ring, just when she's about to end the call. "Hello?"

Zoya clears her throat. "Uh, hello. *Salaam.*"

"*Wa 'Alaikum Salaam.*" Haroun pauses. "Everything okay?"

She blows out a frustrated sigh. "*Yes,* everything's okay. Why? Can't I call you just to talk to you, Haroun?"

For a moment, there is silence on the other end. Then, "Sorry, I didn't mean—"

"It's fine, I just—" She presses her fingers to her temples. "I just wanted to hear your voice."

"Okay." Not until she hears the smile in his voice does Zoya register what she just said.

"Oh, *damn*. Did I say that out loud?"

"Do you want to hear the truth?" If Zoya could see him right now, he would likely be smirking.

"Probably not."

He laughs, and the wrinkles in Zoya's forehead disappear. "Hey, listen—" His voice cuts off as he turns to speak to somebody else away from the phone. "Zoya? I have to go."

"Oh, okay," she says, flustered. "Yeah, of course."

"I'll see you at home, *Insha Allah*. Okay?"

"Okay," she says, but by the time her voice comes out, he's already gone.

~

When Zoya gets home, she sets her purse on the foyer table and trudges into the dining hall. Reaching up to rub her eyes, she stops short when she sees Haroun sitting at the dining table with a blue file in front of him.

Has he been waiting for her?

"Hey," she says cheerfully.

"Hey," he replies in a subdued tone.

"Is . . . everything okay?'

Haroun rubs his forehead. "You're late today. Was everything fine at work?"

He's deflecting, Zoya thinks. *Something's wrong.* She nods, moving closer to him. "Yeah, I just needed to talk to PR about some news after the press conference and . . . ." She freezes suddenly, catching sight of the file in front of him.

The file containing Sumaiya's pictures with Zaki Ahmed.

She has about two seconds to decide whether she will feign ignorance or acknowledge the situation, but her mouth makes the decision for her as the words spill out automatically. "Where did you find that?" she whispers.

When he looks up at her, the purple underneath his eyes seems to darken. Almost bruised, as if he hasn't slept in days. "Were you ever going to tell me about this?" She detects the hurt in his voice.

Zoya swallows, pulling out a chair to sit in front of him. "It's . . . not what it looks like."

"Really?" His eyes are wounded. "What does it look like?"

"Look, just give me a chance to explain . . ." Zoya says. He doesn't interrupt her, just watches her with that look in his eyes, and it crumbles all of her resolve. "I was going to tell you."

Haroun closes his eyes and rubs his temples. When he speaks, there is more despair in his tone than before. Something that nags at Zoya worse than if he were to be angry. "So was I just a ploy in this game? Something else for Zaki Ahmed to exploit? And Sumaiya was a . . . spy?"

"Haroun—"

He interrupts her, signaling the height of his distress. "Was our engagement even real?"

To this, Zoya does not respond. But Haroun must realize that her silence is affirmation, because his eyes widen with grief before he places his head in his hands. Zoya reaches forward to hold his hands, but he flinches away from her touch. Her hand stays suspended in midair, a crestfallen expression on her face.

When Haroun looks back up at her, his eyes are watery. "Why didn't you tell me about this?"

Zoya gestures to his state. "Because I knew it would upset you."

"So you decided on your own that I didn't deserve to know the truth?" Despair seeps through his tone.

"I would rather you believe a lie than know something that would hurt you."

The expression on his face morphs into disbelief. "You would rather nurture our relationship with sugarcoated lies than harsh truths?"

A stab pierces Zoya's heart. If this is how he is reacting to what Sumaiya has done, how will he react if he finds out what Zoya has done?

"Tell me something, Zoya." There is a plea in his eyes. "If it were anybody else, would you have told them?"

She doesn't even have to think about an answer to that. He and her both know the reply. Zoya stands and is about to turn away when Haroun grasps her hand. She whirls back around and says agitatedly, "*Yes*. I would have, okay?"

His lips tremble. "Then *why*?"

Zoya lets out a huff of frustration, turning on her heel to stomp away. But he pulls at her wrist again, and this time Zoya turns at lightning speed with her curls flying around her face, not calculating her next words before she blurts them out, "Because I *love* you."

There is a moment of terrifying silence as Haroun stares up at her, his face rigid with shock. The words hang in the air between them. In the grand room. In the quiet, dark house. In the rapid beating of their hearts.

Zoya takes a deep breath. She has said it. There is no turning back now. "I *love* you, and I couldn't bear to see you upset."

Haroun continues to watch her with that look on his face before he swallows. "*Love* isn't built on lies, Zoya."

She knows he's right. He's always right. But that doesn't stop his words from piercing her heart. An unfamiliar anger flares up within her, anger at *him* for being so good and so pure. The kind of anger she felt when she first met him and was frustrated by his rare righteousness.

"Well, that's the only love I know," Zoya hisses.

And with that, she spins on her heel and rushes up the stairs. This time, he doesn't stop her. This time, he doesn't grasp her hand. And she's not sure she wants him to. She rushes into her room and flings herself on her bed, burying her face in the blanket. She wants to hide. Away from Haroun and the wounded look on his face. Away from the world.

She just wants to disappear.

She tried to do the right thing. And it had still backfired in her unsuspecting face. So why bother to ever do the right thing?

Later, well into the night, as Zoya is sniffing and continuously wiping her tears, she hears footsteps on the stairs. They stop near her room, and Zoya waits with bated breath, thinking Haroun may come in. But he doesn't, and his footsteps fade away into his room before he closes the door.

Whatever little peace she had with Haroun Suleiman is probably gone. He doesn't trust her, and he isn't even aware of the extent of the things she's done. If he ever does, it will destroy him. He is too pure for someone as corrupted as Zoya Zameer.

He will never trust her, never love her.

I love you, she had said. What made her mouth open of its own accord?

Being around him always does that to her. She unfurls with the slightest glance of his eyes, pouring everything out to him in the language of heartbreak.

As Zoya leans against her headboard with fresh tears leaking down her face, in the room across from hers, Haroun settles into his bed, arm behind his head. The two of them stare up at their ceilings.

For the rest of the night.

~

Whatever progress their relationship had taken seems to have disappeared over the course of a night. At the breakfast table, they simply greet each other and exchange pleasantries before digging into their food. Silence presses down on them, thick as a cloud. The ubiquitous cloud follows them as they dress for work, as they bid each other goodbye, as they settle into their cars. Even then, it doesn't leave them. Even as Zoya steps into her office and Haroun enters his workplace, the cloud remains over them.

This continues for days. Not outright anger, but minimal words and accidental glances at each other across the room. At first, Zoya thinks Haroun may be the first to break, because that's just who he is.

But he doesn't. His character won't allow him to cut her off, but he's not exactly pursuing active engagement with her. He is as politely distant as ever, leaving her medication around instead of telling her to take it, texting her what time he'll be home rather than calling her, eating as quickly as he can so that they don't have to be in each other's presence for too long.

It disappoints Zoya more than anything. Is he really so upset about being lied to? Even if it was for his own good?

Perhaps he doesn't like when others make important decisions for him. Or maybe Zoya's obsession with control bothers him.

She doesn't know. And it bothers her not to know.

Countless times, she tries to speak to him for longer than a couple seconds. Casual, weightless conversation. And he replies in the same politely subdued manner, eyes lowered as they used to be. He responds when she speaks, but to her it seems forced. He doesn't make any effort to propel the conversation in a different direction, doesn't provide answers longer than a few words. He barely even looks at her.

And yet, before drinking his warm milk every morning, he silently waits for her to swirl her finger over the top of the mug and lick the froth off. Only then does he proceed to drink it.

It's such a small, small thing. But it's like a candle flame in a dark room, like the light at the end of the tunnel. It gives Zoya the reassurance that hope isn't entirely lost.

Before this candle flame gutters out, Zoya makes all efforts to win him over without directly communicating with him. When he tiredly slips into his room at night, there is a new flower tucked into the vase on his bedside table. When he leaves for work in the morning, there is a new trinket added to his car. First a new steering wheel cover, then an expensive new keychain, then neon rims on the wheels of the car. When he opens his closet to select clothes, new Armani, Guess, and Louis Vuitton shirts are piled at the top.

Zoya peeps around corners, watching his reactions with bated breath. Each time, there is a furrow in his brows before a look of comprehension dawns on his face. And after comprehension, a loud sigh and a rubbing of his temples.

She doesn't know entirely what that means, but a sigh is never a good sign. So she keeps trying, leaving things around for him everywhere.

A couple evenings later, Zoya decides that she has had enough of this aloof courtesy. Especially since Haroun was quieter than normal during dinner. When the two of them have eaten and retreated upstairs, Zoya paces around in front of his room.

She lifts a tentative hand and knocks on his door. It opens moments later, and Haroun leans against the doorframe.

"I, uh . . ." Zoya clears her throat. "I just wanted to see if you were okay."

"I'm okay."

There is something off about his voice. She steps closer. "Mind if I come in?"

He swings the door open, and she follows him inside. He settles on the bed. "Did you need something?" he says.

The words sting her. "No. No, I just wanted to see if you were okay. And you had a job interview today, right? How'd it go?"

"I'm okay. The interview was okay."

Zoya is thrown off by his clipped attitude. It's so unlike him. "I, uh—I noticed you've had trouble sleeping. Do you need any sleep medication?"

When he laughs, it's mirthless. "Zoya, there isn't medicine for every pain."

"Okay," she says slowly. "So that's a no?"

He simply shakes his head and tugs the blanket over himself. "I want to be alone right now, please." There is bare tolerance in his voice. Like a dam is about to crack, and water will gush forth.

"Haroun, is everything—"

"Everything's fine," he says exasperatedly, pressing his palms to his eyelids. "Please. Just go. I *really* don't want to say anything that might upset you."

Zoya's fists clench and unclench. He has never been this way, has never acted like this, and suddenly all her surety is thrown out the window. Zoya dares to move closer, settling at the edge of the bed. Haroun turns his face away, but the rapid blinking of his eyes is unmistakable.

"Hey," Zoya wills her voice to soften. "Hey, what's wrong?" She reaches forward, but he flinches back as if her fingers are made of fire. She retreats like a wounded animal.

"Please," he whispers. "Don't."

"What is this about?"

"I told you. I don't want to upset you. Please just go."

Zoya shifts closer. "No, clearly there's a problem—"

"Yes." Haroun fists his hair in his hands, and it sounds like the dam has exploded and the water is beginning to flood out. "Yes, there is." He looks up, and tears fall down his cheeks. "Something bad happens every time I'm around—" He takes a deep breath, not looking in her eyes. "Zaki's accusation, being *used* in the name of business, and now *this*—" His voice is barely above a whisper, and Zoya freezes. Just what *this* is he doesn't say, but she gauges it means his interview didn't go well. "I don't want to say this. Really, I don't. But I can only take so much. I've tried to make this work for the past two months but I'm exhausted. I—I—" He drops his head in his hands. "Just go. Please."

Zoya's eyes are wide as saucers, heartbeat quick and persistent. She backs away from him as if he's burned her, and he doesn't look up even after she exits the room.

Outside, her fingers tremble as she presses them against her mouth, against her heart. Her body convulses with tremors of shock and denial. He couldn't have said all those things to her. He couldn't have. It's not who he is.

But he did. Meaning Zoya has really pushed him over the edge. It's her fault. It's all her fault.

A sound emerges from her throat, halfway between a cry for help and an attempt at a breath. Her hands find the wall behind her, and she manages to stand upright, even when everything in her seems to have upended.

And then she feels it.

Defeat.

The depth of defeat, such that she has never known. Haroun Suleiman will never love her, will never want to be close to her. It's her fault that he's in pain. She did this to him. She forced everything on him the way people had forced things on her. And now he is crumbling and gasping for air under the weight of her mistakes.

Zoya's back hits a doorknob and she blinks, turning around to register her surroundings. In her aimlessness, she's walked to the other side of the manor and is now standing in front of *that* room.

The room her entire life was destroyed in, the room she suffered the most injuries in, the room in which her emotions were toyed with.

The room where the old Zoya Zameer had died.

It seems only fitting for her to revisit those brutal, violent memories again.

~

Haroun twists and turns in bed, sleep nowhere near finding him.

Of course it won't.

He sighs and turns his face to the ceiling. Guilt dredges around his heart, persistent and prodding.

He should not have said those things to Zoya. No wonder his mother had strictly taught her children never to let anger take control, because when it does, then to hell with a person's character. Anger takes the wheel and allows nobody else any control. Then, when it ebbs away, a person is left baffled, surveying their surroundings. Horrified by the collateral damage they've caused just by allowing anger to take the wheel.

As Haroun feels now. Horrified.

He slips out of bed and runs a hand through his hair. What should he say to her? *I'm sorry I told you that you're the root of all my problems.*

He snorts out loud, shaking his head. He really has screwed up this time. But he just wasn't able to control it when he was rejected from what would've been a really good job because of his "questionable character as proven by Zaki Ahmed" (the interviewer had literally used those words). And then he came home and, lo and behold, witnessed the person around whom all his problems had started.

But it wasn't fair for him to say those things to her. It wasn't fair at all. Especially when she is already so hopeless all the time.

And he needs to stop acting like she is the one who forced him to make certain choices. She did not force him to work at Zameer— that was his own choice. She did not hold a gun to his head and ask him to marry her—he agreed with sound mind (albeit reluctantly).

He sighs and rubs his hands along the length of his face, trudging out of the room. He stops outside Zoya's, just shy of stepping in. The chandelier is lit as always, the room basked in a warm, comfortable glow.

"Zoya, I'm sorry for what I said," Haroun murmurs under his breath. "I was angry and you didn't deserve to hear any of it." He shakes his head. "No, that's not right."

"Zoya, please forgive me. That was way out of line. I want to request you to—" He furrows his brows and shakes his head again, leaning forward to plaster his forehead against the wall. "Why so formal, Haroun? Just say it. Be straightforward."

Haroun takes a deep breath and enters his wife's room, stopping short when she is nowhere to be found. Thinking she may be in the bathroom, he settles on the bed and waits for a few moments. But the silence is odd and unsettling, and soon enough he's knocking on the bathroom door, a quizzical frown upon his brows.

"Zoya?" he says. "Zoya, can you come out, please? I want to talk to you."

Silence.

"Look, I understand that you're mad. You have every right to be. But can you please give me a chance to apologize?"

Still nothing.

Haroun's hand hesitates on the doorknob. "Can I come in?" There isn't a single sound. Deciding he can't take the silence anymore, he pushes the door open.

But there's no trace of Zoya.

He swivels around in confusion, glancing at his watch. "It's ten P.M.," he murmurs. "Where would she go right now?"

Haroun makes his way downstairs, fingers drumming over the railing. He ducks his head into random rooms, darts around the kitchen, peers into the dining hall. But no Zoya.

Just as he's about to panic, Mumtaz appears from the end of the hallway carrying a jug of water. She stops when she sees Haroun, lifting her *dupatta* over her head. Haroun lowers his eyes in front of the elder woman.

"*Beta?*" she says. "What are you doing?"

"Mumtaz *bibi,* have you seen Zoya?"

The woman's brows furrow. "I thought she went up to bed an hour ago. Didn't she?"

"I thought so, too." For a moment, there is a charged silence in the air. "Where could she have gone?"

Now Mumtaz is worried. "*Beta,* I'm afraid I don't know. She's usually in bed by now." She sets the jug down and lifts a hand up to her face. "If she's not sleeping, then where is she? She doesn't usually disappear like this, especially not for this long if you're saying she went to bed an hour ago."

The two of them mull over it for a moment before Haroun says, "Okay. Let me find her. She's probably here somewhere. Where could she have gone, right?" He laughs nervously, turning away from the now-tense woman. Once he's out of her sight, he picks up the pace and breaks into a trot.

Hurtling through the house whilst opening and closing doors, Haroun tries to find Zoya. At one point, he huffs out in frustration. "This house is so big—she could be anywhere. *Think,* Haroun, *think.*" He leans against the wall for support and closes his eyes to concentrate.

Suddenly, a memory prods at him. Zoya—back when she had been Ms. Zoya to him—had asked Haroun to close a door. She had seemed traumatized by looking at the ajar door, voice trembling as she made her request. She only relaxed when the door had been shut.

Haroun's eyes fly open, and for some reason he has a strong feeling that's where she is.

He rushes upstairs and reaches the room, taking a deep breath before twisting the knob.

Sure enough, Zoya Zameer is here. She's sitting in the middle of the room, objects upended all around her. The sheets of the bed have been pulled off, the curtains of the windows hang on one end loosely. Items—broken and shattered—litter the room.

Zoya's eyes are wild, gazing somewhere far, far away. Too far. Somewhere Haroun is unable to reach her. He steps closer. "Zoya?"

She doesn't reply, doesn't even register that she's heard him. Her hair is mussed and tangled, as if she has been swiping her fingers through it angrily.

Haroun's face falls. Did he do this to her?

He gazes at her with a worried expression, unsure of how to help. He moves forward and grasps her hands. Zoya flinches back from his touch and stares at his hands with the same expression on her face. Lost, broken.

Her eyes flit to his face, and Haroun realizes with a shock that she's unable to recognize him. He reaches up to cup her cheek, and she gazes at his hand as if it's foreign.

"Zoya?"

She doesn't respond, her eyes blank and hollow.

"Zoya?" Haroun whispers again. After a moment's hesitation, he says, "Sweetheart?"

At the endearing word, Zoya's eyes widen, recognition flitting in them. Her breath comes in short gasps, but she looks at his hand again and seems to register the touch. She surveys the room, taking in her surroundings, and awareness returns to her features.

Seeing her confusion, Haroun repeats, "Sweetheart. Zoya. Look at me."

Slowly, slowly, she stops trembling. Slowly, her chest rises and falls at a more normal pace. Her breathing is not as harsh anymore.

Haroun reaches forward and wraps his arms around her. She seems awfully small in his embrace, awfully minuscule. This loud, boisterous woman with so much flair, so small in his arms.

After a few seconds, she too wraps her arms around his torso and breaks out into sobs. Her eyes fill with tears, pooling down her face and falling on Haroun's shoulders. Staining his shirt. Her tears speak all that her mouth is unable to stay.

~

Back in Zoya's room, Haroun sits awkwardly in front of her, wringing his hands. "Do you need anything else? Another sweater, maybe?" he murmurs.

Zoya shakes her head, eyes searing into the mattress beneath her.

Silence, then, "Zoya, I am so, so sorry about what I said to you. It just—it came out and I—" Haroun runs a tense hand through his hair. "It was way out of line. I'm really, really sorry. I'll do whatever I can to make it up to you."

Zoya stares out the window at the moon, dry tears caking her cheeks. His words from a few hours ago words flit through her mind. *Zaki's accusation, being* used *in the name of business—*

"Zoya?"

She turns. "It's okay." Her voice comes out raspy. It's the first words she's spoken since they entered her room. She can still feel Haroun's arms around her, comforting her. She had been so relaxed with his touch, so unafraid. She has never felt so safe in her life, not since her father's arms in those rare moments when he used to embrace her.

How long did it take for Haroun to come find her after he had said something he regretted? One hour? Two? And how long does Zoya go before even coming close to regretting any of the words she utters?

A lifetime?

"No, really," Haroun says. "You don't have to say that. I know it's not okay." He blows out a sigh. "I've . . . had a lot of time to think, and I've been wanting to apologize for a couple days now. I just . . . didn't know how.

"About Sumaiya, I understand why you hid the situation from me. I'm not saying it was the right thing to do, just that I understand why you did it." His expression becomes grave. "I just . . . so much love, Zoya?" he asks quietly. "So much that you would rather watch me be gullible and unhurt than upset about the truth?" He stands from the chair across from her and edges closer to the bed. "So much love that you would rather victimize yourself in my eyes in order to protect my heart from a greater pain? *You* made Sumaiya tell me you were the reason for our false engagement breaking off, didn't you?"

Zoya turns away, unable to focus when he is so near her. When the familiarity of his comforting touch is so close.

Haroun cups her cheek and turns her face to his. "Answer me."

Zoya nods briefly.

He scoffs in disbelief. "Why? Why did you risk your reputation in my eyes just to protect me?"

"I told you," Zoya manages to say. "I love you."

At this, the hand cupping Zoya's cheek falters, dropping into Haroun's lap. "You love me." It's a statement, not a question. As if he's trying to make himself believe her response, even though she's already said it before.

Zoya nods. "Yes."

"You do."

She stands, huffing out a sigh. "God, why is it so hard for you to believe?"

Haroun grasps her hand, staring up at her. "I don't know." They stay like this for a moment, staring at each other. Then he says, "Can I tell you something?"

Zoya's heart palpitates against her rib cage so hard that she fears he may hear it. Is he going to proclaim his feelings? "Yes," she says, breathless.

He wounds his hand tighter around hers, then brings it up to his lips to press a kiss to her knuckles. Her breathing halts. "Zoya?" The tone of his voice is placatory. Why should he need to placate her unless what he's about to say is something to be wary of? Immediately, she tenses.

"Yes?"

"Zoya, I think you have an unhealthy attachment towards me," Haroun says softly, looping his fingers through hers. It's as if he's trying to placate her with his touch to lessen the blow of his words.

"What?"

"I think you have an unhealthy attachment towards me," he repeats slowly. "It's not good for you. You're putting all your trust in one place."

She pulls her hand from his grasp, wanting to back away but being rooted in place once again when he wounds his arms around her waist. "Zoya."

"No." Her voice shakes. "Stop."

"You're misunderstanding. I'm not telling you that it's wrong to love me, just that nothing in excess is ever good."

"Why would you ever say no to love?" she asks in a shocked voice.

He sighs. "I'm not saying no to love. I'm trying to tell you not to set yourself up for heartbreak." He lifts a hand and places it under her chin, rubbing his thumb along it. "I have the capability to hurt you, even when I don't want to."

"You—" Zoya grasps his hand on her chin. "You're an angel, Haroun."

"That's the problem, isn't it? You place me on such a high pedestal and forget that I'm human. You forget that I'm just like you. That I have the capability to disappoint you."

She shakes her head. "You will never disappoint me."

He laughs scornfully. "You say that now, but I guarantee you I will, even if it's unintentional. You're putting all your trust in a single place, Zoya, and that's dangerous." He pauses. "If you put the engine of a car anywhere but where it's supposed to go, the car will probably malfunction. Because it wasn't made to hold the engine in a different place. In the same way, your trust is in the wrong place, Zoya. And you *will* be disappointed by me. It's just a matter of when and at what magnitude." There is a profound grief in his eyes.

In response, Zoya runs her hand along his forehead. It is so freeing being able to touch somebody like this. Like being handed the reins and steering whichever way she desires. "Haroun," Zoya pleads softly, trying to understand. "Why are you demonizing yourself in my eyes?"

"Did you not do the same to yourself?"

To this she clamps her lips shut, having no answer.

"Exactly." Haroun lifts a hand and gently twirls one of her curls around his finger. "I care about you, Zoya, and I don't want you setting yourself up for a destruction that you have the ability to avoid. Love me, but with a limit. Trust me, but trust God more. Believe me, humans will always disappoint one another. Even in the name of love. Especially in the name of love."

Zoya simply gazes into his eyes, spellbound. She had always wanted for him to look into her eyes, to *see* her, and now that he is, she's able to read so much more into his words. There is a profound depth in his coal black eyes, a bottomless well for one to helplessly fall into.

"Okay," she whispers, not sure she's okay at all.

"Okay," he echoes. After a pause, he says, "And it's not your fault."

"What's not my fault?"

"That you're so attached." He rubs a hand over his face. "I laid out the groundwork. Even when we weren't married. I allowed you to get emotionally attached to me. I allowed you to get so invested in me. If I knew you were getting attached, I should have started backing away as soon as I realized it. I should have withdrawn.

"But I didn't. Because *I* wasn't getting attached and I assumed *you* weren't, either. Because in my eyes, I was only in your presence when it was absolutely necessary. But—" He laughs bitterly. Zoya can tell it's taxing him to say this; it's as if he's just come to terms with this realization. "It wasn't always necessary, was it? Not when I comforted you when you were upset, not when I asked if you were okay too many times out of habit, but it meant something else to you.

"The implications were all there, Zoya. I just chose to ignore them. But I laid out the framework for this. So don't think you lured me into anything. Because you didn't."

Zoya observes him, from his distressed expression to his hand still wrapped around hers. How does he admit these things to himself, let alone to another person? How does anybody admit their faults without spiraling into the depths of defeat?

She hears Haroun's voice in her head. *By trusting God.*

Her thoughts are interrupted when Haroun says, "Can I ask you for a favor?"

"In the name of love?"

"Just someone who cares about you asking for a favor."

She starts at that. For the second time this night, he is admitting that he cares about her. She thinks this is as close to an *"I love you, too"* that she will get, but it makes her happy nonetheless. "What?"

When he voices his favor, Zoya lets out an angry sigh and turns around. But he tugs at her hand once more, rooting her to the spot.

"Please," he says, and it crumbles all of her steely resolve. "Just try it out. If you don't approve of it or it doesn't help you, we'll stop." He holds his hands up. "Deal? But please just give it a chance."

After a few moments of contemplation, Zoya reluctantly nods, and the look in his eyes is enough to make her glad of her decision.

She settles into bed, and Haroun tucks the blanket around her. Then he, too, settles next to her, much to Zoya's surprise and secret joy. In his hands is one of the Qur'ans from Zoya's library room, the one along with all the others collecting dust in there.

He opens it and begins to recite.

When it becomes clear that he isn't leaving, Zoya allows her eyelids to droop, pushing away thoughts of her past and focusing on the sweet melody of her husband's voice. She stumbles in and out of consciousness, vaguely registering a hand gently massaging her scalp. Every time her eyes open, Haroun is still sitting there. Still reciting, still running his fingers through her hair. At one point in the night, he stands to tuck the Qur'an into the topmost shelf before settling back down. He tucks the blanket around both of them, then lifts his hand and proceeds to run it over her head. Back and forth, back and forth.

It seems to Zoya that he does not sleep the entire night. She too lies awake with closed eyes, too scared she will lose these comforting moments to something as arbitrary as sleep.

Forty-Eight

"Allah is the Protector of those who have faith: from the depths of darkness, He will lead them forth into light." (Qur'an 2:257)

~

TO MAKE GOOD ON her favor to Haroun, Zoya sits in front of the therapist, huffing and sighing and making exaggeratedly loud noises.

Ms. Fray—the therapist—smiles at her, having tried conversation for the past fifteen minutes with minimal answers from Zoya. Especially after Zoya had entered, frozen, and basically *ordered* the therapist to remove the lamp from her table. Zoya's lack of response doesn't seem to faze Ms. Fray at all, though, as she continues to ease Zoya into casual conversation, as well as prod her with carefully worded questions. Questions that seem so well versed and practiced that Zoya can only wonder what kind of training these people receive.

Three days pass with Zoya busying herself in work, going home, and then traveling incognito to her therapy sessions. Ms. Fray gives her an indecipherable smile every time Zoya enters, removes her hood, and snatches the band out of her hair, but the woman says nothing more.

As much as Zoya doesn't want to admit it, the sessions are growing on her. She no longer despises entering the therapist's room; and slowly, slowly, she is learning to be less snarky when Ms. Fray talks to her.

"Okay, Zoya," Ms. Fray says a couple days later, that smile still on her face. "We're going to try something. Are you ready?"

"Do I have a choice?" Zoya replies.

Ms. Fray nods. "Of course you do."

Zoya is surprised by this answer. "Okay," she shrugs.

Ms. Fray gestures to her reclining couch, and Zoya giggles. "*Ah, this is the part where I lie down and you hypnotize me into revealing all of my life's darkest secrets. Like in the movies.*"

The therapist shakes her head and guides Zoya to the couch. "Nope, no hypnosis."

Zoya lies down, fanning her curls over her chest. She pulls her knees up, then stretches them back down, then proceeds to organize the bangles on her wrist.

"Try to relax, Zoya, alright?" Ms. Fray advises. Zoya halts motion, sighing. She stares up at the ceiling, the cool upholstered leather beneath her back calming her down. "Good," comes Ms. Fray's voice. It sounds strangely soft and soothing, like ripples in a cool summer pond. Zoya's muscles loosen.

"Now Zoya, tell me about your day."

Zoya's eyes flit to the clock. "Well, I'm usually at home by now."

"Okay, and how about you tell me what you're thinking? Tell me anything at all. Whatever comes to your mind."

Whatever comes to your mind.

This is more control than Zoya is accustomed to. Too much, all at once. Zoya gains control by snatching it, not by having it handed to her.

Suddenly, she doesn't know how to act.

"Um . . . okay." Zoya swallows. "Anything?"

"Anything."

"Okay. Well, I guess I could start with work. Usually, I'm at home and working on something for the company right now. But strangely enough, even though I don't really want to be here"—Zoya gives the therapist an unapologetic look—"I feel like I would rather be here than doing Zameer work."

Ms. Fray nods, not at all cowed by Zoya's blunt confession.

"I don't know why. Recently, I've been feeling very frustrated with work. It all seems so . . . shallow?" Zoya scrambles for the right words. For some reason, she finds herself *wanting* to speak more. It's a strange feeling, especially in front of someone who isn't Haroun. "I told my husband that I feel like my work serves no purpose, that it's merely something I do to pass time. And even the time that passes doesn't seem like time well spent."

Zoya continues to voice her concerns, continues to ramble on and on, like a thick and stiff spool in her is finally coming undone. Ms. Fray sits there with a clipboard in her lap but pays no heed to it as she hangs on to Zoya's every word, nodding here and there to prod her to continue.

When Zoya has spent her breath, she laughs nervously. "You should've told me to shut up."

Ms. Fray shakes her head. "That is the opposite of what I'm here for." Pause. "When did you get married, Zoya?"

Zoya tenses. *The first time or the second time?* "Um—a little over to months ago. Why?"

"Do you feel like your work has started to seem shallow since you got married?"

Zoya ponders over the question for a moment. "No. No, it started before that."

"Mhm." The therapist nods. "Let me put it this way: Do you think your feelings about your work have changed since you met the man who is now your husband?"

"Yes. Definitely."

"Okay. And do you think this change has been forced on you?"

Zoya furrows her brows. "No. Not at all. On the contrary, I feel like being around him automatically pushes me to be a better person."

Ms. Fray nods. "Encouraging growth and change in one another is an important factor in nurturing a healthy relationship." At these words, Zoya smiles tentatively. "Okay, Zoya. We're going to try something, alright? I'm going to say a word, and you're gonna tell me whichever word first comes to your mind in response to it. Don't think too much—just say whatever comes to your mind. Okay?"

Zoya examines her nails. "M'kay."

"Alright, let's start." Ms. Fray shuffles her papers. "Pain."

"Ubiquitous."

"Happiness."

"Short-lived."

"Politicians."

Zoya's brows knit. "Eloquent."

At this, Ms. Fray's lips quirk, but she continues in a composed, professional manner. "Power."

"Manipulative."

"Love."

Zoya twirls a curl around her finger. "I'm thinking of two words."

"Which word pops out?"

"Consuming."

"And the other word?"

Zoya swallows. "Destructive."

"Okay," Ms. Fray says. "Desire."

"Sickening."

The therapist writes something down on her notepad. Then, before asking Zoya anything else, Ms. Fray leans forward and smiles at her. A sincere, open smile.

Zoya gives her a tentative smile back.

"Zoya, do you have frequent nightmares?" the therapist says.

Zoya blanches. The question throws her off completely, but she attempts to feign indifference. "I'm sorry?"

"Do you have nightmares often?"

She hesitates before replying. "Yes."

"Panic attacks?"

Zoya hesitates. "Sometimes."

Ms. Fray nods. There is no hint of remorse or pity on her face. It is detached and entirely professional, allowing Zoya to relax. "Zoya, when you came in here a couple days ago, you asked me to remove the lamp from my table. Does my lamp in particular bother you, or do you have an aversion to all lamps?"

"All lamps," Zoya whispers.

"Okay, and is there any particular reason you don't like lamps? If so, would you like to share that with me?"

Zoya hesitates, hand frozen in her hair. *Would you like to share that with me?* There's pressure—it's *her* choice whether she wants to answer or not. She has the power to say "no."

Instead, she nods shakily. "They're just . . . a bad reminder of the past."

"Is there anything else in particular that disturbs you? Any object, any place, any person, even?"

"I don't like . . . porcelain dishes. Or darkness." Zoya's eyes dart to the therapist. "Men, sometimes, unless I've known them for a while. And . . . touching people."

Ms. Fray makes a note on her clipboard, not at all fazed. Her eyes flit to Zoya's clenched fists, then back to her clipboard. "Are any of these fears related to one another?"

"They all are." Zoya's breath becomes shallow.

"In what way, if you would like to tell me?"

Zoya stays silent, unable to form words.

"Okay, Zoya, relax. This is a safe space, alright? You're at ease here." At the soothing lilt in the woman's voice, Zoya's shoulders loosen.

"You mentioned human contact," Ms. Fray continues. "You don't like touching people, or you don't like it when people touch you?"

"Isn't it the same thing?"

"In which situation do you have more control?"

Zoya hesitates. "I don't particularly like either, but I really don't like it when people touch me. Women, I'm okay with sometimes, but definitely not men."

Ms. Fray nods. "Do you get uncomfortable when your husband touches you?"

"No. It was difficult to get used to at first, but now it doesn't bother me."

"Did he force contact on you in any way?"

"No. Not at all. He's been so understanding about—" Zoya stops, clamps her lips shut. Briefly she thinks of something that has been surprising her ever since she married Haroun.

Haroun is twenty-eight years old, married for the first time, and a virgin. No matter how patient and gentle and compassionate he is, at the end of the day, he's *human*. He has human desires and human tendencies. It must be extremely difficult for him to be in constant close proximity to a woman he is *allowed* to touch, to kiss, to have an intimate relationship with, yet hold himself back. Zoya is his wife, after all. She's sure that he—as a human being—has dreamt of one day experiencing one of the most beautiful things about marriage (as had she, before Farhan ruined it for her).

Despite knowing what an understanding and caring person Haroun is, Zoya is still, needless to say, pleasantly surprised. That he allows her to initiate contact in most situations, that he only touches her when her eyes give him permission, that he only crosses her boundaries when she clearly lets down her guards. And, above all, that he is so patient with her despite the desires she's sure he harbors.

She does not think most men would harbor the self-control he does, have the ability to be as patient and thoughtful as he is.

"Zoya?" the therapist says, breaking her out of her thoughts. "You were saying?"

Zoya realizes that there is a grin on her face and a pink tinge in her cheeks. She bites her bottom lip, trying to remember what she had been saying.

The therapist gently prods, "You were saying that your husband has been understanding about . . ."

"About it all," Zoya says, shrugging.

The woman nods, having gauged that Zoya is done discussing the topic. "You mentioned being afraid of men sometimes. Is your husband included in this bracket?"

"No. I actually feel safer around him than around women."

"It sounds like you have a great deal of affection for your husband," Ms. Fray remarks.

Zoya's responding smile lights up her eyes. "You couldn't know him and *not* feel affection for him."

Ms. Fray nods. "Okay, Zoya. You mentioned not being fond of

darkness. Would you want to elaborate on that?"

Zoya's smile vanishes as she gulps. "I just . . . bad things used to happen at night."

"Like nightmares?"

"Sometimes." Silence, then, "Like . . . pain." Suddenly, she feels absolutely foolish for saying that. She squeezes her eyes shut.

"Don't worry, Zoya," Ms. Fray coaxes. "Everything's okay in here, alright?" Zoya nods hesitantly, comforted by the woman's soothing tone. After a moment, she asks, "Does your father fall into the bracket of men you fear?"

"No. And I haven't seen him for years now."

"Does he live far?"

Zoya laughs mirthlessly. "Something like that."

Ms. Fray nods, not pushing her. "Okay, Zoya. Thank you for trusting me with all this."

There it is again. Someone thanking her for trust.

The woman continues to ask Zoya questions and converse with her in an entirely relaxed manner, continually reassuring her that she is in a safe space. A while later, she says, "We'll stop here for today, alright?"

Zoya's eyes flit to the wall clock in surprise. "It's been an hour?"

The therapist laughs; a light, comforting tinkle. "Time flies when you're having fun, doesn't it?"

Zoya pushes her palms into the upholstered leather and sits. "Thank you."

"I'm glad you're willing to give yourself a chance."

~

A couple sessions later, Zoya signs consent forms for Haroun to meet with Ms. Fray. As he sits in front of the therapist and listens to her, a line of concern appears between his brows

"Mr. Suleiman, your wife may be showing signs of PTSD, or Post Traumatic Stress Disorder. I would highly suggest seeking the help of an exposure therapy expert so that Zoya can work on controlling some of her fears, since they are disrupting her daily life. But I just wanted to say that I'm so glad you were able to convince her to come here. It has already been so long, there are so many repressed memories and so much going on internally, and she has a lot of baggage to unearth.

"Mr. Suleiman, what I need you to understand is that victims of domestic violence such as your Zoya hesitate to address this pain because it can be overwhelming, understandably. They do not want to go to therapy or accept any sort of help because they may feel embarrassed or ashamed about their experiences. They may also think that nobody will understand the gravity of their situation, or will demand why they didn't 'leave' the relationship sooner. Sadly, these kinds of reactions are often true. This leads victims to repress the events of their past."

The therapist takes a deep breath. "What a lot of trauma victims tend to do is shove everything from their past into a place they don't intend on retrieving it from. They have a tendency to repress all memories of their trauma. Zoya has done the same. What I mean is, she has decided to take her past and shove it all in a suitcase." Ms. Fray pauses. "But just because she hasn't opened that suitcase in a long time doesn't mean she's not still carrying the weight of it. It can be dangerous to hold such feelings in." She folds her hands in front of her.

"I need you to understand that healing takes *time*. And that families of survivors have especially important roles to play in order to ensure that survivors of domestic violence or any kind of trauma can feel safe around others again." The therapist pauses and Haroun listens intently. "That being said, however, it's also important for Zoya to understand that her loved ones are a *step* on the way to recovery, not the entire ladder. Mr. Suleiman, Zoya is incredibly attached to you." She pauses, and Haroun nods slowly, a distressed look on his face. "I have spoken to her about this. Her attachment to you, from an outsider's perspective, can be viewed as a little unstable and unhealthy. She is very codependent, and very reliant upon you to be the solution to her problems. Does that make sense?"

Haroun nods. "Yes. I've tried talking to her about this, too."

"Right. Now when we talk about different attachment styles, we attribute them to the first few months of infancy. But depending on what an infant experiences during that crucial time, the type of attachment can carry on into adulthood. If a child experiences comfort, safety, and quick responses to their needs during infancy, they likely develop safety and security in their attachments. *But* if a child experiences discomfort, confusion, or inconsistency during infancy, they are more likely to develop an insecure or unsuccessful attachment style.

"In Zoya's case, she is very attached to you and feels distressed when you aren't near. We call this type of attachment an anxious-ambivalent attachment. In layman's terms, we would describe this as someone who feels distress when their object of attachment isn't near, but they are not entirely satisfied when it *is* near, either. In adulthood, people with this style of attachment may have fears of abandonment, may have difficulty forming stable relationships, and may possess feelings of anxiety or clinginess in their relationships. They may also crave closeness and intimacy but feel undeserving of it."

Pity flashes across Haroun's face.

"The reason I'm telling you all this is because I want you to understand that Zoya's love towards you stems from a style of attachment she cannot necessarily control. She grew up with a father who constantly neglected her because Zoya's very existence reminded him of his wife's death."

Haroun's brows furrow in confusion.

"Zoya's mother passed away giving birth to her. This affected Zoya's childhood in that she was raised by a father who tried but failed to love his daughter, because she constantly reminded him of the wife he lost."

Haroun runs a hand through his hair. He had always assumed Zoya's mother had died when Zoya was a child. He hadn't realized there was so much more to it.

God, how much more does he not know about his wife?

Appalled, he glances at Ms. Fray for a moment. How do these therapists do it? In the span of a few days, the woman has managed to unearth everything about Zoya's past *and* understand it in its entirety.

"I am sharing this with you because I need you to understand the depth of the situation," Ms. Fray says, breaking Haroun out of his thoughts. "The good thing, Mr. Suleiman, is that she is *here*. When we are physically sick, we go to the doctor, but when we are mentally afflicted, it's equally important to seek professional help."

At this point, Haroun remembers something Zoya had said to him when he first encouraged her to go to therapy. *"Imagine what people would say? The CEO of one of the largest businesses in the fashion industry is mentally afflicted. And that's a nice way to say it; the press won't be that polite. I've already gotten enough labels thrown at me—drama queen, divorcée, now domestic violence victim—I'd much rather do without anything else stamped to my forehead."*

He breaks out of his thoughts when Ms. Fray says, "Sir? Are you okay?"

"Yes. Yes, I'm sorry."

"That's alright." Ms. Fray pauses for a beat, and Haroun wonders whether she is psychoanalyzing him. "I was saying that luckily, the human brain is very capable of change. Since Zoya has been coming here, we've been able to identify a lot of issues. And knowing these will help her challenge her insecurities, develop a more secure attachment style, and maintain stability in her relationships."

Haroun nods shakily. "Okay."

"Do you have any questions for me, sir?"

"Yes, ma'am, I do." The two of them converse for a few minutes before Ms. Fray gives him a referral for an exposure therapy expert.

When Haroun leaves the office, the therapist's words and advice are brimming through his mind. The more he finds out about Zoya, the more he wonders how she has managed to present herself as put together for so long. Anyone in her place would have cracked and shattered, but she has remained erect. Whole. Even though he knows her façade is all for the cameras.

But what happens behind the scenes?

Nobody ever knows.

Forty-Nine

AISHA SULEIMAN STANDS EXCITEDLY in front of the door to the auditorium, her family trailing behind her. She takes a deep breath before walking inside.

Zoya gazes around at the paintings being showcased in the high school's art gala. Never in a million years did she imagine being in a situation like this, but Haroun and his family are so attached to one another that it seemed only fitting for all of them to attend Aisha's special day. And luckily, the gala is after work hours for Zoya and Haroun.

Zoya stops in front of one particularly captivating painting. The painting shows the back of a girl's head, the long tresses of her beautiful black hair abruptly cutting off at the end of the canvas. Zoya cocks her head to the side. "Haroun?" she murmurs. He turns at the sound of her voice. "Doesn't this feel so . . . incomplete?"

He studies it for a moment. "I think it leaves a lot up to interpretation."

"Yeah, but . . ." Zoya makes a sound of frustration. "The hair just . . . stops." She doesn't know how to voice what the painting makes her feel.

"If you like that, check this one out." Haroun nudges her

towards another one, and for a moment Zoya is startled by the casualness of his touch. Then her gaze turns to the painting he is showing her, and her eyes spark. It is both outstanding and tragic—a yellow canary in a black and white cage, its wings clipped. The bird's brilliant yellow plumage is the only burst of color in its otherwise dull environment. There is something so hopeful about the painting despite its melancholy air.

"Wow," Zoya manages to say.

Haroun chuckles softly beside her. "Wow indeed," he says. "Know who the artist is?"

Zoya's eyes trail to the name at the bottom right corner and she lets out a gasp. "Aisha?"

The girl in question pops up behind them, grinning. "You like?" she asks with a waggle of her eyebrows.

Zoya grins. "I love!"

A friend of Aisha's walks by, and she turns around to greet her. The other girl, Amal, compliments Aisha's artwork. The two begin to chatter, talking about shopping and clothes or whatever it is that teenage girls talk about, until Amal says, "I love your dress! Although I wouldn't wear it because it's a bit short for me, but it looks awesome on you."

Zoya's eyes narrow as she looks at the two girls. Aisha laughs nervously and smoothly continues the conversation, but Zoya senses her discomfort. When Amal leaves, Zoya turns to Haroun and says, "Did you hear that?"

He turns away from the painting he's looking at. "Hear what?"

Zoya turns to Aisha, appalled. "She basically called you out for your dressing style. Very directly, at that."

Aisha chuckles nervously. "It's okay, *aapi*. I'm sure she had good intentions."

"*Good intentions*? Is that how somebody with *good intentions* approaches someone else?"

Haroun places a hand at Zoya's elbow but she shrugs out of his grasp. "Does this not make you angry? Aisha's decisions are between *her and God*, are they not?"

"Zoya, relax," he says, trying a placatory tone. "I'm sure there was a better way she could have said it, but like Aisha said, I don't think she had the wrong intentions."

"Oh, really?" Zoya folds her arms. "And what good will you take out of *this* situation, Haroun Suleiman?"

He holds her gaze for a moment, a wariness in his eyes. "Maybe we can talk about this later?"

Zoya wants to disagree, but she takes a look at the crowded auditorium and inhales deeply through her nose. He is probably right. Enough attention has been brought to her already. She doesn't need to add fuel to the fire.

She turns away from him and focuses on Aisha's painting again. She runs a finger over the desolate yellow bird, feeling strangely connected to it.

Zoya begins to circle the auditorium. Ten minutes later, after taking in more artwork and cooling off, she turns back to Haroun. He is watching her with such intensity that she does a double take. "What?"

"Nothing."

"That look is not *nothing*, Haroun Suleiman. What's going on in that pretty little head of yours?"

He blushes slightly, dimple creasing. "I was just thinking of something."

"What were you thinking of?"

"How to approach a fiery dragon without pissing it off."

Zoya throws her head back and laughs, immediately flustered by the way his eyes spark at her glee. "Not very subtle, are you?"

"Subtlety is not my strong suit."

Zoya's eyes rove over him in all his startling beauty and she nods. "So I've noticed." They're quiet for a moment, and she can tell he is trying to dissect her words. It makes her grin.

It's his turn to ask, "What?"

"Nothing."

He smirks. "That look is not *nothing*, Zoya Zameer."

Zoya holds a hand over her heart. "Plagiarism, Haroun Suleiman?"

"I wouldn't even dare."

She holds his gaze for a moment before turning away, unable to contain the wide grin that slides onto her face. She attempts to school her expression into a serious one and says, "So tell me."

"Tell you what?"

"What are your thoughts on what just happened back there?" She tilts her head, referring to Amal's comment.

The playful expression slides off his face and he takes a deep breath. "Are you calmer now?"

Zoya rolls her eyes. "I won't yell at you. I promise."

He watches her for a moment before sweeping his gaze around the auditorium. "I think there are two sides to the coin. We need to . . . be careful with the way we deliver our advice, but we also need to be willing to accept advice. I think there's a difference between people giving you *genuine* advice and people telling you something just to attack you." He gestures to Aisha across the auditorium. "I don't think her friend meant any harm, and maybe that was her way of advising Aisha as politely as possible." When Zoya opens her mouth to argue, he continues quickly, "I understand that there may have been a better way for her friend to say it, but we can't live our entire lives getting angry every time someone tries to advise us, can we?" His voice is gentle. "Otherwise we'll always remain stagnant. There will never be any growth if we stubbornly refuse people's genuine guidance and care for us."

Zoya tries to find reason within his words, but Aisha's friend has reminded her of all the people in her past who ruthlessly called Zoya out for her sins.

Haroun continues, "This doesn't just go for Aisha's case but advising people in general." He pauses when Zoya cocks her head to the side and eyes him intently. "I feel like . . . if you're close to somebody, sometimes it's better to point out something before it snowballs into an avalanche. Before it becomes something you lose the control to fix."

Zoya considers his words, never taking her eyes off of him. Finally, she murmurs, "I guess that makes sense." He gives her a surprised look, and she laughs. "What?"

"Nothing."

"You thought I'd fight you over it?" Zoya turns to the painting of a gray lantern beside her. "A year ago, I probably would have. I would have fought you so much that this whole auditorium would be cleared of people scared of me. But you have a way of speaking that makes people listen, Haroun." He's quiet in response to that, and Zoya knows even without looking that the compliment is making him redden.

"I think"—he pauses, sighs deeply—"you've been taught about a lot of black and white areas, been told about strict rulings, seen everything as either *this* or *that*. But sometimes there's no black. Or white." He gestures to the lantern painting. "Sometimes there's only gray. And we try to look for black and white in an entirely gray area, or gray in an entirely black and white area." He pauses to look at her, sees that she's still willing to listen. "It's all very circumstantial, and we need to take a step back and observe the entire chessboard."

Haroun has once again managed to render Zoya speechless. She takes a deep breath, trying to gain her bearings. "There's no gray on a chessboard, though," she says playfully, trying to conceal the shakiness of her voice.

He rolls his eyes. "You know what I mean."

"I know." Impulsively, she reaches forward and squishes his cheek, shocking them both. "You're just so cute when you're explaining things."

When Zoya lets him go, a sly smile spreads on his face. "Does that mean you understood what I was trying to say?"

"More than understood, sweetheart. *You* are one of those people who is able to give the right advice, in the right way and at the right time. God bless your words."

They both freeze in shock at that last statement, Zoya's eyes widening. *God bless?* She never uses that phrase, doesn't believe in it or the hope it brings people.

But from somewhere deep in her, the words have yearned to be voiced.

When she turns back to Haroun, there is a soft, proud smile on his face.

~

Days later, when Haroun's family is visiting, Zoya shuffles around excitedly before approaching Haroun. Naima and Aisha follow suit, smiles on their faces. Zoya has placed everything in her board of directors' care for a couple of hours so that she can do this today, when Haroun is off from work.

He looks up from the book he's reading, eyeing Zoya and his sisters quizzically. "Can I help you?" he asks, dragging out the "can."

"Yes, in fact, you *can* help me." Zoya says, tucking her curls behind her ear. "Go out with me."

His eyebrows rise. "What?"

Zoya shrugs nonchalantly, playing off the rapid thumping of her heart. "Go out with me. A date."

He looks at her quizzically before his eyes drift to his sisters. "Sure. Of course. But, uh, why are they here?"

Aisha places her hands on her hips. "We were here for moral support." Naima cuts in, "But clearly, *bhabhi* doesn't need it."

Oh, dear Naima, Zoya thinks. *My poor heart is about to fly out of my chest. If only you knew.*

"Ah," Haroun says, smiling. "I should have known that something was up when you took off from work. Where are we going, Zoya?"

She is still not used to hearing her name so tenderly spoken from his mouth. "It's a surprise."

"Okay," he says with a shrug, closing his book and standing. "What should I wear?'

"You look amazing," she reassures him, grabbing his hand to lead him out the door. She turns around and gives the sisters a thumbs-up and a mouthed *thank you.* They grin and excitedly gesture for her to text how it goes.

Outside, Haroun is about to step into the driver's seat when he registers Zoya's outfit. "I'm guessing something recreational?" he says, pointing to her sweatpants and long sweatshirt.

"Yes," she replies. "And I'm driving. It needs to be a surprise until we get there."

He holds his hands up. "Okay, ma'am."

Zoya holds back a grin at his playful attitude.

Since Zoya has started going to therapy, she and Haroun have been playfully bantering with one another so much that it scares Zoya. She is not used to this carefree happiness, and every time she grins, a heavy feeling settles into the pit of her stomach. As if her very body is rejecting the happiness it is so unused to.

She shoves the thought out of her mind and shifts gears, driving out of the gates. Haroun continues glancing at her, a questioning smile on his face. "Can I guess where we're going?"

"No."

"Why not?"

"Because you might get it right. And I'll have to pretend you're wrong. And I'm not a good actress."

He laughs, loud and void of any tension. Zoya bites back a smile at the sound of it. "Are you sure about that?"

"About what?"

"Being a bad actress."

She throws him a side glance, panic flaring throughout her. *Does he know about the lie?* "What is that supposed to mean?"

"Nothing." He settles back into his seat and tries very hard not to smile, but the pop of his dimple gives him away. "Nothing at all." The smile fades from his face. He seems to be lost in thought.

"Everything okay?" Zoya murmurs after a couple minutes of silence.

Haroun lifts his pinky finger and absentmindedly rubs the window. "Yeah . . . I just don't like being like this." The sorrow in his voice causes Zoya to peel her eyes from the road for a moment.

"Like what?"

"I want to be able to enjoy things without thinking of the consequences." He turns to her. "Seems like that's all my heart wants to do, though. It looks for the loopholes, the tricks up the sleeves, the misstep that can pull me under." Zoya stays absolutely silent, knowing how difficult it is for him to voice this out loud. "My heart wants to look out for me in every possible way, but I want to be able to jump without making sure if I'll be safe or not. I want to . . . fly."

The words startle her, hitting a place somewhere deep inside her.

"You're in luck," Zoya replies, handing Haroun a blindfold. He takes it without questioning her, and Zoya has to appreciate his self-control—he must be going crazy with curiosity. Zoya parks and exits the vehicle.

"What do you mean?" Haroun says, shutting the door behind him and staring quizzically at their surroundings.

She bounces over to his side, giddy with excitement, and secures the blindfold around his head. Part of the reason Zoya wants to blindfold him is so that it will remain a surprise until the end; the other reason is so that she can hold his hand and steer him in the right direction like a normal, happy couple. Even when she can't shove the nagging discomfort at what she's done to him away. "You're in luck, because I'm taking you somewhere."

"Where?"

"Somewhere you can fly." She steers him along, and he trudges after her in confusion.

When Zoya meets the organizers—texting them instead of speaking aloud so that Haroun will not hear—and all the arrangements have been made, she whispers "Ready?" in Haroun's ear. He nods, and she pulls his blindfold off in a sweeping motion.

For a moment, he is absolutely silent as he registers his surroundings. Then his eyes light up and he barks out a surprised, exhilarated laugh. *"Parasailing?"*

~

Time flits by in blissful happiness. Zoya spends every day at work thinking about going home and spending time with Haroun, and when she goes home she thinks of how much she doesn't want to be anywhere else. Their quality time has decreased since Haroun has been spending his free time at the orphanage as well as the mosques nearby, meeting with their youth directors. Often, Zoya joins him as well, her old wariness ebbing away when she meets other Muslims and scholars in the mosques, a strange peace settling in her heart when attending a house of God.

Soon, the day of the reception arrives. Zoya and Haroun have basically been kicked out of the manor by the scheming sisters and *Ammi.* When the two of them are off of work, they have a late lunch at a restaurant before Naima picks Zoya up to go to the salon and Farhan whisks Haroun away, promising he'll return him.

Contrary to her usual style, Zoya has opted for a very simple look for the reception. She doesn't want to admit it, but in large part this simplicity is due to a conversation she overheard Haroun having with Aisha. His voice was full of emotion when he said, *"Can you imagine being married to somebody so beautiful?"* He hesitated. *"I wish . . . I could be the only one privileged enough to experience that beauty. Not everyone deserves to see it."*

Now Zoya observes herself in the salon mirror, satisfied by the simplicity of her look. Today everybody will see the real Zoya Zameer, and Haroun will be the only one privileged enough to see Zoya Zameer in all her exquisite beauty.

Once Naima takes Zoya home, she covers her eyes and leads her upstairs, cautioning her to watch her step. Naima tells her to wait in her room until Haroun arrives. Then her phone rings and she rushes out saying, "Yes, please. No, no fireworks. Just sparklers."

Zoya widens her eyes in bewilderment. *Fireworks? Sparklers?*

Five minutes later, Zoya is more antsy than ever. Patience and allowing others control aren't her strong suits, and she keeps wondering what is happening around the house. She needs to be prepared, doesn't she?

So I don't "faint" of shock or something, she thinks bitterly.

Zoya steps out of her room and darts her head this way and that, feeling as if she is trespassing on a crime scene. *I'll just take a quick look,* she thinks. *Just one look and I'll come back upstairs.*

So as not to catch anyone's eye—especially Naima's or Aisha's, who might kill her if they see her out of the room before it's time— Zoya rushes down the spiraling stairs. Her heels make *clop clop* sounds against the marble, and she thanks God that everyone is in too much of a frenzy in the main hall to pay her any heed.

The stairs are decorated marvelously, with candles adorning each step and flowers woven around the railings. Zoya is so entranced by them that she doesn't watch where she's going and crashes into somebody at the bottom of the stairs.

It's Haroun. He uprights her quickly before stepping back, and Zoya is hit with a strong sense of déjà vu from the night he caught her just like this. Long ago, back when she had been Ms. Zoya to him.

Haroun does a double take, eyes widening as he takes in Zoya's appearance. To her surprise, Zoya's cheeks warm. This is exactly the kind of reaction she has elicited from so many men, reveling in the pleasure of the taken aback, shell shocked looks on their faces. She remembers how she had always wanted to elicit the same reaction out of Haroun, only to be disappointed when he looked away or kept his gaze lowered.

Now she realizes with a start that she doesn't want *anyone* but him to look at her this way. That if she could spend the rest of her days locked in his gaze, she would. Maybe this is what he meant when he said that he wanted to be the only one privileged enough to experience his wife's beauty. *Or*, Zoya thinks, *Maybe he kept his gaze lowered all the time because when he would finally raise it for the right woman, he'd leave her breathless.*

Haroun clears his throat—breaking Zoya out of her thoughts—and looks down, rubbing the back of his neck. Which has gone very, very red.

Zoya's lips quirk, but she feigns innocence despite her rapidly beating heart. She twirls one of her curls around her fingers. "Well, don't you look *ravishing*."

"You're welcome. I mean"—he sputters, flushes a deeper red—"thank you. You look"—he pauses, as if trying to think of the right word. Zoya waits with bated breath.

"Buddy!" someone chooses that moment to yell. Zoya closes her eyes in frustration, recognizing that voice all too well. When she reopens them, Farhan is swinging his arm around Haroun's neck, pulling him in for a hug.

Haroun seems almost relieved for the distraction. Zoya turns to Farhan and bats her eyelashes innocently, fury radiating off of her. "Has anyone ever told you what a *colossal* inconvenience you are?" she snaps.

"Hey—" Haroun interrupts in an indignant voice, but Farhan cuts him off.

"*You* have, Ms. Zoya," he says cheerfully. "Multiple times."

Zoya huffs angrily and turns on her heel, walking away from the duo with a heavy heart at what Haroun had been about to say.

You look—

What? She wants to *hear* him say it.

She doesn't have much time to ponder over it, though, because at that moment Aisha spots her and rushes towards her, all flying *hijab* and flaring nostrils. "Farhan *bhai,* you had *one job!*" she whines. Before she can catch up to her sister-in-law, though, Zoya is already dashing up the stairs and out of her sight, not wanting to face the wrath of the eighteen-year-old girl.

After twenty minutes of impatiently sitting in her room, Zoya is saved by *Ammi's* knock on the door. Her mother-in-law leads her down the stairs, where Haroun and Zoya will simply wait before walking into the hall together.

When prompted by *Ammi,* Zoya turns around. She stops short, her breath catching in her throat. Even though she saw him just twenty minutes ago, setting her eyes on Haroun Suleiman at the same time that he sets his gaze on her causes a strange feeling to travel through her heart. They both walk towards one another, turn, and proceed into the great hall, where people have arrived and are continuing to arrive. Haroun holds out his elbow, and Zoya loops her arm through his, trying to control her heart from going into overdrive.

Once they've greeted their guests, thanked them for their gifts, and are comfortably settled on a curved loveseat, Haroun leans in and whispers, "Do you know what I'm most excited about?"

Zoya leans in and replies "What?" as a camera flashes, capturing the couple whispering to one another.

"The food."

Zoya laughs, and a camera flashes once more. Then Haroun's friends come to whisk him away before the two of them can make any more conversation.

Zoya sits awkwardly for a moment, throwing her signature

smile to any guest who catches her eye. She groans in frustration when Farhan gives her an excited wave, blissfully unaware of her annoyance. But her eyebrows rise when she sees him sneak a contemplative glance at gorgeous Naima, who is rolling the tray of cake into the middle of the hall.

Minutes later, Aisha walks up to Zoya, narrowing her eyes. "*Aapi*, don't think you're off the hook for sneaking downstairs before you were called."

Zoya laughs. "Wouldn't even dream of it."

The younger girl places her hands on her hips, but before she can say anything, Zoya points to Sameer and says, "Aha! There's my secretary. If you'll excuse me, Aisha, I have some work-related business." She sidles away from Aisha, who playfully rolls her eyes and smiles.

When Zoya approaches Sameer, he shakes his head, "Uh uh. We're not talking about work at your *wedding*."

"But—"

"Nope." He holds his plate out to her. "Chocolate covered strawberries?"

Zoya rolls her eyes and turns away from him, searching the crowd for Haroun. As she drifts around, she turns a corner and almost falls on him for the second time in the night. She rights herself quickly and lets out a nervous laugh.

"Everything good?" he asks.

"Yeah. I think your sisters might kill me if I try to micromanage anything else, though."

He laughs, and the sound is so heartwarming that Zoya stares at him for a moment, holding her breath. "Thank you, Haroun."

He gives her a quizzical brow. "You're welcome. But for what?"

"For everything." Zoya shrugs, gesturing around. The quizzical brow doesn't go away, but he sticks his tongue out nonetheless.

Zoya lets out a loud, loose laugh full of mirth. She's overwhelmed by the urge to throw her arms around Haroun, bury her head in his chest, close her eyes, and simply have him hold her. To feel absolutely safe again.

She remembers his words then. *I think you have an unhealthy attachment towards me.* And then Ms. Fray's words. *It is always dangerous to be so codependent on one's partner.*

Zoya stands absolutely still for a few moments, the two of them simply staring at one another.

Until someone yells, "Oye, we can't cut the cake without the bride and groom."

Zoya closes her eyes in frustration. It's Farhan—*obviously*—and Haroun suddenly steps back from Zoya, coughing awkwardly. Zoya balls her hand into a fist to refrain from throttling Farhan Malik.

"Oops," Farhan says a moment too late, wiggling his brows suggestively. "Did I interrupt something?"

"Don't you always?" Zoya snaps, and Haroun gives her an exasperated look.

The three of them head into the great hall, and Haroun and Zoya position themselves behind the cake trolley as the guests turn to them. Aisha gives a small speech that has everyone laughing merrily, and Farhan and Sameer give an equally groundbreaking speech together, earning chuckles from the crowd. Naima is last, soothing the audience with her gentle words and prayers for the couple.

Then Zoya picks up the knife, and Haroun wraps his hand around hers. The sparkler candles shoot delicate flames up, and the two of them cut the cake as the crowd applauds and hoots excitedly.

And for a moment, everything is absolutely and entirely okay.

~

At night, when the couple is taking a relaxed walk around the neighborhood, Haroun searches for the cat he has grown extremely fond of. Goldie, he had playfully named her. Zoya had laughed at the irony of it, considering the cat was pure white. When she'd asked Haroun why he chose the name, his warm gaze traveled over the sunlight catching in Zoya's hair. Then he averted his eyes, cheeks growing pink.

He has brought the cat a meal, as he has been doing for the past couple of days. But today, the cat isn't frequenting her normal abode.

Today, she is nowhere to be found.

To distract Haroun from worrying, Zoya says, "Did you enjoy yourself tonight?"

"A lot. You?"

"Yes. Your sisters are amazing at planning this kind of thing."

Haroun's eyes twinkle. "They are."

"Have you guys found anyone for Naima yet? Or has Naima met someone?"

Haroun shakes his head and sighs. "She's anxious about or rejects almost everybody we introduce to her. And she doesn't have her own preference either. Trust issues, you know?" There is a sad smile on his face. "So we've put a hold on searching for a while. Whenever she's comfortable, she'll let us know."

Before Zoya is able to respond to this, loud barks erupt from near them. Haroun rushes towards the sound anxiously, Zoya trailing behind. Too late, the two of them see some rabid-looking pit bulls surrounding a small white ball of fur.

Haroun sprints forward despite Zoya's cries of warning. The dogs scatter at his approach, and Goldie becomes visible. She is breathing hard, blood pooling out of her neck rapidly.

Haroun falls to his knees, and Zoya rushes forward quickly upon hearing his cry of pain. He fists his hair in his hands, a lost look in his eyes, the meal for the cat forgotten at the side. Zoya is too appalled to form words.

The kitten is mewling painfully, chest rapidly rising and falling. Her eyes dart this way and that, settling on Haroun's face. Haroun reaches forward with a shaky hand and softly cradles the cat's paw in his hands.

His shoulders shake, and Zoya leans down to place a trembling hand on them. She has hardly ever seen him this vulnerable, and she doesn't know what to do.

The cat shudders, taking one more breath before blinking wearily. And just like that, Goldie goes still.

For a long time, husband and wife simply sit in silence, staring. Haroun at the cat, Zoya at Haroun. She rubs his shoulder soothingly and gently closes the deceased kitten's eyes.

That's when Haroun's breath hitches and a sob erupts. He

presses a hand over his mouth to keep from letting out more but Zoya rubs his back, reassuring him that it's okay for him to cry. She leans close to him, wanting to whisper words of comfort but failing to do so. She has never been good at expressing the things that matter most out loud, anyway.

Instead, Zoya wraps Haroun in a tight embrace. With a shock, she remembers how just earlier tonight, she had wanted to hug him. But certainly not in this way.

Her cheek touches his ear, and her arms are wrapped securely around his shoulders. Her throat has tightened, making it impossible to form words, so she tries to soothe Haroun with her hands instead, rubbing comforting circles on his back. He sits there shaking for a few moments before wrapping a slow arm around her waist and burying his face in her tangle of curls.

Zoya doesn't understand how Haroun—this pillar of strength—unravels at the most innocent of things. At the death of a mere cat. She is unable to express the depth of her pain in seeing the anchor to her life so disconnected, so broken. It makes guilt pool up like an overflowing well inside her at what she's done to him.

When they stand, Haroun cradles the cat's dead body in his hands. "We have to bury her." His voice trembles. They head back to the manor, where he refuses to let Zoya shovel mud and insists on doing it himself.

Zoya watches him, helpless. Somehow, she is always helpless when it comes to Haroun Suleiman.

Later, he sits and drinks the coffee Zoya makes him, surrounded by the beautiful decorations in the manor. Zoya watches him carefully. She hears footsteps behind her but doesn't dare take her eyes off of Haroun.

Naima sits down next to Zoya. She must have heard the commotion, must know what has happened. Because she simply stands there for a few quiet moments.

"Sometimes we forget that we have to die, too," Naima whispers, watching her brother. Zoya listens quietly. "We forget that this entire world"—she makes a sweeping motion with her hands—"is temporary. That everything we're striving for, everything that won't let us sleep at night, everything we work so hard for, will mean nothing. All that will matter are our deeds, the way we lived, the devotion to our faith." Naima folds her arms across her chest. "We look for so much permanence in this world, *Subhan Allah.* That's why we're always restless and dissatisfied. Because nothing . . ." She stops when Haroun swipes at his eyes. This strong man—who is always ready to look at the good side of things—is unable to control his tears because of an innocent, dead animal.

Finally, Naima says, "Nothing is permanent except God and His mercy."

As Zoya watches Haroun Suleiman, she wonders how she met such a family. How they bounce back and recover from things so quickly. How they manage to build themselves up from pain so quickly. And not just that, but how they turn to God for comfort every single time.

Because it's been years, and Zoya Zameer is only just beginning to learn.

Fifty

The Prophet Muhammad (peace be upon him) said, "The believers who show the most perfect faith are those who have the best behavior, and the best of you are those who are the best to their wives."
(At-Tirmidhi, classed as Hasan)

~

HAROUN'S PHONE RINGS.

Zoya glances at the caller ID, a smirk playing on her face. She picks up the call and turns the speaker on.

"HAROUN!" Farhan bellows. Zoya slaps her palms over her ears, quickly turning the speaker off.

"HAROUN!" he yells again, and the man being called appears from the other room, a quizzical expression on his face. He takes one look at Zoya's giggly features and folds his arms in mock anger. "MY BOY, GUESS WHAT?"

Zoya clears her throat and alters her voice a few degrees deeper. "What?"

"I prayed five times a day this whole week!" His voice is ecstatic, and Zoya can imagine the expression on his face even through the phone.

Haroun rushes forward, grabbing the phone from a silently giggling Zoya. "Really?" he says to Farhan.

"Yes! I did it!"

Haroun strides into the other room. "See? I knew you could do it." Pause. "You're the man. Now we're gonna keep this up, alright?"

Zoya rolls her eyes at the childlike excitement in their voices and turns back to the designer files in her hands.

When Haroun enters the room again, he says, "Just got off the phone with my boss after I spoke to Farhan. He asked me to order a cake for someone in the company. It's for his tenure."

Zoya jumps at this opportunity. Although Haroun has been very glum since Goldie died, she can tell he's trying to get past it. "What kind of cake?"

"Nothing too fancy. He's a simple, homey kinda guy."

Zoya mulls over it before she has a brilliant idea. One that will (hopefully) allow Haroun to loosen up a bit—although she has to admit that he's looking much better after Farhan's call. "Why don't we bake the cake for him?"

Haroun processes this for a moment. "That's . . . actually not a bad idea."

"Litotes, Mr. Suleiman?"

He stares at her as if she's grown another head. Zoya laughs. "It's a literary device. Like when someone says 'not bad' instead of saying 'good.'" Haroun watches her strangely before cracking a smile.

"I didn't know you were the English type," he says amusedly.

Zoya shrugs as they both head to the kitchen. "I did best in English class."

"Really? What class did you do worst in?"

Zoya wrinkles her nose. "History."

Haroun chuckles. "History was definitely boring. But I *really* hated chemistry." Zoya gives him a surprised look, to which he says, "What?"

"I just thought you'd be the chemistry type. You know, helping everyone out with formulas. Wearing extra thick goggles. Smarter than the teacher. Etcetera."

"You think too highly of me." His voice is casual as he reaches into cabinets to pull materials out, but Zoya can sense the distress behind the statement.

"So what was *your* favorite subject?"

Haroun thinks about it for a moment, the jar of baking powder suspended in his hands. "Honestly, I'm not sure. I think in college, since I loved the two subjects enough to double major in them, it was either finance or religion classes. But in high school it may have been . . . Spanish?"

Zoya lets out a gleeful laugh, recalling reading this from his résumé. "*¿Habla español?*"

Haroun flicks her nose before he pours the bakery contents into a mixing bowl. "*Sí, ma chérie.*"

Zoya tuts. "*Eso no es español.*"

"*Hayır, aşkım.*"

Zoya dissects his accent. "That's not Spanish either." Then she backtracks, a smile playing on her lips. "Did you call me *ma chérie?*"

Haroun dodges her question and says, "Can you pass me the eggs?"

"And what was that second thing you said? *Aşkım?*"

"That means lightbulb."

Zoya sputters out a laugh at his attempt to slide her off. "You know I can Google translate it, right?"

"If you figure out how to spell it right, sure." Haroun smiles at her then, and Zoya is relieved that he's momentarily distracted from Goldie.

They start to prepare the cake together, with Zoya cracking jokes and Haroun artfully dodging her questions. She ties an apron around his waist, and in return, he gathers her hair into a bandanna. He watches her curiously when she does all the messy work with her sleeves rolled down as usual, but she continuously redirects his attention to something else.

When Zoya sees that Haroun is busy mixing the ingredients and pouring them into a pan, she sidles to the sink to wash her hands. Instinctively, she pushes her sleeves up and laughs at something he says. She doesn't notice when he comes up behind her.

Zoya's laughter dies down when she realizes that he can see her scars. She darts a quick glance at Haroun and sees him looking at her with an almost curious expression on his face.

Her heart begins to thump wildly.

The atmosphere thickens with tension. Although Zoya is pretty sure Haroun has seen her arms while she's sleeping, she has always consciously worn long sleeves. But this is the first time he's witnessed her imperfections while she is awake and aware.

Haroun is one of the only good things in her life. And when she sees one of the only good things in her life witnessing all the ugliness of it, she has the overwhelming desire to self-destruct.

Zoya suddenly has a hard time breathing, and the spoon in her hand clatters to the floor as she rushes away. Upstairs. Into her room. She bangs the bathroom door open and stands breathlessly in front of the sink, chest heaving up and down.

When Zoya sees herself in the mirror, her eyes trail down to her exposed arms. After therapy, her scars have stopped bothering *her* so much, but to know that *Haroun* has now seen them in front of her tugs at her uncomfortably.

She clutches at her throat, feeling as if she may throw up. She should have known. She should have known that her life only consists of small glimpses of happiness in between everything dreary and horrifying. Zoya claws at herself, rubs her arms, scratches the scars. Wanting them to go away. Wanting them to become invisible.

She doesn't want to see them, doesn't want to be reminded of them. Not when she finally began to forget them.

"Zoya?" Haroun's voice is distant, but his footsteps are coming closer with every second. Zoya halts, breath hitching as she cries. She doesn't want him here. He shouldn't be here. He shouldn't see her like this. She makes a move to close the bathroom door but hears rushed footsteps, and suddenly Haroun is blocking her path, palm flat against the door. His eyes are wide, confused.

Haroun's gaze trails down, and everywhere he looks, Zoya feels as if she is on fire with shame.

She turns her back to him.

"Zoya." His voice is soft, gentle. But she doesn't want that right now. She wants him to go as far away from her as possible so she can drown in her mortification.

Through the mirror, Zoya sees his hand lift but edges away so that he can't touch her. "Zoya," he murmurs. "It's okay."

Zoya shakes her head and wraps her arms around herself, tears streaming down her face. She can't contain the tremors rolling through her. The desire for the ground to open up and swallow her whole intensifies.

She feels Haroun's hand touch her shoulder, and she flinches away from him, wiping her nose of the snot that has accumulated. "Hey." He steps around her to look at her. Zoya turns away once more, feeling awfully bruised and beaten. Like a malfunctioned electronic piece he is trying to put back together.

She wants to short circuit.

"Zoya, look at me." His tone is firm.

She doesn't. But then his fingers come up under her chin and lift her face, and suddenly she is staring into his eyes, strong and tender.

Zoya's chin wobbles, and Haroun shakes his head slowly. "It's okay."

Despite wanting to hold herself together, Zoya fails miserably as more tears come gushing out, trailing down her cheeks and trickling onto his fingers at her chin.

"Let me see," he says quietly. Zoya shakes her head, mortified. She begins to turn away once more, but his hold on her chin—though gentle—is firm. Tears pool down her cheeks endlessly. "Zoya."

His voice unravels her, unspools her as it always does.

Slowly, slowly, without looking into his eyes, Zoya lifts her arms and turns them over to showcase the scars. Looking at them while he is awakens a renewed disgust within her. The urge to itch and scratch at her already reddened skin overtakes her again, but she remains utterly frozen. Waiting for his reaction.

Zoya suddenly remembers something Ms. Fray had said. *"The first step to recovery is your acceptance that something is wrong. That help should be sought. That something is plaguing you. This does not make you in any way a weaker person; in fact, it makes you a stronger person because you are willing to acknowledge and accept your own faults and vulnerabilities. And you're willing to work towards overcoming their effect on you."*

Haroun's fingers trail from her hands to her wrists, then to the crook of her elbows, where he holds her steadily. As if he knows that the world is spinning beneath her feet. As if he senses that she needs an outside force to upright her. Zoya wants to throw his hands off of her, tell him to peel his eyes away from the vermin in front of him.

But he does no such thing. Instead, his fingers trail back to her hands as he loops them through hers. "Do you know what these make you?" he asks her. His voice is a silent thrum in the big, empty house. "A warrior."

At this, a scornful laugh escapes her. "A warrior who lost the battle?" Her voice cracks.

"A warrior who was able to return from the battle alive." Haroun lifts her left hand and brings it up to his cheek. "You may not have thought you won, Zoya, but you survived." Slowly, without taking his eyes off of her, he leans into her hand and presses a kiss to her palm.

At the contact, something in Zoya breaks, and she begins to sob again. "Shh," Haroun coaxes. "You are a warrior because you managed to return from the battlefield. You survived."

Zoya's chin wobbles. She holds his hand then, steady, and simply stares into his eyes. This man who manages to turn every ugly thing in her life into something so tragically beautiful that she is never able to look at it the same way again.

And maybe, maybe, he is teaching her that the heart beating in her chest deserves to love itself just a little bit, too.

~

Weeks pass as the couple transitions into a comfortable phase in their relationship. They make it a point to take out time for one another throughout the week in between Zoya's busy schedule—because of Zameer's new project—and Haroun's tight work schedule at the finance company he's landed a stable job at.

Zoya frequents the mosque with Haroun regularly, and her frozen heart begins to thaw. A place which once gave her nothing but anxiety starts to become a source of comfort. What's more is that the community has taken an incredible liking to Haroun. The youth especially connect with him on a very personal basis.

Despite both Zoya and Haroun dealing with piles of work, they still go out together at least once or twice a week. Sometimes they surprise one another by taking the other out to someplace cool, and sometimes they bring the party home. Fast food and laughter in front of the TV screen. Falling asleep together on the couch wrapped in blankets.

Zoya has discovered many interesting new places, courtesy of Haroun's adventures. Such as the quiet, serene rooftop overlooking New York City; where Haroun had gotten surprisingly emotional and told Zoya that he never brought anyone there before because he felt beauty like that only deserved to be seen by someone equally beautiful. Zoya had turned to him and said, "Like you." But he had shaken his head and responded, "*I* found this place by chance. But *you* are here because this place is a reflection of you." And then he had watched her shyly, and Zoya could have sworn she saw stars in his eyes.

In addition to Haroun's undeniably growing affection towards her, Zoya is benefiting a great deal from her therapy sessions—although she will never admit that out loud. She overhears Mumtaz telling Haroun that there is less of Zoya's hair in the trash cans, that she has lighter eye bags and a more radiant smile.

Despite all of this, however, Zoya can never truly shake off the hollowness within her. The guilt at what she's done. The anxiety at how she will fix it.

And then there's that ever-present feeling. The horrible, aching emptiness. Persistent and prodding. She has everything she wants—business is booming, she is learning to control her fears, and she and Haroun are finally happy and comfortable with one another. Yet it doesn't feel like enough.

There always seems to be something missing.

These thoughts echo in her mind even as she lies on Haroun's chest one night, listening to the telltale beating of his heart. Playing absentmindedly with his fingers. His arm is wrapped around her, and the other hand strokes through her hair softly. Like running fingers through warm water. He untangles her curls and passes his fingers over her forehead, massaging it. Zoya closes her eyes in contentment, a soft smile making its way onto her face.

"Haroun?"

"Hmm?" he replies.

"I'm scared."

He continues to brush his fingers over her forehead. "Do you want me to turn the lights back on?"

Ever since Zoya has been meeting with her exposure therapy expert, she has slowly started practicing things at home as per the therapist's recommendation. Like occasionally turning the lights off at night. And sleeping next to Haroun.

Zoya chuckles softly at his question. "No, not the lights. I'm scared because . . ." She takes a deep breath, afraid to speak her truth. Afraid that somehow saying it will jinx her. Even though this is what Haroun had been hinting at weeks ago as well, except his feelings differ slightly from hers. He is afraid of taking risks; she is afraid of losing what she has risked.

"I'm so happy," Zoya whispers. "And I'm scared of all this happiness."

His fingers halt in her hair, then resume stroking through it. "You're scared of being happy?"

"Yes."

He tightens his arm around her and leans down to kiss her forehead, then rests his head back against the headboard. "Why?"

Zoya turns so she's facing him. Even though she can't see his face clearly in the dark, she can hear the pounding of his heart. The reminder of his humanity. "I'm terrified because this world is crazy. It does things. It's a seesaw, and one way or another, it has to balance. I'm scared that because I'm so happy, one day my happiness will be snatched away from me."

Haroun takes her hand and places a soft kiss on it. "I think about that a lot. Like, a *lot*." He chuckles nervously, then sighs. "I wish I could help you overcome the feeling. But honestly, I struggle with it, too. I talked to my mom about it once . . ." He pauses. "She told me that if I keep worrying so much about what *might* happen, I'll always forget to enjoy the present moment." He shifts so that he's upright and facing her. "She's always telling me to take a deep breath. To relax. She says that my anxiety isn't going to stop whatever's going to happen from coming. But keeping a clear head will help me face it." He lets out a soft chuckle. "Do you remember what you told me once, Zoya? '*Jo ho gaya, so ho gaya.*' Whatever has happened, has happened.

"Keep the same mentality for the future. What's going to happen is going to happen. And worrying about it is only going to make you more uneasy and restless." He lies back down, and they settle back into place.

"But—" Her lips tremble. Zoya Zameer's lips tremble. "I'm so happy, Haroun. You make me so happy and I"—her breath hitches as he hugs her tighter—"Newton once said every action has an equal and opposite reaction. So this much happiness . . . " She trails off. ". . . must have an opposing reaction. It must lead to *some* conflict, *some* trouble. After all, there needs to be balance, right?"

Haroun quiets for a moment, then says, "Zoya, at the end of the day, we have free will. Maintaining balance depends on what *we* make of a situation, too. Like, yes, gravity exists. But if we didn't toy with it, how would planes have been invented?" He sighs, and Zoya can feel the tension in his shoulders. "We're not . . . puppets; we're given choices by God. He's put it in us to have the cognitive sense to make the right or wrong choice."

He twirls one of her curls around his finger, and Zoya senses that he's trying to tell this to himself just as much as he's trying to tell it to her. It awes her how, despite the fact that he struggles with something, he still manages to give her the advice he wishes *he* could listen to. "Allah has written what's best for us, and at the end of the day, that's what we'll get. But even though everything is predestined, Allah has given us the control and the ability to make our own decisions, whether they set the seesaw straight or send it swinging it up and down. Balance is our choice."

Zoya stills. His eloquence always takes her breath away. After a moment, he gently nudges her. "You okay?"

She entwines their fingers. "Yes, you just constrict my vocal cords sometimes."

His answering laugh is deep and throaty. It rumbles against his chest and reverberates throughout Zoya's core. It's such a comforting, homey sound that she snuggles closer. Inhales his clean, calming Dove soap scent.

He kisses her hair. "*So jao, meri jaan.* Go to sleep."

Zoya tilts her head up at him in surprise at the words of endearment. "You know I can't sleep after that."

He laughs. "Why not?"

"Now you have to speak to me in Urdu."

Haroun groans. "Zoya."

"Haroun!"

He sighs theatrically.

"Hmm," Zoya muses. "Tell me . . . tell me a childhood story. All in Urdu, though."

He seems to want to protest but gives in at the longing present in her voice. "*Aik din—*" Zoya immediately squeals, and Haroun chuckles. "I haven't even started yet!"

"I know, but you sound so good!" She wraps an arm around his torso. "Okay, no interruptions now. Go ahead."

"*Aik din, jab mai chaar saal ka tha . . .*"

Zoya holds back another squeal, and they spend the next hour talking and laughing. And Zoya—although immersed in Haroun's stories and his enchanting words—can't ignore the nagging, pressing worry that still weighs down on her.

That so much happiness can only yield to so much pain.

Fifty-One

"On that Day you will be brought to judgment and none of your secrets will remain hidden." (Qur'an 69:18)

~

BEFORE GOING TO THEIR respective offices, Zoya and Haroun go to a coffee shop to eat breakfast together. She settles at a table while he orders at the counter for them. Zoya is about to call Sameer to discuss a work-related matter when she feels a peculiar, prickly feeling at the back of her neck. As if she is being watched.

Zoya Zameer is used to being watched and scrutinized from every angle—under cameras, in written words, all in microscopic detail. But this? This strange feeling? It makes her uncomfortable in a way that she can't describe.

She turns around.

Everything in her stills. A loud, deafening silence presses down on her. One that makes her want to itch her ears until they are raw.

When she sees him, everything in her freezes. Time stops. Her blood stops. Her pulse seems to stop. The air, before alive and bustling with sound and commotion, is now still and frozen. As if gravity has stopped and physics has stopped and the world is one still, deadly kind of silent.

When she sees him, everything in her trembles and threatens to collapse. She is unable to form words on her lips, unable to even move to back the hell away from him. Everything she has done, every recognition on the news, every trade show she has gone to, every campaign she's released, everything that she is, disappears. She seems to have fallen off a very high ledge, scrambling around in the suffocating blackness to grasp onto something.

Because everything that she is is fading away. Every accomplishment, every success, every feature on the news. One look in his eyes and she is back to nineteen-year-old Zoya Zameer. Helpless and powerless. She feels as if somebody has tackled her fortressed walls, the ones she has so precisely been building the past couple of years. So many times, people have itched and scratched at her walls and given up when they've received no entry, but one look at him bulldozes all of her carefully built walls down. Everything that Zoya is comes crashing down, and she is left standing in debris as the ghost of who she is to the world. While in her mind she is back to being nineteen-year-old Zoya Zameer, watery eyes piercing the man in front of her.

Her ex-husband, Farhan Hussain.

He smiles. In that way young Zoya used to be wary about until eventually growing to fear. "Well, well." His voice is exactly as she remembers it, and she fights to keep her insides from combusting. "Zoya."

Speak, Zoya, she urges herself. *Say something.*

But words fail her.

"How have you been?" There is no genuine concern in his voice, no actual regard for how she has been. His tone is full of silent mockery; laughter sparks in his eyes. In front of this man, Zameer Co. is nothing. Zoya Zameer is nobody.

Zoya wills herself to speak. "Fine" is all she can muster. She fears that her heart may stop working, and she cannot display any kind of weaknesses in front of this man.

Farhan tilts his head around the coffee shop, as if searching for something. Or someone. When he finds whatever it is he's looking for, a slow smile spreads across his face. Zoya doesn't dare take her eyes off of him despite the tremors rolling throughout her body.

"Who are you here with?" he asks nonchalantly.

"Nobody," Zoya replies quickly.

"Really?" he muses. "I remember seeing something about a new boy toy on the news—"

"Will you *never* change, Farhan?" Zoya all but spits out, regretting it immediately when his smile widens. He is provoking her. And he is enjoying it.

"I see that *you* certainly have." His eyes rove over her once, and Zoya's insides squirm uncomfortably. This man is not Haroun, and he is looking at her in the most disgusting way.

"Does your *Islam* not teach you to *lower your gaze?*" Zoya barks. At this, anger flares in Farhan's eyes. But it vanishes as he turns away. "Get away from me, Farhan. Or I won't hesitate to call my guards. Or 911. You see, they respond to *my* beck and call now."

"Ah, yes, I have heard of your . . . influence."

Zoya cannot believe his abrasiveness, his cockiness. His open declaration that he doesn't believe he has done anything wrong. She continues to tremble with fear and rage.

Then she feels a tug at her hand, and fingers slip through hers. She turns to see Haroun's confused eyes darting between the two of them, and that is enough. He is enough. The debris she has been trapped in begins to flatten away, the fallen walls begin to reconstruct, and suddenly she is erect again. Whole.

And the intrusive thought makes an appearance again. *I think you have an unhealthy attachment towards me.*

Haroun holds out a hand, still confused as to who he is greeting, but Zoya pushes him back with a force that causes his eyebrows to furrow. "No," she says, voice shaking.

Farhan throws her that awful smile again. His eyes flick to Haroun. "Nice to meet you, Mr. . . ."

"Haroun," he prompts.

"Haroun." Farhan holds his hand out, but Zoya blocks him by standing in front of her husband. She shakes her head, fists clenching and unclenching.

"Zoya," Haroun whispers in her ear. "What are you doing?"

Zoya guesses that Haroun doesn't yet understand who he's standing in front of. He would have difficulty recognizing him, anyway, since the news Zaki released contained a grainy and blurry picture of Zoya and Farhan's *nikah*. This was one of the reasons the press hadn't been able to track down Farhan for questioning.

Farhan chuckles. "Don't mind her, she's still angry at me for something she believes I did."

"If you truly think you did nothing wrong, Farhan"—she feels Haroun tense behind her when he finally realizes who the man in front of him is—"and that I don't have any proof because *nobody was watching*..." Zoya turns to look at Haroun, and merely his face gives her the strength she needs.

She wonders what she should say that will strike Farhan harder than anything. Something he may actually fear despite the shameless person that he is. Something that will shift the ground beneath his feet.

Suddenly, a lightbulb flares to life over her head.

"If you think you did nothing wrong, then I won't meet you in any court here." Zoya pauses for effect, knowing how this will unravel him, even though she herself is not convinced by it. "I'll meet you on the Day of Judgment, in the court of God. The only time I will be provided full justice." She smiles in satisfaction at the taken aback—then horrified—look on Farhan's face. She has hit him where it hurts, and nothing has ever felt better.

Zoya feels Haroun's fingers at the small of her back, gently guiding her away from Farhan. But she doesn't turn away before one last glance at the astonishment on her ex-husband's face.

Outside the restaurant, however, she doesn't feel nearly as brave as she pretended to be. She feels weak and tattered. Ripped apart and upended. The ground beneath her seems to waver, teetering her off the edge of a high cliff.

So many times . . . so many times she has wondered if she will ever see her ex-husband again; and if she will, what display of power she will make that will leave him rattled.

She had wanted to make him feel helpless. She had wanted to make him feel powerless and reduced to nothing around her.

Instead, she has succeeded in nothing but reducing herself to powerlessness.

"Zoya?" Haroun says. "Let's go home, okay?"

She nods, unable to form words. Haroun heads inside to collect their food order before coming back outside to wrap an arm around Zoya.

She shrugs it off, feeling repulsive. She heads into the car before Haroun can say another word.

At home, Zoya calls Sameer and says that she won't be coming to work, hanging up before he can ask why. Moments later, her phone rings with *Bill Nye The Science Guy* flashing across the screen, but she hurls it onto her bed and rushes into the bathroom. Turns the shower on hastily. Grabs a new bar of soap. Enters the shower and scrubs at herself until her skin is red and raw. Haroun continues to bang on the bathroom door, but Zoya pays him no heed. She slips down to the shower floor, water pooling around her feet and drumming against her insistently, and she wishes she could make the disgust roiling throughout her disappear.

And as she hears her husband worriedly knocking on the door—the pure and gentle man that he is—she realizes she *can* make it disappear.

~

That night, Zoya has the manor decorated in soft colors, with rose petals leading up to their room. She waits with bated breath on the bed, surrounded by candles and flickering lights and more rose petals, suddenly unsure of why she's so nervous. She's done this before—why is she scared?

Maybe because this time, it will actually mean something to her.

Footsteps tread the stairs, and Zoya's heartbeat quickens.

"Zoya?" Haroun's voice reveals his confusion, and Zoya covers her mouth to stifle her giggles. It feels good to laugh again. The whole day had been spent with quiet thinking and continuous backtracking and a plethora of second guessing.

And fear. So much fear and confusion and uncertainty.

When Mumtaz had heard Zoya's conversation with herself in the dining hall this afternoon, she had asked if there was anything she could help with. When Zoya reluctantly told the elderly woman, her face had lit up. She had reached forward and tucked a curl behind Zoya's ear, and Zoya had been surprised by the affectionate gesture.

"What's going on, Zoya?" Haroun says from outside the door, interrupting her thoughts. "Where are you?" He opens the door to their room, pausing as he takes in the sight before him. His eyes travel all around the room before stopping on Zoya, after which they widen. "Zoya?" There is uncertainty in his tone.

She steps forward, and Haroun's expression goes from uncertain to even more baffled. "What . . . what's going on, Zoya?"

Zoya stands, then reaches out for his hand. "Haroun." Her voice comes out shaky. "Please."

Comprehension dawns on his face, pure and clear. His eyes take in the room and Zoya's appearance in a new light as he understands the meaning behind it all.

"You . . . really?" he asks shakily.

As confirmation, Zoya steps forward and places her head against his chest, embracing him tightly. Then she steps back, eyes wide with both fear and exhilaration.

Zoya nods.

Awaiting his response, she gazes into his eyes. They are thoughtful, as well as pleasantly surprised.

Then he gives her the smallest, softest smile.

~

When Zoya blinks awake a little before *Fajr* time, she lifts her head to look up at her husband. He's fast asleep, chest rising and falling with the pressure of each breath. She smiles softly as she gazes tenderly at him. She didn't think her love for Haroun Suleiman could have increased, but seeing him asleep—with his arms subconsciously wrapped around her—changes her mind. He gives her new reasons to fall deeper in love with him. Every day.

Zoya reaches up and tickles his chin. His eyebrows furrow and his eyes open, darting around in confusion. When he sees his giggling wife, a smile lights up his face before he snuggles closer to her. His fingers stroke her hair as she rubs soothing circles onto the crook of his elbow.

"Love you," Haroun says almost absentmindedly as he stands to head to the bathroom.

It takes Zoya a few moments to recover from her shock. Her eyes are wide, heartbeat racing at the words.

Then she grins.

And it feels as if everything in the world has been set right.

Fifty-Two

~

HAROUN ENTERS THE ORPHANAGE, greeting the receptionist. He makes his way through the familiar halls to the room he will find the children in. When they see him, they excitedly jump up and rush forward. The manager laughs as the children all grasp at Haroun.

"Hey, *guysss*. Missed me?"

They all nod profusely, reaching up to wrap their arms around him, grab his shirt, give him a hug. A boy at the back pauses, staring at Haroun almost indignantly. He says, "You didn't bring your miss today."

Haroun laughs. "I'm sorry, miss is just a little bit busy."

Another boy turns to the first one and throws him a sly smile. "Zahid thinks your miss is *pretty*, don't you, Zahid?"

Zahid's eyes dart worriedly between Haroun and the second boy. "I didn't say that!"

"Settle down, children, settle down," the manager says.

Haroun chuckles at the worry in the young boy's eyes. "It's okay," he whispers. "I don't mind. She *is* pretty."

The children giggle as Zahid lets out a relieved sigh.

Haroun spends an hour with them before standing to leave. The children pout, and he promises he'll come back soon, since he's switched his hours around. Then he departs for work.

Zahid thinks your miss is pretty.

And who can blame the child? Haroun thinks as he settles in his car. Zoya has such an exquisite, radiant beauty that it's hard to look away from her. Especially when she smiles, or is caught up in her work and furrows her brows, or when she sleeps with a peaceful expression on her face.

Haroun bites his lower lip, trying to contain his smile so other drivers don't think he's crazy for grinning at his steering wheel.

When he gets to work, he decides that he'll surprise Zoya with something this evening. She has frequently mentioned wanting to have a backyard movie night, and that's exactly what Haroun will do for her.

She has been pretty stressed for the past couple of days—especially after seeing her ex-husband at the coffee shop—but every time Haroun asks her what's wrong, she shakes her head and smiles. But Haroun senses that she needs something to take her mind off of things.

The thought of a backyard movie night excites him. Throughout the day, he is in constant communication with Mumtaz to make arrangements. The older woman laughs delightedly when she first hears his idea, saying that Zoya has a surprise for him as well.

One of Haroun's coworkers narrows his eyes at him. "Haroun," he muses. "*You've* been awfully cheerful lately. Smiling at your phone twenty-four seven."

Haroun laughs. "Do you want me to *cry*, Daniel?"

"No, no." He places a palm at Haroun's desk and scrutinizes him carefully. "You're just making me consider getting married."

Haroun's mouth forms an *O* before he laughs again. "Glad I could be the one, O Cynic of Marriage."

Daniel rolls his eyes. "Oh, shut up."

Later, Haroun receives a call from the hospital. The receptionist says that Zoya needs to request a medication refill, and that there's some paperwork that needs to be filled for healthcare purposes. Haroun promises her he'll visit right after work and ends the call.

When he reaches the hospital, he receives a text from Mumtaz that whatever he requested has been organized. He thanks her profusely and makes his way up the elevator and down the hall of the hospital. It's eerily quiet; the only sounds are the occasional beeps and whirs of machinery and his footsteps slapping against the linoleum.

Upon reaching the receptionist in the pharmacy department, Haroun tells her his reason for visiting. After showing his ID and providing Zoya's date of birth, he asks if he can get a prescription for Zoya's medication

"You said Zoya Zameer?"

Haroun nods.

The receptionist types on her computer, then says. "She doesn't need any medication refills."

Haroun's brows furrow. "What? But the pharmacy gave me a call and said that she needs refills for her headaches."

The receptionist's brows furrow as she squints at the screen. Then she leans back and shakes her head. "Nope. She's not in need of any medication for headaches. Actually, she's not in need of *any* medication."

Haroun is starting to become extremely confused. His eyebrows knit as he gazes around quizzically, deep in thought. *Not in need of any medication?* "Are you sure?"

"Yes," she nods briskly. "Zoya Zameer, right?"

"Yes."

She shakes her head again. "None."

"Okay," Haroun murmurs. "Must have been a mistake. Anyway, where can I fill out the paperwork for my wife's healthcare plan?"

The receptionist looks even more baffled. "Zoya already has a solid healthcare plan, with all expenses paid."

"All expenses paid?" Haroun's confusion grows. "Even for the treatment of her concussion?"

The woman blows out a sigh, clearly frustrated. "Sir, your wife doesn't need any medication refills, and there are no expenses to be paid at the moment. In fact"—she squints at the computer screen—"I'm not quite sure what concussion you're talking about. She seems perfectly healthy. There have been no incidents requiring her need for treatment."

Haroun's breath catches in his throat. *What?* "Okay, ma'am, I'm sorry. I think we're both a little confused here. Are you looking at *Zoya Zameer's* file?"

She nods. "Yes, sir. Z-O-Y-A Z-A-M-E-E-R, correct?"

"Correct," Haroun whispers, feeling as if the wind is whooshing out of him. "There seems to be a misunderstanding. Is it possible for me to speak to her doctor?"

The woman sighs. "What is the doctor's name?"

"Dr. Ruth Creek."

She types on her computer before saying, "Dr. Ruth has been posted elsewhere. Weeks ago, actually."

Haroun rubs his forehead, worried. "I don't understand. Have Zoya's medical records just not been updated? Why did I receive a call if she's not in need of meds?"

"I don't know. There may have been a misunderstanding with someone else's paperwork. Sorry for any inconvenience, sir," she replies dismissively.

Haroun steps back and heads to a chair by the wall, feeling lightheaded. He pulls out his phone and logs into the hospital's app to access Zoya's medical records. He realizes that he has never done so before because Zoya always assures him that she will handle it.

Come to think of it, she was reluctant when granting him permission to access her medical records. He had joked that he would use the information to clone her, and she had only smiled weakly, gripping the pen harder than necessary.

When the app logs in, he scrolls through to "patient charts" and to the graphs detailing her health over the years.

There is a consistent, stable line upwards.

Haroun rubs his chin, eyebrows knitted. He clicks through records of immunizations and then down to *medications: active.*

None for headaches. Or nausea. Or faintness.

Haroun stares at it for longer than necessary. He scrolls farther down, seeing that the last active prescription on her file expired six months ago. Before they were married. And it was for minor headaches.

Haroun's hands begin to shake, so he pockets his phone and presses his palms to his eyelids.

Clearly, this is a mistake. Perhaps the doctors haven't updated Zoya's medical records and her latest prescribed medications. It can happen, right? After all, doctors are human, too.

Yeah, he tries to reassure himself. *Probably some mistake.*

A strange mistake.

Haroun stands and departs the hospital, trudging to his car. He's so distracted that he almost trips over a speed bump.

How is it possible for Zoya's records to be so outdated? *Alhamdulillah,* she's still alive and well. And as far as he's known, doctors have never screwed up something as major as this.

As for Dr. Ruth—how weird for her to be posted elsewhere? She didn't even mention anything to Haroun the last time they spoke.

Ah, he thinks. *Let me call her.*

When he dials her number, it goes straight to voicemail. He tries again, and the same thing happens.

Haroun's heartbeat grows more rapid by the second.

Relax. She's probably busy. This is all just a huge misunderstanding.

Driving home, he receives many profuse honks and angry middle fingers. He blinks to keep himself focused.

When he enters through the manor gate and parks outside, Zoya texts him, *"where are you???"* with some silly emojis. Haroun reads the message and squeezes his eyes shut. His head feels as if it may explode.

She texts him again when he finally exits the car to head inside. Aman lets him in.

Zoya stands in front of him, dressed in a royal blue gown and crystal earrings that make her look so beautiful, she is almost unbearable to look at.

Haroun's heart feels strange.

When she looks in his eyes, she must detect something off

because the smile fades from her radiant face.

"Haroun? Is everything okay?"

He gestures for them to proceed into the hall. There is a delicious aroma in the air, but Haroun can't seem to focus on it. His mind is reeling.

When they sit down, Zoya says shakily, "Haroun?"

"I, um . . ." He falters, presses his lips together. "I went to the hospital after work." He glances at her swiftly, and she tenses.

"They gave me a call about some healthcare paperwork. They said you weren't picking up. And they reminded me about medication refills, which you hadn't requested. And . . ." His voice is shaking—he's afraid of what he's about to say. Haroun looks down at his fist, which has started trembling. "The receptionist . . . the receptionist said that you're not in need of meds and they didn't—didn't have any records of your injuries?" The statement comes out as a question, and when Haroun looks up into Zoya's eyes, he's ready for her to refute this absurdity.

Because there cannot possibly be any truth to this.

Silence.

"Zoya?" His voice is small. "This is a mistake, right? Maybe they forgot to update your records?"

Zoya stands from her spot and moves closer to him, reaching forward to grab his hand. But Haroun pulls out of her grasp, confused as to why she won't answer him. Why won't she laugh and tell him that this is all so stupid? "It's a mistake, right?"

"Haroun—"

"I tried to see your doctor to ask her about it but they said she's been posted somewhere else?" He laughs nervously. "Coincidence, right?" Zoya reaches forward again, and Haroun pulls back once more at her silence. "Coincidence, *right*?"

Why is she looking at me like that? Haroun's heartbeat speeds up at an abnormal pace. Zoya's silence is making him nervous, and he stares urgently into her eyes, willing her to give him the answer he needs to hear.

Because if it's anything else, Haroun doesn't know what he'll do. He doesn't know.

"Haroun, I—" Zoya breaks off, avoiding his eyes. He watches her carefully. *Why won't she tell me that this is all a stupid mistake so we can laugh about it?* Haroun's gaze prods her insistently, but she doesn't raise her eyes to his.

He pulls away suddenly, fearing his heart may combust and collapse because of the speed at which it is beating. His eyes widen, and his breaths begin to come in short bursts of air.

Why is she silent?

"Zoya?" he says slowly, voice shaking. "Tell me it's a lie?"

"I—"

"Tell me there's been a mistake?" His eyes pierce hers, begging for an answer.

Zoya stays silent. Haroun's urgent gaze roves over her face, trying to detect the meaning behind her silence and the sudden grief that has encompassed her features.

But he has known this face for a good amount of time now. He has seen it smile, has seen it frown. And cry, and worry, and laugh.

So he understands the crestfallen expression on her face. He understands it all too well.

And he wishes he didn't.

Haroun's heart takes off like helicopter blades. Beating, beating, beating against his chest. Ripping, tearing through the flesh.

"No." Haroun shakes his head back and forth. "No, no." He stands and begins pacing back and forth, rubbing his chin. An anxious laugh escapes him. *This can't be true.* "No, no."

Zoya stands and reaches towards him, but he backs away from her quickly. *This cannot be true.* His hands go up in his hair, fisting it. Maybe if he squeezes hard enough, he'll fly awake and turn to see Zoya sleeping peacefully beside him. And he will thank Allah for making something so horrible exist only in an unfathomable nightmare.

But he senses Zoya's presence beside him. And he hears her sniffles, signaling the tears falling from her beautiful eyes.

Haroun thinks he may collapse. "Oh, no." A strangled cry escapes him. He loses feeling in his legs and falls to the floor, continuously shaking his head back and forth. "No, no, no." *This* cannot *be true. This is all a lie. A scary, stupid lie. There is* no way *that this is true.*

But things begin to reprocess in his mind, and it starts to make sense. How antsy Zoya became with her medication. How quickly she recovered from her concussion. How reluctant she was to talk about her illness or injuries. How aloof her doctor had been around Haroun every time they went to the hospital.

No, no, no, no. Oh, God, *no.*

"Haroun—" Zoya's voice trembles. He feels her hands on his shoulder again but pushes her away. Her fingers feel like fire. They feel like fire.

"No," he murmurs over and over again.

"Please, Haroun," Zoya's voice has a scary urgency to it. "Please, just let me explain."

It all makes awful sense now.

Haroun thinks his vocal cords have stopped working. He cannot seem to formulate words on his tongue. *This is all a lie. This is all a lie. It's not true. It* can't *make sense.*

Zoya touches him once more, and again he automatically flinches away from her.

Haroun has always tried to comfort Zoya with his touch if she has ever been stressed—or even when she has not been stressed. When she cries, he wraps his arms around her. When she laughs, he bounces her curls around in his fingers. When she's angry, he rubs her temples. When she's disappointed, he places her palms at his cheek and makes a fish face until she laughs.

She is doing the same now. Trying to touch him to comfort him.

This can only mean one thing: what he hasn't feared even in his *worst nightmares*, what he never even *fathomed*, what his heart has protected itself against even *thinking* about, has happened.

It was all a lie.

"Please, Haroun—"

"No!" he exclaims, having found his voice. He shakes his head back and forth like a little child's. "No, don't say anything, *please.* Don't tell me any more lies. Don't."

Zoya wipes her cheeks. The mascara has smeared across her beautiful, beautiful face. Tears well in her eyes. "Please listen to me just once—"

"*You lied to me!*" he shouts, pain emerging from somewhere deep inside him. Like a volcano that's been dormant for years has finally erupted. "Again and again and again. From the moment you asked me to marry you." His voice breaks and sobs overtake him. *Everything has been a lie. Every single thing.* "I *loved* you. I loved you."

Zoya's features twist in pain. "You wouldn't have wanted me otherwise!"

"*That doesn't make it okay!*" he yells. The pain, the pain. It's too much to bear. Haroun begins to sob so hard that he breaks out into a fit of coughs, leaning back against the wall. He takes deep, heaving breaths, raising his gaze to Zoya's. The helicopter in his chest is tearing through all of his flesh, causing an illusion of blood to pool down his body and around his feet. "You don't know anything. Just once," he whispers. "Just *once* if you had tried to ask me—"

"You wouldn't have *wanted* me!" Zoya yells again, crying.

"*So you lied to me?*" he stands then, and walks towards her. Her blue gown swirls around her in the wind of the fan. Mascara is smeared under her eyes, but this exquisite woman—his wife—is still the picture of absolute beauty.

This much beauty . . . this much beauty cannot tell such an ugly lie, can it?

Haroun cannot take it. He cannot take it.

"You *lied,*" he says in a low voice. "And not just once. Over and over and over again. Every smile, every hug, *har baat.*" His eyes travel down to her hands. Her soft, beautiful hands that he has held so many times. Her hands that have absentmindedly run through his hair many nights. He takes one of these hands and places it against his cheek. His eyes are wide, darting helplessly between hers. "Every time you did this, it was a lie." His eyebrows furrow, powerlessness overtakes him again. "All of it . . . a lie." He drops her hand, feeling as if the helicopter heart in his ribcage may burst out of his chest and take flight somewhere far, far away.

Somewhere it will never return from.

There is no way this is happening to him again. There is no way he's being brutally exposed to an enormous lie all over again. Like when he belatedly found out about his father's second wife.

Only this time, it's much, much worse.

"No." Zoya's lips tremble. Haroun is not accustomed to seeing her cry this way. If she cries, her sobs shake throughout her whole body. But this? This is quiet crying. Tears are rapidly pooling in her eyes, but no sound leaves her lips.

It makes the truth even more unbearable for Haroun.

Zoya reaches up and tries to cup his cheek, but he pushes her hand away. "It wasn't a lie. I loved you. I *love* you."

"*NO!*" Haroun breaks out into sobs again. "You don't love me. If you loved me, you wouldn't have lied to me. And you wouldn't have lied to me over and over again." He backs away, pressing his palms to his eyelids. They feel like fire. Everything feels like fire. "*Love* isn't built on lies."

"I was going to tell you," she whispers. "I was trying to build the courage."

"That makes it okay?" Haroun removes his hands from his eyes and gives her a look of disbelief. "You requested me to marry a *sick* woman. And I didn't do it out of pity; I did it because I was considering reaching out to you later, anyway. I needed a lot more time to think about it, and I wanted to talk to my mom first." His words blubber together, barely cohesive. "But then you called me to the hospital and told me you were *sick.* And that you didn't want to *die* that way. And then you proposed and you were crying and—"

Suddenly, he stops. His gaze drops to the floor as all the fight leaves him. The helicopter in his chest begins to die down, clicking and whirring slowly as if it will come to a final stop soon. "I can't . . . I can't do it anymore."

His shoulders shake once more as he weeps. Zoya tries to reach forward to comfort him, but Haroun backs away from the contact as if her fingers are made of fire. He falls to the floor with his hands in his hair, continuously murmuring, "No, no, no." He's lost all control.

It seems that his heart is failing him. It's too much. The pain is too much.

Everything is just too much.

Then it all goes black.

~

A few hours earlier

Zoya and her board of directors decide on giving everybody in the company a day off. The recent release of their new campaign has been met with very positive feedback, and it feels only appropriate for the employees to be able to celebrate by taking a break.

While Haroun is at work, Zoya spends the entire day in the kitchen with Mumtaz. She has decided to prepare a special feast for him. Although she is not a fantastic cook, Mumtaz has been helping a great deal to be on par with Zoya's excitement.

The older woman frequently leaves the kitchen to call or text someone in a very secretive fashion. When Zoya asks her what's up, she simply smiles and shakes her head.

In the evening, Zoya changes and does some makeup before calling Haroun to ask when he'll be home. He cheerfully tells her he needs to run a quick errand after work, so he should be home in about an hour. Zoya waits with bated breath, feeling jittery and excited. The food has all turned out great, courtesy of Mumtaz's expert aid, and the aroma wafts from the kitchen throughout the entire hall.

About an hour and a half later, Zoya texts Haroun, *"where are you???"* followed by a bunch of silly face emojis. She checks after a couple minutes, taken aback when it says that the message has been read. Five minutes ago.

Why didn't he reply?

Maybe he's driving, Zoya thinks. Mumtaz catches her worried expression and asks what's wrong, but Zoya shakes her head. She sends another text, again shocked when Haroun reads it immediately. Zoya is about to call him when she hears Aman opening the door, and she rushes to the entrance.

Zoya's eyes rove over Haroun's face. His expression is passive, revealing nothing, which throws Zoya further into confusion.

Then his eyes meet hers, and Zoya is taken aback by the sadness in them.

"Haroun? Is everything okay?"

He doesn't reply, just motions for them to proceed into the hall. When settled, Zoya gives him a worried look. "Haroun?"

"I, um . . ." He hesitates. "I went to the hospital after work."

Zoya's heart seems to stop in her chest. The air whooshes out of her.

"They gave me a call about some healthcare paperwork. They said you weren't picking up. And they reminded me about medication refills, which you hadn't requested. And . . ." There is a tremble in his voice, a tremble in his shoulders. Zoya senses that he's trying to hold himself together, and she fears her heart may fail in anticipation of his next words. "The receptionist . . . the receptionist said that you're not in need of meds and they didn't—didn't have any records of your injuries?" There is disbelief in his voice, reflected in his eyes as well when he looks at her. As if Zoya will say "*pfft*" and they will have a good laugh about it.

He doesn't want to believe what he's saying.

Zoya's heart thumps persistently against her chest in the silent hall. So loud. So very loud in comparison to the dead silence that has settled in the pit of her stomach. Spreading everywhere throughout her body. Immobilizing her limbs.

"Zoya?" Haroun's voice cracks. "This is a mistake, right? Maybe they forgot to update your records?" His eyes seem to pierce hers with the questions in them.

Zoya wills her body to move. She stands and sits next to him, reaching out to hold his hand. But he pulls back, the question in his eyes more insistent. "It's a mistake, right?"

"Haroun—"

"I tried to see your doctor to ask her about it but they said she has been posted somewhere else?" He laughs nervously. "Coincidence, right?" Zoya tries to reach for his hand once more, but he pulls back again. "Coincidence, *right*?" This time, the question is riddled with helplessness. Like if Zoya will answer in anything other than the affirmative, he will lose control.

"Haroun, I—" She opens and closes her mouth like a fish. Her palms are sweating, perspiration beading at her forehead and neck. Haroun watches her carefully, and something in her face must give him the answer he has been fearing because he pulls back suddenly. Eyes wide, breaths laborious.

"Zoya?" he says slowly, voice shaking. "Tell me it's a lie?"

"I—"

"Tell me there's been a mistake?" His eyes pierce hers, begging for an answer.

Zoya stays silent, having no answer that will not destroy him.

"No." Haroun shakes his head back and forth. "No, no." He stands and rubs his chin, pacing to and fro. He laughs anxiously, as if making a joke of his disbelief. "No, no."

And Zoya's first tear falls. Her chin wobbles, and she stands to try to reach for him again. He backs away, fisting his hair in his hands. "Oh, no." A strangled sound escapes him; his knees bend and he falls to the floor, persistently shaking his head. "No, no, no."

"Haroun—" Zoya's voice breaks as she bends down to comfort him. He pushes her hands off and turns away, murmuring "no" numerous times.

"Please, Haroun," Zoya cries. "Please just let me explain." He doesn't reply, doesn't even acknowledge that he's heard her. There is a lost, faraway look in his eyes.

"*Please*, Haroun—"

"No!" he exclaims, shaking his head again and again. "No, don't say anything, *please*. Don't tell me any more lies. Don't."

Zoya wipes her face harshly to clear the tears that have accumulated, but more take their place. "Please listen to me just once—"

"*You lied to me!*" he shouts, sadness and anger contorting his features. "Again and again and again. From the moment you asked me to marry you." He begins to cry again. "I *loved* you. I loved you."

Zoya cries and cries and cries, hands over her weak heart. "You wouldn't have wanted me otherwise!"

"*That doesn't make it okay!*" he yells. By now, guards and

servants have grouped to witness the commotion. Many of them have cutlery and decorations in hand, per Zoya's orders to set the table for dinner. And many others have balloons and blankets in hand, per Haroun's orders to add finishing touches to the backyard. But one look at the scene before them sends them scampering away from the couple.

Haroun cries so roughly that he begins to cough, pressing his back against the wall. He breathes deeply, as if he can't get enough air, and raises his gaze to Zoya's. His eyes, always calm and gentle, are now shattered with grief. "You don't know anything. Just once," he whispers. "Just *once* if you had tried to ask me—"

"You wouldn't have *wanted* me!" Zoya repeats loudly, sobbing.

"*So you lied to me?*" he regains his footing and stumbles towards her. "You *lied.*" His voice becomes deathly quiet. "And not just once. Over and over and over again. Every smile, every hug, *har baat.*" He takes her hand then, and places it against his cheek. His eyes are wide, darting helplessly between hers. "Every time you did this, it was a lie." His eyebrows knit. "All of it . . . a lie." He lets go of her hand.

"No." Zoya's voice shakes. She reaches forward and tries to touch his cheek, but he pushes her away. "It wasn't a lie. I loved you. I *love* you."

"*NO!*" he cries. "You don't love me. If you loved me, you wouldn't have lied to me. And you wouldn't have lied to me over and over again." He steps back, pressing his hands to his eyelids. "*Love* isn't built on lies."

"I was going to tell you," Zoya whispers. "I was trying to build the courage."

"That makes it okay?" He watches her with painful eyes, shoulders shaking. "You requested me to marry a *sick* woman. And I didn't do it out of pity; I did it because I was considering reaching out to you later, anyway. I needed a lot more time to think about it, and I wanted to talk to my mom first." Zoya's hands tremble at his words. He was considering proposing to Zoya? "But then you called me to the hospital and told me you were *sick.* And that you didn't want to *die* that way. And then you proposed and you were crying and—" Suddenly, his shoulders sag. His gaze falls to the floor by her feet. "I can't—I can't do it anymore."

He breaks out into rough sobs. Zoya tries to comfort him, but he flinches back from her touch. He falls once more and buries his head in his hands. "No, no, no." He's spiraling out of control. Out of the rational, logical sphere he always tries to contain himself in. This Haroun is not the Haroun Suleiman Zoya is so familiar with. This Haroun is a mess.

Zoya's unshakeable pillar, now crumbling.

And then her strong pillar collapses. And Haroun faints.

~

Zoya waits with bated breath, pacing the hospital floor. She scrambles forward when a doctor approaches her.

"He's okay. Stress levels were high, but he's better now. You can go see him. He'll be discharged soon."

"Thank you, sir," Zoya murmurs, taking a deep breath before stepping into the room.

Haroun is sitting on the bed and staring outside the window. His eyes are red-rimmed, face pale and drawn. In the span of a couple hours, his strong exterior has been turned weak and sallow.

He seems to be drained of all energy.

He turns at the sound of her footsteps, eyes telling a horrible tale of grief. A mumble comes out of his mouth. Zoya moves closer to hear him. "Leave," he repeats.

Zoya flinches. "Haroun—"

He turns back to the window. "I don't want to listen to anything you say," he snaps in a low voice. So uncharacteristic. So unlike gentle, kind Haroun Suleiman. "I don't want to hear your voice. I don't want to be in your presence." His chin wobbles. "I don't even want to *look* at you." He tries hard to blink away the tears so that Zoya doesn't witness the level of his pain, but to no avail.

She has seen Haroun Suleiman cry only twice—once in the middle of the night during the first few days of their marriage, and the second time when Goldie died. Despite Aisha telling her that Haroun could be equally emotional as he could be rational, Zoya has never witnessed his tears more than twice in the months that she's been married to him.

Haroun's eyes are heavy, dark circles marring his visage. He roughly wipes away tears, refusing to meet Zoya's gaze.

"Haroun—"

"*Don't.*" His fists clench as he squeezes his eyes shut. "I don't want to hear any more lies. *Please.* I can't take it."

"You have to know how *sorry* I am—"

Haroun turns to her, eyes red and wide. "If you had even the slightest bit of regret or sorrow, you wouldn't be here right now." He turns back to the window. "So don't." He pulls his knees up to his chest like a child, settling his chin in between them.

Zoya remains silent, clamping her lips together to keep the sobs from erupting.

After a moment, Haroun whispers, "You built our entire relationship off of a lie—how is anything after that supposed to be the truth? You *wrecked* the foundation"—he laughs bitterly—"and expected the entire building to stay standing. Eventually, everything collapses." He takes a trembling breath. "And it's never the same again."

Zoya's face scrunches up as her tears fall. At the sound of her weeping, Haroun's jaw and fists clench. This is not the Haroun who murmurs sweet nothings in Zoya's ear and makes her laugh every night. This is not the Haroun who can't stand to see a single tear on his wife's face. This is not the Haroun who defends Zoya in her presence as well as her absence.

This Haroun Suleiman is heartbroken. Beyond repair.

And Zoya has done it to him.

"Go," Haroun says with such finality that more tears well in Zoya's eyes. He turns away so that neither can witness the other's tears. So that neither can witness the absolute heartbreak on the other's face as they part. "Leave." His voice breaks. "I don't want to be *near* you. I want you to leave me alone, Zoya." His lips tremble as he wraps his arms tighter around himself, as if he's trying to hold himself together. "*Please.* I need . . . time."

So Zoya leaves.

She rushes out of the room, and out come all the sobs she had tried to repress in front of him. She can't breathe, she can't breathe. She cries so hard that her knees buckle and she falls to the hospital floor. Somebody approaches her but she waves them off, burying her head in her hands. Her poor, stupid heart feels as if it may combust and fail.

And Zoya doesn't think she would mind it one bit.

Fifty-Three

The Prophet Muhammad (peace be upon him) said: "Your love of
something may blind and deafen you."
(Sunan Abu Dawud, classed as Hasan)

~

HAROUN REALIZES HE HAS fallen into the same trap he warned Zoya of. He has loved too much. He has loved too much, and it has cost him. He has made too much room for someone other than God in his heart.

And it has destroyed him.

So Haroun Suleiman falls apart.

~

And Zoya Zameer falls apart.

Fifty-Four

*"O humanity! Indeed, there has come to you a warning from your Lord,
a cure for what is in the hearts, a guide, and a mercy for the believers."*
(Qur'an 10:57)

~

WHEN SHE RETURNS HOME, Zoya cannot stem the flow of her tears. She rushes upstairs and locks her bedroom door, collapsing on the bed. The bed on which she had snuggled into Haroun's arms just this morning.

It seems like ages ago.

She thinks of his eyes at the hospital. Stricken, pooling with grief and disbelief.

Broken.

She screams and screams and screams until her throat turns raw from screaming. Her body convulses with shudders as she cries.

Soon guards quietly step into the room to retrieve Haroun's belongings, prying Zoya off of them with helpless eyes when she begs them to stop. Eventually, she falls back with trembling lips and soundless screams.

Zoya Zameer stays in her room for days, opening it only to receive the food that is placed outside her door. Her maids give up incessantly knocking to ask whether she is okay. She eats numbly, without tasting anything, and throws it all up almost immediately after.

She ignores all calls from the office and picks up her phone only to text Haroun, crying harder when her messages fail to deliver. The doorbell rings frequently and insistently, but she ignores the guards who come to inform her of people's arrivals. People from work, investors, contractors, employees, more people from work.

And when the guards inform her that *Ammi* and the sisters have come, Zoya buries herself deep into the closet. Palms over her ears, muted screams trapped within her.

When her servants approach her door to ask questions, she refuses to reply. Mutely she sits, waiting and waiting with bated breath by her window, hoping to see his car pull in and for him to step out, because there's no way Haroun Suleiman wouldn't come back for her. He's too good to leave anyone in such a broken state.

But days and days and days pass, and there is still no sign of him. It destroys Zoya. Especially to know that *she* has done this to Haroun.

Zoya continues to call and text his number, but every time she reaches his voicemail, she hurls her phone across the room. Hands in her hair, she sits on the prayer mat he frequented the entire day, hoping that if she savors some remnant of him, he will somehow remember her and return.

But he does not return. And Zoya cannot believe it. Living in denial, she avoids all human contact and doesn't speak a single word to anyone. All she does is wake up, pray mechanically, eat, and attempt to sleep at night. In the expensive, mattress-foamed bed that suddenly feels too big for her alone. She constantly reaches around in the blankets to touch another body, but her hands come up empty and again tears spring to her eyes.

She thinks that perhaps two weeks pass. The only way she can tell in her disjointed perception of time is by the envelope she receives at the end of the month. It contains her bank statement and information on all her monthly bills. She throws it to her bed carelessly and later thumbs it open as a distraction, furrowing her brows at the *paid* statement. Electricity, internet, landline, guards, cars—everything has been paid for. Her mouth opens and closes, and her knees begin to crumple. Her feet give way and she falls to the bed, hand covering her mouth.

That's when it really hits her.

He's not coming back. He's asked for his belongings to be delivered to him and he's paid the bills, and he's not coming back.

The reality hits Zoya so strongly that she crashes against the floor, causing a searing pain in her lower back. But the pain is nothing to the storm starting to brew within her.

She stands and slams her room door open, rushing down the stairs. Her head is pounding.

Zoya wants to scream, but after having been unused for so long, her voice doesn't come easily. As she's hurling down the stairs, all the maids and guards rush to her service, glad that she's finally left her room after days but panicked at her explosive nature.

Zoya points to the paper and opens her mouth to scream that Haroun is gone, that he left, that he's never coming back. Tears stream down her face; her expression is the epitome of grief. She tries to speak but her voice cracks, and she attempts to clear her throat.

After seconds of clamping her mouth open and shut, Zoya realizes that her voice is not just aged from disuse—it's really not coming out. She touches her throat and looks up at her worried maids and guards, eyes widening.

Still, no sound escapes her throat.

She falls back and clutches the staircase railing, the bank statement slipping from her hand and fluttering to the floor.

Zoya takes heaving breaths and tries to open her mouth once more to speak, but her voice continues to fail her. All that comes out is a whoosh of air coupled with a rasping sound—the telltale sound of wind before a storm hits. She blinks rapidly, gazing back up at her audience. A looming fear begins to rise over her head and cloud her vision, blurring her sight and arresting her senses. Speechless, she hacks at her throat, as if attempting to procure sound. But to no avail.

Because Zoya Zameer has lost what is most valuable to her.

Zoya Zameer has lost her voice.

Fifty-Five

"Whether you speak secretly or openly—He surely knows (best) what is hidden in the heart." (Qur'an 67:13)

~

DOCTORS COME AND GO, prattling off a series of possible diagnoses and ailments. Mumtaz calls some of the best doctors in the city—even the state—but they cannot seem to figure out what is wrong with Zoya Zameer. Outwardly, she seems entirely okay.

What they don't realize, however, is that she's not suffering from a physical ailment or a psychological affliction.

Zoya Zameer's battle is spiritual.

Mutely, she sits before the doctors as they check her vital signs. As they take scans and run tests on her. They ask her questions, to which she nods or shakes her head silently. When these questions further progress into more complicated ones so that she may have to speak other than nod yes or no, she remains silent. So they hand her a pen and a pad and, in written words, she explains her situation.

She says that she's feeling completely okay, although it burns the blood in her fingers to write this. She tells them to leave because she doesn't need them.

But one psychotherapist is finally able to diagnose her ailment as psychogenic dysphonia, which he explains to Mumtaz is a change in voice quality that emerges as a result of sudden emotional or psychological trauma. He says that her voice is not entirely gone, and the condition is temporary. He prescribes medication—which

Zoya doesn't touch—and makes immediate appointments for vocal therapy.

Then he leaves as well.

Zoya Zameer's mouth—the same that used to puncture and maim and wound others—remains shut.

Her eyes are filled with woe. Whenever someone speaks to her, she raises her eyes to theirs helplessly and tries to respond, but words fail to come out. Her eyes are haunting in their urgent story. She tries to send a message so alert, so persistent, yet is unable to do so. Barely heard whimpers escape her lips and she moves her hands around in a feeble attempt to communicate. Her maids and guards watch helplessly, attempting to gauge what she's trying to say.

Each night, Zoya Zameer's soft whimpers echo throughout the silent manor, penetrating the darkness. She sees Haroun in her dreams—his dark eyes and withering stare, his stiff posture. Still as a statue the last time she saw him. Wells of tears in his eyes.

His grief haunts her every dream, plagues her every thought.

Each night, as Zoya whimpers, Mumtaz wakes suddenly and rushes to her room after hearing her over the monitor. The maid attempts to comfort her by embracing her and stroking Zoya's hair. Guards rush to her room, only to find it the same cycle of haunting dreams and endless tears that afflict her.

Eventually, Mumtaz frequents Zoya's bedroom more and more until she sleeps next to her every night. Pretty soon, the guards stop rushing at the now-familiar whimpers. Doors stop frantically opening. Mumtaz wakes but pats Zoya's back almost absentmindedly.

Zoya Zameer: the woman who had always cried wolf and manipulated others when she was completely safe, now begins to cry for real about the monsters and wolves that haunt her. Yet her agonized calls for help are simply echoes of her past nights reverberating through the walls. Nothing new.

Zameer's shareholders are enraged, to say the least, and her employees are baffled. Reporters swarm her doorstep, attempting to fit into every single place that offers room to breathe. Like ants, they are haphazardly strewn around her entire manor's entrance. There are streams of angry shouts, declarations, protests, demands for answers. Zoya's guards rush to stop them from entering. They maintain control, as is their duty, but even they have trouble fully containing the surging crowd.

Zoya sits in her room on the second floor, watching the scene occurring below her very window with passive eyes. Cameras attempt to scrutinize the manor from every angle. Zoya remains behind sheer curtains, hoping this is enough to cover her from their view.

She can understand their rage. Really, she can.

That doesn't mean she's willing to do anything about it.

Zoya turns away and settles on her bed, staring motionlessly at the wall in front of her.

If only time would stop crawling and begin to speed up. Perhaps then her pain would lessen, and she would be able to control it to some extent. As people say, *time heals all wounds.* So maybe this agonizingly slow crunch of time can hasten to heal her. Maybe, just maybe, she won't be fractured and broken and shattered into a million pieces anymore.

Maybe she won't succumb to the large, gaping chasm of grief that is opening up inside her. Pulling her under with every passing minute, every waking moment, every breath she takes.

Absolute grief.

Zoya doesn't think any dictionary definition gives justice to this emotion. It is everything; it is all-consuming. And she has only experienced this once before, when her father left.

It seems to have increased tenfold this time around.

Whoever said that humans were fifty to sixty percent water had been thoroughly wrong. The human body is nothing but a vessel of emotions, packaged with experience and trials. With emotions such as grief.

An emotion that makes Zoya feel as if lightning and fire are encased in her body. Trying to contain these cyclones of grief is the most difficult task Zoya has ever had to experience. It comes all at once, drowning her, and then it continues to push her deeper into the water. Inch by inch. Bit by bit.

Until grief swallows her completely whole.

Nights she flies awake breathing heavily, feeling as if the air is compressing, determined to suffocate her. Little by little, sleep escapes her. She finds herself frequently awake in the AM, her eyelids drooping yet slumber never finding her. Sometimes she awakens hurriedly as she drifts off to sleep, feeling as if she is being watched. Cold sweats break out all over her body, and excruciating pains numb her head. She throws up frequently, and a strange sort of pain nestles in her stomach. Migraines become normal, and she dines with insomnia every night. Every thought that crosses her mind, every *jhalak*, every single thing that passes through her head causes her to wince.

But she doesn't visit the doctors or go near anyone, not wanting her affliction to further increase by having to communicate with people. The only person allowed in her house is the vocal therapist, whom Mumtaz forces Zoya to sit with every day.

Zoya wakes up to bright sunlight streaming through her windows, having never slept at all. Her prayers are numb and mechanical, each move barely thought out.

Her beautiful auburn curls become lank; strands of fallen hair are littered all around the house. Her eye bags have returned, considerably darker now. Her skin is sallow and sunken.

And when insistent knocks and pleas to open the door come from *Ammi* and the sisters, Zoya finds it hard to breathe. The panic attacks resurface, and Mumtaz has to lead her upstairs and tuck her into bed before Zoya is able to feel her heart again.

Eventually, *Ammi* goes away. And the sisters go away. Only to return again, causing Zoya to press her hands tightly over her ears to cover the sound of their pain through the entrance door.

Zoya cannot look at them. What will she say to them? She has no words. She only knows that if she is to stumble upon them, she will bury herself deeper and deeper into the dark, gaping hole she is falling into.

And this time, she fears that she may never be able to return from it.

~

Mumtaz sets a plate of spaghetti and a glass of water in front of Zoya. "Anything else, *bibi?*"

Zoya shakes her head and grabs her fork. She lifts it to her mouth, chews, and swallows. Raising her eyes to Mumtaz's, Zoya attempts to smile, but it seems distorted on her face. She coughs and opens her mouth, aiming to tell Mumtaz that the spaghetti tastes good.

But no sound comes out.

Zoya clamps her mouth shut and furrows her eyebrows. Her lips begin to tremble, and Mumtaz rushes forward worriedly.

"What's wrong, *bibi?*"

Zoya shakes her head, trying to tell Mumtaz that she's fine and nothing's wrong, but Mumtaz takes this as a sign of affirmation. The maid slides a pen and notepad to Zoya, but Zoya shakes her head again. Mumtaz gestures to the spaghetti. "Is there something wrong with it? Is it too hot? Too cold?" Zoya continues to shake her head and Mumtaz continues to speak hurriedly, fretting over nothing. "I warmed it up for forty-five seconds; I know you don't like having it too hot, so I didn't—"

She stops as Zoya lets out a sudden whimper. A second later, tears spill down her face. She raises a hand to her mouth, to her lips, and makes a pawing motion. Mumtaz watches her helplessly, unsure of what to do. The elderly woman reaches forward and wraps her arm around Zoya's shoulders, and Zoya's shoulders begin to shake as she emits quiet sobs.

The doorman rushes in, the worry which is usually in his eyes even more pronounced now. "What's wrong?"

"I don't know, Aman *beta,*" Mumtaz says, concerned. "She won't even use the pen and paper to tell me."

In response to this, more tears pool in Zoya's eyes, and she presses her wrists against her eyelids. How can she say that she just wanted to compliment mumtaz's spaghetti? She just wanted to say three words: *this tastes good.*

She has been reduced to nothing, like the ashes after a flame.

Perhaps, Zoya thinks as tears stream down her face. *Perhaps this is a punishment from God. For my not saying 'thank you' when I had the chance to. And now, when I so badly want to say these simple words, I'm unable to.* Zoya claws at her mouth and Mumtaz tries to stop her, but she pushes the woman away.

Her maid watches her with a helpless expression on her face.

Fifty-Six

"People, here is an illustration, so listen carefully: those you call on beside God could not, even if they combined all their forces, create a fly, and if a fly took something away from them, they would not be able to retrieve it. How feeble are the petitioners and how feeble are those they petition!" (Qur'an 22:73)

~

THE MANOR IS STILL.

Deafening silence makes a home in all the rooms and halls. It settles on the gold plated decorations and the extravagant furniture and the silently swaying chandeliers.

Zoya sits on a couch; she is as silent as her house. Her eyes trace everything in front of her, drinking it all up hungrily. Imagining another presence roaming the halls. Another figure walking to and fro and settling next to her. Stroking her hair tenderly. Placing a kiss at her forehead.

She blinks constantly to pull herself out of her trances, but the memories come back. Again and again. To tease her, to haunt her.

She once thought that simply the memory of Haroun Suleiman in her manor would be enough for her. That she would remember him here in times of distress, and that would be enough.

It is never enough.

All it does is fill her up to an excruciating point before draining her of everything. Over and over again. Fill up. Drain. Fill up. Drain.

A horrible travesty.

Somehow, this is worse than death. At least with death, she would know with absolute certainty that he would never return, no matter how much she wouldn't be able to accept it.

But this? This disappearance—like her father's—all over again?

This is death while living.

It's slowly poisoning her. The lack of news from Haroun, the restlessness of staying home with the knowledge that he's somewhere out there, his payments and her memories the only proof of his existence.

But in a way, they're not so different at all. Death and departure—with both there are torturous memories haunting one for an entire lifetime, promising to destroy them.

As they are destroying Zoya Zameer.

She had been destroyed once before. But it had never hurt this much. She had divorced her ex-husband and occupied this home for weeks during her *'iddah*. She lived in silence, her heart pleading for her father to come home. However, even then, her father's lack of love her entire life had trained her not to expect anything from him when it mattered most.

It had destroyed her, yet she had been able to rebound from it.

Today, she's standing on the same battlefield, but fighting a different war. Alone with her thoughts all over again, monsters and demons creeping into her life's every crevice, memories tearing her apart.

The same battlefield, but an entirely different war.

All the people in her life that Zoya has cared about have left her. Surely this means that there is something about her which makes people want to leave. Which makes it hard to stay.

It all started with her mother, who birthed her and died the next minute from the pain of labor. Leaving Zoya behind to be raised in the hands of a bitter and heartbroken father, who was unable to even look at his daughter without being reminded of the woman he loved being taken from him.

Then he left, too. Her father, whom Zoya had loved and tried to make him love her. But no matter how hard he tried to maintain his façade, he couldn't shake the anguish from his eyes every time he looked at his daughter.

And when he chose a husband for her and later found out what kind of man Farhan Hussain was, he fled. Too ashamed to show his daughter his face.

Then Haroun. *Oh, Haroun.* Zoya presses a fist against her mouth to contain the sobs. Haroun had entered her storm of life like a ray of sunshine, like the rainbow after rain.

And just as quickly, he had left, too.

She cannot go after him. She cannot. She has spent an entire lifetime running after people; is it not time for someone to hold her dear in their lives? Is it not time for her to discover her importance in other people's lives?

If the one person she has loved so ardently in her life cannot find the strength to run back to her, she will know that she has truly failed. At all of her twisted ideals of sidling up to men to remind them of her importance, to not be neglected.

If the one person she loved with all her heart is gone, who is left to stay?

~

One night, Zoya wakes suddenly, flinging the covers off of herself. She breathes harshly, searching the room in the bright light, but there's no sign of the person in her dream. She begins to cry and Mumtaz wakes, worriedly glancing at her before realizing that Zoya was dreaming. She tries to coax her back to sleep but Zoya opens her mouth, attempting to speak. Mumtaz pushes the pen and pad towards her, but Zoya shakes her head and takes a long, heaving breath.

A strange feeling appears in her throat, one she has stopped growing accustomed to over the past couple of weeks living voiceless. One her vocal therapist continuously tried to instill in her. The feeling tingles in her throat, and she takes another deep breath. Her heart gives permission to her brain and finally, finally, Zoya Zameer speaks.

"Haroun," she whispers hoarsely before she clamps a hand over her mouth, rushes to the bathroom, and throws up in the sink yet again.

Mumtaz hurries after her, patting Zoya's back as she retches. There is a pitiful look on the elderly woman's face—she has become accustomed to this scene over the past couple of weeks. Out of habit, Mumtaz asks if anything was wrong with the food Zoya ate. Zoya shakes her head and presses her forehead against the cool wall, attempting to redirect her body's temperature.

In the morning, Zoya is checked by a doctor, who prods her in various places and asks many strange questions. She runs some tests, observes the results, and returns with a wide smile on her face. The doctor congratulates Zoya, and Mumtaz lets out a happy laugh, kissing Zoya's forehead and resting a gentle hand against her stomach. Zoya sits there mutely, too shocked by the news to react.

Then she cries.

Her hoarse sobs worry the doctor, but Mumtaz simply watches Zoya with grieved eyes, too saddened to explain Zoya's outburst to the doctor.

At night, Zoya absentmindedly looks at the date on the calendar and withers away from it as if it is made of fire. Because this was the day that she married *him* seven years ago—the day that she married Farhan Hussain.

She locks herself in the bathroom, crying and muffling her screams so as not to wake Mumtaz. But the elderly woman wakes and ceaselessly knocks on the door, begging Zoya to come out.

At the breakfast table in the morning, Zoya is picking at her food, her cheek in her hand. Suddenly, she asks Mumtaz in a raspy voice, "Do we have sleeping pills?" She has to clear her throat to help her voice adjust to being used again. Even her maid's eyes are wide; she is unused to hearing Zoya's voice after so long.

Mumtaz eyes the dark circles under Zoya's eyes and says. "Yes, *bibi*."

"Okay. Can I please have one?"

"It might not be best for you to take pills in this state—"

"Mumtaz."

After a moment's hesitation, Mumtaz nods and turns to do as she is told.

"Wait," Zoya says with furrowed brows. "Why do we have sleeping pills?"

"Oh, Aman usually has a hard time falling asleep," Mumtaz says casually as she refers to the doorman.

Zoya's face scrunches up. "Hard time falling asleep? . . ." she mumbles to herself. Mumtaz nods and retreats into the kitchen.

I never knew that, thinks Zoya. *How come I didn't know that?*

Later, when Zoya is leaving the manor to take a walk around her garden, she stops in front of Aman, who gazes at her with the same expression as always. Apologetic, grieved. "You never told me that you have trouble sleeping. For a while now?" she says this accusingly, as if Aman *should* have told her. But there is also an expression of hurt on her face.

A spark of surprise flashes in Aman's eyes upon hearing Zoya's voice again. He raises his eyebrows at her question. "Uh, *bibi*, I didn't think it mattered."

"Didn't think it mattered?" Zoya says tiredly, rubbing her eyes. "Of course it matters." She pauses, calculating her next words. "You're going to the doctor with me. We're going to get you medicine that actually works."

Aman looks baffled. "Uh, thank you, but there's really no need for that. My follow up appointment is next week—"

"We're going now. Come on." She gestures for him to get seated in the car.

He obliges, albeit hesitantly.

He signals to the security guard by the gate to take his post as he settles in Zoya's car. She wraps a scarf around her head and perches sunglasses on her nose in a makeshift disguise.

While Zoya drives, Aman continues to glance confusedly at her. She breaks the thick silence between them. "What is it that won't let you sleep?" The words come out broken and rasped, her throat still unused to sound.

"I'm sorry?"

"What's bothering you?"

"Nothing, *bibi*."

A scornful, hoarse laugh escapes her. Having experienced quite fully the disturbance caused by insomnia, Zoya won't fall for his "nothing."

"Tell me, Aman."

He scratches his beard, expression anxious. "I—"

"Is it me?" Zoya laughs mirthlessly. "I know I've been terrible to all of you."

"No, *bibi*, you're not at fault."

She gives him a curious expression through the rearview mirror. "What do you mean?"

Aman hesitates. "You really don't remember me, do you?"

Zoya has to swerve rapidly to avoid hitting a car—she is so surprised by his words. "Excuse me?"

"You don't remember me?"

Zoya observes him through the mirror again. "What do you mean, '*remember*?' You've been my doorman for like six years, if that's what you mean."

"And before that?"

"Before?" Now Zoya is extremely baffled. "I didn't know you before then."

"I was hired by Farhan *saab* before I was hired by you, *bibi*."

Zoya slams on the brake, earning a honk of disapproval from behind her. "What?"

Aman glances at the surrounding cars warily. "When you got rid of all the servants, you got rid of me, too. But I don't think you remembered me, because you were looking for a doorman and had me hired again."

Zoya's mind is reeling; she can't seem to process his words.

"I can't"—he takes a deep breath—"I have a hard time sleeping because I can't get over what he did to you."

Zoya glances at him in the rear view mirror again, shocked. His face is scrunched up, worry lines etched into his forehead.

"What?" Zoya breathes.

"He hurt you over and over again, and I was too much of a coward to do anything about it." The distress in Aman's voice is plain and clear. Zoya parks in front of the doctor's office and turns to face her doorman.

He looks overcome by anxiety and shame, and a strange, unfamiliar pang of sorrow twists in Zoya's heart. She finally begins to understand why he is always so antsy and upset around her. She's often played it off as fear, but now there's no mistaking the remorse in his eyes.

"Aman, it wasn't your fault," she says quietly, suddenly all too familiar with the guilt twisting the features of his face.

Zoya remembers her own words then, seemingly from ages ago. *Zoya Zameer kabhi kisi ko maaf nahi karti.*

"But I didn't do anything to help," Aman says. "I didn't do anything to try to stop him." He pauses a moment, then whispers, "I heard your screams, and I still didn't do anything."

Zoya fights off the tears pricking her eyes. "And you couldn't have. People in power know nobody will dare confront them." She says this with a bitterness in her mouth as she remembers her own use of power, and the way she has wielded it to harm others.

Aman inhales sharply, lines etched into his forehead.

"Aman, there was really no way you could have done anything about it without risking your own safety. So stop beating yourself up over it." He doesn't seem the least bit less distressed, so Zoya adds, "The fact that you're so anxious about this tells me how guilty you feel, and it's okay. Don't ruin your life over it. *Jao. Maaf kiya.* I've forgiven you. It was never your fault, anyway."

Aman rubs his hand along his beard, anguish marring his features. He shakes his head almost absentmindedly, as if he is unable to dispel what has been haunting him for years with just a few of Zoya's words.

She knows it may take him weeks, months, or years to even come close to forgiving himself. She now knows what that feels like all too well. But if she can do this for somebody else—if she can ease Aman's distress in the slightest after all the horrible things she has done in her life—perhaps her heart will heal. Perhaps God will stop punishing her.

Then Zoya exits the vehicle and opens the car door for her doorman.

Fifty-Seven

~

WHEN *Ammi*, AISHA, AND Naima come again, Zoya rushes upstairs. She cannot speak to them. Not now. Not ever.

The last time she saw them, they had lovingly wrapped their arms around her and told her how happy she made Haroun.

She may die of guilt if she faces them now.

But just to make herself feel better, just to lessen the guilt that coils itself around her like barbed wire every day, she thinks of why she had to do it. Of why she had to take Haroun Suleiman.

In the past several years of her life, she has only taken, taken, taken by force. She has bribed people with her money, has mocked them with her wealth and status, has manipulated them into giving her what she wants.

And she has always ended up getting what she wants.

Zoya never attained anything without force, she realizes. She constantly manipulated her way into fulfilling her desires, starting with taking Farhan's investments and the *mahr* he gave her upon marriage to build herself up quicker than most people would be able to. Using Zaki Ahmed as a stepladder for her career before she disposed of him. Building a career and manipulating her way into making her employees faithful to her and her company.

Integrity, integrity, integrity. She had always drilled this into her employees' heads, constantly lashing out at them if they didn't hold integrity in their work ethic.

And *her* work ethic? What about all the things *she* had done? What about the threats she made to her workers to cut from their paychecks if they didn't work properly? What about the bribes she made, the people she fired without reason, the way she treated her employees?

Even the way she used Zaki Ahmed to make herself a name?

Zoya blinks then, coming to a forceful realization. One that hits her like a ton of bricks.

She has been a hypocrite.

Always doing what she had hated being done to her. Treating people needlessly harsh, using her past as an excuse for her attitude, toying with people's emotions.

Then, *ah.* Then Haroun came along, and she toyed with him the most. She did things she thought were good for him, never stopping to consider his ideals. She played around with him and his morals when he first started working, when she gave him a promotion to keep him closer to her even when he flinched at her overly friendly nature towards him, when she threatened managers to get his sisters better jobs.

Then she manipulated him worst of all by taking his love by force. By coercing him into marrying a 'dying' woman. By forcing his love for her, even when she knew he was not ready. Even when she knew he was emotionally unstable and reeling from the after effects of his broken engagement. She took advantage of his brokenness and yanked him towards her.

Like a puppeteer would to a helpless, unwitting puppet.

Zoya told herself that she had to do it, that she couldn't bear the thought of life without Haroun. And she knew no one would ever know her and love her by choice, so she felt that she had to do the next best thing.

Forcefully take and take and take. And be okay with taking and never receiving.

At first, Zoya felt that she had fallen in love with Haroun Suleiman.

Now that she looks back at it, it was more than just love. In her there had been a growing desire to protect, maintain, and nurture what she felt was the last remnant of purity in her cruel world; and the only way she felt she could do that was by keeping him all to herself.

Zoya had never felt like she *needed* anybody until she met Haroun. Her life had been filled with rage and fire and anger and harshness, and Haroun was the softness and gentleness that she never had the opportunity to experience. She needed him like she needed air.

He was the water to her fire. The calm to her rage. He was hope, love, compassion—all things she had been robbed of in life.

He was the eye of her storm.

So of course she had to have him. Of course she did—even if it was by force. Even if in the end, it was by breaking his pure and gentle heart.

Zoya drove Haroun to his breaking point. For all the threats she gave him that the world was an evil place and held no mercy for good people like him, for all her warnings for him to stop being so good because this cruel world would rob him of it, *she* had been the one to destroy him.

Zoya Zameer drove the man who seldom broke to the point of no return.

Fifty-Eight

~

ZOYA CANNOT STOP THINKING about what Aman told her. The guilt on his face as he finally admitted what had been plaguing him for years is toying with her emotions. What makes it worse is that she has always treated him nastily, criticizing him every day as she passes by, just for the sake of it.

She finally understands the meaning of the agonized look in his eyes every time looked at her.

Zoya stares outside the window of her room and thinks of what a horrible person she has been. Rubbing circles on her stomach, she ponders over what a terrible example she will be for anyone who comes into this world.

As she is drowning in self-loathing, Zoya Zameer—CEO of Zameer Co. and one of the most renowned women in the United States of America—passes out on her bedroom floor. She only wakes when a freaked out Mumtaz splashes water over her face and shoves medicine down her throat.

The next morning, Zoya's heart squeezes painfully as she watches Mumtaz. This elderly woman—whom Zoya has never respected and has always harshly reprimanded—has been forced to become Zoya's mother.

"I deserve this," Zoya rasps, eyes on the floor. "For all the bad things I've done, I deserve all that is happening to me."

Mumtaz throws her a look of pure shock, then shakes her head. "No, *bibi*. You're a good person."

Zoya's eyes widen in bewilderment. "No, Mumtaz. You're wrong. I've hurt so many people. I've even hurt *you* and you're still being nice to me after I've continuously put you down." She grabs Mumtaz's sleeve. "It's because there is goodness in *you,* too." Her voice breaks. She pulls Mumtaz closer to her. "There is goodness in everyone except for me."

Zoya lifts Mumtaz's arm and begins to examine it. The maid's expression contorts in sadness as she witnesses her once-strong mistress unraveling so destructively.

"Is there good blood that flows in you that doesn't flow in me?" Zoya whispers, turning Mumtaz's arm over.

Mumtaz's lips begin to tremble.

Zoya continues, "Maybe he poisoned me with his evil nature, so now I can never be good again."

"Who, *bibi?*" Mumtaz asks shakily.

"That devil. Farhan," Zoya explains. "He injected his poison in me every time he beat me and yelled at me, then sweet talked me in front of everyone. That's why *Haroun* left me, too," Zoya says quietly, finally letting go of Mumtaz's arm as she comes to this realization. She begins to examine her own arms and hands, which have begun to tremble.

"If I were to count on each hand, on each finger, on each part of all my fingers, I wouldn't even come close to counting the people I've wronged, the people I've ruthlessly hurt." Zoya's hands begin to shake violently, and Mumtaz's features crumple in concern. "For all my talk of not tolerating injustice, I wouldn't even be able to come *close* to counting all the wrongs I've committed. *I* was the one committing injustice, hypocritically claiming I couldn't tolerate it." Zoya's face contorts in pain as she begins to sob, staring at her hands accusingly.

Mumtaz reaches forward and grabs her shaking hands, trying to calm her down. "God would never forgive me for all the things

I've done," Zoya blubbers. "I've hurt too many people."

Gently, Mumtaz says, "That's not true. Allah forgives anyone who is willing to turn to Him and ask for forgiveness."

Zoya shakes her head. "Not me. Not me. I'm a devil. He turned me into a devil. Farhan made me a devil. And now, like the devil, I'll always be away from God's mercy."

"Allah's name *Ar-Raheem* means The Most Merciful," Mumtaz says, smiling softly. "Allah will forgive you. Allah forgives anyone who turns to Him in repentance."

Zoya begins to cry loudly. "I'll never go to paradise, either. Paradise lies under the feet of our mothers, right? Maybe that's why mine birthed me and passed away. So that all my avenues to paradise are closed, because paradise doesn't want people like me."

"That's not true," Mumtaz says. "There is never a single way to get to paradise, sweetheart. Paradise will be full of people who were once sinners and then turned to Allah in repentance. That's what this *dunya* is for."

"Haroun left me, too," Zoya wails, her voice rising in hysteria. Mumtaz's words don't seem to have the intended effect, because Zoya begins clawing at her arms. "He left me because there is good blood in him but there is no good blood in me!" Mumtaz tries to stop her, but Zoya continues to strike her arms. "He has so much good blood, and he transfers it to everyone he meets, but somehow he missed me and I'm still poisoned by the bad blood Farhan put in me. And Haroun left me because I have no good blood!"

Zoya turns hysterical, continuously shaking her head and rocking back and forth. Aman rushes inside at the commotion and attempts to calm Zoya down, but she pushes his arms away and grasps Mumtaz's sleeve. Zoya looks up at her maid with pain-stricken eyes and says, "Please ask God to forgive me." before she collapses on the floor.

~

Later, when Zoya has calmed down, she stares at the smoke rising from the chamomile tea in front of her. "Mumtaz," she begins hesitantly. "How does someone ask for forgiveness?"

Her maid glances at her. "From God or from people?"

Zoya is not ready to face God. She doesn't think that God will not want to see her after all that she's done. So she says, "People."

"Be sincere. *Mukhlis.* And if they get angry at you, acknowledge that their emotions are valid. It takes courage and time for people to forgive, just as it takes time for people to ask for forgiveness."

"What if . . . what if they never forgive?"

Mumtaz ponders over this for a moment. "If anyone has even the smallest ounce of goodness in their heart, *eventually* they will forgive. That doesn't mean they'll forget what happened or be on good terms with the person they've forgiven again, just that they'll acknowledge that it's time to let go of their bitterness. Because it takes a lot of strength to forgive." Her voice is wise, carrying years of experience. "And of course, it takes time."

Hearing such wisdom from the woman reminds Zoya of Haroun, and how he used to advise Zoya in the same gentle manner.

She fights to keep her tears at bay.

"What if you have done too many wrongs and hurt too many people?" Zoya murmurs, her voice breaking. "My faults are as great as . . . the water in the sea. If I wanted to fix every wrong I've committed, I would spend an entire lifetime chasing after people, some of whom are not even around anymore."

Mumtaz smiles. "Do you know how forgiving Allah is? How easy He makes it for us? If we say four words after each prayer twenty times—*Subhan Allah wa bi hamdihi*—our sins, even if they are as great as the foam of the sea, will be forgiven."

Shock envelops Zoya; she didn't know this. Has God made it so simple for humans to repent?

The more she learns about Islam, the more terrified she becomes. She doesn't know how she will rectify all the errors she's committed—with herself, with others, and with her relationship with God.

"I want to make a list," Zoya says quietly. "A list of all the people I've hurt or wronged. And I want to ask them for forgiveness."

Mumtaz gives her a soft smile. "Okay, *bibi.*"

"And I want you to stop calling me *bibi*—I'm about half your age. Call me Zoya." She hesitates. "Or . . . *beta.*"

A smile blooms on the maid's face. "Of course."

Zoya works on her list all morning, stopping only to eat and use the bathroom. She spends hours reflecting on all the people she has hurt.

Initially, she comes up with a very small list of people—Haroun, Aisha, Naima, and *Ammi*. But after some more contemplation, she adds more names, eyebrows scrunching as she works. The first name she writes after her in-laws is Farhan Malik. Then Sameer, Flora, Mumtaz, Aman, her other maids and security guards, people from work, the two managers of Haroun's sisters . . . and many more people.

As Zoya works, Mumtaz unobtrusively makes her presence known from time to time. She dusts the furniture, replaces the wilting flowers in the vases, settles plates of food here and there.

And every time her eyes fall on Zoya, there is a proud smile on the maid's face.

Fifty-Nine

"Say, 'O Allah, Owner of Authority, You give authority to whoever You please and remove it from who You please; You honor whoever You please and disgrace who You please—all good is in Your Hands. Surely You (alone) are Most Capable of everything.'" (Qur'an 3:26)

~

AT NIGHT, ZOYA TAKES a different route through the manor. She circles back to one of the older rooms, one she doesn't usually frequent. When she enters, she sees storage boxes piled in one corner. Drifting over to them, Zoya opens the flap to check the contents.

Photographs.

Photographs on photographs of the prestigious Zoya Zameer in all her expensive, eye-catching clothing. Clothing that forces the onlooker to keep their eyes on her, to undress her with their gaze.

Zoya shivers as she looks at these photographs now, wondering how she ever felt comfortable in these clothes.

How brazen she had been! She took every opportunity to flirt with every man she met just to prove her own sick perceptions of humanity to herself. To prove that every man was as Farhan Hussain had been: lustful and manipulative.

Then Haroun had walked into her life and made her stumble upon every breath, question every thought she ever had about the male species. He never did any of the things she believed were innate in every man, never showed even an inkling of the destructive lust she believed every man couldn't control.

She had deprived every man of human emotion, until Haroun Suleiman had stumbled into her life. He silently objected to her perceptions of men, as well as her perceptions of Muslims.

How stupid had she been? In testing mankind's capacity for lust, she flushed her dignity and self-respect down the toilet. She shamelessly bat her lashes at every man she met, using their muddled senses as an opportunity to walk closer, place a finger at her chin, and cock her head to the side—the way she knew drove men crazy.

How insanely stupid she had been!

Zoya picks up a photograph that catches her attention. It's from the Desi World Fashion Show, seemingly ages ago. Zoya is talking to a distressed-looking Haroun, whose gaze is lowered to the ground.

His posture brings tears to her eyes. How she had mocked him for his morals and ideals! How she had thought it comical to test his patience by walking closer to him and behaving indecently every time he was in her presence, just to set him on edge.

It's a wonder he even agreed to marry her.

And when he told her numerous times that Zameer Co. and the parties and the free mixing were just not his scene, Zoya had become amused. Who wouldn't love a lively, vibrant, and action-packed life full of entertainment, drama, and flurry?

As Zoya stares at the photographs, she finally understands why Haroun had been the way he was. He had been lied to by his father and had such a hard time finding faith again—life hadn't been easy on him—but he remained steadfast on his path.

Yet Zoya manipulated him as well.

She recalls how he had worn a casual t-shirt on the day of his interview, probably hoping that even though he needed it, he wouldn't receive the job because it was not the kind of life he wanted.

When he got the job anyway, he had been politely aloof for the first few days, probably hoping that this would make people not like him, and thus he would be told to take his leave.

But when he realized that there was probably no other way out, he threw himself into his work as much as he could without compromising his values. He supposed that if he was doing the job, then he might as well do it properly. He worked as hard as he could to secure money for his mother's operation. He tried to maintain all the dignity and morality that he could, even while his environment was constantly testing him.

He had been distant with his CEO, hoping that she would dislike him. But Zoya hadn't—in fact, his behavior had only piqued her interest.

So Haroun stayed. And the bags under his eyes became considerably darker, and he exuded even more exhaustion. His unexpected promotion brought him no joy.

Because his work at Zameer—his idle work which lacked purpose—went against his very core. It went against what he stood for, what he felt that the driving factor of his existence was. And he couldn't take it.

Zoya only now understands.

She wishes that she could hear his voice. Just once. She wishes that she could tell him how sorry she is—for being so selfish and for not understanding his position. She wishes that she could stroke the hair away from his tired eyes every time he tried to explain to her— in guarded and concealed words—that he needed something more invigorating, that his life's purpose was not being met.

She wishes that she could see Haroun Suleiman just one more time.

Sixty

"He breaks you to build you. Deprives you to give you. This pain in your heart was created to make you yearn less for this life. And to yearn more for Jannah." —Reclaim Your Heart by Yasmin Mogahed

~

THAT NIGHT, ZOYA TRAILS around the prayer room Haroun used to frequent. She rubs circles over her stomach absentmindedly, glancing around at the furniture. It's almost as if she can feel his presence, see the light in his eyes, feel his hands in her hair. Gently stroking.

She trails over to the prayer mat a friend gifted to Haroun. It's blue and gold, with an embroidery of the *Ka'bah* on it that brought tears to his eyes. Zoya never understood why he was so emotional over it.

She settles on the prayer mat, leaning down to attempt to inhale Haroun's smell. Fighting off tears when she discovers that it's long gone, just like him.

Everywhere that Zoya turns is torture. She sees ghosts of him flitting around corners, occupying the places he frequented most, appearing briefly when she is at her worst.

Zoya's lips tremble.

She has probably cried more in the past few weeks than she has cried in her entire life. Strong-willed Zoya Zameer, brought to her knees by an ache in her heart.

Suddenly feeling as if she's not alone, Zoya raises her head to look around the room. There is no fear in her heart; only confusion.

Her eyes zero in on a painting hung on the wall, which contains the same shade of gold embossed on the prayer mat. In Arabic calligraphy, it reads, *Al-Muhaymin*.

Haroun had said that this one word had pulled him out of the depths of faithlessness and despair. What had it meant?

The Guardian, The Protector, The Overseer.

Zoya presses her lips together to contain herself, but to no avail. It has been too long. She has fought this growing feeling inside her for too long—this feeling of needing something more, something greater. Even her body is tired of constantly struggling; all it wants now is to give up, all it wants now is to let go.

To return home.

Zoya bends down, feeling as if a gravitational force pulls her forehead to the ground. A whimper escapes her.

And finally, finally, with a deep, heaving breath, Zoya opens up to her Lord.

The proud, arrogant, successful CEO Zoya Zameer—in a heap on the floor, bowed down before her *Rabb*, her Lord, her Master

Who would ever imagine the angry, haughty Zoya Zameer to prostrate in *sujood* to her Creator? Who *could* ever imagine?

Zoya is made from dirt, just like the rest of humanity.

She's quite a sight to behold—her head bent down in *sujood*, tears pouring out of her eyes, all of her accomplishments and successes behind her.

She doesn't care that she is *the* Zoya Zameer, the face of the contemporary fashion industry. *The* Zoya Zameer with the elegant dresses and the impeccable makeup. *The* Zoya Zameer no one dares speak up in front of . . . except for one person.

That one person is gone, and who knows if he's ever coming back.

At this moment, she is only a slave to her Master. She is only a creation of her Lord. Like eight billion other people on earth, she is only human. She is nothing more.

Abruptly touched by her insignificance in the vast universe,

Zoya's shoulders begin to shake with the force of her emotions. She has been put in her place by her *Rabb*. Yet He's so forgiving, so merciful, that He still allowed her this sweet moment of time in her life where she was absolutely happy.

She deserves the loss—she knows she does.

And now she finally understands.

He took from her what she loved the most to force her to turn to Him. She has been fighting a connection with Him for so long, and her Lord finally turned her heart to Him.

Zoya weeps and weeps.

The world doesn't *need* her. The one person she had cared about so deeply, the one person whom she had willingly loved after her father left, has also left her.

How ironic.

With her head touching the ground, Zoya is suddenly hit by the thought that she is nothing. If she dies at this moment, no one will *need* her. What has she done to make anyone need her? Nothing. All she has been successful in doing is using her assets to hurt others.

What a shame. What a shame.

Zoya is not *needed* by anyone. Only her Creator loves her, she realizes with a loud sob. Only He listens. She cries even more as she makes the prayer that has been plaguing her heart for a while, "Lord, p-please forgive me."

She cannot say more; how is she to ask her Lord for forgiveness for all the horrible things she's done? She remembers Preeti, whom she had so mercilessly fired in front of everyone, fanning herself with her *dupatta* as she did. She remembers Flora, whom she was fond of and threw out primarily to look good in front of Haroun (which didn't work out anyway). She remembers Farhan Malik, whom she had publicly humiliated him on live TV simply because he carried the same name as her abusive ex-husband—a trait which he had absolutely no control over. She remembers the managers she bribed, the young girl Jadyn whom she ruthlessly ridiculed, the countless people she fired without reason, the people she brought to tears with her arrogance.

The countless things *she* deemed insignificant, which she can neither name nor remember now, but they had hurt others beyond measure

Most of all, she is truly sorry to Haroun Suleiman. For falling in love with him and deceiving him. For making him fall in love with her, then breaking his heart.

Zoya Zameer lifts her head and raises her hands to the sky, tears streaming down her face like rivers. "God," she cries. "Allah. I have done horrible, speechless things. Forgive me, Lord. Forgive me, *please*—"

Unable to say any more, she touches her head to the ground again, humbling herself. It has taken her years and breaking a strong man's heart to realize that she means nothing to no one, and only God knows the state of her heart. Only *He* has stayed through all the turbulence in her life—she has just been too blind to see Him.

Zoya will never be able to face anyone again after the crimes she has committed. She spent too much time justifying her behavior, claiming that she was heartbroken from her father's lack of love and from her ex-husband's abusive nature. "They made me like this," she frequently said.

But what had Haroun told her? That God is the ultimate Sovereign, but He's given humanity free will. Zoya has blamed God for all the bad that has happened in her life, not pausing for a single second to reflect on her own actions, as well as the consequences of those actions.

Haroun told her that humans have the ability to make choices.

Haroun had been through a lot, but he didn't let that change his character. He made choices that forced him to become a better version of himself, every day. He didn't let his experiences change his heart.

Zoya Zameer curls into a ball on the floor, in one of the rooms of her big, big manor. Who can tell that she is the CEO of one of the largest businesses in the United States of America?

She has finally understood her place.

Sixty-One

~

SLOWLY, SLOWLY, ZOYA ZAMEER'S prayers become less mechanical. The ache in her heart is slowly soothed by her conviction in *Al-Muhaymin*. Her hands rise more frequently and with more purpose on the prayer mat. She begins to take interest in learning the other names of Allah. She reads about His attributes, which she has been too stubborn to recognize. Learning them, she only grows more amazed by Him.

Of course, there is still a wariness in her heart around Him; it's been so long since she's felt a connection with Him, and Zoya is unaccustomed to trying to close the distance after such a long time. Not just with Allah, but with humans, too. She has often brushed people off after a single bad experience.

Rectifying an abandoned relationship definitely requires effort, but Zoya is determined. She feels that her Lord has been waiting for her to turn to Him, to cry in front of Him, to be vulnerable in front of Him.

Zoya ponders over what a strange relationship it is. She has avoided God for years, but after one night of crying in front of Him and opening up to Him, a strange tranquility has descended in her heart.

The peace she felt that she was always missing.

Now, when her tears fall, they are not full of pain. Instead, they are full of relief.

She finally has some One to let the pain out on.

One morning, when Zoya is eating breakfast, she thinks of how Haroun used to split his omelet in fours and spread ketchup over it. He frequently fed her with his own hands, telling her that the Prophet Muhammad said feeding one's wife was an act that would be rewarded in and of itself. At the memory, the ache returns to her heart—the searing ache she has become all-too-familiar with. It teases her by prodding at her barely stitched wounds.

But as soon as the pain comes, something else happens as well.

The pain dulls.

That same strange tranquility settles in her heart, blanketing her pain.

She suddenly thinks of how she always regarded Haroun as her unshakeable mountain, her pillar of strength.

Was she wrong? Mountains don't shake. Pillars don't crumble.

Yet Haroun Suleiman broke down in the worst way possible. He didn't shake; he disintegrated entirely. He didn't crumble; he fell apart entirely.

Can any human be utterly unshakeable? A column of absolute strength?

No, Zoya realizes suddenly. It's not possible, and she's only now recognized it. She used to think of herself—of the *incredible* Zoya Zameer—as someone who possessed these qualities.

But she fell apart.

Then she thought that Haroun Suleiman—sweet, patient, strong Haroun—possessed these qualities.

But he fell apart as well.

So who is left to harbor these attributes? Who is left to be her unwavering strength? Who is she supposed to turn to in times of pain and distress, as well as happiness and elation?

Zoya recalls another name of God: *Al-Qawwiy*, The All-Strong.

Her eyes prick with sharp tears as she finally understands Who truly provides and Who truly supports and Who truly stays.

God. Allah.

She feels as if her Lord is giving her a chance at redemption. She feels as if Haroun's absence is not a punishment but a test, an opportunity for her to grow closer to her Lord. To hope that with His mercy, he will forgive her sins.

So she grasps the rope of opportunity hovering midair in front of her, and she hopes that the climb won't leave her too breathless.

And even if it does, only when she gets to the top will she tend to her injuries.

~

Taking a deep breath, Zoya pulls out the list of people she wants to ask forgiveness from. Her eyes rove over the names, settling on the one whose house she will go to first.

Not *Ammi* and the sisters. Not Haroun. To face them, she needs much more courage than she has right now. And she doesn't know if she's ready to hear about Haroun—about where he is and whether anyone has seen him.

Instead, she is going to someone she has done a lot of wrong to.

She exits her manor, greets Aman, and begins to walk towards her car. Raheem rushes forward to drive, but Zoya waves him off. "No need today. I want to do this all on my own."

Zoya enters the directions on Google Maps and drives off. Her hands tremble on the steering wheel, but she's determined to do this, no matter how difficult it will be and no matter how ashamed she will be to face this person.

His house has a cozy appearance; it's light brown, with bright bouquets of flowers potted along the steps. Zoya rings the doorbell, clasping her hands in front of her as she waits.

Farhan Malik appears ten seconds later. He takes one look at Zoya, eyes bulging out of his head, and stammers, "M-Ms. Zoya?

Zoya takes him in. Disheveled hair, scruffy beard, worry lines. Perhaps what is most unsettling is the shock and fear in his eyes.

Fear.

She has done nothing but make this man tremble and cower in front of her. Like a tyrant forcing the helpless to grovel, she has endlessly browbeaten Farhan Malik with her poisonous words and merciless behavior.

"Ms. Zoya?" he repeats, one hand on the door. "Uh . . . do you want to come in?" He is hesitant, unsure of how to engage with the Zoya Zameer standing in front of him. The Zoya he hasn't seen in two months—the Zoya *nobody* has seen in two months.

Zoya nods. "Yes," she manages to say. "Please."

She enters, and he closes the front door before leading her into the living room. His voice shakes when he tells her to sit while he gets her a drink. Before he leaves, she detects the mixed emotions on his face—curiosity, shock, anxiety, and confusion. Zoya has to give him credit—he tries to remain composed.

When he returns with a tray of haphazardly strewn cookies and apple cider, Zoya takes one look at his trembling hands and bursts into tears.

"Oh, no," Farhan says uncomfortably. "Uhh . . ."

Zoya continues to cry, wiping her cheeks hastily. She attempts to speak, but her throat tightens.

"You don't like apple cider? I think we have orange juice, too," Farhan says nervously, setting the tray down and sitting across from her. When Zoya continues to cry, he mumbles a curse and gestures to the tray. "Would you prefer other cookies? We have Oreos, too, if you like those better."

Zoya shakes her head back and forth, and eventually Farhan's nervous rambling dies down. He breathes a deep sigh. "Ms. Zoya, what's going on? Where have you been?"

Zoya rubs her eyes, cursing the tears that have come at the most inopportune of times. "I wanted to talk to you."

"Okay," he states, still confused. "Where have you *been,* though?"

"Home," she replies simply. "I haven't gotten the courage to leave. And I'm not sure I want to anymore."

"You know, everyone at the company has been worried sick. And people are *angry* . . . I'm not sure if you've been keeping up with the news . . ." He pauses, the look on his face telling her that he doesn't know if he should continue. But this is Farhan Malik, so he barrels forward. "Protests, strikes, all that stuff. The media's in a frenzy. Bill's been going crazy—he and Ibitoye are the unofficial COO's. *Everybody's* been going crazy; we're practically jobless." He pauses once more, regret flashing across his face. "I mean, I'm not sure what's been going on with you. I'm sure you had . . . your reasons," he ends lamely.

Zoya furrows her brows and shifts the conversation. "Have you not been in contact with Haroun?" Saying his name out loud stabs her heart; she doesn't think that she deserves to talk about him after what she has done to him.

An immediate wariness takes over Farhan. "Barely," he says. "He told me he was leaving for a bit and that he didn't know when he would be back. And that he's keeping his distance from everybody."

Zoya's shoulders shake. She has done this to a man who visited his family constantly and made it a point to spend time with his friends frequently. "When was the last time you spoke to him?"

Farhan scratches his beard. "Probably a couple weeks ago. He said he needed time. And that he wanted to be alone." He rubs a hand across his face. "Haven't talked to him since."

Zoya doesn't know if she's imagining it, but she detects an accusatory tone in Farhan's voice. And why shouldn't it be accusatory? She took his best friend away from him. She took Haroun Suleiman away from everybody who cared about him.

That's why she needs to say what she's here to say.

Farhan interrupts her thoughts. "Have you really not left your house this entire time?"

Zoya shakes her head.

"So . . . you left your house to meet *me*?" There is clear bafflement in his voice. "Can I ask"—he hesitates—"what happened between you and Haroun?"

Zoya raises her eyes to his. There is genuine concern and curiosity on his face. He truly has no idea what went down between them.

Which means that even though Zoya destroyed Haroun

Suleiman, he still found it in himself to guard her honor and remain silent about her betrayal.

Truly, Zoya does not deserve that man.

Her eyes lower to the ground. "I broke his trust. In a really bad way."

Farhan is quiet for a few moments, then, "What could have been *so bad* . . ." He trails off, probably realizing that he is invading her privacy.

Zoya sighs. "I lied to him about myself. He thought he was marrying . . . somebody else." This is the most she can say without burying herself deeper in quicksand.

"To make Haroun want to go away for such a long time . . . it must have been really bad." There's an edge to Farhan's voice.

Zoya begins to cry again. Loud, heaving sobs that bring the discomfort back on Farhan's face. "I didn't have a choice," she weeps. "I didn't have a choice."

"There's always a choice before ruining somebody's life," he says quietly.

His words send shock waves throughout Zoya. They throw her back into a different time, when she was extremely haughty and arrogant. When she rubbed her power in people's faces to get what she wanted, or to prove a point.

Farhan's words remind her of when she told Sumaiya the very same thing. When the two of them had been sitting in her car, a weeping Sumaiya told Zoya that *she had no other choice.* Zoya had screamed that there was always a choice before ruining somebody's life.

Another person to add to the forgiveness list, Zoya thinks solemnly.

She raises her eyes to Farhan's, wanting to say words that will erase the distress from his face. But she doesn't know how to. "Farhan," she begins, sniffing. "I'm . . . so sorry, Farhan."

He looks at her for a moment, wariness flitting across his features, before he sighs.

"Really, Farhan," Zoya forces herself to continue. "I think I could spend an entire lifetime and still never be able to express how *sorry* I am for everything I've done to you. For treating you the way I did, for keeping you constantly on your toes around me. All because of a name that was never your fault to begin with." Farhan's brows knit, but Zoya continues. "I'm sorry. I'm so sorry. For everything I've said to you and done to you. You didn't deserve any of it." She quiets then, unable to say more without her throat clogging up painfully.

Farhan doesn't say anything for a few moments. He simply fidgets, staring at the floor with strict intensity. He is so quiet that Zoya eventually murmurs, "Won't you say anything?"

He sighs, rubs his temples. "I know what you *want* me to say, Ms. Zoya." His eyes are guarded. "But . . . honestly, I'm not sure I can."

Zoya nods. She had expected this much from him—she had even expected him to chase her out with pitchforks and holler that she didn't deserve to show up at his doorstep after the way she had treated him.

Although his reaction is much less severe than she anticipated, it still pierces her heart—especially since this is the first time Zoya Zameer is putting aside her pride and her arrogance and actively seeking forgiveness.

Yet tranquility descends once more in her heart at having finally said the words Farhan deserves to hear. It feels as if a crushing weight has been lifted off of her.

"I understand that," Zoya finally says. "I know it's not going to be easy for you to overlook everything I've done to you. But if you find it in your heart . . ." Tears leak out of her eyes, and her quiet crying must make Farhan uncomfortable because he tightens his fists. "Please forgive me. If you find it in your heart. Please."

She stands to leave. Farhan follows suit, still quiet, and leads her out the door. When Zoya steps onto the porch, he suddenly mumbles from behind her, "Ms. Zoya?"

She turns.

Farhan hesitates, shifting his guarded eyes. "Thank you. For coming."

The words send both unexpected warmth and pleasant surprise

through Zoya. She has done so much to this man, and has mistreated him in so many ways. But he's still generous enough to offer her words of comfort, even though he's unable to forgive her right away.

Truly, she has been missing out on this goodness for a very long time.

Zoya nods, unable to speak without her voice shaking, and heads back to her car.

Farhan Malik stands with folded arms on his porch, eyes following the boss who made his life a living hell.

Yet tears still prick his eyes.

~

Zoya realizes that she has been unjust to many men in the past several years of her life. She has held them at very low standards because of the men she's known before them.

So she visits Sameer next.

Sameer freaks out when he sees her, asking a million questions and demanding a million answers. She quietly sits in front of him, and his questions only die down when she presses her palms to her eyes and begins to cry yet again.

She tells Sameer that she's sorry for constantly forcing him to do things which may have tested his limits. She tells him that she's sorry for manipulating his loyalty towards her by burdening him with questionable tasks, especially with the entire Sumaiya ordeal.

Sameer sits in front of her quietly, and when she's done blubbering, he shakes his head and tells her to pull herself together. It must have a strange effect on him to see his boss this way because he addresses her in a logical and almost angry manner, saying that he will only forgive her if she shapes up and stops crying. He tells her that life goes on even when the worst calamities hit, and she cannot afford to self-destruct every time she experiences a trial.

Zoya wipes her tears away and even manages a warped smile, but it's at odds with how she really feels. Especially since she doesn't think she deserves to be addressed this way by somebody she has challenged many times.

Sameer asks Zoya whether she will return to work, and she tells him that she's not ready yet, and swears him into secrecy about meeting her.

Zoya calls it a day and heads home, marveling over how much asking for forgiveness from only two people has taken such a toll on her.

Where will she find the strength to talk to the rest of the people on her list? How will she even approach them when just thinking of doing so causes her to tremble uncontrollably?

"*Al-Qawiyy*," she murmurs in her car over and over and over again, recalling one of Allah's names. *The Strong. The Strong. The Strong.*

Rain begins to patter against her windshield. Zoya flicks the wipers on so that it becomes easier to see the road.

For a moment, she ponders over how Allah—*Al-Qawiyy*—has given her the shelter of faith from the storm of disbelief and anger she was so caught up in before. Only when she escaped the storm did she realize why she couldn't see. Only when she witnessed the eye of the storm did she realize that she was trapped.

She suddenly remembers something that Naima once said. When Goldie died, the younger girl sat next to Zoya and shared some surprisingly intelligent insights, but there had been one thing she'd said that Zoya hadn't understood.

Until she had experienced it herself.

Naima had said, "I don't really think you can begin to establish a strong relationship with Allah unless He tests you. In times of ease, it's easy to forget Allah. But when calamity hits, that's when we realize that we need Him the most, and we want to get closer to Him then."

Zoya ponders over these words, analyzing them in microscopic detail. Indeed, there is a shocking truth to these words. Zoya had been living a luxurious, extravagant life. She had *everything*. Money, status, power, influence, beauty. All the things she thought she needed.

But she didn't have God.

She had forgotten God. So He had pulled her back to Him. He had introduced worldly, materialistic love to her, and when it was taken away from her, she discovered that only God stayed.

She had first thought that Haroun's departure was simply proof of how little luck she had in her life. But no, this had been written for her. If it hadn't happened, Zoya wouldn't have discovered her purpose, wouldn't have recognized all the wrongs she had committed in her life.

So many times, God had tried to teach her a lesson. And so many times, she had not heeded His message.

So He took what she valued the most. He took Haroun from her.

But even in gaping loss, there is gain. What had Haroun once said? *I trust that there's khair in this, too.*

She lost Haroun, but she gained faith. She gained trust in God. She came to know that only He stayed.

God did not deliberately want to cause Zoya pain; God simply wanted her to come back to Him.

So after losing Haroun, Zoya had finally opened up to her Lord.

But at what price? By destroying a gentle man's innocence, by robbing him of his goodness.

With a shock, Zoya reaches a sudden epiphany. One that had constantly afflicted Haroun, and one that her therapist had tried working on with Zoya many times as well.

But Zoya had been stubborn and upset both times, because her heart did not want to accept the truth.

She realizes that just like everyone else, Haroun Suleiman is *human*. She had placed him on an unrealistically high pedestal, had forgotten that he was just like eight billion other people on earth. She had too severely relied on his sincerity. Not that he proved her wrong, but she forgot that he was simply human and nothing more.

And *Al-Muhaymin*—The Guardian, The Protector, The Overseer—gave her this bitter yet truthful reminder of Haroun's humanity by causing him to leave. He opened her eyes to the fact that no matter how great of a person Haroun was, he was still human. His ribcage still harbored a beating human heart, one that was able to be hurt and angered and tested.

Thus, Zoya realized that only God stays. Only Allah stays

during times of sorrow and happiness and everything in between.

As Zoya drives, this jumble of thoughts makes her want to set herself in motion. It makes her want to erase everything and start on a clean slate, just as the windshield wipers wipe away the patter of the raindrops in order for her to see more clearly where she is headed.

Zoya realizes how incredibly lucky she has been. How—despite being one of the most notoriously arrogant and excessively power-hungry people in the nation—God had shown her mercy by placing her on the slow, arduous, but determined journey to Him.

Otherwise, she would have grown old and wasted away in her million dollar manor, being given no chance to right her wrongs or ask for the forgiveness she so direly needed.

God—Allah, *Ar-Raheem*—has been so merciful with Zoya Zameer.

Sixty-Two

ZOYA PICKS AT THE food Mumtaz has laid out on the breakfast table, lost in thought.

Once, she and Haroun had been talking about divine predestination. Zoya had argued that if everything was predestined, what role did free will play in a person's life?

Haroun had chuckled and told her that she'd be surprised by how many people asked that question. And she *was* surprised— people doubted faith as she did?

Apparently, yes. Very frequently. *It's the essence of being human,* Haroun had said. *The test is how you'll let these thoughts affect your faith.*

Zoya had probably not passed her test, then. She was constantly hanging onto faith by a thread, threatened by any doubt that entered her mind. Even that fragile thread of faith would have been clipped off if not for Haroun. He always tried to explain things to her and address her doubts, even if she wasn't always entirely satisfied.

She recalls the conversation the two of them had that day. Haroun had explained that while God had prewritten everything, He had also given humans the ability to make choices, which would set them on the path that they had been destined to tread. Zoya had argued that it wasn't really *choosing* if they were to tread that path anyway, but Haroun had shaken his head and given her an example.

He said that the starting point and ending point of two places would always remain constant, but there were various ways in which the end destination could be accessed. He said that getting from home to work would lead her from one constant to another constant, but the journey in between would consist of multiple routes and exits on the highway, giving her various options to choose from to reach the same destination at the end.

Zoya had asked him something that had been haunting her, attempting to remain as secretive as possible because he hadn't yet discovered her deceit. She said, "So do you think I was written for you or that I made a choice and forced myself to be written for you?"

Haroun had looked up at her then, dark eyes shining. "Zoya, you were always written for me. No matter which way it happened, the destination for marriage was always you."

As Zoya ponders over these memories, she thinks of the choices she has made that have led her to God. She adamantly avoided Him for so long, but at the end of the day, He still brought her back to Him. Despite her rebelliousness and her stubborn refusal to connect with Him—she had ended up helplessly staggering back to Him.

And He had been waiting for her. Because He knew these were the choices she would eventually make.

A small smile forms on her face, the first real one since Haroun left. And who brought it to her face? Who managed to haul her out of the depths of her despair and set her on track again?

The same One she had constantly and wrongfully blamed for putting her through all her suffering. The same One she had been running from all along. The same One she had denied and adamantly refused over and over again.

God.

~

When Zoya knocks on the door of the next person on her list, she has half a mind to make a run for it. But the thought occurs to her too late; the chain lifts on the other side of the door and it creaks open.

There she stands—Sumaiya Akhtar. There are bags under her eyes, and a few scars marring the right side of her face.

Zoya takes one look at her and inhales sharply. The ache returns to her chest.

Sumaiya's eyes widen when she sees Zoya. She stands there unsurely, one hand rising to her chest. Footsteps approach from inside the house, and an older woman appears. She takes one look at Zoya, and angry lines settle into the planes of her face.

The woman—who must be Sumaiya's mother—screams at Zoya. Tells her that she has no right to show up at their doorstep, that she has *some audacity* even showing her face. This means her mother knows of everything that went down—of all the lies and deceit and the mess her daughter was caught up in between Zaki Ahmed and Zoya Zameer.

She knows Sumaiya's car accident was not an accident.

Zoya takes it all silently, head bent in acceptance. When the shouts die down, she quietly asks, "Can I please come in?"

The woman throws her a baffled look. She gestures around angrily and repeats that Zoya has some audacity showing up and asking for entrance as if this is "*tumhari phuphi ka ghar.*"

Sumaiya is standing behind her mother, and she must see something on Zoya's face because she places a hand on her mother's shoulder. The older woman turns to her daughter, and Sumaiya gestures shakily to allow Zoya entry.

Reluctantly, Sumaiya's mother does as she is told, but the anger never leaves her face. She retreats upstairs, muttering harsh words under her breath.

When Zoya is settled in the living room, Sumaiya says, "How are you? You look . . . awful."

Zoya laughs mirthlessly. "I could say the same thing to you."

"What happened?"

Zoya shakes her head. "Never mind that." She observes Sumaiya carefully, noticing how each breath of hers comes out shallow and careful, requiring much effort. "How are you?"

At this question, Sumaiya's eyebrows rise in surprise. "Um . . . I'm okay?" Pause. "How about you?"

Zoya shrugs. "I wanted to come see you."

"Okay," Sumaiya says slowly, as if waiting for Zoya to explain.

"I—" Zoya stops, sighs, rubs her temples. "I wanted to say sorry to you."

Sumaiya's brows furrow.

"What . . . happened to you"—*what I did to you*—"was highly unjust. And it happened because I was . . . too bloodthirsty. Too vengeful. I didn't even give a damn that your *life* was possibly on the line." Zoya shakes her head in disgust. "You warned me. You told me that Zaki Ahmed would make you pay, and that he would do it without giving a damn about your life. But I didn't listen to you." Distress seeps through her tone. Zoya thinks that all she has been feeling lately is distress, worry, and regret. A torturous, never ending cycle.

Sumaiya fingers a pattern on her shirt.

"I'm . . ." Zoya turns to look at her. "I'm *so* sorry."

Sumaiya remains quiet for a few moments before turning back to Zoya. "Ms. Zoya—"

"Just Zoya. Please."

"Okay . . . Zoya . . . I wanted to tell you that I'm sorry, too," Sumaiya whispers. Zoya's jaw slackens in surprise. "I've been wanting to apologize to you. I was trying to build up the courage to come to you." Zoya realizes that there is an uncomfortable parallel between this conversation and her confrontation with Haroun, on the day that all hell broke loose.

Sumaiya's voice breaks her out of her thoughts. "*Boht zyaati ki mene Zameer k saath*. Please, please forgive me for it." She shifts, wincing in pain. Zoya watches her with woeful eyes, knowing that Sumaiya's condition is her fault. "I've learned the hard way that there is always another choice to make."

Zoya laughs bitterly. "So have I."

"I wanted to ask . . ." Sumaiya hesitates. "I've been seeing you all over the news. About how you haven't left your house in weeks. And that everyone at Zameer is in an uproar but you're . . . nowhere to be found. What . . . happened, if I may ask?"

Zoya drops her head in her hands. "I realized all my mistakes is what happened. I broke a good man's heart."

"I never got to congratulate you on your marriage," Sumaiya says. There is an awkward silence. "But right now, you and Haroun . . ." Sumaiya trails off.

"He . . . he left."

Sumaiya sucks in a sharp breath, wincing when the action pierces her chest. "Oh, no. What happened?"

"I lied to him," Zoya repeats the line she is becoming tortuously accustomed to. "Majorly. He couldn't handle being so . . . betrayed."

Moments of tense silence pass before a warm hand comes down to clasp Zoya's. Zoya flinches and looks up with a start. Sumaiya is watching her with that familiar pity in her eyes, and Zoya wants to bury herself deeper into the quicksand she's trapped in.

"There's always another choice," Sumaiya says sadly. "And we've both learned that the hard way."

The two women sit for a few silent moments, hands clasped together. Then Zoya says once more, "I'm really sorry. You have no idea how sorry I am."

Sumaiya shakes her head. "I've had some of my own time to reflect." She breathes out a shallow sigh, an indent appearing in her forehead. "I shouldn't have made the choices that I did."

"And neither should have I," Zoya replies. For a moment, she ponders over how humans think that lessons are learned only from those they look up to; yet here she is, learning a great deal from someone who harmed her company.

"God's plan . . . is perfect in every way," Sumaiya murmurs. "Perfect plan, perfect execution, perfect timing, perfect *everything*. Who would have thought that we would be sitting together like this one day?" She raises their clasped hands. "I guess we both had lessons to learn."

Zoya thinks of the wariness she still feels around God, the wrongs she still has to make right. She laughs sadly. "I'm not sure I've fully learned mine."

Sumaiya shifts again, her face creasing with pain. As Zoya watches her struggle with the simple act of breathing and moving, even after about seven months of the car accident, her guilt intensifies. Especially when Sumaiya says, "You are here. And that makes all the difference in the world."

How is Sumaiya able to comfort Zoya after what Zoya has done to her? It would have been more appropriate for her to react like her mother, but it seems to Zoya that everybody harbors this goodness except for her.

Nevertheless, Zoya smiles tentatively at her words.

"Besides, if lessons were meant to be learned all at once and never again, Allah wouldn't have given us entire lifetimes to witness them and eventually fix our mistakes. So while understanding that He ultimately decrees and has knowledge of all that we do, *we* choose what to do with the time that He's given us."

There it is again—the element of choice. The emphasis on free will.

Zoya thinks she finally understands what Haroun had tried explaining to her about predestination and free will coinciding.

She may be standing in the midst of a battlefield, a war cry rising up her throat. She may feel as if she is being rained on with debris and hardships. She may feel trapped and suffocated.

But the key to winning the battle is wielding her weapon and shield. The key is guarding herself against all odds, while simultaneously knowing that some One has her back and is aware of every action she will take.

The key to winning every battle is trusting God, and knowing that despite the outcome being predestined by a Sovereign above, the weapon required to win is still enclosed in her very fist.

Sixty-Three

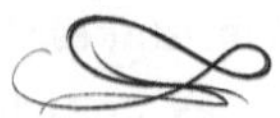

ZOYA BEGINS TO READ about other names of Allah, pondering over the way they feel on her tongue. She murmurs them quietly as she visits people to ask for forgiveness, as she walks around her manor, as she busies herself in helping her maids clean or cook, as she lies in bed at night. Saying Allah's names brings that strange sense of peace back into her heart. She has searched for this peace for too long; there is no way she will ever let it go now.

One of the names of Allah that Zoya comes across is *Al-Wali*: The Protecting Friend, The Supporter. Interestingly, as she learns more about this name, she sees that a similar status is given to a woman's father as well.

She had learned this in passing when she was marrying Haroun and needed a *wali* for her *nikah*. But she hadn't paid much attention to the word, much less cared about the meaning of it.

Now when she thinks of it as she lies in bed, a bitter smile makes its way onto her face.

Her father was to be her *wali*—her guardian, her protector, her supporter. One of *God's* names has been given to a man for his daughters; it is such an important attribute for a father to have. Her father was to guard her and protect her—it was *divinely* given to him as a responsibility.

Zoya chokes out a bitter laugh. Mumtaz—lying on the bed next to her—turns to her with a quizzical brow. Zoya simply shakes her head.

Her father made a mockery of one of the names of *God*. When Zoya thinks about him now, an uneasiness settles in her heart. If she ever sees him again, what will she say to him? What is a daughter supposed to say to her absentee father? How is she supposed to ask him why he didn't follow through with such an important attribute? How will the words form on her tongue to ask him why he didn't take heed of one of God's names?

Zoya rolls over to her right side and clasps her hands under her head. She may never see her father again—a very realistic possibility—but how is she to make this bitterness in her heart go away? It has already taken her so long to free herself of the cage of arrogance and resentment she had been trapped in. She doesn't want to end up in that same cycle again.

She wants to let go.

Whether she sees her father again or doesn't see her father again, Zoya wants the bitterness to leave her heart and make room for forgiveness instead.

Interestingly, when she thinks of bitterness and forgiveness, she also often thinks of her ex-husband Farhan. How will she (if ever) forgive him for being the cause of her anger towards God? For robbing her of so many years of a relationship with Him, as well as the irreplaceable *sukoon* associated with Him? Does she have it in her to let go and potentially forget what Farhan Hussain did to her? Does she have the courage to extract all the anger and hostility and pain from her heart, and leave him up to God?

All Zoya knows is that—as with her father—she wants to be rid of the animosity against Farhan that weighs her down every day, the resentfulness that exhausts her every second. If that means leaving her ex-husband up to *Al-Hakam*—The Judge, The Giver of Justice, The One who always delivers justice to everyone in every situation—then so be it.

There is no one who will deliver justice to Zoya better than God will.

Zoya sighs, closing her eyes and attempting to sleep.

But tonight, sleep doesn't find her. Nausea climbs up her throat again and again, forcing her to rush to the bathroom and bend over the sink. Fatigue consumes her; her eyelids droop despite her body's discomfort.

However, instead of feeling disgusted or frustrated, Zoya feels something else entirely. Every time her body experiences another upheaval or another discomfort, Zoya forces herself to spread her fingers gently across her stomach and think of one thing only.

Honor.

What an honor it is that her Lord has chosen her. He has chosen her as a means through which to produce life. He has given her the chance to give somebody else a chance. He has made her body a secure, protective vessel through which He will provide life and security to another. He has chosen her body as the fort, the castle that guards protect. *Zoya Zameer's* womb has been chosen to shield the life of the next generation.

What an honor, a blessing, a beautiful responsibility it is.

With this thought in mind, she trudges back to bed and lifts the covers gently so as not to wake Mumtaz. Settling back against the headboard, she stares at the extravagant chandelier hanging from the ceiling.

Zoya breathes a deep sigh. Tomorrow, she will have to do what she has been dreading. She will have to do what has been plaguing her heart and causing sheens of sweat to rise along her neck for days.

She will visit *Ammi,* Naima, and Aisha.

~

In the morning, Zoya takes a walk around her neighborhood. Her heart is protesting wildly to what she's about to do today, thudding against her chest in fearful anticipation.

Days or weeks ago, if she had opened the door when her mother-in-law and sister-in-laws had come knocking, she would have been destroyed in the worst way possible, because she would have been charging into battle alone.

Now, however, she *knows* she's not alone. She knows she has *Al-Wali.*

It's a foggy, chilly morning, but the fresh air serves as a balm to

Zoya's distressed state. As she walks, she sees a figure ahead of her in the fog. Another person taking a walk.

She squints. Something about that gait is surprisingly familiar . . .

With a gasp, Zoya's hand flies to her heart. *Haroun?*

No. It can't be.

He's gone, Zoya. He's not here. Stop thinking about him.

But as Zoya continues to squint at the figure, the gait seems unmistakably familiar.

Zoya breaks out into a trot with a sole focus in mind—to follow the figure ahead of her. She rushes into the fog, inhaling the chilly morning air. After a minute, she stops to catch her breath.

When she looks back up, he's gone.

Zoya's breath catches in her throat. She swivels her head this way and that, searching for turns in the sidewalk that may have led him off path. But the sidewalk trails straight ahead.

Yet he's gone.

There's no one there, Zoya realizes with a start. There was never anyone there.

The world around her seems to dim and become eerily silent, every noise and movement arresting her senses.

She stands motionlessly in the absolute stillness for a moment. Then slowly, ever so gently, a leaf falls from the tree to her right.

Something in her shifts at seeing the leaf; something vulnerable in her teeters, then falls helplessly off the edge of the cliff inside her.

A sob emits from her throat as she leans down to pick up the leaf. Haroun used to talk about one of his favorite verses in the Qur'an, something about how even a leaf couldn't fall without God's knowledge.

She never gave much thought to it. But now, she feels as if she is incredibly close to Allah. She feels as if He is sending tranquility down to her, easing the shudders in her body. Restoring her heart to a regular pace.

She feels as if He is giving her a sign.

What had Haroun said once? He tapped his chest and said, "This is the secret to knowing Allah." The heart.

Zoya cradles the leaf against her heart and allows the tears to escape. They are not tears of anguish; they are tears of happiness. They testify that the One most surely has her back. The One who is her *Wali*, her Protecting Friend, her Supporter. Allah is reassuring her before she visits her in-laws that He will be there every step of the way, Guarding and Protecting her.

And who could ever protect her better than God?

As Zoya stands in the foggy stillness, clutching a leaf against her chest, she wonders why she never paid attention to all the signs that had been dangling in front of her face all along.

~

After praying *Dhuhr* and holding her hands up in *du'a* for a few minutes, Zoya stands and folds the prayer mat, getting ready to meet her in-laws. She sweeps the scarf off of her head and is about to stow it away when she catches her reflection in the mirror and stops. A memory prods at her.

She wraps a scarf around her head and adjusts it while looking in the mirror. Satisfied with her appearance, she starts heading to the prayer mat when she catches Haroun eyeing her.

When their gazes lock, he looks away almost shyly, but not before she sees the expression in his eyes. The tenderness, the adoration.

She grins at him. "What?"

He shakes his head and looks down, smiling. "Nothing . . ." But when he looks back up at her with the same gentle expression, he says, "You just look really pretty."

Wind rushes through Zoya's ears and she stills for a moment, forgetting how to breathe. Somehow, he always manages to unhinge her with a few simple words.

When she looks in his eyes, she sees a reflection of herself but also . . . someone she isn't. She sees a woman he respects and holds in such high regard, increased tenfold because of the scarf on her head.

Zoya breaks out of the memory, examining herself in the mirror. She is holding that same blue *hijab*, the one associated with her memory. Why had Haroun revered the piece of cloth on her head so much? Surely it held some kind of importance for which he held it in such high esteem. For which millions of women across the globe willingly wrap it around their heads every day.

Zoya hesitates, holding up the *hijab* in front of her. Her fingers tremble.

Does she deserve to wear this?

People wear this as an act of devotion to God and faith, do they not? As a symbol of their love and dedication to their Lord. Zoya has done horrible things in her life, for which she has only just started to repent. Does she deserve to put this on her head as a marker of her faith and her devotion to Allah? Or is she too messed up to do so?

Then she remembers something—something Sumaiya had said a long time ago. Her voice rings in Zoya's head, loud and clear. *"I'm not wearing this because of who I am. I'm wearing this because of Allah and because of the person that I want to become."*

Back then, Zoya had laughed this statement off scornfully. She had rolled her eyes and thought Sumaiya to be a blubbering, bumbling fool. Someone attempting redemption with meaningless words.

Now, these words have been given a new meaning. These words show her what Sumaiya truly meant that day.

That she wasn't perfect, but she was willing to give it a try.

Zoya is far from perfect—she has painstakingly realized this over the past three months. But should she try as Sumaiya tried? Should she hope that this act will bring her closer to God, and closer to the person that she wants to become?

Zoya watches herself in the mirror, immobilized by the piece of blue cloth resting in her hands.

She doesn't know if she's ready. Perhaps it's better for her to wait until she knows with absolute certainty that this is what she wants.

Zoya is about to put the scarf back in her closet when another thought nags at her and roots to the ground.

What if she dies tomorrow?

What then? She will harbor this hesitant desire in her heart and never be able to implement it in her life. She will lie six feet under, regretting the choices she didn't make.

Zoya doesn't want to wait for the time she can never be

guaranteed of, the time she will be confident *enough*. She wants to do this now, in case she dies tomorrow. She wants it to be the last good thing she does if she dies tomorrow. She wants to have a glimpse of this goodness in her life despite not being ready . . . because who knows if she will ever be ready?

Doesn't the devil love to prey on insecurities? Won't *Shaitan* rejoice that she is putting aside an act of goodness that she had the ability to do?

There will always be obstacles set in her path by *Shaitan* to unhinge and divert her. He will always try to stop her from following the path of goodness, the Right Path—as it is said in the *surah* she recites in every prayer—the *Sirat al-Mustaqeem*.

So she has to do this. She has to defeat *Shaitan* and do something that holds the possibility of bringing her closer to the God she is learning to love and trust. Maybe this will make her the person she wants to become, as Sumaiya had said.

Zoya takes a deep breath and settles the blue cloth lightly over her head.

Sixty-Three

"Indeed, Allah will not change the condition of a people until they change what is in themselves." (Qur'an 13:11)

~

WHEN ZOYA KNOCKS ON the door of her in-laws' apartment, she feels as though her heart will explode.

She would prefer that to having to face these three women. These women who did so much for her, only for Zoya to betray them.

For this meeting, she has brought Mumtaz with her. Although Zoya now knows that she has her *Muhaymin*, her *Qawiyy*, her *Wali*, she still needs the comfort of human contact. Mumtaz rubs her hand soothingly as they hear footsteps approaching the other side of the door.

The door that Naima opens.

The softness on her tired face disappears the moment she sees Zoya. For a second, there is nothing but pure shock—pure shock at seeing her sister-in-law almost three months later. Then her face takes on an expression of absolute fury, as if the blood beneath her skin is boiling to the surface.

"Amma," she shouts sharply behind her, causing Zoya to flinch. "Look who *finally* showed up." Her voice is too high, too shaky.

Zoya stands motionlessly, rattled by Naima's uncharacteristic sharpness. The younger woman watches her with fierce, wide eyes.

Ammi appears behind Naima. Zoya's heart rate seems to slow and the lights seem to dim. The older woman is frail and weak, head full of gray hair, bags underneath her eyes as dark as shadows. Her eyes widen considerably upon seeing Zoya.

Aisha follows, freezing in the doorway when she catches sight of her absentee sister-in-law. The sister-in-law who murdered a man's heart, then fled from the crime scene.

It breaks Zoya's already fragile heart to see people so close to Haroun. Their presence teases her, reminding her of his absence.

"*Aa jaye,*" Naima breaks the silence in that same sharp voice, gesturing to the inside of the apartment. "*Hum aapke hi muntazir hai.*" Sarcasm drips heavily from her voice.

Ammi's eyes rove over Zoya's weakened form, sallow skin, and hollow eyes. Her mother-in-law reaches forward unsurely before stepping back. "Zoya?" she mumbles feebly.

Zoya's voice fails in front of these women, whom she has robbed of happiness. Her eyes trail to Naima's, again surprised to find them cold and unrelenting. Then to Aisha's, which are confused and disbelieving.

"I'm—" Zoya's lips tremble. "I'm so sorry." Her legs crumple, and she falls to her knees, crying. *Ammi* and Aisha reach down to help her up, but Naima stays by the door. Cold and stoic.

The two women help her to her feet but step back immediately, eyes wary. Finally, *Ammi* says, "I . . . wanted to believe it wasn't true when we pulled it out of Haroun." Her shoulders begin to shake. "But you've been ignoring us. And now seeing your state . . ." An indent forms between her brows, grief pools in her eyes.

Silence settles among them for a few long moments. *Ammi* continues to watch her daughter-in-law, and the constantly shifting expressions in her eyes scare Zoya. As if *Ammi* can't decide which part of her emotions to put on full display. The shock, the denial, or the utter grief.

Finally she murmurs, "Why didn't you ever open the door when we came knocking? Hiding yourself away like that . . . it only made you look more guilty. Lying about your health . . ." Her chest heaves as she takes a shaky breath. "Do you have any idea what you've put us through? We didn't know if you were alive, if you were okay. We found out about you from the news, not knowing what's true and what's a lie."

Ammi walks forward slowly, reaching up to capture one of the curls that has escaped from underneath Zoya's *dupatta*. She watches it carefully before flicking her eyes back to Zoya. "I told you to call me *Ammi*. I made you my *daughter*." The older woman's lips tremble. "*Koi maa k saath aise karta hai?*"

Can anyone do this to a mother?

Ammi drops her hand. "*Koi maa k saath itni bari zyaati karta hai? Koi maa ko itna pareshan rakhta hai k us ko pata hi na ho us ki beti kahan hai, kis haal me hai? Koi maa k saath is tarha ka sulook karta hai?*"

Zoya's chin wobbles at the words. *Can anyone commit such an injustice against a mother? Can anyone keep a mother so worried that she does not even know where her daughter is, in what state she is in? Can anyone treat a mother in this way?*

Ammi begins to cry. "*Koi bhi beti maa k saath is tarha kar sakti hai?*"

Can any daughter do this to a mother?

Zoya shakes her head, tears streaming down her face. She reaches forward to grab her mother-in-law's hand, but *Ammi* backs away, shaking her head. "*Tumhe andaaza bhi hai k tum ne apni maa ko kitna pareshan rakha hai in teen maheeno me? Tum dono ne— tum ne aur Haroun ne.*"

Do you have any idea of how worried you've kept your mother these past three months? Both of you—you and Haroun.

Zoya's lips barely move to mouth the words "I'm sorry, I'm sorry" over and over again.

"What is a mother for?" *Ammi's* question pierces Zoya somewhere deep. "Hmm? *Maa ka haq nahi hai k wo apne bacho ke maslihaat me un ka saath de?* Is it not a mother's right to support her children through their hardships?" She backs away, sagging against Naima. "*Tum dono ne mujhe maa ka haq nahi adaa karne diya. Nahi adaa karne diya.*"

The last two sentences pierce Zoya somewhere deep. *You two have not allowed me to maintain the rights of a mother. You have not allowed me to.*

Zoya's heart begins to tremble. What is worse about *Ammi's* words is that they display her heartbreak not primarily over what Zoya has done to Haroun, but of Zoya's avoidance of *Ammi* after her lie was exposed. Of hiding herself away from the only woman apart from Mumtaz who was willing to be her mother.

Naima laughs scornfully, cutting off her mother's pained confession. "You really played us all, didn't you, *bhabhi*?" Aisha throws her sister a furtive glance, but Naima barrels onwards relentlessly. "Played with my brother. Made him marry a woman *on the brink of death* and made him fall in love with you. And then you broke his heart. You know what, though?" She wipes angry tears away. "May God ask you. May *Allah* ask you for what you've done to him."

Zoya breaks out into sobs at these words, and Mumtaz—responding to her cries immediately—rubs her side, trying to calm her down.

Ammi watches them both carefully, the grief never leaving her eyes.

Only Aisha stands by the door, eyes darting warily between all the women.

"You shouldn't have done this," *Ammi* whispers, crestfallen. "You really should *not* have done this."

Zoya's lips tremble.

"Where is he?" she finally whispers, voicing the question that has been plaguing her for weeks.

Naima laughs mirthlessly. "You don't get to ask that now. You don't. Not after what you've done to him."

Zoya is appalled by Naima's behavior, not because Zoya doesn't deserve it but because she was not expecting this from *Naima*.

But Naima has always been the softer one—so much like her brother in character. Zoya knew she had trust issues, knew she was reluctant to open up, knew about all of her insecurities. And she still hurt her.

The softest are always the most anguished when they break.

"Please," Zoya whispers, reaching forward to hold Naima's hand. The younger woman steps back, folding her arms across her chest unyieldingly.

Then Zoya turns to *Ammi,* trying to place her hands on the older woman's shoulders. But *Ammi* holds a hand up quietly, eyebrows scrunched together in pain. Somehow, her silence is worse than if she had been angry. Zoya wishes *Ammi* would yell, scream that Zoya is a horrible person, threaten to make her life a living hell. Instead, she remains mute, which pierces Zoya's heart in the worst way possible.

Finally, Zoya turns to Aisha. The prestigious Zoya Zameer, rendered helpless in front of these women she has lied to. Begging them for forgiveness like a pauper begs for food on the streets.

Zoya looks into Aisha's confused, worried eyes and says, "Please, Aisha. Tell your brother to come back." She came here wanting to ask for forgiveness, but seeing their unyielding states, Zoya has been rendered helpless again. "*Please—*"

"How can you even dare to say that after what you've done to him?" Naima snaps, causing Zoya to flinch again. "Besides, we barely have any contact with him." When Zoya gives her a bewildered look, Naima nods. "Yeah. You took him away from us, too. All he said before he left was that he needed time and that he'd be safe. And not to worry." Naima's breath hitches. "Since then, he's just been sending us money and talking to us *once every few days.*" She clears her throat and stands up straighter, trying to hold herself together. "So thank you for that, *bhabhi.*" She spits out the last word bitterly. "Thank you for forcing a responsible man to abandon his family."

Zoya's eyebrows knit in worry. Even *they* are not in constant contact with Haroun? *Oh, God.*

She stumbles back, and Mumtaz catches her. She whispers words of comfort in Zoya's ear, "*Hosla karo.* This is not good for your condition."

Ammi raises her eyes to theirs at these words. "Condition?" she whispers, baffled. "What condition?"

Naima laughs scornfully. "Haven't you heard, *Amma?* She's *terminally ill,* remember? On the *brink of death.*"

Zoya's breath heaves at these words. They seem to pierce into her skull like knives. Constant, persistent. Reminding her of her awful mistake over and over again.

As she deserves.

Mumtaz shakes her head at Naima. "No, *beta*. There's . . . something else."

Mumtaz tells the women the news. *Ammi* staggers backwards in shock. Aisha raises a hand to her mouth. Even the hard planes in Naima's face shift, and her merciless eyes soften as they travel down to Zoya's stomach.

After what seems like ages, *Ammi* reaches forward slowly, placing her hand on Zoya's stomach. "Oh, Allah," she says tiredly, heaving a breath. "Oh, Allah."

Zoya takes this as an opening and staggers forward, wrapping her arms around her mother-in-law. "I'm sorry," she says, throat burning from the tears. "I'm sorry, I'm sorry, I'm sorry." She cannot see their faces through the blurry tears, but she can make out the outlines of Naima and Aisha, motionlessly watching her.

For a few moments as Zoya cries, *Ammi* simply stands. Then, almost helplessly, she embraces her daughter-in-law. The two women cry against one another. And they are a strange sight to behold—the betrayer hugging the betrayed, the liar hugging the deceived, the inflictor of pain hugging the wounded.

When Zoya pulls back, *Ammi* cups her cheek. Her eyes are so full of grief that Zoya fears she may lose herself in them forever and never witness another happy day.

"Why?" the older woman cries. "Why?"

In response, Zoya simply whimpers and shakes her head. "I'm sorry. I'm so sorry."

Later, the five women are sitting in the living room. Haroun's grandparents, whom the three women have been living with, have joined them. They speak to Zoya more calmly than she would have expected. They advise her, scold her, question her. Zoya knows that it must take an incredible amount of effort for them to restrain their anger and approach her with caution instead. She attempts to address their concerns as best as she can, but after a certain point all

Zoya can manage is shaky "yeses" or "nos." The grandparents momentarily cease their questions, and a heavy silence settles over the family.

There is a thick tension in the air; one that promises forgiveness will not come soon and when it comes, it will not come easy; one that brings the hard planes back in Naima's face and the wrinkles back in *Ammi's* forehead. Only Aisha remains neutral, having not said a word since Zoya arrived.

Ammi's eyes are sad when she asks Zoya whether she would like to come stay with them. But Zoya shakes her head profusely. She knows how much it costs the woman to make the offer, despite *Ammi's* good heart. "I need to be home if . . . when Haroun comes back," she mumbles, earning a scoff from Naima.

Just when Zoya and Mumtaz are leaving, Aisha approaches Zoya, twisting the cloth of her dress around her fingers. Zoya stops, eager to hear even one word from the girl's mouth, *something* to testify how she must be feeling.

"*Aapi* . . ." Aisha starts, unable to meet Zoya's gaze. Strong-willed, confident, bubbly Aisha, unable to look her brother's heartbreaker in the face. "Why did you do it?"

Zoya cannot give the girl a satisfactory answer. It grieves her, because she senses that Aisha has always been more attached to her. Zoya had noticed this from the start, when the younger girl opted to call Zoya the more personal *aapi* rather than the formal *bhabhi*. Zoya always saw the admiration in Aisha's eyes every time she spoke to her, always noticed the laughter that came easily to her when they both conversed.

Zoya has not been good to these people.

"Come on." Naima reaches for her sister's arm. "You're not going to get your answer."

Zoya watches them one last time before she goes, once again thinking of how much destruction she has wrought in the lives of those around her.

And as for the people she has come to care about, she has destroyed them worst of all.

~

Zoya visits them every day after that. Naima seldom speaks to her and clenches her jaw whenever Zoya approaches her. *Ammi* seems to be on the fence, one day watching her daughter-in-law with grieved eyes and another day managing to crack a small smile. Aisha seems to be the only one who speaks to Zoya almost normally, which earns her angry stares from her sister.

Haroun's grandparents, at the end of the day, are older and have had more experience with the cruelties of life. They advise Zoya, caution her, and even tell her not to worry.

Their kindness soothes her.

Zoya knows that it will take time for all of them to recover. She knows it will take weeks and months and maybe even years for them to be able to just look at her without their hearts cracking. But she knows that eventually, even a heart of ice melts.

She knows because this very same thing happened to her. And if her heart of ice was able to melt to *God*, what are humans?

Along with seeking redemption, Zoya decides to finally return to work.

She hasn't kept up with anything going on, hasn't spoken to anybody from work other than Farhan and Sameer, and is aware that the company has been in an upheaval since her absence.

She is ready for all of this.

What she is not ready for, however, are the questions. The looks in the eyes of her employees when they see her. Their wariness around harsh Zoya Zameer—the only Zoya Zameer they know.

When she proceeds to Zameer's headquarters the next day, the security guards sitting at the entrance bolt upright. They don't even try to hide their shock; they simply stare at her with slackened jaws and widened eyes.

Zoya stops walking, eyes darting between them. With a pang, she realizes that she doesn't know their names, having never bothered to learn them or having forgotten them immediately after being told.

She clears her throat. "Hello."

The security guard on the right tips his head at her as the one on the left says, "Hello, Ms. Zoya."

"How are you?"

They are quiet for a couple seconds, probably shocked by the uncharacteristic question. Then Left mutters, "Good, Ms. Zoya. What about—what about you?"

She nods, "Good, thank you." She waits, wondering if they will say anything else to her. They remain silent, so she walks past them into the building.

Her eyes travel across the lobby, capturing the familiarity of it with new eyes. The extravagant furniture, the top tier technology, the lights and screens.

And of course, the open-mouthed receptionist Sarah and the frozen employees.

"*Zoya?*" someone screeches from behind her. Ibitoye materializes, her face as beautiful as Zoya remembers, if not more. "Oh, my God. Zoya, where the *hell* have you been?" Her eyes rake over Zameer's CEO, settling confusedly on the blue scarf loosely draped over her head.

Zoya manages to crack a smile. "Hello to you, too."

"Oh, my *God*," Ibitoye huffs, leaning forward to wrap her arms around Zoya. Zoya returns the embrace, smiling at her perplexed onlookers. When Ibitoye pulls back, she says, "Do you know how worried *sick* we've been? No word from you for like *half a year*—"

"Three months."

"—*whatever*. We've been going crazy wondering what happened to you and . . . and trying to keep Zameer functioning."

Zoya smiles. "Looks like you've been doing an okay job."

"*Barely*. The first few weeks were *insane*. Protests, strikes, angry shareholders, Bill and the board and I going crazy trying to handle everything. Tried getting in contact with Haroun and—" Ibitoye stops, sighs as she looks at Zoya, as she really takes her in. "What *happened*, Zoya?"

At that moment, a shout emerges from behind them, followed by rushed footsteps. "Did somebody say *Zoya damn Zameer* is here?"

Everyone turns to see Bill rushing towards them. His eyes widen, and he staggers to a stop in front of Zoya, who quirks a smile at him. She isn't surprised that only five minutes after her return, the entire staff is aware of her presence. They probably have a group chat where they gossip and complain about her.

"Zoya *damn* Zameer?" she echoes amusedly. "Has a nice ring to it, I'll admit."

"Where have you *been*?" he says with a mix of exasperation and relief.

Zoya clamps her lips shut, eyes darting between everyone. "I will answer all of your . . . queries. But at one time. I don't want to have to say it over and over again." She takes a deep breath. "I will do it on camera, for everyone to hear." Zoya turns to Ibitoye. "Where's Sameer?"

"He's with Lucas and the rest of PR on the fifth floor."

"Can you ask him to arrange a meeting room for me? And direct everyone there, please."

Ibitoye nods and disappears into the elevator, taking one last look at Zoya, as if to make sure she's still real.

Bill watches her closely, and Zoya almost flinches under his gaze. He gestures to her simple white dress and plain blue scarf. "New look?"

She tugs at some flyaway curls uncomfortably. "You could say that."

He shakes his head. "I didn't mean it like that. You look . . . good."

"Thank you, Bill Nye."

There is an awkward silence before he blurts out, "Have you really not left your house all this time?"

Zoya turns her eyes skyward. "I will answer all of your questions to the best of my ability and sanity. I promise. Just give me some time."

He nods. "Of course."

Zoya turns to the rest of the employees in the lobby, who are still gawking at her. She notices the wariness and terror they exude in her presence, and the smile vanishes from her face.

Is this what she has been reduced to? A symbol of fear in the hearts of those who toiled for her?

"Why . . ." she begins slowly, eyes darting between all of them. "Why didn't any of you ever say anything to me? Why didn't you stop my rash behavior? Why did you tolerate my . . . injustices?"

Their eyebrows rise at her uncharacteristic questions. Zoya watches them earnestly, willing someone to give her an excuse that will make her feel less guilty. But they remain silent, darting glances at one another and waiting for someone else to answer and take the brunt of her wrath.

But they don't, because there isn't any.

She sighs, turning away from them. "It's okay. You don't have to answer me." She laughs scornfully. "I know I don't deserve your answers."

Bill gives her a surprised look, a pucker appearing between his brows. Zoya gauges from his reaction that it will be tough for her employees to become used to the new Zoya Zameer. But what will be even more difficult is for Zoya not to spiral back into the depths of despair every time she sees the shock on their faces.

~

During the meeting, staff members pass by the glass walls rear back in shock, whispering to one another, "Zoya Zameer is *actually* here!" The whispers rise to a fever pitch, and within the hour, reporters swarm the building entrance, trying to fight their way in. Zoya is distracted by the uproar outside the windows, unprepared to step into it. She tries to speak to her board of directors and PR team, but her attention continues to stray to the noise outside.

"Zoya?" Ibitoye questions when the CEO trails off for a moment.

"Sorry," she replies. "As I was saying, I've had a lot of time to think over the past couple of weeks and . . ." She takes a deep breath. "I want to propose a change to the business model. Start off fresh. Not only because we've been going downhill the past couple of months—which is entirely my fault and will require many, many meetings to discuss—but also because I think we need this."

The board of directors all turn to one another, exchanging wary glances. Ibitoye speaks up after a charged moment. "What kind of change, exactly?"

"Nothing too drastic, hopefully. Or maybe it is. I just feel like . . . we need to rethink our values and propositions." Zoya absentmindedly traces circles on the desk. "Why do we manufacture the clothing that we manufacture?"

"High demand," Bill replies.

"Customer satisfaction," someone else pipes up.

"Prevalent usage."

More workers throw out more reasons. Zoya nods, keeping her eyes on the desk. "Notice how none of you said that it's because it holds a certain value in people's lives, or anything along those lines."

The executives dart confused glances at one another. "I mean"—Bill shrugs—"that's a given, I think."

Zoya smiles. "But it's not the first thing that comes to your minds." She sighs, stands, and turns to the board behind her. "I understand if you do not want to stay at Zameer after this, I truly do. But I need you to hear me out."

She uncaps a marker and writes four words on the board: *Affordable everyday modest wear.*

Zoya turns back to her audience. "I think what is severely lacking in the market"—she taps the board—"is modest wear. And not just bridal modest wear but everyday, essential modest wear. *Affordable* wear." She pauses for a moment, watching the myriad of expressions on her workers' faces. They rub their chins in contemplation, scratch notes onto their papers.

Zoya continues, "The difference in value is that ethnic bridal wear can be found in many, many places. But everyday modest wear is very difficult to find and even more difficult to *continue* to find at prices the average person can afford." She begins to walk around the room, animatedly gesturing with her hands and occasionally referring to the stack of statistics lying on the desk, which she researched the past couple of days. When she finishes, she turns to everybody and raises her eyebrows. "What do you guys think?"

They exchange glances with one another. This time, there is not only confusion but surprise on their faces as well. She never asked for their opinions *this* earnestly.

Then Ibitoye turns to her and says, "I . . . think I'll need some time to consider this."

Zoya nods. "You guys don't need to give me an answer right now. And I promise that I'll understand if you will want to take your leave after this. But . . . your opinions matter to me."

Bill coughs awkwardly, trying to cover up the shock written so clearly all over his face. Zoya calls an end to the meeting, and everyone begins to shuffle around to exit the room. Sameer approaches her, a wide smile on his face.

Zoya cocks her head to the side. "What's that look, Sameer Mirza?"

He salutes. "I'm proud of you, soldier."

Zoya smiles and turns to the window, where she can see the crowds of people outside. "Not yet. There are still many battles to fight."

Sameer begins to back away to exit the room. "Something tells me you'll be okay."

And despite the crowds demanding answers outside the headquarters, despite the personal and professional losses Zoya has incurred, despite the long list of people she still needs to ask forgiveness from, and despite the press conference scheduled later today, for the first time in a long time, Zoya isn't too scared.

For the first time, she believes Sameer's assertion that she will be okay.

Sixty-Four

~

DURING THE PRESS CONFERENCE, Zoya addresses her absence as implicitly as possible, stating that her mental health was at stake. Afterwards, countless articles and news reports are released; the media does a full blow-by-blow of the press conference and makes many speculations (seldom nicely) about her absence.

Zoya may be able to handle everything else that will accompany her return, but under no circumstances may the media find out that she's pregnant. They will go ballistic, and she will not be able to handle the ensuing chaos.

Before, she seldom gave a damn what the press said about her. Now, she worries that wrongful accusations and speculations may end up wounding the new reputation she is trying to build.

No wonder Haroun had always been so anxious in this environment.

The press doesn't take the business pivot lightly, either. Shock and anger follow her announcement, as well as many meetings with investors and contractors. At one point, Zoya has to lock herself in her office to take deep, heaving breaths and escape it all—she'd forgotten the pressures of her job.

After a long and hectic week, Zoya tiredly makes her way to her car. She rubs her eyes and inhales sharply when a sudden pain shoots up her stomach. Leaning against the car door for support, she takes deep breaths.

A sudden tingling sensation appears at the back of her neck. The unmistakable feeling of being watched.

Zoya whirls around, narrowing her eyes to stare into the still, silent night. There seems to be a figure at the far end of the parking lot. Too far for Zoya to clearly see but close enough for her to squint and make out the shape of a man.

She staggers backwards, hurriedly getting in her car and revving the engine. Zoya takes the opposite route from the figure, dashing onto the highway to race home. She taps her fingers against the steering wheel, feeling uneasy.

When she reaches home, Aman greets her with a small smile and gestures for her to enter. She returns the smile, asks him how his day went, and hurries inside.

Mumtaz appears. "*Salaam*, Zoya. Go get freshened up and I'll set out dinner for you."

Zoya nods, reaches forward to peck her cheek, and heads upstairs to shower and change. Fifteen minutes later, she is walking down the stairs while rubbing a towel through her hair. Even though she has male servants at home, Zoya is taking the *hijab* slowly, wearing it loosely outdoors before eventually properly covering herself with it.

Zoya stops short when she sees Mumtaz and Aman. They are standing in the middle of the hall, warily glancing at her. Zoya furrows her brows at them.

Mumtaz steps forward. "Um, Zoya *beta* . . ."

"What? What's wrong?" Zoya says, her eyes darting between the two of them, towel suspended midair in her hands.

Mumtaz exchanges a helpless glance with Aman.

"Is there mascara under my eyes or something?" Zoya jokes, trying to lighten the increasingly tense mood.

They don't laugh.

Finally, Aman clears his throat. "Um, someone's here . . ." He gestures to the living room. Zoya follows him, confused by both of their behavior.

But when she steps into the living room, all of her confusion dissipates, replaced by utter shock. Shock that roots her to the ground and immobilizes her.

Because standing in front of her is none other than Haroun Suleiman.

~

Zoya faints.

And she doesn't gain consciousness.

So they rush her to the hospital.

~

Her eyes seem to be sewn shut, eyelids heavy and warm. Zoya tries to open them, but to no avail. She tries to say something, but everything in her seems to be sealed tight.

She falls back into unconsciousness, thinking of one word over and over again.

Al-Qawiyy. The Strong.

~

Zoya wakes to the sound of her heart monitor. It beeps at a steady rhythm by her head, prodding her to open her eyes.

Finally, Zoya's eyes flutter open.

She squints against the harsh hospital light. IV's are plugged into her arms; there is a hospital band around her wrist. Her eyes survey the room, and when she turns her head to the right, a gasp escapes her.

The monitor showcases the sudden shift in her heartbeat when she looks at Haroun Suleiman. When she takes in his appearance— rough stubble, dark eye bags, pallid skin.

Haunted, grieved eyes.

He's watching her with warring emotions passing across his face, folded hands resting underneath his chin. From his disheveled appearance, it seems that he has been there for quite a while.

Seeing him, a strange feeling overtakes Zoya. The ghost of who she used to be around him flits past her—the aching, longing girl who loved him as if he was the breath of air for her drowning soul. As if he was the only solace in the world.

The husband and wife simply stare at one another after three long months, eyes attempting to communicate what their mouths can't. Haroun's eyes rove over Zoya's form before a deep concern settles over his face. Zoya watches the myriad of expressions in his eyes, wishing she could turn away to avoid being haunted by them.

She has learned that true intimacy does not lie in the act of touch alone. It lies also in the exchange of glances across a crowded room, the smiles shared over the dinner table, the whispered words of comfort in the darkness of the night.

Especially in the lock of eyes, a testimony that nothing but the two souls gazing intently at each other matter in that moment, as Zoya and Haroun are gazing at one another now.

Their eyes holds the weight of the world.

Haroun has changed. There is a ubiquitous wariness about him, a constant gray cloud hovering over him.

He continues to watch her, and he is not the first to turn away.

Zoya raises her eyes to the ceiling, taking a deep breath before turning back to him. "Are you real?" she rasps. He watches her silently for a moment before nodding slowly. "Please," Zoya whispers. "Say something. Say something so I know I'm not imagining you again."

His eyes fill with grief at the word "again" before he murmurs, "I'm real."

Oh, God. That voice.

How I've missed it.

Haroun leans forward warily. "Are *you* real?"

Zoya cracks a smile, shifting her palms beneath her to push herself up into a sitting position. His hands reach out and hover awkwardly around her before dropping back into his lap.

Out of habit, Zoya's hand trails down to rub her stomach. Haroun's eyes track her movements, zeroing in on the place her hand rests. He stands up to sit next to her on the hospital bed, and again Zoya is stricken by the fact that Haroun Suleiman is actually *here*. Not a flitting memory, not a hallucination, but *real*. In front of her and in the flesh.

Haroun looks at her for a moment before reaching forward to

place his hand over hers. Zoya tries not to display the shock roiling throughout her at the contact, remembering that the last time she touched him was to beg him to stay.

Haroun's hand shifts to rest directly over her stomach, where he traces slow circles. Zoya watches him warily.

Suddenly, his face crumbles. "I didn't know," he whispers shakily. "I didn't know."

The thick cord of distance between them snaps, and Zoya reaches forward to wrap her hand around the back of his head and pull him close. He cries messily, head buried in her neck and tears staining her collarbone. Zoya rubs her hands through his hair, murmuring "shh" and "it's okay" over and over again. He shakes his head back and forth, continuously whispering, "I didn't know, I didn't know."

As Zoya rubs her hands soothingly over him, she thinks of how strange time is. Just three months ago, she had been sobbing in front of him, begging him to listen to her and alleviate her guilt. And three months later, he is the one crying, reiterating his own regret.

They have each dealt with a lot of baggage and learned many difficult lessons over the past few weeks. There is such a large gap between them; so much has changed in their hearts since they last saw each other.

Zoya continues to rub Haroun's back softly and leans down to kiss his forehead. "Shh. Quiet now, okay? We don't want little Haroun or little Zoya to hear their daddy crying, do we?"

He cries harder at this, shaking his head against her chest.

Later, after she wipes his tears, they settle at a considerable distance from one another again. "I wanted to come back," Haroun begins, eyes trained to the floor. "But . . . I couldn't bring myself to. Even when I knew that in some ways, it was only getting worse by being away.

"But . . ." He breathes a deep sigh. "I've had a lot of time to think." He stops suddenly, as if unsure of how to continue.

"So have I," replies Zoya, resting her chin on her knees and watching him intently.

He begins to trace circles on the bed. "When I found out that you were sick . . . instead of being sympathetic or feeling like I should come back, I became . . . angry." His eyes flick to hers, and Zoya has to contain her gasp. It will take them so much time to be able to look at one another without witnessing the immense grief in each other's eyes. "I became angry and told myself that I wouldn't let you manipulate me like that again. I wouldn't let you guilt trip me like that again. The more I heard you were sick . . . the more determined I became on not coming back." He shakes his head and reaches up to shove a hand through his hair. "I haven't been making the best decisions."

And it's all my fault, Zoya thinks, looking at him with regret seeping through her bones. She doesn't know what makes her do it, but Zoya reaches forward and cups Haroun's cheek. "I love you," she murmurs simply.

Haroun gazes at her with that heavy wariness back in his eyes— although Zoya can't testify that it ever left.

Then she says, "But I love the *Rabb* Who gave you to me more. And He didn't give you to me just once, but twice." Her thumb circles over his face, passing over his eyelids and his cheeks and his lips, just to give herself the reassurance that he's actually real and not some figment of her imagination.

Under her thumb, a corner of Haroun's lips turns up. It's a strange smile, as if his face has forgotten how to procure it. Zoya senses that it will be this way for a while for both of them.

But they each have the most powerful Sovereign on their side to guide them. Being apart from one another to turn to Him has truly made them realize this in depth.

Zoya settles back against her pillows. She fumbles with the the strings of her hospital gown, daring to voice the question that has been plaguing her. "So . . . where were you?"

Haroun turns to the window, jaw clenching. They are sitting in front of one another, but both of them seem to be in so many different places at once.

Finally, he says, "A friend of mine from college was visiting family overseas. He had an apartment upstate, and I stayed there for a while. Needed to be . . . alone."

Zoya's smile is bittersweet. He had been *so* close geographically, *so* incredibly close, but the metaphorical distance seemed to have crossed both time and space. There had been so much grief and pain and hurt—it had made everything seem so far away.

Here Allah is teaching her another lesson. Despite the short miles between them, Zoya and Haroun's hearts had been as distant from one another as galaxies in the universe. She thinks of how, when Allah wants two people to meet, there is no force on earth that can stop them. Even if they are poles apart from one another—as she and Farhan Hussain had been but still met at a coffee shop almost seven years later.

But when Allah wants two people to remain apart from one another, then no amount of human effort can bring the two people together.

How bittersweet, Zoya thinks, continuing to watch her husband with a poignant smile. A smile which testifies that her Creator has been there all along, and she has only just realized.

Any traces of happiness fade, however, when she realizes that she will have to address the elephant in the room.

She will have to talk about what she did to Haroun.

Zoya clears her throat, cheeks tingeing pink with apprehension. She lowers her gaze to the hospital room's tile floors, inhaling the oddly comforting, clinical smell of the atmosphere to ground herself.

"Haroun," she begins. "I need you to know why I did it."

She peeks a glance at him, almost losing her nerve when his posture becomes rigid and his expression tenses. Gingerly, Zoya reaches for his hand, but he pulls back, jaw clenching.

Wounded but understanding his reaction, Zoya sits back and takes a deep breath.

"I'm not going to say that my actions were justified. They were obviously not. I had every opportunity to make a better choice, and I did not. That's entirely my fault, and I've suffered the consequences of it." Quietly she adds, "And so have you. You were the collateral, and you sustained injuries that could have been avoided if *I* hadn't been selfish and arrogant." Zoya swallows the thick tears that have accumulated in her throat.

Haroun's jaw is working, but he remains quiet.

"But I just . . . I need you to know why I lied to you."

Haroun laughs bitterly. "I thought you weren't going to justify your actions."

"No," Zoya says quietly. "I won't. I simply want to explain what led me to make my awful decisions."

He looks as if he wants to counter her statement, but changes his mind. He turns his face to the hospital window.

"My mother . . . my mother died during labor." Zoya wraps her arms around her knees. "I spent the first nineteen years of my life pining for my father's love. He maintained his duties as a father, but he didn't have it in him to love me. In his eyes, I was not the last mark of the woman he loved; I was what had taken his love away from him. By surviving when my mother didn't, I had earned his disapproval forever, even when he tried so hard not to show it."

Haroun's jaw is still clenched, but his face has turned from the window to Zoya.

Zoya tilts her head and rests it on her knees, unwilling to continue but knowing that she has to say this. "So when my father sat me down and told me he found a potential spouse for me, all my rationality flew out the window. He hugged me, stroked my hair, and didn't pressurize me at all. That was one of the few times he was openly affectionate with me, and I was willing to sacrifice anything to have a loving relationship with him. To have him hug me and genuinely smile at me again." Zoya shrugs. "So I said yes to the proposal, without a single ounce of hesitation."

She tightens her hands around her knees. "Of course, neither of us could have imagined what kind of man Farhan Hussain would be. In front of all other eyes, he was the perfect Muslim. It was only behind closed doors . . ." She swallows, and finally Haroun looks into her eyes, his gaze harboring a guarded sympathy.

"Anyway, when I got a divorce from him, and when my father found out what Farhan had done to me while we were married, he was so ashamed to have 'chosen' Farhan for me that he packed up and left. I never saw him or heard from him after that, and I still have no idea where he is." Zoya quiets, tracing a circle on her knee. The customary ache that always accompanies her father's memory returns. "Now that I think about it, though, I feel like it became too much for him. He was overcome by the guilt of neglecting his daughter for nineteen years . . ." She swallows, tears pricking her eyes. "And the last straw was finding out what the man of his choosing had done to his daughter."

Haroun turns away once more, an emotion Zoya can't decipher filling his eyes. His hands are fists in his lap.

"The reason I'm telling you all this, Haroun, is because my life has been full of abandonment and twisted love. I . . . when I met you and got to know you—and I say this with absolute conviction—you were the best thing that ever happened to me." Zoya pauses to take a deep breath, and Haroun shakes his head with a bitter smile at her words. "You were kind, gentle, and forgiving. And somehow, you thought that *I,* Zoya Zameer, had goodness in my heart, too. And nobody has ever made me feel that way.

"So, manipulative person that I was, I didn't think I could just . . . let you go. Not after everything I went through. You were . . . the candle flame in my dark, dark room. I couldn't extinguish that." Zoya's breaths become shallow. "So I felt like the only way I could keep you was by"—her voice cracks—"forcing you to marry me and love me."

Haroun lets out a dark chuckle. "You didn't think you could just *ask* me?" His voice is high-pitched, raw with emotion. "You didn't think you could just approach me and wonder if I would be willing to marry you?" He stands and settles at the edge of her bed, and even though Zoya had wanted to hold his hand minutes ago, she has the sudden, distinct impression that if he touches her, she'll burst into tears.

"How much did you loathe yourself?" he whispers angrily, lifting her chin so that she has nowhere to look but in his haunted gaze. True to her instinct, tears pool in her eyes at his gentle touch. "To think that nobody would want you unless you manipulated them into it?" His eyes dart between hers, the persistence in them only making his question more difficult to answer.

"How strongly did you believe that there was nothing good about you"—he rubs his thumb along her jaw, capturing a fallen tear and staring irately at it—"for you to *lie* to me about your health, and be willing to suffer the consequences of your deception, just to assure yourself that someone could love you?"

He releases her and looks away, swallowing hard. His voice is much quieter when he says, "And then you continued to allow me to be caught up in your web of deception, and refused to confess your lies even after we . . ." He hesitates, facial muscles tensing. "Even after we started to love each other. Even after we slept together."

Zoya's voice comes out a weak whisper. "I wanted to tell you. Believe me, I did. But with each passing day, my courage . . . plummeted. Until even just thinking of my actions threw me into a panic."

He shakes his head, scoffing.

Seeing his attitude, Zoya feels both a deep understanding of his pain as well as an intense loathing for herself.

"I know that these words will never be enough," she says carefully. "But I'm *so* sorry, Haroun." Her breath hitches. "I'll never be able to fully express it; there aren't enough letters in the alphabet or words in the world. I will never be able to describe the extent of my guilt; I can only hope that as God has been merciful with me, so too will He be merciful with you." She inhales a quick, sharp breath. "I hope that someday, your heart softens towards me, and that you'll find it in yourself to forgive me."

Haroun turns to her then, eyes full of sorrow. His Adam's apple bobs up and down as he swallows, and again Zoya wants so badly to reach forward and provide him with some semblance of comfort. She wants to loop her fingers through his and trace the shape of his hands. She wants to caress his cheeks until his eyes flutter closed in contentment.

But she knows that her touch is the last thing he needs right now. So she remains silent, satisfied in simply watching him.

As Zoya observes Haroun, as her eyes rake over the features that she has come to love without an ache pulsing in her heart, she thinks of something.

Why has he come back? Why has Allah given Haroun back to her?

Because Zoya had learned to live without him, she realizes with a start. She had learned to love him without it being a physical ache in her heart. She had learned to love him with a *part* of her heart, not the entirety of it. Thus, she had freed herself from the dangerous, unhealthy attachment she had towards him. She had freed herself from the pain and anguish she felt when he wasn't near her, and which never quite went away even when he was close by.

She had freed herself from her dependency on him. From her dependency on anyone other than God.

Allah gave Haroun back to her because He knew Zoya didn't *need* him anymore—she only wanted him.

And this difference makes all the difference in the world.

Sixty-Five

"So put your trust in Allah." (Qur'an 27:79)

~

RAMADAN IS ALMOST UPON them, bringing with it festive lights, deep reflections, and a serene aura. Servants bustle around the manor, decorating in preparation for the month.

Zoya has never before given much importance to Ramadan. She has fasted, remaining her cruel self throughout the thirty days with no intention to change, and has always anxiously waited for the month to be over.

Now, however, she feels as if she can finally join in on the excitement; can finally feel the peace filtering through the environment; can finally prepare for the month in which redemption and mercy and forgiveness are such large concepts.

All three things Zoya direly needs.

The new business startup is also steadily gaining recognition from the media, as well as from organizations in the fashion industry which Zoya had never before acknowledged. After the pivot, many employees had chosen to leave—as Zoya had expected—but many more, to her surprise, eagerly lined up at Zameer to fill the empty spots. Despite knowing that business was still unstable and risky. Despite knowing that it would take weeks for their new direction to solidify and succeed.

But people wanted to do something with a purpose.

Zoya had smiled after interviewing a number of people in just one day. Now that she relied on her *Wali,* she was recognizing all the paths He made for her, which she had previously been too blind to notice.

The interviewees had initially been wary around her, having heard of her reputation. But everyone was slowly beginning to understand that cruel Zoya Zameer was gone, replaced by someone who had an intense desire to change.

Slowly, people began to appreciate the new Zoya Zameer.

Zoya also made the very difficult decision of approaching Zaki Ahmed. Whatever he had done to her had been in response to her very first ruse—when she used her feminine wiles to manipulate him and fool him into thinking that she was making a commitment.

Her purpose in becoming acquainted with him had only been to use his stronghold in the industry so that she could build her own company, then cast him off when the business skyrocketed.

When Zoya showed up to Zaki's office, he was livid, of course. It reminded Zoya of how she once told him that she upheld strong *zameer.*

And yet.

She had not. She had repeatedly lied and cheated and deceived him and many others. And although Zaki's retaliation had been dangerous and insane, he had done it *because* he had been frauded by her first.

Zoya had not upheld the attributes of the word *zameer,* of her last name. She had not upheld the morality, the conscience, the scruples, the distinction between right and wrong which the word implied. She had made a joke of her name.

Zaki Ahmed had reminded her of it when she went to visit him. He had pointed his finger in her face and said "*Boht fakhar hota tha na tumhe apne zameer pe?* You were so damn proud, weren't you?" He had sworn at her, cursed at her, screamed at her, and Zoya stayed quiet throughout it all. When he paused to recover his breath, Zoya said, "You're right. *Mene apne zameer ka mazaak uraaya.* I made a joke of my name. And I'm here to apologize for that. What I did to you wasn't right."

Zaki had laughed in disbelief. "What's with this new act, huh? This whole *'holier than thou'* thing? Another trick up your sleeve?"

Zoya had suddenly been reminded of the same attitude she once harbored towards Haroun—of thinking his goodness disguised an ulterior motive.

Zoya shook her head. "No. I'm truly sorry. It wasn't right of me." Then, seeing that Zaki didn't believe a word that came out of her mouth and wasn't willing to further listen, Zoya made to leave his office.

"Oh, and Zaki?" She turned around. "You still need to learn to talk to women with respect. I understand your anger, which is why I didn't say anything to you, but I will not tolerate it if you ever talk to me like that again." Zoya had been as polite as possible, but when she exited the room, she saw the vein throbbing in his temple.

The entire ordeal made her realize that some battles are won, and some battles are lost.

And some are best left up to God.

During Ramadan, Zoya and Haroun frequently have *iftaar* with his family. Naima has softened considerably towards Zoya, thanks to Ramadan. Everyone is determined to forgive and forget during the beautiful month.

Although Naima still watches her warily, the bite in her voice has disappeared. She seems to have realized that Zoya is relentless in trying to win her back, and she makes the job slightly easier for her. She forces herself to laugh, sits next to Zoya even when she doesn't say anything, and tries to smile. Zoya senses that Naima is doing this more for herself than for anyone else—she is too soft and too serene to become so permanently icy.

Aisha is the same old Aisha—bubbly and loud and making everybody laugh to dissipate the unavoidable tension.

Ammi is quiet sometimes. But, after all, she is a mother. Her love is incomparable, even as she tries to conceal her pain.

Every time Zoya and Haroun stand to head back home, *Ammi* hugs them a little too fiercely, kisses their foreheads a little too forcefully. As if she believes she won't see them again for a while, as if she's trying to reassure herself by embracing them tightly, in case she doesn't see them again.

Even Haroun's father visits them, spurred by Ramadan's aura of forgiveness as well as the desire to reconnect with his children after Naima's outburst. Haroun and his family soften towards him, despite his negligence of his children for years. Haroun had always been respectful, but now he begins to chuckle with his father occasionally. Eventually, he laughs without any wariness in his eyes.

All in all, fractured relationships are mending. Slowly, but surely. Everyone has not only time but *Al-Wadood* by their side, The Most Loving.

Each day of Ramadan is spent with Zoya and Haroun going to their respective offices for work, and eating *iftaar* together in the evening. The meals are a quiet occurrence, in which both of them frequently look up at the other, as if to make sure they're still there.

Some nights, they pray *taraweeh* in congregation at the mosque. Other nights, the two of them pray *taraweeh* at home. Haroun leads the prayer, and Zoya follows his lead. The first few times she hears his Qur'an recitation, she is tearful. When he asks her why, she simply shakes her head, unable to say, "I still can't believe you're here."

They are quiet and wary around one another, but there is no more hostility between them. They simply can't seem to figure out how to act or what to say. Space flows and ebbs between them like a wave, one day forcing them far apart and another attempting to bring them close together.

Like when Zoya tries reading the Qur'an but stumbles over the words, and Haroun sits next to her—close—and guides her along, correcting her when she makes a mistake. Sometimes he points to a symbol or a word and explains it so that she is better able to understand and read it. She nods along as he speaks, always silently thanking Allah for bringing them back together.

In this way, the distance between them begins to dissipate—still present but malleable. It's able to be tampered with and coerced into disappearing altogether. There is room for healing—slow, quiet healing.

Sometimes, when Zoya watches Haroun, or when she listens and follows along as he leads prayer, she thinks of something she once said to him. Back when she had been broken and confused and her heart had been aching.

She had said that she wanted a North Star. She wanted constancy. And she had told him this hoping he would understand that she wanted *him*.

But what had he said to her? He had directed her towards God, urging her to open up to Him so that she could find constancy.

At the time, she hadn't understood this. She had been avoidant of God and didn't think opening up to Him would solve any of her issues.

Now, the more she observes Haroun, the more the memory brings a smile to her face.

She thinks of how a compass consists of four cardinal directions—cardinal north, south, east, and west—and cardinal north points to the north direction on a map.

But true north is another thing entirely. True north is a fixed point. True north is home.

Zoya had always thought of Haroun to be her North Star—to be her true north. She had thought *he* was the direction she was supposed to be heading towards.

Only now does she realize—Haroun is not her true north. Haroun is not home.

Haroun has simply been her cardinal north. He has simply been the direction on the map that is guiding her towards where she is supposed to be heading.

Her true north, however?

Her true north has been God all along.

~

The bustle of people is accompanied by the sound of the *adhaan* in *Masjid al-Haraam*, which resonates loudly throughout Makkah. Men in white and women in black shuffle around, preoccupied by their joint motive of getting closer to the *Ka'bah*.

Zoya and Haroun join the crowd, walking together silently amidst the people. Every few seconds they turn towards one another, in awe of the beauty and peace surrounding them.

They stop when they are close enough to the *Ka'bah,* staring at the incredible sight before them.

As they stand in front of the house of God, Zoya and Haroun are each occupied by their own thoughts. They are seemingly so close to one another, but still healing from their individual wounds.

This is why they are here—at the house of God—to grow closer to Him and heal their wounds. Because surely, as they have both realized, true happiness and peace can only be found in Him.

They have both made mistakes, have both fallen into traps they could have avoided had they made better choices. But everything was set in place by the One above; the One who knew that they both needed these trials and experiences in order for their hearts to change direction. In order for them to know and experience pain.

Only then would they turn to Him for solace. Only then would they remember Him. Only then would they learn to trust Him above all else.

They have not entirely recovered from their wounds and perhaps never will, but they are both on the journey to healing and redemption. They both have errors to rectify, mindsets to change, pain to overcome. They both have faults to acknowledge, pasts to forget, futures to look to with hope.

This is not the end for them.

As Haroun unfolds his arms and drops his hands, they brush against Zoya's. She turns her head slightly, acknowledging the contact. Since their reunion, they have rarely touched each other— as if doing so would renew their pain

Haroun doesn't break contact.

Instead of looping her fingers through his, however, Zoya remains still. They both do, allowing their knuckles to brush against each other gently.

This is what they need in order to heal. God and small increments of each other's love.

They know that this is not the end for them. This is just the beginning.

Small gestures of affection will blossom into a healthy love. A love that will urge them to keep turning back to God. A love that will bring smiles to their faces and coolness to their eyes.

They will heal—all they need for it is God and time.

And for those who are with Allah, there are no sad endings.

So—with their hands softly brushing against one another—they set out to embark on the lifelong Journey to Hidaya.

Epilogue

"HAROUN!" ZOYA WHINES, STRUGGLING to figure something out on her laptop. Zameer's new website is befuddling her, and she has called in Sameer to work with Haroun and figure out the new cataloging system.

Meanwhile, a small boy with curly black hair dashes around the room, causing the papers on the table to flutter in the air every time he rushes by. "I didn't do it, I didn't do it!" the little boy insists, grabbing at his mother's hands.

Zoya lifts her head to the ceiling in exasperation. "Please make him stop," she begs her husband.

"Zameer, come here." Haroun stands, holding his hands out.

The little boy follows his father's voice to the far end of the room. Haroun picks him up, tickling him lovingly. "Why are you bothering your mom? Hmm?" Haroun walks towards Zoya with Zameer in his arms.

The little boy gazes at his father with wide eyes, grabbing at his curls. His tiny features coil in tension. "I—I was just tewwing her dat I'm not wying. I didn't dwop da waundwy," he jumbles with a baby lisp.

Haroun smiles at him. "It's okay. I believe you. I know you

didn't drop the laundry." Zoya raises an eyebrow at her husband, and he winks at her. "I know you would never in a hundred thousand years lie to me. Right, Zameer?"

The little boy looks conflicted now. His eyes dart between his mother and father.

"Right, Zameer?" Haroun repeats gently, tugging at his son's curls.

Zameer nods reluctantly. "Yes . . . Papa." He avoids his father's gaze, looking inordinately guilty.

Haroun breaks out into boisterous laughter, and Sameer can't help but crack a smile at the father and son. He turns towards Zoya and shrugs as if to say, "*Is Haroun ka koi hal nahi hai.*" Zoya rolls her eyes in agreement.

But as she watches Haroun gently explain to their son why he shouldn't lie, Zoya's eyes soften. She breathes a long, deep sigh of relief when she sees the now-giggling boy and the father making funny faces.

In moments like this, it's easy to forget the time in their lives when they had been so distant from one another, because what is a few months to many years?

But other times, those few months of turmoil seem to haunt them everywhere they go—every time someone mentions a sickness, every time old reports emerge of the once-arrogant Zoya Zameer, every time family members shuffle around the topic awkwardly. The two of them become tense, waiting with bated breath for the moment to pass.

Sometimes, the moment passes. Other times, a shadow passes over them both instead, settling in their hearts. Weighty and suffocating.

But on other occasions, they forget the entire distressing ordeal. Like when they sit in the backyard during starry nights, sipping tea and huddling close together. When they smile and gaze into one another's eyes like newlyweds. When they fuss over their son and tickle him as he giggles, "Mama! Papa!" When they turn to one another while studying *tafsir*, discussing topics that particularly intrigue them. When they attend mosques to pray and meet other Muslims and listen to lectures together. In times like these, it's easy to forget the pain that had taken root between them years ago.

Despite the dark moments that often intrude their remodeled lives, they realize that God's mercy is of the essence. His mercy to soften their hearts towards one another and vanquish the negative feelings, the bad memories. Allowing them to turn the old, darkened pages of their book and start fresh on pristine, clean ones.

Because with Allah on their side, they will never be disappointed.

~

When Farhan gets married two years after Zameer's birth, he makes it a point to bring up his marriage in every conversation. Even when the topic at hand has nothing to do with it—*especially* when the topic at hand has nothing to do with it.

After all, with a wife like Naima, it would be hard for him *not* to brag.

Whenever the couple visits Zoya and Haroun, everyone erupts into boisterous laughter—Farhan and Naima's banter is too amusing. One day, the mansion echoes with the sound of merriment as Zoya makes sandwiches and Haroun works on his computer.

Haroun's father is busy making *chai* in the kitchen, having insisted on doing so despite Zoya's and the servants' protests.

Leaning over Naima, Farhan lets out a dramatic gasp. "Oh, my *God*. Is that *gray hair* I see?" He fingers a single strand in her braid.

Naima swats his hand away playfully, trying to read her book. "Oh, stop it."

Zoya sets the sandwiches on the table and heads to Haroun, who murmurs a "thank you" and kisses her hand.

"No, no, no." Farhan strokes his chin with exaggerated concern while Zoya and Haroun watch the scene with mirth and affection in their eyes.

"I can't be married to somebody with *gray hair!*" Farhan declares. "I'm too young to become so *old!*"

Naima looks up from her book with narrowed eyes. "Well, it's not like *you're* Tom Holland."

Farhan clasps his hands to his chest in mock hurt. "*Oh*, so *Tom Holland* is the standard now?"

Naima smiles up at her husband sweetly. "I'm sorry, was there ever any other standard?"

"Oh, I'll show *you* Tom Holland!" Farhan sweeps Naima into his arms, spinning her around as she shrieks in alarm. Zameer, who is racing two toy cars against one another on the floor, looks up at the commotion. His confused eyes follow his aunt and uncle, and Zoya and Haroun laugh even more at the little boy's bafflement.

"Put me *down*, you good-for-nothing—"

Farhan spins his wife around faster. "I'm sorry, what was that?"

"Okay, okay! Put me down, you"—Naima hesitates—"amazing . . . human being." She grimaces, though her eyes are shining with laughter.

Farhan stops for a moment, contemplating. "Come on, you can do better than that."

"Yeah, come on, Neemee," Zameer suddenly says, clapping his hands together gleefully. Farhan gives the little boy a wink.

"Fine!" Naima huffs. "Fine, um . . . you . . . incredibly handsome, extremely charming . . . human being?"

Farhan hesitates for a second before he says, "Good enough." He sets his wife down breathlessly, who blows out a sigh and pushes him back, laughing. "I'm *pregnant*, Farhan," she scolds.

Farhan flicks her nose and rubs her stomach affectionately. "No life-threatening stunts were conducted." Then he turns to Zameer and says, "Glad to know you're on my side, little king." He reaches down and swoops the boy up on his shoulders, who shrieks in delight.

Farhan carries him to the back door before turning to a still-giggling Zoya. "Permission to kidnap, *bhabhi*?"

"No," Haroun replies, chuckling.

"Is your name *bhabhi*?" Farhan asks, raising an eyebrow as Zameer tugs at his hair to lead him in the other direction.

Haroun rolls his eyes playfully. Zoya turns to Farhan and smiles. "Permission granted."

~

Five years after Zoya's son's birth, an envelope shows up at her doorstep, emblazoned with a name that makes her heart stop.

Zameer Arsalan.

Zoya rips open the envelope, Haroun at her side, watching her with concern.

Inside the envelope lies a death certificate.

A startled cry escapes her, but other than that she remains mute. Zoya's eyes become wet as she stares at the paper, willing the words to change. Quietly, Haroun murmurs, "*Inna lillahi wa inna ilayhi rajioon.* To God we belong and to Him we shall return. I'm sorry. I'm so sorry."

There is a will inside the envelope, too, and a letter addressed to Zoya in handwriting both foreign and familiar.

Zoya shakes her head, leaning against Haroun. She cannot read the letter. She cannot. There is not enough strength in her to open it, despite having waited the past ten years for something like it.

Maybe someday she will read it. Maybe when she is a stronger version of the person that she is today.

But right now, she doesn't have the willpower to read her father's last letter.

Zoya simply leans against Haroun as he rubs her shoulder and kisses her hair. He murmurs the same words over and over again.

I'm sorry. I'm sorry. I'm sorry.

~

One year later, Zoya huffs and puffs in the labor room, eyes rolling into the back of her head.

"No, no, no," Haroun murmurs fiercely, clasping Zoya's hand. "Stay with me, Zoya." He smooths the hair over her head as she takes deep, heaving breaths.

"Heart rate one thirty-five," the nurse announces, snapping latex gloves onto her hands. "BP rising."

The obstetrician positions herself at Zoya's feet, smiling at her comfortingly. "Come on, Zoya," she says. "Push."

With Haroun whispering *Bismillah* by her side, Zoya pushes.

Later, when the sound of the baby's cry releases exhales and smiles all around the room, Zoya lets out a laugh mingled with tears. She reaches forward feebly, and the doctor gently places the now swaddled baby in the mother's arms.

Zoya and Haroun stare down at the baby adoringly—Haroun with uncontrollable tears of joy—as the doctor says, "An 8-pound healthy baby girl. Congratulations."

As Zoya watches the infant, tears escape her eyes as well. But they are not only tears of happiness; they are also tears of anguish.

"Oh," she exhales with a sob. "Oh, my beautiful, sweet little girl. If you were a boy—"

Haroun rears back and stares angrily at Zoya, having had this conversation with her numerous times before. "Zoya," he says sharply.

Zoya continues to cry as she watches the baby and caresses her face. "*Allah na kare tumhe kabhi bhi dunya ki pithkaare khaani pare.* God forbid you *ever* have to go through *any* trials, my love, my sweetheart, *meri jaan.*"

"And she will not," Haroun says fiercely, turning Zoya's face to him by placing his finger under her chin. "She will *not.* What did I tell you?"

The two stare into one another's eyes, Zoya's unspoken sentence charging between them electricity.

I don't want her to grow up like I did.

"You cannot protect her from everything," Zoya murmurs.

"As long as I am alive, I will, *Insha Allah.*" There is ferocity in his eyes, the kind that emerges when he becomes exceptionally emotional. He cradles the baby girl with Zoya. "*Us ke pas us ka baap hai,* and I will never let anything happen to her." He wipes a tear from Zoya's face. "*Mai hoon, na?* And we have Allah—who is a better Protector and Sustainer than Him?"

A tentative smile blooms on the exhausted mother's face. Her daughter will surely experience the love and adoration of the best father in the world.

The two of them stare down at the wriggling bundle of joy with tears of happiness streaming down their faces. This beautiful baby girl will be cherished beyond measure by her family, be the coolness of her parent's eyes, and become the *laadli*—the most beloved—of her father especially.

And during times of sadness and distress, she will never feel alone.

As Haroun said, who is a better Protector and Sustainer than Allah?

Haroun's Letters

Zoya Zoya Zoya.

I told you not to let me become the focus of your heart I warned you not to get too attached.

I didn't warn myself.

Oh beautiful Zoya Zameer oh cruel Zoya Zameer.

I did this to myself I unintentionally shifted my focus from God to a human.

A human who had the ability to break me.

Oh Zoya.

That morning I told you I loved you.

You have no idea how much it took me to say that. To free myself of the worry and guilt that appeared every time I began to trust you. I didn't want it to turn out like every other time . . . every other time that I trusted somebody and they gave me reasons not to.

Oh Zoya beautiful sweet Zoya your beauty should not be able to tell such a terrible lie.

I should not have trusted you.

I've become a little boy again I can't stop crying.
We consummated our marriage for God's sake!
How did you lie to me the whole time?
I can't stop crying.

How could you do it? Every time we embraced each other or laughed together or spent time with one another how did it not hang above your head how did you not think that I am lying to this man every second that we are together how how how?

How could you let me love you and love you and love you and let it all be a sick lie?

Lies lies lies why does this world have to consist of something as ugly as lies?

I don't know how to think of you anymore without falling apart.

They are saying on the news that something is going on with Zoya Zameer that you are not leaving your house that you haven't gone to work in days and nobody has seen you and nobody knows what's going on.

I know what's going on I know you feel guilty now I know you regret what you did I know everything about you oh beautiful cruel Zoya Zameer.

But I can't handle it I can't handle it when they say you must be sick because it makes me want to throw up all over again. Such a lie such a horrible lie . . . how could you do it?

You are not sick you are ashamed don't do this to me again don't think you can play with me and my heart again don't think you can make them say on the news that you're sick and it will make me come back I don't have the strength to look at you.

Without falling apart.

Zoya Zoya Zoya.

Allah is teaching me a lesson because every time I say your name or think of your beautiful face there is a searing pain in my chest and it doesn't go away.

Allah is telling me that I filled too much of my heart with you and He's right I did even if it was unknowingly. This was the first time I have ever loved someone like this and I thought opening my heart up to you was the right thing to do but I opened up too much of me and now I've torn myself apart.

There is not enough room in my heart as there is pain.

Sometimes I sit by the window and hear your laugh. I see your smile. I feel your curls between my fingers. Sometimes I hear your voice whispering in my ear and it sounds like the mornings you used to wake up and plead with me to make breakfast claiming you would burn the kitchen down if you did. And the times when we would bake together flour in your hair flour on my hands.

Sometimes I think of coming back because I would never have done something like this even in my worst nightmares I would never have left my wife and my mother and my sisters but oh Allah I have turned into the very person I despised.

I have become my worst nightmare.

At night when I go to sleep the bed feels cold and empty.

I remind myself of your deceit.

But then in the morning when I wake up I reach for your hand and come up empty.

I used to make du'a to Allah for so many things I used to ask for guidance and mercy and health and happiness but now I only want to be rid of this agony.

Oh God please make the pain go away. I can't take it anymore.

Some days it gets better and some days . . . Zoya I think of your beautiful grief-stricken face in that royal blue dress and the tears return to my eyes and the ache returns to my heart. How could such beauty tell such a lie how how how?

Every time I pray or read the Qur'an my vision blurs. Oh Allah please ease my pain and suffering please.

Nothing is difficult for you O Qawiyy please end my agony.

Oh Allah oh Allah.

It is not so horrible now, two months later. Allah listened to my du'as about easing my pain and now when I think of you or when I see your pictures, I am able to control the ache.

The ache that won't leave me because I keep remembering your lie and I keep remembering the defeat on your face when I asked you if it was true.

Your love does not hurt nearly as much as your lies do.

But I can control the ache now.

To some extent.

I should come back I need to come back this isn't right. This has never been right.

Last night I dreamt about you again. I keep dreaming about you.

In my dream, you kept lying to me and I covered my ears to shield myself, but you pulled my hands away and whispered your lies in my ears.

*I talk to my mom and my sisters sometimes and they say you don't let
them in every time they come to visit and how could you?
How could you let them in after what you've done?*

I wouldn't let them in either if I were you.

I hope I never hear a single lie in my life again.

Zoya?

I saw you on the news today. It's been three months. You were wearing a white dress and a blue scarf on your head.

You looked tired, so tired. Eyes dark and hollow and your beautiful radiant skin dimmed by weakness.

I had a dream about you again. I've been having more dreams about you the past few days.

In the dream, you smiled at me. In the way that always made me avert my eyes because you made me flush like a ten year old boy.

And then you turned around, walking towards the light.

Maybe it's time to come back. Maybe it's time to let go of this bitterness in my heart.

I hate it. I hate that I've become this person. This person who resents and resents and resents.

No more. I want my heart back.

I'm packing my bags. It's time to end this. I don't want to be this person anymore.

Oh Allah, guide me to the straight path.
Guide me to You.

Translations

URDU

Words/Terms

Jhumkas: South Asian cultural earrings

Dupatta: Cultural (and often religious) scarf or stole

Sherwani: Formal South Asian clothing for men

Lehenga: Formal South Asian clothing for women

Shalwar kameez: South Asian cultural clothing

Biryani: South Asian cultural rice

Samosa: South Asian cultural food

Dahi bhare: South Asian cultural food

Chipkali: Lizard

Yaar: Dude / bro

Bibi: Ma'am

Gup shup: Chit-chat

Bichaare: Poor guy

Masoom: Innocent

Jaan: Literally translates to life / soul; also often used as a term of endearment

Meri jaan: My life / my love

Bakwaas: Nonsense

Acha: Okay

Phir: Again

Majboori / majbooriyan: Something you do either when you don't have another choice or feel like you don't have another choice

Sharam: Shame

Beta: Child / son; commonly used to address someone younger than you

Ghairat: Honor, dignity, pride, or shamefacedness. Used chiefly among men to describe the dignity and respect they hold, especially in regards to women.

Bhai: Used to address an older brother or a male older than you

Insaaniat: Humanity

Besharam: Shameless

Behaya: A synonym for *besharam* referring to a lack of *hayaa,* or modesty

Dharkan: Heartbeat / palpitations

Chai: Tea

Zameer: Conscience / dignity / strong morals and character

Chalo: Go / let's go / okay

Aapi: Used to address an older sister or a female older than you

Bhabhi: Typically refers to one's sister-in-law

Jhalak: Glimpse

Saab: Sir

Mukhlis: Sincere

Ammi / Amma: Mother

Laadli: Beloved one / dearest one

Phrases/Sentences

Oh, and kabhi kabhi meri Urdu nikal jaati hai: Oh, and sometimes my Urdu (the language) comes out.

Mene tumse bola, to tum hi karo ge. Samaj aai?: I've asked you, so you will be the one to do it. Do you understand?

Urdu me jawab de sakte ho, meri jaan?: Can you reply in Urdu, my love?

G, samaj aai: Yes, I understand.

Koi baat nahi: It's nothing / it's alright.

Koi chakkar chal raha hai?: Is there something (an affair) going on?

Meri marzi: My choice.

Kya hua hai, Zoya?: What happened / what's wrong?

Kya hai?: What is it?

Paaghal hai sab aaj kal, yaar: Everyone is crazy nowadays, dude.

Jo ho gaya, so ho gaya: Whatever happened, has happened.

Nikamme log: Useless people.

Apne kaam se kaam rakho: Mind your own business.

Mera maghaz na chaato: Literally translates to "don't lick my brain." Contextually translates to "don't bother me" or "don't irritate me."

Meri naak na katwa de na: Literally translates to "don't cut my nose off." Contextually translates to "don't rid me of my respect and dignity" or "don't embarrass me."

These heels mujhe maar dalein gi: These heels are going to kill me.

Aap mujhe Zoya bulaa sakti hai: You can call me Zoya.

And mai apne naam par qaaim rehti hun, to mujh par jhoota aur ghatiya ilzaam lagaane se pehle is naam ka soch kar lehaaz kar liya kare, please. Kyun ke I'm the daughter of Zameer, and I am Zameer: And I am steadfast on my name, so before placing a false and foolish blame on me, think of and respect this name, please. Because I'm the daughter of Zameer. And I am Zameer.

Agar mera naam Zoya Zameer hai: If my name is Zoya Zameer.

Nikamma aadmi. Seriously, is ne kabhi zindagi me koi acha decision liya bhi hai ya nahi?: Useless man. Seriously, has he ever made a good decision in his life or not?

Tumhari izzat aur ghairat pe koi daagh lagane ki koshish kare, ye mere se bardaasht nahi hota. Jis tarha tumhe istemaal kia gaya hai, ye mere se bardaasht nahi hota: That somebody has tried to lay a hand on your honor and dignity is unbearable for me. The way you have been used is unbearable for me.

Zaalim taaqat-war nahi hota, hum us se dar ke us ko taaqat-war bana dete hain: The oppressor is not powerful; we fear him and thus make him powerful.

Aur Zoya Zameer kabhi kisi ko maaf nahi karti: And Zoya Zameer never forgives anyone.

Tumhe bari hasee aa rahi hai, huh? Chalo, tum bhi niklo. Jao: You're finding this really funny, aren't you? Okay, you get out, too. Go.

So jao, meri jaan: Go to sleep, my love.

Aik din, jab mai chaar saal ka tha: One day, when I was four years old.

Har baat: Every talk / every thing.

Jao. Maaf kiya: Go. I've forgiven you.

Tumhari phuphi ka ghar: The house of your *phupho* (dad's sister);

used as an expression of comedy or anger when telling somebody that they are becoming too comfortable in a place which isn't theirs.

Boht zyaati ki mene Zameer k saath: I did a lot of injustice to Zameer.

Aa jaye, hum aapke hi muntazir hai: Come; after all, we've been waiting for you.

Koi maa k saath aise karta hai?: Can anyone do this to a mother?

Koi maa k saath itni bari zyaati karta hai?: Can anyone commit such an injustice against a mother?

Koi maa ko itna pareshan rakhta hai k us ko pata hi na ho us ki beti kahan hai, kis haal me hai?: Can anyone keep a mother so worried that she does not even know where her daughter is, in what state she is in?

Koi maa k saath is tarha ka sulook karta hai?: Can anyone treat a mother in this way?

Koi bhi beti maa k saath is tarha kar sakti hai?: Can any daughter do this to a mother?

Tumhe andaaza bhi hai k tum ne apni maa ko kitna pareshan rakha hai in teen maheeno me? Tum dono ne—tum ne aur Haroun ne: Do you have any idea of how worried you've kept your mother these past three months? Both of you—you and Haroun.

Maa ka haq nahi hai k wo apne bacho ke maslihaat me un ka saath de?: Is it not a mother's right to support her children through their hardships?

Tum dono ne mujhe maa ka haq nahi adaa karne diya. Nahi adaa karne diya: You two have not allowed me to maintain the rights of a mother. You have not allowed me to.

Hosla karo: Maintain yourself / have patience.

Boht fakhar aata tha na tumhe apne zameer pe?: You were very proud of your *zameer* (conscience / morality), weren't you?

Mene apne zameer ka mazaak uraaya: I have made a joke of my zameer.

Is Haroun ka koi hal nahi hai: There is no solution about this Haroun (expressed in a joking manner).

Allah na kare tumhe kabhi bhi dunya ki pithkaare khaani pare: God forbid you ever have to suffer the trials and tribulations of this world.

Us ke pas us ka baap hai: She has her father.

Mai hoon, na?: I'm here, right? (Often expressed to let someone know that you are there for them and will support them).

Arabic

Words/Terms

Fajr: First of five daily prayers for Muslims

Dhuhr: Second of five daily prayers for Muslims

Maghrib: Fourth of five daily prayers for Muslims

'Isha: Fifth of five daily prayers for Muslims

Wudu: Ablution / a form of purification that Muslims complete before praying

Du'a: Supplication

Insha Allah: If God wills / God willing

Adhaan: Call to prayer

Sunnah: Lifestyle of the Prophet Muhammad / the way of the Prophet

Nafl: Optional / extra form of worship

Abaya: A simple, loose over-garment or gown worn by Muslim women

Tasbeeh: Looks like a beaded necklace and is used to perform *dhikr,* which is the remembrance and glorification of God

Hayaa: Modesty

Astaghfirullah: A form of *dhikr* (remembrance of God) used to seek forgiveness from God

Masjid: Mosque

Musallah: Prayer area

Alhamdulillah: A form of *dhikr* (remembrance of God) meaning "all praise and thanks be to God"

Halal: Permissible / what is allowed for Muslims

'Iddah: A period of time that must elapse before a Muslim widow or divorcée remarries. This period of time is meant to allow a Muslim woman privacy and a break from society so that she can grieve properly, as well as take care of her personal responsibilities without interference from others who are not immediately related to her.

Dunya: Refers to this temporary world (as opposed to the hereafter)

Hidaya: Guidance (often divine)

Hikmah: Wisdom when referring to humans; ultimate wisdom when referring to God

Bismillah: In the name of God

Sukoon: Peace

Hadith: Prophetic sayings

Da'wah: The practice or policy of conveying the message of Islam to non-Muslims.

Hijab: The word *hijab* refers to "barrier" or "partition." Many Muslim women wear the *hijab* to practice modesty and show submission to Allah (God) and their faith. Although broadly understood as the head covering / veil, the word is meant to refer to physical modesty, as well as modesty in one's character and behavior.

Khair: Good

Shaitan: Satan / evil spirit

Imam: Islamic leadership position

Wali: Guardian, protector, supporter; typically a male responsible for the caretaking and protection of his female ward. (In the context of this novel, if a father is absent from his daughter's life, and if she has no brothers, grandfathers, or paternal / maternal uncles, an *imam* is allowed to serve as her *wali*).

Nikah: Islamic marriage ceremony

Mahr: Dowry given by husband to wife upon Islamic marriage

Walima: Marriage feast / banquet; typically occurs after the *nikah* or marriage ceremony

Surah: A chapter in the Qur'an

Ayah: A verse in the Qur'an

Subhan Allah: A form of *dhikr* (remembrance of God) meaning "Glory to God / God is perfect"

Rabb: Lord / Master

Ka'bah / Masjid al-Haraam: Most sacred site in Islam; located in Makkah, Saudi Arabia

Sujood: The act of low bowing or prostration to God in the direction of the Ka'bah

Sirat al-Mustaqeem: The Straight Path / the Right Path which pleases God

Iftaar: Meal eaten to break the fast

Taraweeh: Optional night prayer during the month of Ramadan

Tafsir: Exegesis / in-depth study of the Qur'an

Sahih: Used to describe a *hadith* (Prophetic saying) that has been preserved and transmitted accurately.

Hasan: Used to describe a *hadith* (Prophetic saying) whose authenticity is not as well-established as that of *sahih hadith*, but sufficient for use as supporting evidence.

Bukhari, Muslim, Tirmidhi, Abu Dawud, Sunan an-Nasa'i: Five of the six canonical collections of *ahadith* (Prophetic sayings) recognized by *Sunni* Muslims.

Phrases / Sentences

Assalaamu 'Alaikum: Muslim greeting meaning "peace be upon you"

Salaam: Short version of Muslim greeting meaning "peace be upon you"

Wa 'Alaikum Salaam: Response to Muslim greeting meaning "and may peace be upon you"

Inna lillahi wa inna ilayhi rajioon: A prayer meaning "Truly we belong to God and truly to Him shall we return"

Spanish

Words/Terms

Pobrecito: Poor thing!

Nada: None / nothing

Adios: Goodbye

Phrases / Sentences

Qué será, será: Whatever will be, will be

Sal de aquí: Get out of here

¿Habla español?: You speak Spanish?

Eso no es español: That's not Spanish

French

Phrases/Sentences

Sí, ma chérie: Yes, my darling / sweetheart

Turkish

Phrases/Sentences

Hayır, aşkım: No, my love

References

Chapter 10

On Haroun and Zoya's conversation about power and free will:

Anas ibn Malik reported: A man said, "O Messenger of Allah, should I tie my camel and trust in Allah, or should I untie it and trust in Allah?" The Messenger (peace be upon him) said, "Tie it, and trust in Allah." (At-Tirmidhi, classed as Hasan)

This hadith indicates the concept of *tawakkul* in Islam, which refers to relying on God and trusting in his plan. Prophet Muhammad's response, to "tie it, and trust in Allah," signifies that alongside having strong faith and *tawakkul*, humans have personal responsibility as well.

Chapter 11

On Haroun and Zoya's conversation about retaliating against Farhan or forgiving him:

"We ordained therein for them life for life, eye for eye, nose for nose, ear for ear, tooth for tooth, and wounds equal for equal. But if anyone remits the retaliation by way of charity, it is an act of atonement for him." (Qur'an 5:45)

This verse mentions two different concepts: the concept of justice and the concept of forgiveness. The first part of the verse refers to the fact that the world needs balance to function. Newton once said that for every action, there is an equal and opposite reaction. The Qur'an states that someone who has been wronged has the fundamental right to react, if that's what they desire. Justice cannot otherwise be obtained.

The second part of the verse adds that, despite a person's right to react in an identical manner, they have the option to forgive. To be merciful. Which God says yields a greater reward.

Chapter 14

On Haroun's conversation with his coworkers about Islam and the misrepresentation of it:

"Whoever kills an innocent person, it is as if he has killed all of humanity." (Qur'an 5:32)

"Whether you speak in secrecy or aloud, (it is all the same to Allah). He even knows the secrets that lie hidden in the breasts of people." (Qur'an 67:13)

"Judgment lies with Allah alone. He declares the Truth, and He is the best judge." (Qur'an 6:57)

"Be a community that calls for what is good, urges what is right, and forbids what is wrong: those who do this are the successful ones." (Qur'an 3:104)

On the authority of Abu Sa'eed al-Khudree (may Allah be pleased with him) who said: I heard the Messenger of Allah (peace and blessings of Allah be upon him) say, "Whosoever of you sees an evil, let him change it with his hand; and if he is not able to do so, then (let him change it) with his tongue; and if he is not able to do so, then with his heart—and that is the weakest of faith." (Sahih Muslim)

Chapter 25

On Haroun's conversation with Zoya about guarding people's reputations:

Abdullah ibn 'Amr ibn al-'As narrated that the Prophet Muhammad (peace be upon him) said: "The Compassionate One has mercy on those who are merciful. If you show mercy to those who are on the earth, He Who is in the heaven will show mercy to you." (Sunan Abu Dawud, classed as sahih)

On Haroun retelling the story of the slander against 'Aisha (may Allah be pleased with her):

"Verily those who brought forth the slander (against 'Aishah) are a group among you. Consider it not a bad thing for you. Nay, it is good for you. Unto every man among them will be paid that which he had earned of the sin, and as for him among them who had the greater share therein, his will be a great torment (11). Why then, did not the believers, men and women, when you heard it (the slander), think good of their own people and say: 'This (charge) is an obvious lie?' (12). Why did they not produce four witnesses? Since they (the slanderers) have not produced witnesses! Then with Allah they are the liars (13). Had it not been for the Grace of Allah and His Mercy unto you in this world and in the Hereafter, a great torment would have touched you for that whereof you had spoken (14). When you were propagating it with your tongues, and uttering with your mouths that whereof you had no knowledge, you counted it a little thing, while with Allah it was very great (15). And why did you not, when you heard it, say: 'It is not right for us to speak of this. Glory be to You (O Allah)! This is a great lie' (16)." (Qur'an 24:11-16)

Chapter 28

On Haroun and Zoya's conversation about seeking contentment:

"Verily, with every difficulty, there is ease. With every difficulty, there is ease." (Qur'an 94:5-6)

"And your Lord is going to give you, and you will be satisfied." (Qur'an 93:5)

"Your Lord did not abandon you, nor did He forget." (Qur'an 93:3)

Chapter 58

On Mumtaz and Zoya's conversation about repenting to God:

The Prophet Muhammad (peace be upon him) said, "Whoever says, *'Subhan Allah wa bi hamdihi'* one hundred times a day, will be forgiven all his sins even if they were as much as the foam of the sea.'" (Sahih Bukhari)

Chapter 58

On Mumtaz and Zoya's conversation about good deeds, sins, heaven, and hell:

It was narrated from Mu'awiyah bin Jahimah As-Sulami, that Jahimah came to the Prophet (peace be upon him) and said:

"O Messenger of Allah! I want to go out and fight (in Jihad) and I have come to ask your advice." He said: "Do you have a mother?" He said: "Yes." He said: "Then stay with her, for Paradise is beneath her feet." (Sunan an-Nasa'i, classed as sahih)

Chapter 61

On Zoya remembering when Haroun fed her with his own hands:

The Prophet Muhammad (peace be upon him) said: "You will be rewarded for whatever you spend for Allah's sake even if it were a morsel which you put in your wife's mouth." (Sahih Bukhari)

Acknowledgements

Oh, Lord, how do I even begin?

First and foremost, *Alhamdulillah.* All praise and thanks be to God, for providing me with the strength to write this story. Without You, nothing is possible.

A heartfelt thank you to my skilled copy editor, line editor, and developmental editor—Zainab bint Younus—for showing me all the ways a single sentence could be written, and for ensuring that my story would be as cohesive as possible. Your feedback was exceptionally helpful, and allowed me to significantly improve my story.

To my incredibly kind and supportive developmental editor Ustadha Sarah Ahmed, for pointing out glaring plot holes and areas of improvement. Thank you for helping me refine certain concepts to better reflect the journey of faith.

To my copy editor Zephanasia Lewis, for giving my story a final read before I whisked it off to my interior book designer. Thank you for your feedback and encouragement.

A deeply, deeply sincere and heartfelt thank you to my book cover designer, Melisa Labra. For months, you witnessed the extent of my panic and anxiety, and delivered a spectacular cover that erased all my concerns and addressed all elements of the story. Thank you for so energetically fulfilling my vision.

I'm grateful to my interior book designer Lorna Reid, for bringing my words to life on the page. Thank you for the care and attention you put into designing my text, and for making sure it aligned with my vision for the story.

To *mami* Ayesha Bashiruddin, Marah Siyam, Judith Kristen, and F.S. Yousaf. You were all witnesses of my frazzled and panicked state, and I'm incredibly grateful to you for helping me navigate the daunting publishing process.

I'm beyond appreciative of my lovely friend and beta reader Sarah Siddiqui. Thank you for discovering inconsistencies and errors in the storyline that I hadn't noticed, and for being so eager and passionate about the novel.

To Mariam Insanally, Nabihah Rashid, Muskan Subhani, Heba Safiullah, Aleena Aslam, and Duaa Ali—friends who literally kept me sane throughout the publishing and book cover design procedures, and without whose support I may have lost heart a long time ago. Thank you for believing in me—what would I do without you guys?

To my entire Wattpad community and friend group, especially these girls: Aisha Zahid, Ifrah Rindani, Zainab Nisar, Elizah Ahmad, Tanisha Anirin, Zoya Farooqui, Summaiya Amer, Sumaiya Thaseen, Kabeer Kalam, Amal Wasti, and Sarwat Boota. You all saw this story first, and have supported me consistently throughout this entire endeavor. Thank you, thank you, thank you. For your love and support over the past three years, and for inspiring me to make my publishing dream a reality. I'm forever grateful to each and every one of you.

Thanks to Ustadha Sumara Khan, for triple-checking the Arabic translations and references to make sure they're accurate and authentic.

To Professor Belinda McKeon, for advising me not to lose heart over harsh criticism, and to push through with the story that I want to tell the world.

And, of course, the fam:

To my mom, Saima Uppal. Mama, Mama, Mama. I don't have the words to express the amount of love and support you've provided me with. Thank you for answering all my questions regarding religion, for constantly reassuring me that I could do this (even when I felt close to giving up), for continuously pushing me to achieve my potential, and for being just as excited as me (if not more) about publishing *Journey to Hidaya*. Your care and encouragement drove me to continue writing. I love you (and I'm sorry that all I've been doing at home for the past couple of months is typing maniacally away on my laptop).

To my Papa, Azhar Chughtai: People always say that dads have special, different ways of expressing their love, and I've realized the truth of this statement. Thank you for your excitement at my publishing a novel, for your constant mantra of "It doesn't matter how much the process costs; you don't need to worry about that. I'll take care of it." I hope that you see this book and are proud of me. I love you.

To my sisters Rimsha and Fatima: for listening to me rant day after day, for patiently giving me suggestions, for telling me which word sounded better in a sentence after I would shout it at you guys across the room, and for being my pillars of strength throughout the entire strenuous publishing journey. Rimsha, thanks for matching my energy and planning book parties months beforehand. Fatima, thanks for being my unofficial agent and creating a promotional Instagram account for my writing all on your own. You guys are the best; I couldn't have done this without you.

To my brother Fasiih: you showed your love and support in your own way. By constantly calling me "author, author, author" (which meant more to me than I could ever express), and by joking about how I'd become famous one day and forget you guys (of course I wouldn't). You're pretty amazing (I don't tell you that enough, do I?).

To Fakhar, for making sure the Urdu translations were accurate, and for supporting me and advising me (this is the only time I'll ever be nice to you :P). To Noor, for her love and encouragement—thank you for being so excited about my book. And to Khadeeja, for being the first person in my family to read and love and squeal over *Journey to Hidaya*.

And thank *you*, wonderful reader, for picking up this book. You've greatly impacted my life, and have played an essential role in my dream coming true. I'm forever grateful to you.

About the Author

Kainat Azhar is a Pakistani-American Muslim. She has always been interested in the various experiences of religion and culture, and the roles that they play in a person's life. An avid reader and writer, Kainat loves exploring the complexities of relationships and emotions through her work. She primarily writes fiction, but enjoys writing poetry as well. When not immersed in a book or animatedly typing stories on her laptop, Kainat can probably be found passionately studying, obsessively eating noodles, or wishfully adding new destinations to her travel bucket list. And if she's holding this book (her debut novel) in her hands and reading her bio, she's probably bursting into tears of joy.

You can find her at **kainatazharchughtai.com**, on Instagram @kainatazharr, @kainatazharwrites, & @everyunspokenstory, and by email at **kainatcazhar@gmail.com**.